NO GOOD DEED

Southerly Buster's pinnace slammed down alongside the parent ship in a flurry of dust and small debris. The door opened and Knger wearing his gaudy fi... ...rian gray coveralls.

Dreebly, his hea... He stood there, droopi... ...m a merciless dressing down. Then, slowly, the two ... alked all around the crippled hulk, with the mate pointing out details of exterior damage.

Grimes already knew what the damage was like inside—the Mannschenn Drive torn from its housing, the hydroponics tanks a stinking mess of shattered plastic and shredded greenery, most of the control room instruments inoperable if not completely ruined.

Saul came to stand by his captain's side. The first lieutenant said happily, "You certainly put paid to *his* account, sir."

Grimes said, not so happily, "I only hope that he doesn't put paid to mine. . . ."

"But, sir, the man's a slave trader! You've wrecked his ship—but that was the only way that you could stop the commission of a crime."

"Strong measures, Mr. Saul—especially if there were no crime being committed."

"But he fired on us, sir."

"At, not on. And we fired at him first."

"But he still hasn't a leg to stand on. . . ."

"Hasn't he? I've checked up on the Non-Citizen Act. I'm afraid that the Morrowvians do not qualify for citizenship. They have no rights whatsoever."

Baen Books by
A. Bertram Chandler

))((( )))((

FIRST COMMAND

A. Bertram Chandler

BAEN

FIRST COMMAND

This is a work of fiction. All the characters and events portrayed in this book are fictional, and any resemblance to real people or incidents is purely coincidental.

Spartan Planet, copyright © 1969 by A. Bertram Chandler.
The Inheritors, copyright © 1972 by A. Bertram Chandler.
The Big Black Mark, copyright © 1975 by A. Bertram Chandler.
The Far Traveler, copyright © 1979 by A. Bertram Chandler.

A Baen Books Original

Baen Publishing Enterprises
P.O. Box 1403
Riverdale, NY 10471
www.baen.com

ISBN: 978-1-4516-3850-9

Cover art by Stephen Hickman

First Baen paperback printing, August 2011

Distributed by Simon & Schuster
1230 Avenue of the Americas
New York, NY 10020

Library of Congress Cataloging-in-Publication Data
2011020088

Printed in the United States of America

10 9 8 7 6 5 4 3 2 1

⁕⁎⟪⟪CONTENTS⟫⟫⁎⁕

SPARTAN PLANET

DEDICATION

For Susan,
Whose Idea It Was

))((Chapter 1))((

There was that sound again—thin, high, querulous, yet audible even above the rhythmic stamp and shuffle of the dance that beat out through the open windows of the Club. It sounded as though something were in pain. Something was.

Brasidus belched gently. He had taken too much wine, and he knew it. That was why he had come outside—to clear his head and, he hoped, to dispel the slight but definitely mounting waves of nausea. The night air was cool, but not too cool, on his naked body, and that helped a little. Even so, he did not wish to return inside just yet.

He said to Achron, "We may as well watch."

"No," replied his companion. "No. I don't want to. It's . . . dirty, somehow . . ." Then with a triumphant intonation he delivered the word for which he had been groping. "Obscene."

"It's not. It's . . . natural." The liquor had loosened Brasidus' tongue; otherwise he would never have dared to

5

speak so freely, not even to one who was, after all, only a helot. "It's we who're being obscene by being unnatural. Can't you see that?"

"No, I can't!" snapped Achron pettishly. "And I don't want to. And I thank Zeus, and his priesthood, that we don't have to go through what that brute is going through."

"It's only a scavenger."

"But it's a sentient being."

"And so what? I'm going to watch, anyhow."

Brasidus walked briskly to where the sound was coming from, followed reluctantly by Achron. Yes, there was the scavenger, struggling in the center of the pool of yellow light cast by a streetlamp. The scavenger—or scavengers . . . had either of the young men heard of Siamese twins, that would have been the analogy to occur to them—a pair of Siamese twins fighting to break apart. But the parallel would not have been exact, as one of the two linked beings was little more than half the size of the other.

Even in normal circumstances the scavengers were not pretty animals, although they looked functional enough. They were quadrupedal, with cylindrical bodies. At one end they were all voracious mouth, and from the other end protruded the organs of excretion and insemination. They were unlovely but useful, and had been encouraged to roam the streets of the cities from time immemorial.

Out on the hills and prairies and in the forests, their larger cousins were unlovely and dangerous, but they had acquired the taste for living garbage.

"So . . . messy," complained Achron.

"Not so messy as the streets would be if the beasts didn't reproduce themselves."

"There wouldn't be the same need for reproduction if you rough hoplites didn't use them as javelin targets. But you know what I'm getting at, Brasidus. It's just that I . . . it's just that some of us don't like to be reminded of our humble origins. How would you like to go through the budding process, and then have to tear your son away from yourself?"

"I wouldn't. But we don't have to, so why worry about it?"

"I'm not worrying." Achron, slightly built, pale, blond, looked severely up into the rugged face of his dark, muscular friend. "But I really don't see why we have to watch these disgusting spectacles."

"You don't have to."

The larger of the scavengers, the parent, had succeeded in bringing one of its short hind legs up under its belly. Suddenly it kicked, and as it did so it screamed, and the smaller animal shrieked in unison. They were broken apart now, staggering over the cobbles in what was almost a parody of a human dance. They were apart, and on each of the rough, mottled flanks was a ragged circle of glistening, raw flesh, a wound that betrayed by its stench what was the usual diet of the lowly garbage eaters. The stink lingered even after the beasts, rapidly recovering from their ordeal, had scurried off, completing the fission process, in opposite directions.

That was the normal way of birth on Sparta.

»«(Chapter 2)»«

That was the normal way of birth on Sparta—but wherever in the universe there is intelligence there are also abnormalities.

Achron looked at his wristwatch, the instrument and ornament that marked him as something more than a common helot, as almost the social equal of the members of the military caste. He said, "I have to be getting along. I'm on duty at the créche at 2400 hours."

"I hope you enjoy the diaper changing and the bottle feeding."

"But I do, Brasidus. You know that I do." His rather high voice dropped to a murmur. "I always feel that one or two of them might be . . . yours. There are a couple in this new generation that have your nose and eyes."

Brasidus put a large, investigatory and derisory hand to his face. "Impossible. I've still got them."

"Oh, you know what I mean."

"Why not keep a lookout for your own offspring, Achron?"

"It's not the same, Brasidus. In any case, it's not often I'm called upon to contribute . . ."

The two friends walked back to the Club House, but did not go farther inside than the cloakroom. Brasidus watched Achron slip into his tunic and sandals, then, on an impulse, Brasidus followed suit. Somehow he was no longer in the mood for the dance, and his prominent nose wrinkled a little at the acrid smell of perspiration, the sweet-sour reek of vomit and spilled wine that drifted into the anteroom from the main hall. The thudding of bare feet on the polished floor, in time to the drums and the screaming, brassy trumpets, usually excited him, but this night it failed to do so, as even did the confused shouting and scuffling that told him that the inevitable brawl had just broken out. On other occasions he had hurled himself gleefully into the press of struggling, sweating naked bodies—but this, too, had lost its attraction for him.

More and more he was feeling that there was something missing, just as there had been something missing when he had been a guest at Achron's Club. He had thought, at the time, that it was the boisterous good fellowship, the hearty food and the strong, rough wine. Now he had sated himself with all of these, but was still unsatisfied.

He shrugged his heavy shoulders, then tugged the hem of his tunic down to its normal midthigh position. He said, "I'll stroll down to the créche with you, Achron. I don't feel like going back to the barracks just yet. And, anyhow, tomorrow's my free day."

"Oh, thank you, Brasidus. But are you sure? Usually you hate to leave while there's any wine left in the jars."

"Just don't feel like any more drinking or dancing. Come on."

It was dark outside the building. The sky, although clear, was almost starless, and Sparta had no moons. The widely spaced streetlamps on their fluted columns seemed to accentuate the blackness rather than to relieve it, and the glimmering white pillars of street-fronting buildings appeared to be absorbing rather than reflecting what little light there was. In their shadows there was furtive movement, but it was no more than the scavengers going about their appointed tasks. Then, overhead, there was the drone of engines.

Brasidus stopped abruptly, laid a detaining hand on Achron's upper arm. He looked up, staring at the great, shadowy bulk that drove across the night sky, its course set for the blinking beacon atop the Acropolis, its tiers of ports strings of luminous beads, its ruby and emerald navigation lights pendants at the end of the necklace.

Achron said impatiently, "Come on. I don't want to be late clocking in. It's only the night mail from Helos. You must have seen it dozens of times."

"At least," agreed Brasidus. He fell into step again beside his companion. "But . . ."

"But you always wanted to join the Air Navy yourself, Brasidus. But you're too big, too heavy. A pity." There was a hint of spite in Achron's voice.

Brasidus recognized it, but ignored it. He murmured, "And there are even better things to be than an airman. I've often wondered why we didn't build any more space-ships after we colonized Latterhaven, why we allowed the Latterhaveneers to have the monopoly of the trade between the two worlds. We should own and operate our own spaceships."

Achron laughed unkindly. "And what chance do you think you'd have of being a spaceman? Two ships are ample for the trade, and the spice crop's only once a year. What would you do between voyages?"

"We could . . . explore."

"Explore?" Achron's slim arm described an arc against the almost empty sky. "Explore what? And on the other side of the world there's the Lens—and we all know that it's no more—or less—than a vast expanse of incandescent gases."

"So we've been told. But . . . I've managed an occasional talk with the Latterhaven spacemen when I've been on spaceport guard duty, and they don't think so."

"They wouldn't. Anyhow, you could be a lot worse things than a soldier—and in the Police Battalion of the Army at that. And as far as the possibility or otherwise of other worlds is concerned, I'd sooner listen to our own priests than to that atheistical bunch from Latterhaven."

They were almost at the créche now, a huge, sprawling adjunct to the still huger temple. Its windows glowed with soft yellow light, and above the main doorway, in crimson neon, gleamed the insignia of the State Parenthood Service, the red circle from which, at an angle, a barbed arrow jutted up and out. Brasidus wondered, as he had wondered before, how the créche had come to take for its own the symbol of Ares, the God of War. It was, he supposed, that the highest caste into which a child could grow was, after the priesthood, the military. Then he thought about his own alleged parenthood.

"These babies like me . . ." he said abruptly.

"Yes, Brasidus?"

"I . . . I think I'll come in with you, to see for myself."

"Why not? It's outside visiting hours—not that anybody does ever visit—but you're a police officer. Old Telemachus at the desk won't know if you're on duty or not."

Telemachus, bored by his night duty, welcomed the slight deviation from normal routine. He knew Brasidus slightly but, nonetheless, insisted that he produce his identity card. Then he asked, his wrinkled head protruding turtle-like from his robes, "And what is the purpose of your visit, Sergeant? Has some criminal taken refuge within our sacred precincts?"

"Achron tells me that two of his charges might be . . . mine."

"Ah. Potential criminals." The old man cackled at his own humor. "But seriously, Sergeant, it is a great pity that more of our citizens do not evince greater interest in their sons. Even though the direct physical link was abolished ages ago, there should still be responsibility. Yes. Responsibility. Before I was asked to resign from the Council, I succeeded in having the system of regular visiting hours introduced—not that anybody has taken advantage of them . . ."

"Phillip will be waiting for his relief," broke in Achron sulkily.

"So he will. But it will not hurt that young man to be kept waiting. Do you know, at the 2200-hours feed he failed to ensure that the bottles were at the correct temperature! I could hear Doctor Heraklion carrying on, even out here. Luckily the Doctor came into the ward at just the right time." Telemachus added spitefully, "I honestly think that Phillip will make a better factory hand than a children's nurse."

"Is the correct temperature so important, sir?" asked Brasidus curiously. "After all, we can eat hot things and cold things, and it never seems to do us any harm."

"But we are fully developed, my dear boy. The children are not. Before the priests learned how to improve upon nature, a child, up to quite an advanced age, would be getting his nourishment directly from the father's bloodstream. So—can't you see?—these immature digestive organs must be coddled. They are not ready to handle what we should consider normal food and drink."

"Phillip will be in a bad temper," complained Achron. "I hate him when he's that way."

"All right then, you can relieve your precious Phillip. Are you sure you don't want to stay on for a talk, Brasidus?"

"No, thank you, Telemachus."

"Off you go, then. And try not to make any arrests."

Brasidus followed his friend through long corridors and then into the softly lighted ward where he was supposed to be on duty. They were met at the door by Phillip, a young man who, save for his dark coloring, was almost Achron's twin. He glowered at his relief. "So you've condescended to show up at last. I should give you something to help you to remember to get here on time."

"Do just that," said Brasidus roughly.

Phillip stared insolently at the Sergeant and sneered, "A pity you brought your friend with you. Well, I'm off, dearie. It's all yours, and you're welcome to it."

"What about the handover procedure?" demanded Achron sharply.

"What is there to hand over? Fifty brats, slumbering peacefully—until they all wake up together and start yelling their heads off. Thermostat in the dispenser's on the blink, so you'll have to check bottle temperatures before you break out rations for the little darlings. Clean nappy bin was replenished before the change of watch— or what should have been the change of watch. I'm off."

He went.

"Not really suitable for this profession, is he?" asked Achron softly. "I sometimes think that he doesn't like children." He gestured toward the double row of white cots. "But who couldn't love them?"

"Not you, obviously."

"But come with me, Brasidus. Leave your sandals by the door and walk softly. I don't want them woken." He tiptoed on bare feet over the polished floor. "Now," he whispered, "I'll show you. This is one of them." He paused at the foot of the crib, looked down lovingly.

And Brasidus looked down curiously. What he saw was just a bud, a baby, with a few strands of wispy black hair plastered across the overlarge skull, with unformed features. The eyes were closed, so he could not tell if there were any optical resemblance between himself and the child. The nose? That was no more than a blob of putty. He wondered, as he had often, how Achron and the other nurses ever told their charges apart. Not that it much mattered, not that it would matter until the boys were old enough for aptitude tests—and by that time all characteristics, psychological and physiological, would be well developed.

"Isn't he like you?" murmured Achron.

"Um. Yes."

"Don't you feel . . . proud?"

"Frankly, no."

"Oh, Brasidus, how can you be so insensitive?"

"It's a gift. It goes with my job."

"I don't believe you. Honestly, I don't. But quiet. Heraklion's just come in."

Brasidus looked up and saw the tall, white-robed figure of the Doctor at the end of the aisle. He bowed stiffly, and the salutation was returned. Then Heraklion beckoned. Remembering to walk softly, the young man made his way between the rows of cots.

"Brasidus, isn't it?" asked Heraklion.

"Yes, Doctor."

"What are you doing here, Sergeant?"

"Just visiting, with Achron."

"I really don't approve, you know. Our charges are very . . . delicate. I shall appreciate it if you don't go wandering all over the building."

"I shan't be doing that, Doctor."

"Very well. Goodnight to you, Sergeant."

"Goodnight to you, Doctor."

And as he watched the tall, spare figure of Heraklion striding away along the corridor, Brasidus, the policeman in his makeup suddenly in the ascendant, asked himself, What is he hiding? And then the first of the babies awoke, and almost immediately after the other forty-nine of them. Brasidus bade a hasty farewell to Achron and fled into the night.

⅏«Chapter 3»⅏

There was an odd, nagging suspicion at the back of
Brasidus' mind as he walked slowly through the almost
deserted streets to the police barracks. Normally he would
have been attracted by the sounds of revelry that still
roared from the occasional Club—but the mood that had
descended upon him earlier still had not left him, and to
it was added this new fretting surmise. Crime was not rare
on Sparta, but it was usually of a violent nature and to
cope with it required little in the way of detective ability.
However, crime against the state was not unknown—and
the criminals were, more often than not, highly placed
officials, better educated and more intelligent than the
commonalty. There was a certain smell about such
malefactors—slight, subtle, but evident to the trained
nose.

Brasidus possessed such an organ, and it had twitched
at the odor that lingered about Doctor Heraklion.

Drugs? Could be—although the man himself did not
appear to be an addict. But, in his position, he would have

access to narcotics, and the peddlers had to get their supplies from somebody.

Even so, Brasidus was reluctant to pass his suspicions on to his superiors. To begin with, there was no proof. Secondly—and this was more important—he had witnessed what had happened, more than once, to overzealous officers who had contrived to trample on the toes of the influential. To present his captain with a *fait accompli*, with all the evidence (but of what?) against Heraklion neatly compiled, would be one thing, would almost certainly lead to promotion. To run to him with no more than the vaguest of suspicions, no more than a hunch, actually, could well result in permanent banishment to some dead-end hamlet in the bush.

Nonetheless, an investigation could bring rewards and, if carried out discreetly and on his own time, would not be too risky. After all, there was no law or regulation to debar any citizen from entry to the créche. Now and again, at the instigation of members like Telemachus, the Council had attempted to encourage visits, although with little success. Perhaps a sudden access of parental feeling would look suspicious—but calling to see a friend, one of the children's nurses, would not. Too, Achron himself might have noticed something odd, might even be induced to remember and to talk about it.

"What's biting you, Sergeant?" asked the bored sentry on duty at the barracks gate.

Brasidus started. "Nothing," he said.

"Oh, come off it!" The man who had served with Brasidus for years and was shortly due for promotion himself, could be permitted liberties. "Anybody'd think you had a solid

week's guard duty ahead of you, instead of your free day."
The sentry yawned widely. "How was the dance, by the
way? It's unlike you to be back so early, especially when
you've a morning's lay-in for recuperation."

"So-so."

"Any good fights?"

"I don't know. There seemed to be one starting just as
I left."

"And you didn't join in? You must be sickening for
something. You'd better see a doctor."

"Maybe I'd better. Good night, Leonidas—or should it
be good morning?"

"What does it matter to you? You'll soon be in your
scratcher."

On his way to his sleeping quarters Brasidus had to pass
the duty sergeant's desk. That official looked up as he
approached. "Oh, Brasidus . . ."

"I'm off duty, Lysander."

"A policeman is never off duty—especially one who is
familiar with the routine for spaceport guard duties." He
consulted a pad on his desk. "You, with six constables, are
to present yourself at the port at 0600 hours. The men have
already been checked off for the duty, and arrangements
have been made to have you all called. You'd better get
some sleep."

"But there's no ship due. Not for months."

"Sergeant Brasidus, you and I are policemen. Neither
of us is an expert on astronautical matters. If the
Latterhaveneers decide to send an unscheduled ship, and
if the Council makes the usual arrangements for its
reception, who are we to demand explanations?"

"It seems . . . odd."

"You're a creature of routine, Brasidus. That's your trouble. Off with you now, and get some sleep."

Once he had undressed and dropped onto the hard, narrow bed in his cubicle he did, rather to his surprise, fall almost at once into a dreamless slumber. And it seemed that only seconds had elapsed when an orderly called him at 0445 hours.

A cold shower completed the arousing process. He got into his black and silver uniform tunic, buckled on his heavy sandals and then, plumed helmet under his arm, made his way to the mess hall. He was the first one there. He looked with some distaste at the already laid table—the crusty bread, the joints of cold meat, the jugs of weak beer. But he was hungry, and pulled up a form and began his meal. As he was eating, the six constables of his detail came in. He nodded in greeting as they muttered sullenly, "Morning, Sergeant." Then, "Don't waste any time," he admonished. "They'll be waiting for us at the spaceport."

"Let 'em wait," growled one of the latecomers. He threw a gnawed bone in the general direction of the trash bucket, missed.

"That's enough from you, Hector. I hear that there's a vacancy for village policeman at Euroka. Want me to recommend you?"

"No. Their beer's lousier even than this, and they can't make wine."

"Then watch your step, that's all."

The men got slowly to their feet, wiping their mouths on the back of their hands, halfheartedly dusting the crumbs from the fronts of their tunics. They took their

helmets from the hooks on the wall, put them on, then
filed slowly from the mess hall to the duty sergeant's desk.
He was waiting for them, already had the armory door
unlocked. From it he took, one by one, seven belts, each
with two holsters. So, thought Brasidus, this is an actual
spaceship landing. Staves and short swords were good
enough for ordinary police duties. As the belts were being
buckled on, the duty sergeant produced the weapons to
go with them. "One stun gun," he muttered, passing them
out. "One projectile pistol. To be used only in extreme
urgency. But you know the drill, Sergeant."

"I know the drill, Sergeant," replied Brasidus.

"We should," grumbled Hector, "by this time."

"I'm telling you," explained the duty sergeant with
ominous patience, "so that if you do something silly, which
is all too possible, you won't be able to say that you
weren't told not to do it." He came out from behind the
desk, inspected the detail. "A fine body of men, Sergeant
Brasidus," he declaimed sardonically. "A credit to the
Army. I don't think. But you'll do, I suppose. There'll be
nobody there to see you but a bunch of scruffy
Latterhaven spacemen."

"What if they aren't from Latterhaven?" asked
Brasidus. He was almost as surprised by his question as
was the duty sergeant.

"Where else can they be from? Do you think that the
gods have come all the way from Olympus to pay us a call?"

But if the gods came, it would be, presumably, on the
wings of a supernal storm. It would not be a routine spaceship arrival—routine, that is, save for its unscheduled
nature.

The men were silent during the ride to the spaceport.

Air-cushioned, the police transport sped smoothly over the cobbled streets of the city, the rough roads of the countryside. Dawn was not far off and already the harpies were uttering their raucous cries in the branches of the medusa trees. One of the birds, its wings whirring about its globular body, swept down from its perch and fluttered ahead of the driver's cab, squawking discordantly. The vehicle swerved. Hector cursed, pulled his projectile pistol, fired. The report was deafening in the still air. The harpy screamed for the last time and fell, a bloody tangle of membrane and cartilage, by the side of the road.

"Was that necessary, hoplite?" asked Brasidus coldly.

"You heard what Sergeant Lysander told us, Sergeant." The man leered. "This was an emergency."

Only a bird, thought Brasidus. Only a stupid bird. Even so . . . He asked himself, Am I getting soft? But I can't be. Not in this job. And in all my relationships I'm the dominant partner.

The spaceport was ahead now, its latticework control tower looming starkly against the brightening yellow of the eastern sky. Atop the signal mast there was flashing the intense green light that warned of incoming traffic. A ship was due. *Latterhaven Venus* or *Latterhaven Hera*? And what would either of them be doing here off season?

The car halted at the main gates, sitting there on the cloud of dust blown up and around it by its ducts. The guard on duty did not leave his box, merely actuated the mechanism that opened the gateway, waved the police through. As they drove to the Spaceport Security Office, Brasidus saw that the inner barrier was being erected on the concrete apron. He noticed, too, that only one conveyor belt had been rigged, indicating that there would be very little cargo either to load or to discharge. That, at this time of the year, made sense. But why should the ship be coming here at all?

They were outside the office now. The car stopped, subsided to the ground as its fans slowed to a halt. The constables jumped out, followed Brasidus into the building. To meet them there was Diomedes—corpulent, pallid, with a deceptively flabby appearance—the security captain. He returned Brasidus' smart salute with a casual wave of his pudgy hand. "Ah, yes. The guard detail. The usual drill, Sergeant. You're on duty until relieved. Nobody, Spartan or spaceman, to pass through the barrier either way without the Council's written authority." He glanced at the wall clock. "For your information, the ship is due at 0700 hours. You may stand down until 0650."

"Very good, sir. Thank you, sir," snapped Brasidus. "If I may ask, sir, which of the two ships is it?"

"You may ask, Sergeant. But I'm just Security. Nobody ever tells me anything." He relented slightly. "If you must know, it's neither of the two regular ships. It's some wagon with the most unlikely name of *Seeker III.*"

"Not like the Latterhaveneers to omit the name of their precious planet," muttered somebody.

"But, my dear fellow, the ship's not from Latterhaven. That's the trouble. And now, Sergeant, if you'll come with me I'll try to put you into the picture. It's a pity that nobody's put me into it first."

»))«Chapter 4»))«

The ship not from Latterhaven was no more than a glittering speck in the cloudless morning sky when Diomedes, followed by Brasidus and the six hoplites, marched out from the office onto the apron, to the wire mesh barrier that had been erected to define and enclose the strange vessel's landing place. It was no more than a speck, but it was expanding rapidly, and the rhythmic beat of the inertial drive, faint to begin with, was becoming steadily louder.

Old Cleon, the port master, was there, his long white hair streaming out in the breeze. With him were other officials, one of whom carried a portable transceiver. Brasidus could overhear both ends of the conversation. He learned little; it was no more than the exchange of messages to be expected with standard landing procedure. Cleon himself did not seem to be very interested. He turned to Diomedes. "Most unprecedented!" he complained. "Most unprecedented. Had it not been for the

Council's direct orders I should have refused permission to land."

"It's not a very large ship," said Diomedes, squinting upwards.

"Large enough. Too large, for an intruder. Those rebels on Latterhaven might have let us know that they've discovered and colonized other habitable planets."

"They, too, must have a security service," said Diomedes. "Secrets, secrets! How can I run a spaceport when nobody ever tells me anything? Answer me that, Captain!"

"Descending under full control, to area designated," reported the man with the transceiver.

Diomedes turned to his men. "I've told Sergeant Brasidus all that I know, and he's passed it on to you. So keep alert. We're not expecting any hostile action—but be ready for it. That's all."

Brasidus checked the freedom of his weapons in their holsters. The others followed his example.

Lower dropped the ship, lower. Even with nothing against which to measure her, it could be seen that she was small—only half the size, perhaps, of *Latterhaven Venus* or *Latterhaven Hera*. The gold letters embossed on her side were now readable. "*SEEKER III.*" (And what, wondered Brasidus, of *Seeker I* and *Seeker II?*) And above the name there was a most peculiar badge or symbol. A stylized harpy it looked like—a winged globe surmounted by a five-pointed star. It was nothing like the conventional golden rocker worn on Latterhaven uniforms.

The ship came at last between the waiting men and the rising sun, casting a long, chill shadow. The throbbing of its engines made speech impossible. And then, suddenly augmenting their beat, there was the drone of other machinery. Slowly, majestically, no less than six of the great airships of the Spartan Navy sailed over the spaceport and then, in line ahead, circled the landing field. Their arrival was clearly not fortuitous. Should *Seeker*'s crew attempt any hostile action they, and their ship, would be destroyed by a shower of high-explosive bombs—as would be, Brasidus realized, the military ground party and the port officials. The same thought must have occurred to Diomedes. The portly captain looked even unhappier than usual and muttered, "Nobody ever tells me anything."

With a crunch of metal on concrete the ship landed, an elongated ovoid quivering on her vaned landing gear, in spite of its bulk somehow conveying the impression that the slightest puff of wind could blow it away. Then, as the engines were shut down, it ceased to vibrate, settled down solidly. There was a loud crack and a jagged fissure appeared in the scarred concrete of the apron. But the strange vessel was not especially heavy. The initial damage had been caused by a clumsy landing of *Latterhaven Hera*, and Cleon, with months in which to make the necessary repairs, still hadn't gotten around to it.

Slowly an airlock door toward the stern of the ship opened. From it, tonguelike, an extensible ramp protruded, wavered, then sought and found the ground. There were beings standing in the airlock chamber. Were they human? Brasidus had read imaginative stories about odd, intelligent lifeforms evolved on other planets—and, after all, this ship could be proof that there were more habitable planets than Sparta and Latterhaven in the universe. Yes, they seemed to be human. Nevertheless, the Sergeant's hands did not stray far from the butts of his holstered weapons.

Somebody was coming down the ramp, a man whose attire bore no resemblance to the carelessly informal rig of the Latterhaven spacemen. There was gold on his visored cap, and a double row of gold buttons on his odd tunic, and bands of gold on the sleeves of it. His black trousers were not the shapeless coverings worn for warmth and protection in the hill country, but were shaped to his legs and sharply creased. His black, highly polished footwear afforded complete coverage—and must be, thought Brasidus, wriggling his toes, extremely uncomfortable. He reached the ground, turned and made a gesture toward the open doorway. Another man came out of the airlock, followed the first one to the ground. He, although his uniform was similar, was dressed more sensibly, with a knee-length black kilt instead of the constricting trousers.

But was it a man, or was it some kind of alien? Brasidus once again recalled those imaginative stories, and the assumption made by some writers that natives of worlds with thin atmospheres would run to abnormal (by Spartan standards) lung development. This being, then, could be deformed, or a mutant, or an alien. Somebody muttered, "What an odd-looking creature!"

Walking with calm deliberation the two men approached the barrier. The one with the trousered legs called, "Anybody here speak English?" He turned to his companion and said, "That was a silly question to which I should get a silly answer. After all, we've been nattering to them on RT all the way in."

"We speak Greek," answered Diomedes.

The spaceman looked puzzled. "I'm afraid that I don't. But your English is very good. If you don't mind, it will have to do."

"But we have been speaking Greek all the time."

"Something odd here. But skip it. Allow me to introduce myself. I am Lieutenant Commander John Grimes, Interstellar Federation Survey Service. This lady is Doctor Margaret Lazenby, our ethologist . . ."

Lady, thought Brasidus. Then he must be a member of some other race. The Ladies? I wonder where they come from . . . And such odd names—Johngrimes, Margaretlazenby. But the Latterhaveneers go in for odd names, too.

Diomedes was making his own self-introduction. "I am Diomedes, Captain of Spaceport Security. Please state your business, Johngrimes."

"I've already done so. And, as you must know, I received clearance to land."

"Then state your business again, Johngrimes."

"All right. We're carrying out the census in this sector of space. Of course, your cooperation isn't compulsory, but it will be appreciated."

"That is a matter for the King and his Council, Lieutenant Commander."

"We can wait. Meanwhile, I'd like to comply with all the usual regulations and clear my ship inwards. I'm ready to receive the officers from Port Health and Customs as soon as you like."

"We have no need for them here, Lieutenant Commander Johngrimes. My orders are that you and your crew stay on your side of the barrier until such time as you lift off."

The strange-looking man was talking to the spaceship commander in a high, angry voice. "But this is impossible, Commander. How can we carry out any sort of survey in these conditions? They distinctly told us that we could land—and now they turn their spaceport into a prison camp just for our benefit. Do something, Commander."

Brasidus saw the Captain's prominent ears redden. Nonetheless, he replied mildly enough, "But this is their world, Miss Lazenby. We're only guests."

"Guests? Prisoners, you mean. A wire barrier around us, and a fleet of antique gasbags cruising over us. Guests, you say!"

Strange, thought Brasidus, how this peculiar-looking spaceman appears attractive when he's in a bad temper, while poor Achron and his like just get more and more repulsive . . . And why do I compare him to Achron and the others? A finer bone structure, perhaps, and a more slender body—apart from that shocking deformity—and a higher voice?

"Quiet, please!" The owner of the shocking deformity subsided. Johngrimes turned again to the barrier. "Captain Diomedes, I request that you get in touch with some higher authority. I am here on Federation business."

"What federation?" asked Diomedes.

"You don't know? You really don't know?"

"No. But, of course, I'm Security, so nobody ever tells me anything."

"What a bloody planet," murmured Margaretlazenby. "What a bloody planet!"

"That will do, Peggy," admonished Johngrimes.

And how many names do these people have? Brasidus asked himself. Through the wire mesh of the barrier he stared curiously at the Lady. He must be some sort of alien, he thought. And yet . . . Margaretlazenby, suddenly conscious of his stare, blushed, then returned his gaze in a cool, appraising manner that, fantastically, brought the blood flooding to the skin of his own face.

≫«Chapter 5»«≪

Brasidus flushed as he met the spaceman's appraising—and somehow approving—stare. He heard him murmur to his captain, "Buy that one for me, Daddy," and heard Johngrimes reply, "Peggy, you're incorrigible. Get back on board at once."

"But I am the ethologist, John."

"No need to get wrapped up in your work. Get back on board."

"Yes, sir. Very good, sir. Aye, aye, sir."

He looked at Brasidus for a long, last time and then turned with a flounce of kilts. The movement of his hips and full buttocks as he mounted the ramp was disturbing.

"Now, perhaps," said the Commander, "we can get down to business. I may be old-fashioned, but I've never cared much for a mixed crew."

"So it's true, Lieutenant Commander," Diomedes said. "So you aren't from Latterhaven."

"Of course not. We shall be calling there after we've

finished here. But tell me, what made the penny drop so suddenly?" He grinned. "Or should I have said 'obol'?"

"You speak strangely, Johngrimes. What do you mean?"

"Just a figure of speech. Don't you have automatic vendors? No? What I meant was this: Why should my mention of a mixed crew suddenly convince you that my claim that this is a Federation ship is correct?"

Diomedes did not answer at once. He glared around at Cleon and his aides, at Brasidus and his men. He growled, "You all of you have ears—unluckily. You all of you have heard far too much. But you will not speak of it. To anybody. I need not remind you of what has happened in the past to men who have breached Security." He turned back to the space captain. "Your arrival here, Lieutenant Commander, has rather upset our notions of cosmogony. It is now a matter for the Council—and for the Council only."

"But why did the penny drop?" persisted Johngrimes.

"Because you have brought evidence that there is more than one intelligent race in the universe. At first we thought that your Margaretlazenby was deformed—on this world, of course, he would have been exposed immediately after birth—and then you told us that you have a mixed crew."

The Commander stared at Diomedes incredulously. He said at last, "Of course, it has been said more than once, not altogether in jest, that they aren't really human . . . But tell me, Captain Diomedes, do you actually mean what I think you mean? Haven't you anybody like her on your Planet?"

"Like what, Lieutenant Commander?"

"Like her. Like Doctor Lazenby."

"Of course not. We are all human here. As we should be, Sparta being the birthplace of the human race."

"You really mean that?"

"Of course," replied Diomedes.

But does he? wondered Brasidus, who had worked with the Security Captain before.

"And you have no . . . ?" began the spaceman, then pulled himself up abruptly. Brasidus recognized the signs. Find out all you can, but give nothing away yourself.

"We have no what?" prompted Diomedes.

Johngrimes made a quick recovery. "No Immigration, no Customs, no Port Health?"

"I've already told you that, Lieutenant Commander. And I've already told you that you and your crew must remain confined to your ship."

"Then perhaps you would care to come aboard, Captain Diomedes, to talk things over."

"Not by myself—and not unarmed."

"You may bring one man with you," said Johngrimes slowly. "But both of you will leave your weapons this side of the barrier."

"We could board by force," said Diomedes.

"Could you? I think not. *Seeker* may be carrying out the Census, but she's still a frigate, with a frigate's armament. In a matter of seconds we could sweep this field—and the sky over the field—clear of life. This is not a threat, merely a statement of fact." The words carried conviction.

Diomedes hesitated. "Very well," he said at last. He looked up to the circling airships as though for reassurance, shook his head doubtfully. He addressed Cleon, "Port Master, please have your radioman inform the Flight Admiral of my movements." He turned to Brasidus, "Sergeant, you may come with me. Leave Leading Hoplite Hector in charge."

Brasidus got close enough to Diomedes so that he could speak in a low, urgent whisper. "But, sir, the standing orders . . . the passes, to be signed by a member of the Council . . ."

"And who do you think drew up those standing orders, Sergeant? I am Security." Diomedes unlocked the gate with a key from his belt pouch. "Come with me."

"Your weapons," reminded Johngrimes.

Diomedes sighed, unbuckled his belt with its two holstered pistols, passed it to one of the men. Brasidus followed suit. The Sergeant felt naked, far more so than when stripped for the dance or for field sports. He knew that he still retained one weapon in the use of which he was, as were all members of the police branch of the Army, superbly trained—his body. But he missed those smooth, polished wooden butts that fitted so snugly into his hands. Even a despised sword or spear would have been better than nothing.

Ahead of them, Johngrimes was walking briskly toward the open airlock door, toward the foot of the ramp. Diomedes and Brasidus followed. They could see, as they neared the vessel, that the odd excrescences on its skin were gun turrets, that from at least two of them slender barrels were trained upon them, following them, that from others heavier weapons tracked the circling airships.

Johngrimes was taking no chances.

Although he had been often enough on spaceport guard duties, this was the first time that Brasidus had been aboard a spaceship; usually it was only Diomedes who boarded visiting vessels. Mounting the ramp, the Sergeant eyed professionally the little group of officers waiting just inside the airlock. They all carried sidearms, and they all looked competent enough. Even so, thought Brasidus, they'll not be able to use their pistols for fear of hitting each other. The knee to the groin, the edge of the hand to the neck . . .

"Better not," said Diomedes, reading his subordinate's face.

"Better not," said Johngrimes, turning back to look at the pair of them. "An incident could have unfortunate—for your planet—repercussions."

Better not, thought Brasidus.

Soldierlike, he approved the smartness with which the spacemen saluted their commander. And soldierlike, he did not like the feel of a deck under his feet instead of solid ground. Nonetheless, he looked about him curiously. He was disappointed. He had been expecting, vaguely, vistas of gleaming machines, all in fascinating motion, banks of fluorescing screens, assemblages of intricate instruments. But all that there was was a little metal-walled room, cubical except for the curvature of its outer side, and beyond that another little room, shaped like a wedge of pie with a bite out of its narrow end.

But there must be more to the ship than this.

An officer pressed a button on the far, inwardly curved wall of the inside room. A door slid aside, revealing yet another little compartment, cylindrical this time.

Johngrimes motioned to his guests—or hostages? Diomedes (but he was familiar with spaceships) entered this third room without any hesitation. Apprehensively Brasidus followed him, with Johngrimes bringing up the rear.

"Don't worry," said Diomedes to Brasidus. "This is only an elevator."

"An . . . an elevator?"

"It elevates you. Is that correct, Lieutenant Commander?"

"It is, Captain Diomedes." Johngrimes turned to Brasidus. "At the moment, we are inside the axial shaft— a sort of hollow column running almost the full length of the ship. This cage that we've just entered will carry us up to my quarters. We never use it, of course, in free fall— only during acceleration or on a planetary surface."

"Do you have machines to do the work of your legs, sir?"

"Why not, Sergeant?"

"Isn't that . . . decadent?"

The spaceship commander laughed. "Men have been saying that ever since the first lazy and intelligent bastard invented the wheel. Tell me, did you march out from the city to the spaceport, or did you ride?"

"That's different, sir," said Brasidus lamely.

"Like hell it is." Johngrimes pressed a button. The door slid shut. And almost immediately Brasidus experienced an odd, sinking sensation in his stomach. He knew that the cage was in motion, felt that it was upward motion. Fascinated, he watched the lights flashing in succession on the panel by the door—and almost lost his balance when the elevator slowed to a stop.

The door slid open again, revealing a short stretch of alleyway. Still there were no machines, no instruments— but the air was alive with the subdued murmur of machinery.

Brasidus had likened the ship to a metallic tower, but this was not like being inside a building. It was like being inside a living organism.

⫷⫸《Chapter 6》⫷⫸

"Come in," said John Grimes, pushing a button that opened another sliding door. "As a very dear friend of mine used to say, this is Liberty Hall. You can spit on the mat and call the cat a bastard."

"Cat?" asked Brasidus, ignoring an admonitory glare from Diomedes. "Bastard? What are they?" He added, "It's the second time you've used that last word, sir."

"You must forgive my Sergeant's unmannerly curiosity, Lieutenant Commander," said Diomedes.

"A healthy trait, Captain. After all, you are both policemen." He smiled rather grimly. "So am I, in a manner of speaking . . . But sit down, both of you."

Brasidus remained standing until he received a grudging nod from his superior. Then he was amazed by the softness, by the comfort of the chair into which he lowered himself. On Sparta such luxury was reserved for the aged—and only for the highly placed aged at that, for Council members and the like. This lieutenant commander was not an old man, probably no older than Brasidus himself. Yet here he was, housed in quarters that the King might envy. The room in which Johngrimes was entertaining him and Diomedes was not large, but it was superbly appointed. There were the deep easy chairs, fitted with peculiar straps, there was a wall-to-wall carpet, indigo in color, with a deep pile, there were drapes, patterned blue, that obviously concealed other doorways, and there were pictures set on the polished paneling of the walls. They were like no paintings or photographs that Brasidus had ever seen. They glowed, seemingly, with a light of their own. They were three-dimensional. They were like little windows on to other worlds.

Brasidus could not help staring at the one nearest to him. It could have been a typical scene on his own Sparta—distant, snow-capped peaks in the background, blue water and yellow sand, then, in the foreground, the golden-brown bodies of naked athletes.

But . . .

Brasidus looked more closely. Roughly half of the figures were human—and the rest of them were like this mysterious Margaretlazenby. So that was what he must look like unclothed. The deformity of the upper part of the body was bad enough; that of the lower part was shocking.

"Arcadia," said Johngrimes. "A very pleasant planet. The people are enthusiastic nudists—but, of course, they have the climate for it."

"We," said Diomedes, turning his attention to the picture from the one that he had been studying, a bleak, mountain range in silhouette against a black sky, "exercise naked in all weathers."

"You would," replied Johngrimes lightly.

"So," went on Diomedes after a pause, "this Margaretlazenby of yours is an Arcadian." He got to his feet to study the hologram more closely. "H'm. How do they reproduce? Oddly enough, I have seen the same deformation on the bodies of some children who have been exposed. Coincidence, of course."

"You Spartans live up to your name," said Johngrimes coldly.

"I don't see what you mean, Lieutenant Commander. But no matter. I think I begin to understand. These Arcadians are a subject race—intelligent but nonhuman, good enough to serve in subordinate capacities, but temperamentally, at least, unqualified for full command."

"Doctor Lazenby was born on Arcadia. It's a good job she's not here to listen to you saying that."

"But it's true, isn't it? H'm. What amazes and disgusts me about this picture is the way in which humans are mingling with these . . . these aliens on terms of apparent equality."

"I suppose you could look at it that way."

"Here, even though we are all Men, we are careful not to be familiar with any but privileged helots. And these Arcadians are aliens."

"Some time," said Johngrimes, "I must make a careful study of your social history. It should be fascinating. Although that is really Peggy's job."

"Peggy?"

"Doctor Lazenby."

"And some time," said Diomedes, "I must make inquiries as to your system of nomenclature. I have heard you call this Margaretlazenby by his rank and profession, with the first part of his name missing. And I have heard you call him Peggy."

Johngrimes laughed. "I suppose that it is rather confusing to people who have only one name apiece. We have at least two—the surname, or family name . . ."

"But there is only one family. The State."

"On Sparta, perhaps. But let me finish, Captain Diomedes. We have the family name, which, with us, comes last, although some human races put it first. Then we have one, if not more, given name. Then we have nicknames. For example, Margaret, one word, Lazenby, one word. Peggy, which for some obscure reason is a corruption of Margaret. Of course, she could also be called Maggie or Meg. Or Peg. In my own case—John Grimes. But that 'John' can be changed to 'Jack' or 'Johnnie' by people who really know me."

"Like Theo for Theopompus," contributed Brasidus.

"Yes. Some of our nicknames are curtailments, like Margie or Margo for Margaret."

"How many names has that being got?" exploded Diomedes.

"I've heard her called other things—and called her them myself. But you wouldn't know what a bitch is, would you?"

"Doubtless some exotic beast you've run across on your travels. But, Lieutenant Commander, you keep on using these odd pronouns—'she' and 'her.' Are they confined to Arcadians?"

"You could say that." Grimes seemed to he amused by something. "Now, gentlemen, may I offer you refreshment?

The sun's not yet over the yardarm, but a drop of alcohol won't kill us. Or would you rather have coffee?"

"Coffee? What's that?"

"Don't you have it here? Perhaps you would like to try some now."

"If you partake with us," said Diomedes cautiously.

"But of course." Grimes got to his feet, went to his desk, picked up a telephone. "Pantry? Captain here. I'd like my coffee now, please. Large pot, with all the trimmings. Three cups."

He took an oddly shaped wooden . . . instrument (?) off the desk top, stuffed a hollow bowl at the end of it with what looked like a dried brown weed, put the thin stem in his mouth, applied a flame from a little metal contraption to the open top of the bowl. He inhaled with apparent pleasure, then expelled from between his lips a cloud of fragrant fumes. "Sorry," he said, "do you smoke?" He opened an ornamental box, displaying rows of slim cylinders obviously rolled from the brown weed.

"I think that one strange luxury will be enough for one day, Lieutenant Commander," said Diomedes, to Brasidus' disappointment.

The door to the outside alleyway opened. A spaceman came in, by his uniform not an officer, carrying a large silver tray on which rested a steaming silver pot, a silver jug and a silver bowl filled with some white powder, and also three cups of gleaming, crested porcelain each standing in its own little plate. But it was not the tray at which Diomedes and Brasidus stared; it was at the bearer.

He was obviously yet another Arcadian.

Brasidus glanced from him to the picture, and back

again. He realized that he was wondering what the spaceman would look like stripped of that severe, functional
clothing.

"Milk, sir? Sugar?" the man was asking.

"I don't think that they have them on this planet,
Sheila," said Grimes. "There's quite a lot that they don't
have."

﹒⫻⫻Chapter 7⫻⫻﹒

Slowly Diomedes and Brasidus made their way down the ramp from the airlock. Both were silent, and the Sergeant, at least, was being hard put to sort and to evaluate the multitude of new impressions that had crowded upon him. The coffee—could it be a habit-forming drug? But it was good. And that burning weed the fumes of which Lieutenant Commander Grimes had inhaled with such enjoyment. And the un-Spartan luxury in which Grimes lived—luxury utterly unsuitable for a fighting man. And this Interstellar Federation, an officer of whose navy—although it was called the Survey Service—he claimed to be.

And those oddly disturbing Arcadians (if they were Arcadians)—the doctor Lazenby, the steward Sheila, and one or two more whom the Spartans had glimpsed on their way ashore . . .

They were out of earshot of the ship now, halfway between the airlock and the gate, outside which Hector and the other hoplites had stiffened to attention.

Diomedes said, "Come to my office, Sergeant. I want to talk things over with you. There's a lot that I don't understand, but much of it strengthens my suspicions."

"Of whom, sir? This Lieutenant Commander Grimes?"

"No. He's just a spaceman, the same as Captain Bill and Captain Jim of the Venus and the Hera. If his service prefers to tack a double-barreled label on him, that's his worry. Oh, I want to find out where the ship is from and what's the real reason for its visit, but my main suspicions are much nearer home."

They passed through the gate, opened for them and locked after them by Hector. Old Cleon approached them, was brushed off by Diomedes. They continued their march to the office, although in the case of Diomedes it was more of a waddle.

"In my job," went on the Security Captain, buckling on his pistol belt as he walked, "I'm no respecter of persons. I shouldn't be earning my pay if I were." He gestured upwards. "Flight Admiral Ajax up there, for example. He holds his rank—and his life—only because I do not choose to act yet. When I do . . ." He closed his pudgy fist decisively and suggestively. "You're an ambitious man, Brasidus. And an intelligent one. I've had my eye on you for some time. I have been thinking of asking to have you transferred to Security. And when Diomedes asks, people hurry to oblige him."

"Thank you, sir."

"With promotion to lieutenant, of course."

"Thank you, sir."

"Think nothing of it. I need a young assistant for the . . . the legwork." He smiled, showing all his uneven, discolored teeth, obviously pleased with the expression that he had just coined. "The legwork," he repeated.

The two men entered the Spaceport Security Office, passed through into Diomedes' private room. At the Captain's order, Brasidus sat down. The chair was hard, comfortless, yet he felt far happier on it than he had felt in the luxury of Lieutenant Commander Grimes' day cabin. Diomedes produced a flagon of beer, two mugs. He poured. "To our . . . partnership," he said.

"To our partnership, sir."

"Now, Lieutenant Brasidus, what I am saying to you is strictly confidential. I need not remind you of the consequences to yourself if you abuse my confidence. To begin with, I played along with this man Grimes. I asked the silly questions that he'd assume that I would ask. But I formed my own conclusions."

"And what were they, sir?"

"Oh, I'm not telling you yet, young Brasidus. I could be wrong—and I want your mind to remain uninfluenced by any theories of mine. But they tie in, they tie in. They tie in with the most heinous crime of all—treason to the State. Now, tell me, who're the most powerful men on Sparta?"

"The most powerful man is the King, sir."

Diomedes' thin eyebrows lifted, arching over his muddy eyes. "Is he? But no matter. And I said 'the most powerful men'."

"The Council, sir."

"H'm. Could be. Could be. But . . ."

"What are you driving at, sir?"

"What about the doctors, our precious medical

priesthood? Don't they control the birth machines? Don't they decide who among the newly born is to live, and who, to die? Don't they conduct the fatherhood tests? Don't they say, in effect, that there shall be so many members of the military caste, so many helots—and so many doctors?"

"Yes. That's so, sir. But how could they be traitors?"

"Opportunity, dear boy. Opportunity. Opportunity for a betrayal of the principles upon which our State was founded. Frankly, although I have long harbored suspicions, I did not really think that it was possible until the man Grimes landed here with his ship and his mixed crew. Now I realize the evil spell that can be exerted by those . . . creatures."

"What creatures?" demanded Brasidus as impatiently as he dared.

"The Arcadians? Yes—that's as good a name as any." He refilled the mugs. "Now, I have to make my report and my recommendations to the Council. When Grimes made his first psionic contact with the spaceport authorities, before he reentered normal Space-Time, he requested permission to land and to take a census, and also to carry out ecological and ethological surveys. Ethology, by the way, is the science of behavior. I learned that much, although I've been making use of its principles for years. Later he confirmed this by normal radio—psionic reception at this end was rather garbled as our telepaths were completely unfamiliar with so many new concepts.

"As you well know, after your many spells of spaceport guard duty, it has always been contrary to Council policy to allow visiting spacemen to mingle with our population. But I shall recommend that in this case an exception be made, arguing that Grimes and his men are quite harmless, also that the Federation—yes, I'm afraid that there is one—is obviously powerful and might take offense if its servants are not hospitably received.

"My real reason for the recommendation I shall keep to myself."

"And what is it, sir?"

"When a pot boils, Brasidus, all sorts of scum comes to the top. A few . . . Arcadians running around on Sparta might well bring the pot to the boil. And who will get scalded? That is the question."

"You don't like the doctors, Captain?"

"That I do not. I am hoping that those whom I suspect of treason will be forced to act—and to act rashly."

"There is something suspicious about them—or about some of them." Briefly, but omitting nothing, Brasidus told Diomedes of his encounter with Heraklion in the créche. "He was hiding something," he concluded. "I am sure of that."

"And you're ideally situated to find out what it was, Brasidus." Diomedes was thoughtful. "This is the way that we shall play it. Officially you are still a sergeant in the Police Battalion. Your pay will be made up, however, to lieutenant's rates out of Security funds. You will be relieved of spaceport guard duties. You will discover, in fact, that your captain will be allowing you considerable free time—free insofar as he is concerned. As far as I am concerned, it will not be so free. Off duty, you will be able to visit your friend Achron at the créche. I already knew of your friendship with him, as a matter of fact—that was one of the reasons why I was considering having you transferred to my Branch. One of the nurses might have been a better recruit—but their loyalties are so unreliable. On duty, you will act as escort to Lieutenant Commander Grimes and his officers.

"And you will report to me everything—and I mean everything—you learn."

"And what shall I learn, sir?"

"You'll be surprised. It could be that I shall be, too." He picked up the telephone on his desk, ordered his car brought round to the office. Then he said to Brasidus, "Give Hector his instructions. He can carry on until relieved. Then you can ride with me back to the city."

»«(Chapter 8»)«

Back in the city, Diomedes had his driver proceed directly to the police barracks. There, with no trouble, he obtained an interview with Brasidus' commanding officer. Brasidus, sitting on the hard bench outside the captain's office, wondered what was being said about him. Then the door opened and he was called in.

He looked at the two men confronting him—the squat, somehow squalid Diomedes, the tall, soldierly Lycurgus. Diomedes looked smugly satisfied, Lycurgus, resentful. There could be no doubt as to how things had gone—and, suddenly, Brasidus hoped that he would not regret this change of masters.

"Sergeant—or should I say Lieutenant?" growled Lycurgus. "I think that you already know of your transfer. Officially, however, you are still a sergeant and you are still working for me. Your real orders, however, will come from Captain Diomedes." He paused, then went on, "You are relieved from duty until 0800 hours tomorrow

49

morning, at which time you are to report to the spaceport."
He turned to Diomedes. "He's all yours, Diomedes."

"Thank you, Lycurgus. You may accompany me,
Brasidus."

They left the office. Diomedes asked, "And when is
your friend Achron on duty again, young man?"

"He has the midnight to 0600 shift for the rest of this
week, sir."

"Good. Then I propose that you spend the rest of the
day at leisure; after all, this was supposed to be your
free time, wasn't it? Get some sleep this evening before
midnight—you might visit Achron again then. Of course,
you will report to me at the spaceport tomorrow morning.
I have no doubt that I shall be able to persuade the
Council to accede to Lieutenant Commander Grimes'
requests, so you will be required for escort duties."

"And when I visit Achron, sir? Am I to carry out any
investigations?"

"Yes. But cautiously, cautiously. Find out what you can
without sticking your neck out. But I must leave you now.
I have to report to my lords and masters." His sardonic
intonation left no doubt in Brasidus' mind as to who was
the real lord and master.

Brasidus went to the mess hall for a late and solitary
luncheon of bread, lukewarm stew and beer. Then,
conscious of his new (but secret) rank and his new
responsibilities, he decided to visit the library. There were
books, of course, in the recreation hall of the barracks,
but these were mainly works of fiction, including the
imaginative thrillers that were his favorite reading. (But
none of the writers had imagined monsters so fantastic as

these Arcadians—fantastic because of similarities to as well as differences from normal humankind.) He was in uniform still, but that did not matter. However, there was his belt, with its holstered pistols. He went to the desk sergeant to turn it in.

"Keep it, Brasidus," he was told. "Captain Lycurgus said that you were on instant call as long as the spaceship's in port."

It made sense—just as the regulation forbidding the carrying of firearms when not on duty made sense; they might be used in a drunken brawl at one of the Clubs. However, Brasidus always felt happier when armed and so did not inquire further. He went out into the street, his iron-tipped sandals ringing on the cobbles. He stood on the sidewalk to watch a troop of armored cavalry pass, the tracks of the chariots striking sparks from the paving, the gay pennons whipping from the slender radio masts, the charioteers in their plumed helmets standing tall and proud in their turrets.

Cavalry in the city. The Council must be apprehensive.

Brasidus continued his walk when the chariots had gone by. He strode confidently up the wide stone steps to the white-pillared library entrance, but inside the cool building diffidence assailed him. An elderly man behind a big desk surveyed him disapprovingly, his gaze lingering on the weapons. "Yes, Sergeant?" he demanded coldly.

"I . . . I want to do some reading."

"Unless you've come here to make an arrest, that's obvious. What sort of reading? We do have a thriller section." He made "thriller" sound like a dirty word.

"No, not thrillers. We've plenty of those in our own recreation hall. History."

The bushy white eyebrows lifted. "Oh. Historical thrillers."

"No. Not thrillers." Brasidus was finding it hard to keep his temper. "History."

The old man did not get up from his seat, but turned and pointed. "Through there, Sergeant. That door. If you want to take a book out, you'll have to sign for it and pay a deposit, but there are tables and benches if you want to read on the premises."

"Thank you," said Brasidus.

He went through the door, noted the sign "HISTORICAL SECTION" above it. He stared at the book-lined walls, not knowing where to begin. He walked to the nearer shelves, just inside the doorway, the clatter of his uniform sandals on the marble floor drawing disapproving glares from the half dozen or so readers seated at the tables. But they were only helots, by the looks of them, and their feelings did not matter.

He scanned the row of titles. A History of Sparta, by Alcamenes. That would do to start with. He pulled it from its place on the shelf, carried it to a vacant table, sat down. He adjusted the reading lamp.

Yes, he had been lucky in his random choice. This seemed to be a very comprehensive history—starting, in fact, in prehistorical days. The story it told should not have been new to Brasidus. After all, he had been exposed to a normal education. But he had not paid much attention to his teachers, he had known that he was destined to be a soldier. So, apart from the study of past campaigns, of what value was education to him?

But here it all was. The evolution of a biped from a big-headed quadruped, with forelimbs modified to arms and hands. The slow, slow beginnings of civilization, of organized science. And then, at last, the invention of the birth machine by Lacedaemon, the perfection of the technique by which the father's seed could be brought to maturity apart from his body. No longer hampered by the process of budding, men went ahead by leaps and bounds. Aristodemus, the first King of Sparta, organized and drilled his army and navy, subjugated the other city-states, imposed the name of his capital upon the entire planet, although (even to this day, as Brasidus knew) there were occasional armed revolts.

And there were the scientific advancements. The mechanical branch of the priesthood advanced from aeronautics to astronautics and, under Admiral Latterus, a star fleet was launched, its object being the colonization of a relatively nearby planet. But Latterus was ambitious, set up his own kingdom, and with him he had taken the only priests who knew the secret of the interstellar drive. After many generations the people of Latterhaven—as Latterus' colony had been called—revisited Sparta. A trade agreement was drawn up and signed, complying with which the Latterhaveneers sent two ships every year, bringing various manufactured goods in exchange for shipments of the spices that grew only on Sparta.

Impatiently Brasidus turned to the index. Interstellar Federation. No. Not listed. Interstellar ships, interstellar drive, but no Federation. But that would have been too much to expect. Latterhaven had a history, but its people kept it to themselves. This Admiral Latterus had his ships and, no doubt, one planet had not been enough for him. He had his birth machines—and, even though Brasidus was no biologist, he was sure that it would be possible to accelerate production. The natural way—intercourse between two beings and, possibly, each one budding—was slow and wasteful. Suppose that all the seed were utilized. Then how long would it take to build up teeming populations on a dozen worlds?

Terra, for example.

And Arcadia?

No. Not Arcadia.

But were the Arcadians human? Could they be the result of a malfunction of the birth machine set up on their planet? If this was the case, how could they, with their obvious physical deficiencies, reproduce?

Brasidus looked up Arcadia in the index. It was not, of course, listed.

He put Alcamenes' book back on the shelf, went out to see the old librarian. "Have you," he asked, "anything on the Interstellar Federation? Or on a world called Arcadia?"

"I told you," buffed the ancient man, "that it was fiction you wanted. Science fiction, at that."

"Suppose I told you that there is an Interstellar Federation? Suppose I told you that there are, at present, Arcadians on Sparta?"

"I'd say, young man, that you were quite mad—if it wasn't for your uniform. And it's not that I'm afraid of that, or of the guns you wear into my library. It's because that I know—as who doesn't?—that a strange, unscheduled ship has made a landing at the spaceport. And you're a sergeant in the Police Battalion of the Army, so you know more about what's going on than we poor scholars." He cackled. "Go on, Sergeant. Tell me more. I am always willing to acquire new knowledge."

"What rumors have you heard?" asked Brasidus. After all, he was a Security officer now and might as well start acting like one.

"They say that this ship's a battleship—and, with the Air Navy hanging over the spaceport like a bad smell and the streets full of cavalry, it could well be. They say that the President of Latterhaven has demanded our instant surrender. They say, too, that the ship's not from Latterhaven at all, that it's manned by robots with twin turrets on their chests from which they shoot lethal rays."

"They must be functional . . ." mused Brasidus, "I suppose."

"What must be?" demanded the librarian.

"Those twin turrets. Good day to you."

He clanked out through the wide doorway, down the stone steps.

»《Chapter 9》«

Brasidus walked back to his barracks, thinking over what he had read and what the librarian had told him. It all tied in—almost. But how did it tie in with Diomedes' suspicions of the medical priesthood? Perhaps tonight he would be able to find something out.

In the mess hall he partook of an early evening meal—and still his active brain was working. The spices exported to Latterhaven were a luxury, so much so that they were used but rarely in Spartan cookery. And you can say that again, Brasidus told himself, chewing viciously on his almost flavorless steak. Obviously they were also a luxury on the other planet; otherwise why should the Latterhaveneers find it worthwhile to send two ships every year for the annual shipment? But what did the Latterhaveneers bring in return for the spices? Manufactured goods. But what manufactured goods?

Brasidus, as a spaceport guard, had watched the Latterhaven ships discharging often enough. He had seen the unmarked wooden crates sliding down the conveyor belts into the waiting trucks, had vaguely wondered where these same trucks were bound when, escorted by police chariots, they had left the spaceport. He had made inquiries once, of one of the charioteers whom he knew slightly. "We just convoy them into the city," the man had told him. "They're unloaded at that big warehouse—you know the one, not far from the créche. Andronicus Imports."

And what did Andronicus import?

Diomedes might know.

Finishing his meal, Brasidus wandered into the recreation hall. He bought a mug of sweet wine from the steward on duty, sat down to watch television. There was the news first—but there was no mention of the landing of *Seeker III*. Fair enough. The Council had still to decide what to say about it as well as what to do about it. The main coverage was of the minor war in progress between Pharis and Messenia. Peisander, the Messenian general, was something of an innovator. Cleombrotus of Pharis was conservative, relying upon his hoplites to smash through the Messenian lines, and his casualties, under the heavy fire of the Messenian archers, were heavy. There were those who maintained that the bow should be classed as a firearm and its use forbidden to the ordinary soldiery, those not in the Police Battalion. Of course, if the hoplites, with their spears and swords, got loose among the archers, there would be slaughter. Against that, the archers, lightly armored, far less encumbered, could run much faster. The commentator, hovering above the battlefield, made this same comment, and Brasidus congratulated himself upon his grasp of military principles.

Following the news came a coverage of the games at Helos. Brasidus watched the wrestling bouts for a while, then got up and left the hall. After all, the games were no more than a substitute for war—and war, to every Spartan worth his salt, was the only sport for a man. Nonlethal sports were only for helots.

Finding the duty orderly, the Sergeant gave instructions to be called at 2330 hours.

He was almost at the crèche when he saw a slight form ahead of him. He quickened his pace, overtook the other pedestrian. As he had thought it would be, it was Achron.

The nurse was pleased to see him. He said, "I rang the barracks, Brasidus, and they told me that you were on duty all day."

"I was, but I'm off the hook now."

"You were at the spaceport, weren't you? Is it true that this ship is from outside, with a crew of monsters?"

"Just a ship," Brasidus told him.

"But the monsters?"

"What monsters?"

"Horribly deformed beings from outer space. Mutants."

"Well, Diomedes and myself were entertained on board by the commander, and he's human enough."

"More than you can say for Diomedes," commented Achron spitefully. "I used to like him once, but not any more. Not after what he did."

"What did he do?"

"I'll tell you sometime. Are you coming in, Brasidus?"

"Why not?"

"Telemachus will be pleased. He was saying to me what a fine example you are to the average Spartan."

"Back again, Sergeant?" the old man greeted him. "I shall soon think that you would welcome a return to the bad old days of budding."

"Hardly," said Brasidus, trying to visualize the difficulties that would be experienced in the use of weapons when encumbered by undetached offspring.

"And were you out at the spaceport today, Brasidus?"

"Yes."

"What are they really like, these monsters?"

"Captain Diomedes bound us all to secrecy."

"A pity. A pity. If you were to tell me what you saw, it would never go beyond the walls of this building."

"I'm sorry, Telemachus. You'll just have to wait until the news is released by the Council."

"The Council." The old man laughed bitterly. "In my day there were men of imagination serving on it. But now . . ." He looked up at the wall clock. "Well, in you go. Phillip is waiting for his relief. He was most unpleasant when he discovered that I had detained you this time yesterday."

Brasidus followed his friend to the ward where he was on duty. This time Phillip was in a better mood—and he, too, tried to pump the Sergeant about the day's events at the spaceport. Finally he gave up and left the two friends. As before, Brasidus allowed himself to be led to the sons who might be his own. Yet again he was unable to detect any real resemblance. And then—it was what he had been waiting for—all the babies awoke.

He retreated hastily, as any normal man would have done, leaving Achron to cope. But he did not go to the door by which he had entered, but to the farther doorway.

He waited there for a minute or so, thinking that Doctor Heraklion or one of his colleagues might be attracted by the uproar—but, after all, such noises were common enough in the créche.

But neither Heraklion nor anybody else appeared in the long, dimly lit corridor, and Brasidus decided to venture further afield. He was barefooted, so could walk silently. He was wearing a civilian tunic, which was advantageous. Should anybody who did not know him see him, his appearance would be less likely to cause alarm than if he was in uniform.

Cautiously he advanced along the corridor. His own was the only movement. If there were any sounds, he could not hear them for the bawling behind him. On either side of the corridor there were numbered doors. Storerooms? Laboratories? Cautiously he tried one. It was locked.

He continued his prowl. It was a long corridor, and he did not wish to get too far from the ward—yet this was a golden opportunity to find something out. He came to a cross passageway, hesitated. He saw that a chair was standing just inside the left-hand passage. Presumably it had just been evacuated—there was a book open, face down, on the seat, a flagon and a mug beside it. A guard? If so, not a very good one. No doubt he had some pressing reason for deserting his post—but he would never have done so, at no matter what cost to personal dignity, had he been a member of the military caste. A helot, then—or even a doctor? Heraklion? Brasidus did not know what the man's hours of duty were, but they could coincide with or overlap Achron's.

He picked up the book, looked at the title. *Galactic Spy*, by Delmar Brudd. Yet another of those odd double names. He turned to the title page, saw that the novel had been published by the Phoenix Press, Latterton, on the planet of Latterhaven. So this was a sample of the manufactured goods exported by that planet. But why should these books not be put into general circulation? If it were a question of freight, large editions could easily be printed here on Sparta.

He was suddenly aware that a door was opening. He heard someone say, "I must leave you, dear. After all, it is my turn for sentry duty."

A strange voice replied. It was too high-pitched, held an odd, throaty quality. Yet it was oddly familiar. What—who—did it remind Brasidus of? Even as he slid silently back around the corner—but not before he had replaced the book as he had found it—he had the answer. It sounded like the voice of the Arcadian, Margaret Lazenby. It was certainly not the voice of any native of Sparta.

Still, Brasidus was reluctant to retreat. He continued to peer around the corner, ready to jerk back in a split second. "I prefer you to the others, Heraklion," the Arcadian was saying.

"I'm flattered, Sally. But you shouldn't have come to me. It's very dangerous. If Orestes found that I'd deserted my post, there'd be all hell let loose. And besides . . ."

"Besides what?"

"Only last night—or, rather, yesterday morning—that revolting young pansy Achron had his boyfriend with him in the ward—and this same boyfriend is a police sergeant. A dumb one, luckily. Even so, we have to be careful."

"But why, Heraklion, why? You're priests as well as doctors. You control this planet. It would be easy for you to engineer a rough parity of the numbers of men and women—and then just let Nature take its course."

"You don't understand . . ."

"That's what you're always saying. But you saw to it that we were educated and drew some farfetched analogy between ourselves and the hetaerae of ancient Greece. I know that we're petted and pampered—but only within these walls. We've never seen outside them. Is that how women live on Latterhaven, on Terra, on all the Man-colonized planets?"

"You don't understand, Sally."

"No. Of course not. I'm only a woman. And it's obvious that you don't want me, so I'm getting back to my own quarters. To the harem." This final word, dripping contempt, was strange to Brasidus.

"As you will."

"And the next time you come to me, I shall be busy."

The door opened properly, but still Brasidus did not withdraw his head. The couple who emerged from the storeroom or whatever it was had their backs to him. The shorter of the pair was dressed in a brief, black tunic woven from some transparent material. His lustrous, auburn hair hung to his smooth, gleaming shoulders and his rounded buttocks gleamed through the flimsy garment. He walked with a peculiarly provocative swing of the hips. Brasidus stared after him—and so, luckily, did Heraklion. Before the doctor could turn, Brasidus withdrew, hurried silently back along the corridor. There were no shouts, no pursuit. The only noise came from the ward, where

Achron—and what was a pansy?—still had not pacified his charges.

Conquering his repugnance, Brasidus went in. "Can I help?" he asked the nurse.

"Oh, you're still here, Brasidus. I thought you'd have run away ages ago. Bring me some bottles from the dispenser, will you? You know how."

Brasidus obeyed. While he was so engaged, Doctor Heraklion strode through the doorway. "Really, Sergeant," snapped, "I can't have this. This is the second time that you've come blundering in here, disturbing our charges. I shall have to complain to your superior."

"I'm sorry, Doctor."

"That isn't good enough, Sergeant. Leave, please. At once."

Brasidus left. He would gain nothing by staying any longer. And perhaps he should telephone Diomedes to tell him what he had learned. But what had he learned? That there was a nest of Arcadian spies already on Sparta? Spies—or infiltrators? Infiltrators—and the doctors working in collusion with them?

And how did that tie in with the visit of *Seeker III*, a vessel with Arcadians in its own crew?

Very well indeed, Brasidus told himself. Very well indeed.

He rang Diomedes from the first telephone booth he came to, but there was no answer. He rang again from the barracks, and there was still no answer. He looked at the time, shrugged his shoulders, went to his cubicle and turned in.

While he was having his breakfast, prior to going out to

the spaceport, Captain Lycurgus sent for him. "Sergeant," he said, "I've received a complaint. About you. From Doctor Heraklion, at the créche. In future, leave his nurses alone in duty hours."

"Very good, sir."

"And one more thing, Brasidus . . ."

"Yes, sir?"

"I shall pass the Doctor's complaint on to Captain Diomedes. I understand that he gives you your real orders these days."

»)«(Chapter 10)»)«

Diomedes sent his car round to the barracks in the morning to pick up Brasidus. It was another fine day, and the drive out to the spaceport was pleasant. The driver was not disposed to talk, which suited Brasidus. He was turning over and over in his mind what he would tell Diomedes and was wondering what conclusions Diomedes would draw from the events in the créche. Meanwhile, there was the morning air to enjoy, still crisp, not yet tainted by the pungency from the spice fields on either side of the road.

Above the spaceport the ships of the Air Navy still circled and, as the car neared the final approaches, Brasidus noted that heavy motorized artillery as well as squadrons of armored cavalry had been brought up. Whatever John Grimes had in mind, the Police Battalion would be ready for him. But Brasidus did not regret that he had not, as a recruit, been posted to a mechanized unit. A hoplite such as himself was always fully employed, the armored cavalry, but rarely, the artillery, almost never.

The main gates opened as the car, without slackening speed, approached them. The duty guard saluted smartly—the vehicle rather than himself, Brasidus guessed. There was a spectacular halt in a column of swirling dust outside the Security office. Diomedes was standing in the doorway. He sneezed, glared at the driver, withdrew hastily into the building. Brasidus waited until the dust had subsided before getting out of the car.

"That Agis!" snarled the Captain as he sketchily acknowledged Brasidus' salute, "I'll have him transferred to the infantry!"

"I've seen him do the same when he's been driving you, sir."

"Hmph! That's different, young man. Well, he got you here in good time. Just as well, as I've instructions for you."

"And I've a report for you, sir."

"Already, Brasidus? You've wasted no time." He smiled greasily. "As a matter of fact, I've already had a call from Captain Lycurgus, passing on a complaint from Doctor Heraklion. What did you learn?"

Brasidus, who possessed a trained memory, told his superior what he had seen and heard. Diomedes listened intently. Then he asked, "And what do you think, Brasidus?"

"That Arcadians were already on Sparta before *Seeker* landed, sir."

"Arcadians? Oh, yes. The twin-turreted androids. Did you hear that rumor, too? And how do you think they got here?"

"There could have been secret landings, sir. Or they

could have been smuggled in aboard *Latterhaven Venus* and *Latterhaven Hera*."

"And neither of these theories throws Security in a very good light, does it? And the smuggling one rather reflects upon the spaceport guards."

"They needn't be smuggled in as adults, sir. Children could be hidden in some of those crates discharged by the Latterhaven ships. They could be drugged, too, so that they couldn't make any noise."

"Ingenious, Brasidus. Ingenious. But I've been aboard the Venus and the Hera often enough and, believe me, it would be impossible for either ship to carry more than her present complement. Not even children. They're no more than cargo boxes with a handful of cubicles, cells that we should consider inadequate for our criminals, perched on top of them."

"The cargo holds?"

"No. You can't have a man—or a child—living in any confined space without his leaving traces."

"But they didn't just happen, sir. The Arcadians, I mean."

"Of course not. They either budded from their fathers or came out of a birth machine." Diomedes seemed to find this amusing. "No, they didn't just happen. They were either brought here or came here under their own power. But why?"

"Heraklion seemed to like the one that he was with last night. It was . . . unnatural."

"And what were your feelings toward him? Or it?"

Brasidus blushed. He muttered, "As you said yourself, sir, these beings possess a strange, evil power."

"So they do. So they do. That's why we must try to foil

any plot in which they're engaged." He looked at his watch. "Meanwhile, my own original plan still stands. The Council has approved my suggestion that *Seeker*'s personnel be allowed to leave their ship. Today you will, using my car and driver, escort Lieutenant Commander Grimes and Doctor Lazenby to the city, where an audience with the King and the Council has been arranged for them. You will act as guide as well as escort, and—you are armed—also as guard."

"To protect them, sir?"

"Yes. I suppose so. But mainly to protect the King. How do we know that when they are in his presence they will not pull a weapon of some kind? You will be with them; you will be situated to stop them at once. Of course, there will be plenty of my own men in the Council Chamber, but you would be able to act without delay if you had to."

"I see, sir."

"All right. Now we are to go aboard the ship to tell them that everything has been organized."

A junior officer met them in the airlock, escorted them up to the commander's quarters. Grimes was attired in what was obviously ceremonial uniform—and very hot and uncomfortable it must be, thought Brasidus. Professionally he ran his eye over the spaceman for any evidence of weapons. There was one, in full sight, but not a very dangerous one. It was a sword, its hilt gold-encrusted, in a gold-trimmed sheath at his left side. More for show than use, was Brasidus' conclusion.

John Grimes grinned at his two visitors. "I hate this rig," he confided, "but I suppose I have to show the flag.

Doctor Lazenby is lucky. Nobody has ever gotten around to designing full dress for women officers."

There was a tap at the door and Margaret Lazenby entered. He was dressed as he had been the previous day, although the clothing itself, with its bright braid and buttons, was obviously an outfit that was worn only occasionally. He said pleasantly, "Good morning, Captain Diomedes. Good morning, Sergeant. Are you coming with us, Captain?"

"Unfortunately, no. I have urgent business here at the spaceport. But Brasidus will be your personal escort. Also, I have detailed two chariots to convoy you into the city."

"Chariots? Oh, you mean those light tanks that we've been watching from the control room."

"Tanks?" repeated Diomedes curiously. "A tank is something you keep fluids in."

"There are tanks and tanks. Where we come from, a tank can be an armored vehicle with caterpillar tracks."

"And what does 'caterpillar' mean?"

Grimes said. "Over the generations new words come into the language and old words drop out. Obviously there are no caterpillars on Sparta, and so the term is meaningless. However, Captain Diomedes, you are welcome to make use of our microfilm library; I would suggest the Encyclopedia Galactica."

"Thank you, Lieutenant Commander." Diomedes looked at his watch. "But may I suggest that you and Doctor Lazenby proceed now to your audience?"

"And will the rest of my crew be allowed ashore?"

"That depends largely upon the impression that you make upon the King and his Council."

"Where's my fore-and-aft hat?" muttered Grimes. He got up, went through one of the curtained doorways. He emerged wearing an odd, gold-braided, black cloth helmet. He said, "Lead on, MacDuff."

"It should be 'Lay on, MacDuff,'" Margaret Lazenby told him.

"I know, I know."

"And who is MacDuff?" asked Diomedes.

"He's dead. He was the Thane of Cawdor."

"And where is Cawdor?"

Grimes sighed.

Brasidus, although he could not say why he did so, enjoyed the ride to the city. He, Grimes and Margaret Lazenby were in the back seat of the car, with the Arcadian (it was as good a label as any) sitting between the two humans. He was stirred by the close proximity of this strange being, almost uncomfortably so. When Margaret Lazenby leaned across him to look at a medusa tree swarming with harpies, he realized that those peculiar fleshy mounds, which even the severe uniform could not hide, were deliciously soft. So much for the built-in weapon theory. "What fantastic birds!" exclaimed the Arcadian.

"They are harpies," said Brasidus.

"Those round bodies do look like human heads, don't they? They could be straight out of Greek mythology."

"So you have already made a study of our legends?" asked Brasidus, interested.

"Of course." Margaret Lazenby smiled. (His lips against the white teeth were very red. Could it be natural?) "But they aren't just your legends. They belong to all Mankind."

"I suppose they do. Admiral Latterus must have carried well-stocked libraries aboard his ships."

"Admiral Latterus?" asked Margaret Lazenby curiously.

"The founder of Latterhaven. I am surprised that you have not heard of him. He was sent from Sparta to establish the colony, but he made himself King of the new world and never returned."

"What a beautiful history," murmured the Arcadian. "Carefully tailored to fit the facts. Tell me, Brasidus, did you ever hear of the Third Expansion, or of Captain John Latter, master of the early timejammer *Utah*? Come to that, did you ever hear of the First Expansion?"

"You talk in riddles, Margaret Lazenby."

"And you and your world are riddles that must be solved, Brasidus."

"Careful, Peggy," warned John Grimes.

The Arcadian turned to address his commander— and, as he did so, Brasidus was acutely conscious of the softness and resilience of the rump under the uniform kilt. "They'll have to be told the truth sometime, John— and I'm sure that Brasidus will forgive me for using him as the guinea pig for the first experiment. But I am a little drunk, I guess. All this glorious fresh air after weeks of the canned variety. And look at those houses! With architecture like that, there should be real chariots escorting us, not these hunks of animated ironmongery. Still, apart from his sidearms, Brasidus is dressed properly."

"The ordinary hoplites," said Brasidus with some pride, "those belonging to the subject city-states, are armed only with swords and spears."

"They didn't have wristwatches in ancient Sparta," Grimes pointed out.

"Oh, be practical, John. He could hardly wear an hour-glass or a sundial on his arm, could he?"

"It's . . . phony," grumbled Grimes.

"It should be as phony as all hell, but it's not," Margaret Lazenby told him. "I wish I'd known just how things are here, though. I'd have soaked up Hellenic history before we came here . . . What are those animals, Brasidus? They look almost like a sort of hairless wolf."

"They are the scavengers. They keep the streets of the city clean. There is a larger variety, wild, out on the hills and plains. They are the wolves."

"But that one, there. Look! It's Siamese twins. It seems to be in pain. Why doesn't somebody do something about it?"

"But why? It's only budding. Don't you reproduce like us—or like we used to, before Lacedaemon invented the birth machine?" He paused. "But I suppose you have birth machines, too."

"We do," said Grimes—and Margaret Lazenby reddened. It was obviously a private joke of some kind.

"The glory that was Greece, the grandeur that was Rome," murmured the Arcadian after a long pause. "But this isn't—forgive me, Brasidus—quite as glorious as it should be. There's a certain . . . untidiness in your streets. And this absence of women seems . . . odd. As I recall it, the average Greek housewife was nothing much to write home about, but the hetaerae must have been ornamental."

"Did they have hetaerae in Sparta?" asked Grimes. "I thought that it was only in Athens."

We do have hetaerae in Sparta, Brasidus thought but did not say, recalling what he had seen and heard in the créche. Sally (another queer name!) had admitted to being one. But what were hetaerae, anyhow?

"They had women," said Margaret Lazenby. "And some of them must have been reasonably good-looking, even by our standards. But Sparta was more under masculine domination than the other Greek states."

"Is that the palace ahead, Brasidus?" asked Grimes.

"It is, sir."

"Then be careful, Peggy. Watch your step—and your tongue."

"Aye, aye, Cap'n."

"And I suppose that you, Brasidus, will report everything that you've heard to Captain Diomedes?"

"Of course, sir."

"And so he should," Margaret Lazenby said. "When it gets around, these pseudo-Spartans might realize all that they are missing."

"And is the fact that they're missing it grounds for commiseration or congratulation?" asked Grimes quietly.

"Shut up!" snapped his officer mutinously.

»)«Chapter 11»)«

It was not the first time that Brasidus had been inside the palace, but, as always, he was awed (although he tried not to show it in front of the foreigners) by the long, colonnaded, high-ceilinged halls, each with its groups of heroic statuary, each with its vivid murals depicting scenes of warfare and the chase. He marched along beside his charges (who, he was pleased to note, had fallen into step), taking pride in the rhythmic, martial clank of the files of hoplites on either side of them, the heralds, long, brazen trumpets already upraised, ahead of them. Past the ranks of Royal Guards—stiff and immobile at attention, tiers of bright-headed spears in rigid alignment—they progressed. He realized, with disapproval, that John Grimes and Margaret Lazenby were talking in low voices.

"More anachronisms for you, Peggy. Those guards. Spears in hand—and projectile pistols at the belt . . ."

"And look at those murals, John. Pig-sticking—those animals aren't unlike boars—on motorcycles. But these people do have good painters and sculptors."

"I prefer my statues a little less aggressively masculine. In fact, I prefer them nonmasculine."

"You would. I find them a pleasant change from the simpering nymphs that are supposed to be decorative on most planets."

"You would."

Brasidus turned his head. "Quiet, please, sirs. We are approaching the throne."

There was a sharp command from the officer in charge of the escort. The party crashed to a halt. The heralds put the mouthpieces of their instruments to their lips, sounded a long, discordant blast, then another. From a wide, pillared portal strode a glittering officer. "Who comes?" he demanded.

In unison the heralds chanted, "John Grimes, master of the star ship *Seeker*. Margaret Lazenby, one of his officers."

"Enter, John Grimes. Enter, Margaret Lazenby."

Again a command from the leader of the escort, and with a jangle of accouterments, the march resumed, although at a slower pace. Through the doorway they passed, halted again. There was another prolonged blast from the heralds' trumpets, a crash of grounded spear butts.

There was the King, resplendent in golden armor (which made the iron crown somehow incongruous), bearded (the only man on Sparta to be so adorned), seated erect on his high, black throne. There, ranged behind him on marble benches, was the Council—the doctors in their scarlet robes, the engineers in purple, the philosophers in black, the generals in brown and the admirals in blue. There was a small group of high-ranking helots—agronomists robed in green, industrialists in gray. All of them stared curiously at the men from the ship, from whom the guards had fallen away. But, Brasidus noted, there was more than curiosity on the faces of the scarlet-robed doctors as they regarded Margaret Lazenby. There was recognition, puzzlement and . . . guilt?

Grimes, at heel-clicking attention, saluted smartly.

"You may advance, Lieutenant Commander," said the King.

Grimes did so, once again drawing himself to attention when within two paces from the throne.

"You may relax, John Grimes. At ease." There was a long pause, then, "We have been told that you come from another world—another world, that is, beyond our polity of Sparta and Latterhaven. We have been told that you represent a government calling itself the Interstellar Federation. Assuming that there is such an entity, what is your business on Sparta?"

"Your Majesty, my mission is to conduct a census of the Man-colonized planets in this sector of space."

"The members of our Council concerned with such matters will be able to give you all the information you need. But we are told that you and your officers wish to set foot on this world—a privilege never accorded to the crews of Latterhaven ships. May we inquire as to your motives?"

"Your Majesty, in addition to the census, we are conducting a survey."

"A survey, Lieutenant Commander?"

"Yes, Your Majesty. There are worlds, such as yours, about which little is known. There are worlds—and yours is one of them—about which much more should be known."

"And this Federation of yours"—Brasidus, watching the King's face, could see that he had not been surprised by any of Grimes' answers, that he accepted the existence of worlds other than Sparta and Latterhaven without demur, that even the mention of this fantastic Federation had been no cause for amazement—"it has considerable military strength?"

"Considerable strength, Your Majesty. My ship, for example, is but a small and unimportant unit of our fleet."

"Indeed? And your whereabouts are known?"

"The movements of all vessels are plotted by Master Control."

"And so . . . and so, supposing that some unfortunate accident were to happen to your ship and your crew on Sparta, we might, just possibly, expect a visit from one or more of your big battleships?"

"That is so, Your Majesty."

"And we could deal with them, sire!" interpolated a portly, blue-robed Council member.

The King swiveled around in his throne. "Could we, Admiral Philcus? Could we? We wish that we possessed your assurance. But we do not. It does not matter how and by whom the planets of this Federation were colonized— what does matter is that they own spaceships, which we do not, and even space warships, which even Latterhaven does not. We, a mere monarch, hesitate to advise you upon naval tactics, but we remind you that a spaceship can hang in orbit, clear of the atmosphere—and therefore beyond reach of your airships—and, at the same time, release its shower of bombs upon our cities. Consider it, Philcus." He turned back to Grimes. "So, Lieutenant Commander, you seek permission for you and your men to range unhindered over the surface of our world?"

"I do, Your Majesty."

"Some of our ways and customs may be strange to you. You will not interfere. And you will impart new knowledge only to those best qualified to be its recipients."

"That is understood, Your Majesty."

"Sire!" This time it was one of the doctors. "I respectfully submit that permission to leave this outworld ship be extended only to human crew members."

"And what is your reason, Doctor? Let Margaret Lazenby advance so that we may inspect him."

The Arcadian walked slowly toward the King. Looking at his face, Brasidus could see that the being had lost some of his cockiness. But there was a certain defiance there still. Should this attitude result in punishment ordered by the King, thought Brasidus, there will be a large measure of injustice involved. The major portion of the blame would rest with Grimes who, after all, had so obviously failed to maintain proper disciplinary standards aboard his ship.

Cresphontes, King of All Sparta, looked long and curiously at the alien spaceman. He said at last, "They tell us that you are an Arcadian."

"That is so, Your Majesty."

"And you are a member of a space-faring race."

"Yes, Your Majesty."

"Turn around, please. Slowly."

Margaret Lazenby obeyed, his face flushing.

"So . . ." mused the King. "So . . ." He swiveled in his throne so that he faced the Council. "You have all seen. You have all seen that this Arcadian is smaller than a true man, is more slightly built. Do you think that he would be a match for one of our warriors, or even for a helot? A thousand of these creatures, armed, might be a menace. But . . ." He turned to address Grimes. "How many of them are there in your crew, Lieutenant Commander?"

"A dozen, Your Majesty."

"A mere dozen of these malformed weaklings, without arms . . . No, there can be no danger. Obviously, since they are members of *Seeker*'s crew, they can coexist harmoniously with men. So, we repeat, there is no danger."

"Sire!" It was the doctor who had raised the objection. "You do not know these beings. You do not know how treacherous they can be."

"And do you, Doctor Pausanias? And if you do know, how do you know?"

The Councilman paled. He said, lamely, "We are experienced, sire, in judging who is to live and who is not to live among the newborn. There are signs, reliable signs. She"—he pointed an accusing finger at Margaret Lazenby—"exhibits them."

"Indeed, Doctor Pausanias? We admit that a child emerging from the birth machine with such a deformed chest would be among those exposed, but how is that deformity an indication of character?"

"It is written in her face, sire."

"In *her* face? Have you suddenly learned a new language, Doctor?"

"Sire, it was a slip of the tongue. His face."

"So . . . Face us, Margaret Lazenby. Look at us." The King's right hand went up to and stroked his short beard. "We read no treachery in your countenance. There is a softness, better suited to a children's nurse than to a warrior, but there is courage, and there is honesty."

"Sire!" Pausanius was becoming desperate. "Do not forget that sh—that he is an alien being. Do not forget that in these cases expression is meaningless. A woods boar, for example, will smile, but not from amiability. He smiles when at his most ferocious."

"And so do men at times." The King grinned, his teeth very white in his dark, bearded face. "We become ferocious, and we smile, when councilmen presume to tell us our business." He raised his voice. "Guards! Remove this man."

"But, sire . . ."

"Enough."

There was a scuffle at the back of the chamber as the doctor was hustled out by four hoplites. Brasidus noticed, with grim satisfaction, that none of the man's scarlet-robed colleagues made any move to defend him. He thought, *Cresphontes knows where his real strength lies. With us, the military.*

"Lieutenant Commander Grimes!"

"Your Majesty?"

"We have decided that you may carry out your survey. You and your officers and men, both human and Arcadian, may leave your ship—but only as arranged with our Captain Diomedes, and only under escort. Is that quite clear?"

"Quite clear, Your Majesty. We shall see only what we are allowed to see."

"You have made a correct assessment of the situation. And now, as we have matters of import to discuss with our Council, you are dismissed."

Grimes saluted and then, slowly, he and Margaret Lazenby backed from the royal presence. Brasidus accompanied them. Beyond the door to the throne room the escort fell in about them.

As they marched out of the palace to the waiting car, Grimes asked, "Brasidus, what will happen to that doctor? The one who was dragged out of the chamber?"

"He will he beheaded, probably. But he is lucky."

"Lucky?"

"Yes. If he were not a doctor and a councilman, he could have his arms and legs lopped off before being exposed on the hillside with the defective children."

"You're joking, Brasidus!" exclaimed Margaret Lazenby.

"Joking? Of course not."

The Arcadian turned to Grimes. "John, can't we do something?"

Grimes shook his head. "Anything that we could do would mean the death of more than one man. Besides, our strict orders are not to interfere."

"It is expedient," said Margaret Lazenby bitterly, "that one man should die for the good of the people."

"Careful, Peggy. This place may be bugged. Remember that we aren't members of the Council."

"Spoken like a true naval officer of these decadent days. I often think that the era of gunboat diplomacy had much to recommend it."

»《Chapter 12》«

They rode back to the spaceport almost in silence. Brasidus realized that the two foreigners had been shocked when told of the probable fate of Pausanius. But why should they be? He could not understand it. Surely on their world, on any world, insolence toward the King himself must result in swift and drastic punishment. To make their reaction even stranger, the doctor had spoken against them, not for them.

They sped through the streets of the city, one chariot rattling ahead of the hovercar, the second astern of it. There were more people abroad now, more sightseers; word must have gotten around that aliens from the ship were at large. Citizen and helot, every man stared with avid curiosity at the Arcadian.

Margaret Lazenby shuddered. He muttered, "John, I don't like this planet at all, at all. I'd have said once that to be one woman in a world of men would be marvelous. But it's not. I'm being undressed by dozens of pairs of eyes.

Do you know, I was afraid that the King was going to order me to strip."

"That shouldn't worry an Arcadian," John Grimes told him. "After all, you're all brought up as nudists."

"And I don't see why it should worry him," Brasidus put in, "unless he is ashamed of his deformities."

Margaret Lazenby flared, "To begin with, Sergeant, I'm not deformed. Secondly, the correct pronouns to use insofar as I am concerned are 'she' and 'her.' Got it?"

"And are those pronouns to be used when talking of the other spacemen who are similarly . . . malformed?" asked Brasidus.

"Yes. But, as a personal favor, will you, please, stop making remarks about the shape of my body?"

"All right." Then he said, meaning no offense, "On Sparta nobody is deformed."

"Not physically," remarked Margaret Lazenby nastily, and then it was the Sergeant's turn to lapse into a sulky silence, one that remained unbroken all the rest of the way to the ship.

Brasidus left the spacemen at the barrier, then reported to Spaceport Security. Diomedes was seated in his inner office, noisily enjoying his midday meal. He waved the Sergeant to a bench, gestured toward the food and drink on the table. "Help yourself, young man. And how did things go? Just the important details. I already know that the King has agreed to let Grimes carry out some sort of survey, and I've just received word that Pausanius has lost his head. But what were your impressions?"

Deliberately Brasidus filled a mug with beer. Officers were allowed stronger liquor than the lower-ranking hoplites, even those with the status of sergeant. He rather hoped that the day would soon come when he would be able to enjoy this tipple in public. He gulped pleasurably. Then he said, "It must be a funny world that they come from. To begin with, they didn't seem to have any real respect for the King. Oh, they were correct enough, but ... I could sense, somehow, that they were rather looking down on him. And then ... they were shocked, sir, really shocked when I told them what was going to happen to Pausanius. It's hard to credit."

"In my job I'm ready and willing to credit anything. But go on."

"This Margaret Lazenby, the Arcadian. She seems to have a terror of nudity."

"She, Brasidus?"

"Yes, sir. She told me to refer to her as 'she'. Do you know, it sounds and feels right, somehow."

"Go on."

"You'll remember, sir, that we saw a picture in Lieutenant Commander Grimes' cabin of what seemed to be a typical beach scene on Arcadia. Everybody was naked."

"H'm. But you will recall that in that picture humans and Arcadians were present in roughly equal numbers. To know that one is in all ways inferior is bad enough. To be inferior and in the minority—that's rather much. His—or her—attitude as far as this world is concerned makes sense, Brasidus. But how did it come up?"

"She said, when we were driving back through the city, that she felt as though she were being undressed by the eyes of all the people looking at her. (Why should she have that effect on humans? I'm always wondering myself what she is like under her uniform.) And she said that she was afraid that King Cresphontes was going to order her to strip in front of him and the Council."

"Men are afflicted by peculiar phobias, Brasidus. You've heard of Teleclus, of course?"

"The Lydian general, sir?"

"The same. A very brave man, as his record shows. But let a harpy get into his tent and he's a gibbering coward." He picked up a meaty bone, gnawed on it meditatively. "So don't run away with the idea that this Arcadian is outrageously unhuman in his—or 'her'—reactions." He smiled greasily. "She may be more human than you dream."

"What are you getting at, sir? What do you know?"

Diomedes waved the bone playfully at Brasidus. "Only what my officers tell me. Apart from that—I'm Security, so nobody tells me anything. Which reminds me, there's something I must tell you. Your little friend Achron has been ringing this office all morning, trying to get hold of you." He frowned. "I don't want you to drop him like a hot cake now that you've acquired a new playmate."

"What new playmate, sir?"

"Oh, never mind, never mind. Just keep in with Achron, that's all. We still want to find out what's going on at the créche, alien ships or no alien ships. As I've said—and I think you'll agree—it seems to tie in."

"But, sir, wouldn't it be simple just to stage a raid?"

"I like my job, Brasidus—but I like the feel of my head on my shoulders much better. The doctors are the most powerful branch of the priesthood. This Pausanius, do you think that the King would have acted as he did if he hadn't known that he, Pausanius, was in bad with his own colleagues? All that happened was that he got himself a public execution instead of a very private one."

"It all seems very complicated, Captain."

"You can say that again, Brasidus." Diomedes tossed his bone into the trash basket. "Now . . ." He picked up a sheaf of crumpled, grease-stained papers from the untidy table. "We have to consider your future employment. You'll not be required for escort duties this afternoon. I shall be arranging his itinerary with Lieutenant Commander Grimes. And tomorrow the bold space commander and his Arcadian sidekick will not be escorted by yourself."

"And why not, sir?"

"Because you'll be working—working with your hands. You've plainclothes experience. You can mix with helots as one of them and get away with it. This afternoon you pay a call on Alessis, who is both an engineer and—but let it go no further—on our payroll. Tomorrow Alessis with a gang of laborers will carry out the annual overhaul of the refrigerating machinery in the Andronicus warehouse. You will be one of the laborers."

"But I don't know anything about refrigeration, sir."

"Alessis should be able to teach you all that a common laborer should know this afternoon."

"But the other helots, sir. They'll know that I'm not a regular member of the gang."

"They won't. Alessis has just recruited green labor from at least half a dozen outlying villages. You'll be the one big-city boy in the crowd. Oh, this will please you. Your friend Heraklion will not be in the crèche. He has been called urgently to his estate. It seems that a fire of unknown origin destroyed his farm outbuildings."

"Unknown origin, sir?"

"Of course."

"But what has the Andronicus warehouse to do with the créche?"

"I don't know yet. But I hope to find out."

Brasidus returned to the barracks in Diomedes' car, changed there into civilian clothes. He had been given the address of Alessis' office, walked there briskly. The engineer—a short, compact man in a purple-trimmed tunic—was expecting him. He said, "Be seated, Lieutenant. And I warn you now that tomorrow, on the job, I shall be addressing you as 'Hey, you!'"

"I'm used to plainclothes work, sir."

"As a helot?"

"Yes. As a helot."

"As a stupid helot?"

"If that is what's required."

"It will be. You're going to wander off by yourself and get lost. You'll be tracing the gas-supply main—that will be your story if anybody stumbles on you. I was supposed to be giving you an afternoon's tuition in refrigeration techniques, but that will not be necessary. All I ask of my helots is that they lift when I tell them to lift, put down when I tell them to put down, and so on and so forth. They're the brawn and I'm the brain. Get it?"

"Yes, sir."

"Good. Can you read a plan?"

"I can."

"Splendid." Alessis got up, opened a drawer of his desk

and pulled out a large roll of tough paper. He flattened it out. "Now, this is the basement of the Andronicus warehouse. Power supply comes in here," his stubby forefinger jabbed, "through a conduit. Fans here, compressors here—all the usual. The cold chambers are all on the floor above—with the exception of this one. Deep freeze—very deep freeze, in fact."

"There's no reason why it shouldn't be in the basement."

"None at all. And there's no reason why it shouldn't be up one floor, with the other chambers. But it's not its location that's odd."

"Then what is?"

"It's got two doors, Brasidus. One opening into the basement, the other one right at the back. I found this second door, quite by chance, when I was checking the insulation."

"And where does it lead to?"

"That is the question. I think, although I am not sure, that there is a tunnel behind it. And I think that the tunnel runs to the créche."

"But why?"

Alessis shrugged. "That's what our mutual friend Diomedes wants to find out."

))«(Chapter 13)»((

A black windowless cube, ugly, forbidding, the Andronicus warehouse stood across the cobbled street from the gracefully proportioned créche complex. To its main door, a few minutes before 0800 hours, slouched the gang of workmen employed by Alessis, among them Brasidus. He was wearing dirty, ill-fitting coveralls, and he was careful not to walk with a military stride, proceeded with a helot's shamble.

The other men looked at him, and he looked at them. He saw a bunch of peasantry from the outlying villages, come to the city to (they vaguely hoped) better themselves. They saw a man like themselves, but a little cleaner, a little better fed, a little more intelligent. There were grunted self-introductions. Then, "You'll be the foreman?" asked one of the workmen.

"No," admitted Brasidus. "He'll be along with Alessis."

The engineer arrived in his hovercar, his foreman riding with him. They got out of the vehicle and the foreman went to the doorway, pressed the bell push set to one side of it. Then he said, "Jump to it. Get the tools out of the car." Brasidus—his years of training were not easily sloughed off—took the lead, swiftly formed an efficient little working party to unload spanners, hammers, gas cylinders and electrical equipment. He heard the foreman say to his employer, "Who's that new man, sir? We could use a few more like him."

Slowly the door opened. It was thick, Brasidus noted. It appeared to be armored. It looked capable of withstanding a chariot charge, or even the fire of medium artillery. It would have been more in keeping with a fortress than a commercial building. In it stood a man dressed in the gray tunic of an industrialist. That made him a helot, although one of a superior class. Nonetheless, his salutation of Alessis was not that of an inferior to a superior. There could even have been a hint of condescension.

The maintenance gang filed into the building—the engineer and his foreman unhampered, Brasidus and the others carrying the gear. So far there was little to be seen—just a long, straight corridor between featureless metal walls, terminating in yet another door. But it was all so clean, so sterile, impossibly so for Sparta. It reminded Brasidus of the interior of John Grimes' ship, but even that, by comparison, had a lived-in feel to it.

The farther door was heavily insulated. Beyond it was a huge room, crowded with machinery, the use of which Brasidus could only guess. Pumps, perhaps, and compressors, and dozens of white-faced gauges. Nothing was in motion; every needle rested at zero.

"Have you everything you want, Alessis?" asked the industrialist.

"I think so. Nothing's been giving any trouble since the last overhaul?"

"No. I need hardly tell you that the deep freeze is, as always, top priority. But Hera's not due for another couple of months."

"Not to worry, what's the hurry?" quipped the engineer. Then, to his foreman, "O.K., Cimon, you can start taking the main compressor down. One of you"—he looked over his workmen carefully as though making a decision—"come with me to the basement to inspect the deep freeze. You'll do, fellow. Bring a hammer and a couple of screwdrivers. And a torch."

Brasidus opened the hatch in the floor for Alessis and then, as he followed the engineer down to the lower level, managed to shut it after himself. It was not difficult; the insulation, although thick, was light. In the basement there was more machinery seeming, thought Brasidus, to duplicate the engines on the floor above. It, too, was silent. And there was the huge, insulated door that he, as instructed by Alessis, opened.

The chamber beyond it was not cooled, but a residual chill seemed to linger in the still air. Physical or psychological? Or psychic? There was . . . something, some influence, some subtle emanation, that resulted in a slight, involuntary shudder, a sudden, prickly gooseflesh. It was as though there were a million voices—subsonic? supersonic? on the verge of audibility—crying out to be heard, striving, in vain, to impart a message. The voices of the dead? Brasidus must have spoken aloud, for Alessis said, "Or the not yet born."

"What do you mean?" demanded Brasidus. "What do you mean?"

"I . . . I don't know, Lieutenant. It seemed that the words were spoken to me by someone, by something outside."

"But this is only a deep-freeze chamber, sir."

"It is only a deep-freeze chamber—but it has too many doors."

"I can't see the second one."

"No. It is concealed. I found it only by accident. You see that panel? Take your screwdriver and remove the holding screws."

In spite of his unfamiliarity with power tools, with tools of any kind, Brasidus accomplished the job in a few seconds. Then, with Alessis' help, he pried the insulated panel out from the wall, lifted it to one side. There was a tunnel beyond it, high enough so that a tall man could walk without stooping, wide enough so that bulky burdens could be carried along it with ease. There were pipes and conduits on the roof of the tunnel, visible in the light of the torches.

"An alternative freezing system," explained Alessis. "Machinery in the créche itself. I'm not supposed to know about it. The tunnel's insulated, too—and I've no doubt that when it's in use it can be brought down to well below zero."

"And what am I supposed to do?" Brasidus asked.

"You take your orders from Captain Diomedes, not from me. You're supposed to snoop—that's all that I know. And if you are caught, I risk my neck by providing you with some sort of a cover story. You thought—and I thought—that all these wires and pipes are supposed to be doing something. As, in fact, they are. Well, you'll find another door at the end, a proper one, and with dogs that can be operated from either side." His hand rested briefly on Brasidus' upper forearm. "I don't like this business. It's all too hasty; there's far too much last-minute improvisation. So be careful."

"I'll try," Brasidus told him. He stuck the hammer and the screwdriver into his belt—after all, he was supposed to be a workman, and if it came to any sort of showdown they would be better than no weapons at all—and, without a backward glance, set off along the tunnel.

The door at the far end was easy enough to open, and the screw clamps were well greased and silent. With the thick, insulated valve the slightest crack ajar, Brasidus listened. He could hear nothing. Probably there was nobody on the farther side. He hoped. The door opened away from him into whatever space there was on the other side. It was a pity, as anybody waiting there—the possibility still had not been ruled out—would be hidden from Brasidus as he emerged. But if the door were flung open violently, he would be not only hidden, but trapped.

Brasidus flung the door open violently, catching it just before it could thud noisily against the wall of the corridor.

So far, so good.

But what was there to see? Across the corridor there was yet another door, looking as though it, too, were insulated. And it was locked. To his left stretched a long, long passageway, soft ceiling lights reflected in the polished floor. To his right stretched a long, long passageway, similarly illuminated. On both sides there were doors, irregularly spaced, numbered.

Brasidus stood, silent and motionless, every sense

tuned to a high pitch of sensitivity. There was the faintest hint of perfume in the air, merged with other hints—antiseptics, machinery, cooking—noticeable only by reason of its unusualness. A similar fragrance had lingered around Margaret Lazenby. And, remembered Brasidus, around that other Arcadian in this very building—Sally. And, oddly enough, around Heraklion. (Normally the only odors associated with doctors were those of the various spirits and lotions of their trade.)

So, he thought, there are Arcadians here.

So, he told himself, I knew that already.

So what?

His hearing was abnormally keen, and he willed himself to ignore the mutter of his own heartbeats, the susurus of his respiration. From somewhere, faint and faraway, drifted a murmur of machinery. There were voices, distant, and a barely heard tinkle of that silvery laughter he already associated with the Arcadians. There was a whisper of running water, evocative of a hillside rill rather than city plumbing.

He did not want to stray too far from the door, but realized that he would learn little, if anything, by remaining immobile. He turned to his left, mainly because that was the direction from which the Arcadian laughter and the faint splashing sounds were coming. He advanced slowly and cautiously, his hand hovering just clear of the haft of his hammer.

Suddenly a door opened. The man standing there was dressed in a long, soft, enveloping robe. He had long, blonde hair, and the fine features and the wide, red mouth of an Arcadian. There was about him—about her,

Brasidus corrected himself—more than just a hint of that disturbing perfume. "Hello," she said in a high, pleasantly surprised voice. "Why, hello! A fresh face, as I live and breathe! And what are you doing in this abode of love?"

"I'm checking the refrigeration, sir."

"Sir!" There was the tinkling laughter, amused but not unkind. "Sir! That's a giveaway, fellow. You don't belong here, do you?"

"Why, sir, no."

The Arcadian sighed. "Such a handsome brute—and I have to chase you off. But it's getting on for the time when our learned lovers join us for . . . er . . . aquatic relaxation in the pool. And if they find you wandering around where you shouldn't be . . ." She drew the edge of her hand across her throat in an expressive gesture. "It's happened before—and, after all, who misses a helot? But where did you come from? Oh, yes, I see. You could be a refrigeration mechanic . . . My advice to you is to get back into your hole and to pull it shut after you." Then she said, as Brasidus started to turn to retreat to the tunnel, "No so fast, buster. Not so fast." A slim hand, with red-painted nails, caught his right shoulder to swing him so that he faced her; the other hand came up to rest upon his left shoulder. Her face was very close to his, the lips parted.

As though it were the most natural thing in the world, Brasidus kissed her. Unnatural, said a voice in his mind, flatly and coldly. Unnatural, to mate with a monster from another world, even to contemplate such a sterile coupling. Unnatural. Unnatural.

But his own arms were about her and he was returning her kiss—hotly, avidly, clumsily. That censor in his mind was, at the moment, talking only to itself. He felt the mounds of flesh on her chest pressing against him, was keenly aware of the softness of her thighs against his own.

Suddenly, somehow, her hands were between their upper bodies, pushing him away. With a twist of her head she disengaged her mouth. "Go, you fool!" she whispered urgently. "Go! If they find you, they'll kill you. Go. Don't worry—I'll say nothing. And if you have any sense, you'll not say anything either."

"But . . ."

"Go!"

Reluctantly, Brasidus went. Just as he closed the door he heard footsteps approaching along the alleyway.

But there was no alarm raised; his intrusion had been undetected.

Back in the deep-freeze chamber, Alessis looked at him curiously. "Have you been in a fight? Your mouth . . . there's blood."

Brasidus examined the back of his investigatory hand. "No," he said. "It's not blood. I don't know what it is."

"But what happened?"

"I don't know," replied Brasidus truthfully. Still he was not feeling the shame, the revulsion that should have been swamping him. "I don't know. In any case, I have to make my reports only to Captain Diomedes."

))«Chapter 14»((«

"So it was not the same one that you saw before?" asked Diomedes.

"No, Captain. At least, I don't think so. Her voice was different."

"H'm. There must be an absolute nest of Arcadians in that bloody créche . . . And all . . . she did was to talk to you and warn you to make yourself scarce before any of the doctors came on the scene?"

"That was all, Captain."

"You're lying, Brasidus."

"All right." Brasidus' voice was sullenly defiant. "I kissed him, her, it. And it—or she—kissed me back."

"You what?"

"You heard me, sir. Your very vague instructions to me were that I should find out all that I could. And that was one way of doing it."

"Indeed? And what did you find out?"

"That these Arcadians, as you have said, exercise a sort

97

of hypnotic power, especially when there is physical contact."

"Hypnotic power? So the touch of mouth to mouth almost put you to sleep?"

"That wasn't the way I meant it, sir. But I did feel that, if I weren't very careful, I should be doing just what she wanted."

"And what did she want?"

"Do I have to spell it out for you, sir? Oh, I know that intercourse with an alien being must be wrong—but that was what she wanted."

"And you?"

"All right. I wanted it, too."

"Brasidus, Brasidus . . . You know that what you have just told me could get you busted down to helot. Or worse. But in our job, as you are learning, we often have to break the law in order to enforce it."

"As a policeman, sir, I am reasonably familiar with the law. I cannot recall that it forbids intercourse with aliens."

"Not yet, Brasidus. Not yet. But you will recall that contact with the crews of visiting ships is prohibited. And I think that the preliminaries to making love may be construed as contact."

"But are these Arcadians in the créche crew members of visiting ships?"

"What else can they be? They must have got here somehow." Diomedes looked long and hard at Brasidus, but there was no censure in his regard. "However, I am not displeased by the way in which things are turning out. You are getting to know something about these . . . . things. These Arcadians. And I think that you are strong

enough to resist their lure . . . Now, what have we for you?
This evening, I think, you will visit your friend Achron at
the créche. Keep your eyes and ears open, but don't stick
your neck out. Tomorrow I have an assignment for you
that you should find interesting. This Margaret Lazenby
wishes to make a sightseeing trip, and she especially asked
for you as her escort."

"Will Lieutenant Commander Grimes be along, sir?"

"No. He'll be consorting with the top brass. After all,
he is the commander of *Seeker* and, to use spaceman's
parlance, seems to pile on rather more G's than the master
of a merchantman . . . Yes, Brasidus, have yourself a nice
visit with your boyfriend, and then report to me here
tomorrow morning at 0730 hours, washed behind the ears
and with all your brasswork polished."

Brasidus spent the evening with Achron before the
latter reported for duty. It was not the first time that he
had been a guest at the nurse's Club—but it was the first
time that he had felt uncomfortable there. Apart from his
own feelings, it was no different from other occasions.
There were the usual graceful, soft-spoken young men,
proud and happy to play host to the hoplites who were
their visitors. There was the usual food—far better cooked
and more subtly seasoned than that served in the army
messes. There was the usual wine—a little too sweet,
perhaps, but chilled and sparkling. There was music and
there was dancing—not the strident screaming of brass
and the boom and rattle of drums, not the heavy thud of
bare feet on the floor, but the rhythmic strumming of
lutes and, to it, the slow gyrations of willowy bodies.

But . . .

But there was something lacking.

But what could be lacking?

"You are very thoughtful tonight, Brasidus," remarked Achron wistfully.

"Am I?"

"Yes. You . . . you're not with us, somehow."

"No?"

"Brasidus, I have to be on duty soon. Will you come with me to my room?"

The Sergeant looked at his friend. Achron was a pretty boy, prettier than most, but he was not, he could never be, an Arcadian . . .

What am I thinking? he asked himself, shocked. Why am I thinking it?

He said, "Not tonight, Achron."

"But what is wrong with you, Brasidus? You never used to be like this." Then, with a sort of incredulous bitterness, "It can't be one of the men from the ship, can it? No, not possibly. Not one of those great, hairy brutes. As well consort with one of those malformed aliens they've brought with them!" Achron laughed at the absurdity of the idea.

"No," Brasidus told him. "Not one of the men from the ship."

"Then it's all right."

"Yes, it's all right. But I shall have a heavy day tomorrow."

"You poor dear. I suppose that the arrival of this absurd spaceship from some uncivilized world has thrown a lot of extra work on you."

"Yes. It has."

"But you'll walk with me to the créche, won't you?"

"Yes. I'll do that."

"Oh, thank you. You can wait here while I get changed. There's plenty of wine left."

Yes, there was plenty of wine left, but Brasidus was in no mood for it. He sat in silence, watching the dancers, listening to the slow, sensuous thrumming. Did the Arcadians dance? And how would they look dancing, stripped for performance, the light gleaming on their smooth, golden skins? And why should the mere thought of it be so evocative of sensual imaginings?

Achron came back into the hall, dressed in his white working tunic. Brasidus got up from the bench, walked with him out into the night. The two friends made their way through the streets in silence at first, but it was not the companionable silence to which they had become used. Finally Brasidus spoke, trying to keep any display of real interest out of his voice.

"Wouldn't it be better if you nurses lived in at the créche? The same as we do in the barracks."

"Then we shouldn't have these walks, Brasidus."

"You could visit me."

"But I don't like your barracks. And your Club's as bad."

"I suppose that the cooking could be improved in both. Just who does live in at the créche?"

"All the doctors, of course. And there are some engineers who look after the machinery."

"No helots?"

"No. Of course not." Achron was shocked at the idea. "Even we—but, after all, Brasidus, we are helots—have to live outside. But you know all that. Why are you asking me?"

That was a hard counterquestion to answer. At last Brasidus said, "There have been rumors . . ."

"Rumors of what?"

"Well, it's a very large building. Even allowing for the wards and the birth machine, there must be ample space inside. Do you think that the staff doctors and engineers could have . . . friends living with them?"

It was Achron's turn to hesitate. "You could be right, Brasidus. There are so many rules telling us that we must not stray away from our wards. Now that you raise the point, I can see that there has always been an atmosphere of . . . of secrecy . . ."

"And have you ever seen or heard anything?"

"No."

"And do the staff doctors and engineers have any friends among the nurses?"

"They wouldn't look as us." Resentment was all too evident in Achron's voice. "They're too high and mighty. Keep themselves to themselves, that's what they do. And their own accommodation, I've heard, the King himself might envy. They've a heated swimming pool, even. I've never seen it, but I've heard about it. And I've seen the food and the wine that come in. Oh, they do themselves well—far better than us, who do all the work."

"There might be inquiries being made," said Brasidus cautiously.

"There are always inquiries being made. That Captain Diomedes wanted me to work for him. But he's not . . . he's not a gentleman. We didn't get on. Why should I help him?"

"Would you help me?"

"And how can I, Brasidus?"

"Just look and listen. Let me know of anything out of the ordinary in the créche."

"But the doctors can do no wrong," said Achron. "And even if they did, they couldn't. You know what I mean."

"In your eyes, you mean?"

"In my eyes," admitted the nurse. "But for you, and only for you, I'll . . . I'll look and listen. Does it mean promotion for you?"

"It does," said Brasidus.

"Are you coming in?" asked Achron as they reached the entrance to the créche.

"No. I shall have a long and wearing day tomorrow."

"You . . . you don't give me much inducement to help you, do you? If I do, will things be the same between us again?"

"Yes," lied Brasidus.

⽒«Chapter 15»⽒«

Brasidus drove out to the spaceport in the car that had been placed at his disposal. He realized that he was looking forward to what he had told Achron would be a long and wearing day. He enjoyed the freshness of the morning air, looked up with appreciation at the Spartan Navy still, in perfect formation, circling the landing field. But now he did not, as he had done so many times in the past, envy the airmen. He was better off as he was. If he were up there, a crew member of one of the warships, even the captain of one of them, he would not be meeting the glamorous, exotic spacefarers—and most certainly would not, in the course of duty, be spending the entire day with one of them.

Margaret Lazenby was already ashore, was waiting in Diomedes' office, was engaged in conversation with the Security captain. Brasidus heard his superior say, "I'm sorry, Doctor Lazenby, but I cannot allow you to carry weapons. The cameras and recording equipment—yes. But not that pistol. Laser, isn't it?"

"It is. But, damn it all, Diomedes, on this cockeyed world of yours my going about unarmed degrades me to the status of a helot."

"And the Arcadians are not helots?"

"No. It should be obvious, even to a Security officer. Would a helot hold commissioned rank in the Federation's Survey Service?"

"Then if you possess warrior's status, your being let loose with a weapon of unknown potentialities is even worse insofar as we are concerned." The fat man, facing Margaret Lazenby's glare with equanimity, allowed himself to relent. "All right. Leave your pistol here, and I'll issue you with a stun gun."

"I shall not leave my weapon here. Will you be so good as to put me through to the ship so that I can tell the duty officer to send somebody ashore to pick it up?"

"All right." Diomedes punched a few buttons on his board, picked up the handset, spoke into it briefly, then handed it to the Arcadian. He turned to Brasidus. "So you've arrived. Attention!" Brasidus obeyed with a military crash and jangle. "Let's look at you. H'm, brass not too bad, but your leatherwork could do with another polish . . . But you're not going anywhere near the palace, so I don't suppose it matters. At ease! Stand easy! In fact, relax."

Meanwhile, Margaret Lazenby had finished speaking into the telephone. She returned the instrument to its rest. She stood there, looking down at the obese Diomedes sprawled in his chair—and Brasidus looked at her. She was not in uniform, but was wearing an open-necked shirt with a flaring collar cut from some soft, brown material, and below it a short kilt of the same color.

Her legs were bare, and her slim feet were thrust into serviceable-looking sandals. At her belt was a holstered weapon of unfamiliar design. The cross straps from which depended her equipment—camera, sound recorder, binoculars—accentuated the out-thrusting fleshy mounds on her chest that betrayed her alien nature.

She was, obviously, annoyed, and when she spoke it was equally obvious that she was ready and willing to transfer her annoyance to Brasidus. "Well, Brasidus," she demanded. "Seen enough? Or would you like me to go into a song and dance routine for you?"

"I . . . I was interested in that weapon of yours."

"Is that all?" For some obscure reason Brasidus' reply seemed to annoy her still further. And then a junior officer from *Seeker* came in, and Margaret Lazenby unbuckled the holstered pistol from her belt, handed it to the young spaceman. She accepted the stun gun from Diomedes, unholstered it, looked at it curiously. "Safety catch? Yes. Firing stud? H'm. We have similar weapons. Nonlethal, but effective enough. Oh, range?"

"Fifty feet," said Diomedes.

"Not very good. Better than nothing, I suppose." She clipped the weapon to her belt. "Come on, Brasidus. We'd better get out of here before he has me stripped to a peashooter and you polishing your belt and sandals."

"Your instructions, sir?" Brasidus asked Diomedes.

"Instructions? Oh, yes. Just act as guide and escort to Doctor Lazenby. Show her what you can of the workings of our economy—fields, factories . . . you know. Answer her questions as long as there's no breach of security involved. And keep your own ears flapping."

"Very good, sir. Oh, expenses . . ."

"Expenses, Brasidus?"

"There may be meals, an occasional drink . . ."

Diomedes sighed, pulled a bag of coins out of a drawer, dropped it with a clank on to the desk. "I know just how much is in this and I shall expect a detailed account of what you spend. Off with you. And, Doctor Lazenby, I expect you to bring Brasidus, here, back in good order and condition."

Brasidus saluted, then followed the spaceman out through the doorway.

She said, as soon as they were outside the building, "Expenses?"

"Yes, Doctor . . ."

"Call me Peggy."

"I have rations for the day in the car, Peggy, but I didn't think they were . . . suitable. Just bread and cold meat and a flagon of wine from the mess at the barracks."

"And so . . . and so you want to impress me with something better?"

"Why, yes," admitted Brasidus with a certain surprise.

"Yes." (And it was strange, too, that he was looking forward to buying food and drink for this alien, even though the wherewithal to do so came out of the public purse. On Sparta every man was supposed to pay for his own entertainment, although not always in cash. In this case, obviously, there could be no reciprocation. Or could there be? But it did not matter.)

And then, with even greater surprise, Brasidus realized that he was helping Margaret Lazenby into the hovercar. Even burdened as she was, she did not need his assistance, but she accepted it as her due. Brasidus climbed in after her, took his seat behind the control column. "Where to?" he asked.

"That's up to you. I'd like a good tour. No, not the city—shall be seeing plenty of that when I accompany John—Commander Grimes—on his official calls. What about the countryside and the outlying villages? Will that be in order?"

"It will, Peggy," Brasidus said. (And why should the use of that name be so pleasurable?)

"And if you'll explain things to me as you drive . . ."

The car lifted on its air cushion in a flurry of dust, moved forward, out through the main gateway, and for the first few miles headed toward the city.

"The spice fields," explained Brasidus with a wave of his hand. "It'll soon be harvest time, and then the two ships from Latterhaven will call for the crop."

"Rather . . . overpowering. The smell, I mean. Cinnamon, nutmeg, almond, but more so . . . And a sort of mixture of sage and onion and garlic. But those men working in the fields with hoes and rakes, don't you have mechanical cultivators?"

"But why should we? I suppose that machines could be devised, but such mechanical tools would throw the helots out of employment."

"But you'd enjoy vastly increased production and would be able to afford a greater tonnage of imports from Latterhaven."

"But we are already self-sufficient."

"Then what do you import from Latterhaven?"

Brasidus creased his brows. "I . . . I don't know, Peggy,"

he admitted. "We are told that the ships bring manufactured goods."

"Such as?"

"I don't know." Then he recalled the strange book that he had seen in the créche. "Books, perhaps."

"What sort of books?"

"I don't know, Peggy. The doctors keep them for themselves. But we turn off here. We detour the city and run through the vineyards."

The road that they were now following was little more than a track, running over and around the foothills, winding through the terraced vineyards on either side. As far as the eye could see the trellises were sagging under the weight of the great, golden fruit, each at least the size of a man's head, the broad, fleshy leaves. Brasidus remarked, "This has been a good year for grapes."

"Grapes? Are those things grapes?"

"What else could they be?" Brasidus stopped the car, got out, scrambled up the slope to the nearest vine. With his knife he hacked through a tough stem, then carried the ripe, glowing sphere back to Peggy. She took it, hefted it in her two hands, peered at it closely, sniffed it. "Whatever this is," she declared, "it ain't no grape—not even a grapefruit. Something indigenous, I suppose. Is it edible?"

"No. It has to be . . . processed. Skinned, trodden out, exposed to the air in open vats. It takes a long time, but it gets rid of the poison."

"Poison? I'll take your word for it." She handed the fruit back to Brasidus, who threw it onto the bank. "Oh, I should have kept that, to take to the ship for analysis."

"I'll get it again for you."

"Don't bother. Let the biochemist do his own fetching and carrying. But have you any of the . . . the finished product? You did say that you had brought a flagon of wine with you."

"Yes, Peggy." Brasidus reached into the back of the car, brought up the stone jug, pulled out the wooden stopper.

"No glasses?" she asked with a lift of the eyebrows.

"Glasses?"

"Cups, goblets, mugs—things you drink out of."

"I . . . I'm sorry. I never thought . . ."

"You have a lot to learn, my dear. But show me how you manage when you haven't any women around to exercise a civilizing influence."

"Women?"

"People like me. Go on, show me."

Brasidus grinned, lifted the flagon in his two hands, tilted it over his open mouth, clear of his lips. The wine was rough, tart rather than sweet, but refreshing. He gulped happily, then returned the jug to an upright position. He swallowed, then said, "Your turn, Peggy."

"You can't expect me to drink like that. You'll have to help me."

You wouldn't last five minutes on Sparta, thought Brasidus, not altogether derisively. He turned around in his seat, carefully elevated the wine flagon over Peggy's upturned face. He was suddenly very conscious of her red, parted lips, her white teeth. He tilted, allowing a thin trickle of the pale yellow fluid to emerge. She coughed and spluttered, shook her head violently. Then she gasped, "Haven't the knack of it—although I can manage a Spanish wineskin. Try again."

And now it was Brasidus who had to be careful, very careful. He was acutely aware of her physical proximity, her firm softness. "Ready?" he asked shakily.

"Yes. Fire at will."

This time the attempt was more successful. When at last she held up her hand to signal that she had had enough she must have disposed of at least a third of the flagon. From a pocket in her skirt she pulled a little square of white cloth, wiped her chin and dabbed her lips with it. "That's not a bad drink," she stated. "Sort of dry sherry and ginger . . . but more-ish. No—that's enough. Didn't you ever hear the saying, 'Candy is dandy, but liquor is quicker'?"

"What is candy?" asked Brasidus. "And liquor is quicker for what?"

"Sorry, honey. I was forgetting that you have yet to learn the facts of life. Come to that, there're quite a few facts of life that I have to learn about this peculiar fatherland of yours. What is home without a mother?" She laughed. "Of course, you're lucky. You don't know how lucky. A pseudo-Hellenic culture and nary an Oedipus complex among the whole damn boiling of you!"

"Peggy, please speak Greek."

"Speak English, you mean. But I was using words and phrases that have dropped out of your version of our common tongue." She had slipped a little tablet into her mouth from a tube that she had extracted from her pocket. Suddenly her enunciation was less slurred. "Sorry, Brasidus, but this local tipple of yours is rather potent. Just as well that I brought along some soberer-uppers."

"But why do you need them? Surely one of the pleasures of drinking—the pleasure of drinking—is the effect; the . . . the loosening up."

"And the drunken brawl?"

"Yes," he said firmly.

"You mean that you'd like to . . . to brawl with me?"

Brasidus glimpsed a vivid mental picture of such an encounter and, with no hesitation, said, once again, "Yes."

"Drive on," she told him.

»«Chapter 16»«

They drove on, through and over the foothills, always climbing, the snowcapped peak of Olympus ever ahead, until, at last, Brasidus brought the car to a halt in the single street of a tiny village that clung precariously to the mountainside.

"Kilkis," he announced. "The tavern here could be worse. We halt here for our midday meal."

"Kilkis." The Arcadian repeated the name, gazed around her at the huddle of low but not ungraceful buildings, and then to the boulder-strewn slopes upon which grazed flocks of slow-moving, dun-colored beasts, many of them almost ready to reproduce by fission. "Kilkis," she repeated. "And how do the people here make a living? Do they take in each other's washing?"

"I don't understand, Peggy."

"Sorry, Brasidus. What are those animals?"

"Goats," he explained. "The major source of our meat supply." He went on, happy to be upon more familiar ground, "The only helots allowed to carry arms are the goatherds—see, there's one by that rock. He has a horn to summon assistance, and a sword, and a spear."

"Odd-looking goats. And why the weapons? Against rustlers?"

"Rustlers?"

"Cattle thieves. Or goat thieves."

"No. Goat raiding is classed as a military operation, and, in any case, none of the other city-states would dare to violate our borders. We have the Navy, of course, and firearms and armored chariots. They do not. But there're still the wolves, Peggy, and they're no respecters of frontiers."

"H'm. Then I think that you should allow your goatherds to carry at least a rifle. Is it a hazardous occupation?"

"It is, rather. But the schools maintain a steady flow of replacements, mainly from among those who have just failed to make the grade as hoplites."

"I see. Failed soldiers rather than passed veterinarians."

They got out of the car and walked slowly into the inn, into a long room with rush-strewn floor, tables and benches, low, raftered ceiling, and a not unpleasant smell of sour wine and cookery. At one end of the room there was an open fire, upon which simmered a huge iron cauldron. The half dozen or so customers—rough-looking fellows, leather-clad, wiry rather than muscular—got slowly to their feet at the sight of Brasidus' uniform, made reluctant and surly salutation. And then, as they got a proper look at his companion, there was more than a flicker of interest on their dark, seamed faces.

"You may be seated," Brasidus told them curtly.

"Thank you, Sergeant," replied one of them, his voice only just short of open insolence.

The taverner—fat, greasy, obsequious—waddled from the back of the room. "Your pleasure, lords?" he asked.

"A flagon of your best wine. And," added Brasidus, "two of your finest goblets to drink it from. What have you to eat?"

"Only the stew, lord. But it is made from a fine, fat young goat, just this very morning cast off from its father. Or we have sausage—well-ripened and well-seasoned."

"Peggy?" said Brasidus, with an interrogative intonation.

"The stew will do very nicely. I think. It smells good. And it's been boiled, so it should be safer . . ."

The innkeeper stared at her. "And may I be so impertinent as to inquire if the lord is from the strange spaceship?"

"You've already done so," Margaret Lazenby told him, then relented. "Yes. I am from the ship."

"You must find our world very beautiful, lord."

"Yes. It is beautiful. And interesting."

Roughly, Brasidus pulled out a bench from a vacant table, almost forced Peggy down onto the seat. "What about that wine?" he growled to the innkeeper.

"Yes, lord. Coming, lord. At once."

One of the goatherds whispered something to his companions, then chuckled softly. Brasidus glared at the men, ostentatiously loosened the flap of the holster of his projectile pistol. There was an uneasy silence, and then, one by one, the goatherds rose to their feet and slouched out of the room. The Arcadian complained, "I had my recorder going." She did something to the controls of one of the instruments slung at her side. An amplified voice said loudly, "Since when has the Army been playing nurse to offworld monsters?"

"Insolent swine!"

"Don't be silly. They're entitled to their opinions."

"They're not. They insulted me." Then, as an afterthought, "And you."

"I've been called worse things than 'offworld monster' in my time. And you've ruined their lunchtime session, to say nothing of my chances of making a record of a typical tavern conversation."

Reluctantly, "I'm sorry."

"So you damn well should be."

The innkeeper arrived with a flagon and two goblets. They were mismatched, and they could have been cleaner, but they were of glass, not of earthenware or metal, and of a standard surprising in an establishment such as this. He placed them carefully on the rough surface of the table, then stood there, wine jug in hand, awaiting the word to pour.

"Just a minute," Margaret Lazenby said. She picked up one of the drinking vessels, examined it. "H'm. Just as I thought."

"And what did you think, Peggy?"

"Look," she said, and her pointed, polished fingernail traced the design of the crest etched into the surface of the glass. "A stylized Greek helmet. And under it, easy enough to read after all these years, 'I.T.T.S. DORIC.'"

"I.T.T.S.?"

"Interstellar Transport Commission's Ship."

"But I thought that your ship belonged to the Interstellar Federation's Survey Service."

"It does."

"But apart from the Latterhaven freighters, no ships but yours have ever called here."

"Somebody must have. But what about getting these . . . these antiques filled?"

Brasidus gestured to the innkeeper, who, after a second's hesitation, filled the Arcadian's glass first. One did not have to be a telepath to appreciate the man's indecision. Here was a sergeant—and a sergeant in the Police Battalion of the Army at that. Here was an alien, in what might be uniform and what might be civilian clothing. Who ranked whom?

Brasidus lifted his goblet. "To your good health, Peggy."

"And to yours." She sipped. "H'm. Not at all bad. Of course, in this setting it should be retsina, and there should be feta and black olives to nibble . . ."

"You will speak in riddles, Peggy."

"I'm sorry, Brasidus. It's just that you're so . . . so human in spite of everything that I keep forgetting that your world has been in isolation for centuries. But suppose we just enjoy the meal?"

And they did enjoy it. Brasidus realized that his own appreciation of it was enhanced by the Arcadian's obvious delight in the—to her—unfamiliar food and drink. They finished their stew, and then there were ripe, red, gleaming apples—"Like no apples that I've ever seen or tasted," commented Peggy, "but they'll do. Indeed they will"— and another flagon of wine. When they were done, save for the liquor remaining in the jug, Brasidus wiped his mouth on the back of his right hand, watched with tolerant amusement as his companion patted her lips with a little square of white cloth that she brought from one of her pockets.

She said, "That was good, Brasidus." From a packet that she produced from a shoulder pouch she half shook two slim brown cylinders. "Smoke?"

"Is this the same stuff that Commander Grimes was burning in that wooden thing like a little trumpet?"

"It is. Yours must be about the only Man-colonized world that hasn't tobacco. Commander Grimes likes his pipe; I prefer a cigarillo. See—this is the striking end. Just a tap—so. Put the other end in your mouth." She showed him how, then remarked, as she exhaled a fragrant blue cloud, "I hope that the same doesn't happen to us as happened to Sir Walter Raleigh."

"And what did happen?" Brasidus inhaled, then coughed and spluttered violently. He hastily dropped the little cylinder onto his plate. Probably this Sir Walter Raleigh, whoever he was, had been violently ill.

"Sir Walter Raleigh was the Elizabethan explorer who first introduced tobacco into a country called England. He was enjoying his pipe after a meal in an inn, and the innkeeper thought that he was on fire and doused him with a bucket of water."

"This fat flunkey had better not try it on you!" growled Brasidus.

"I doubt if he'd dare. From what I've observed, a sergeant on this planet piles on more G's than a mere knight in the days of Good Queen Bess." She laughed through the wreathing, aromatic fumes—then, suddenly serious, said, "We have company."

Brasidus swung round, his right hand on the butt of

his pistol. But it was only the village corporal—a big man in slovenly uniform, his leather unpolished, his brass tarnished. His build, his broad, heavy face were indicative of slowness both physical and mental, but the little gray eyes under the sandy thatch of the eyebrows were shrewd enough.

"Sergeant!" he barked, saluting and stiffening to attention.

"Corporal—at ease! Be seated."

"Thank you, Sergeant."

"Some wine, Corporal?"

The corporal reached out a long arm to one of the other tables, grabbed an earthenware mug, filled it from the flagon. "Thank you, Sergeant. Your health, Sergeant. And yours, sir." He drank deeply and noisily. "Ah, that was good. But, Sergeant, my apologies. I should have been on hand to welcome you and . . ." he stared curiously at the Arcadian. "You and your . . . guest?"

"Doctor Lazenby is one of the officers of the starship *Seeker*."

"I thought that, Sergeant. Even here there are stories." The man, Brasidus realized, was staring at the odd mounds of flesh that were very obvious beneath the thin shirt worn by the alien.

"They aren't concealed weapons," remarked the Arcadian wryly. "And, in the proper circumstances, they are quite functional."

The corporal flushed, looked away and addressed himself to his superior. "I was absent from the village, Sergeant, as today is Exposure Day. I had to supervise. But as soon as I was told of your arrival, I hastened back."

"Exposure Day?" asked Margaret Lazenby sharply.

"Yes," Brasidus told her. "One of the days on which the newly born—those newly born who are sickly or deformed, that is—are exposed on the mountainside."

"And what happens to them?"

"Usually the wolves finish them off. But without food or water they'd not last long."

"You're joking." It was an appeal rather than a statement or a question.

"But why should I joke, Peggy? The purity of the race must be maintained."

She turned to the corporal, her face white, her eyes blazing. "You. Had the wolves come when you left the . . . the Exposure?"

"No, sir. But they're never long in hearing the cries and winding the scent."

She was on her feet, pushing her bench away so violently that it toppled with a crash. "Get a move on, Brasidus. If we hurry, we may still be in time."

Brasidus was sickened by her reactions, by her words. Exposure was necessary, but it was not something to take pictures of, to make records of. As well join the scavengers in their filth-eating rounds of the city streets.

"Come on!" she flared.

"No," he said stubbornly. "I'll not help you to make a film that you and your shipmates can gloat over."

"Make a film?" Her voice was incredulous. "You fool. We may be in time to save them."

And then it was Brasidus' turn to experience a wave of incredulity.

›»《Chapter 17》«‹

"No!" said Brasidus.

"Yes!" she contradicted him. But, incongruously, it was not the borrowed pistol that she was leveling at the two men, but a camera. Brasidus laughed—and then the slim hands holding the seemingly innocuous instrument twitched ever so slightly, and from the lens came an almost invisible flicker of light and, behind the policemen, something exploded. There was a sudden, acrid stench of flash-boiled wine, of burning wood.

That deadly lens was looking straight at Brasidus again.

"Laser," he muttered.

"Laser," she stated.

"But . . . but you were supposed to leave all your weapons behind."

"I'm not altogether a fool, honey. And, oddly enough, this is a camera, with flash attachment. Not a very good one, but multipurpose tools are rarely satisfactory. Now, are you going to drive me out to the Exposure?"

She'll have to bring along the corporal, thought Brasidus. And the two of us should be able to deal with her.

And now the deadly camera was in her left hand only, and the borrowed stun gun was out of its holster. She fired left-handed, and at this short range she could hardly miss. The corporal gasped, made one tottering step forward, then crashed untidily to the floor. The belled muzzle swung slightly and she fired again. There was the sound of another heavy fall behind Brasidus. That, he guessed, would be the innkeeper. There would be no telephone calls made to the city for several hours. The goatherds were notorious for their reluctance to assist the forces of law and order.

"Get into the car," she said. "I'll ride behind. And make it snappy."

He walked out of the inn, into the afternoon sunlight, deliberately not hurrying. He consoled himself with the thought that, even though he was falling down on the job as a sergeant of Police, he was earning his keep as a lieutenant of Security. He had been told to find out what made these aliens tick—and he was finding out. In any case, if the wolf packs were as ravenous as usual, there would be nothing left but a scatter of well-gnawed bones.

He climbed into the driver's seat, thought briefly about making a dash for it, then thought better of it. He could never get out of range in time. He heard her clambering in behind him. He wished that he knew which way that so-called camera was pointing—and then he succeeded in catching a glimpse of it in the rear mirror. If the firing stud were accidentally pressed, it would drill a neat, cauterized hole through his head. Or would the water content of his brains explode? In that case, it would not be so tidy.

"Get going," she said. And then, as an afterthought, "I suppose you know the way."

"I know the way," he admitted. The car lifted on its air cushion and proceeded.

"Faster. Faster."

"This is only a goat track," he grumbled. "And this isn't an armored chariot we're riding in."

Even so, deliberately taking the risk of fouling the fan casings on projecting stones, he managed to increase speed. Rather to his disappointment, the vehicle still rode easily, sped over the rough terrain without making any crippling contacts.

And then, ahead of them, seemingly from just over the next rise, sounded the ominous howling and snarling of the wolf pack, and with it, almost inaudible, a thin, high screaming.

"Hurry!" Margaret Lazenby was shouting. "Hurry!"

They were over the rise now. Once before, Brasidus had watched an Exposure, and the spectacle had sickened him, even though he had realized the necessity for it, and appreciated the essential justice of allowing Nature to erase its own mistakes in its own way. But to rescue one or more of these mewling, subhuman creatures—that was unthinkable.

The car was over the rise.

And then it was bearing down on the snarling, quarreling pack, on the carnivores too engrossed in their bloody business to notice the approach of potential enemies. But perhaps they heard the whine of the ducted fans and, even so, remembered that, on these occasions, Men never interfered with them.

The car was sweeping down the slope toward the mêlée, and Margaret Lazenby was firing. Brasidus could feel the heat of the discharges, cursed as the hair on the right side of his head crisped and smoldered. But he maintained a steady course nonetheless, and experienced the inevitable thrill of the hunt, the psychological legacy from Man's savage ancestors. Ahead there was a haze of vaporized blood; the stench of seared flesh was already evident. The howling of the pack rose to a frenzied crescendo but the animals stood their ground, red eyes glaring, slavering, crimsoned jaws agape. Then—an evil, gray, stormy tide—they began to surge up the hillside to meet their attackers.

Brasidus was shooting now, the control column grasped in his left hand, the bucking projectile pistol in his right. Between them, he and Margaret Lazenby cleared a path for their advance, although the car rocked and lurched as it passed over the huddle of dead and dying bodies. Then—"Stop!" she was crying. "Stop! There's a baby there! I saw it move!"

Yes, there, among the ghastly litter of scattered bones and torn flesh, was a living child, eyes screwed tight shut, bawling mouth wide open. It would not be living much longer. Already two of the wolves, ignoring the slaughter of their companions, were facing each other over the tiny, feebly struggling body, their dreadful teeth bared as they snarled at each other.

Margaret Lazenby was out of the car before Brasidus could bring it to a halt. Inevitably she lost her balance and fell, rolling down the slope, almost to where the two carnivores were disputing over their prey. She struggled somehow to her knees just as they saw her, just as they abandoned what was no more than a toothsome morsel for a satisfying meal. Somehow, awkwardly, she managed to bring her camera-gun into firing position, but the weapon must have been damaged by her fall. She cried out and threw it from her, in a smoking, spark-spitting arc that culminated in the main body of the pack. Even as it exploded in a soundless flare of raw energy she was tugging the borrowed stun gun from its holster.

Once she fired, and once only, and one of the two wolves faltered in the very act of leaping, slumped to the ground. The other one completed its spring and was on her, teeth and taloned hind paws slashing. Brasidus was out of the car, running, a pistol in each hand. But he could not use his guns—animal and alien formed together a wildly threshing tangle, and to fire at one would almost certainly mean hitting the other. But the Arcadian was fighting desperately and well, as yet seemed to be undamaged. Her hands about the brute's neck were keeping those slavering jaws from her throat, and her knee in the wolf's belly was still keeping those slashing claws at a distance. But she was tiring. It would not be long before sharp fangs found her jugular or slashing talons opened her up from breastbone to groin.

Dropping his weapons, Brasidus jumped. From behind he got his own two hands around the furry throat, his own knee into the beast's back. He exerted all of his strength, simultaneously pulled and thrust. The animal whined, then was abruptly silent as the air supply to the laboring lungs was cut off. But it was still strong, was still resisting desperately, was striving to turn so that it could face this fresh enemy.

Margaret Lazenby had fallen clear of the fight, was slowly crawling to where she had dropped her pistol.

She never had to use it. Brasidus brought his last reserves of strength into play, heard the sharp snap of broken vertebrae. The fight was over.

He got groggily to his feet, ready to face and to fight a fresh wave of carnivores. But, save for the Arcadian, the squalling child and himself, the hillside was bare of life. There were charred bodies, human and animal, where the laser weapon had exploded; the other wolves, such of them as had survived, must have fled. The stench of burning flesh was heavy in the air.

At a tottering run, Margaret Lazenby was hurrying to the child, the only survivor of the Exposure. More slowly, Brasidus followed, looked down at the little naked body. He said, "It would have been kinder to let it die. What sort of life can it expect with that deformity?"

"Deformity? What the hell do you mean?"

Wordlessly he pointed to the featureless scissure of the baby's thighs.

"Deformity? This, you fool, is a perfectly formed female child."

She got down to her knees and tenderly picked up the infant. And, as she did so, it became somehow obvious that the odd mounds of flesh on her chest, fully revealed now that her shirt had been torn away, were, after all, functional. The baby stopped crying, groped greedily for an erect pink nipple.

Peggy laughed shakily. "No, darling, no. I'm sorry, but the milk bar's not open for business. I'll make up a bottle for you when we get back to the ship."

"So," muttered Brasidus at last, "so it is one of your race."

"Yes."

"And those . . . lumps are where you fission from."

She said, "You've still a lot to learn. And now give me your tunic, will you."

"My tunic?"

"Yes. Don't just stand there, looking as though you've never seen a woman before." Brasidus silently stripped off his upper garment, handed it to her. He expected that she would put the child back on the ground while she covered her own seminudity. But she did not. Instead, she wrapped the baby in the tunic, cooing to it softly. "There, there. You were cold, weren't you? But Mummy will keep you warm, and Mummy will see that you're fed." She straightened, then snapped in a voice of command, "Take me back to the ship, as fast as all the Odd Gods of the Galaxy will let you!"

»)«(Chapter 18»)«

So they drove back to the ship swiftly, bypassing Kilkis—Brasidus had no desire to meet again the village corporal—taking roads that avoided all centers of population, however small. Peggy was in the back of the car, making soft, soothing noises to the querulous infant. Achron, thought Brasidus sullenly, would have appreciated this display of paternal solicitude—but I do not. And what did he feel? Jealousy, he was obliged to admit, resentment at being deprived of the Arcadian's company. Perverts the doctors in the créche might be, but these aliens could and did exert a dangerous charm. But when it came to a showdown, as now, they had no time for mere humans, lavished their attentions only upon their own kind.

Suddenly the child was silent. The car was speeding down a straight stretch of road, so Brasidus was able to risk turning his head to see what was happening. Peggy had the stopper out of the wine flask, was dipping a corner of her handkerchief into it, then returning the soaked scrap of rag to the eager mouth of the baby. She grinned ruefully as she met Brasidus' stare. "I know it's all wrong," she said. "But I haven't a feeding bottle. Too, it will help if the brat is sound asleep when we get back to the spaceport."

"And why will it help?" demanded Brasidus, turning his attention back to the road ahead.

She said, "It's occurred to me that we have probably broken quite a few laws. Apart from anything else, armed assault upon the person of a police officer must be illegal."

"It is. But you carried out the armed assault. We did not."

She laughed. "Too true. But what about our interference with the Exposure? It will be better for both of us if your boss doesn't know that the interference was a successful one."

"I must make my report," said Brasidus stiffly.

"Of course." Her voice was soft, caressing. "But need it be a full report? We got into a fight with the wolf pack— there's too much evidence littered around on the hillside for us to lie our way out of that. I've a few nasty scratches on my back and my breasts."

"So that's what they're called. I was wondering."

"Never mind that now. I've got these scratches, so it's essential that I get back on board as soon as possible for treatment by our own doctor."

"I thought that you were the ship's doctor."

"I'm not. I have a doctorate in my own field, which is not medicine. But let me finish. We had this fight with these four-legged sharks you people call wolves. I fell out of the car, and you jumped out and saved my life, although not before I was mauled a little. And that's near enough to the truth, isn't it?"

"Yes."

"Now, the child. She'll fit nicely into the hamper you brought the provisions in. The poor little tot will be in a drugged stupor by the time we get to the spaceport, so she'll be quiet enough. And with your tunic spread over her, who will know?"

"I don't like it," said Brasidus.

"That makes two of us, my dear. I don't like having to conceal the evidence of actions that, on any world but this, would bring a public commendation."

"But Diomedes will know."

"How can he know? We were there, he was not. And we don't even have to make sure that we tell the same story, exact in every detail. He can question you, but he can't question me."

"Don't be so sure about that, Peggy."

"Oh, he'd like to, Brasidus. He'd like to. But he knows that at all times there are sufficient officers and ratings aboard *Seeker* to handle the drive and main and secondary armaments. He knows that we could swat your gasbags out of the sky in a split second, and then raze the city in our own good time." There was a long silence. Then, "I'm sorry to have gotten you into quite a nasty mess, Brasidus, but you realize that I had no choice."

"Like calls to like," he replied with bitter flippancy.

"You could put it that way, I suppose, but you're wrong. Anyhow, I'm sure that I shall be able to persuade John—Commander Grimes—to offer you the sanctuary of our ship if you're really in a jam."

"I'm a Spartan," he said.

"With all the Spartan virtues, I suppose. Do you have

that absurd legend about the boy who let the fox gnaw his vitals rather than cry out? No matter. Just tell Captain Diomedes the truth, but not the whole truth. Say that it was all my fault, and that you did your best to restrain me. Which you did—although it wasn't good enough. Say that you saved me from the wolves."

They drove on in silence while Brasidus pondered his course of action. What the Arcadian had said was true, what she had proposed might prevent an already unpleasant situation from becoming even more unpleasant. In saving Peggy's life, he had done no more than his duty; in helping to save the life of the deformed—deformed?—child he, an officer of the law, had become a criminal. And why had he done this? With the destruction of the laser-camera the alien had lost her only advantage.

And why had he known, why did he still know that his part in the rescue operations had been essentially right?

It was this strange awareness of rightness that brought him to full agreement with his companion's propositions. Until now, he had accepted without question the superior intellectual and moral stature of those holding higher rank than himself, but it was obvious that aboard *Seeker* there were officers, highly competent technicians with superbly trained men and fantastically powerful machinery at their command, whose moral code varied widely from the Spartan norm. (Come to that, what about the doctors, the top-ranking aristocrats of the planet, whose own morals were open to doubt? What about the doctors, and their perverse relations with the Arcadians?)

Peggy's voice broke into his thoughts. "She's sleeping now. Out like a light. Drunk as a fiddler's bitch. I think that we shall be able to smuggle her on board without trouble." She went on, "I appreciate this, Brasidus. I do. I wish . . ." He realized that she must be standing up in the back of the car, leaning toward him. He felt her breasts against the bare skin of his back. The contact was like nothing that he had ever imagined. He growled, "Sit down, damn you. Sit down—if you want this wagon to stay on the road!"

»《Chapter 19》«

They encountered no delays on their way back to the spaceport, but, once they were inside the main gates, it was obvious that their return had been anticipated. Diomedes, backed by six armed hoplites, was standing, glowering, outside his office. A little away from him was John Grimes—and it was not a ceremonial sword that depended from his belt but two holstered pistols. And there was another officer from the ship with him, wearing a walky-talky headset. The Commander glared at Brasidus and his companion with almost as much hostility as did Diomedes.

Diomedes raised an imperious arm. Brasidus brought the car to a halt. Grimes said something to his officer, who spoke into the mouthpiece of his headset. Brasidus, looking beyond the young man to the ship, saw that the turrets housing her armament were operational, the long barrels of weapons, fully extruded, waving slowly like the questing antennae of some giant insect.

"Brasidus." Diomedes' voice was a high-pitched squeal, a sure sign of bad temper. "I have received word from the village corporal at Kilkis. I demand your report—and your report, Doctor Lazenby—immediately. You will both come into my office."

"Captain Diomedes," said Grimes coldly, "you have every right to give orders to your own officers, but none whatsoever to issue commands to my personnel. Doctor Lazenby will make her report to me, aboard my ship."

"I have means of enforcing my orders, Commander Grimes."

As one man, the six hoplites drew their stun guns.

Grimes laughed. "My gunnery officer has his instructions, Captain Diomedes. He's watching us from the control room through very high-powered binoculars and, furthermore, he is hearing everything that is being said."

"And what are his instructions, Commander?"

"There's just one way for you to find out, Captain. I shouldn't advise it, though."

"All right." With a visible effort, Diomedes brought himself under control. "All right. I request, then, Commander, that you order your officer to accompany Brasidus into my office for questioning. You, and as many of your people as you wish, may be present."

Grimes obviously was giving consideration to what Diomedes had said. It was reasonable enough. Brasidus knew that, if he were in Grimes' shoes, he would have agreed. But suppose that somebody decided to investigate the contents of that food hamper on the back seat, some thirsty man hopeful that a drink of wine might remain in the flagon. Or suppose that the effects of the alcohol on the presently sleeping baby suddenly wore off.

Margaret Lazenby took charge. She stood up in the back of the car—and the extent of her dishevelment was suddenly obvious. The men stared at her, and Grimes, his fists clenched, took a threatening step toward Brasidus, growling, "You bastard."

"Stop it, John!" The Arcadian's voice was sharp. "Brasidus didn't do this."

"Then who did?"

"Damn it all! Can't you see that I want at least another shirt, as well as medical attention for these scratches? But if you must know, I made Brasidus take me to watch the Exposure."

"So the village corporal told me," put in Diomedes. "And between you, the pair of you slaughtered an entire wolf pack."

"We went too close, and they attacked us. They pulled me out of the car, but Brasidus saved me. And now, Captain Diomedes, I'd like to get back on board as soon as possible for an antibiotic shot and some fresh clothing." Before leaving the car, she stooped to lift the hamper from the back seat, handed it to Grimes' officer.

"What's in that basket?" demanded Diomedes.

"Nothing that concerns you!" she flared.

"I'll decide that," Grimes stated. "Here, Mister Taylor. Let me see."

The officer turned to face his captain, with his body hiding the hamper from Diomedes and his men. It was not intentional—or was it? Grimes, his face emotionless, lifted Brasidus' torn tunic from the open top of the wickerwork container. He said calmly, "One wine flagon. About six inches of gnarled sausage. The heel of a loaf of crusty bread. You decide, Captain, what may be brought off the ship onto your world, I decide what may be brought from your world onto my ship. Mister Taylor, take this hamper to the biochemist so that its contents may be analyzed. And you, Doctor Lazenby, report at once to the surgeon. I'll receive your report later."

"Commander Grimes, I insist that I inspect that hamper." Three of the hoplites stepped forward, began to surround Mister Taylor.

"Captain Diomedes, if any of your men dare to lay hands upon my officer the consequences will be serious."

Diomedes laughed incredulously. "You'd open fire over a mug of wine and a couple of scraps of bread and sausage?"

"Too right I would."

Diomedes laughed again. "You aliens . . ." he said contemptuously. "All right, you can have your crumbs from the sergeants' mess. And I'd like a few words with your Doctor Lazenby as soon as she can spare me the time. And I'll have rather more than a few words with you, Brasidus, now!"

Reluctantly Brasidus got out of the car.

"And you let her threaten you with a laser weapon—and, furthermore, one that you had allowed her to carry . . ."

Brasidus, facing Diomedes, who was lolling behind his desk, said rebelliously, "You, sir, checked her equipment. And she told me herself that the thing did function as a camera."

"All right. We'll let that pass. You allowed her to use a stun gun on the village corporal and the innkeeper, and then you drove her out to the Exposure. Why, Brasidus, did you have to stop at Kilkis, of all villages, on this day, of all days?"

"Nobody told me not to, sir. And, as you know, the dates of the Exposures are never advertised. You might have been informed, but I was not."

"So you drove her out to see the Exposure. And you got too close. And the wolves attacked you, and pulled her out of the car."

"That is correct, sir."

"Surely she could have used this famous laser-camera to defend herself."

"It was damaged, sir. She had to throw it away in a hurry. It blew up."

"Yes. I've been told that there's an area on the hillside that looks as though some sort of bomb had been exploded." He leaned back in his chair, looked up at the standing Brasidus. "You say that the wolves attacked her. Are you sure that it wasn't you?"

"And why should it have been me, sir?"

"Because it should have been. You let an alien order you around at gun point, and then you ask me why you should have attacked her! And now . . ." the words came out with explosive violence, "What was in the hamper?"

"Wine, sir. Bread. Sausage."

"And what was your tunic doing there?"

"I lent it to her, sir, to replace her own shirt."

"So, instead of wearing it, she put it in the hamper."

"The air was warm, sir, when we got down from the

mountains. She asked me if she could have it so that the fibers from which it is woven could be analyzed by the . . . the biochemist."

"H'm. All in all, Brasidus, you did not behave with great brilliance. Were it not for the fact that these aliens—or one alien in particular—seem to like you, I should dispense with your services. As it is, you are still useful. Now, just what were this Margaret Lazenby's reactions when she learned of the Exposure?"

Lying, Brasidus knew, would be useless. The village corporal at Kilkis would have made a full report. He said, "She was shocked. She wanted to get to the site in time to rescue the deformed and defective children."

"You were not in time, of course."

"No, sir. We were not in time." He added virtuously, "I made sure of that."

"How, Brasidus?"

"I knew the way, she did not. I was able to make a detour."

The answer seemed to satisfy Diomedes. He grunted, "All right. You may sit down." For a few seconds he drummed on the desktop with his fingertips. "Meanwhile, Brasidus, the situation in the city is developing. Commander Grimes allowed his Arcadians, as well as the human members of his crew, shore leave. There was an unfortunate occurrence in the Tavern of the Three Harpies. An Arcadian, accompanied by a human spaceman, went in there. They got drinking with the other customers."

"Not the sort of place that I'd drink in by choice," Brasidus said, the other's silence seeming to call for some sort of comment.

"They were not so fortunate as to have a guide, such as yourself, to keep them out of trouble." (You sarcastic swine, thought Brasidus.) "Anyhow, there was the usual crowd in there. Helots of the laboring class, hoplites not fussy about the company they keep. It wouldn't have been so bad if the two spacemen had just taken one drink and then walked out, but they stayed there, drinking with the locals, and allowed themselves to be drawn into an argument. And you know how arguments in the Three Harpies usually finish."

"There was a fight, sir?"

"Brilliant, Brasidus, brilliant. There was a fight, and the human spaceman was laid out, and the Arcadian was beaten up a little, and then stripped. There was, you will understand, some curiosity as to what her body was like under her uniform."

"That was bad, sir."

"There's worse to follow. At least four hoplites had sexual intercourse with her by force."

"So it is possible, sir, in spite of the malformation."

Diomedes chuckled obscenely. "It's possible, all right. Everybody in the tavern would have had her if the other spaceman hadn't come round and started screaming for help on a little portable transceiver he wore on his wrist. A dozen men from the ship rushed in, real toughs—and I wish that my own personnel could learn their techniques of unarmed combat. Then the police condescended to intervene and laid everybody out with their stun guns, and then Commander Grimes, who'd heard about it somehow, came charging into my office threatening to devastate the city, and . . . and . . .

"Anyhow, you can see why I had to handle this Lazenby creature with kid gloves. Even though Grimes admits that his own crew were at fault—he had issued strict orders that no sightseeing party was to consist of fewer than six people—he was furious about the 'rape,' as he called it. You saw how he reacted when he thought that you had been doing something of the kind. He demanded that the rapists be punished most severely."

"But they were hoplites, sir, not helots. They had the right . . ."

"I know, I know. When I need instruction in the finer points of Spartan law, I'll come to you. The conduct was discourteous rather than criminal. The culprits will, by this time, have been reprimanded by their commanding officer, and will, in all probability, he back in the Three Harpies, telling anybody who cares to listen what intercourse is like with an Arcadian. It is, I gather, quite an experience. Are you quite sure that you didn't . . .?"

"Quite sure, sir."

"That's your story, and you stick to it." Again there was a pause, and the muffled drumming of Diomedes' fingers on the top of his desk. Then he went on, "Even on Sparta we have experienced occasional mutiny, infrequent rebellion. Tell me, Brasidus, what are the prime causes of mutiny?"

"Discontent, sir. Overly strict discipline. Unjust punishments . . ."

"And . . .?"

"That's about all, sir."

"What about envy, Brasidus?"

"No sir. We all know that if we show ability we shall

become officers, with all the privileges that go with rank."

"But what if there's a privilege out of reach to everybody except a few members of one aristocratic caste?"

"I don't see what you mean, sir."

"Brasidus, Brasidus, what do you use for brains? What about that nest of Arcadians in the créche? What do you suppose the doctors use them for?"

"I . . . I can guess."

"And so they have something that the rest of us haven't. And so"—Diomedes' voice dropped almost to a whisper—"the power that they've enjoyed for so long, for too long, may be broken."

"And you," said Brasidus, "envy them that power."

For long seconds the Captain glared at him across the desk. Then, "All right, I do. But it is for the good of the State that I am working against them."

Perhaps, thought Brasidus. Perhaps. But he said nothing.

")((Chapter 20))(("

Clad in a laboring helot's drab, patched tunic, his feet unshod and filthy, his face and arms liberally besmeared with the dirt of the day's toil, Brasidus sat hunched at one of the long tables in the Tavern of the Three Harpies. There were hoplites there as well as manual workers, but there was little chance that any of them would recognize him. Facial similarities were far from uncommon on Sparta.

He sat there, taking an occasional noisy gulp from his mug and listening.

One of the hoplites was holding forth to his companions. "Yes, it was on this very table that I had him. Or it. Good it was. You've no idea unless you've tried it yourself."

"Must've been odd. Wrong, somehow."

"It was odd, all right. But wrong nohow. This face-to-face business. And those two dirty great cushions for your chest to rest on . . ."

"Is that what they're for?"

"Must be. Pity the doctors can't turn out some of those creatures from their birth machine."

"But they do. Yes. They do."

Everybody turned to stare at the man who had just spoken. He was a stranger to Brasidus, but his voice and his appearance marked him for what he was. This was not the sort of inn that the nurses from the créche usually frequented—in an establishment such as this they would run a grave risk of suffering the same fate as the unfortunate Arcadian from the ship. "They do," he repeated in his high-pitched sing-song, and looked straight at Brasidus. There was something in his manner that implied, And you know, too.

So this was the fellow agent whom Diomedes had told him that he would find in the tavern, the operative to whom he was to render assistance if necessary.

"And what do you know about it, dearie?" demanded the boastful hoplite.

"I'm a nurse . . ."

"That's obvious, sweetie pie."

"I'm a nurse, and I work at the créche. We nurses aren't supposed to stray from our wards, but . . ."

"But with a snout like yours, you're bound to be nosy," said the hoplite laughing.

The nurse stroked his overlong proboscis with his right index finger, grinned slyly. "How right you are, dearie. I admit it. I like to know what's going on. Oh, those doctors! They live in luxury, all right. You might think that practically all of the créche is taken up by wards and machinery and the like, but it's not. More than half the building is their quarters. And the things they have! A heated swimming pool, even."

"Decadent," grunted a grizzled old sergeant.

"But nice. Especially in midwinter. Not that I've ever tried it myself. There's a disused storeroom, and this pool is on the other side of its back wall. There're some holes in the wall, where there used to be wiring or pipes or something. Big enough for a camera lens." The nurse fished a large envelope from inside the breast of his white tunic, pulled from it a sheaf of glossy photographs.

"Lemme see. Yes, those are Arcadians, all right. Top-heavy, ain't they, when you see them standing up. Wonder how they can walk without falling flat on their faces."

"If they did, they'd bounce."

"Look sort of unfinished lower down, don't they?"

"Let me see!"

"Here, pass 'em round, can't you?"

Briefly, Brasidus had one of the prints in his possession. He was interested more in the likeness of the man standing by the pool than in that of his companion. Yes, it was Heraklion, all right, Heraklion without his robe but still, indubitably, the supercilious doctor.

"Must have come in that ship," remarked somebody.

"No," the nurse told him. "Oh, no. They've been in the créche for years."

"You mean your precious doctors have always had them?"

"Yes. Nothing but the best for the guardians of the purity of our Spartan stock, dearie. But who are we to begrudge them their little comforts?"

"Soldiers, that's who. It's we who should be the top caste of this world, who should have the first pickings. After all, the King's a soldier."

"But the doctors made him, dearie. They made all of us."

"Like hell they did. They just look after the birth machine. And if there wasn't a machine, we'd manage all right, just as the animals do."

"We might have to," the nurse said. "I heard two of the doctors talking. They were saying that the people were having it too soft, that for the good of the race we should have to return to the old ways. They're thinking of shutting the machine down."

"What! How can you be a fighting man if you have to lug a child around with you?"

"But you said that we could manage all right without the doctors."

"Yes. But that's different. No, the way I see it is this. These doctors are getting scared of the military, but they know that if most of us are budding we shan't be much good for fighting. Oh, the cunning swine! They just want things all their way all the time instead of for only most of the time."

"But you can't do anything about it," the nurse said.

"Can't we? Who have the weapons and the training to use 'em? Not your doctors, that's for certain. With no more than the men in this tavern, we could take the créche—and get our paws on to those Arcadians they've got stashed away there."

"More than our paws!" shouted somebody.

"You're talking mutiny and treason, hoplite," protested the elderly sergeant.

"Am I?" The man was on his feet now, swaying drunkenly. "But the King himself had one of the doctors executed. That shows how much he thinks of 'em!" He paused, striving for words. They came at last. "Here, on

Sparta, it's fair shares for all—excepting you poor damn helots, of course. But for the rest of us, the rulers, it should be share an' share alike. Oh, I know that the colonel gets better pay, better grub an' better booze than I do—but in the field he lives the same as his men, an' all of us can become colonels ourselves if we put ourselves to it, an', come to that, generals. But the colonels an' the generals an' the admirals don't have Arcadians to keep their beds warm. Not even the King does. An' now there's some of us who know what it's like. An' there's some of us who want more of it."

"They're plenty of Arcadians aboard the spaceship," somebody suggested.

"I may be drunk, fellow, but I'm not that drunk. The spaceship's a battlewagon, and I've heard that the captain of her has already threatened to use his guns and missiles. No, the créche'll be easy to take."

"Sit down, you fool!" ordered the elderly sergeant. "You got off light after you assaulted the Arcadian space-man, but he was only a foreigner. Now you're inciting to riot, mutiny, and the gods alone know what else. The police will use more than stun guns on you this time."

"Will they, old-timer? Will they? And what if they do? A man can die only once. What I did to that Arcadian has done something to me, to me, do you hear? I have to do it again, even though I get shot for it." The man's eyes were crazy and his lips, foam-flecked. "You don't know what it was like. You'll never know, until you do it. Don't talk to me about boys, or about soft, puling nurses like our long-nosed friend here. The doctors have the best there is, the best that there can ever be, and they should be made to share it!"

"The police . . ." began the sergeant.

"Yes. The police. Now let me tell you, old-timer, that I kept my ears flapping while they had me in their barracks. Practically every man has been called out to guard the spaceport—the spaceport, do you hear? That alien captain's afraid that there'll be a mob coming out to take his pretty Arcadians by force, and fat old Captain Diomedes is afraid that the space commander'll start firing off in all directions if his ship and his little pets are menaced. By the time that the police get back to the city, every Arcadian in the créche'll know what a real man is like, an' we shall all be tucked up in our cots in our quarters sleeping innocently."

"I didn't see a single policeman on my way here," contributed the nurse. "I wondered why." And then, in spurious alarm, "But you can't. You mustn't. You mustn't attack the créche!"

"And who says I mustn't? You, you feeble imitation of a . . . a . . ." He concluded triumphantly, "of an alien monster! Yes, that's a point. All this talk of them as alien monsters. It was only to put us off. But now we know. Or some of us know. Who's with me?"

The fools, thought Brasidus, the fools! as he listened to the crash of overturned benches, as he watched almost all the customers of the tavern, helots as well as hoplites, jump to their feet.

"The fools," he muttered aloud.

"And you would have been with them," whispered the nurse, "if I hadn't slipped a capsule into your drink." And then Brasidus saw the thin wisp of almost invisible vapor that was still trickling from the envelope in which the photographs had been packed. "I have access to certain drugs," said the man smugly, "and this one is used in our schoolrooms. It enhances the susceptibility of the students."

"Students," repeated Brasidus disgustedly.

"They have a lot to learn, Lieutenant," the nurse told him.

"And so have I. I want to see what happens."

"Your orders were to protect me."

"There's nobody here to protect you from, except that old sergeant. But why wasn't he affected?"

"Too old," said the nurse.

"Then you're quite safe."

Brasidus made his way from the tavern out into the street.

»《Chapter 21》«

He would have retreated to the safety of the inn, but he was given no opportunity to do so. A roaring torrent of men swept along the street, hoplites and helots, shouting, cursing and screaming. He was caught up by the human tide, buffeted and jostled, crying out with pain himself when a heavy, military sandal smashed down on one of his bare feet. He was sucked into the mob, made part of it, became just one tiny drop of water in the angry wave that was rearing up to smash down upon the créche.

At first, he was fighting only to keep upright, to save himself from falling, from being trampled underfoot. And then—slowly, carefully and, at times, viciously—he began to edge out toward the fringe of the living current. At last he was able to stumble into a cross alley where he stood panting, recovering his breath, watching the rioters stream past.

Then he was able to think.

It seemed obvious to him that Diomedes must have

planted his agents in more than one tavern. It was obvious, too, that Diomedes, ever the opportunist, had regarded the unfortunate incident in the Three Harpies as a heaven-sent opportunity for rabble-rousing—and as an excuse for the withdrawal of all police from the city. And that is all that it was—an excuse. It was doubtful, thought Brasidus, that Grimes had demanded protection. The spaceman was quite capable of looking after himself and his own people—and if the situation got really out of hand he could always lift ship at a second's notice.

But there were still puzzling features in the situation. The military police were under the command of General Rexenor, with the usual tally of colonels and majors subordinate to him. Diomedes was only a captain. How much power did the man wield? How much backing had he? Was he—and this seemed more than likely—answerable only to the palace?

The mob was thinning out now; there were only the stragglers half-running, stumbling over the cobblestones. And already the first of the scavengers were emerging from their hiding places, sniffing cautiously at the crumpled bodies of those who had been crushed and trampled. Brasidus fell in with the tattered rearguard, kept pace with a withered, elderly man in rough and dirty working clothes.

"Don't . . . know . . . why . . . . we . . . bother . . ." grunted this individual between gasping breaths. "Bloody . . . hoplites . . . 'll . . . be . . . there . . . first. All . . . the . . . bloody . . . pickings . . . as . . . bloody . . . usual."

"What pickings?"

"Food . . . wine . . . Those . . . bloody . . . doctors . . .

worse . . . 'n . . . bloody . . . soldiers . . . Small . . . wonder
. . . the . . . King . . . has . . . turned . . . against . . . 'em."

"And . . . the Arcadians?"

"Wouldn't . . . touch . . . one . . . o' . . . them . . . wi' . . .
barge . . . pole. Unsightly . . . monsters."

Ahead, the roar of the mob had risen to an ugly and
frightening intensity. There were flames, too, leaping
high, a billowing glare in the night sky. The crowd had
broken into a villa close by the créche, the Club House of
the senior nursing staff. They had dragged furniture out
into the roadway and set fire to it. Some of its unfortunate
owners fluttered ineffectually about the blaze and, until
one of them had the sense to organize his mates into a
bucket party, were treated with rough derision only. And
then the crowd turned upon the firemen, beating them,
even throwing three of them into the bonfire. Two of them
managed to scramble clear and ran, screaming, their robes
ablaze. The other just lay there, writhing and shrieking.

Brasidus was sickened. There was nothing that he
could do. He was alone and unarmed—and most of the
soldiers among the rioters carried their short swords and
some of them were already using them, hacking down the
surviving nurses who were still foolish enough to try to
save their property. There was nothing at all that he could
do—and he should have been in uniform, not in these
rags, and armed, with a squad of men at his command,
doing his utmost to quell the disorder.

Damn Diomedes! he thought. He knew, with sudden
clarity, where his real loyalties lay—to the maintenance of
law and order and, on a more personal level, to his friend
Achron, on duty inside the créche and soon, almost

inevitably, to be treated as had been these hacked and incinerated colleagues of his.

The Andronicus warehouse . . .

Nobody noticed him as he crossed the road to that building; the main body of the rioters was attempting to force the huge door of the crèche with a battering ram improvised from a torn-down streetlamp standard. And then, looking at the massive door set in the black, feature-less wall of the warehouse, he realized that he was in dire need of such an implement himself. He could, he knew, enlist the aid of men on the fringes of the crowd eager for some violence in which they, themselves, could take part—but that was the last thing that he wanted. He would enter the crèche alone, if at all.

But how?

How?

Overhead, barely audible, there was a peculiar throbbing noise, an irregular beat. He thought, So the Navy is intervening, then realized that the sound was not that of an airship's engines. He looked up, saw flickering, ruddy light reflected from an oval surface. And then, in a whisper that seemed to originate only an inch from his ear, a familiar voice asked, "Is that you, Brasidus?"

"Yes."

"I owe you plenty. We'll pick you up and take you clear of this mess. I had to promise not to intervene—I'm just observing and recording—but I'll always break a promise to help a friend."

"I don't want to be picked up, Peggy."

"Then what the hell do you want?"

"I want to get into this warehouse. But the door is

locked, and there aren't any windows, and I haven't any explosives."

"You could get your friends to help. Or don't you want to share the loot?"

"I'm not looting. And I want to get into the créche by myself, not with a mob."

"I wouldn't mind a look inside myself, before it's too late. Hold on, I'll be right with you." Then, in a fainter voice, she was giving orders to somebody in the flying machine. "I'm going down, George. Get the ladder over, will you? Yes, yes, I know what Commander Grimes said, but Brasidus saved my life. And you just keep stooging around in the pinnace, and be ready to come a-runnin' to pick us up when I yell for you . . . Yes, yes. Keep the cameras and the recorders running."

"Have you a screwdriver?" asked Brasidus.

"A screwdriver?"

"If you have, bring it."

"All right."

A light, flexible ladder snaked down from the almost invisible hull. Clad in black coveralls, Peggy Lazenby was herself almost invisible as she rapidly dropped down it. As soon as she was standing on the ground, the pinnace lifted, vanished into the night sky.

"What now, love?" she asked. "What now?"

"That door," Brasidus told her, pointing.

"With a screwdriver? Are you quite mad?"

"We shall need that later. But I was sure that you'd have one of your laser-cameras along."

"As it happens, I haven't. But I do have a laser pistol—which, on low intensity, is a quite useful electric torch."

She pulled the weapon from its holster, made an adjustment, played a dim beam on the double door. "Hm. Looks like a conventional enough lock. And I don't think that your little friends will notice a very brief and discreet fireworks display."

She made another adjustment, and the beam became thread thin and blinding. There was a brief coruscation of sparks, a spatter of incandescent globules of molten metal.

"That should be it. Push, Brasidus."

Brasidus pushed. There was resistance that suddenly yielded, and the massive valves swung inwards.

Nobody noticed them enter the warehouse—the entire attention of the mob was centered on the door of the créche, which was still holding. When they were inside, Brasidus pushed the big doors shut. Then he asked, "How did you find me?"

"I wasn't looking for you. We knew about the riot, of course, and I persuaded John to let me take one of the pinnaces so that I could observe the goings-on. Our liftoff coincided with a test firing of the auxiliary rocket drive— even your Captain Diomedes couldn't blame Commander Grimes for wanting to be all ready for a hasty getaway. And the radar lookout kept by your Navy must be very lax—although, of course, our screen was operating. Anyhow, I was using my infrared viewer, and when I saw a solitary figure slink away from the main party, I wondered what mischief he was up to. I focused on him, and, lo and behold, it was you. Not that I recognized you at first. I much prefer you in uniform. Now, what is all this about?"

"I wish that I knew. But the mob's trying to break into the créche, and I've at least one friend in there whom I'd like to save. Too . . . oh, damn it all, I am a policeman, and I just can't stand by doing nothing."

"What about your precious Diomedes? What part is he playing in all this?"

"Come on," he snarled. "Come on. We've wasted enough time already." He found the light switch just inside the door, pressed it, then led the way to the hatch in the floor. They went through it, down into the basement, and then to the big chamber. Peggy helped him to open the door, followed him to the far insulated wall. Yes, that was the panel beyond which lay the tunnel—the slots of the screw-heads glittered with betraying bright metal.

At the far end of the tunnel the door into the créche was not secured, and opened easily.

»«Chapter 22»«

It was quiet in the passageway, but, dull and distant, the ominous thudding of the battering ram could be heard. And there was the sound of crying, faint and faraway, the infants in the wards screaming uncontrollably.

"Which way?" Peggy was asking. "Which way?"

"This way, I think." He set off at a run along the corridor, his bare feet noiseless on the polished floor. She followed at the same pace, her soft-soled shoes making an almost inaudible shuffle. They ran on, past the closed, numbered doors. At the first cross alleyway Brasidus turned right without hesitation—as long as he kept the clangor of forcible entry as nearly ahead as possible, he could not go far wrong.

And then one of the doors opened. From it stepped the tall, yellow-haired Arcadian whom Brasidus had encountered during his first trespass. She was dressed, this time, in a belted tunic, and her feet were shod in heavy sandals. And she carried a knife that was almost a short sword.

"Stop!" she ordered. "Stop!"

Brasidus stopped, heard Margaret Lazenby slither to a halt behind him.

"Who are you? What are you doing here?"

"Brasidus. Lieutenant, Police Battalion of the Army. Take us to whoever's in charge here."

"Oh, I recognize you—that painfully shy workman who strayed in from the warehouse . . . But who are you?"

"I'm from the ship."

"What I thought." The blonde stood there, juggling absently with her knife. And she'll be able to use it, thought Brasidus. "What I thought," repeated the woman. "So, at long last, the Police and the outworld space captain are arriving in the nick of time to save us all from a fate worse than death."

"I'm afraid not," Peggy Lazenby told her. "Our respective lords and masters have yet to de-digitate. We're here in our private capacities."

"But you're hung around with all sorts of interesting-looking hardware, dearie. And I can lend Brasidus a meat chopper if he wants it."

Brasidus said that he did. It was not his choice of weapons, but it was better than nothing. The Arcadian went back through the door, through which drifted the sound of excited, high-pitched voices, returned with the dull-gleaming implement. Brasidus took it. The haft fitted his right hand nicely, and the thing had a satisfying heft to it. Suddenly he felt less helpless, less naked.

"And what's your name, by the way?" the blonde Arcadian was asking.

"Lazenby. Peggy Lazenby."

"You can call me Terry. Short for Theresa, not that it matters. Come on."

With her as a guide, they found their way to the vestibule without any delays, bypassing the wards which the infants were making hideous with their screams. But the noise in this entrance hall was deafening enough; it was like being inside a lustily beaten bass drum. Furniture had been piled inside the door, but with each blow of the battering ram, some article would crash to the floor.

There were doctors there, white-faced but, so far, not at the point of panic. There were nurses there, no braver than their superiors, but no more cowardly. They were armed, all of them, after a fashion. Sharp, dangerous-looking surgical instruments gleamed in tight-clenched fists, rude clubs, legs torn from furniture, dangled from hands that had but rarely performed rougher work than changing a baby's diaper.

"Heraklion!" Terry was calling, shouting to make herself heard above the tumult. "Heraklion!"

The tall doctor turned to face her. "What are you doing here, Terry? I thought I told you women to keep out of harm's way." Then he saw Brasidus and Peggy. "Who the hell are these?" He began to advance, the scalpel in his right hand extended menacingly.

"Lieutenant Brasidus. Security."

"Looks like a helot to me," muttered somebody. "Kill the bastard!"

"Wait. Brasidus? Yes, it could be . . ."

"It is, it is!" One of the nurses broke away from his own group, ran to where Heraklion was standing. "It is. Of course, it's Brasidus!"

"Thank you, Achron. You should know. But who are you, madam?"

"Doctor Margaret Lazenby, of the starship *Seeker*."

Heraklion's eyes dwelt long and lovingly on the weapons at her belt. "And have you come to help us?"

"I let myself get talked into it."

"I knew you'd come," Achron was saying to Brasidus. "I knew you'd come." And Brasidus was uncomfortably aware of Peggy Lazenby's ironic regard. He said to Heraklion, more to assert himself than for any other reason, "And what is happening, Doctor?"

"You ask me that, young man? You're Security, aren't you? You're Captain Diomedes' right-hand man, I've heard. What is happening?"

Brasidus looked slowly around at the little band of defenders with their makeshift armament. He said, "I know what will happen: massacre, with ourselves at the receiving end. That door'll not hold for much longer. Is there anywhere to retreat to?"

"Retreat?" demanded Heraklion scornfully. "Retreat, from a mob of hoplites and helots?"

"They—the hoplites—have weapons, sir. And they know how to use them."

"Your Doctor Lazenby has weapons—real weapons."

"Perhaps I have," she said quietly. "But ethology happens to be my specialty. I've studied the behavior of mobs. A machine gun is a fine weapon to use against them—but a hand gun, no matter how deadly, only infuriates them."

"There's the birth-machine room," suggested somebody. "I've heard said that it could withstand a hydrogen-bomb blast."

"Impossible!" snapped Heraklion. "Nobody here is sterile, and to take the time to scrub up and break out robes at this time . . ."

"The birth machine won't be much use with nobody around to operate it," said Brasidus.

Heraklion pondered this statement, and while he was doing so a heavy desk crashed from the top of the pile of furniture barricading the door. Halfheartedly, three of the nurses struggled to replace it, and dislodged a table and a couple of chairs. "All right," he said suddenly. "The B-M room it is. Terry, run along and round up the other women and get them there at once. Doctor Hermes, get along there yourself with all these people."

"And what about the children?" Achron, in his agitation, was clutching Heraklion's sleeve. "What about the children?"

"H'm. Yes. I suppose that somebody had better remain on duty in each ward."

"No, Doctor," said Brasidus. "It won't do at all. Those wild animals out there hate the nurses as much as they hate you. To the hoplites, they're helots who live better than soldiers do. To the helots, they're overprivileged members of their own caste. Those nurses with the villa outside of the créche have all been killed. I saw it happen."

"But the children . . ." Achron's voice was a wail.

"They'll be safe enough. They might miss a meal or a diaper change, but it won't kill 'em."

"And if there's no other way out of it," put in Peggy Lazenby, "we'll make them our personal charge." She winced as an uproar from the nearer ward almost drowned out the heavy thudding of the battering ram. "I sincerely hope that it never comes to that!"

One of the nurses screamed. The pile of furniture was tottering. The men below it tried to shore it with their bodies, but not for long. A spear probed through the widening gap between the two valves, somehow found its mark in soft human flesh. There was another scream, of pain, this time, not terror. There were other spearheads thrusting hopefully and not altogether blindly. There was a scurrying retreat from the crumbling barricade. Suddenly it collapsed, burying the wounded man, and the great valves edged slowly and jerkily inwards, all the pressure of the mob behind them, pushing aside and clearing a way through the wreckage. And through the widening aperture gusted the triumphant howling and shouting, and a great billow of acrid smoke.

The mob leaders were through, scrambling over the broken furniture, their dulled weapons at the ready. There were a half dozen common soldiers, armed with swords. There was a fat sergeant, some kind of pistol in his right hand. He fired, the report sharp in spite of the general uproar. He fired again.

Beside Brasidus, Peggy Lazenby gasped, caught hold of him with her left hand as she staggered. Then her own pistol was out, and the filament of incandescence took the sergeant full in the chest. But he came on, still he came on, still firing, the hoplites falling back to allow him passage, while the Arcadian fumbled with her gun, trying to transfer it from her right hand to her left. He came on, and Brasidus ducked uselessly as two bullets whined past his head in quick succession.

Then he fell to his knees as Achron shoved him violently to one side. The nurse's frail body jerked and shuddered as the projectiles thudded into him, but he, like the sergeant, refused to die. He lifted the table leg with which he had armed himself, brought it smashing down with all his strength onto the other's head. The wood splintered, but enough remained for a second blow, and a third. No more were necessary. The sergeant sagged to the floor, and Achron, with a tired sigh, collapsed on top of the gross body.

"He's dead," muttered Brasidus, kneeling beside his friend. "He's dead."

But mourning would have to wait. Hastily he shifted Achron's body to one side so that he could get at the sergeant's pistol. And then he saw the face of the dead man, recognizable in spite of the blood that had trickled down it.

It was Diomedes.

He got to his feet, ready to use the pistol. But he did not have to. Firing left-handed, Peggy Lazenby had shot down the other mob leaders, then used the weapon to ignite the tangle of wrecked furniture and the floor itself.

"That should hold 'em," she muttered. "Now lead us out of here, Doctor."

"But you're wounded," Brasidus cried, looking for telltale patches of wetness on the dark material of her clothing.

"Just bruised. I'm wearing my bulletproof undies. But come on, you two. Hurry!"

»《Chapter 23》《«

Suddenly the sprinklers came on, saturating the air of the vestibule with aqueous mist and choking, acrid steam. But this was a help to the retreating defenders, a hindrance to the mob. Frightened, the rioters drew back. They had been ready enough to charge barefooted through and over blazing wreckage; now (but too briefly) the automatic fire-fighting system instilled in them the fear of the unknown. An acid spray, they must have thought, or some lethal gas. When their shouts made it obvious that they were inside the créche, Heraklion and his party were already halfway along the first of the lengthy corridors.

The Doctor, it was obvious, knew his way. Without him, Brasidus and Peggy Lazenby would have been hopelessly lost. He turned into cross alleyways without hesitation, finally led them up a ramp, at the head of which was a massive door. It was shut, of course. Heraklion cursed, wrestled with the hand wheel that obviously actuated the securing device. It refused to budge.

163

Peggy Lazenby pulled out her laser pistol. Heraklion stared at her ironically. "Sure," he said. "Go ahead—if you've all day to play around in. But long before you've made even a faint impression, you'll wish that you'd kept the charge in that weapon for something more useful."

The mob was closer now. They did not know the direction their quarry had taken, but they were spreading through the vast building, looting and smashing. Sooner or later some of them would stumble upon the ramp leading up to the room housing the birth machine. Sooner, thought Brasidus, rather than later. He examined the pistol that he had taken from Diomedes. It was a standard officers' model Vulcan. One round up the spout, four remaining in the magazine. He regretted having dropped the cleaver that Terry had found for him.

"Here they are," announced Peggy unemotionally. She fired down the ramp, a slashing beam that scarred the paint work of the walls at the foot of the incline. There was a scream, and, shockingly, there was the rapid, vicious chatter of a machine carbine. But whoever was using it was not anxious to expose himself, and the burst buried itself harmlessly in the ceiling.

"I thought that only your people were allowed firearms," said Heraklion bitterly to Brasidus. Brasidus said nothing. If Diomedes, armed, had been among the mob leaders, how many of his trusted lieutenants were also involved?

Still Heraklion wrestled with the hand wheel, and still Peggy and Brasidus, pistols ready, kept their watch for hostile activity. But everything was quiet, too quiet—until at last, from the alleyway that ran athwart the foot of the ramp, there came an odd shuffling, scraping sound. Slowly, slowly the source of it edged into view. It was a heavy shield mounted on a light trolley. Whoever had constructed it had known something about modern weaponry; a slab of concrete, torn up from a floor some- where, was its main component. Of course, it could not withstand laser fire indefinitely, but long before it crumbled and disintegrated, the riflemen behind it would have disposed of the laser weapon and its user.

There was a small, ragged hole roughly in the center of the slab. Brasidus nudged Peggy, drew her attention to it. She nodded. Suddenly something metallic protruded from the aperture, something that flared and sputtered as the laser beam found it. But Brasidus, at the last moment, switched his own attention from the decoy to the rim of the shield, loosed off two hasty but accurate shots at the carbine that was briefly exposed, at the hands holding it.

Then Heraklion cried out. Under his hands the wheel had moved, was moving of its own accord. The enormously thick door was opening. The Doctor grabbed his com- panions, pulled them through the slowly widening gap, pushed them clear of the narrow entrance as a deadly hail of bullets splattered around it. Then he turned on the colleague who had, at last, admitted them. "Shut it! At once!" And, as the man obeyed, he demanded coldly, "You were a long time opening up. Why?"

"We had to be sure that it was you. We couldn't get the closed-circuit TV working."

"Even on this primitive planet," commented Peggy Lazenby, "one can find oneself at the mercy of a single fuse."

The little crowd of refugees, with their nervous chatter, seemed out of place in these surroundings. There was an air of mystery—of holy mystery, even—that could not be dispelled by the intrusion. Tier upon tier towered the vats, empty now, but spotlessly clean and gleaming. Mile after convoluted mile ran the piping—glittering glass, glowing plastic, bright-shining metal. Bank upon bank stood the pumps, silent now, but ready, in perfect order, awaiting the touch of a switch to carry out their functions as mechanical hearts and lungs and excretory organs.

"There's no place like womb," remarked Margaret Lazenby.

"What was that, Peggy?"

"Never mind. You're too young to understand." Then, crisply official, "Doctor Heraklion, what now?"

"I . . . I don't know, Doctor Lazenby."

"You're in charge. Or are you?"

"I . . . I suppose that I am. I'm the senior doctor present."

"And Brasidus is the senior Security officer present, and I'm the senior Interstellar Federation's Survey Service officer present. And what about you, Terry? Are you the senior anything?"

"I don't know. But the other girls usually do what I tell them to."

"So we're getting some place. But where? Where? That's the sixty-four-dollar question." She took two nervous strides forward, two nervous strides back. "I suppose that this glorified incubator is on the phone, Doctor Heraklion?"

"It is, Doctor Lazenby. Unluckily the main switchboard for the créche is just off the vestibule."

"A pity. I was thinking that you might get through to the military. Or even to the palace itself."

"We tried that as soon as we were warned that the mob was heading our way. But we got no satisfaction. In fact, we gained the impression that the top military brass was having its own troubles."

"They could be, at that," contributed Brasidus. "That sergeant who was leading the rioters, the one with the pistol—it was Diomedes."

"What!"

Heraklion was incredulous. Margaret Lazenby was not. She said, "It makes sense, of a kind. This wouldn't be the first time that an ambitious, comparatively junior officer has organized a coup. And I think I know what makes him tick—or made him tick. There was the lust for power, of course. But, with it, there was a very deep and very real patriotism. I'm a woman, and I had to talk to him officially. I could tell, each time, how much he hated me and feared me. No, not personally, but as a member of the opposite sex.

"There are some men—and he was one of them—to whom a world like yours would be the ultimate paradise. Men Only. There are some men to whom the stratified social system of yours—cribbed, with improvements, from the real Spartans—would seem the only possible way of running a planet.

"But . . .

"But, Doctor Heraklion, there are other men, such as you, who would find the monosexual, homosexual setup rather unsatisfying. And you, my good Doctor, were in a position to do something about it."

Heraklion smiled faintly. "It's been going on for a very long time, Doctor Lazenby. It all started long before I was born."

"All right. The doctors were able to do something about it. I still don't know how this birth machine of yours works, but I can guess. I suppose that all approved Spartans make contributions of sperm cells."

"That is so."

"And the most important contribution—correct me if I am wrong—will be the annual shipments made by the aptly named *Latterhaven Venus* and *Latterhaven Hera*. Venus and Hera were Greek goddesses, by the way, Brasidus. Women—like me, and like Terry and the other playmates. How did the ships get their names, Heraklion?"

"We have always suspected the Latterhaveneers of a warped sense of humor."

"I wonder what the mob is doing?" asked somebody anxiously.

"We're safe enough here," said Heraklion curtly.

Are we? thought Brasidus, suddenly apprehensive. Are we? It seemed to him that the floor under his bare soles had become uncomfortably warm. He shifted his stance. Yes, the floor was heating up. He looked down, saw a crack in the polished surface. Surely it had not been there before. And, if it had been, there had not been a thin wisp of smoke trickling from it.

He was about to tell Heraklion when a device on Peggy Lazenby's wrist—it looked like a watch but obviously was not—buzzed sharply. She raised her forearm to her face. "Doctor Lazenby here."

"Captain here. What the hell are you doing? Where are you?"

"Quite safe, John. I'm holed up in the créche, in the birth-machine room."

"The créche is an inferno. Admiral Ajax requested my aid to evacuate the children and to restore order in the city. We're on the way now."

The floor tilted, slightly but sharply. One of the vats shattered loudly and the piping dependent from it swung, clattering and tinkling, against the vessels in the tier below, breaking them. The smell of smoke was suddenly very strong.

"Is there only one way out of this place?" demanded Peggy sharply.

"No. There's a hatch in the roof. Through the records room," Heraklion told her.

"Then that's the way that we have to go to escape from this alleged H-bombproof shelter of yours." Into her wrist transceiver she said, "You'll have to pick us off the roof, John. And while you're about it, you can send a squad of Marines down to save the firm's books. No, I'm not joking."

Luckily the hatch was clear, and luckily the ladder was readily available. Through the little room they passed— the women, the surviving nurses and doctors, then, last of all, Heraklion, Peggy and Brasidus. Brasidus had almost to pull her away from the shelves of microfilmed records, and from the glass case in which was displayed the big, flat book on the cover of which, in tarnished gold, were the words, Log of Interstellar Colonization Ship DORIC. First Captain Deems Harris.

They were on the roof then—the tilting, shuddering roof, swept by scorching eddies and black, billowing smoke. The night sky above them was alive with the noise of engines, and from below sounded, ever louder and more frightening, the roar of the fire. Cautiously Heraklion made his way down the listing surface to the low parapet. Brasidus followed him. The two men cautiously peered over, flinching back when a sudden gust of flame seared their faces, crisping their hair and eyebrows.

Grimes had sent down a landing party. Disciplined, uniformed men and women were handling chemical fire extinguishers, others, in a chain, were passing the children out of the blazing building. And still others had set up weapons to protect the rescuers; the rattle of heavy automatic fire was loud and insistent above the other noises.

Peggy Lazenby had joined the two men. "Intervention," she murmured. "Armed intervention. Poor John. He'll be in the soup over this. But what else could he do? He couldn't let those babies burn to death . . ."

"As we shall do," stated Heraklion grimly, "unless your captain does something about it, and fast." As he spoke the roof tilted another few degrees.

But the peculiar, irregular throbbing of the inertial drive was louder now, was deafening. Directly overhead, the glare of the fire reflected from the burnished metal of her hull, *Seeker* dropped through the vortex of smoke and sparks. Lower she sagged, and lower, until men and women cried out in fear and ran in panic to escape from the inexorably descending pads of her vaned landing gear. Lower she sagged, and lower—and from her open main airlock the boarding ramp was suddenly extruded, the lower end of it scant millimeters only from the heaving, cracking surface of the roof. Even Brasidus knew that he was privileged to watch an exhibition of superb spacemanship.

Down the extended ramp ran six men. Peggy Lazenby met them, cried, "This way!" and led them to the still open hatchway. And a vastly amplified voice was booming from the ship, "Board at once, please! Board at once!"

Heraklion hustled his people into some sort of order, got them onto the gangway, the women first. He stayed with Brasidus, making sure that the evacuation proceeded in an orderly manner. Still the two men waited, although the loudspeaker was blaring, "Get a move on, there! Get a move on!"

At last the six men and Peggy Lazenby were emerging from the hatch, she last of all. They were heavily burdened, all of them, and she, clasping it to her as tenderly as she had clasped the rescued child, carried the antique log book. "What are you waiting here for?" she demanded of Heraklion.

He said, "We have no spaceships, but we have read books. We know of the traditions. This créche is my ship, and I shall be the last to leave."

"Have it your own way," she told him.

She and Brasidus went up the ramp after the six marines. Heraklion followed them. Just as he reached the airlock, a geyser of flame erupted from the open hatch and the once flat surface of the roof cracked and billowed and, as *Seeker* hastily lifted, collapsed.

"That was my ship," whispered the Doctor.

"You can build another," Peggy told him.

"No," he said. "No. No longer do we have any excuse not to revert to the old ways."

"And your old ways," she said, "are not the old ways of Diomedes and his party. That is why he hated and feared you. But can you do it?"

"With your help," he said.

"That," she said, "is a matter for the politicians back home. But let's get out of this damned airlock and into the ship, before we fall out. It's a long way down."

Brasidus, looking at the burning building far below, shuddered and drew back hastily. It was, as she had said, a long way down.

»«(Chapter 24»)«

The Night of the Long Knives was over, the Night of the Long Knives and the four action packed days and nights that had followed it. The power had fallen into the streets, and Admiral Ajax, warned by his own intelligence service of the scheduled assassinations of himself and his senior captains, had swooped down from the sky to pick it up. The birth machine was destroyed, the caste system had crumbled, and only the patrolling airships of the Navy kept Sparta safe from the jealous attentions of the other city-states. Cresphontes—a mere figurehead—skulked in his palace, dared make no public appearances.

Grimes and his *Seeker* had played little active part in quelling the disturbances, but always the spaceship had been there, hanging ominously in the clouds, always her pinnaces had darted from one trouble spot to another, her Marines acting as ambulance men and firemen—but ambulance men and firemen backed by threatening weaponry to ensure that they carried out their tasks unmolested.

173

Brasidus had rejoined his own police unit, and, to his surprise, had found that greater and greater power and responsibilities were being thrust upon him. But it made sense. He knew the spacemen, had worked with them—and it was obvious to all that, in the final analysis, they and the great Federation that they represented were the most effective striking force on the planet. They did not strike, they were careful not to fire a single gun or loose a single missile, but they were there, and where they had come from there were more and bigger ships with even heavier armaments.

The universe had come to Sparta, and the Spartans, in spite of centuries of isolationist indoctrination, had accepted the fact. Racial memory, Margaret Lazenby had said, long and deep-buried recollections of the home world, of the planet where men and women lived and worked together in amity, where the womb was part of the living female body and not a complex, inorganic machine.

And then there was the last conference in John Grimes' day cabin aboard *Seeker*. The Lieutenant Commander sat behind his paper-littered desk, making a major production of filling and lighting his pipe. Beside him was Margaret Lazenby, trim and severe in uniform. In chairs facing the desk were the rotund little Admiral Ajax, the tall, saturnine Heraklion, and Brasidus. A stewardess brought coffee, and the four men and the woman sipped it appreciatively.

Then Grimes said, "I've received my orders, Admiral. Somewhat garbled, as messages by psionic radio too often are, but definite enough. I have to hand over to the civil authorities and then get the hell out." He smiled bleakly.

"I've done enough damage already. I fear that I shall have to do plenty of explaining to my lords Commissioners."

"No, Commander." Heraklion's voice was firm, definite. "You did not do the damage. The situation, thanks to Diomedes, was already highly explosive. You were only the . . . the . . ."

"The detonator," supplied Ajax.

"Just how explosive was it?" inquired Grimes. "I'd like to know. After all, I shall have a report to make." He switched on a small recorder that stood among the litter on his desk.

"Very explosive. Some of us at the créche had decided to make women, not only for ourselves but for every man on Sparta. We had decided to revert to the old ways. Diomedes knew of this. I still think that he was actuated by patriotism—a perverted patriotism, but patriotism nonetheless."

Peggy Lazenby laughed scornfully. "Fine words, Doctor. But what about that female baby who was exposed, the one that Brasidus and I rescued?"

"Yes, the Exposure. That was a custom that we intended to stamp out. But the unfortunate child, as well as being female, was mentally subnormal. She'd have been better off dead."

"So you say. But you forget that the planets of the Federation have made great strides in medical science during the centuries that you have been stagnating."

"Enough, Peggy. Enough," said Grimes tiredly. He put his pipe into a dirty ashtray, began to sort his papers. "As I told you, my orders are to hand over to the civil authorities. Who are they? The King? The Council?" The Spartans smiled scornfully. "All right. I suppose that you gentlemen will have to do. You, Doctor Heraklion, and you, Admiral Ajax, and you—just what rank do you hold these days? I've rather lost track, Brasidus. But before I hand over, I want to be sure that the Admiral and friend Brasidus know what it's all about. Heraklion knows, of course, but even the most honest of us is liable to bend the facts.

"This ship, as you know, is a unit of the fleet of the Federation's Survey Service. As such she carries, on microfilm, a most comprehensive library. One large section of it is devoted to colonizing ships that are missing. We're still stumbling upon what are called the Lost Colonies, and it's helpful if we have more than a vague idea as to their origin. This Sparta of yours is, of course, a Lost Colony. We've been able to piece together your history both from our own reference library and from the records salvaged from the créche.

"So far, the history of colonization comes under three headings, the First Expansion, the Second Expansion and the Third Expansion. The First Expansion was initiated before there was a practicable FTL—faster than light— drive. The Second Expansion was carried out by vessels fitted with the rather unreliable Ehrenhaft Drive, the so-called gaussjammers. The Third Expansion made use of timejammers, ships with the almost foolproof Mannschenn Drive.

"The vessels of the First Expansion, the deep-freeze ships, went a long way in a long time, a very long time. They carried at least three full crews—captains, watch-keeping officers, maintenance engineers and the like. The colonists, men and women, were in stasis, just refrigerated cargo, in effect. The crews spent their off-duty months in stasis. But there was, of course, always one full crew on duty.

"As a result of some incredible stupidity on somebody's part, the crews of many of the early ships were all male. In the later ones, of course, the balance of the sexes was maintained. Doric—the ship from which this Lost Colony was founded—had an all male crew, under First Captain— he was the senior of the four masters—Deems Harris. This same Captain Harris was, probably, a misogynist, a woman hater, when the voyage started. If he were not, what happened probably turned him into one.

"Third Captain Flynn seems to have exercised little control over his officers—or, perhaps, he was the ringleader. Be that as it may, Flynn decided, or was persuaded, to alleviate the monotony of his tour of duty by reviving a dozen of the more attractive colonist girls. It seems to have been quite a party while it lasted—so much so that normal ship's routine went by the board, vitally important navigational instruments, such as the Very Long Range Radar, were untended, ignored. The odds against encountering a meteoric swarm in deep space are astronomical—but Doric encountered one. Whether or not she would have been able to take avoiding action is doubtful, but with some warning something could have been done to minimize the effects of the inevitable collision. A collision there was—and the sphere in which the female colonists were housed was badly damaged, so badly damaged that there were no survivors. I should have explained before that these deep-freeze ships didn't look anything like a vessel such as this one; they consisted of globes held together by light girders. They were assembled in orbit and were never intended to make a landing on any planetary surface.

"Anyhow, Captain Flynn aroused Captain Harris and the other masters and their officers after the damage had been done. Captain Harris, understandably, took a somewhat dim view of his junior and formed the opinion that if Flynn had not awakened those women the collision would not have occurred. Oddly enough, as his private journal indicates, he blamed the unfortunate wenches even more than he blamed Flynn. He despised Flynn for his weakness and irresponsibility—but those poor girls he hated. They were thrown into some sort of improvised brig.

"Meanwhile, Doric was far from spaceworthy. Apart from the slow leakage of precious atmosphere, much of her machinery was out of kilter, the automated 'farm,' upon which the crew depended for their food and their atmospheric regeneration, especially. Although the world that you know as Sparta was not the ship's original objective—oddly enough, long-range instrumental surveys had missed it—Doric's quite excellent equipment picked it up, made it plain to Captain Harris that he could reach it before air and food and water ran out. So, putting all hands save himself and one officer back into stasis, he adjusted his trajectory and ran for this only possible haven.

"His troubles were far from over. The shuttles— relatively small rocket craft used as ferries between the big ship in orbit and the world below—had all been ruined by that meteoric shower. Nonetheless—it was a remarkable feat of spacemanship—he succeeded in getting that unhandy, unspaceworthy and unairworthy near wreck down through the atmosphere to a relatively soft landing.

"At first glance, the survivors were not too badly off. The planet was habitable. The fertilized ova of various animals—sheep, pigs, cattle, dogs and cats, even—had all been destroyed by the crash landing, but the local fauna was quite edible. And the ship had carried a large stock of seed grain.

There was a decided imbalance of the sexes—the only women were Captain Flynn's hapless ones, and there were all of five thousand men—but even that would right itself in time. The ship—as did all ships of that era—carried equipment that was the prototype of your birth machine, and there were supplies of deep-frozen sperm and ova sufficient to populate a dozen worlds.

"But . . .

"Twelve women, and five thousand and forty-eight men.

"Rank, said Captain Flynn and some of the other officers, should have its privileges. It most certainly should not, said the colonists—among them, of course, the twelve men whose wives the women had been.

"There was trouble, starting off with a few isolated murders, culminating in a full-scale revolt against the officers and those loyal to them. Somehow the twelve girls were . . . eliminated. Deems Harris doesn't say as much in his journal, but I gained the impression that he was behind it.

"Now, this Deems Harris. It is hard for us in this day and age of quick passages to get inside the skins, the minds of those old-time space captains. Probably none of them was quite sane. Most of them were omnivorous, indiscriminating readers, although some of them specialized. This Deems Harris seems to have done so. In history. By this time, with his colony off to a disastrous beginning, he seems to have hankered after some sort of culture in which women played a very small part—or no part at all. One such culture was that of Sparta, one of the ancient Greek city-states back on Earth. Greek women were little more than childbearing, housekeeping machines—and the Spartan women suffered the lowest status of them all. Sparta was the state that specialized in all the so-called manly virtues—and little else. Sparta was the military power. Furthermore, the original Spartans were a wandering tribe called Dorians. Dorians—Doric—See the tie-up? And their first King was Aristodemus. Aristodemus—Deems Harris.

"The first Aristodemus, presumably, kept women in their proper place—down, well down. This latter-day Aristodemus would go one better. He would do without women at all." Grimes looked at Margaret Lazenby. "At times I think that he had something."

"He didn't have women, that's for certain. But go on."

"All right. Aristodemus—as we shall call him now—was lucky enough to command the services of like-minded biochemists. The sperm, of course, was all neatly classified—male and female being among the classifications. Soon that first birth machine was turning out a steady stream of fine, bouncing baby boys. When the adult populace started to get a bit restive, it was explained that the stock of female sperm had been destroyed in the crash. And somebody made sure that the stock was destroyed."

"But," Brasidus interrupted, "but we used to reproduce

by fission. Our evolution from the lower animals has been worked out in detail."

"Don't believe everything you read," Peggy Lazenby told him. "Your biology textbooks are like your history textbooks—very cunningly constructed fairy tales."

"Yes," said Grimes. "Fairy tales. Aristodemus and his supporters were able to foist an absolutely mythical history upon the rising generations. It seems fantastic, but remember that there was no home life. They—like you, Brasidus, and like you, Admiral—knew only the Spartan state as a parent. There were no fathers and mothers, no grandfathers and no grandmothers to tell them stories of how things used to be. Also, don't forget that the official history fitted the facts very neatly. It should have done— after all, it was tailor-made.

"And so it went on, for year after year, for generation after generation, until it became obvious to the doctors in charge of the birth machine that it couldn't go on for much longer. That bank of male sperm was near exhaustion. This first crisis was surmounted—ways and means were devised whereby every citizen made his contribution to the plasm bank. A centrifuge was used to separate X-chromosome-bearing sperm cells from those carrying the Y-chromosome. Then the supply of ova started to run out. But still the race was in no real danger of extinction. All that had to be done was to allow a few female children to be born. In fact, this did happen now and again by accident—but such unfortunates had been exposed on the hillside as defective infants. Even so, the doctors of those days were reluctant to admit female serpents into this all-male paradise.

"And now Latterhaven comes into the story. I'm sorry to have to disappoint you all, but there never was a villainous Admiral Latterus. And, apart from the ill-fated *Doric*, there never were any spaceships owned by Sparta. But while Aristodemus was building his odd imitation of the original, Terran Sparta, the First Expansion ran its course. Then, with the perfection (not that it ever was perfect) of the Ehrenhaft Drive came the Second Expansion. Finally, there was the Third Expansion, and there was the star ship *Utah*, commanded by Captain Amos Latter. It was Latter and his people who founded the colony—one run on rather more orthodox lines than yours—on Latterhaven, a world only a couple of light years from this one.

"The Latterhaveneers made explorations of the sector of space around their new home. One such expedition stumbled upon Sparta. The explorers were lucky not to be slaughtered out of hand—the records indicate that they almost met such a fate—but they were not, and they dickered with the Spartan top brass, and all parties eventually signed a trade agreement. In return for the spice harvest, Latterhaven would send two ships each Spartan year with consignments of unfertilized ova.

"The situation could have continued indefinitely if we hadn't come in—or if Diomedes hadn't found out about the doctors' secret harem."

"The situation would not have continued," stated Heraklion. "As I've told you, Commander, it was our intention to introduce a reversion to—the normal way of birth."

"That's your story and you stick to it. It could be true, I

suppose; it would account for the way that Diomedes hated you." He refilled and relit his pipe. "The question is, what happens now?"

"What does happen?" asked Admiral Ajax.

"To begin with, I've been recalled to base. I shall have to make my report. It is possible that the Federation will replace your birth machine—although, come to that, you should be able to import materials and technicians from Latterhaven. You might even be able to build a new one for yourselves. But . . .

"But the Federation is apt to be a little intolerant of transplanted human cultures that deviate too widely from the norm. Your monosexual society, for example—and, especially, your charming custom of Exposure. This is your world and, as far as I'm concerned, you're welcome to it. I'm a firm believer in the fifth freedom—the freedom to go to hell your own way. But you've never heard a politician up on his hind legs blathering about the Holy Spirit of Man. If you want to reconstruct your society in your own way, in your own time, you'll have to fight—not necessarily with swords and spears, with guns and missiles— for the privilege.

"I advise strongly that you send a representative with us, somebody who'll be able to talk sense with my lords and masters, somebody who'll be able to take a firm line."

"There's Brasidus," said Peggy Lazenby softly, looking directly at him. You and I have unfinished business, her eyes said.

"Yes, there's Brasidus," agreed Grimes. "After all, he knows us."

And he'll get to know us better. The unspoken words,

her unuttered thought, sounded like a caressing voice in Brasidus' mind.

"But we need him," said Heraklion.

"A first-class officer," confirmed Ajax. "He has what's left of the Police eating out of his hand."

"I think that one of my colleagues would be a better choice as emissary," said Heraklion.

"So," murmured Grimes. "So . . ." He looked steadily across his desk at the Spartans. "It's up to you, Lieutenant or Colonel or whatever you are. It's up to you. I'm sure that Admiral Ajax will be able to manage without you—on the other hand, I'm sure that Doctor Heraklion's friend will prove a quite suitable envoy.

"It's up to you."

It's up to me, Brasidus thought. He looked at the woman sitting beside the space commander—and suddenly he was afraid. Diomedes' words about the frightening powers wielded by this sex lingered still in his mind. But, in the final analysis, it was not fear that prompted his answer, but a strong sense of responsibility, of loyalty to his own world. He knew—as the aliens did not, could never know—how precarious still was the balance of power. He knew that, with himself in command—effective if not titular—of the ground forces, peace might be maintained, the reconstruction be commenced.

"It's up to you," said Peggy Lazenby.

He said firmly, "I'd better stay."

She laughed, and Brasidus wondered if he alone were aware of the tinkling malice that brought an angry flush to his face. "Have it your own way, sweet. But I warn you, when those tough, pistol-toting biddies of the

Galactic Peace Corps get here, you'll wonder what's struck you."

"That will do, Peggy." Grimes' voice snapped with authority. "That will do. Now, gentlemen, you must excuse us. We have to see our ship secured for space. How soon can you get your envoy here, Doctor Heraklion?"

"About an hour, Commander."

"Very good. We shall lift ship as soon as he's on board." He got to his feet, shook hands with the three Spartans. "It's been a pleasure working with you. It's a great pity that it was not in pleasanter circumstances."

This was dismissal. Ajax in the lead, the three men walked out of Grimes' cabin. Brasidus, bringing up the rear, heard Peggy Lazenby say softly, "The poor bastard!"

And he heard Grimes reply, in a voice that held an unexpected bitterness, "I don't know. I don't know. He could be lucky."

For a long while Brasidus wondered what they meant, but the day came at last when he found out.

THE
INHERITORS

DEDICATION

For my favorite aelurophobe

Grimes was on the carpet—neither for the first nor the last time.

He stood stiffly in front of the vast, highly polished desk behind which sat Admiral Buring, of the Federation's Survey Service. His prominent ears were angrily flushed but his rugged face was expressionless.

The admiral's pudgy hands played with the bulky folder that was before him. His face, smooth and heavy, was as expressionless as Grimes'. His voice was flat.

He said, "Commodore Damien warned me about you when you were transferred to my command. Not that any warning was necessary. For one so young you have achieved a considerable degree of notoriety." He paused expectantly, but Grimes said nothing. Buring continued, but now with a hint of feeling in his voice. "My masters—who, incidentally, are also yours—are far from amused at your latest antics. You know—you *should* know—that interference, especially by junior officers, in the internal affairs of any world whatsoever, regardless of the cultural or technological level of the planet in question, is not tolerated. I concede that there were extenuating circumstances, and that the new rulers of Sparta speak quite highly of you . . . ." The thick eyebrows, like furry, black caterpillars, arched incredulously. "Nonetheless . . ."

The silence was so thick as to be almost tangible. Grimes decided that it was incumbent upon himself to break it.

"Sir?"

"Nonetheless, Lieutenant Commander, your continued presence at Base is something of an embarrassment, especially since a party of VIPs, political VIPs at that, is due here very shortly. Some commission or other, touring the galaxy at the taxpayer's expense. I don't want you around so that politicians can ask you silly questions—to which, I have no doubt, you would give even sillier answers.

"Furthermore, this whole Spartan affair has blown up into a minor crisis in interplanetary politics. Both the Duchy of Waldegren and the Empire of Waverley are talking loudly about spheres of influence."

The admiral allowed himself the suspicion of a smile. "In any sort of crisis, Grimes, there is one thing better than presence of mind . . . ."

"And that is, sir?" asked Grimes at last.

"Absence of body. Ha. So I'm doing you a good turn, sending you out in *Seeker*, on a Lost Colony hunt. There have been persistent rumors of one out in the Argo Sector. Go and find it—or get lost yourself. I'm easy."

"Maintenance, sir . . ." said Grimes slowly. "Repairs . . . stores . . . manning . . . ."

"They're your business, Captain. No, I'm not promoting

you, merely according you the courtesy title due to the commanding officer of a ship. You look after those no doubt boring details. And"—he made a major operation of looking at his watch—"I want you off Lindisfarne by sixteen-hundred hours local time tomorrow."

Grimes looked at his own watch. He had just seventeen hours, twelve minutes and forty-three seconds in which to ensure that his ship was, in all respects, ready for space. Maintenance, he knew, was well in hand. There were no crew deficiencies. Taking aboard essential stores would not occupy much time.

Even so . . .

"I'd better be getting on with it, sir," he said.

"You'd bloody well better. I'll send your orders down to you later."

Grimes put on his cap, saluted smartly and strode out of the admiral's office.

∿(((**2**)))∿

She was a survey ship rather than a warship, was *Seeker*. The Survey Service, in its first beginnings, had been just that—a survey service. But aliens being what they are— and humans being what *they* are—police work, on large and small scales, had tended to become more important than mere exploration and charting. The Survey Service, however, had not quite forgotten its original function. It maintained a few ships designed for peaceful rather than warlike pursuits, and *Seeker* was a member of this small squadron. Nonetheless, even she packed quite a wallop.

Lieutenant Commander John Grimes was her captain. His last assignment, during which he had stumbled upon a most peculiar Lost Colony, had been census taking. Now he had been actually sent out to *find* a Lost Colony. He suspected that *anything* might happen, and probably would. It wasn't that he was accident prone. He was just a catalyst.

Nothing had happened yet; after all, it was early in the voyage. He had lifted from Lindisfarne exactly on time,

194

driving through the atmosphere smoothly and easily, maintaining his departure trajectory until he was clear of the Base Planet's Van Allens. Then, with the inertial drive shut down, the ship had been turned about her short axis until she was lined up, with due allowance for drift, on the target star. The Mannschenn Drive had been started, the inertial drive restarted—and passage was commenced.

Satisfied, he had filled and lit his pipe, and when it was going well had ordered, "Deep space routine, Mr. Saul." He had made his way to his quarters below and abaft the control room and then, ensconced in his easy chair, had opened the envelope containing his orders.

The first sheet of the bundle of papers had contained nothing startling. *You will proceed to the vicinity of the star Gamma Argo and conduct a preliminary survey of the planets in orbit about same, devoting especial attention to any of such bodies capable of supporting human life.* "Mphm . . ." he grunted. The rest of the page consisted of what he referred to as "the usual guff."

At the head of the next page was the sentence that brought an expression of interest to his face.

We have reason to believe that there is a humanoid— or possibly human—settlement on the fourth planet of this system. Should this settlement exist it is probable that it is a hitherto undiscovered Lost Colony. You are reminded that your duties are merely to conduct an investigation, and that you are not, repeat not, to interfere in the internal affairs of the colony.

"Mphm," grunted Grimes again. Noninterference was all very well, but at times it was hard to maintain one's status as a mildly interested spectator.

Appended hereto are reports from our agents at Port
Llangowan, on Siluria, at Port Brrooun, on Drroomoorr,
at Port Mackay, on Rob Roy, at Port Forinbras, on
Elsinore, at . . .

"Mphm." The Intelligence Branch seemed to be earning its keep, for a change. Grimes turned to the first
report and read:

From Agent X1783 (Commander, I.B.,F.S.S.)
Dated at Port Llangowan, May 5,
    Year 171 Silurian (17113157 TS)
To O.I.C. Intelligence, Federation's Survey Service,
    Port Woomera, Centralia, Earth.

Sir,
    POSSIBLE LOST COLONY IN ARGO SECTOR
    I have to report the possibility that there is a hitherto
undiscovered Lost Colony in the Argo Sector, apparently
on a planet in orbit about Gamma Argo.
    It is my custom, whilst stationed on this world, to spend
my evenings in the Red Dragon tavern, a hostelry that seems
to be the favorite drinking place of whatever merchant
spacemen are in port.
    On the evening of May 3 several officers from the Dog
Star Line's Pomeranian were lined up at the bar, and were
joined there by officers of the same company's Corgi,
newly berthed. As was to be expected, the personnel of the
two vessels were old friends or acquaintances.
    The table at which I was seated was too far from the
bar for me to overhear the conversation, but I was able to
make use of my Mark XVII recorder, playing the recording

back later that night in the privacy of my lodgings. The spool has been sent to you under separate cover, but herewith is a suitably edited transcript of what was said, with everything of no importance—e.g. the usual friendly blasphemies, obscenities and petty company gossip—deleted.

First Mate of Pomeranian: *And where the hell have you been hiding yourselves? You should have been in before us. I suppose that you got lost.*

Second Mate of Corgi: *I never get lost.*

First Mate of Pomeranian: *Like hell you don't. I remember when you got your sums wrong when we were together in the old Dalmatian, and we finished up off Hamlet instead of Macbeth . . . But what's twenty light-years between friends?*

Second Mate of Corgi: *I told you all that the computer was on the blink, but nobody would listen to me. As for this trip, we had to deviate.*

First Mate of Corgi: *Watch it, Peter!*

Second Mate of Corgi: *Why?*

First Mate of Corgi: *You know what the old man told us.*

Second Mate of Corgi: *Too bloody right I do. He's making his own report to the general manager, with copies every which way. Top Secret. For your eyes only. Destroy by fire before reading. He's wasted in the Dog Star Line. He should have been in the so-called Intelligence Branch of the clottish Survey Service.*

First Mate of Pomeranian: *What did happen?*

First Mate of Corgi: *Nothing much. Mannschenn Drive slightly on the blink, so we had to find a suitable planet on which to park our arse while we recalibrated.*

Second Mate of Corgi: *And what a planet! You know how I like sleek women . . . .*

First Mate of Corgi: *Watch it, you stupid bastard!*

Second Mate of Corgi: *Who're you calling a bastard? You can sling your rank around aboard the bloody ship, but not here. If I'd had any sense I'd a skinned out before the bitch lifted off. Morrowvia'll do me when I retire from the Dog Star Line! Or resign . . .*

First Mate of Corgi: *Or get fired—as you will be, unless you pipe down!*

Second Mate of Corgi: *You can't tell me . . .*

First Mate of Corgi: *I can, and I bloody well am telling you! Come on, finish your drink, and then back to the ship!*

At this juncture there are sounds of a scuffle as Corgi's *chief officer, a very big man, hustles his junior out of the* Red Dragon.

Third Mate of Pomeranian: *What the hell was all that about?*

First Mate of Pomeranian: *Search me.*

The rest of the recorded conversation consists of idle and futile speculation by Pomeranian's *officers as to the identity of the world landed upon by* Corgi.

To date I have been unable to identify this planet myself. There is no Morrowvia listed in the catalogue, even when due allowance is made for variations in spelling. Also I have checked the Navy List, and found that the master of Corgi *is not, and never has been, an officer in the FSS Reserve. None of his officers hold a Reserve commission. It may be assumed, therefore, that the master's report on the discovery of what appears to be a Lost*

Colony will be made only to his owners. Corgi, when she deviated, was bound from Darnstadt to Siluria. Her normal trajectory would have taken her within three light-years of Gamma Argo. The planetary system of Gamma Argo was surveyed in the early days of the Second Expansion, and no indigenous intelligent life was found on any of its worlds . . . .

"Mphm . . ." Grimes refilled and relit his pipe. This was interesting reading.

He turned to the report from the agent at Port Brrooun. He, the shipping advisor to the Terran Consul, had been spending most of his free evenings in an establishment called the Beer Hive. Brrooun had been *Corgi*'s next port of call after Llangowan. Her second officer had confined his troubles to a sympathetic Shaara drone. At Port Mackay, on Rob Roy, he had gotten fighting drunk on the local whiskey and had beaten up the chief officer and publicly abused the master. Normally such conduct would have led to his instant dismissal—but Captain Danzellan, *Corgi*, had been most reluctant to leave the objectionable young man behind, in the hands of the civil authorities. The Intelligence Officer at Port Mackay, although knowing nothing of the Lost Colony, had been intrigued by the failure of the master to rid himself of an obvious malcontent and had wondered what was behind it. His own theories, for what they were worth, included a Hanoverian plot against the Jacobean royal house of Waverley . . . . It was from Port Fortinbras, on Elsinore, that the next really interesting report came. The agent there was a woman, and worked as a waitress in the Poor Yorick, a tavern famous for its funereal decor. The agent, too, was famous insofar as the Intelligence Branch of the Survey Service was concerned, being known as the Bug Queen. Her specialty was recorders printed into the labels on bottles.

Transcript of conversation between Harold Larsen, owner-manager of Larsen's Repair Yard, and Peter Dalquist, owner of Dalquist's Ship Chandlery:

Dalquist: An' how are things at the yard, Harald?

Larsen: Can't complain, Pete, can't complain. Southerly Buster's havin' a face lift.

Dalquist: Drongo Kane . . .

Larsen: You can say what you like about Drongo—but he always pays his bills . . .

Dalquist: Yeah. But he drives a hard bargain first.

Larsen: You can say that again.

Dalquist: An' what is it this time? General maintenance? Survey?

Larsen: Modifications. He's havin' his cargo spaces converted into passenger accommodation—of a sort. An' you remember those two quick-firin' cannon I got off that derelict Waldegren gunboat? Drongo's havin 'em mounted on the Buster.

Dalquist: But it ain't legal. Southerly Buster's a merchant ship.

Larsen: Drongo says that it is legal, an' that he's entitled to carry defensive armament . . . . Some o' the places he gets to, he needs it! But I checked up with me own legal eagles just to make sure that me own jets are clear. They assured me that Drongo's within his rights.

Dalquist: But quick-firin' cannon, when every man-o'-war is armed to the teeth with laser, misguided missiles an' only the Odd Gods of the Galaxy know what else! Doesn't make sense.

Larsen: Maybe it doesn't—but Drongo's got too much sense to take on a warship.

Dalquist: What if a warship takes on him?

Larsen: That's his worry.

Dalquist: But he must be thinkin' of fightin' somebody . . . . Any idea who it might be?

Larsen: I haven't a clue. All that I know is that his last port, before he came here, was Brrooun, on one o' the Shaara worlds. He told me—he'd had rather too much to drink himself—that he'd fed a couple of bottles of Scotch to a talkative drone. He said that he'll buy drinks for anybody—or anything—as long as he gets information in return. Anyhow, this drone told Drongo what he'd been told by the drunken second mate of a Dog Star tramp.

Dalquist: Which was?

Larsen: Drongo certainly wasn't telling me, even though he'd had a skinful. He did mutter something about Lost Colonies, an' finders bein' keepers, an' about the Dog Star Line havin' to be manned by greyhounds if they wanted to get their dirty paws into this manger . . .

Dalquist: An' was that all?

Larsen: You said it. He clammed up.

Unfortunately Captain Kane and his officers, unlike the majority of spacemen visiting Port Fortinbras, do not frequent the Poor Yorick, preferring the King Claudius. On the several occasions that I have been there as a customer, at the same times as Southerly Buster's personnel, I have been unable to learn anything of importance. Attempts *made by myself to strike up an acquaintance with Captain Kane, his mates and his engineers have failed.*

Grimes chuckled. He wondered what the Bug Queen looked like. It seemed obvious that she owed her success as an agent to her skill with electronic gadgetry rather than to her glamour. But Kane? Where did *he* come into the picture? The man was notorious—but, to date, had always managed to stay on the right side of the law.

But it was time that he, Grimes, put his senior officers into the picture.

They were all in Grimes's day cabin—his departmental heads and his senior scientific officers. There was Saul, the first lieutenant, a huge, gentle, very black man. There was Connery, chief engineer. The two officers in charge of communications were there—Timmins, the electronicist, and Hayakawa, the psionicist. There were Doctors Tallis, Westover and Lazenby—biologist, geologist and ethologist respectively—all of whom held the rank of full commander. Forsby—physicist—had yet to gain his doctorate and was only a lieutenant. There were Lieutenant Pitcher, navigator, Lieutenant Stein, ship's surgeon and biochemist, and Captain Philby, officer in charge of *Seeker*'s Marines.

Grimes, trying to look and to feel fatherly, surveyed his people. He was pleased to note that the *real* spacemen— with the exception of Hayakawa—looked the part. Ethnic origins and differentiation of skin pigmentation were canceled out, as it were, by the common uniform. With the exception of Maggie Lazenby the scientists looked their part. They were, of course, all in uniform—though it wasn't what they were wearing but how they were wearing it that mattered. To them uniform was just something to cover their nakedness, the more comfortably the better. And to them beards were merely the means whereby the bother of depilation could be avoided. The growths sprouting from the faces of Tallis, Westover and Forsby contrasted shockingly with the neat hirsute adornments sported by Connery and Stein. The only one of the scientists at whom it was a pleasure to look was Doctor Lazenby—slim, auburn-haired and wearing a skirt considerably less than regulation length.

Grimes looked at her.

She snapped, "Get on with it, John." (Everybody present knew that she was a privileged person.)

"Mphm," he grunted as he carefully filled his pipe. "Help yourselves to coffee—or to something stronger from the bar, if you'd rather." He waited until everybody was holding a glass or a cup, then said, "As you all know by this time, this is a Lost Colony expedition . . . ."

Forsby raised his hand for attention. "Captain, forgive my ignorance, but I've only just joined the Survey Service. And I'm a physicist, not a historian. Just what *is* a Lost Colony?"

"Mphm," grunted Grimes again. He shot a dirty look at Maggie Lazenby as he heard her whispered *"Keep it short!"* He carefully lit his pipe. He said, "The majority of the so-called Lost Colonies date from the days of the Second Expansion, of the gaussjammers. The gaussjammers were interstellar ships that used the Ehrenhaft Drive. Cutting a long and involved story short, the Ehrenhaft generators produced a magnetic current—a current, not a field—and the ship in which they were mounted became, in effect, a huge magnetic particle, proceeding at a speed which could be regulated from a mere crawl to FTL along the 'tramlines,' the lines of magnetic force. This was all very well—but a severe magnetic storm could throw a gaussjammer light-years off course, very often into an unexplored and uncharted sector of the galaxy . . . ."

"FTL?" demanded Forsby in a pained voice. "FTL?"

"A matter of semantics," Grimes told him airily. "You know, and I know, that faster-than-light speeds are impossible. With our Mannschenn Drive, for example, we cheat—by going astern in time as we're going ahead in space. The gaussjammers cheated too—by coexisting with themselves all along the lines of magnetic force that they were on. The main thing was—it worked. Anyhow, visualize a gaussjammer after a magnetic storm has tangled the lines of force like so much spaghetti *and* drained the micro-pile of all energy. The captain doesn't know where he is. But he has got power for his main engines."

"You said that the micro-pile was dead."

"Sure. But those ships ran to emergency generators— diesel generators. They churned out the electricity to drive the Ehrenhaft generators. The ship's biochemist knew the techniques for producing diesel fuel from whatever was available—even though it meant that all hands would be on short rations. So, for as long as she could, the ship either tried to make her way back to some known sector or to find a planet capable of being settled. . . ."

"Analogous," contributed Maggie Lazenby, "to the colonization of many Pacific islands by Polynesians in

Earth's remote past. But this colony that we're supposed to be looking for, John . . ."

"Yes. I was getting around to that. It's supposed to be in the Argo Sector. It was stumbled upon by a Dog Star Line ship that made a deviation to recalibrate her Mannschenn Drive controls. It won't be a Lost Colony for much longer."

"Why not?" asked Forsby.

"To begin with, the Dog Star Line people know about it. The Shaara know about it. *We* know about it. And Drongo Kane knows about it."

"Drongo Kane?" This was Forsby again, of course. "Who's he?"

Grimes sighed. He supposed that his physicist knew his own subject, but he seemed to know very little outside it. He turned his regard to his officers, said, "Tell him."

"Drongo Kane . . ." murmured Saul in his deep, rich voice. "Smuggler, gunrunner . . ."

"Pirate . . ." contributed Timmins.

"That was never proven," Grimes told him.

"Perhaps not, sir. But I was on watch—it was when I was a junior in *Scorpio*—when *Bremerhaven*'s distress call came through."

"Mphm. As I recall it, *Bremerhaven*'s own activities at the time were somewhat dubious . . . ."

"Slaver . . ." said Saul.

"Somebody had to take the people off Ganda before the radiation from their sun fried them. Whatever ships were available had to be employed."

"But Kane *was paid* by the Duke of Waldegren for the people he carried in *Southerly Buster*."

"Just a fee," said Grimes, "or commission, or whatever, for the delivery of indentured labor."

"What about this bloody Lost Colony?" demanded Maggie Lazenby.

"We're supposed to find it." Grimes gestured toward the folder on his desk with the stem of his pipe. "I've had copies made of all the bumf that was given to me. It consists mainly of reports made by agents on quite a few worlds. Our man at Port Llangowan, on Siluria, recorded a conversation between officers of *Corgi* and *Pomeranian* in one of the local pubs. *Corgi* had found this world—which seems to be called Morrowvia—quite by chance. Our man at Port Brrooun, on Drroomoorr, recorded a conversation between the second mate of *Corgi* and a Shaara drone; once again Morrowvia was mentioned. The same young gentleman— the second mate, not the drone—got into trouble at Port Mackay on Rob Roy. Normally he'd have been emptied out there and then by *Corgi*'s master—but keeping him on board must have been the lesser of two evils."

"Why?" asked Forsby.

"Because," Grimes told him patiently, "the master of *Corgi* didn't want word of a new world that could well be included in the Dog Star Line's economic empire spread all over the galaxy. Where was I? Yes. Our woman at Port Fortinbras, on Elsinore, recorded a conversation between the owner of a repair yard and the owner of a ship chandlery. The repair yard was doing some work on Drongo Kane's ship, *Southerly Buster*—the mounting of armament, among other things. Kane had told the owner of the yard something—not much, but something—about a Lost Colony found by a Dog Star tramp. . . ."

"And what are *we* supposed to do, Captain?" asked Forsby. "Plant the Federation's flag, or something?"

"Or something," said Maggie Lazenby. "You can rest assured of that."

Or something, thought Grimes.

))((4))((

As far as Grimes knew there was no real urgency—
nonetheless he pushed *Seeker* along at her maximum safe
velocity. This entailed acceleration slightly in excess of 1.5
G, with a temporal precession rate that did not quite, as
Maggie Lazenby tartly put it, have all hands and the cook
living backward. But Maggie had been born and reared on
Arcadia, a relatively low gravity planet and, furthermore,
disliked and distrusted the time-twisting Mannschenn
Drive even more than the average spaceman or -woman.
However, Lieutenant Brian Connery was an extremely
competent engineer and well able to maintain the delicate
balance between the ship's main drive units without
remotely endangering either the vessel or her personnel.

Even so, Grimes suffered. *Seeker* had a mixed crew—
and a ship, as Grimes was fond of saying, is not a Sunday
School outing. On past voyages it had been tacitly
assumed that Maggie was the captain's lady. On this voyage
it was so assumed too—by everybody except one of the
two people most intimately concerned. Grimes tried to
play along with the assumption, but it was hopeless.

"I suppose," he said bitterly, after she had strongly resisted a quite determined pass, "that you're still hankering after that beefy lout, Brasidus or whatever his name was, on Sparta . . . ."

"No," she told him, not quite truthfully. "No. It's just that I can't possibly join in your fun and games when I feel as though I weigh about fourteen times normal."

"Only one and a half times," he corrected her.

"It *feels* fourteen times. And it's the psychological effect that inhibits me."

Grimes slumped back in his chair, extending an arm to his open liquor cabinet.

"Lay off it!" she told him sharply.

"So I can't drink now."

"You will not drink now." Her manner softened. "Don't forget, John, that you're responsible for the ship and everybody aboard her . . . ."

"Nothing can happen in deep space."

"Can't it?" Her fine eyebrows lifted slightly. "Can't it? After some of the stories I've heard, and after some of the stories you've told me yourself . . ."

"Mphm." He reached out again, but it was a half-hearted attempt.

"Things will work out, John," she said earnestly. "They always do, one way or the other . . . ."

"Suppose it's the wrong way?"

"You'll survive. I'll survive. We'll survive." She quoted, half seriously, " 'Men have died, and worms have eaten 'em—but not for love . . .'"

"Where's that from?" he asked, interested.

"Shakespeare. You trade school boys—you're quite

impossible. You know nothing—*nothing*—outside your own field."

"I resent that," said Grimes. "At the Academy we had to do a course in Twentieth Century fiction . . ."

Again the eyebrows lifted. "You surprise me." And then she demanded incredulously, "What sort of fiction?"

"It was rather specialized. Science fiction, as a matter of fact. Some of those old buggers made very good guesses. Most of them, though, were way off the beam. Even so, it was fascinating."

"And still trade-school-oriented."

He shrugged. "Have it your way, Maggie. We're just Yahoos. But we do get our ships around." He paused, then delivered his own quotation. "'Transportation is civilization.'"

"All right," she said at last. "Who wrote that?"

"Kipling."

"Kipling—and science fiction?"

"You should catch up on your own reading some time. . . ." The telephone buzzed sharply. He got up and went rapidly to the handset.

She remarked sweetly, "*Nothing* can happen in deep space . . . ."

"Captain here," said Grimes sharply.

Lieutenant Hayakawa's reedy voice drifted into the day cabin. "Hayakawa, Captain sir . . . ."

"Yes, Mr. Hayakawa?"

"I . . . am not certain. But I think I have detected psionic radiation—not close, but not too far distant."

"It is extremely unlikely," Grimes said, "that we are the only ship in this sector of space."

"I . . . I know, Captain. But—it is all vague, and the other telepath is maintaining a block . . . I . . . I tried at first to push through, and he knew that I was trying. . . . Then, suddenly, I relaxed. . . ."

Psionic judo . . . thought Grimes.

"Yes . . . You could call it that . . . But there is somebody aboard that ship who is thinking all the time about . . . Morrowvia . . . ."

"Drongo Kane," said Grimes.

"No, Captain. Not Drongo Kane. This is a . . . young mind. Immature . . . ."

"Mphm. Anything else?"

"Yes . . . . He is thinking, too, of somebody called Tabitha . . . ."

"And who's *she* when she's up and dressed?"

"She is not dressed . . . not as *he* remembers her."

"This," stated Maggie Lazenby, "is disgusting. I thought, in my innocence, that the Rhine Institute took a very dim view of any prying by its graduates into private thoughts. I was under the impression that telepathy was to be used *only* for instantaneous communications over astronomical distances."

"If every Rhine Institute graduate who broke the Institute's rules dropped dead right now," Grimes told her, "there'd be one helluva shortage of trained telepaths. In any case, the Institute allows some latitude to those of its people who're in the employ of a recognized law enforcement agency. The Federation's Survey Service is one such. Conversely, the Institute recognizes the right of any telepath, no matter by whom employed, to put up a telepathic block."

"I still don't like it. Any of it."

"Mr. Hayakawa," said Grimes into the telephone, "you heard all that?"

"Yes, Captain."

"And what are *your* views?"

In reply came a thin chuckle, then, "I try to be loyal, sir. To the Institute, to the Service, to my shipmates, to my captain. Sometimes it is hard to be loyal to everybody at once. But, also, I try to be loyal to myself."

"Putting it briefly," said Maggie Lazenby, "you know on which side your bread is buttered."

"Butter is an animal-derived food, Miss Commander, which I never touch."

"Mr. Hayakawa," asked Grimes, "do you hear anything further from the strange ship?"

"No, Captain. The block has been reestablished."

"Let me know when you do hear anything more." He punched buttons, then spoke again into the instrument. "Captain here, Mr. Timmins. Mr. Hayakawa has reported a vessel in our vicinity, apparently heading for Morrowvia. Have you picked anything up?"

"Just the normal commercial traffic, sir. A Shaara freighter, *Mmoorroomm,* Rob Roy to ZZrreemm. *Empress of Scotia,* Dunedin to Darnstadt. *Cutty Sark,* Carinthia to Lorn. *Schnauzer,* Siluria to Macbeth. And, according to Sector Plot, the following ships not fitted with Carlotti equipment: *Sundowner,* Aquarius to Faraway, *Rim Eland,* Elsinore to Ultimo. . . ."

"Thank you." Then, speaking more to himself than to anybody else, "*Schnauzer* . . . Dog Star Line . . . cleared for Macbeth. . . . She might finish up there eventually. . . ."

He ignored Maggie's questioning look and went to his playmaster. As its name implied, the device provided entertainment, visual and audio—but this one, a standard fitting in the captain's quarters in all FSS ships, was also hooked up to the vessel's encyclopedia bank. "Get me Lloyd's Register," he ordered. "I want details on *Schnauzer*. Sirian ownership. Dog Star Line . . . ."

The screen lit up, displaying the facsimile of a printed page.

Schnauzer—a new ship, small, exceptionally fast for a merchantman, defensively armed. (The Dog Star Line had long insisted that its vessels were capable of conducting their own defense on some of the trade routes where piracy still persisted.)

"Mphm," he grunted. Back at the telephone he ordered Timmins to send a coded message to the FSS agent at Port Llangowan, on Siluria, to ask the names of *Schnauzer*'s personnel when she cleared outward.

He strongly suspected that the master would be Captain Danzellan.

))(((5))))((

"Master, Roger Danzellan," the Federation's man on Siluria replied eventually. "First mate, Oscar Eklund. Second mate, Francis Delamere. Third mate, Kathryn Daley. Chief engineer, Mannschenn Drive, Evan Jones. Chief engineer, Interplanetary Drives, Ian Mackay. Juniors, H. Smith, B. Ostrog, H. Singh. Purser/catering officer, Glynis Trent . . ." The message went on to say that Captain Danzellan and Mr. Delamere had both been among *Corgi*'s complement when she had last been at Port Llangowan. The last piece of information that it contained was that Francis Delamere was the nephew of the Dog Star Line's general manager.

So—obviously, the Dog Star people were interested in Morrowvia. On receiving the report from *Corgi*'s master they had acted, and fast. A suitable ship had been shunted off her doubtlessly well-worn tramlines, and Danzellan had been transferred to her command. Probably he had not wished to have Delamere as one of his Officers—but Delamere had pull. Nepotism, as Grimes well knew, existed in the Survey Service. In a privately owned shipping company the climate would be even more suitable to its flourishing.

There was only one thing for Grimes to do—to pile on the Gs and the lumes, to get to Morrowvia before Danzellan. Fortunately, the merchant vessel was not fitted with a Mass Proximity Indicator—the Dog Star Line viewed new navigational aids with suspicion and never fitted them to its ships until their value was well proven. Sooner or later—sooner, Grimes hoped—*Seeker* would pick up *Schnauzer* in her screen and, shortly thereafter, would be able accurately to extrapolate her trajectory. *Schnauzer* would know nothing of *Seeker*'s whereabouts or presence.

And Drongo Kane in his *Southerly Buster?* A coded request for information to the Bug Queen brought the news that he had lifted from Port Fortinbras, his refit completed, with a General Clearance. Such clearances were rarely issued. This one must have cost Kane plenty.

Grimes was spending more and more time in his control room. There was nothing that he could *do*—but he wanted to be on hand when *Schnauzer* was picked up. At last she was there—or *something* was there—an almost infinitesimal spark in the screen, at extreme range. Grimes watched, concealing his impatience, while his navigator, hunched over the big globe of utter darkness, delicately manipulated the controls set into the base of the screen. Slowly a glowing filament was extruded from the center of the sphere—*Seeker*'s track. And then, from that barely visible spark just within the screen's limits, another filament was extended.

"Mphm," grunted Grimes.

The display was informative. Relatively speaking, *Schnauzer* was on *Seeker*'s port beam, a little ahead of the beam actually, and steering a converging course. Morrowvia was out of range of the M.P.I., but there was little doubt that both ships were headed for the same destination.

"Have you an estimate of her speed yet, Mr. Pitcher?" asked Grimes.

"Only a rough one, sir," replied the tall, thin, almost white-haired young man. "Give me an hour, and . . ."

"Extrapolate now, if you will."

"Very good, sir."

Two beads of light appeared, one on each filament. "Twenty-four hours," said Pitcher. The range had closed slightly but the relative bearing was almost unaltered. "Forty-eight hours." The bearing was *changing*. Seventy-two hours." *Schnauzer* was slightly, very slightly, abaft *Seeker*'s beam. "Ninety-six hours." There was no doubt about it. At the moment *Seeker* had the heels of the Dog Star ship.

Grimes was relieved. He did not want to drive his ship any faster. An almost continuous sense *of déjà vu* is an uncanny thing to have to live with. The temporal precession field had not yet reached a dangerous intensity, but it had been increased to a highly uncomfortable one. Already there was a certain confusion when orders were given and received. Had they been made? Had they been acted upon?

Grimes waited for Pitcher to answer his question, then realized that he had not yet asked it. "Assuming," he said, "that your first estimate of *Schnauzer's* speed is correct, how much time do we have on Morrowvia before she arrives?"

"Sixty hours Standard, sir. Almost exactly two Morrowvian days."

Not long, thought Grimes. Not long at all for what he had to do. And not knowing what he had to do didn't help matters. He'd just have to make up the rules as he went along.

He said, "We'll maintain a continuous watch on the M.P.I. from now on. Let me know at once if there's any change in the situation, and if any more targets appear on the screen."

"Drongo Kane?" asked Saul.

"Yes, Mr. Saul. Drongo Kane."

The first lieutenant's eyes and teeth were very white in his black face as he smiled mirthlessly. He said, his deep voice little more than a whisper, "I hope that Drongo Kane *is* bound for Morrowvia, Captain."

"Why, Mr. Saul?" Grimes essayed a feeble jest. "Two's company, three's a crowd."

"Racial hatreds die very hard, Captain. To my people, for many, many years, 'slaver' has been an especially dirty word. Ganda, as you know, was colonized by my people . . . . And some hundreds of them, rescued by Kane's *Southerly Buster* before their sun went nova, were sold by him to the Duke of Waldegren . . . ."

"As I said before," Grimes told him, "they weren't *sold*. They entered the duke's service as indentured labor."

"Even so, sir, I would like to meet Captain Drongo Kane."

"It's just as well," said Grimes, "that he's not a reincarnation of Oliver Cromwell—if he were, Mr. Connery would be after his blood too . . . ."

He regarded his first lieutenant dubiously. He was a good man, a good officer, and Grimes liked him personally. But if *Southerly Buster* made a landing on Morrowvia he would have to be watched carefully. And—who would watch the watchman? Grimes knew that if he wished to reach flag rank in the Service he would have to curb his propensity for taking sides.

"Mphm," he grunted. Then, "I'll leave Control in your capable hands, Mr. Saul. And keep a watchful eye on the M.P.I., Mr. Pitcher. I'm going down to have a few words with Hayakawa."

Lieutenant Hayakawa was on watch—but a psionic communications officer, as any one such will tell you, is *always* on watch. He was not, however, wearing the rig of the day. His grossly obese body was inadequately covered by a short kimono, gray silk with an embroidered design of improbable looking flowers. Scrolls, beautifully inscribed with Japanese ideographs, hung on the bulkheads, although space had been left for a single hologram, a picture of a strikingly symmetrical snow-capped mountain sharp against a blue sky. The deck was covered with a synthetic straw matting. In the air was the faint, sweet pungency of a burning joss stick.

Hayakawa got slowly and ponderously to his feet. "Captain san . . ." he murmured.

"Sit down, Mr. Hayakawa," ordered Grimes. The acceleration—now more than two Gs—was bad enough for him; it would be far, far worse for one of the telepath's build. He lowered himself to a pile of silk cushions. Not for the first time he regretted that Hayakawa had been allowed to break the regulations governing the furnishing of officers' cabins—but PCOs, trading upon their rarity, are privileged persons aboard any ship.

He settled down into a position approximating comfort—and then had to get up and shift the cushions and himself to another site. From the first one he had far too good a view of Hayakawa's psionic amplifier, the disembodied dog's brain suspended in its globe of cloudy nutrient fluid. The view of Mount Fujiyama was much more preferable.

He said, "We have *Schnauzer* on the M.P.I. now."

"I know, Captain."

"You would," remarked Grimes, but without rancor. "And you still haven't picked up any further . . . emanations from her?"

"No. Her PCO is Delwyn Hume. I have met him. He is a good man. What you called my judo technique worked just once with him. It will never work again." Then Hayakawa smiled fatly and sweetly. "But I have other news for you."

"Tell."

"*Southerly Buster,* Captain. Myra Bracegirdle is the CPO. *She* is good—but, of course, we are all good. Her screen is as tight as that maintained by Hume or myself. But . . .

"She is emotional. During moments of stress her own thoughts seep through. She hates the *Buster's* mate. His name is Aloysius Dreebly. Now and again—often, in fact—he tries to force his attentions on her."

"Interesting," commented Grimes. He thought, *This is building up to one of those situations where everybody hates everybody. Mr. Saul hates Captain Kane, although he's never met him personally. Myra hates Aloysius. The way Maggie's been carrying on lately I'm beginning to think that she hates me. And I doubt very much if Captain Danzellan feels any great affection for Mr. Francis Delamere . . . .* He grinned. *But Frankie loves Tabbie . . . .*

He said, "And is *Southerly Buster* bound for Morrowvia?"

"I cannot say, Captain. But she is around. And just before you came in I 'heard' Myra Bracegirdle think, 'Thank the gods there're only seven more days to go before we arrive!'"

And that, Grimes told himself, *means that she gets there at the same time as us . . . .*

He clambered laboriously to his feet, went to Hayakawa's telephone. He punched, first of all, for Lieutenant Connery's quarters, but the engineering officer was not there. He called the engine room, and found him.

"Captain here, Chief. Can you squeeze out another half lume?"

"I can't." Connery's voice was sharp. "The governor's playing up, an' we're havin' to run the Drive on manual control. If I try to push her any more we'll finish up last Thursday in the middle of sweet fuck all!"

"Can't you fix the governor?"

"Not without stoppin' her an' shuttin' down. If you want to carry on, it'll have to wait until we get to Morrowvia."

"Carry on the way you're doing," said Grimes.

))(((6)))(((

Seeker saw nothing at all of *Southerly Buster* until both vessels were in orbit about Morrowvia, just prior to landing. This was not surprising, as Drongo Kane's ship had been approaching the planet from the Shakespearian Sector, whilst Grimes had been coming in from Lindisfarne. The angle subtended by these points of origin was little short of 180∞. Furthermore, once Morrowvia itself had come within MPI range the instrument, insofar as bodies of less than planetary mass were concerned, was practically useless. And radar had been useless until the shutting down of the time-space twisting interstellar drive.

There was *Seeker,* hanging in equatorial orbit three hundred miles up from the surface, and below her was Morrowvia, an Earth-type world, but unspoiled. There were blue seas and vast expanses of green prairie and forest land, yellow deserts and polar icecaps as dazzlingly white as the drifting cloud masses. There were snow-peaked mountain ranges, and long, winding rivers, on the banks of which, sparsely scattered, were what seemed to be towns and villages—but from a range of hundreds of miles, even with excellent telescopes, human habitations can look like natural formations, and natural formations like buildings, and telltale industrial smog was altogether lacking.

On the night hemisphere the evidence was more conclusive. There were clusters of lights, faint and yellowish. Said Grimes, "Where there's light there's life, intelligent life. . . ."

"Not necessarily," Maggie Lazenby told him. "There are such things as volcanoes, you know . . ."

"On this hemisphere only? Come off it, Maggie."

"*And* there are such things as luminescent living organisms."

"So what we're seeing are glowworm colonies? And what about the reports from our agents on Siluria and Elsinore and Drroomoorr? Would either the Dog Star Line or Drongo Kane be interested in glowworms?"

"They might be," she said. "They might be."

"Yeah?"

"Yeah. It's high time, Commander Grimes, that you cured yourself of your habit of jumping to conclusions, that you adopted a scientific approach."

Grimes decided against making some cutting retort. The other officers in the control room were looking far too amused by the exchange. He grunted, then demanded of Lieutenant Saul, "Any sign yet of *Southerly Buster*, Number One?"

"No, sir. Perhaps Mr. Hayakawa . . ."

"I've already asked him. As far as his Peke's brain in aspic and he are concerned, the *Buster*'s maintaining absolute psionic silence."

"*Peke's* brain?" asked Maggie.

"Can *you* think of any definitely *Japanese* dog at a second's notice?"

And then a voice came from the NST transceiver. It was a man's voice, harsh, yet not unpleasant, strongly accented. "*Southerly Buster* to Aero-Space Control. *Southerly Buster* to Aero-Space Control. Do you read me? Over."

"But there's not any Aero-Space Control here," announced Lieutenant Timmins. "We've already found that out."

"Kane knows that as well as we do," Grimes told him. "But, to judge by his record, he always maintains a facade of absolute legality in everything he does. This fits in."

"And I suppose," said Saul, "that he's already tried to establish communication with the local telepaths, if any, just as we did."

"Not necessarily. His PCO will have 'heard' our Mr. Hayakawa doing just that, and she'll have learned that Morrowvia is lousy with telepaths, but none of them trained . . . . Oh, they *know* we're here, in a vague sort of way . . . ."

"*Southerly Buster* to Aero-Space Control. *Southerly Buster* to Aero-Space Control. Do you read me? Over."

"There she is!" shouted Pitcher suddenly.

There she was, in the radar screen, a tiny yet bright blip. There she was, a new star lifting above the dark limb of the planet, a tiny planetoid reflecting the rays of Gamma Argo.

"If we can see her, she can see us," commented Grimes. He went to the transceiver, ordered, "Put me on to him, Mr. Timmins." He said sternly, "FSS *Seeker* to *Southerly Buster*. FSS *Seeker* to *Southerly Buster*. Come in, please, on audio-visual."

"Comin' in, *Seeker,* comin' in . . ." drawled the voice. There was a swirl of light and color in the little screen, coalescing into a clear picture. Grimes and his officers looked into a control room not unlike their own—even to a weapons control console situated as it would have been in the nerve center of a warship. And this *Southerly Buster* was a merchantman . . . . Drongo Kane calmly regarded Grimes from the screen—bleak yet not altogether humorless blue eyes under a thatch of straw colored hair, in a face that looked as though at some time it had been completely smashed and then reassembled not over carefully. He said, "I see you, *Seeker*. Can you see me?"

"I see you," snapped Grimes.

"Identify yourself, please, *Seeker*. Can't be too careful once you're off the beaten tracks, y'know."

"Grimes," said the owner of that name at last. "Lieutenant Commander in command of FSS *Seeker*, Survey Vessel."

"Pleased to meet you, Commander Grimes. An' what, may I ask, brings you out to this neck o' the woods?"

"You mayn't ask. That's Federation business, Captain Kane."

The pale eyebrows lifted in mock surprise. "So you know me, Commander! Well, well. Such is fame."

"Or notoriety . . ." murmured Maggie Lazenby.

"Did I hear the lady behind you say somethin'?" inquired Kane.

Grimes ignored this. "What are your intentions, Captain Kane?" he demanded.

"Well, now, that all depends, Commander Grimes. Nobody owns this world 'cepting its people. I've asked if I could make a landing, but got no reply. I s'pose you heard me. But nobody's told me not to land . . . ."

"What are your intentions?" demanded Grimes again.

"Oh, to set the old *Buster*'s arse down onto somethin' safe an' solid. An' after that . . . Fossick around. See what we can buy or barter that's worth liftin'. There're some spacemen, Commander—an' I'm one of 'em—who have to *earn* their livin's . . . ."

"It is my duty—and the way that I earn *my* living—to afford protection to all Federation citizens in deep space, interplanetary space, in planetary atmospheres and on planetary surfaces," said Grimes, with deliberate pomposity.

"You needn't put yourself out, Commander."

"I insist, Captain. After all, as you said, one can't be too careful when off the beaten track."

Kane's lips moved. Grimes was no lip-reader, but he would have been willing to bet a month's salary that grave doubts were being cast upon his legitimacy—and, were this a less tolerant day and age, his morals. "Suit yourself," said Kane aloud. "But you're only wastin' your time."

"I'm the best judge of that."

"Suit yourself," growled Kane again.

Meanwhile, *Seeker*'s inertial drive had stammered into life and the ship was both slowing and lifting under the application of thrust, being driven into a powered, unnatural orbit so that *Southerly Buster* could pass beneath her.

"I thought you'd be landing first," complained Kane.

"After *you*, Captain," Grimes told him politely.

And just where would Kane be setting his ship down? If *Seeker* had arrived by herself Grimes would have adhered to orthodox Survey Service practice—a dawn landing at the terminator, with the full period of daylight for the initial exploration. And should it be considered safe to establish contact with the indigenes at once, a landing near to an obvious center of population.

Kane had never been an officer in the Survey Service, but he had done his share of exploring, had made first landings on planets upon which he had been the first man to set foot. Slowly, steadily *Southerly Buster* dropped through the atmosphere, with *Seeker* following a respectable distance astern. All *Seeker*'s armament was ready for instant use; Grimes had no doubt that the other ship was in a similar state of readiness. *Corgi*'s people had been hospitably treated on Morrowvia—but this was a large planet, probably divided among tribes or nations. Even though all its populace shared a common origin there had been time for divergence, for the generation of hostilities.

Down dropped *Southerly Buster*—down, down. Down dropped *Seeker,* her people alert for hostile action either from the ground or from the other ship. Grimes let Saul handle the pilotage; this was one of those occasions on which the captain needed to be able to look all ways at once.

Down dropped the two ships—down, down through the clear morning air. Kane's objective was becoming obvious—an expanse of level ground, clear of trees, that was almost an island, bounded to north, west and south by a winding river, to the east by a wooded hill. To north and west of it were villages, each with a sparse sprinkling of yellow lights still visible in the dawn twilight. It was the sort of landing place that Grimes would have selected for himself.

Then the viewscreen, with its high magnification, was no longer necessary, and the big binoculars on their universal mounting were no longer required. And the sun was up, at ground level, casting long shadows, pointing out all the irregularities that could make the landing of a starship hazardous.

Kane was down first, setting the *Buster* neatly into the middle of a patch of green that, from the air at least, looked perfectly smooth. Saul looked up briefly from his controls to Grimes, complaining. "The bastard's picked the best place. . . ."

"To the west of him . . ." Grimes said. "Almost on the river bank. . . . It doesn't look too bad."

"It'll have to do, Captain," murmured the first lieutenant resignedly.

It had to do—and, as Grimes had said, it wasn't too bad.

Only one recoil cylinder in the tripedal landing gear was burst when *Seeker* touched the ground, and there was no other damage.

7

This was not the occasion for full dress uniforms, with fore-and-aft hat, decorations, ceremonial sword and all the other trimmings. This was an occasion for comfortable shorts-and-shirt, with heavy boots and functional sidearms.

So attired, Grimes marched down *Seeker*'s ramp, followed by Captain Philby, the Marine officer, and a squad of his space soldiers. Maggie Lazenby and the other scientists had wished to accompany him, but he had issued strict orders that nobody excepting himself and the Marines was to leave the ship until such time as the situation had been clarified. And this clarification depended upon the local inhabitants as well as upon Drongo Kane. Meanwhile, Grimes had said, no foolish risks were to be taken.

As he marched toward the towering hulk of *Southerly Buster* he regretted his decision to land to the west of that ship; he had put himself at a disadvantage. The light of the still-low sun was blinding, making it difficult for his men and him to avoid the lavish scattering of quartzite boulders that protruded through the short, coarse grass. And it made it impossible to see if Drongo Kane had any weapons aimed at him and his party. Probably he had— but *Seeker*'s main armament was trained upon Kane's ship and ready to blow her off the face of the planet at the slightest provocation.

It was a little better once he and the Marines were in the shadow of the other ship. Grimes's eyes adjusted themselves and he stared upward at the blunt, metallic spire as he walked toward it. *Defensively armed!* he thought scornfully. Those two famous quick-firing cannon reported by the Bug Queen were merely an addition to what the *Buster* already had. Even so, in terms of laser and missiles, *Seeker* had the edge on her.

Southerly Buster's ramp was down. At the foot of it an officer was standing, a skeletal figure attired in gray coveralls with shoulder-boards carrying first mate's braid. The man was capless, and bald, and the wrinkled skin of his face was yellow, almost matching the long teeth that he showed when he smiled at the men from *Seeker*.

"Commander Grimes?" he asked in an overly ingratiating voice.

"Mr. Dreebly?" countered Grimes.

"Aloysius Dreebly, sir, at your service."

And so this, thought Grimes, was Aloysius Dreebly. Small wonder that Myra Bracegirdle, *Southerly Buster*'s PCO, hated him. He matched his name—as people with ugly names so very often do. They, as it were, grow to fit the labels that misguided parents bestow upon them at birth. *And this Dreebly,* Grimes continued thinking, *I wouldn't trust him behind me. He'd either kiss my arse or stab me in the back—or both.*

"And will you come aboard, Commander? Captain Kane is waiting for you."

"Certainly, Mr. Dreebly. Lead the way, please."

"Oh, sir, I'm afraid I cannot allow these other men aboard the ship . . . ."

"And I'm afraid that I can't board unless I have an escort of my own people. Captain Philby!"

"Sir!"

The young Marine officer had his pistol out, pointing at Dreebly. His sergeant and the six privates held their rifles at the ready.

"But, sir . . . what are you thinking of? This is *piracy!*"

"Hardly, Mr. Dreebly. All the way from our ship to yours we were tracked by the muzzle of one of your quick-firers. Surely you will allow us to show *our* teeth."

"Let the bastards aboard, Dreebly!" boomed Kane's voice from a loudspeaker. "But put your guns away first, Commander. I don't expect my guests to check in their pocket artillery at the door—but, on the other hand, I take a dim view if it's waved in my face."

At a word from Grimes Philby reholstered his pistol, the Marines slung their machine rifles. Dreebly shambled up the ramp to the after airlock, followed by the party from *Seeker.* Inside the compartment, Grimes looked about him curiously. He had been expecting something squalid—but, at first glance at least, this seemed to be a reasonably well-kept ship. There was a distinct absence of Survey Service spit-and-polish—but such is found only in vessels where there is a superfluity of ratings to do the spitting and polishing. There was shabbiness—but everything looked to be in excellent working order.

The elevator from the stern to the control room would accommodate only four men. Grimes decided to take Philby and one private with him, told the captain to tell his sergeant and the remaining Marines to stand guard in the airlock and at the foot of the ramp. (The Marines were apt to sulk if anybody but one of their own officers gave them a direct order.) Dreebly led the way into the cage and, as soon as the others were standing there with him, pressed a button.

She was quite a hunk of ship, this *Southerly Buster*, thought Grimes, as they slid rapidly upward, deck after deck. She had probably started life as an Interstellar Transport Commission's *Gamma Class* cargo liner but, under successive ownership, had been modified and remodified many times. A vessel this size, even with a minimal crew, would be expensive to run. Whatever Kane's activities were, they must show a profit.

The cage came to a gentle halt. "*This* way, please, gentlemen," said Dreebly. He led the way into a short alleyway, to a door with a sign, captain, written above it. The door opened, admitting them into a spacious day cabin. Drongo Kane rose from an easy chair to greet them, but did not offer to shake hands.

He was as tall as his lanky bean pole of a mate, but there was a little more flesh on his bones. He moved with a decisive sort of grace, like an efficient hunting animal. He wasted no time on courtesies.

"Well, Commander Grimes?" he demanded.

"Captain Kane, I thought that we might combine forces. . . ."

"Did you, now? You've very kindly seen me down to the surface in one piece—not that I needed you—an' now you can go and play soldiers off by yourself, somewhere."

Grimes's prominent ears flamed. He was aware that Captain Philby and the Marine were looking at him, were thinking, *What's the old man going to say (or do) now?* Well, what *was* the old man (Grimes) going to say (or do) now?

He said, "I represent the Federation, Captain."

"An' this planet, Commander, is not a Federated World."

"Yet," said Grimes.

"If ever," said Kane.

"I was sent here by the Federation . . ." Grimes began again.

"To claim this planet—possibly against the wishes of its people?"

"To conduct a survey."

"Then conduct your survey. I'm not stoppin' you."

"But I'm responsible for your safety, and that of your ship, Captain. You're a citizen of Austral, a Federated World, and your vessel's port of registry is Port Southern, on that planet."

"I don't need any snotty nosed Space Scouts to see me across the road."

"Maybe you don't, Captain Kane—but you're here, and I'm here, and I am obliged to carry out my duties to the best of my ability."

"Cor stiffen the bleedin' crows!" swore Kane disgustedly.

Then, to somebody who had come in silently and was standing behind Grimes, "Yes, Myra?"

Grimes turned. So this was the Myra Bracegirdle of whom Hayakawa had talked. She was a tall girl, but thin rather than slender (this *Southerly Buster* must be a poor feeding ship), her face with its too prominent bones, too wide mouth and too big, dark eyes framed by silky blonde hair.

She said, "A word with you, Captain. Alone."

"Oh, don't worry about the Space Scouts, Myra. They're here to look after us. We have no secrets from *them*."

"*They* are on the way here, Captain. They saw the ships land. They have heard about spaceships, of course, but have never seen one . . . ."

And what about Corgi? Grimes asked himself. *But she could have landed on the other side of the world from here.*

He said, "Captain Kane, do you mind if I call my ship?"

"Go ahead, Commander. This is Liberty Hall; you can spit on the mat and call the cat a bastard."

But as Grimes was raising his wrist transceiver to his mouth it buzzed sharply, then Saul's voice issued from the little instrument. "First lieutenant here, Captain. Mr. Hayakawa reports that parties of natives are approaching the landing site from both villages."

"I'll be right back," said Grimes.

"Don't let me keep you," said Kane. "Mr. Dreebly, please show these gentlemen off the premises."

"Oh, Captain," Grimes said, pausing in the doorway, "I

shall take a very dim view if you act in a hostile manner toward the natives."

"And what if they act in a hostile manner toward me?"

"That," said Grimes, "will be different."

)))(((8)))(((

Grimes did not hurry back to his own ship, neither did he dawdle. He would have liked to have hurried, but was aware that Kane would be watching him. He walked at a moderately brisk pace, with Philby at his side and the other Marines marching after them.

"Sir," asked Philby, "do you think they'll be hostile?"

"*Corgi*'s crew didn't find them so, Captain Philby. But she landed on another part of the planet, among different people. We'll just have to play it by ear . . . ."

"A show of force . . ." murmured the young officer, as though he were looking forward to it.

And he was, thought Grimes. He was. He glanced at Philby's face—young, unlined, features, save for the strong chin, indeterminate. A Marine Corps recruiting poster face . . . . There was no vice in it—neither was there any sensitivity, or imagination. It was the face of a man who could have written those famous lines—and without ironical intention: *Whatever happens, we have got The Maxim gun—and they have not.*

"Don't forget," said Grimes, "that this is *their* world, and that we're interlopers."

"Yes, sir, but we're civilized. Aren't we?"

"Mphm."

"And these people, out of the mainstream for so long, need to be taught the Federation's way of life . . . ."

Was Philby joking? No, Grimes decided, he was not. He said mildly, "The Federation's way of life as exemplified by whom? By the crew *of Seeker?* By Captain Drongo Kane and *his* crew? Or by Captain Danzellan and *Corgi's* or *Schnauzer's* people? Kane and Danzellan are Federation citizens, just as we are."

"Yes, sir. I suppose so. But . . ."

"But we have the superior fire power. Not all that superior. From what we saw aboard *Southerly Buster* I'd say she packs the wallop of a young battleship. And I should imagine that *Schnauzer* could show her teeth if she had to."

"What are your orders, sir?" asked Philby stiffly, obviously regretting having initiated the conversation.

"Just keep handy while I meet the natives. Better call another half dozen of your men down. Have your weapons ready—but not too obviously."

"With your permission, sir." Philby raised his wrist transceiver to his mouth. "Mr. Saul? Captain Philby here. Would you mind telling Corporal Smithers to detail six men for EVA? Yes, number three battle equipment. Over."

Then Grimes gave his orders. "Mr. Saul, Captain here. Do as Captain Philby says. And ask Dr. Lazenby if she'll join me at the after airlock. Yes. At once. All other officers and all ratings, with the exception of the six Marines, to remain on board. Yes, main and secondary armament to remain in a condition of readiness."

He heard the sergeant, who was a pace or two behind him, whisper something to one of the Marines about a show of force. He smiled to himself. He was not showing the force at his disposal—but it was nice to know that it was handy.

He beckoned Maggie down from the open airlock door. She walked gracefully down the ramp, despite the fact that she was hung around with all manner of equipment— cameras, recorders, even a sketch block and stylus.

She said, "We've had a good look at them through the control room telescope and binoculars. They seem to be human. . . ."

"Are they armed?"

"Some are carrying spears, and a few have longbows. . . ."

The additional Marines clattered down the ramp. Grimes looked at the automatic weapons they carried and hoped that they would not be used. He was pleased to see that each man had a couple of sleep gas grenades at his belt, and that one of them was carrying extra respirators; these he handed out to Grimes, Philby and to the other members of the party that had gone to *Southerly Buster*.

There was activity just by the boarding ramp of that ship, too. Grimes borrowed Maggie's binoculars, saw that Kane, Dreebly and three more men had come outside and that a folding table had been set up. The wares spread upon it glittered in the strong sunlight. Trade goods, Grimes decided. Bright, pretty baubles. . . . And did he hope to buy a territory, a continent, a planet, even, for a string of glass beads? Why not? Things as strange had happened in Man's long history.

The first of the party of natives, that from the north, was now in sight from ground level. They moved with catlike smoothness over the grass, threading their way around the outcropping boulders. There were twenty of them—ten males and ten females. *Ten men and ten women,* Grimes corrected himself. Six men, carrying long spears, were in the lead, advancing in open order. Then came the women, eight of whom carried bows and who had quivers of arrows slung over their shoulders. This appeared to be their only clothing. The remaining four men brought up the rear.

Humans, thought Grimes, studying them through Maggie's glasses. Exceptionally handsome humans. That all of them were unclothed was no indication of their cultural level—naturism was the rule rather than the exception on several highly civilized planets, such as Arcadia. Their skins varied in color from pale gold to a dark brown, the hair of their heads and their body hair—which was normally distributed—was of a variety of colors, black, white, gray, brown, a coppery gold. . . . Grimes focused his attention on a girl. The short hair of her head was parti-colored, stripes of darker and lighter gray alternating. The effect was odd, but not unpleasing. He grunted. There was something odd about her eyes, too. But this offshoot of humanity, cut off from the main stem for generations, must have tended to grow apart from the generality of humankind.

The natives came to a halt by *Southerly Buster*'s ramp. The men stood aside to let two of the women, the two who

carried no weapons, advance slowly to where Drongo Kane
was standing by his table of trade goods. These two women
were a little taller, a little larger than their companions, but
no less graceful. They wore an air of maturity, but they
were no less beautiful. They were talking to Kane and he
seemed to be having no trouble understanding them,
and they seemed to be having no trouble in understanding
him.

"Here they come, sir," said Philby. *"Our* lot."

Grimes lowered the glasses, turned to face the visitors.
This was a smaller party, only six people. Once again there
was an equal division of the sexes.

Their leader, flanked by a spearman on either side of
her, advanced slowly to where Grimes, with Maggie
Lazenby beside him, was standing. Grimes saluted with a
flourish—and a part of his mind stood back and laughed
wryly at his according this courtesy to a naked savage. But
a savage she was not. Savages tend to be dirty, unkempt;
she was fastidiously clean. Her short hair was snowy,
gleaming white, her lustrous skin was brown, the lips of
her generous mouth a red that seemed natural rather than
the result of applied cosmetics. The overall effect was
definitely erotic. Grimes heard one of the Marines whistle,
heard another whisper, "Buy that one for me, Daddy. . . ."
He could not blame either of them—but felt definitely
censorious when Maggie murmured, "And you can buy
either—or both—of her boyfriends for me . . . ."

The two men were tall. Both were golden skinned; one
had orange-colored hair, the other was black-haired. Of
their essential maleness there was no doubt. Each, however,
was built more on the lines of an Apollo than a Hercules,

and each moved with a fluid grace as pronounced as that with which the woman walked.

To her, not at all reluctantly, Grimes returned his attention. He knew that the slow inspection that he was making was not mannerly, but he could not help himself. He told himself that it was his duty, as captain of a survey ship, to make such an inspection. Her eyes, he saw, were a peculiar greenish-yellow, and the tips of her ears were pointed. Her cheekbones were prominent, more so than the firm chin. His regard shifted slowly downward. Beneath each full but firm breast there was a rudimentary nipple. But she was human, human—even though the bare feet, which should have been long and slender, were oddly chubby.

She was human when she spoke. She said, "Welcome to Morrowvia." The accent was strange (of course) and the timbre of her voice held a quality that was hard to define.

"Thank you," replied Grimes. Then, "And whom do I have the honor of addressing?" The words, he realized as soon as he gave them utterance, were too formal, too far removed from everyday speech. But she understood them. Evidently the vocabulary had not become impoverished during the long years between first settlement and rediscovery.

She said simply, "My name is Maya. I am the queen."

So I'm saved the trouble of saying, "Take me to your leader," Grimes thought smugly. *Drongo must be doing his dickering with some very minor court official . . . .* He asked suavely, "And what is the name of your country, Your Majesty? Is it, too, called Morrowvia?"

Puzzle lines creased her rather broad face. And then

she smiled. Her teeth were very white and looked sharp, the teeth of a carnivore rather than of an omnivore. She said, "You do not understand. The captain of the ship called *Corgi* made the same mistake when he landed at Melbourne, many kilometers from here. I have been told that he called the Queen of Melbourne 'Your Majesty.' He explained, later, that this is a title given to queens on your world, or worlds . . . ." She added modestly, yet not without a touch of pride, "I am the elected Queen of Cambridge, the town to the south of where you have landed."

"Melbourne . . ." echoed Grimes. "Cambridge . . ." But it made sense. Homesick colonists have always perpetuated the names of their home towns.

"*He*—Morrow—left us a book, a big book, in which he had written all the names that we are to use for our towns . . . ." Maya went on.

Yes, it made sense all right. It was all too probable that the people of a Lost Colony would deviate from the human norm—but if they still spoke a recognizable major Earth language, and if their centers of population were named after Earth cities, whoever rediscovered them would have no doubt as to their essential humanity.

"Then what shall I call you," asked Grimes, "if 'Your Majesty' is not correct?"

"Maya," she told him. "And I shall call you . . ."

"Commander Grimes," he said firmly. It was not that he would at all object to being on given name terms with this rather gorgeous creature—but not in front of his subordinates."Have you a second name, Maya?" he asked.

"Yes, Commander Grimes. It is Smith."

Maya Smith, thought Grimes, a little wildly. *Maya Smith, the Queen of Cambridge . . . And not a rag to cover her, not even any Crown Jewels . . . And escorted by henchmen and henchwomen armed to the teeth with spears and bows and arrows . . .*

Spears and bows and arrows . . . they could be just as lethal as more sophisticated weaponry. Grimes looked away hastily from the Queen of Cambridge to her people, saw, with relief, that there was no immediate cause for worry. The Morrowvians were not using the time-honored technique of enthusiastic fraternization, of close, ostensibly friendly contact that would make the snatching of guns from their owners' hands all too easy when the time came. There was a certain stand-offishness about them, in fact, an avoidance of too close physical proximity. Some of the Marines, to judge by the way that they were looking at the native women, would have wished it otherwise—but Philby and his sergeant were keeping a watchful eye both on their men and on the visitors.

Grimes felt free to continue his conversation with Maya. He gestured toward *Southerly Buster,* where the people from the other village were still clustered about Kane and his officers."And your friend . . . what is she called?"

"*She* is no friend of mine. That *cat!*"

"But who is she?"

"Her name is Sabrina. She is the Queen of Oxford." The woman turned away from Grimes, stared toward Kane's vessel and the activity around her boarding ramp. She said, in a rather hurt voice, "The other ship has brought gifts for the people. Did you bring no gifts?"

"Mphm," Grimes grunted. He thought, *There must be something in my storerooms that she'd fancy* . . . .He said, "We did not know what you would like. Perhaps you would care to come on board, to take refreshments with us. Then we shall be able to discuss matters."

Maggie Lazenby snorted delicately.

"Thank you, Commander Grimes," said Maya Smith. "And my people?"

"They may come aboard too. But I must request that they leave their weapons outside."

She looked at him in some amazement. "But we never bring weapons into another person's home. They are for hunting, and for defense. There will be nothing to hunt in your ship—and surely we shall not need to defend ourselves against anything!"

You have *been away from the mainstream of civilization a long time!* thought Grimes.

He called the first lieutenant on his wrist transceiver to warn him to prepare to receive guests, then led the way up the ramp, into the ship.

»«((**9**))«

The Survey Service has procedures laid down for practically everything, and as long as you stick to them you will not go far wrong. Grimes didn't need to consult the handbook titled *Procedures For Entertaining Alien Potentates*. He had entertained Alien Potentates before. Insofar as the milking of such beings of useful information was concerned he had conformed to the good old principle—candy is dandy, but liquor is quicker. Of course, it was at times rather hard to decide what constituted either candy or liquor for some of the more exotic life forms. . . .

The majority of the natives had been shown into the wardroom, there to be entertained by the first lieutenant and—with the exception of Maggie Lazenby—the senior scientific officers. In his own day cabin Grimes had Maya Smith, the two men who constituted her bodyguard, and Maggie. He knew that it was foolish of him to feel ill at ease sitting there, making polite conversation with a naked woman and two naked men. Maggie took the situation for granted, of course—but her upbringing had been different from his. On Arcadia, the planet of her birth and upbringing, clothing was worn only when the weather was cold enough to justify the inconvenience.

"Tea, Maya?" asked Grimes. "Coffee?"

"What's tea?" she asked him. "What's coffee?"

"What do you drink usually?" he asked.

"Water, of course," she told him.

"And on special occasions?"

"Water."

"Mphm." He got up, opened his liquor cabinet. The light inside it was reflected brightly from the labels of bottles, from polished glasses.

Maya said, "How pretty!"

"Perhaps you would like to try . . . What would you like to try?"

"Angels' Tears," she said.

So she could read as well as speak Anglic. Grimes set out five liqueur glasses on the counter, uncorked the tall, beautifully proportioned bottle and filled them. He handed one to Maya, then served Maggie, then the two men. He lifted the remaining glass, said, "Here's mud in your eye!" and sipped. Maya sipped. The two men sipped. Maya spat like an angry cat. The men looked as though they would have liked to do the same, but they were too overawed by their unfamiliar surroundings.

"Firewater!" ejaculated the Morrowvian woman at last.

Grimes wondered what the distillers on Altairia would think if they could hear their most prized product so denigrated. This liqueur was almost pure alcohol—but it was smooth, smooth, and the cunning blend of spices used for flavoring could never be duplicated off the planet of its origin. Then he remembered a girl he had known on Dunsinane. He had not minded buying her expensive drinks, but he had been shocked by the way in which she misused them. The ending of what promised to be a beautiful friendship had come when she had poured Angels' Tears over a dish of ice cream . . . .

He said, "Perhaps this drink is a little strong to those who are not accustomed to it. But there is a way of making it less . . . fiery." He pressed the button, and in seconds a stewardess was in the cabin. The girl blushed furiously when she saw the nudity of the two Morrowvian men, but she tried hard to ignore their presence.

"Jennifer," said Grimes, "bring three dishes of ice cream."

"What flavor, sir?"

What flavor ice cream had that girl used for her appalling concoction? "Chocolate," said Grimes. "Very good, sir."

She was not gone long. Grimes took the tray from her when she returned; he was afraid that she might drop it when attempting to serve the naked bodyguards . He set it down on the table, then took Maya's glass from her. He poured the contents over one of the dishes of ice cream, handed it to her. "Now try it," he said.

She ignored the spoon. She raised the dish in her two hands to mouth level. Her pink tongue flickered out. There was a very delicate slurping sound. Then she said to her bodyguards, "Thomas, William—this is *good!*"

"I'm glad you like it," said Grimes, handing their portions to the two men. Then—"The same again?"

"If I may," replied Maya politely.

Alcohol, even when mixed with ice cream, is a good lubricant of the vocal cords. Maya, after her second helping, became talkative. More than merely talkative . . . she became affectionate. She tended to rub up against Grimes whenever he gave her the opportunity. He would have found her advances far more welcome if Maggie had not been watching amusedly, if the two bodyguards had not been present. Not that the bodyguards seemed to mind what their mistress was doing; were it not for her inhibiting presence they would have behaved toward Maggie Lazenby as she, Maya, was behaving toward Grimes . . . .

"Such a long time . . ." gushed Maya. "Such a long, long time. . . . We knew we came from the stars, in a big ship . . . . Not *us*, of course, but our first fathers and mothers . . . . We hoped that some time some other ship would come from the stars . . . . But it's been a long, long time . . . .

"And then, after the ship called *Corgi* came, we thought that the next ships would land at Melbourne, and that it'd be *years* before we saw one . . . . The Queen of Melbourne, they say, now has a cold box to keep her meat and her water in, and she has books, *new* books, about all sorts of marvelous things . . . . And what are *you* giving *me*, Commander Grimes?"

I know what I'd like to give you, he thought. The close proximity of smooth, warm woman-flesh was putting ideas into his head. He said, trying to keep the conversation under control, "You have books?"

"'Course we have books—but we can't make any new ones. Every town has a copy of The History; it was printed and printed and printed, years ago, when the machines were still working. . . ."

"The History?" asked Grimes.

"Yes. The History. All about Earth, and the first flights away from Earth, and the last voyage of the *Lode Cougar* . . ."

"The ship that brought you here?"

"Of course. You don't suppose we *walked,* do you?"

"Hardly. But tell me, how do you get about your world? Do you walk, or ride, or fly?"

"There were machines once, for riding and flying, but they wore out. We walk now. Everywhere. The Messengers are the long walkers."

"I suppose that you have to maintain a messenger service for the business of government."

"What business?" She pulled away from Grimes, stood tall and erect. It was a pity that she spoiled the effect by wavering lightly. "What government? *I* am the government."

"But surely," Grimes persisted, "you must have some planetary authority in overall charge. Or national authorities. . . ."

"But why?" she asked. "But why? I look after the affairs of my town, Sabrina looks after the affairs of *her* town, and so on. Who can tell me how much meat is to be dried or salted before the onset of winter? Who can tell me how the town's children are to be brought up? *I* am the government, of my own town. What else is needed?"

"It seems to work, this system of theirs . . ." commented Maggie Lazenby.

"'Course it works. Too many people in one town—then start new town."

"But," persisted Grimes, "there's more to government

than mayoral duties—or queenly duties. Public health, for example. . . ."

"Every town has its doctor, to give medicine, set broken bones and so on . . ."

Grimes looked appealingly at Maggie. She looked back at him, and shrugged. So he plodded on, unassisted. "But you must have a capital city . . ."

Maya said, "We have. But it does not rule us. We rule ourselves. It is built around the landing place of the *Lode Cougar*. The machines are there, although they have not worked for *years*. There are the records—but all we need to know is in The History. . . ."

"And the name of this city?"

"Ballarat."

So Morrow—presumably he had been master of *Lode Cougar*—was an Australian. There was a Ballarat, on Earth, not far from Port Woomera.

"And how do we get to Ballarat?" asked Grimes.

"It is many, many days' walk . . ."

"I wasn't thinking of walking."

"The exercise wouldn't do you any harm," Maggie told him.

"In my house there is a map . . ."

The telephone buzzed sharply. Grimes answered it. Saul's deep voice came from the speaker, "Captain, our orbital spy eyes have reported the arrival of another ship. Mr. Hayakawa says that it is *Schnauzer*."

So—*Schnauzer* had arrived, earlier than expected. Presumably Captain Danzellan's PCO had picked up indications that other vessels were bound for Morrowvia. And presumably he would make his landing in the same location that he had used before, in *Corgi*. Where was it again? Melbourne. Grimes tried to remember his Australian geography. The Ballarat on Earth wasn't far from Melbourne. He hoped that this would also be the case on this planet, so that he could kill two birds with one stone.

Lieutenant Saul could look after the shop in his, Grimes's, absence.

Somebody would have to keep an eye on Drongo Kane.

Grimes would have liked to have been able to fly at once to Melbourne, to be there and waiting when *Schnauzer* arrived. But there was so much to be done first—the delegation of authority, the pinnace to be readied and stocked for an absence from the mother ship of indefinite duration and, last but not least, to determine the location of Captain Danzellan's arrival point with accuracy. The orbiting spy eyes would do this, of course—provided that *Schnauzer* was not using some device to render their data erroneous. She was not a warship—but it was safe to assume that she was fitted with electronic equipment not usually found aboard a merchantman.

So, early in the afternoon, Grimes and Maggie Lazenby accompanied Maya and her people back to their town. Fortunately their intake of fortified ice cream had slowed the Morrowvians down, otherwise Grimes would have found it hard to keep up with them. Even so, he was soon sweating in his tropical uniform, and his bare knees were scratched by the long, spiky grass that grew on the bank of the river, and he had managed to twist his right ankle quite painfully shortly after the departure from *Seeker* . . . .

Lethargic though they were, the Morrowvians made good time. Their bare skins, Grimes noted enviously, seemed proof against the razor-edged grass blades—or it could be that they, somehow, avoided painful contact. And Maggie, once they were out of sight of the ship, removed her uniform shirt and gave it to Grimes to carry. She was as unself-conscious in her semi-nudity as the natives were in their complete nakedness. Grimes wished that he dare follow her example, but he did not have the advantage of her upbringing.

There was one welcome halt on the way. One of the bow-women called out, and pointed to a swirl that broke the otherwise placid surface of the slow-flowing river. She unhitched a coil of line from the belt that encircled her slim waist, bent the end of it to a viciously barbed arrow. She let fly, the line snaking out behind the missile. When it hit there was a mad, explosive flurry as a creature about half the size of a full grown man leaped clear of the water. Two of the men dropped their spears, grabbed the line by its few remaining coils. Slowly, with odd growling grunts, they hauled it in, playing the aquatic creature like an angler playing a fish, towing it to a stretch of bank where the shore shelved gently to a sandy beach.

Grimes and Maggie watched as the thing was landed— she busy with her camera.

"Salmon," announced Maya. "It is good eating."

"*Salmon?*" thought Grimes. It was like no salmon that he had ever seen. It was, he supposed, some kind of fish, or some kind of ichthyoid, although it looked more like a scaly seal than anything else. But what it was called made sense. Long, long ago somebody—Morrow?—had said, "Give *everything* Earth names—and then, when this world is rediscovered, nobody will doubt that we're an Earth colony."

A slash from a vicious looking knife killed the beast, and it was slung from a spear and carried by two of the men. The journey continued.

They reached the town at last. It was a neat assemblage of low, adobe buildings, well spaced along dirt streets, with trees, each a vivid explosion of emerald foliage and crimson blossom, growing between the houses. Maya's house (palace?) was a little larger than the others, and atop a tall post just outside the main entrance was a gleaming five pointed star, wrought from silvery metal.

There were people in the streets, men, women and children. They were curious, but not obtrusively so. They were remarkably quiet, except for a group of youngsters playing some sort of ball game. These did not even pause in their sport as the queen and her guests passed them.

It was delightfully cool inside Maya's house. The small windows were unglazed, but those facing the sun were screened with matting, cutting out the glare while admitting the breeze. The room into which she took Grimes and Maggie was large, sparsely furnished. There was a big, solid table, a half dozen square, sturdy chairs. On one wall was a map of the planet, drawn to Mercatorial projection. The seas were tinted blue, the land masses either green or brown except in the polar regions, where they were white.

Maya walked slowly to this map. Her fingers stabbed at it. "This," she said, "is the River Thames. It flows into the Atlantic Ocean. Here, on this wide bend, is Cambridge...."

"Mphm." *And this Cambridge,* thought Grimes, *is about in the middle of a continent, an island continent that straggles untidily over much of the equatorial belt, called—of all names!—England ... And where the hell is Melbourne?* He studied the map closely. There was a North Australia, another island continent, roughly rectangular, in the northern hemisphere. And there was a River Yarra. His right forefinger traced its winding course from the sea, from the Indian Ocean, to the contour lines that marked the foothills of the Dandenongs. Yes, here was· Melbourne. And to the north of it, still on the river, was Ballarat.

He asked, "How do your people cross the seas, Maya? You said that all the machines, including the flying machines, had broken down years ago."

"There are machines and machines, Commander Grimes. We have the wind, and we have balloons, and we have sailing boats. The balloons can go only with the wind, of course, but the sailing boats—what is the expression?— can beat to windward. . . ." Then she said abruptly, "I am a poor hostess. You must be thirsty. . . ."

Not as thirsty as you *must be,* thought Grimes, *after gorging yourself on that horrid mixture.*

"I could use a drink, Maya," said Maggie.

The Morrowvian woman went to the shelved cupboard where pottery, brightly and pleasingly glazed, was stacked. She took out six shallow bowls, set them on the table. Then she took down a stoppered pitcher that was hanging on the wall. This was not glazed, and its porous sides were bedewed with moisture. She poured from this into three of the bowls. The remaining vessels she filled with food from a deep dish that she extracted from the depths of a primitive refrigerator, a large unglazed earthenware box standing in a small bath of water. She used her hands to transfer cubes of white flesh from the dish to the bowls. There was no sign of any knives, forks or spoons.

She lifted her bowl of water to her mouth. She grinned and said "Here's mud in your eye!" She *lapped* the liquid, a little noisily. Grimes and Maggie drank more conventionally. The water was pleasantly cool, had a faint vegetable tang to it. Probably it was safe enough—but, in any case, all of *Seeker*'s people had been given wide spectrum antibiotic shots before landing.

Maya, using one hand only, quite delicately helped herself to food from her bowl. Without hesitation Maggie followed suit. Her fine eyebrows arched in surprised appreciation. Grimes took a cautious sample. This, he decided after the first nibble, was *good*. It reminded him of a dish that he had enjoyed during his last leave on Earth, part of which he had spent in Mexico. This had been fish—raw, but seasoned, and marinaded in the juice of freshly squeezed limes. He would have liked some more, but it would be a long time, he feared, before he would be able properly to relax and enjoy whatever social amenities this planet afforded.

Maggie, having followed Maya's example in licking her hands clean, had unslung one of her cameras, was pointing it at the map. She explained, "We have to have a copy of this, so that we can find our way to Melbourne."

"It will not be necessary. I can send a Messenger with you. But I warn you, it is a long journey, unless you go in your ship."

"We shall not go in the ship, Maya," Grimes told her. "But we shall not be walking, either. We shall use a pinnace, a relatively small flying boat."

"I have never flown," said Maya wistfully. "Not even in a balloon. Do you think that I . . . ?"

"Why not?" said Grimes. *Why not?* he thought. *She'll be able to introduce me to her sister queen in Melbourne.*

"When do we leave?" she asked him.

"In the morning, as soon after sunrise as possible." That would be a good time; Melbourne was only a degree or so west of Cambridge. The flight would be made in daylight, and arrival would be well before sunset.

She said, "You will excuse me. I must make arrangements for my deputy to run affairs during my absence."

"I must do likewise," said Grimes.

They looked at each other gravely, both monarchs of a small kingdom, both with the cares of state heavy on their shoulders. It was unkind of Maggie to spoil the effect by snickering.

"I shall send an escort with you," said Maya.

"It is not necessary. All we have to do is to follow the river."

"But wolves have been reported along the river bank. . . ."

And if the "wolves" of Morrowvia bore the same relationship to Terran wolves as did the Morrowvian "salmon" to Terran salmon, Grimes didn't want to meet them. He said so to Maya.

So he and Maggie, escorted by four spearmen and two bow-women, walked back to the ship. The members of the escort were too awestricken by the visitors from Outside to talk unless spoken to, and after ten minutes or so of very heavy going no attempt was made at conversation.

))((11))((

Grimes did not get much sleep that night.

He did not want to leave his ship until he was reasonably sure that the situation was under control. Drongo Kane was the main problem. Just what were his intentions? *Southerly Buster* had been kept under close observation from *Seeker*, and all the activity around her airlock had been filmed. Highly sensitive long-range microphones had been trained upon her—but Kane had set up some small noise-making machine that produced a continuous *whup, whup, whup* . . . . Hayakawa, disregarding the Rhine Institute code of ethics, had tried to pry, but Myra Bracegirdle, Kane's PCO, was maintaining an unbreakable block over the minds of all the *Buster*'s personnel. He had then tried to pick up the thoughts of the people in the town of Oxford, with little more success.

Grimes studied the film that had been made. He watched, on the screen, Kane talking amicably with Sabrina, the Queen of Oxford. He seemed to be laying on the charm with a trowel, and the Morrowvian woman was lapping it up. She smiled smugly when Drongo hung a scintillating string of synthetic diamonds about her neck, and her chubby hand went up to stroke the huge ruby that formed the pendant of the necklace, that glowed with crimson fire between her ample, golden-skinned breasts. She looked, thought Grimes, like a sleek cat that had got its nose into the cream. If it had not been for that annoying *whup, whup, whup* he would have heard her purring. It was shortly after her acceptance of this gift that Kane took her into the ship. Dreebly and two others—a little, fat man who, to judge by his braid, was the second mate and a cadaverous blonde in catering officer's uniform— remained by the table, handing out cheap jewelry, hand mirrors, pocket knives (a bad guess, thought Grimes amusedly, in this nudist culture), pairs of scissors and (always a sure way of buying goodwill) a quite good selection of children's toys. But it was the books that were in the greatest demand. The lens of one of the cameras that had been used zoomed in to a close-up of the display. Their covers were brightly-colored, eye-catching. They were, every one of them, handouts from the Tourist Bureaus of the more glamorous worlds of the galaxy.

Did Kane intend opening a travel agency on this world? It was possible, Grimes conceded. After all, the man was a shipowner. And his ship, according to the report from Elsinore, had been modified to suit her for the carriage of passengers.

"I don't like the looks of this, Captain," said the first lieutenant.

"What don't you like about it, Mr. Saul?" asked Grimes.

"I still remember what he did on Ganda."

"He can hardly do the same here. These people aren't being evacuated from their world before it's destroyed. They're quite happy here. In any case, the Gandans were skilled workmen, technicians. These people, so far as I can see, are little better than savages. *Nice* savages, I admit, but . . ."

"Forgive me for saying so, Captain, but you're very simple, aren't you?"

Grimes's prominent ears reddened. He demanded sharply, "What do you mean, Mr. Saul?"

"You've seen even more of these people than I have, sir. Have you seen an ugly man or woman?"

"No," admitted Grimes.

"And there are worlds where beautiful women are in great demand . . . ."

"And there are the quite stringent laws prohibiting the traffic in human merchandise," said Grimes.

"Kane is bound to find some loophole," insisted Saul. "Just as he did on Ganda." Then his racial bitterness found utterance. "After all, he's a *white* man."

Grimes sighed. He wished, as he had wished before, that Saul would forget the color of his skin. He said tiredly, "All right, all right—Whitey's to blame for *everything*. But, from my reading of history, I seem to remember that it was the fat black kings on the west coast of Africa who sold their own people to the white slave traders. . . ."

"Just as that fat yellow queen whom Kane entertained will sell her people to the white slave trader."

"I wouldn't call her *fat* . . ." objected Grimes, trying to bring the conversation to a lighter level.

"Just pleasantly plump, dearie," said Maggie Lazenby.

"But, as you say, Drongo won't be able to pull off a coup like the Gandan effort twice running. And even if he makes a deal with some non-Federated world, *he's* still a Federation citizen and subject to Federation law."

"Yes, Commander Lazenby," agreed Saul dubiously. "But I don't trust him."

"Who does?" said Grimes. "During my absence you'll just have to watch him, Mr. Saul, like a cat watching a mouse." He added, "Like a black cat watching a white mouse."

"A white rat, you mean," grumbled Saul.

»)((12))((

Before sunrise the pinnace was ready.

Grimes was taking with him Pitcher, the navigator, Ensign Billard who, as well as being assistant communications officer (electronic), was a qualified atmosphere pilot, and Commander Maggie Lazenby. All of them carried sidearms. The pinnace, too, was armed, being fitted with a laser cannon and two 20-mm machine guns.

Just as the sun was coming up, Grimes, Pitcher, Billard and Maggie stood outside the ship, watching as the small craft, its inertial drive muttering irritably, was eased out of its bay high on the ship's side, maneuvered down to the ground. It landed rather clumsily. Saul stepped out of the pilot's cabin and saluted with rather less than his usual snap. (He had been up, working, all night.) He said, "She's all yours, Captain."

"Thank you, Number One." Grimes looked at his watch, the one that had been adjusted to keep Morrowvian time. "Mphm. Time Maya was here."

"And here she is," said Maggie. "Enter the Queen of Cambridge, singing and dancing . . . ."

Maya was not singing and dancing, but she looked well rested, alert, and as though she were looking forward to the outing. She was escorted by a half a dozen bow-women and a like number of spearmen, two of whom were carrying a large basket between them. Curiously, Grimes looked into the basket. There were bowls of the raw fish that he had enjoyed the previous day, other bowls of what looked like dried meat. He looked away hastily. All that he had been able to manage for breakfast was a large cup of black coffee.

Maya looked with interest at the pinnace. "How does this thing fly?" she asked. "I don't see any wings or gasbag. . . ."

"Inertial drive," Grimes told her briefly. "No, I'm sorry, but I can't explain it at this hour of the morning." He turned to Saul. "All right, Number One. I'm getting the show on the road. I leave *Seeker* in your capable hands. Don't do anything you couldn't do riding a bicycle."

"What *is* a bicycle?" asked Maya.

"Remind me to bring you one some time. . . ." He visualized the tall, lush, naked woman astride such a machine and felt more than a little happier.

Pitcher and Billard clambered into the pinnace. They stood in the open doorway and took the hamper of Maya's provisions as the two Morrowvian spearmen handed it up to them. Then, Maggie, disdaining the offer of a helping hand from Grimes, mounted the short ladder into the doorway. Grimes, however, was courteously able to assist Maya to board. He glared coldly at Saul when he noticed the sardonic look on the first lieutenant's face. Then he boarded himself.

Pitcher, with a chart made from Maggie's photographs, and young Mr. Billard occupied the forward compartment. Grimes sat with Maggie and Maya in the after cabin. As soon as the women were comfortable—although Maya was sitting on the edge of her seat like a young girl at her very first party—Grimes ordered, "Take her up."

"Take her up, sir," acknowledged Billard smartly. He was little more than a boy and inclined to take himself seriously, but he was able and conscientious. The noise of the restarted inertial drive was little more, at first, than a distant whisper. The pinnace lifted so gently that there was no sense of motion; even Grimes was surprised to see the sleek hull of *Seeker* sliding past and downward beyond the viewports. She ascended vertically, and then her passengers were able to look out and down at the two ships—*Southerly Buster*'s people were sleeping in; there were no signs of life around her—at the winding river, at the little towns spaced along its banks.

Maya ran from one side to the other of the small cabin. There was rather much of her in these confined quarters. "Oh, look!" she said, pointing. "There's *Cambridge*! Doesn't it look *small* from up here! And that town on the next bend is Kingston, and there's Richmond. . . . And there's the weekly cargo wherry, there, with the sail. . . ."

Grimes could not appreciate the distant view as it was obscured by Maya's breasts, but he did not complain.

"Sir," called Pitcher, "do you want us to steer a compass course, or shall we navigate from landmark to landmark? That way we shall not put on much distance."

"From landmark to landmark," said Grimes. "We may as well enjoy the scenery."

"You look as though you're doing that right now," commented Maggie.

"Would you mind getting back to your seat, Maya?" asked Grimes. "We shall be accelerating soon, and you may lose your balance. . . ."

"Make sure you don't lose yours . . ." Maggie murmured.

The irregular beat of the inertial drive was louder now, and its vibration noticeable. The pinnace turned in a wide arc, and then the landing site was astern of them, and the two tall ships were dwindling to the size of toys. Ahead of them, and a little to starboard, was a snowcapped mountain, Ben Nevis. Below them was a wide prairie over which surged a great herd of dun colored beasts. "Bison," said Maya, adding that these animals constituted the main meat supply of her people. She offered strips of dried flesh from her basket to Grimes and Maggie, much as a Terran woman would offer chocolates. Grimes took one and chewed it dubiously. It wasn't bad, but it would not worry him much if he never tasted any more of it.

He took a pair of binoculars from their rack and stared down at the so-called bison. From almost directly above them he could not get much of an idea of their general appearance—but he knew that the Terran animals of that name had never run to six legs, whereas these brutes did.

The gleaming peak of Ben Nevis hung in their starboard viewports for long seconds, then dropped slowly astern. The pinnace, now, was following the course of another river, the Mersey, and Maya was pointing out the towns along its meandering length. "Yes, that must be Lancaster. . . . I visited there two years ago, and I remember that thickly wooded hill just by it. . . . Most of the people living along the Mersey banks are Cordwainers . . . ."

"Cordwainers?" asked Grimes, thinking that she must be referring to some odd trade.

"It is their name, just as Smith is the name of most of us along the Thames . . . ."

"And what names, how many names, do you have on this world?" asked Maggie.

"There's Smith, of course. And Wells. And Morrow. And Cordwainer. That's all."

"Probably only four male survivors when *Lode Cougar* got here," said Grimes. "And polygamous marriages . . ."

"Chester," announced Maya, pointing to another town. "Brighton, and the shipbuilding yards . . . That schooner looks almost finished . . . Manchester, I *think* . . . Oh, this is the way to travel! It took me weeks, many weeks, when I did it by foot and by wherry!"

"And why do you travel?" asked Maggie.

"Why do *you* travel?" the other woman countered. "To . . . to see new things, new people."

"And what new things have you seen?"

"Oh, the workshops at Manchester. You must have noticed the smoke as we flew over them. They smelt metal there, after they've dug the ore from the ground. They say that for years and years, before the process was discovered, we had to use scraps of metal from the ship to tip our spears and arrows."

"And so your weapons are made from this iron—I suppose it's iron—from Manchester?" asked Maggie.

"Yes."

"And what do you buy it with? What do you barter for it?"

"The salmon are caught only in the Thames. Their pickled flesh is a great delicacy."

"And tell me," Maggie went on, "don't some of you Smiths and Morrows and Wellses and Cordwainers get the idea, sometimes, that there are other ways of getting goods besides barter?"

"There are no other ways, Commander Maggie."

"On some worlds there are. Just suppose, Maya . . . just suppose that it's been a bad year for salmon. Just suppose that you need a stock of new weapons and have nothing to give in exchange for them. Just suppose that you lead a party of spearmen and archers to, say, Oxford, to take the people by surprise and to take their bows and spears by force . . ."

"Are you mad?" demanded Maya. "That would be impossible. It is not . . . human to intrude where one is not wanted. As for . . . *fighting* . . . that is not human either. Oh, we fight the wolves, but only to protect ourselves from them. We fight the eagles when we have to. But to fight each other . . . unthinkable!"

"But you must fight sometimes," said Maggie.

"Yes. But we are ashamed of it afterward. Our young men, perhaps, over a woman. Sometimes two women will quarrel, and use their claws. Oh, we have all read The History. We know that human beings have fought each other, and with weapons that would make our spears and bows look like toys. But we *could* not." There was a long silence, broken when she asked timidly, "And can you?"

"I'm afraid we can," Grimes told her. "And I'm afraid that we do. Your world has no soldiers or policemen, but yours is an exceptional world . . . ."

"And are *you* a soldier, Commander Grimes?"

"Don't insult me, Maya. I'm a spaceman, although I am an officer in a fighting service. I suppose that you could call me a policeman of sorts . . . ."

"The policeman's lot is not a happy one . . ." quoted Maggie solemnly.

"Mphm. Nobody press-ganged me into the Survey Service."

Then they were approaching the coast, the mouth of the river and the port town of Liverpool. North they swept, running low over the glittering sea, deviating from their course to pass close to a large schooner, deviating again to make rings around a huge, unwieldy balloon, hovering over a fleet of small fishing craft whose crews were hauling in nets alive with a silvery catch, whose men stared upward in wonder at the alien flying machine.

Pitcher called back from the pilot's cabin, "We're setting course for the mouth of the Yarra, sir—if you're agreeable."

"I'm agreeable, Mr. Pitcher. You can put her on automatic and we'll have lunch."

Maya enjoyed the chicken sandwiches that had been packed for them, and Pitcher and Billard waxed enthusiastic over the spiced fish that she handed around.

))((13))((

It was an uneventful flight northward over the ocean. They sighted no traffic save for a large schooner beating laboriously to windward; the Morrowvians, Grimes learned from Maya, were not a sea-minded people, taking to the water only from necessity and never for recreation.

As the pinnace drove steadily onward Maya, with occasional encouragement from Grimes and Maggie, talked. Once she got going she reminded Grimes of a Siamese cat he had once known, a beast even more talkative than the generality of its breed. So she talked, and Grimes and Maggie and Pitcher and Billard listened, and every so often Maggie would have to put a fresh spool in her recorder.

This Morrowvia was an odd sort of a planet—odd insofar as the population was concerned. The people were neither unintelligent nor illiterate, but they had fallen surprisingly far from the technological levels of the founders of the colony—and, even more surprisingly, the fall had been arrested at a stage well above primitive savagery. On so many worlds similarly settled the regression to Man's primitive beginnings had been horridly complete.

So there was Morrowvia, with a scattered population of ten million, give or take a few hundreds of thousands, all of them living in small towns, and all these towns with good old Terran names. There was no agriculture, save for the cultivation of herbs used medicinally and for the flavoring of food. Meat was obtained by hunting, although halfhearted attempts had been made at the domestication of the so-called bison and a few of the local flying creatures, more reptilian than anything else, the flesh and the eggs of which were palatable. The reason why more had not been done along these lines was that hunting was a way of life.

There was some industry—the mining and smelting of metals, the manufacture of weapons and such few tools as were required, shipbuilding. Should more ever be required, said Maya, the library at Ballarat would furnish full instructions for doing everything, for making anything at all.

Government? There was, said the Morrowvian woman, government of a sort. Each town was autonomous, however, and each was ruled—although "ruled" was hardly the correct word—by an elected queen. No, there were no kings. (Maya had read The History and knew what kings were.) It was only natural that women, who were in charge of their own homes, should elect a woman to be in overall charge of an assemblage of homes. It was only natural that the men should be occupied with male pursuits such as hunting and fishing—although women, the younger ones especially, enjoyed the hunt as much as the men did. And it was only natural that men should employ the spear as their main weapon, while women favored the bow.

No, there were no women engaged in heavy industry, although they did work at such trades as the manufacture of cordage and what little cloth was used. And women tended the herb gardens.

Maya confirmed that there were only four families— although "tribes" would be the better word—on Morrowvia. There were Smiths, Cordwainers, Morrows and Wellses. There was intermarriage between the tribes, and in such cases the husband took his wife's surname, which was passed on, also, to the children of such unions. It was not quite a matriarchal society, but it was not far from it.

Grimes steered the conversation on to the subject of communications. There had been radio—but many generations ago. It had never been required—"After all," said Maya reasonably enough, "if I die and my people elect a new queen it is of no real concern to anybody except themselves. There is no need for the entire planet to be informed within seconds of the event."—and transmitters and receivers had been allowed to fall into desuetude. There was a loosely organized system of postmen—men and women qualified by powers of endurance and fleetness of foot—but these carried only letters and very light articles of merchandise. Heavier articles were transported in the slow wherries, up and down the rivers—which meant that a consignment of goods would often have to be shipped along the two long sides of a triangle rather than over the short, overland side.

There was a more or less—rather less than more—regular service by schooner between the island continents.

The seamen, Grimes gathered, were a race apart, males and females too incompetent to get by ashore—or, if not incompetent, too antisocial. Seafaring was a profession utterly devoid of either glamor or standing. Grimes was rather shocked when he heard this. He regarded himself as being in a direct line of descent from the seamen and explorers of Earth's past, and was of the opinion that ships, ships of any kind, were the finest flower of human civilization.

The airmen—the balloonists—were much more highly thought of, though the service they provided was even more unreliable than that rendered by the sailors. Some of the airmen, Maya said, were wanting to fit their clumsy, unmaneuverable craft with engines—but Morrow (he must have been quite a man, this Morrow, thought Grimes) had warned his people, shortly before his death, of the overuse of machinery.

He had said (Maya quoted), "I am leaving you a good world. The land, the air and the sea are clean. Your own wastes go back into the soil and render it more fertile. The wastes of the machines will pollute everything—the sky, the sea and the very ground you walk upon. Beware of the machine. It pretends to be a good servant—but the wages that it exacts are far too high."

"A machine brought you—your ancestors—here," pointed out Grimes.

"If that machine had worked properly we should not be here," said Maya. She smiled. "The breaking down of the machine was our good luck."

"Mphm." But this was a *good* world. It could be improved—and what planet could not? But would the reintroduction of machinery improve it? The reintroduction not only of machinery but of the servants of the machine, that peculiar breed of men who have sold their souls to false gods of steam and steel, of metal and burning oil, who tend, more and more, to degrade humanity to the status of slaves, to elevate the mindless automata to the status of masters.

Even so . . . what was that quotation he had used in a recent conversation with Maggie? "Transportation is civilization."

More efficient transportation, communications in general, would improve Morrowvia. He said as much. He argued, "Suppose there's some sort of natural catastrophe . . . a hurricane, say, or a fire, or a flood. . . . If you had radio again, or efficient aircraft, the survivors could call for help, almost at once, and the help would not be long in reaching them."

"But why?" Maya asked. "But why? Why should *they* call for help, and why should *we* answer? Or why should *we* call for help, and why should *they* answer? We—how shall I put it? We go our ways, all of us, with neither help or hindrance, from anybody. We . . . cope. If disaster strikes, it is *our* disaster. We should not wish any interference from outsiders."

"A passion for privacy," remarked Maggie, "carried to extremes."

"Privacy is our way of life," Maya told her. "It is a good way of life."

Grimes had been wondering how soon it would be before the pair of them clashed; now the clash had come. They glared at each other, the two handsome women, one naked, the other in her too-skimpy uniform, somehow alike—and yet very unlike each other. Claws were being unsheathed.

And then young Billard called out from the forward compartment. "Land on the radar, sir! Looks like the coastline, at four hundred kilometers!"

Rather thankfully Grimes got up and went into the pilot's cabin. He looked into the screen of the radarscope, then studied the chart that had been made from the original survey data and from Maggie's photographs of that quite accurate wall map in Maya's "palace." Yes, that looked like Port Phillip Bay, with the mighty Yarra flowing into it from the north. He thought, *North Australia,* here we come! Then, with an affection of the Terran Australian accent, *Norstrylia, here we come!*

That corruption of words rang a faint but disturbing bell in his mind—but he had, as and from now, more important things to think about.

He said to the navigator, "A very nice landfall, Mr. Pitcher," and to Billard, "Better put her back on manual. And keep her as she's going."

Maya was by his side, looking with pleased wonderment at the glowing picture in the radar screen. Grimes thought, *I wish she wouldn't rub up against me so much. Not in front of Pitcher and Billard, anyhow. And not in front of Maggie, especially.*

))((14))((

It was summer in the northern hemisphere, and when the pinnace arrived over Melbourne, having followed the winding course of the Yarra to the foothills of the Dandenongs, there were still half a dozen hours of daylight left. The town, as were all the towns, was a small one; Grimes estimated that its population would run to about four thousand people. As they made the approach he studied it through powerful binoculars. It was neatly laid out, and the houses seemed to be of wooden construction, with thatched roofs. Beyond the town, on a conveniently sited patch of level, tree-free ground, towered the unmistakable metal steeple of a starship. There was only one ship that it could be.

Suddenly the pinnace's transceiver came to life. "*Schnauzer* calling strange aircraft. *Schnauzer* calling strange aircraft. Do you read me?"

"I read you," replied Grimes laconically.

"Identify yourself, please."

"*Schnauzer,* this is Number One Pinnace of FSS *Seeker*. Over."

There was a silence. Then, "You may land by me, Number One Pinnace."

Grimes looked at Pitcher and Billard. They looked back at him. He raised an eyebrow sardonically. Pitcher said, "Uncommonly decent of him, sir, to give permission to land . . . ."

"Mphm. I suppose he was here first—although I don't think that planting a shipping company's flag makes a territorial claim legally valid."

"They could rename this world Pomerania . . ." suggested Pitcher.

"Or Alsatia . . ." contributed Billard.

"Or NewPekin . . ." continued Pitcher. "Or some other son-of-a-bitching name . . . ."

"Or Dogpatch," said Grimes, with an air of finality. And then, into the microphone, an edge of sarcasm to his voice. "Thank you, *Schnauzer*. I am coming in."

Acting on his captain's instructions Billard brought the pinnace low over the town. People stared up at them— some in the by now familiar state of nudity, some clothed. Those who were dressed were wearing uniform, obviously personnel from the Dog Star ship. The small craft almost grazed the peaked, thatched roofs, then settled down gently fifty meters to the west of *Schnauzer*, on the side from which her boarding ramp was extended.

"Well," remarked Maggie, "we're here. I don't notice any red carpet out for us. What do we do now?"

"We disembark," Grimes told her. "There'll be no need to leave anybody aboard; the officers of major shipping companies are usually quite law-abiding people." *Ususally*, he thought, *but not always*. He remembered suddenly the almost piratical exploits of one Captain Craven, the master *of Delta Orionis*, to which he, Grimes, had been an accessory.

"What about Drongo Kane?" asked Maggie.

"You can hardly call *him* a major shipping company," said Grimes.

Three men were walking slowly down the merchant ship's ramp. In the lead was a bareheaded, yellow-haired giant, heavily muscled. Following him was a tall and slender, too slender, young man. Finally—last ashore and first to board—was a portly gentleman, clothed in dignity and respectability as well as in master's uniform. All of them wore sidearms. Grimes frowned. As a naval officer he did not like to see merchant officers going about armed to the teeth—but he knew that the Dog Star Line held quite strong views on the desirability of the ability of its ships and its personnel to defend themselves.

The door of the pinnace opened and the short ladder extended itself to the grassy ground. Grimes buckled on his belt with the holstered pistol, put on his cap and, ignoring the steps, jumped out of the small craft. He turned to assist Maggie but she ignored his hand, jumped also. Maya followed her, leaping down with feline grace. Pitcher was next, then Billard, who spoiled the effect by tripping and sprawling untidily.

Schnauzer's master had taken leading place now, and was advancing slowly, with his two officers a couple of paces to the rear. Unlike them he was not wearing the comfortable, utilitarian gray shorts, shirt and stockings but a white uniform, with tunic and long trousers—but portly men look their best in clothing that conceals most of the body.

He acknowledged Grimes's salute stiffly, while his rather protuberant brown eyes flickered over the young man's insignia of rank. He said, in a rather reedy voice, "Good afternoon, Commander." Then, "You are the commanding officer of *Seeker*?"

"Yes, Captain. Lieutenant Commander Grimes. And you, sir, are Captain Roger Danzellan, and the two gentlemen with you are Mr. Oscar Eklund, chief officer, and Mr. Francis Delamere, second officer."

"How right you are, Commander. I realize that there is no need for me to introduce myself and my people. But as a mere merchant captain I do not have the resources of an Intelligence Service to draw upon. . . ."

Grimes took the hint and introduced Maggie, Maya, Pitcher and Billard.

"And now, Commander," asked Danzellan, "what can I do for you?"

"If you would, sir, you can tell me what you are doing here."

"Trade, Commander, trade. This is a competitive galaxy, although you ladies and gentlemen in the Survey Service may not find it so. My employers are not in business for the state of their health . . . ."

"Aren't they?" inquired Maggie. "I would have thought that the state of their *financial* health was their main concern."

"A point well taken, Commander Lazenby. Anyhow, the Dog Star Line is always ready and willing to expand its sphere of operations. When a Dog Star ship, *Corgi*—but I imagine that you know all about *that*—stumbled upon this world, quite by chance, the reports made by her master, myself, were read with great interest by the Board of Directors. It was realized that we, as it were, have one foot well inside the door. It was decided to strike the iron while it is hot. Do you read me, Commander Grimes?"

"Loud and clear, Captain Danzellan. But tell me, what sort of trade do you hope to establish with the people of Morrowvia?"

"There are manufactured goods from a score of planets on our established routes for which there will be a demand here. For example, I have in my hold a large consignment of solar-powered refrigerators, and one of solar cookers. On the occasion of my first visit here a refrigerator was left with the, er, Queen of Melbourne. I was pleased to discover on my return that it is still working well, and even more pleased to learn that other, er, queens have seen it, and that still others have heard about it . . ."

"You will remember, Commander Grimes," said Maya, "that I told you about the cold box."

"So even this lady, from Cambridge, many miles from here, has heard about it."

"Mphm. But how are the people going to pay the freight on these quite unnecessary luxuries—and for the luxuries themselves?"

"Unnecessary luxuries, Commander? I put it to you— would *you* be prepared to sip your pre-prandial pink gin without an ice cube to make it more potable? Do *you* enjoy lukewarm beer?"

"Frankly, no, Captain. But—the question of payment . . ."

"These are sordid details, Commander. But I have no doubt that something will be worked out."

"No doubt at all," commented Maggie Lazenby. "When people want something badly enough they find some way of paying for it."

"In a nutshell, Commander Lazenby. In a nutshell." Danzellan beamed upon her benignly. Then, "I am sorry that I cannot ask you aboard my ship, but we are rather cramped for space. In a merchant vessel carrying capacity for money-earning cargo is of greater importance than luxurious accommodation for personnel."

"I understand," said Grimes. Such merchant vessels as he had been aboard housed their officers in far greater comfort than did the Survey Service. He went on, "Maya, here, wishes to pay her respects to her sister queen. We will accompany her."

"I'll show you the way, Commander," volunteered Mr. Delamere eagerly.

Danzellan frowned at his second officer and the young man wilted visibly. Then the captain relented. "All right," he said. "You may take the party from *Seeker* to Queen Lilian's palace." He added sternly, "See that they don't get lost."

))((15))((

Delamere led the way from the landing site to the town, walking fast. He did not pause when he took the party past a survey team from *Schnauzer*, busily engaged with tapes, rods and theodolite, working under the direction of a young woman with third officer's braid on her shoulder-boards. He acknowledged her wave absently. Watching the surveyors was a large group of children, with a smaller number of adults. These people, Grimes saw, were very similar to those whom he had encountered at *Seeker*'s landing place—well formed, beautiful rather than merely handsome. He was interested to note, however, that here the rudimentary nipples below the true breasts were the exception rather than the rule, whereas among Maya's people almost every woman—as she herself—was so furnished.

The dirt roads between the houses were level and tidy. The wooden buildings were well spaced and these, unlike those in Cambridge, had glazed windows—but, probably, the winters on this continent would be relatively severe.

There was an amplitude of trees and flowering shrubs in every open space.

Lilian's palace was larger than the other houses. It had, like Maya's, a tall staff standing outside its main entrance, a pole surmounted by a star fabricated from glittering metal rods. Also, in the full light of the westering sun, there stood just outside the door a metallic box, mounted on small wheels. Grimes had seen such contraptions before; this was the famous sun-powered refrigerator.

A tall woman came out to meet them. Her skin was creamy; the hair of her head and body was a glowing orange color. She said to Maya, "Welcome, sister. My house is yours."

"Thank you, sister," replied Maya. Then, "We have corresponded, but I did not think that we should ever meet."

"You are . . . ?"

"Maya, from Cambridge, Lilian."

"I know of you, Maya. Now I have the pleasure of knowing you."

"Lilian . . ." said Delamere.

"Yes, Francis?"

"How is Tabitha?"

"She is well, Francis."

"Can I see her, Lilian?"

"It will be well if you do not, Francis. Unless you are willing to abide by our customs."

The young man looked desperately unhappy. His long nose quivered like that of a timid rabbit. He said, "But you know . . ."

"What do I know, Francis? Only what I am told. Only

what I see with my own eyes." (*And those green eyes,* thought Grimes, *will see plenty.*)

"Lilian," Maya said, "I have brought friends with me."

"So I see." The woman was regarding the people from *Seeker* with a certain lack of enthusiasm. Her attitude seemed to be, *If you've seen one stranger from beyond the stars, you've seen them all.*

"Lilian, this is Commander Grimes, captain of the ship called *Seeker*. The lady is Commander Maggie Lazenby. The gentlemen are Lieutenant Pitcher and Ensign Billard."

Grimes saluted. Lilian Morrow inclined her head gravely, then said, "Be pleased to enter."

They followed her into the palace. Inside it was very like Maya's official residence, the big wall map being the most prominent decoration on a wall of the room into which she led them. She saw them seated, then excused herself and went back outside. While she was gone Grimes asked Delamere, "Who is Tabitha, Mr. Delamere?"

The second mate flushed angrily and snapped, "None of your business, Commander." Then, obviously regretting his display of temper, he muttered sulkily, "She's Lilian's daughter. I . . . I met her when I was here before, in *Corgi*. Now her mother won't let me see her again unless . . ."

"Unless what?" prompted Maggie. "Unless what, Francis?"

That's right, thought Grimes. *Turn on the womanly charm and sympathy.*

Delamere was about to answer when Lilian returned. She was carrying a tray on which was a rather lopsided jug of iced water, a dish of some greenish looking flesh cut into cubes, glass drinking bowls. She filled a bowl for each of them from the jug.

The water was refreshing, the meat tasted how Grimes imagined that the flesh of a snake would taste. He supposed—he hoped—that it was non-poisonous. Maya seemed to be enjoying it.

"And now, Commander Grimes," asked Lilian, after they had all sipped and nibbled, "what do you here?"

"I represent the Federation, Lilian . . . ."

"Just as Captain Danzellan represents the Dog Star Line. Captain Danzellan hopes to make money—and Morrow warned us about *that*—for his employers and himself. And what do *you* hope to make for yourself and your employers?"

"We are here to help you, Lilian."

"Do we need any help, Commander Grimes?"

"The Survey Service, Lilian, is like a police force. You know what a police force is. You have read The History. We protect people from those who would exploit them, rob them, even."

"Have we asked for protection?"

"You may do so."

"But we have not done so."

"Yet."

"Lilian knows that she has nothing to fear from us," said Delamere, more than a little smugly.

"Indeed, Francis?" The look that she gave him drove him back into sullen silence. Then she addressed Grimes again. "Commander Grimes, the relationship established between ourselves and Captain Danzellan is, on the whole, a friendly one. Captain Danzellan, in exchange for certain concessions, will bring us goods that we cannot make for ourselves. Before anything is decided, however, it will be necessary to convene a Council of Queens. I, of course, speak only for Melbourne—but Morrow foresaw that a time would come when matters affecting the entire continent, the entire world, even, would have to be discussed. Word has gone to my sisters of Ballarat, Alice, Darwin, Sydney, Perth, Brisbane—but there is no need for me to recite to you the names of all the towns of North Australia—that decisions affecting us all must soon be made. It is fortunate that our sister of Cambridge is with us; she will be able to report to her own people on what we are doing."

"These concessions . . ." began Grimes.

"They are none of *your* business, Commander."

Grimes looked appealingly at Maggie. She was supposed to know what made people tick. She was supposed to know which button to push to get which results. She looked back at him blandly.

Damn the woman! thought Grimes. *Damn* all *women*. He floundered on, "But perhaps I should be able to advise you. . . ."

"We do not need your advice, Commander."

"Mphm." Grimes fished his battered pipe from his pocket, filled it, lit it.

"Please!" said Lilian sharply, "do not smoke that filthy thing in here!"

"So your great ancestor warned you about smoking. . ."

"He did so. He warned us about all the vices and unpleasant habits of the men who, eventually, would make contact with us."

"Oh, well," muttered Grimes at last. Then, "I suppose that there is no objection to our visiting Ballarat, to look at your library, your records . . . ."

"That is a matter for the Queen of Ballarat."

And there isn't any radio, thought Grimes, *and there aren't any telephones, and I'm damned if I'll ask Her Majesty here to send a messenger.* He said, "Thank you for your hospitality, Lilian. And now, if you will excuse us, we'll get back to our pinnace and set up camp for the night."

She said, "You are excused. And you have my permission to sleep on the outskirts of the town."

"Shall we set up a tent for you, Maya?" Grimes asked.

"Thank you, no. Lilian and I have so much to talk about."

"Can I see Tabitha?" pleaded Delamere.

"No, Francis. You may not."

Schnauzer's second officer got reluctantly to his feet. He mumbled, "Are you ready, Commander? I'm getting back to my ship."

He led the way out of the palace and back to the landing site, although his services as a guide were hardly necessary. *Schnauzer,* dwarfing the trees that grew around the grassy field, stuck up like a sore thumb.

Back at the pinnace Grimes, Pitcher and Billard unloaded their camping gear, with Maggie watching and, at times, criticizing. The little air compresser swiftly inflated the four small sleeping tents, the larger one that would combine the functions of mess-room and galley. Then Billard went to the nearby stream for two buckets of water. A sterilizing tablet was dropped into each one, more as a matter of routine than anything else. If the broad spectrum antibiotic shots administered aboard *Seeker* had not been effective it would have been obvious by now. The battery-powered cooker was set up, and in a short time a pot of savory stew, prepared from dehydrated ingredients, was simmering and water was boiling for coffee.

The four of them sat around the collapsible table waiting until the meal was ready.

Grimes said, "What do you make of it, Maggie?"

"Make of what?" she countered.

"The whole setup."

She replied thoughtfully. "There's something *odd* about this world. In the case of Sparta there were all sorts of historical analogies to draw upon—here, there aren't. And how shall I put it? Like this, perhaps. The Morrowvians rather resent the violation of their privacy, but realize that there's nothing much that they can do about it. They certainly aren't mechanically minded, and distrust of the machine has been bred into them—but they do appreciate that the machine can contribute greatly to their comfort. I imagine that Danzellan's 'cold boxes' will be *very* popular. . . . As for their attitude toward ourselves—there's distrust again, but I think that they are prepared to like us as individuals. Maya, for example, has taken quite a shine to you. I've been expecting to see you raped at any tick of the clock . . . ."

"Mphm."

"You could do worse, I suppose—though whether or not she could is another matter . . . ."

"Ha, ha," chuckled Pitcher politely.

"Hah. Hah," growled Grimes, inhibiting any further mirth on the part of his subordinates.

"Anyhow, as far as behavior goes they do tend to deviate widely from the norm. The *human* norm, that is . . ."

"What do you mean?" asked Grimes.

"I rather wish that I knew, myself," she told him.

))((16))((

Grimes had Pitcher work out the local time of sunrise, then saw to it that everybody had his watch alarm set accordingly. Before retiring he called Saul aboard *Seeker*— his wrist transceiver was hooked up to the much more powerful set in the pinnace—and listened to his first lieutenant's report of the day's activities. Mr. Saul had little to tell him. Maya's people had made considerable inroads into the ship's supply of ice cream. Sabrina's people had been coming and going around *Southerly Buster* all day, but neither Sabrina nor Captain Kane had put in an appearance. Saul seemed to be shocked by this circumstance. Grimes shrugged. Drongo's morals—or lack of them—were none of his concern.

Or were they?

Grimes then told Saul, in detail, of his own doings of the day, of his plans for the morrow. He signed off, undressed, wriggled into his sleeping bag. Seconds after he had switched off his portable light he was soundly asleep.

The shrilling of the alarm woke him just as the almost level rays of the rising sun were striking through the translucent walls of his tent. He got up, went outside into the fresh, cool morning, sniffed appreciatively the tangy scent of dew-wet grass. Somewhere something that probably was nothing at all like a bird was sounding a series of bell-like notes. There were as yet no signs of life around *Schnauzer,* although the first thin, blue drift of smoke from cooking fires was wreathing around the thatched rooftops of Melbourne.

Grimes walked down to the river to make his toilet. He was joined there by Pitcher and Billard. The water was too cold for the three men to linger long over their ablutions, although the heat of the sun was pleasant on their naked bodies. As they were walking back to the camp Maggie passed them on her way to her own morning swim. She told them that she had made coffee.

Soon the four of them were seated round the table in the mess tent to a breakfast of reconstituted scrambled egg and more coffee. Rather surprisingly they were joined there by Maya. The Morrowvian woman put out a dainty hand and scooped up a small sample of the mess on Grimes's plate, tasted it. She complained, "I don't like this."

"Frankly, neither do I," admitted Grimes, "but it's the best we can offer." He masticated and swallowed glumly. "And what can we do for you this morning?"

She said, "I am coming with you."

"Good. Do you know the Queen of Ballarat?"

"I know of her. And Lilian has given me a letter of introduction." With her free hand she tapped the small bag of woven straw that she was carrying.

"Then let's get cracking," said Grimes.

While Maggie, with Maya assisting rather ineffectually, washed the breakfast things Grimes, with Pitcher and Billard doing most of the work, struck and stowed the sleeping tents. Then the furniture and other gear from the mess tent was loaded aboard the pinnace, and finally the mess tent itself was deflated and folded and packed with the other gear.

From the pinnace Grimes called *Seeker,* told Saul that he was getting under way. While he was doing so Billard started the inertial drive, and within seconds the small craft was lifting vertically. As she drew level with *Schnauzer's* control room Grimes could see figures standing behind the big viewports. He picked up his binoculars for a better look. Yes, there was the portly figure of Captain Danzellan, and with him was Eklund, his mate.

"Take her south for a start, sir?" asked Pitcher. "And then, once we're out of *Schnauzer's* sight, we can bring her round on the course for Ballarat . . . ."

"No," decided Grimes. The same idea had occurred to him—but Lilian knew his destination, and she was at least on speaking terms with Danzellan and his officers. In any case—as compared with Drongo Kane—the Dog Star people were goodies, and if anything went badly wrong they would be in a position to offer immediate help. "No," he said again. "Head straight for Ballarat."

Ballarat was different from the other towns that they had seen. It was dominated by a towering structure, a great hulk of metal, pitted and weathered yet still gleaming dully in the morning sunlight. It was like no ship that

Grimes or his officers had ever seen—although they had seen pictures and models of such ships in the astronautical museum at the Academy. It was a typical gaussjammer of the days of the Second Expansion, a peg-top-shaped hull with its wide end uppermost, buttressed by flimsy looking fins. To land her here, not far from the magnetic equator, her captain must have been a spaceman of no mean order—or must have been actuated by desperation. It could well have been that his passengers and crew were so weakened by starvation that a safe landing, sliding down the vertical lines of force in the planet's solar regions, would have been safe for the ship only, not for her personnel. Only the very hardy can survive the rigors of an arctic climate.

Hard by the ship was a long, low building. As seen from the air it seemed to be mainly of wooden construction, although it was roofed with sheets of gray metal. No doubt there had been cannibalization; no doubt many nonessential bulkheads and the like were missing from the gaussjammer's internal structure.

Billard brought the pinnace in low over the town. There were people in the streets, mainly women and children. They looked upward and pointed. Some of them waved. And then, quite suddenly, a smoky fire was lit in a wide plaza to the east of the gaussjammer. It was a signal, obviously. The tall streamer of smoke rose vertically into the still air.

"That's where we land," said Grimes. "Take her down, please, Mr. Billard."

"Aye, aye, sir!"

Quietly, without any fuss or bother, they landed. Even

before the door was open, even before the last mutterings of the inertial drive had faded into silence, they heard the drums, a rhythmic thud and rattle, an oddly militaristic sound.

"Mphm?" grunted Grimes dubiously. He turned to Maya. "Are you sure the natives are friendly?"

She did not catch the allusion. "Of course," she said stiffly. "*Everybody* on Morrowvia is friendly. A queen is received courteously by her sister queens wherever she may go."

"I'm not a queen," said Grimes. "I'm not a king, even . . ."

"The way you carry on sometimes, aboard your ship, I'm inclined to doubt the validity of that last statement," remarked Maggie Lazenby.

"Open up, sir?" asked Billard.

"Mphm. Yes. But nobody is to go outside—except myself—until I give the word. And you'd better have the twenty millimeters ready for use, Mr. Pitcher."

He belted on his pistols—one projectile, one laser— then set his cap firmly on his head. Maya said, "I am coming with you."

Grimes said, "I'm not in the habit of hiding behind a woman's skirts."

"What skirts?" asked Maggie Lazenby. Then, "Don't be silly, John. Maya's obviously one of *them.* When they see her with you they'll know that you're friendly."

It made sense.

Grimes jumped down from the open door to the packed earth of the plaza, clapping each hand to a pistol butt as soon as he was on the ground. Maya followed him. They stood there, listening to the rhythmic *tap-tappity-tap* that was, with every second, louder and louder.

And then a women—a girl—appeared from around the end of the long, low building. She was naked save for polished high boots and a crimson sash, and was carrying a flag on a staff, a black flag with a stylized great cat, in gold, rampant over a compass rose. Behind her marched the drummers, also girls, and behind them a woman with a silver sash and with a silver crown set on her silvery hair. She was followed by six men, with spears, six female archers, and by six more men, each of whom carried what was obviously an automatic rifle of archaic design.

Abruptly the drums fell silent and the drummers divided their ranks to let the queen pass through. She advanced steadily, followed by her standard bearer. Her skin was black and gleaming, but there was no hint of negroid ancestry in her regular features. Apart from the absence of rudimentary nipples she was what Grimes was coming to consider a typical Morrowvian woman.

Grimes saluted.

The standard bearer dipped her flag.

The queen smiled sweetly and said, "I, Janine Morrow, welcome you to Ballarat—the landing place of *Lode Cougar* and of our forebears. I welcome you, spaceman, and I welcome you, sister."

"Thank you," said Grimes. (Should he call this definitely regal female "Your Majesty" or not?)

"Thank you, Janine," said Maya. "I am Maya, of Cambridge."

"Thank you, Janine," said Grimes. "I am John Grimes, of the Federation Survey Service ship *Seeker*."

)(((17)))((

Grimes called the others down from the pinnace and introductions were made. Then Janine led the way to her palace, which was the long, low building hard by the ancient spaceship. In a room like the other rooms in which they had been similarly entertained there was the ritual sharing of food and water, during which the Queen of Ballarat read the letter that Maya had brought. Grimes was about to get a glimpse of it during her perusal; the paper was coarse-textured and gray rather than white, and the words had been scrawled upon it with a blunt pencil.

Janine said, "Lilian is favored. Twice she has been visited by Captain Danzellan, and now Commander Grimes is calling on her."

"Now Commander Grimes is calling on *you*," Maya pointed out.

"And so he is." Janine smiled sweetly, her teeth very white and her lips very red in her dark brown face. "And so he is. But what brings you to Ballarat, Commander Grimes? Do you have gifts for me?"

"I shall have gifts for you—but I have nothing at the moment. You will appreciate that we cannot carry much in a small craft such as my pinnace."

"That is true," agreed Janine. "But every time that Captain Danzellan has wished to look for information in the museum or the library he has brought me something." She gestured toward one of the walls where a new-looking clock, with a brightly gleaming metal case, was hanging. "That is a *good* clock—far better than the old one with its dangling weights. This one does not have a spring even— just a power cell which Captain Danzellan tells me will be good for centuries."

"From the way that you greeted us," said Grimes, "I thought that you were pleased to see visitors from the home world of your ancestors."

"But I am, I am! Too, it pleases me to try to—what is the word?—to reconstruct the old rituals. I have studied The History, as have we all. Also, I have access to records which my sisters elsewhere have not. I received you as important visitors must be received on Earth. . . ."

"Mphm."

"I am sorry that I could not fire a salute, but we have no big guns. In any case, the supply of ammunition for our rifles is limited."

"You did very nicely," said Grimes.

"Bring on the marching girls . . ." muttered Maggie.

Grimes, surreptitiously, had eased his watch off his wrist. The instrument was almost new; he had purchased it from the commissary just prior to departure from Lindisfarne. He said, "Perhaps you will accept this, Janine. It is a personal timekeeper."

"Just what I've always wanted," she said, pleased.

"I take it, then," said Grimes, "that you are the custodian of the books, the records, the . . ."

"Of everything," she told him proudly. "Perhaps, while Maya and I have a gossip, you would care to be shown around?"

"We should," said Grimes.

Their guide was the young woman who had carried the banner. Her name was Lisa Morrow. She vouchsafed the information that it was usually she who conducted visiting queens from other towns through the palace, but that it was the first time that she had been responsible for a party of outworlders. She did not seem to be greatly impressed by the honor, or even to regard it as such.

The palace was more than a palace. It was a library, and it was a museum. They were taken first of all into the Earth Room, a huge chamber devoted to Earth as it had been when *Lode Cougar* had lifted from Port Woomera on her last voyage. This had been the overcrowded planet dominated, in its northern and southern hemispheres respectively, by the short-lived Russian and Australian Empires.

Lode Cougar, concluded Grimes, had carried a lot of junk—but even in the days of the Third Expansion a ticket out to the stars was very often a one-way ticket; it was even more so in the days of the First and Second Expansions. Those first colonists had been so reluctant to break every tie with their home world.

Here, in the Earth Room, were maps and photographs, reproductions of famous works of art, even files of newspapers and magazines. These latter had been chemically treated to make the paper impervious to normal wear and tear, but now were practically unreadable—and Lisa Morrow took good care her charges did not, as they would have loved to have done, leaf through them. Grimes could make out the headlines on the front page of one of the papers, The Australian. "*Lode Tiger* missing, feared lost." No doubt the same paper had carried similar headlines regarding *Lode Cougar*. This had been long before the days of trained telepaths or the time-and-space-twisting Carlotti Communications System, but the established colonies had maintained a reasonably fast mail service with Earth. Grimes had read somewhere that it had taken less time for a letter to get from Port Southern, on Austral, to Sydney, in Australia, than it did to get through the post offices at either end. This state of affairs had persisted until the introduction of Carlotti radio transmission of all correspondence.

There were books, too—*real* books, properly bound, although with very thin, lightweight covers and paper. There were shelves of *How To* volumes. House building, boat building, aircraft building . . . mining, smelting, casting . . . navigation . . . surveying. . . Useful, Grimes supposed, if you did not, as you were supposed to do, finish up at an established colony but, instead, made a forced landing on a hitherto undiscovered world.

There was fiction—but, in spite of their age, these books looked almost fresh from the printers. Grimes had suspected that the Morrowvians were oddly lacking in imagination. Anything factual—such as the famous History—they would read, or any book that would aid them to acquire necessary skills. But the products of the storyteller's art left them cold. This attitude was not uncommon, of course, but it seemed more pronounced here than elsewhere. What books had Danzellan given to Lilian on the occasion of his first visit? Grimes asked Lisa the question.

She told him, "One by a man called Blenkinshop on first aid. And one about the fisheries on a world called Atlantia. We are having copies made for the library."

"So you have a printing press?"

"Yes, Commander Grimes. It is used only when a book is almost worn out or when there is something new that has to be printed."

"Is it hand operated?"

"No. We have an engine, driven by steam. Shall I show it to you now, or would you rather see the *Lode Cougar* room?"

"The *Lode Cougar* room," Grimes told her.

This adjoined the Earth Room, but was not as large. It contained relics of the ship herself. There were cargo manifests, log books, crew and passenger lists. There was a large photograph of the *Cougar*'s officers taken at Port Woomera, presumably shortly prior to lift-off. It was typical of this sort of portraiture, whatever the day and age. The captain, his senior officers on either side of him, was seated in the front row, his arms folded across his chest (as were the arms of the others) to show the braid on his sleeves. Standing behind the row of seated seniors were the juniors. Grimes stopped to read the legend below the photograph.

The captain's name was not, as he had expected that it

would be, Morrow. (But in an emergency, such as a forced landing on an unexplored world, anybody at all is liable to come to the fore.) The name of Morrow was not among those of the officers. A passenger, then? Examination of the ship's passenger list would supply the answer.

Lisa was pointing to a shelf of volumes. "And these," she was saying, "were Morrow's own books . . ."

Grimes paused on his way to the display cases in which the ship's documents were housed. Books told one so much about their owner's makeup. His eye swept over the fiction titles. He realized, with pleased surprise, that he had read most of them, when he was a cadet at the Academy. Early Twentieth Century—and even late Nineteenth Century—science fiction aboard a starship! But it was no more absurd than to find the same science fiction required reading for future officers of a navy whose ships, even though they had yet to penetrate to The Hub, fared out to The Rim. *The Planet Buyer* . . . that had been good, as he remembered it. *The Island Of* . . .

His wrist transceiver was buzzing. He raised the instrument to his mouth. "Captain!" Saul's voice was urgent. "Captain, I would have called you before, but we've been having transmitter trouble. Drongo Kane left in his pinnace at first light this morning, heading north. He's got Sabrina with him and three of his own people, all armed."

"You heard that?" Grimes demanded of his officers.

They nodded.

"Thank you for your attention," Grimes said to Lisa, "but we must get back to our pinnace."

"Is Drongo Kane a friend of yours, that you are so

eager to greet him?" she asked innocently, and looked bewildered when Grimes replied, "That'd be the sunny Friday!"

))((18))((

Grimes paused briefly in the room where Janine was still gossiping with Maya. As he entered he heard Maya ask, "And how do *you* deal with the problem of the uncontrollable adolescent?"

He said, "Excuse me, ladies. I've just received word that Drongo Kane is on his way here . . . ."

"Drongo Kane?" asked Janine, arching her silver brows.

"The captain of a ship called the *Southerly Buster*," Maya told her. "A *most* generous man."

"Goodie goodie," exclaimed her sister queen. She looked rather pointedly at Danzellan's gleaming clock on the wall, then at Grimes's watch that was strapped around her slim, brown wrist.

"Perhaps he'll give you an egg timer . . ." suggested Maggie Lazenby.

"What is that?" asked Janine.

"It's not important," said Grimes impatiently. "Excuse us, please."

He led the way out of the palace, to where his pinnace was grounded in the middle of the plaza, looking like a huge, stranded silver fish. He looked up at the clear sky. Yes—there, far to the southward, was a tiny speck, a dark dot against the blueness that expanded as he watched. Then he was aware that the two queens had followed him outside.

"Is that Drongo Kane?" asked Janine.

"I think it is," he replied.

"Then I must prepare a proper reception," she said and walked rapidly back to her palace. Maya stayed with Grimes.

She said, "Janine prides herself on doing things properly."

"If she were doing things properly," Grimes told her, "she would have a battery of ground to air missiles standing by."

"You must be joking!" she exclaimed, shocked.

"Have our own armament in readiness, sir?" asked the navigator.

"Mphm. I *was* joking, Mr. Pitcher. But it will do no harm to have the twenty millimeters cocked and ready."

Two women were building another fire in the brazier that had served Grimes for a beacon. One of them produced a large box of oversized matches from the pouch that she wore slung from her shoulder, lit the kindling. Almost immediately the column of gray smoke was climbing skyward.

Kane's pinnace was audible now as well as visible, the irregular beat of its inertial drive competing with the more rhythmic efforts of Janine's drummers, warming up behind the palace. It was coming in fast, and it seemed that it would overshoot the plaza. But Kane—presumably it was he at the controls—brought the craft to a spectacular, shuddering halt when it was almost directly over *Seeker*'s pinnace, applying maximum reverse thrust. That would not, thought Grimes disapprovingly, do his engines any good—but he, himself, had often been guilty of similar showmanship.

Oddly enough no crowd had gathered—but no crowd had gathered to greet Grimes. There were only a few deliberately uninterested bystanders, and they were mainly children. On no other world had Grimes seen such a fanatical respect for privacy.

Drongo Kane was dropping down now—not fast, yet not with extreme caution. His vertical thrust made odd patterns in the dust as the pinnace descended, not unlike those made in an accumulation of iron filings by a magnetic field. When there was little more than the thickness of a coat of paint between his landing gear and the ground he checked his descent, then cut his drive.

The door in the side of the pinnace opened. Drongo Kane stood in the opening. He was rigged up in a uniform that was like the full dress of the Survey Service—with improvements. An elaborate gold cockade ornamented his cocked hat, and his sword belt was golden, as was the scabbard. A score of decorations blazed over the left breast of his frock coat. Grimes thought he recognized the Iron Cross of Waldegren, the Golden Wings of the Hallichek Hegemony. Anybody who was highly regarded by those two governments would be *persona non grata* in decent society.

Kane jumped lightly to the ground, seemingly unhampered by his finery. He extended a hand to help Sabrina from the pinnace. Jewels glittered on her smooth, golden skin, and a coronet ablaze with emeralds was set on her head. She was inclined to teeter a little in her unaccustomed, high-heeled sandals.

"Cor stone me Aunt Fanny up a gum tree!" whispered Maggie.

"Captain Kane is *generous*," murmured Maya.

"Mphm," grunted Grimes.

Inside the pinnace two of Kane's officers—and they were dressed only in their drab working uniforms—were setting up some sort of machine, an affair of polished brass, just within the doorway. Grimes stared at it in amazement and horror.

"Captain Kane," he shouted, "I forbid you to terrorize these people!"

Kane grinned cheerfully. "Keep your hair on, Commander! Nobody's goin' to terrorize anybody. Don't you recognize a salutin' cannon when you see one? Sabrina, here, has told me that this Queen Janine is a stickler for etiquette. . ." Then his eyes widened as, to the rattle of drums, the procession emerged from around the corner of the palace. He licked his lips as he stared at the high-stepping girl with the *Lode Cougar* flag—that sash and those boots—especially the boots—did something for her. He muttered to himself, "And you can say *that* again!"

With a last ruffle of drums Janine and her entourage came to a halt. Kane drew himself to attention and saluted grandly. "Fire one!" snapped somebody inside the pinnace. The brass cannon boomed, making a noise disproportionate to its size. "Fire two!" Again there was the gout of orange flame, the billowing of dirty white smoke. "Fire three!"

At first it looked as though the spearmen, archers and riflemen would either turn and run—or loose their weapons off against the spacemen—but Janine snapped a sharp order and, drawing herself up proudly, stood her ground.

"Fire four!" *Boom!*

"Fire five!"

Janine was enjoying the show. So was Kane. Sabrina, at his side, winced every time the gun was fired, but tried to look as though this sort of thing was an everyday occurrence. Maya whispered urgently to Grimes, "This *noise* . . . can't you make him stop it?"

"Fire nine!" *Boom!*

"Fire ten!"

Janine's bodyguards had recovered their composure now and were standing at stiff attention, and there was a certain envy evident in the expressions on the faces of the drummer girls—but the standard bearer spoiled the effect when the drifting fumes of the burning black powder sent her into a fit of sneezing.

"Fire sixteen!" *Boom!*

Surely not, thought Grimes dazedly. *Surely not. A twenty-one gun salute for somebody who, even though she is called a queen, is no more than the mayor of a small town . . . .*

"Fire twenty!" *Boom!*

"Fire twenty-one!" *Boom!*

"A lesson," remarked Maggie, "on how to win friends and influence people . . . ."

"He certainly influenced me!" said Grimes.

Kane, accompanied by Sabrina, marched to where Janine was standing. He saluted again. Janine nodded to him regally. The standard bearer, recovered from her sneezing fit, dipped her flag toward him. The spearmen and riflemen presented arms. Grimes watched all this a little enviously. He was sorry that Maya had not briefed him regarding Janine's love of the ceremonial, as obviously Sabrina had briefed Kane. But it could be that Kane knew Sabrina far better than he, Grimes, knew Maya. There are more things to do in a shared bed than talking—but talking in bed is quite a common practice . . . .

"Shall I fire a burst from the twenty millimeters," asked Pitcher wistfully, "just to show that we can make a noise too?"

"*No*," Grimes said sternly.

"Sir," called Billard, "here comes another pinnace!"

Danzellan's arrival on the scene was anticlimactic. When he came in to a landing the queen, together with Kane, Sabrina and two of *Southerly Buster*'s officers carrying a large chest of trade goods, had returned to her palace and was staying there.

))(((19)))(((

Captain Danzellan was in a bad temper.

He demanded, "Commander Grimes, why didn't you tell me that Drongo Kane was on this planet? I learned it, only by chance, from Lilian after you had left Melbourne—and then my radio officer monitored the conversation you had with your first lieutenant. . . ."

"To begin with," said Grimes tartly, "you didn't ask me. In any case, I gained the impression that you wanted nothing at all to do with me or my people." He was warming up nicely. "Furthermore, sir, I must draw your attention to the fact that the monitoring of Survey Service signals is illegal, and that you are liable to a heavy fine, and that your radio officer may have his certificate dealt with."

Danzellan was not awed. "A space lawyer!" he sneered.

"Yes, Captain. And a space policeman."

"Then why don't you arrest Kane?"

"What for?" asked Grimes. "He has broken no laws— Federation or local. I can neither arrest him nor order him off Morrowvia."

"Commander Grimes, I am paid to look after my owners'

309

interests. I cannot do so properly while this man Kane is running around loose, corrupting the natives. To be frank, if you were not here I should feel justified in taking the law into my hands. Since you *are* here—I appeal to you, as a citizen of the Federation, for protection."

"Captain Danzellan, Captain Kane is cooking up some sort of deal with the natives. He, like you, is a shipmaster. *You* represent your owners, Kane *is* an owner. You allege that he is corrupting the natives and imply that he is queering your pitch. Meanwhile, *I* am wondering if whatever sort of deal *you* are cooking up will corrupt the natives . . . ."

"Of course not!" snorted Danzellan. "The Dog Star Line will always have their best interests at heart!"

"And the best interests of the management and shareholders . . . ?" put in Maggie.

Danzellan smiled in a fatherly way. "Naturally, Commander Lazenby. After all, we are businessmen."

"Mphm," Grimes grunted. He said, "Kane is a businessman too."

"But I was here first, Commander Grimes."

"*Lode Cougar* was here first, Captain Danzellan. Get this straight, sir—unless or until either you or Captain Kane steps out of line I am merely here as an observer."

"Then may I suggest, sir, that you start doing some observing? That is what I intend to do. I am going to call on Janine, now, to see if I can find out what line of goods Kane is peddling."

"I'll come with you," Grimes told him. "Maggie, you'd better come too. And you, Maya, if you wouldn't mind. Mr. Pitcher and Mr. Billard—stay by the pinnace."

The two men and the two women walked across the plaza to the main entrance of the palace. Four natives were standing in the doorway, spearmen of Janine's ceremonial bodyguard. They held their weapons not threateningly but so as to bar ingress.

"Let me pass!" huffed Danzellan.

"The queen insists on privacy," said one of the men.

"But I know Janine. We are good friends."

"The queen said, sir, that she and Captain Kane and her other guests were not to be disturbed."

Grimes nodded to Maya. Possibly she would be admitted while the offworlders were not. The Morrowvian woman walked forward until her breasts were pressing against the haft of one of the spears. She said indignantly, "You know who I am. Let me in!"

The spearman grinned. His teeth were sharp and very white. He said, "I am sorry, lady, but I cannot. Janine mentioned you especially."

"And what did she say?" demanded Maya.

"Do you really want to know, lady?" The man was enjoying this.

"Yes!"

"She said, lady, 'Don't let Commander Grimes or any other foreigners in here while I am in conference. And the same applies to that cat from Cambridge.'"

"Cat from Cambridge . . ." muttered Maya indignantly. "You can tell Janine that should she ever visit *my* town she will not be received hospitably."

"Well, Commander Grimes," asked Danzellan, "what are you doing about this?"

"What can I do?" countered Grimes irritably.

"We can talk things over," suggested Maggie Lazenby.

"Talk, talk!" sneered Danzellan, "while that damned pirate is raping a planet!"

"It's all that we can do at the moment," Grimes told him. "I suggest that we return to our pinnace. And I suggest that you, sir, do some talking."

"All right," said the shipmaster at last.

"The Dog Star Line's interest in this world will bring nothing but good to the people," stated Danzellan.

"Mphm," grunted Grimes skeptically.

"But it is so, Commander. If we are allowed to run things our way the planet will remain virtually unspoiled. There will be no pollution of the air, the soil or the seas. Unless the Morrowvians so desire it—and I do not think they will—there will be no development of heavy industries. The small luxuries that we shall bring in will demand power, of course—but solar power will be ample for their requirements."

"It all sounds very nice," admitted Grimes, "but what do your employers get out of it?"

"Oh, they'll make a profit—but not from the Morrowvians."

"From whom, then?"

"From passengers. Tourists. As you know, we have been, for many years, primarily freight carriers—but there is no reason why we should not break into the passenger trade, the tourist trade specifically. Trans-Galactic Clippers have been doing very nicely at it for some years now. But TG has the game sewn up insofar as the worlds on their itinerary are concerned.

"Now we, the Dog Star Line, have a new planet of our very own. We can build our own hotels and vacation camps, we can run cruises over the tropical seas in big schooners that we shall build and man—already recruiting for their crews is being opened on Atlantia." He smiled sympathetically at Maya. "I'm afraid that's necessary, my dear. Your people aren't very sea-minded."

"And you think that this scheme will work?" asked Grimes, interested.

"Why shouldn't it work, Commander? The advertising need only be truthful. Think of the posters, the brochures with photographs of all the beautiful, naked women—and, come to that, of the equally beautiful naked men. Visit Morrowvia—and shed your clothing, your cares, your inhibitions! Why, it'll have Arcadia licked to a frazzle!"

Maggie looked very coldly at Captain Danzellan. She said, "Arcadia is not a holiday resort for the idle rich, nor does it wish to be one. Our naturism is a way of life, not an advertising gimmick."

"Are you an Arcadian, Commander Lazenby? But what you said about naturism being a way of life on Arcadia applies equally well to Morrowvia. And we, the Dog Star Line, will do nothing to destroy that way of life. I have studied history, and I know how very often a superior race, a supposedly superior race, has ruined a simple people by forcing upon them unnecessary and unsuitable clothing. We shall not make that mistake."

"No, you won't," said Maggie. "It might affect your profits."

Grimes said, "I still think, Captain Danzellan, that you will ruin this world, whether or not you force the women into Mother Hubbards and the men into shirts and trousers."

Danzellan shrugged. "There's ruin *and* ruin, Commander Grimes. Which is the lesser of two evils—a flourishing tourist trade, or the introduction of heavy industry? Come to that—will the tourist trade be an evil?"

"And the tourists will *pay*?" asked Maya. "They will bring us things like the sun-powered cold boxes, and the clocks and the watches, and jewels like the ones that Captain Kane gave to Sabrina? Not that *I* want jewels," she added virtuously, "but I should like a cold box, and a clock that does not have to have the weights wound up every night."

"Maya is talking sense," said Danzellan.

"Yes, I am talking sense. You people have so many things to make life comfortable that we cannot make for ourselves, that we should not care to go to the trouble of making for ourselves. If offworlders are willing to pay for the pleasure of breathing our air, basking in our sunshine— then let them pay!"

"And there," said Danzellan smugly, "you have the attitude of a typical Morrowvian."

"But she's so simple," expostulated Grimes. "Her people are so simple."

Before Maya could answer Maggie stepped in. She said, "Perhaps not so simple, John. Apart from anything else, they have The History and Morrow's dictums to guide them. Too, there's an odd streak in their makeup. . . . I wish I knew . . ."

"I wish I knew what Kane was up to," said Danzellan.

"Don't we all," agreed Grimes.

))((20))((

They sat in the main cabin *of Seeker*'s pinnace—talking, smoking (even Maya tried one of Maggie's cigarillos and said that she liked it) and waiting for something to happen. Danzellan was in touch with his own ship by his wrist transceiver and also, of course, with Mr. Delamere, who had piloted *Schnauzer*'s boat to Ballarat and was remaining inside the craft. Grimes used the pinnace's radio to tell Mr. Saul what had happened so far and, meanwhile, all transceivers not otherwise in use were tuned to a variety of wavebands, in the hope that Drongo Kane's messages (if any) to *Southerly Buster* could be monitored.

At last Kane's voice sounded from Maggie's transceiver. He said simply, "Blackbird." The reply was almost immediate. "Pinnace to Captain. Blackbird." Then, "Pinnace to *Southerly Buster*. Blackbird." Finally, faintly, "*Southerly Buster* to pinnace. Acknowledge Blackbird."

"Blackbird?" echoed Grimes.

"I don't like it," said Maggie. "I don't like it. That word rings some sort of a bell . . ."

"Captain to *Seeker*," said Grimes into the microphone of the main transceiver. "Captain to *Seeker*. Do you read me?"

"Loud and clear, Captain."

"That you, Mr. Saul? Keep your eyes open for any activities around *Southerly Buster*. Kane has just sent a message to his ship. It must be a code. Just one word. Blackbird."

"Blackbird . . ." repeated Saul. Then, "Have I your permission to use force?"

"What are you talking about, Saul?"

"Operation Blackbird, Captain. Didn't you know that blackbirding was a euphemism for slave trading?"

"He's right . . ." whispered Maggie. "And there are worlds where women such as these would fetch a good price— some of the Waldegren mining colonies, for example . . ."

Grimes was thinking rapidly. If he departed at once it would be all of seven hours before he was back aboard *Seeker*. In seven hours a lot could happen. Saul, as second in command, was in full charge of the ship until her captain's return. Saul, normally, was a most reliable officer—but could Saul, with all his racial prejudices and bitternesses, be trusted to deal with the situation that was developing? Kane would scream to high heaven if a single shot were fired at his precious *Southerly Buster,* and he would not be the first pirate to have friends in high places—although heaven would not be one of them. Even so, if Kane were about to do something illegal he would have to be stopped.

The situation, Grimes realized, was made to order for Drongo Kane. *Seeker*'s captain was hours away from his ship—and so was *Southerly Buster*'s captain, but it didn't matter. The obnoxious Mr. Dreebly could embark the passengers, quote and unquote, and then lift ship into orbit, where Kane's pinnace could rendezvous with her. And once the Morrowvians were aboard the *Buster* she would be virtually untouchable insofar as hostile action by *Seeker* was concerned.

"Mr. Saul," ordered Grimes, "do all you can to prevent the natives from boarding *Southerly Buster*. Do not use arms unless there is absolutely no alternative. I am returning at once." He turned to Danzellan. "You heard all of that, Captain?"

"Of course, Commander."

"Good. Then I'll ask you to keep an eye on Drongo Kane for me."

"I'll do that, with pleasure." Maggie said, "I'll stay with Captain Danzellan, John. I want to have another look at *Lode Cougar*'s records—if Janine will condescend to let me back into her palace after Kane has left. I have an idea that what I find may have some bearing on this situation. If it's what I'm afraid it might be—then be careful. Be bloody careful."

"I'll try," said Grimes.

"You always do, but . . ." She followed Danzellan as the shipmaster returned to his own pinnace.

Pitcher asked, "Take her up, sir?"

"Yes, Mr. Pitcher. And flog your horses. Put her on a direct Great Circle; we've no time for sightseeing."

While the navigator busied himself with charts and instruments Billard did his best to make the pinnace behave like a guided missile.

⧗⧗⧗⧗⧗

They wasted no time, screaming southward high over the countryside, over the sea. Maya was awed, a little frightened, even, and sat there in silence. Pitcher and Billard exchanged occasional monosyllables, while Grimes stuck to the transceiver. Timmins, the senior radio officer, was at the other end. He reported, "*Southerly Buster* seems to be ready for immediate lift-off, sir. All ports, save for the main airlock, have been sealed." Then, a little later, "Two officers have left the ship and are walking toward the town of Oxford. Mr. Saul and Captain Philby have followed them, with six Marines." Later still, "Mr. Saul reports that the way was barred to him and his party by a dozen spearmen and a dozen archers. He is returning to the ship. I'll put him on to you as soon as he's here."

Grimes studied Saul's face in the tiny screen. The man was struggling to repress his smoldering fury. "Captain," he said, "these damned people don't *want* to be helped. They were there on the river bank, with the spears and bows and arrows, and some damned woman, the deputy queen she said she was, ordered me back. She said, "We don't want you and the likes of you here. Captain Kane warned Sabrina about you.""

"So."

"So what are your instructions, Captain?"

"Get a boat out, to keep a watch over the town and to report what the people are doing. Have *Seeker* in a state of instant readiness for lift-off . . . ."

"I've already given the orders, sir. But the armament . . ."

"I've already told you not to go firing guns off

indiscriminately. But . . . mphm. Have the belts for the sixty millimeters loaded with sleep gas shells. And if you use 'em—and you'll have to justify their use to me—make bloody sure that you don't *hit* anybody. Understood?"

"Understood, Captain."

"Good. Then keep me informed."

Grimes turned to Maya. "Can *you* tell me," he asked, what *is* going on?"

"I don't know. We have always kept ourselves to ourselves, Sabrina and I. We have never been close friends. We have never been friends. But Captain Kane gave many gifts to Sabrina's people. There were books, with beautiful pictures of other worlds, with accounts of other worlds. There were . . . catalogues, giving details of all the goods that may be purchased on other worlds . . ."

"First Lieutenant to Captain." It was Saul again. "Number Three boat is in position over Oxford. We are trying to get a picture to you."

And there, on the screen, was the picture of the town as seen from the air. The boat was hanging almost directly over the central plaza and transmitting a magnified image. The two men from *Southerly Buster,* being clothed, were easily identifiable.

They were busily marshaling about two hundred Morrowvians into an orderly column. Even from above it was obvious that they were all women. To one side of the plaza a half dozen light handcarts had been loaded with possessions—cushions, pieces of pottery, longbows and quivers of arrows. One of Kane's men went to inspect the cart that was loaded with weapons, called a woman to him and was obviously telling her that these would have to be left. Then whoever was in charge of the boat got a long-range microphone working.

"I'm sorry, Peggy. These will have to be left behind."

"But the girls must have them, Bill. What will they do for sport on Caribbea if they have no bows?"

Caribbea? wondered Grimes. Probably it was the most glamorous world depicted in the brochures that Kane had distributed—but Essen would be a more likely destination for this shipment of female slaves.

"You can't use bows and arrows underwater," explained the man Bill patiently. "In the seas of Caribbea they use spear guns."

"But we don't *like* water. None of us likes water. Nobody will *make* us go into the water, will they?"

There's not much water on Essen, thought Grimes. *Only enough for washing and drinking—not that those Waldegren miners wash much, and they don't believe in diluting their schnapps . . .*

"Nobody will *make* you do anything," lied Bill.

His companion called to him, "Dump that junk, and we'll get the show on the road!"

"Our ETA, Mr. Pitcher?" asked Grimes.

"We're doing the best we can, sir, but we can't make it before nineteen-hundred Local—another four and a half hours."

"Mr. Saul, do you read me?"

"Sir?"

"Lay a barrage of sleep gas on the bank of the river as soon as that column from Oxford gets under way."

"Very good, sir."

"And be *careful.*"

"Of course, sir." Saul's voice was hurt.

"Let me know as soon as you open fire, and give me a picture if you can."

"Very good sir." Grimes could almost read the first lieutenant's thoughts: *Get off my back, Whitey!*

It is not only the black races who hate slavery, thought Grimes, *and it is not only the black races who've been enslaved. But what the hell is Kane playing at? Pressing ahead with his blackbirding under the very nose of a Survey Service ship . . . He's always prided himself on being able to keep just on the right side of the law.*

He said, "Get me Mr. Hayakawa, please."

"Yes, Captain?" asked the psionicist at last. His picture did not appear on the screen; that was being reserved for the transmissions from the lookout boat. "Yes, Captain?"

"Mr. Hayakawa, I know that your opposite number aboard the *Buster* is maintaining a block, but have you been able to pick up *anything*?"

"Yes, Captain. A few minutes ago there were stray thoughts from the mate of *Southerly Buster.* They ran like this, 'And the beauty of it is that the stupid Space Scouts can't touch us!'"

"That remains to be seen, Mr. Hayakawa," said Grimes. "That remains to be seen."

))((21))((

The trouble with radio as a means of communication is that anybody can listen. Grimes, in his later conversations with his ship, had employed a scrambler. He did not know whether or not *Southerly Buster* ran to a descrambling device. Apparently she did not. Dreebly appeared to be proceeding with his embarkation procedure as planned.

In an orderly march the two hundred young women streamed out of Oxford, a score of spearmen at the head of the column, another twenty male warriors bringing up the rear, behind the carts laden with small possessions. Kane's two men were in the lead. Grimes, remembering the general layout of the country, knew that once the van of the procession passed a low, tree-crowned hill it would be in the field of fire of *Seeker*'s guns. With an effort he restrained himself from taking over the fire control from Saul. He knew that a direct hit from a nonlethal gas shell can kill just as surely—and messily—as one from a high explosive projectile. But Saul was on the spot, and he was not. All he could do was to watch the marchers proceeding slowly along the bank of the winding river.

He heard Saul say quietly, "Bearing one hundred and seventy-five true. Range three thousand. Shoot."

"Bearing one hundred and seventy-five. Range three thousand. *Fire!*"

Even over the radio the hammering of the heavy automatics was deafening. Watching the screen Grimes saw a neat seam of explosions stitched across the line of advance of the Morrowvian women, saw the billowing clouds of greenish vapor pouring from each bursting shell.

"Traverse, traverse! Now—ladder!"

Nice gunnery, thought Grimes. Saul was boxing his targets in with the gas shells.

A new voice came from the transceiver. It was Dreebly's. "*Southerly Buster* to *Seeker.* What the hell are you playing at?"

"*Seeker* to *Southerly Buster.* What the hell are *you* playing at?"

Grimes decided that he had better intervene; Mr. Saul was not in a diplomatic mood. He said quietly, "Commander Grimes to *Southerly Buster.* What is the nature of your complaint, please?"

Dreebly spluttered, then, "What is the nature of my complaint, you ask? Some butterfly-brained ape aboard your ship is firing off guns. There're shells whistling past our control room."

"Routine weekly practice shoot, Mr. Dreebly," said Grimes. "Don't worry; we never hit anything unless we want to."

"But you're firing toward Oxford!"

"Are we? But our range setting is well short of the town."

"I know what you're firing at, Commander Grimes. You've a boat up, spotting for you!"

"What am I firing at, Mr. Dreebly?"

"Pah! You make me sick!" Dreebly broke off the conversation. Grimes returned his attention to the screen. The gas was slowly thinning, and through its translucent veil he could see the untidily sprawling figures of the Morrowvians—and of Kane's two officers.

Maya demanded, "You haven't killed them? You haven't killed them?"

"Of course not!" Grimes told her. "They'll wake in a few hours' time, without even a headache. I've just put them to sleep, that's all. . . ."

Meanwhile Timmins had succeeded in tuning in to the conversation between Dreebly and Kane. Kane was saying, "Get them aboard, and then get off-planet! Yes, I *know* they can't walk—but you've ground cars, haven't you? And there are respirators in the stores. Pull your finger out, Dreebly, and get cracking! What do you think I pay you for?"

Saul was back on the air. "Sir, you heard all that. What do I do now?"

I could answer that question a lot more easily, thought Grimes, *if I knew that Kane was breaking Federation law. But he seems to have the idea that he is not . . . .*

"What do I do now?" repeated Saul.

"Mphm. Carry on with your practice shoot, Mr. Saul. Use H.E. Chew up the ground between *Southerly Buster* and the . . . er . . . intending emigrants."

"Emigrants! *The slaves,* you mean, Captain."

"They aren't slaves yet. Just make a mess of the terrain so that it's impassable to Kane's ground cars."

"But he's got boats, sir. He can use them."

"He has two boats—a pinnace, which is still at Ballarat, and one lifeboat. The lifeboat is just big enough for his crew. It will take it a long time to ferry two hundred people—especially as they will have to be lifted aboard it, and lifted off."

"I see, sir. . . . But what if *Southerly Buster* fires at us?"

"They won't dare, Mr. Saul. At least, I hope they won't. If they do—*if* they do—it is your duty to take every possible measure for the protection of *Seeker.*"

No, he thought, *Kane won't open fire, or order his mate to do so. Apart from anything else, he's the injured, innocent citizen and I'm the big, bad, gun-toting villain. I'm not happy about things at all, at all. But I* must *stop him.*

Meanwhile, he wished that he were back aboard his ship. He *liked* guns. He knew that this was childish of him, and that it was high time that mankind outgrew its love for noisy pyrotechnics. He knew that a gun pleads to be pointed at something—and then begs to have its trigger pulled. He hoped that Saul would remain content merely to wreak havoc on the landscape.

))((22))((

Saul wreaked havoc on the landscape. Grimes, watching on his screen, thought, relishing the play on words, *He's wrecking* the landscape. What had been grassland was now a crater-pitted desolation over which drifted acrid fumes, and the copses had been reduced to jagged, blackened stumps.

Kane came on the air. His voice, despite the fact that it had been relayed through at least two stations, was loud and clear. He said, "Commander Grimes, this is Captain Kane. My mate tells me that your first lieutenant's runnin' amok."

"Running amok, Captain Kane? What do you mean?"

"He's shootin' off his guns—*your* guns—like a madman. Wastin' the taxpayers' money. He's interferin' with the embarkation of my passengers."

"Passengers, Captain Kane?"

"Yeah. Passengers. I own me own ship, an' if I decide to go into the passenger trade, that's my business."

"I'm sure it is, Captain. I'm sorry that my arrangements

clashed with yours, but we were due for a practice shoot. . . ."

"Oh, you were, were you? An' did you promulgate a warnin'?"

"Unfortunately the facilities for so doing don't exist on this planet."

"Listen, Grimes, keep your nose out of my business or you'll get it bloodied."

"I'm inclined to think, Kane, that your business is *my* business. I represent the Federation. . . ."

"An' the Federation is supposed to encourage honest trade, not interfere with it."

"*Honest* trade?"

"You heard me. Honest *and* legal."

"All right, Kane. I have your word for it—for what it's worth. Where are you taking those women?"

"It's no concern of yours, Grimes. But it's only natural that after generations of isolation they'll want to see new worlds."

"Mphm. And how are they paying their fares? You never impressed me as being a philanthropic institution."

Kane laughed. "Have you never heard of *Travel Now, Pay Later?* TG Clippers do a lot of business that way, an' so does Cluster Lines."

"But these people don't have money."

"There're more important things in life than money— not that I can think of any right now."

Grimes realized that he was being talked into a corner. He said firmly, "I have to know where you intend taking your . . . er . . . passengers."

"I've already told you that it's none of your business."

"Would it be . . . Essen?"

"I'm not sayin' that is is—but what if it is Essen?"

"All right, Captain Kane. *If* you don't mind, I'll just assume that it is Essen. There'd be a good market there for women, wouldn't there? And Federation law definitely prohibits any kind of traffic in human beings."

"Yeah. It does. I know the law as well as you do, Commander. Probably better. An' I'm tellin' you flat that I'm breakin' no laws. So I'll be greatly obliged if you'll tell your Jimmy The One to get out of *my* mate's hair."

"I'm sorry, Captain Kane, but I just can't take your word for it."

"No, you wouldn't, would you? We couldn't have a spick-an'-span Survey Service commander takin' the word of Drongo Kane, a poor, honest workin' stiff, master of a scruffy little star tramp, could we? Oh, no. But I'll tell you this. One of your own officers, that Commander Maggie Lazenby, is in Janine's palace now, an' that stuffed shirt Danzellan is with her. Janine's lettin' 'em look at the secret records, the ones that she showed me. I'm not kiddin' you, Grimes. She'll tell you that you can't touch me."

"That remains to be seen, Captain Kane."

"Why don't you call her now?"

"Why not?" agreed Grimes tiredly. He got on to Timmins, ordered him to arrange a hookup. After a few minutes Maggie's voice came through the speaker of the pinnace's transceiver.

"Commander Lazenby here, *Seeker.*"

"Stand by, please, Commander Lazenby. I'm putting you through to the captain."

"Captain here," said Grimes.

"Yes, John?"

"I've been talking with Captain Kane. . . ."

"Yes. I know. He's just come into the Records Room."

"He assures me that whatever he's doing is quite legal, and that you'll bear him out."

"Yes, but . . . I've just unearthed some very old records. . . . And from what Captain Danzellan tells me . . ."

"She says yes," put in Kane. "An' until the law is changed, if it ever is. . . ."

"I said yes, *but* . . ." insisted Maggie.

"And if Tabitha is not lying . . ." contributed Danzellan.

"She said *yes!*" snapped Kane, his customary drawl forgotten.

"Maggie!" said Grimes forcibly. "Report, at once, in detail what you have discovered."

But there was no report. Kane used his wrist transceiver to jam the signals from those worn by Maggie and Danzellan, and before either or both of them could take any action the far more powerful transceiver of Kane's pinnace blocked all further transmissions from Ballarat.

)))(((23)))(((

Yes . . . *but*.

Yes . . . *but*.

But *what?*

Meanwhile, Mr. Saul had made the terrain between the landing site and Oxford quite impassable to any ground vehicle, and would have to be restrained before he blew away all *Seeker*'s 60 mm ammunition. Grimes told the first lieutenant to cease fire, at once.

But what loophole in Federation law had Kane discovered? What possible means of stopping that loophole had Maggie discovered? Where did Francis Delamere's local girlfriend, Tabitha, come into it?

Grimes decided that *Southerly Buster*'s lift-off from Morrowvia must be, at the very least, delayed. Could he stop the *Buster*'s boat from ferrying, a dozen or so at a time, the unconscious women to the ship? Yes, he could— but only at grave risk to the boat's passengers. Embarkation would have to be allowed to continue; by the time that it was complete he, Grimes, would be back aboard *Seeker* and would be able to take full charge.

Seeker's cannon were silent now, and *Southerly Buster*'s one remaining boat had nosed cautiously out of its bay and was flying to where the victims of the gas shell barrage were sprawled in the long grass. *Seeker*'s boat transmitted pictures of all that was going on. The small craft from the *Buster* dropped to a landing among the sleeping bodies and two men, wearing respirators, scrambled out of it. Working fast, they dragged fifteen of the women into the boat, careless of any abrasions or contusions they might inflict. They were equally careless with their two anesthetized mates—but that was no excuse. Kane's men were clothed and the risk of painful damage to their skins was so much less.

"Do I have to watch this, Captain?" the first lieutenant was raging.

"I'm afraid you have to, Mr. Saul," Grimes told him. "Of course, if you can think of any way of stopping it without hurting any innocent people . . ."

Saul did not reply.

The first load was carried to *Southerly Buster*, the boat landing at the foot of the boarding ramp. Its passengers were dragged out and dumped on the ground, and almost immediately the boat began its return journey. Meanwhile a cargo hatch had been opened high on the side of the ship and the arm of a crane swung out. A net was lowered and the women, together with the two unconscious men, were piled into it, swiftly hoisted up an inboard. It was obvious that Kane was blessed with an efficient second-in-command.

Seeker's boat followed the one from *Southerly Buster* back to her loading site. There was a repetition of the

callously efficient handling of the unknowing passengers—
and then another, and then another.

But Grimes's pinnace had crossed the coastline now,
was rushing inland. Grimes hoped to be back aboard *Seeker*
before *Southerly Buster*'s embarkation was completed,
although he could not hope to make it before sunset.
Dusk was sweeping over the countryside as the two ships
came into view, Kane's vessel towering brightly in the
harsh glare of working lights. Saul had the hatch of the
pinnace's bay open and waiting, and Billard expertly jock-
eyed the craft into the opening. Grimes was out through
the door and running up to the control room before the
pinnace had settled to her chocks. He found Saul staring
sullenly out of a viewport.

"That's the last boatload," said the first lieutenant
morosely. "Recall our boat, sir?"

"Do just that, Mr. Saul. I want the ship buttoned up for
lift-off."

"Yes . . ." Saul gestured toward the *Buster*. "She's
buttoning up."

The boom of the crane was withdrawn, the cargo hatch
was shut. *Southerly Buster*'s boat lifted from the ground
where she had discharged her last load, nosed up the
mother ship's side to her bay. The ramp folded up and
inward. The airlock door slid shut. Faintly there came the
clangor of starting machinery, the unmistakable broken
rhythm of the inertial drive.

Grimes ordered, "Use your sixty millimeters again, Mr.
Saul. Tracer, time fused. I want every shell bursting
directly over her—not too close, but close enough so they
can hear the shrapnel rattling around their control room."

"Aye, sir!"

The automatics rattled deafeningly, the tracers streaked out from the muzzles in a flat trajectory, the bursting shells were spectacular orange flowers briefly blossoming against the dark sky.

Not at all surprisingly Dreebly's voice came screaming from the transceiver. "Stop firing! Stop firing, you idiots, before you hurt somebody!"

"Then shut down your engines!" commanded Grimes. "I am grounding you."

"By what authority? You have no authority here. This is not a Federated world."

"Shut down your engines!"

"I refuse."

Dreebly did more than merely refuse. Winking points of blue flame appeared from a turret on *Southerly Buster's* side. The streams of tracer from the two ships intersected, forming a lethal arch. Freakishly there were explosions at its apex as time- and impact-fused projectiles came into violent contact with each other—but the majority of *Seeker's* shells still burst over *Southerly Buster,* and those from the *Buster's* guns burst directly over *Seeker.*

"The bastard's hosepiping!" exclaimed Saul.

Yes, Dreebly was hosepiping, slowly and deliberately lowering the trajectory of his stream of fire. Would he have the nerve to fire at rather than over a Federation ship? Grimes knew that *he* did not have the nerve to fire directly at *Southerly Buster.* Should he do so there would inevitably be casualties—and those casualties might well be among the *Buster's* innocent passengers.

He said to Saul, "Cease fire."

"But, sir, I could put that turret out of action. . . ."

"I said, cease fire."

Seeker's hammering guns fell silent. There was a last burst from the Buster's automatics, a last noisy rattle of shrapnel around Seeker's control room. From the transceiver came Dreebly's taunting voice, "Chicken!"

"She's lifting," said Pitcher.

"She's lifting," echoed Saul disgustedly.

"Secure all," ordered Grimes, hurrying to the pilot's chair. "Secure all! There will be no further warning!"

He heard the coded shrilling of the alarms as he belted himself in. He checked the telltale lights on the control panel before him. By the time that the inertial drive was ready to lift Seeker clear of the ground Southerly Buster would be beyond pursuit range.

Was everything secure? It would be just too bad if it wasn't. The trained spacemen he could trust to obey orders promptly, the scientists were a different kettle of fish. But he couldn't afford to worry about them now, could not afford to indulge in the archaic, time-consuming, regulation ritual of the countdown.

He pushed the button for full emergency rocket power—and almost immediately tons of reaction mass exploded from the Venturis in incandescent steam. The giant hand of acceleration slammed him deep down into the padding of his seat. Seeker was lifting. Seeker was up and away, shooting skyward like a shell fired from some gigantic cannon. She overtook the slow-climbing Southerly Buster, roared past her as though she were standing still, left her well astern.

On the console the telltale light of the inertial drive was now glowing green. Grimes cut his rockets and the ship dropped sickening until the I.D. took hold, then brought up with a jar. She shuddered in every member as Grimes applied lateral thrust, as she lurched sideways across the sky. Pitcher, who had realized what the captain was trying to do, was doing, had stationed himself by the radar. "A little more, sir," he called. "Easy, now, easy. . . ." Then, "hold her at that!"

"Hold her!" repeated Grimes.

The ship shuddered and groaned again, but he was holding her in position relative to the ground below, to the still-climbing *Southerly Buster*. Then—slowly, but not so slowly as to conceal his intentions—he reduced vertical thrust. Dreebly tried, but in vain, to wriggle past *Seeker*. Grimes anticipated every move. (Later he learned that Hayakawa had been feeding him information, that Myra Bracegirdle, loyal rather to her sex than to her ship, had worked with and not against her fellow telepath.) It seemed that he could not go wrong—and every time that Dreebly attempted a lateral shift *Southerly Buster* fell victim to the parallelogram of forces, inevitably lost altitude.

At last it was obvious to Mr. Dreebly that he had only two choices. Either he could return to the surface, or he could commit suicide by crushing his control room and everybody in it against *Seeker*'s far less vulnerable stern. He was not in a suicidal mood.

Grimes could not resist the temptation. He called for a microphone and for a hookup to the *Buster*'s transceiver. He said just one word, and that with insufferable smugness.

"Chicken!"

Slowly the two ships dropped through the night—
Southerly Buster cowed and inferior. Apart from that one
taunt there had been no exchange of signals. Slowly they
dropped, the defeated Dreebly and the overconfident
Grimes.

It was this overconfidence that led, at the finish, to
disaster. Just before Dreebly's landing Grimes miscalculated,
and his stern made brief contact with the *Buster*'s stem,
doing her no great damage but throwing her off balance.
With all his faults, Dreebly was a superb shiphandler. He
fought to correct the topple, and had he not been inhibited
by the ominous bulk of the other vessel hanging immediately above his control room he might well have done
so. *Southerly Buster*'s fall was not completely catastrophic, but it was a fall, nonetheless. Visibly shuddering, she
tilted, further and further, until her long axis was parallel
to the ground.

It was then that Dreebly lost control, and there was a
tinny crash as she dropped the last half meter.

⑷⑷ 24 ⑺⑺

It was, Grimes admitted glumly, quite a mess. Just how big a mess it was depended upon the legality or otherwise of his actions, the illegality or otherwise of Kane's operations. Legalities and illegalities notwithstanding, he was obliged to give assistance to the damaged—the wrecked—ship.

She was not a total write-off, although on a world with no repair yards it would be months before she could be made spaceworthy; she would probably have to be towed off-planet to somewhere where there were facilities. (And who would have to pay the bill? Kane would certainly take legal action against the Federation.)

Fortunately everybody aboard *Southerly Buster* had escaped serious injury, although the unfortunate women from Oxford, who had just been recovering consciousness at the time of the crash, were badly bruised and shaken. Them Grimes sent back to their town in *Seeker*'s boats.

He said to Saul, "I've done enough damage for one day. I'm turning in—for what's left of the night."

"The report to Base, sir . . . ."

Grimes told him coarsely what he could do to the report, then, "It will have to wait, Number One. I don't want to stick my neck out in writing until I have a few more facts."

"But you put down an attempt at slave trading, sir."

"Mphm. I hope so. I sincerely hope so. But I'm afraid that the bastard Drongo has some dirty big ace up his sleeve. Oh, well. Sufficient unto the day is the evil thereof. I'm getting some shut-eye. Good night, Number One."

"Good night, sir."

Grimes went up to his quarters. He paused briefly in his day cabin, poured himself a stiff drink, downed it in one swallow. He felt a little better. He went through into his bedroom, and stiffened with astonishment in the doorway. Maya was there, curled up on the bed, her back to him. She was snoring gently—and then immediately was wide awake, rolling over to face him.

"Maya . . ." he said reprovingly.

"I had to sleep somewhere, John," she told him, even more reprovingly. "And you seemed to have quite forgotten all about me."

"Of course I hadn't," he lied.

"Of course you had," she stated, without rancor. "But you had much more important things on your mind." She was off the bed now and was sagging enticingly against him. She said, in a very small voice, "And I was frightened. . . ."

The scent of her was disturbing. It was not unpleasant but it was strange—yet somehow familiar. It was most definitely female. He said, "But you can't sleep here. . . ."

"But I have been sleeping here, John. . . ." (So, she

had begun to use his first name, too.) She pleaded, "Let me stay. . . ."

"But . . ."

Her hands, with their strangely short fingers, were playing with the seal-seam of his shirt, opening the garment. They were soft and caressing on the skin of his back, but her nails were very sharp. The sensation was stimulating rather than painful. He could feel her erect nipples against his chest. She pleaded again, "Let me stay. . . ." Against his conscious will his arms went about her. He lowered his head and his lips down to hers. Oddly, at first she did not seem to understand the significance of this, and then she responded avidly. All of her body was against him, and all of his body was vividly aware of it. He walked her slowly backward toward the bed, her legs moving in time with his. Through the thin material of his shorts he could feel the heat of her thighs. She collapsed slowly, almost bonelessly, onto the nest that she had made for herself with pillows and cushions. He let her pull him down beside her, made no attempt to stop her as she removed the last of his clothing. (For a woman who had never worn a garment in her life she was learning fast.)

Their mating was short, savage—and to Grimes strangely unsatisfying. What should have been there for him was not there; the tenderness that he had come to expect on such occasions was altogether lacking. There was not even the illusion of love; this had been no more than a brief, animal coupling.

But she, he thought rather bitterly, *is not complaining.* She was not complaining.

She, immediately after the orgasmic conclusion of the act, was drifting into sleep, snuggled up against him.

She was purring.

))((25))((

Dog tired, his nerves on edge after a sleepless night, Grimes stood in his control room and watched Drongo Kane come roaring in from the northward. He had been expecting Kane; Mr. Timmins had monitored the radio signals exchanged by Mr. Dreebly and his irate captain. He was expecting Maggie, too, but not for at least another hour. She had told him that Captain Danzellan was bringing her back to *Seeker*. She had refused to tell him what it was that she has discovered in the ancient records kept in Janine's palace, saying, "It will keep."

"Damn it all!" he had exploded, "I shall have Kane to deal with. And if what I suspect is true, legally I won't have a leg to stand on. Not unless you can pull a rabbit out of the hat."

"Not a rabbit," she told him. "Most definitely not a *rabbit*."

And that was all that he could get from her.

He had made use of the ship's memory bank encyclopedia facilities. In a Survey Service vessel these, of course, were continually kept up to date. He learned that although a committee was considering revisal, or even repeal, of the Non-Citizen Act this piece of legislation was still law. As far as he could see the act applied most specifically to the natives of Morrowvia—and that left him well and truly up the well known creek, without a paddle.

And here was Kane, dropping down from the morning sky, a man who knew Federation law so well that he could always bend it without actually breaking it. Here was Kane, a shipmaster *and* a shipowner who had learned that his vessel had been as good as (as bad as) wrecked by the officious actions of a relatively junior Survey Service officer. Here was Kane, more than a little annoyed about the frustration of his highly profitable activities.

Here was Kane.

Southerly Buster's pinnace slammed down alongside the parent ship in a flurry of dust and small debris. The door opened and Kane jumped out. He was no longer wearing his gaudy finery but had changed into utilitarian gray coveralls. Sabrina, still aglitter with jewelry, appeared in the doorway but Kane, irritably, motioned her back inside.

Dreebly, his head bandaged, came out of the ship. He stood there, drooping, while Kane obviously gave him a merciless dressing down. Then, slowly, the two men walked all around the crippled hulk, with the mate pointing out details of exterior damage. Grimes already knew what the damage was like inside—the Mannschenn Drive torn from its housing, the hydroponics tanks a stinking mess of shattered plastic and shredded greenery, most of the control room instruments inoperable if not completely ruined.

Saul came to stand by his captain's side. They watched as Kane and Dreebly clambered into the near-wreck through an amidships cargo hatch. The first lieutenant said happily, "You certainly put paid to *his* account, sir."

Grimes said, not so happily, "I only hope that he doesn't put paid to mine . . . ."

"But, sir, the man's a blackbirder, a slave trader! You've wrecked his ship—but that was the only way that you could stop the commission of a crime."

"Strong measures, Mr. Saul—especially if there were no crime being committed."

"But he fired on us, sir."

"At, not on. And we fired at him first."

"But he still hasn't a leg to stand on . . . ."

"Hasn't he? I've checked up on the Non-Citizen Act. I'm afraid that the Morrowvians do not qualify for citizenship. They have no rights whatsoever."

"I don't see it, sir. They're backward, I suppose—but they're as human as you or I."

"They're not," Grimes told him. "They're not, and that's the bloody trouble. What do you know of the Non-Citizen Act, Mr. Saul?"

"Not much, sir. But I can check up on it."

"Don't bother. I'll fill you in. That particular piece of legislation dates back to the bad old days when, briefly, the genetic engineers had far too much say. Although they were concerned primarily with the life sciences their outlook was that of engineers. You know, as well as I do, the peculiarities of the engineering outlook. If human beings and machines can't work together with maximum efficiency—then modify the human to suit the machine, not the other way round. A planet, like a house, is a machine for living in. If it is not suited to its intending occupants—then modify the occupants to fit. Then the generic engineers took things further. They manufactured, in their laboratories, androids—beings of synthetic flesh and blood that were, in effect, artificial men and women. Then they made 'underpeople'; the word was coined by a Twentieth Century science fiction writer called Cordwainer Smith and later, much later, used in actual fact. These underpeople were even less human than the androids, their very appearance making obvious their animal origins. They could not interbreed with true humans any more than the androids could—but they could breed, although they could not crossbreed. Put it this way—a dogman could mate with a dogwoman and fertilize her, or a catman with a catwoman. Only dogs—or ex-dogs—with dogs. Only cats—or ex-cats—with cats.

"Then there was the Android Revolt on Dancey. There was the virtual take-over of Tallis by the underpeople, although without bloodshed. The Federation Government put its foot down with a firm hand. No more androids were to be manufactured. No more underpeople were to be bred. All existing androids and underpeople were deprived of citizenship. And so on.

"It was quite some time before I realized the nature of the situation here, on Morrowvia. Kane, somehow, twigged it long before I did. But, last night, the final pieces of the jigsaw puzzle fell into place with a quite deafening *click!*. I should have seen it before. There are so many clues . . . ."

"What do you mean, sir?"

"You did the science fiction course at the Academy, Mr. Saul."

"But I never cared for that wild stuff. I can't remember much of it."

"You must remember some of it. Anyhow, we all assumed that this planet was named after the captain of *Lode Cougar*. But I saw some of the records in the museum at Ballarat. Morrow was not *Lodge Cougar's* master, neither was he one of her officers. He must have been one of the passengers—and a genetic engineer. I don't know yet how many survivors there were of *Lode Cougar's* original complement when she landed, although Commander Lazenby will no doubt be able to tell us. I don't think that there could have been many. I don't think that there were any women of childbearing age among them. But, like all the ships of her period, she carried banks of fertilized ova—both human and animal. Perhaps the human ova had been destroyed somehow—or perhaps Morrow just didn't want to use them. Perhaps the ova of all the usual useful animals—with no exception—had been somehow destroyed—or perhaps Morrow was an aelurophile. I rather think that he was. He was also a science fiction addict—there are shelves of his books on display in the museum at Ballarat. He also had a rather warped sense of humor. The clues that he left!"

"What clues, sir?" asked Saul.

"In the names he gave—to the continent where *Lode Cougar* landed, to the four families that he . . . founded, to the planet itself. The planet of Doctor Morrow . . . the island of Doctor Moreau. . . ."

"You're way beyond me, sir."

"Mr. Saul, Mr. Saul, you should have read that Twentieth Century rubbish while you had the chance. One of Morrow's books was *The Island of Doctor Moreau*, by a writer called Wells. Wells' Doctor Moreau was a rather mad scientist who converted animals into imitation humans by crude surgical means. Morrow . . . Moreau . . . see the connection? And one of the four family names on Morrowvia is Wells, another is Morrow.

"Another book was *The Planet Buyer*, by Cordwainer Smith. It was Cordwainer Smith who invented the under-people. One of his favorite planets—he wrote, of course, before men had landed on Earth's moon—was Old North Australia, shortened to Norstrilia. So Morrow called the continent on which he landed North Australia, and made Cordwainer and Smith the other two family names.

"Meanwhile, he was having fun. He was breeding a people to fit in with all his own pet ideas. Evidently he disapproved of the nudity taboo, just as Commander Lazenby's people do on Arcadia. His political ideas bordered on anarchism. Possibly he was an anarchist. I seem to recall from my reading of history that there was quite a powerful, or influential, Anarchist Party on Earth, in both hemispheres, at the time of the Second Expansion. It worked underground, and it contributed to the decline and fall of the Russian Empire. And we see here the results of Morrow's ideas. Utterly unselfconscious nudism, no central government, no monetary system. . . .

"It's a pity that this Lost Colony was ever discovered. Its people are more human than many who are officially so—but they have no rights whatsoever."

There was a silence, then Saul said, "We, our people,

know what it was like . . . ." Grimes looked at him rather nastily so he hastily changed the subject. "But tell me, sir, what did you mean when you said that the pieces of the puzzle fell into place last night?"

"You've served in *Pathfinder*, with Captain Lewis," said Grimes. "So have I. You know his taste in pets. You know how obvious it is, once you step inboard through the airlock. . . .

"Well, since you ask, my quarters stink of *cat*."

))((26))((

Maya joined the two men in the control room. She looked as though she had slept well. She glanced incuriously through the viewports at the disabled *Southerly Buster*, then said plaintively, "I'm hungry . . . "

Go down to the galley and see if the cook can find you some fish heads . . . thought Grimes—and then despised himself for thinking it. He said, "Mr. Saul, would you mind taking Maya to the wardroom for breakfast?"

"But what does she *eat*, sir?" asked the first lieutenant desperately.

"I'll try anything, everything," she said sweetly, "until I find something I like."

Grimes watched her as she followed Saul out of the control room. There should have been, he thought, a tail ornamenting those shapely buttocks. A nice, furry, striped tail . . . He shrugged.

The officer of the watch reported, "Sir, an unidentified craft is approaching from the north."

"That will be *Schnauzer*'s pinnace," said Grimes. He

went to the transceiver, selected the most probable wave-band. "Commander Grimes to Captain Danzellan. Do you read me? Over."

"Loud and clear, Commander. Danzellan here. My ETA your landing site is thirty minutes Standard, twenty-four minutes Local, from now. I have your Commander Lazenby with me. Over."

"Thank you, Captain Danzellan." Should he ask to speak with Maggie? No. She had made no attempt to speak with him. And Grimes was in a misogynistic mood. *Women! Cats!*

He returned to the viewport. He passed the time by mentally composing the sort of report—or complaint—that he would write if he were Drongo Kane.

To: Flag Officer in Charge of Lindisfarne Base
From: Drongo Kane, master and owner of s/s Southerly Buster

Subject: Piratical action by Lieutenant Commander John Grimes, Captain of FSS Seeker.

Sir,
I regret to have to report that while my vessel was proceeding on her lawful occasions she was wantonly attacked by your Seeker, *under the command of your Lieutenant Commander Grimes. Commander Grimes not only used his armament to impede the embarkation of fare-paying passengers, subjecting them to a sleep gas barrage, but also fired upon* Southerly Buster *herself. Later he attempted to ram my ship after she had lifted off, and only the superlative skill of my chief officer, who was in charge of the vessel at the time, averted a collision.*

Although contact between the two ships was avoided contact with the ground was not. As a result of this, Southerly Buster *sustained severe structural damage . . .*

"Pinnace in sight visually, sir," reported the O. O. W.

"Thank you, Mr. Giles."

Danzellan came in more slowly and cautiously than Kane had done, but he wasted no time, setting his craft down at the foot *of Seeker's* ramp. Grimes watched *Schnauzer's* master get out, then help Maggie Lazenby to the ground. He told Giles to telephone down to the airlock sentry, instructing the man to inform Captain Danzellan and Maggie that he would be waiting for them in his quarters. He went down to his day cabin, hastily shutting the door between it and his bedroom. The smell of cat was still strong.

He found and filled his foulest pipe, lit it. When Danzellan and Maggie came in he was wreathed in an acrid, blue smog.

"What a fug!" she exclaimed.

The intercom telephone buzzed. It was the O.O.W. calling. "Sir, Captain Kane and his chief officer are at the airlock. They wish to speak to you."

"Send them up," said Grimes.

"What in the universe have you been *doing,* Commander?" asked Danzellan. "Fighting a small war?"

"Or not so small," commented Maggie.

"I," Grimes told them bitterly, "was attempting to prevent the commission of a crime. Only it seems that slave trading is not a crime, insofar as this bloody world is concerned."

"The underpeople . . ." said Maggie softly. "Underpeople—and the still unrepealed Non-Citizen Act. . . . But how did you find out? It took me hours after I was able to get my paws on the records. . . ."

"I added two and two," Grimes told her, "and came up with three point nine recurring. All the clues are so obvious. Rudimentary nipples, paw-like hands and feet, the way in which the people eat and drink, and the use of 'cat' as a term of opprobrium when, apart from the Morrowvians themselves, there isn't a single animal of Terran origin on the planet. . . ."

Danzellan grinned. "I see what you mean. I've been known to refer to particularly stupid officers as 'pathetic apes.'"

"Those same points had *me* puzzled," admitted Maggie. "But I'm surprised that *you* noticed them."

"And Morrow's books," went on Grimes. "*The Island of Doctor Moreau*. The Cordwainer Smith novels. The names of the four families—Wells, Morrow, Cordwainer and Smith. And North Australia. . . ."

"You're losing me there," admitted Maggie.

A junior officer knocked at the door. "Captain Kane to see you, sir. And Mr. Dreebly."

Kane blew into the room like the violent storm after which his ship was named. He blustered, "I'll have your stripes for this, Grimes! As soon as your bloody admiral hears my story he'll bust you right down to Spaceman Sixteenth Class—unless he decides to shoot you first!"

"Slave trading," said Grimes, "is prohibited by Federation law."

"Yeah. It is. But, Mr. Commander Grimes, such laws

exist only for the protection of Federation citizens. The Morrowvians are non-citizens."

"How do you make that out?"

"How do I make that out? Because they're under-people, Commander—which means that they have the same status as androids, which means that they have no bloody status at all. They're no more than cattle—with the accent on the first syllable!" He laughed briefly at his own play on words, turned to glare at Dreebly when he essayed a snicker. "The only protection they can claim is that of the S.P.C.A.—and there's no branch of that society on Morrowvia!"

Grimes looked at Maggie appealingly. She flashed him a fleeting smile of encouragement. He looked at Danzellan. The portly shipmaster winked at him.

"Slavery," said Grimes firmly, "is still a crime, ethically if not legally."

"So is piracy, Grimes. Ethically *and* legally."

"I seem to recall past occasions in your own career. . . ."

"We're not talking about them. We're talking about *this* occasion in *your* career. The unprovoked attack upon an innocent merchantman. To begin with, Grimes, you can place your artificers at my disposal. *If* they make a good job I just might tone my report to your bosses down a little." He laughed lightly. "A stiff note on paper, instead of a stiff note on cardboard . . . ."

"Mphm," grunted Grimes thoughtfully.

"In fact, Commander," went on Kane, speaking quite quietly now, his exaggerated accent gone, "I think that you could help me considerably. . . ."

And Kane, thought Grimes, *owes his survival to the*

number of friends he has in high places. And Kane is an opportunist. For all he knows I might be an admiral myself one day. He's debating with himself, "Shall I put the boot in, or shall I let bygones be bygones?" Too, he's probably not quite sure if he is altogether in the right, legally speaking. . . .

"Don't trust him, Commander," said Danzellan.

"Keep your nose out of this!" snarled Kane.

"*I* discovered this planet," stated Danzellan. "The Dog Star Line . . ."

". . . can go and cock its leg against a lamp post," Kane finished the sentence.

"Gentlemen," said Grimes soothingly. "Gentlemen. . . ."

"I can't see any round here," remarked Maggie.

"You shut up for a start," he told her. But he realized that her flippancy had broken the tension.

"What do you say, Commander?" persisted Kane. "You have a workshop, and skilled technicians. . . . Get the old *Buster* back into commission for me and you can write your own report to your superiors." He grinned. "After all, I'm just a semiliterate tramp skipper. Paperwork's beyond my capabilities."

"And what about me?" asked Danzellan interestedly.

"The Dog Star Line's big enough to look after itself, Captain, as I have no doubt that it will. My own activities, for quite some time, anyhow, will be confined to this continent of New England. You," he said generously, "can have North Australia."

"Thank you, Captain. I appreciate the gesture. But I feel obliged to tell you that my employers are not quite the soul-less bastards that they have often been alleged to be. They would not wish to share a planet with a slaver. Not," he added, "that it will ever come to that."

"So you're pulling out?" asked Kane.

"No."

"I warn you, Captain Danzellan, that if you or your people try to make things awkward for me, I shall make things even more awkward for the Dog Star Line. They'll finish up by buying me out, at my price. It will not be a low one." He turned to Grimes. "And what do you say, Commander, to my proposition to you?"

"No," said Grimes. "No, repeat no."

"You'll be sorry. My report—and it's a damning one— has already been written. My Carlotti transmitter is quite powerful, and will be able to raise the Lindisfarne Base station with ease. You'd better have your letter of resignation ready."

He turned to go.

"Hold your horses," said Maggie sweetly. "Hold your horses, Captain Kane. I haven't said my party piece yet."

⸎⟨⟨ 27 ⟩⟩⸎

She said, "You'd better all sit down and make yourselves comfortable, as this is quite a long story. You, John, just read the very beginnings of it. You, Captain Kane, read enough to convince you that slaving activities, with Federation law as it stands at present, would be quite legal. And I was able to do more research than either of you.

"The story of *Lode Cougar* is not, in its early stages, an unusual one. There was the gaussjammer, lifting from Port Woomera, bound for the newly established colony on Austral—*your* home world, Captain Kane. As well as the intending colonists she carried cargo, among which was a shipment of fertilized ova. Dogs were required on Austral, and cats, to deal with the numerous indigenous vermin. There were cattle too, of course, and horses—oh, all the usual. And there were human ova, just in case the ship got thrown off course by a magnetic storm and had to start a new colony from scratch, in some utterly uncharted sector of the galaxy. Quite a number of colonies were started that way.

"*Lode Cougar* was unlucky—as so many of the old gaussjammers were. A magnetic storm threw her thousands of light-years off course. Her navigators were unable to determine her position. Her pile was dead, and her only source of power was her diesel generators. The engineers kept these running—which meant that the ship's biochemist was having to produce fuel for the jennies rather than food for the crew and passengers.

"But all they could do was to stand on and stand on, from likely star to likely star, pulling their belts ever tighter, finding that some suns had no planetary systems, that other suns had worlds in orbit about them utterly incapable of supporting any kind of life, let alone life as *we* know it.

"Almost inevitably there was a mutiny. It came about when a gang of starving passengers was caught foraging in the cargo spaces—*the refrigerated cargo spaces.* Is it cannibalism when you gorge yourself on fertilized human ova? A rather doubtful legal point . . . Anyhow, the master of the *Cougar* decided that it was cannibalism, and ordered the offenders shot. In the consequent flareup there was rather too much shooting and then an orgy of *real* cannibalism. . . . Things went from bad to worse after that, especially since the captain, his senior officers and most of the more responsible passengers were killed. Among the survivors was a professional genetic engineer, a Dr. Edward Morrow. He wrote despairingly in his private journal, 'Will this voyage never end? Men and women are behaving like wild beasts. No, I must not say that, because my fellow passengers are worse than beasts. No decent animal could ever sink to such depths.' That passage sticks in my memory. It explains so much. Sometime later he wrote that the ship was approaching yet another sun, and that Bastable, the liner's third officer, hoped that it would run to a habitable planet. 'If it does not,' Morrow wrote, 'that is the finish of us. Soon there will be only one survivor, gnawing the last shreds of human flesh from the last bone.'

"*Lode Cougar* cautiously approached the world that was still to be named. It looked to be habitable. There was a meeting of crew and passengers—what was left of them—and Bastable told them that the landing would have to be made in high magnetic latitudes, for the obvious reason. The others told Bastable that the landing would have to be made in some region with a hospitable climate; nobody was in fit condition to undertake a long trek over ice fields. Bastable acceded to their demands, after a long argument. Had he not been the only man capable of handling the ship he would have been murdered there and then.

"He got her down, as we know. He got her down, in one piece. The experience shattered him. He went to his quarters immediately after the landing, got out the bottle of alcohol that he had been jealously hoarding, and drank himself into insensibility. In his weakened condition—like all the rest he was more than half starved—it killed him. Regarding his death, Morrow made more unkind remarks in his journal about the human race.

"With the very few survivors a colony of sorts could have been started, might possibly have survived. There were ten men—nine of them, including Morrow, passengers, one of them a junior engineer. There were six women, four of them young. Morrow persuaded his companions that they would have a far better chance if they had underpeople to work for them. The only ova that had survived the trouble were those of cats—but Morrow was expert in his profession. With the aid of the engineer he was able to set up incubators and then—all that was required was in the ship's cargo—a fully equipped laboratory.

"He wrote again in his journal, 'The first batch is progressing nicely, in spite of the acceleration. I feel . . . paternal. I ask myself, why should these, my children, be *underpeople!* I can make them more truly human than the hairless apes that may, one day, infest this new world. . . .'

"Regarding the deaths of his fellow *Lode Cougar* survivors he says very little. One suspects that he knew more than he wrote about the food poisoning that killed Mary Little, Sarah Grant and Delia James. One wonders if Douglass Carrick fell off that cliff, or was pushed. And how did Susan Pettifer and William Hume come to get drowned in the river? It is interesting to note, too, that Mary, Sarah, Delia and Susan were the potential child bearers. And, as well as working in his laboratory, Morrow set up a still and soon had it in operation, turning out a very potent liquor from a fermented mash of berries and wild grain. The surviving men and the two remaining women didn't care much then what happened, and as Morrow had succeeded in activating a team of robots from the cargo he was independent of them.

"He didn't bother to kill them as his first batch of 'children' was growing to forced maturity. He just let them die—or be killed by wild animals when they went out hunting for meat."

"Yes," said Kane. "I know all that. The Morrowvians are non-citizens."

"I haven't finished yet, Captain Kane. There was something of the Pygmalion in Morrow—as there must have been in quite a few of those genetic engineers. He fell in love with one of his own creations—his Galatea. He even named her Galatea."

"Touching . . ." commented Kane.

"Yes, wasn't it? And he married her; he'd decided that his people couldn't live in a state of complete anarchy, and must have a few, necessary laws. So he made the union legal."

"Uncommonly decent of him," sneered Kane.

"But that didn't stop him from having quite a few concubines on the side. . . ."

"So the Morrowvian idol had his feet of clay."

"Don't we all, Captain, don't we all?"

"So the records prove that true humans can have sexual relations with these underpeople. I'd found that out long before I saw the precious records. Judging by the stink in here, Commander Grimes has found it out too."

"John! What have you been doing? Don't tell me that you and Maya . . ."

"I won't tell you if you tell me not to."

"So you did. I hope you enjoyed it, that's all."

Kane laughed patronizingly. "So I'll leave you people to your family squabbles, and get back to my ship and send my report off to Lindisfarne. A very good day to you all."

"Wait!" Maggie snapped sharply. "I haven't finished yet."

"I don't think that anything further you can say will

change my mind. Underpeople are underpeople. Underpeople are property. Period."

"There is a ruling," said Maggie slowly, "that any people capable of fertile union with true people must, themselves, be considered true people."

"And so, to coin a phrase, what?"

"Morrow's unions were fertile."

"So he says. How many glorified tomcats were sneaking into his wife's or his popsies' beds while he was elsewhere?"

"The Morrow strain is strongest in North Australia, among the people who bear his name."

"What evidence is there?"

"The Morrows are a little more 'human' than the other Morrowvians. Very few of their women have supplementary nipples. Their general outlook is more 'human'—as you know yourself. That show you put on for Janine with the saluting cannon. . . . And the show she put on for us."

"Yeah. I grant you that. But I think the words of the ruling you mentioned are, 'a fertile, *natural* union.' Old Doc Morrow was a genetic engineer. I've heard it said that those boys could crossbreed an ant and an elephant. . . . I'm sorry. I' m really sorry for you all. You've tried hard, but by the time the Federation reaches a decision I'll have made my pile."

"I," said Danzellan, "can supply more proof for Commander Lazenby's arguments."

"You, Captain? You're no biologist, you're just a shipmaster like myself."

"Even so. . . ." The master of *Schnauzer* was obviously finding something highly amusing. "Even so. . . . You know, it's just over two hundred and twenty days that I first landed on Morrowvia—and that's about two hundred and seventy days Standard . . . ."

"I can do sums in my head as well as you can."

"I am sure you can, Captain Kane. And are you married? Have you a family?"

"No—to both questions."

"It doesn't matter. Well, on the occasion of my first visit, my second officer, Mr. Delamere, got Tabitha, the daughter of the Queen of Melbourne, into trouble, as the saying goes. The young idiot should have taken his contraceptive shots before he started playing around, of course. He's really smitten with her, and managed to get himself appointed to *Schnauzer,* rather against my wishes. Now he wants to make an honest woman of the girl—once again, as the saying goes—but Lilian, Tabitha's mother, will not allow him to marry her unless he complies with local law. This means that he will have to change his name to Morrow, which he does not want to do. He will, of course. The Dog Star Line wants a resident agent on this planet. And even though the queenships are not hereditary in theory they usually are in practice."

"What are you driveling about?" asked Kane crudely.

Danzellan flushed. He said stiffly, "Tabitha has presented young Delamere with a son."

"And how many local boyfriends has she had?" demanded Kane.

"She says that she has none. Furthermore, I have seen the baby. All the Morrowvians have short noses—except this one, who has a long nose, like his father. The resemblance is remarkable. . . ."

Kane refused to concede defeat.

"Paternity tests . . ." he mumbled.

"I can soon arrange those, Captain," Grimes told him. "Don't forget that I have my own biologists, as well as other scientists." He turned to Danzellan. "Did Mr. Delamere come with you, Captain? Call him up, and we'll wet the baby's head!"

"You can break a bottle of champagne over it!" growled Kane, pushing his way out of the day cabin, brushing past Maya who was just coming in, and complaining, "I'm *still* hungry, John. They say that all the ice cream is finished. . . ."

"Go on," said Maggie. "Do the decent thing. Buy the girl a popsicle to show her how much you love her."

"I'll have some more ice cream made, Maya," promised Grimes, looking at her with combined pity and irritation, noticing that Danzellan was regarding her with condescending amusement.

The Morrowvians, thanks to the long-dead Morrow's skill—he had even imposed the right gestation period on his people—were safe from Drongo Kane and his like, but had no defenses against Big Business as represented by the Dog Star Line.

Or had they?

Grimes suspected that they, with their innate feline charm combined with selfishness, would not do at all badly in the years to come.

))((( )))((

THE BIG
BLACK MARK

))((( )))((

DEDICATION

To William Bligh

⟫⟪Last Chance⟫⟪

"Now, Grimes, I'm going to be frank," said the admiral. "There are many people in the Service who don't like you, and who did not at all approve of your last two promotions. I didn't altogether approve of them myself, come to that, although I do admit that you possess one attribute that might, in the fullness of time, carry you to flag rank. You're lucky, Grimes. You could fall into a cesspit and come out not only smelling of roses but with the Shaara Crown Jewels clutched in your hot little hands. You've done it, figuratively, more than once. But I only hope that I'm not around when your luck runs out!"

"You mean, sir," asked Grimes, "that this is some sort of last chance?"

"You said it, commander. *You* said it. . . ."

))((Chapter 1))((

Commander John Grimes, Federation Survey Service, should have been happy.

Rather to his surprise he had been promoted on his return, in the Census Ship *Seeker*, to Lindisfarne Base. He now wore three new, gleaming stripes of gold braid on his shoulder boards instead of the old, tarnished two and a half. Scrambled egg—the stylized comets worked in gold thread—now adorned the peak of his cap. And not only had he been promoted, from lieutenant commander to commander, he had been appointed to the command of a much bigger ship.

He should have been happy, but he was not.

The vessel, to begin with, was not a warship, although she did mount some armament. Grimes had served in real warships only as a junior officer, and not at all after he had reached the rank of lieutenant. As such he had commanded a Serpent Class courier, a little ship with a small crew, hardly better than a spacegoing mail van. Then, as a lieutenant commander, he had been captain of *Seeker,* and in her had been lucky enough to stumble upon not one, but two Lost Colonies. It was to this luck that he owed his promotion; normally it was the officers in the fighting ships, with the occasional actions in which to distinguish themselves, who climbed most rapidly up the ladder of rank.

Now he was captain of *Discovery,* another Census Ship.

And what a ship!

To begin with, she was old.

She was not only old; she had been badly neglected.

She had been badly neglected, and her personnel, who seemed to be permanently attached to her, were not the sort of people to look after any ship well. Grimes, looking down the list of officers before he joined the vessel, had recognized several names. If the Bureau of Appointments had really tried to assemble a collection of prize malcontents inside one hapless hull they could not have done better.

Or worse.

Lieutenant Commander Brabham was the first lieutenant. He was some ten years older than Grimes, but he would never get past his present rank. He had been guilty of quite a few Survey Service crimes. (Grimes, too, had often been so guilty—but Grimes's luck was notorious.) He was reputed to carry an outsize chip on his shoulder. Grimes had never been shipmates with him, but he had heard about him.

Lieutenant Commander (E) MacMorris was chief engineer. Regarding him it had been said, in Grimes's hearing, "Whoever gave that uncouth mechanic a commission should have his head examined!" Grimes did not know him personally. Yet.

Lieutenant (S) Russell was the paymaster. Perhaps "pay-mistress" would have been a more correct designation. Ellen Russell had been one of the first female officers of the Supply Branch actually to serve aboard a ship of the Survey Service. From the very beginning she had succeeded in antagonizing her male superiors. She was known—not affectionately—as Vinegar Nell. Grimes had, once, been shipmates with her. For some reason or other she had called him an insufferable puppy.

Lieutenant (PC) Flannery was psionic communications officer. He was notorious throughout the Service for his heavy drinking. He owed his continuing survival to the fact that good telepaths are as scarce, almost, as hens' teeth.

So it went on. The detachment of Federation Marines was commanded by Major Swinton, known as the Mad Major. Swinton had faced a court-martial after the affair on Glenrowan. The court had decided, after long deliberation, that Swinton's action had been self-defense and not a massacre of innocent, unarmed civilians. That decision would never have been reached had the Federation not been anxious to remain on friendly terms with the king of Glenrowan, who had requested Federation aid to put down a well-justified rebellion.

Officers . . . petty officers.

Grimes sighed as he read. All were tarred with the same brush. He had little doubt that the ratings, too, would all be Federation's bad bargains. It occurred to him that his own superiors in the Service might well have put him in the same category.

The thought did not make him any happier.

"Those are your officers, Commander," said the admiral.

"Mphm," grunted Grimes. He added hastily, "Sir."

The admiral's thick, white eyebrows lifted over his steely blue eyes. He frowned heavily, and Grimes's prominent ears flushed.

"Don't *grunt* at me, young man. We may be the policemen of the galaxy, but we aren't pigs. Hrrmph. Those are your ship's officers. You, especially, will appreciate that there are some people for whom it is difficult to find suitable employment."

The angry flush spread from Grimes's ears to the rest of his craggy, somewhat unhandsome face.

"Normally," the admiral went on, "*Discovery* carries on her books some twenty assorted scientists—specialist officers, men and women dressed as spacemen. But she is not a very popular ship, and the Bureau of Exploration has managed to find you only one for the forthcoming voyage."

Maggie Lazenby? Grimes wondered hopefully. Perhaps she had relented. She had been more than a little cold toward him since his affair with the cat woman, but surely she couldn't bear a grudge this long.

"Commander Brandt," the admiral went on. "Or Dr. Brandt, as he prefers to be called. Anthropologist, ethologist, and a bit of a jack-of-all-trades. He'll be under your orders, of course.

"And, talking of orders—" The admiral pushed a fat, heavily sealed envelope across his highly polished desk. "Nothing very secret. No need to destroy by fire before reading. I can tell you now. As soon as you are ready for Deep Space in all respects you are to lift ship and proceed to New Maine. We have a sub-Base there, as you know. That sub-Base will be your Base. From New Maine you will make a series of exploratory sweeps out toward the Rim. A Lost Colony Hunt, as you junior officers romantically put it. Your own two recent discoveries have stimulated interest, back on Earth, in that sort of pointless exercise. Hrrmph."

"Thank you, sir." Grimes gathered up his papers and rose to leave.

"Not so fast, Commander. I haven't finished yet. *Discovery*, as I can see that you suspect, is not a happy ship. Your predecessor, Commander Tallis, contrived to leave her on medical grounds. The uniformly bad reports that he put in regarding *Discovery*'s personnel were partly discounted in view of his nervous—or mental—condition. Hrrmph.

"Now, Grimes, I'm going to be frank. There are many people in the Service who don't like you, and who did not at all approve of your last two promotions. I didn't altogether approve of them myself, come to that, although I do admit that you possess one attribute that just might, in the fullness of time, carry you to flag rank. You're lucky, Grimes. You could fall into a cesspit and come up not only smelling of roses but with the Shaara Crown Jewels clutched in your hot little hands. You've done it, figuratively, more than once.

"But I only hope that I'm not around when your luck runs out!"

Grimes started to get to his feet again.

"Hold it, Commander! I've some advice for you. Don't put a foot wrong. And try to lick that blasted *Discovery* into some sort of shape. If you do find any Lost Colonies play it according to the book. Let's have no more quixotry, none of this deciding, all by your little self, who are the goodies and who are the baddies. Don't take sides.

"That's all."

"You mean, sir," asked Grimes, "that this is some sort of last chance?"

"*You* said it, Commander. *You* said it. But just don't forget that the step from commander to captain is a very big one." The admiral shot out a big hand. Grimes took it, and was surprised and gratified by the warmth and firmness of the old man's grip. "Good hunting, Grimes. And good luck!"

))((Chapter 2))((

Grimes dismounted from the ground car at the foot of *Discovery*'s ramp. The driver, an attractive blonde spacewoman, asked, "Shall I wait for you, Commander?"

Grimes, looking up at the towering, shabby bulk of his new command, replied, "No, unfortunately."

The girl laughed sympathetically. "Good luck, sir."

"Thank you," he said.

He tucked his briefcase firmly under his arm, strode toward the foot of the ramp. He noted that the handrails were long unpolished, that a couple of stanchions were missing and that several treads were broken. There was a Marine sentry at the head of the ramp in a khaki uniform that looked as though it had been slept in. The man came to a rough approximation to attention as Grimes approached, saluted him as though he were doing him a personal favor. Grimes returned the salute with unwonted smartness.

"Your business, Commander?" asked the sentry.

"My name is Grimes. I'm the new captain."

The man seemed to be making some slight effort to smarten himself up. "I'll call Commander Brabham on the PA, sir."

"Don't bother," said Grimes. "I'll find my own way up to my quarters." He added, rather nastily, "I suppose the elevator is working?"

"Of course, sir. This way, sir."

Grimes let the Marine lead him out of the airlock chamber, along a short alleyway, to the axial shaft. The man pressed a button, and after a short interval, the door slid open to reveal the cage.

"You'll find all the officers in the wardroom, sir, at this time of the morning," volunteered his guide.

"Thank you." Then, "Hadn't you better be getting back to your post?"

"Yes, sir. Of course, sir."

Grimes pushed the button for CAPTAIN'S FLAT.

During the journey up he was able to come to further conclusions—none of them good—about the way in which the ship had been run. The cage was not quite filthy, but it was far from clean. The gloss of the panel in which the buttons were set was dulled by greasy fingerprints. On the deck Grimes counted three cigarette butts and one cigarillo stub. Two of the indicator lights for the various levels were not working.

He got out at the Captain's Flat, the doughnut of accommodation that surrounded the axial shaft, separated from it by a circular alleyway. He had a set of keys with him, obtained from the admiral's office. The sliding door to the day room opened as soon as he applied the appropriate strip of magnetized metal. He went in.

An attempt, not very enthusiastic, had been made to clean up after Commander Tallis' packing. But Tallis had not packed his art gallery. This consisted of a score of calendars, of the type given away by ship chandlers and ship-repair firms, from as many worlds, utterly useless as a means of checking day and date except on their planets of origin. Evidently *Discovery*'s last census run had consisted of making the rounds of well-established colonies. Grimes stared at the three-dimensional depiction of a young lady with two pairs of overdeveloped breasts, indubitably mammalian and probably from mutated human stock, turned from it to the picture of a girl with less spectacular upperworks but with brightly gleaming jewelry entwined in her luxuriant pubic hair. The next one to catch his attention showed three people in one pose.

He grunted—not altogether in disapproval—then found the bell push labeled PANTRY over his desk. He used it. He filled and lit his pipe. When he had almost finished it he pushed the button again.

At last a spacewoman, in slovenly uniform, came in. She demanded surlily, "Did you ring? Sir."

"Yes," answered Grimes, trying to infuse a harsh note into his voice. "I'm the new captain. My gear will be coming aboard this afternoon some time. Meanwhile, would you mind getting this . . . junk disposed of?" He waved a hand to indicate the calendars.

"But *if* Commander Tallis comes back—"

"If Commander Tallis comes back, you can stick it all back up again. Oh, and you might give Lieutenant

Commander Brabham my compliments and ask him to come to see me."

"The first lieutenant's in the wardroom. Sir. The PA system is working."

Grimes refrained from telling her what to do with the public-address system. He merely repeated his order, adding, "And I mean *now*."

"Aye, aye, sir, Captain, sir."

Insolent little bitch, thought Grimes, watching the twitching rump in the tight shorts vanishing through the doorway.

He settled down to wait again. Nobody in this ship seemed to be in any hurry about anything. Eventually Brabham condescended to appear. The first lieutenant was a short, chunky man, gray-haired, very thin on top. His broad, heavily lined face wore what looked like a perpetual scowl. His faded gray eyes glowered at the captain. The colors of the few ribbons on the left breast of his shirt had long since lost their brilliance and were badly frayed. Grimes could not tell what decorations—probably good attendance medals—they represented. But there were plenty of canteen medals which were obvious enough—smudges of cigarette ash, dried splashes of drinks and gravies—to keep them company. The gold braid on Brabham's shoulder boards had tarnished to a grayish green.

A gray man, thought Grimes. *A gray, bitter man.* He said, extending his hand, "Good morning, Number One."

"Good morning. Sir."

"Sit down, Number One." Grimes made a major operation out of refilling and lighting his pipe. "Smoke, if you wish." Brabham produced and ignited an acrid cigarette. "Mphm. Now, what's our condition of readiness?"

"Well, sir, a week at the earliest."

"A *week?*"

"This isn't an Insect Class Courier, sir. This is a *big* ship."

Grimes flushed, but held his temper in check. He said, "Any Survey Service vessel, regardless of size, should be ready, at all times, for almost instant liftoff."

"But, to begin with, there's been the change of captains. Sir."

"Go on."

"And Vinegar Nell—Miss Russell, I mean—isn't very cooperative."

"Mphm. Between ourselves, Number One, I haven't been impressed by the standard of efficiency of her staff." *Or,* he thought, *with the standard of efficiency of this ship in general. But I shall have to handle people with kid gloves until I get the feel of things.*

Brabham actually grinned. "I don't think that Sally was overly impressed by you, sir."

"Sally?"

"The captain's tigress. She used to be Commander Tallis' personal servant." Brabham grinned again, not very pleasantly. "Extremely personal, if you get what I mean, sir."

"Oh. Go on."

"And we're still trying to get a replacement for Mr. Flannery's psionic amplifier. He insists that only the brain of an Irish setter will do."

"And what happened to the old one?"

Brabham permitted himself a small chuckle. "He thought that it should share a binge. He poured a slug of Irish whiskey into its life-support tank. And then he tried to bring it around with black coffee."

"Gah!" exclaimed Grimes.

"Then he blamed the whiskey for the demise of the thing. It wasn't *real* Irish whiskey, apparently. It was some ersatz muck from New Shannon."

Grimes succeeded in dispelling the vision of the sordidly messy death of the psionic amplifier from his mind. He said firmly, "To begin with, Miss Russell will just have to pull her finger out. You're the first lieutenant. Get on to her."

"I'd rather not, sir."

Grimes glared at the man. "I'm not being funny, Mr. Brabham. Shake her up. Light a fire under her tail. And as for Mr. Flannery, he'll just have to be content with whatever hapless hound's brain the Stores Department can dig up—even if it comes from an English bulldog!"

"Then there are the engines, sir."

"The engines? What about them?"

"The chief has taken down both inertial drive-units. There're bits and pieces strewn all over the engine room deck."

"Was the port captain informed of this immobilization?"

"Er, no, sir."

"And why not?"

"I didn't know what the chief had done until he'd already done it."

"In the captain's absence you were the officer in charge. You should have known. All right, all right, the chief should have come to you first. Apparently he didn't. But as soon as you knew that this rustbucket was immobile you should have reported it."

"I—I suppose I should, sir."

"You suppose! Why didn't you?"

A sullen flush spread over the grayish pallor of Brabham's face. He blurted, "Like the rest of us in this ship, MacMorris has been in quite enough trouble of various kinds. I didn't want to get him into any more. Sir."

Grimes repressed a sigh. It was obvious that this ship was a closed shop, manned by the No Hopers' Union, whose members would close ranks against any threatened action by higher authority, no matter how much they bickered among themselves. And what was he, Grimes? A No Hoper or a pillar of the Establishment? In his heart of hearts, which side was he on? While he was sorting out a reply to make to Brabham a familiar bugle call, amplified, drifted through and over the ship's PA system.

Brabham shifted uneasily in his chair.

"Are you coming down to lunch, sir?" he asked.

"No," decided Grimes. "You carry on down, and you can ask—no, *tell*—Miss Russell to send me some sandwiches and a pot of coffee up here. After lunch I shall see Lieutenant Commander MacMorris, Miss Russell, and Mr. Flannery, in that order. Then I shall see you again.

"That is all."

⑅⟨Chapter 3⟩⑅

It was the little blonde stewardess, Sally, who brought up Grimes's lunch. While he was eating it she set about stripping Tallis' calendars from the bulkheads, performing this task with a put-upon air and a great deal of waste motion. Grimes wondered if she had made the sandwiches and the coffee in the same sullenly slapdash way. No, he decided after the first nibble, the first sip. She must have gone to considerable trouble with the simple meal. Surely all the available bread could not have been as stale as the loaf that had been used. Surely it must have been much harder to spread butter so extremely thinly than in the normal manner. And where had she found that stringy, flavorless cold mutton? The coffeepot must have been stood in cold water to bring its weak contents to the correctly tepid stage.

"Will that be all? Sir?" she asked, her arms full of calendars.

"Yes," Grimes told her, adding, "Thank you," not that

she deserved it. He decided that he would tell Miss Russell to let him have a male steward to look after him. Obviously this girl would give proper service only to those who serviced her, and she was too coarse, too shop-soiled for his taste, apart from the obvious disciplinary considerations.

Almost immediately after she was gone there was a knock at the door. A big man entered. He was clad in filthy, oil-soaked overalls. A smear of black grease ran diagonally across his hard, sullen face. More grease was mixed with his long, unruly yellow hair. His hot blue eyes glared down at Grimes.

"Ye wanted to see me, Captain? I'm a busy man, not like some I could mention."

"Lieutenant Commander MacMorris?"

"Who else?"

"Commander MacMorris, I understand that this ship is immobilized."

"Unless ye intend to take her up on reaction drive, she is that."

"By whose authority?" demanded Grimes coldly.

"Mine, o' course. Both the innies was playin' up on the homeward passage. So I'm fixin' 'em."

"Didn't you inform the first lieutenant before you started taking them down? He was in charge, in the absence of a captain."

"Inform *him*? He looks after whatever control room ornaments look after. I look after my engine room."

"As long as I'm captain of this ship," snapped Grimes, "it's my engine room. How long will it take you to reassemble the inertial drive-units?"

Grimes could almost read MacMorris' thoughts as the engineer stood there. Should he or should he not angrily protest the captain's assumption of proprietorial rights? He muttered at last, "If I do all that has to be done, a week."

"A week? Just to put things together again?"

"A week it will be."

"Normal in-port routine, I suppose, Commander MacMorris . . . 0800 to 1700, with the usual breaks . . . I see. But if you work double shifts . . . ?"

"Look, Captain, you're not suggesting—"

"No, Commander MacMorris. I'm not suggesting. I'm ordering."

"But we all have friends on the Base, and the last cruise was a long one."

"You will work double shifts, Chief, longer if necessary. I'll want this vessel ready for Space no more than three days from now."

MacMorris grunted wordlessly, turned to go.

"Oh, one more thing," said Grimes.

"Yes? Sir."

"In the future you are to ask me for permission before you immobilize the engines. That is all."

The engineer left sullenly. Grimes carefully filled and lit his battered pipe. What was it that somebody, some girl, had called it, some time ago? *The male pacifier.* Well, he needed pacifying. He disliked having to crack the whip, but there were occasions when it was unavoidable. MacMorris was known to be a good engineer—but he was one of those engineers to whom a ship is no more than a platform existing for the sole purpose of supporting machinery. Grimes thought, not for the first time, that captains had it much better in the days of sail. Even then there were technicians—such as the sailmaker—but a competent wind ship master would be able to repair or even to make a sail himself if he absolutely had to.

There was another knock at the door.

"Come in!" he called.

"I see you're still smoking that filthy thing!" sniffed Vinegar Nell

She had hardly changed at all, thought Grimes, since when they had last been shipmates—and how many years ago was that? She was slim, still, almost to the point of thinness. Her coppery hair was scraped back severely from her broad brow. Green eyes still glinted in the sharp, narrow face. Her mouth was surprisingly wide and full. She could have been very attractive were it not for her perpetually sour expression.

Grimes said stiffly, "Must I remind you, Miss Russell, that I am the captain of this ship?"

"And so you are, sir. *And* a full commander. I never thought you'd make it."

"That will do, Miss Russell." Belatedly he remembered his manners. "Sit down, will you?" The legs displayed when her short uniform skirt rode up were excellent. "Now, Miss Russell, I want *Discovery* ready for Space in three days."

"You're asking a lot, Captain."

"I'm not, Paymaster. You know the regulations as well as I do. At least as well." He quoted, "All fleet units shall be maintained in a state of instant readiness."

"But there are provedore stores to be loaded. The farm

needs a thorough overhaul; the yeasts in numbers two and three vats went bad on me last trip, and I'm not at all happy about the beef tissue culture. The pumping and filtration systems for the hydroponic tanks need a thorough clean out."

"You can write, can't you?"

"Write?" The fine eyebrows arched in puzzlement.

"Yes. Write. It's something you do on a piece of paper, such as an official form, with a stylus. Make out the necessary requisitions. Mark them *urgent*. I'll countersign them."

"Commander Tallis," she told him, "always wanted all repairs and maintenance carried out by the ship's personnel."

"One way of making sure that you get longer in port. But my name is Grimes, not Tallis. I don't like to loaf around Base until the stern vanes take root. Make out those requisitions."

"All right," she said flatly.

"Oh, and that stewardess . . . Sally, I think her name is."

"Your servant."

"My ex-servant. Have her replaced by a male steward." A smile that was almost a sneer flickered over her full mouth as she looked around at the bulkheads, bare now, stripped of their adornment of blatantly bare female flesh. "Oh, I see. I never thought that you were *that* way in the old days, Captain."

"And I'm not now!" he snarled. "It's just that I don't like insolent sluts who can't even make a decent sandwich. On your way down, tell Mr. Flannery that I want him, please."

"Nobody wants Mr. Flannery," she said. "But we're stuck with him."

Flannery finally put in an appearance. He looked as though he had been dragged out from a drunken slumber. He was red-haired, grossly fat, and his unhealthily pale face was almost featureless. His little eyes were a washed-out blue, but so bloodshot that they looked red. The reek of his breath was so strong that Grimes, fearing an explosion, did not relight his pipe.

"Mr. Flannery?"

"An' who else would it be, Captain?"

"Mphm." The temperamental telepaths had always to be handled carefully and Grimes did not wish to provoke the man into insubordination, with its inevitable consequences. It would take much too long to get a replacement. Once the ship was up and away, however—"Mphm. Ah, Mr. Flannery, I believe that you're unable to get a suitable psionic amplifier to replace the one that, er, died."

"An' isn't that the God's truth, Captain? Poor Terence, he was more than just an amplifier for me feeble, wanderin' thoughts. He was more than just a pet, even. He was a brother."

"Mphm?"

"A dog from the Ould Sod, he was, a sweet Irish setter. They took his foine body away, bad cess to 'em, but his poor, naked brain was there, in that jar o' broth, his poor, shiverin' brain an' the shinin' soul o' him. Night after night we'd sit there, out in the dark atween the stars, just the pair of us, a-singin' the ould songs. The Minstrel Boy to the war has gone. . . . *An' ye are that Minstrel Boy, Paddy,* he'd say to me, he'd *think* to me, *an' you an' me is light-years from the Emerald Me, an' shall we iver see her again?"* Grimes noted with embarrassed disgust that greasy tears were trickling from the piggy eyes. "I'm a sociable man, Captain, an' I niver likes drinkin' alone, but I'm fussy who I drinks with. So ivery night I'd pour a drop, just a drop, mind ye, just a drop o' the precious whiskey into Terence's tank . . . he liked it, as God's me guide. He loved it, an' he wanted it. An' wouldn't ye want it if the sweet brain of ye was bare an' naked in a goldfish bowl, a-floatin' in weak beef tea?"

"Mphm."

"An one cursed night me hand shook, an' I gave him half the bottle. But he went happy, a-dreamin' o' green fields an' soft green hills an' a blue sky with little, white fleecy clouds like the ewe lambs o' God himself. . . . I only hope that I go as happy when me time comes."

If you have anything to do with it, thought Grimes, *there's a very good chance of it.*

"An' I've tried to get a replacement, Captain, I've tried, an' I've tried. I've haunted the communications equipment stores like a poor, shiverin' ghost until I thought they'd be callin' one o' the Fathers to exorcise me. But what have they got on their lousy shelves? I'll tell ye. The pickled brains o' English bulldogs, an' German shepherds an'—yell niver believe me!—an Australian dingo! But niver an honest Irish hound. Not so much as a terrier."

"You have to settle on something," Grimes said firmly.

"But you don't understand, Captain." Suddenly the heavy brogue was gone and Flannery seemed to be speaking quite soberly. "There must be absolute empathy between a telepath and his amplifier. And could *I* achieve empathy with an *English* dog?"

Balls! thought Grimes. *I'll* order *the bastard to take the bulldog, and see what happens.* Then a solution to the problem suddenly occurred to him. He said, "And they have a dingo's brain in the store?"

"Oh, sure, sure. But—"

"But what? A dingo's a dog, isn't he? As a dog he possesses a dog's telepathic faculties. And he's a peculiarly Australian dog."

"Yes, but—"

"And what famous Australians can you call to mind? What about the Wild Colonial Boy? Weren't all the bushrangers—or most of 'em—Irish?"

"Bejabbers, Captain, I believe ye've got it!"

"You've got it, Mr. Flannery. Or you will get it. And you can call it Ned, for Ned Kelly."

And so that's that, thought Grimes, when Flannery had shambled off. *For the time being, at least. It still remains to be seen if my departmental heads can deliver the goods.* But he was still far from happy. Unofficially and quite illegally a captain relies upon his psionic communications officer to keep him informed when trouble is brewing inside his ship. "Snooping" is the inelegant name for such conduct, which runs counter to the Rhine Institute's code of ethics.

For such snooping to be carried out, however, there must be a genuine trust and friendship between captain and telepath. Grimes doubted that he could ever trust

Flannery or that he could ever feel friendly toward him.

And, to judge by his experience to date, similar doubts applied to everybody in this unhappy ship.

⫷Chapter 4⫸

Surprisingly, the ship was ready for liftoff in three days.

Had the Survey Service been a commercial shipping line the refitting operations would have been uneconomical, with swarms of assorted technicians working around the clock and a wasteful use of materials. It was still a very expensive operation in terms of goodwill. *Discovery's* people were robbed of the extra days at Lindisfarne Base to which they had all been looking forward, and the officers in charge of the various Base facilities grew thoroughly sick and tired of being worried by Grimes, all the time, about this, that, and the other.

But she was ready, spaceworthy in all respects, and then Grimes shook Brabham by saying that he was going to make an inspection.

"Commander Tallis only used to make inspections in Space," objected the first lieutenant.

"Damn Commander Tallis!" swore Grimes, who was becoming tired of hearing about his predecessor. "Do you really think that I'm mug enough to take this rustbucket upstairs without satisfying myself that she's not going to fall apart about my ears? Pass word to all departmental heads that I shall be making rounds at 1000 hours. You, Miss Russell, and Major Swinton will accompany me. Every other officer and petty officer will be standing by whatever he's responsible for."

"Ten hundred is morning smoko, sir."

"And so what? Smoko is a privilege, and not a right. Report to me at 1000 hours with Miss Russell and the major. Oh, and you might polish your shoes and put on a clean uniform shirt."

If looks killed, Brabham would have had to organize a funeral, not captain's rounds. Had he been too harsh? Grimes asked himself as the first lieutenant walked stiffly out of the day cabin. *No,* he thought. *No. This ship needs shaking up, smartening up.* He grinned. *And I've always hated those captains who pride themselves on a taut ship. But I don't want a taut ship. All I want is something a few degrees superior to a flag of convenience star tramp.*

Meanwhile his own quarters were, at least, clean. The steward who had replaced Commander Tallis' pet, Sally, was a taciturn lout who had to be told everything, but once he was told anything, he did it. And the service of meals in the wardroom had been improved, as had been the standard of cookery. Also, under Grimes's prodding, Brabham was beginning to take a little pride in his appearance and was even seeing to it that his juniors did likewise. MacMorris, however, was incorrigible. The first time that Grimes put in an appearance in the wardroom, for dinner on the evening of his first day aboard, the engineer was already seated at the table, still wearing his filthy coveralls. On being taken to task he told the captain that *he* had to work for a living. Grimes ordered him either to go and get cleaned up or to take his meal in the duty engineers' mess. Rather surprisingly, MacMorris knuckled under, although with bad grace. But was it, after all, so surprising? Like all the other people in this ship he was regarded as being almost unemployable. If he were paid off from *Discovery* he would find it hard, if not impossible, to obtain another spacegoing appointment in the Survey Service. In a ship, any ship, he was still a big frog in a small puddle and, too, was in receipt of the active-duty allowance in addition to the pay for his rank. As one of the many technicians loafing around a big Base he would be a not too generously paid nobody.

The steward brought in Grimes's coffee. It was the way that he liked it, very hot and strong. He poured a cup of the steaming brew, sipped it appreciatively. There was a knock at the door. It was Brabham, accompanied by Major Swinton and Vinegar Nell.

"Rounds, sir?" asked the first lieutenant.

Grimes glanced at the bulkhead clock. "A little early yet. Be seated, all of you. Coffee?"

"No, thank you, sir. We have just finished ours."

The three officers sat in a stiff line on the settee, the woman in the middle. Grimes regarded them over the rim of his cup. Brabham looked, he thought, like a morose bloodhound.

The Mad Major, with his wiry gray hair and bristling moustache, his hot yellow eyes, looked like a vicious terrier. Grimes had never liked terriers. And Vinegar

Nell? More cat than dog, he decided. A certain sleekness
. . . but sleek cats can be as bad tempered as the rougher
ones. He finished his coffee, got to his feet, reached for
his cap. "All right," he said. "We'll get the show on the
road."

They started in the control room. There was little to
find fault with there. Lieutenant Tangye, the navigator,
was a man who believed in maintaining all his instruments
in a highly polished state. Whether or not Tangye was
capable of using these instruments Grimes had yet to
discover. Not that he worried much about it; he was quite
prepared to do his own navigation. (He, while serving as
navigator in a cruiser, had been quite notorious for his
general untidiness, but no captain had ever been able to
complain about any lack of ability to fix the ship's position
speedily and accurately.)

The next deck down was Grimes's own accommodation,
with which he was already familiar. He devoted more
time to the two decks below in which the officers, of all
departments, were accommodated. The cabins and public
rooms were clean, although not excessively so. The
furnishings were definitely shabby. Miss Russell said,
before he could make any comment, "*They* won't supply
anything new for this ship."

Perhaps They wouldn't, thought Grimes, but had
anybody bothered to find out for sure?

The Marines' quarters were next, housing twenty men.
Here, as in the control room, there was some evidence of
spit and polish. Grimes decided that the sergeant, a
rugged, hairless black giant whose name was Washington,

was responsible. Whatever the crimes that had led to his appointment to *Discovery* had been, he was an old-timer, convinced that the space soldiers were superior to any mere spaceman, ships' captains included. The trouble with such men was that, in a pinch, they would be loyal only to their own branch of the Survey Service, to their own officers.

Petty officers' quarters next, with the bos'n—another old-timer—coming to stiff attention as the inspection party entered the compartment. Grimes decided that he wouldn't trust the man any farther than he could throw him—and, as the bos'n was decidedly corpulent, that would not be very far. Langer . . . yes, that was his name. Hadn't he been implicated in the flogging of ship's stores when the heavy cruiser *Draconis* had been grounded on Dingaan for Mannschenn Drive recalibration?

Provedore ratings, deck ratings, engine room ratings . . . everything just not quite clean, with the faint yet unmistakable taint of too-long-unwashed clothing and bedding permeating the ship's atmosphere.

Storerooms—now well stocked.

The farm decks, with their hydroponic tanks, the yeast and algae and tissue culture vats—everything looked healthy enough. Grimes expressed the hope that it would all stay that way.

The cargo hold, its bins empty, but ready for any odds and ends that *Discovery* might pick up during the forthcoming voyage.

The boat bays . . . Grimes selected a boat at random, had it opened up. He satisfied himself that all equipment was in good order, that the provisions and other supplies were according to scale. He ran the inertial drive-unit for a few seconds in neutral gear. The irregular beat of it sounded healthy enough.

Engine spaces, with the glowering MacMorris in close attendance. In the Mannschenn Drive room, ignoring the engineer's scowl, Grimes put out a ringer to one of the finely balanced rotors. It began to turn at the slightest touch and the other rotors, on their oddly angled spindles, moved in sympathy. There was the merest hint of temporal disorientation, a fleeting giddiness. MacMorris growled, "An' does he want us all to finish up in the middle o' last week?" Grimes pretended not to have heard him.

The inertial drive room, with the drive-units now reassembled, their working parts concealed beneath the casings . . . reaction drive . . . nothing to see there but a few pumps. And there was nothing to see in the compartment that housed the hydrogen fusion power plant; everything of any importance was hidden beneath layers of insulation. But if MacMorris said that it was all right, it must be.

"Thank you," said Grimes to his officers. "She'll do." He thought, *She'll have to do.*

"You missed the dogbox, sir," Brabham reminded him, with ill-concealed satisfaction.

"I know," said Grimes. "I'm going there now. No, you needn't come with me."

Alone, he made his way to the axial shaft, entered the elevator cage. He pushed the button for the farm deck. It was there that the psionic amplifier was housed, for no other reason than to cut down on the plumbing requirements. Pumps and pipes were essential to the maintenance of the tissue culture vats; some of the piping and one of the pumps were used to provide the flow of nutrient solution through the tank in which floated the disembodied canine brain.

On the farm deck he made his way through the assemblage of vats and tanks and found, tucked away in a corner, a small, boxlike compartment. Some wit had taped a crudely printed notice to the door: BEWARE OF THE DOG. *Very funny*, thought Grimes. *When I was a first trip cadet it always had me rolling on the deck in uncontrollable paroxysms of mirth*. But what was that noise from inside the room? Someone singing? Flannery, presumably.

> *"I'll die but not surrender*
> *Cried the Wild Colonial Boy. . . ."*

Grimes grinned. It sounded as though the psionic communications officer had already established rapport with his new pet. But wouldn't a dingo prefer the eerie music of a didgeridoo? What if he were to indent for one? He grinned again.

He knocked at the door, slid it open. Flannery was sitting—sprawling, rather—at and over his worktable. There was a bottle, open, ready to hand, with a green label on which shone a golden harp. There was no glass. The PCO, still crooning softly, was staring at the spherical tank, at the obscene, pallid, wrinkled shape suspended in translucent brown fluid.

"Mr. Flannery!"

Flannery went on singing.

"*Mr. Flannery!*"

"Sorr!" The man got unsteadily to his feet, almost knocked himself down again with a flamboyant parody of a salute. "Sorr!"

"Sit down before you fall down!" Grimes ordered sharply. Flannery subsided gratefully. He picked up the bottle, offered it to Grimes, who said, "No, thank you," thinking, *I daren't antagonize this fat, drunken slob. I might need him.* He remarked, "I see you have your new amplifier."

"Indeed I have, Captain. An' he's good, as God's me witness. Inspired, ye were, when ye said I should be takin' Ned."

"Mphm. So you don't anticipate any trouble?"

"Indeed I do not. Ask me to punch a message through to the Great Nebula of Andromeda itself, an' me an' Ned'll do it."

"Mphm." Grimes wondered how he should phrase the next question. He was on delicate ground. But if he had Flannery on his side, working for him, he would have his own, private espionage system, the Rhine Institute's code of ethics notwithstanding. "So you've got yourself another pal. Ha, ha. I wonder what he thinks of the rest of us in this ship . . . me, for example."

"Ye want the God's own truth, Captain?"

"Yes."

"He hates you. If he had his teeth still, he'd be after bitin' you. It's the uniform, ye see, an' the way ye're wearin' it. He remembers the cowardly troopers what did for the Ned who's his blessed namesake."

"Not to mention the jolly swagman," growled Grimes. "But that's all nonsense, Mr. Flannery. You can't tell me that *that's* the brain of a dingo who was around when the Kelly Gang was brought to book!"

Flannery chuckled. "What d'ye take me for, Captain? I don't believe that, an' I'm not expectin' you to. But he's a dog, an' all dogs have this race memory, goin' back to the Dream Time, an' farther back still. And now, Captain, will ye, with all due respect, be gettin' out of here? Ye've got Ned all upset, ye have."

Grimes departed in a rather bad temper, leaving Flannery communing with the whiskey bottle and his weird pet.

»)«Chapter 5»)«

Six hours before liftoff time Grimes received Brandt, the only scientific officer who was making the voyage, in his day cabin. From the very start they clashed. This Dr. Brandt—he soon made it clear that he did not wish to be addressed as "Commander" and that he considered his Survey Service rank and uniform childish absurdities— was, Grimes decided, a typical case of small-man-itis. He did not need to be a telepath to know what Brandt thought about him. He was no more than a bus driver whose job it was to take the learned gentleman to wherever he wished to go.

And then Brandt endeared himself to Grimes still further by putting his thoughts into words. "It's a high time, Captain," said the little, fat, bald, black-bearded man, "that contacts with Lost Colonies were taken out of the clumsy hands of you military types. You do irreparable damage with your interferences. *I* should have been on hand to make a thorough and detailed study of the

New Spartan culture before you ruined it by aiding and abetting revolution."

"Mphm," grunted Grimes.

"And you did the same sort of thing on Morrowvia."

"Did I? I was trying to save the Morrowvians from Drongo Kane—who, in case you don't know, is a slave trader—and from the Dog Star Line, who wanted to turn the whole damn planet into a millionaires' holiday camp."

"Which it is now well on the way to becoming, I hear."

"The Morrowvians will do very nicely out of it. In any case, on neither occasion was I without scientific advice."

"Dr. Lazenby, I suppose you mean. Or Commander Lazenby, as she no doubt prefers to be called. Pah!"

"Wipe the spit off your beard, Doctor," admonished Grimes, his prominent ears flushing angrily. "And, as far as Commander Lazenby is concerned, the advice she gave me was consistentlygood."

"*You* would think so. An ignorant spaceman led up the garden path by a flashily attractive woman."

Luckily Brabham came in just then on some business or other, and Grimes was able to pass Brandt on to the first lieutenant. He sat down at his littered desk and thought, *That cocky little bastard is all I need.* He remembered a captain under whom he had served years ago, who used to exclaim when things went wrong, "I am surrounded by rogues and imbeciles!"

And how many rogues and imbeciles was he, Grimes, surrounded by? He began to make calculations on a scrap of paper.

Control room officers—six.

Electronic communications officers—two.

Psionic communications officer—one (and that was more than ample!).

Supply branch officers—two.

Engineer officers—six.

Medical officer—one.

Marine officer—one.

Scientific officer—one.

That made twenty, in the commissioned ranks alone.

Cooks—four.

Stewards—two.

Stewardesses—four.

That made thirty.

Marines, including the sergeant and corporal—twenty-two.

Fifty-two was now the score.

Petty officers—four.

General purpose ratings—twenty.

Total, seventy-six. Seventy-six people who must have ridden to their parents' weddings on bicycles.

Grimes had done his figuring as a joke, but suddenly it was no longer funny. Normally he enjoyed the essential loneliness of command, but that had been in ships where there was always company, congenial company, when he felt that he needed it. In this vessel there seemed to be nobody at all with whom he could indulge in a friendly drink and a yarn.

Perhaps things would improve.

Perhaps they wouldn't.

Growl you may, he told himself, but go you must.

))((Chapter 6))((

It is always an anxious moment when a captain has to handle a strange ship, with strange officers and crew, for the first time. Grimes, stolidly ensconced in the pilot's chair, tried, not unsuccessfully, to convey the impression that he hadn't a worry in the whole universe. He made the usual major production of filling and lighting his pipe while listening to the countdown routine. "All hands," Brabham was saying into the intercom microphone, "secure ship for liftoff. Secure ship. Secure ship." Lieutenant Tangye, the navigator, was tense in the co-pilot's seat, his hands poised over the duplicate controls. No doubt the slim, blond, almost ladylike young man was thinking that he could make a far better job of getting the old bitch upstairs than this new skipper. Other officers were standing by radar and radar altimeter, NST transceiver, drift indicator, accelerometer, and all the rest of it. It was unnecessary; all the displays were visible to both pilot and co-pilot at a glance—but the bigger the ship the more people for whom jobs must be found.

From the many compartments the reports came in. "All secure."

"All secure for liftoff."

"All secure."

"All secure."

"Any word from Commander Brandt yet?" asked Grimes. "After all, he is a departmental head."

"Nothing yet, sir," replied Brabham.

"Shake him up, will you, Number One."

"Control to Commander Brandt. Have you secured yet? Acknowledge."

Brandt's voice came through the speaker. "*Doctor* Brandt here. Of course I'm secure. This isn't my first time in Space, you know."

Awkward bastard, thought Grimes. He said, "Lifting off."

"Lifting off," repeated Brabham.

At Grimes's touch on the controls the inertial drive, deep in the bowels of the ship, muttered irritably. Another touch—and the muttering became a cacophonous protest, loud even through the layer after layer of sonic insulation. *Discovery* shook herself, her structure groaning. From the NST speaker came the bored voice of Aerospace Control. "You are lifting, *Discovery*. You are clear of the pad. *Bon voyage.*"

"Acknowledge," said Grimes to the radio officer. He didn't need to be informed that the ship was off the ground. His own instruments would tell him that if he bothered to look at them—but the *feel* of the ship made it quite obvious that she was up and clear, lifting faster and faster. In the periscope screen he could see the spaceport area—the clusters of white administration buildings, the foreshortened silvery towers that were ships, big and little, dropping away, diminishing. The red, flashing beacons marking the berth that he had just left were sliding from the center of the display, but it didn't matter. He had been expecting drift, the wind the way it was. If he had been coming in to a landing it would have been necessary to apply lateral thrust; during a liftoff all that was required was to get up through and clear of the atmosphere.

A hint of yaw—

Only three degrees, but Grimes corrected it, more to get the feel of the ship than for any other reason. With the same motivation he brought the red flashers back to the center of the periscope screen. Mphm. The old bitch didn't handle too badly at all. He increased acceleration from a half gee to one gee, to one and a half, to two.

The intercom speaker squawked. "Dr. Brandt, here. What the hell are you playing at up there?"

"Minding our own bloody business!" snapped Grimes into his microphone. "Might I suggest that you do the same?"

Brabham sniggered loudly.

"Emergency rocket drill," ordered Grimes quietly. That, as he had suspected it would, took the grin off the first lieutenant's face. But the reaction drive was here to be used, wasn't it? "Number One, pass the word."

"Attention, all hands," growled Brabham into the intercom. "Stand by for testing of reaction drive. Sudden variations in acceleration are to be expected. Stand by. Stand by."

Grimes pushed a button, looked down at his console.

Under ROCKETS the READY light glowed vivid green. With all his faults, MacMorris kept every system in a state of go. Decisively Grimes cut the inertial drive. His stomach tried to push its way up into his throat as acceleration abruptly ceased. He brought a finger down to the FIRE button, pushed it down past the first, second, and third stops. He felt as well as heard the screaming roar as the incandescent gases rushed through the Venturis, and then the renewal of acceleration pushed him downward into the thick padding of his chair.

"Aerospace Control to *Discovery*. Are those pyrotechnics really necessary?"

"Tell him testing, testing," said Grimes to the radio officer. He succeeded in restarting the inertial drive and cutting the rockets at exactly the same instant. The ship continued to drive upward with no reduction of velocity.

Brabham loudly sighed his relief. "You're lucky," he commented. "Sir. Come to that, we're all lucky."

"What do you mean, Number One?" demanded Grimes.

The first lieutenant laughed sourly. "This is the first time that the reaction drive has been tested within the memory of the oldest man. Commander Tallis would *never* use it."

"How many times must I tell you that I am not Commander Tallis?"

The intercom speaker crackled, then, "Dr. Brandt here. I'm speaking from my laboratory. What the hell is going on? Do you know that you've smashed thousands of credits worth of valuable equipment?"

"You saw it stowed?" Grimes asked Brabham.

"Yes, sir. There was no chance of its shifting."

Grimes signaled to Tangye to take over the controls. "Keep her going as she is, pilot." Then he said into his microphone, "Captain here, Dr. Brandt. Did anything shift?"

"No. But I heard glass breaking in the cases. Delicate apparatus can't stand up to your needlessly violent maneuvers."

"Did you see the stuff packed, Doctor?"

"Of course."

"Then might I suggest that next time you see that your bits and pieces are packed properly? There are excellent padding materials available."

"I hold you entirely responsible for the breakages, Captain."

"You knew that you were embarking in a spaceship, Doctor."

"Yes. I did. But rockets went out generations ago."

"Reaction drive is still fitted to all Survey Service vessels, as you should have known, *Commander* Brandt."

"Pah!"

Grimes returned his attention to ship handling, taking over from Tangye. Overhead—or forward—the sky seen through the control room dome was a dark purple, almost black. In the periscope screen Lindisfarne was assuming a spherical aspect. Outside the ship there was still atmosphere—but atmosphere in the academic sense of the word only. On the dial of the radar altimeter the decades of kilometers were mounting up steadily and rapidly.

There was nothing to do now but to run out and clear of the Van Allens, while the globe that was Lindisfarne dwindled steadily in the periscope screen, a diminishing half-moon, the sunlit hemisphere opalescently aglow.

The stars were bright and unwinking in the black sky, and the polarizers were automatically dimming the harsh glare of the Lindisfarne sun on the beam. Grimes looked at the magnetometer. The bright red warning light was dimming. It gave one last flicker, then turned to green.

"Clear of the Van Allens, sir," announced Tangye belatedly.

Slow reaction time, thought Grimes. He said, "So I see. Cut the inertial drive and line her up on the target star, will you?"

"Aye, aye, sir," replied the young man, smartly enough.

The engines grumbled to a stammering halt. Only then did Tangye busy himself with a star chart, looking through the ports frequently to check the relative positions of the constellations. Grimes refrained from pointing out the sun that he wanted to head for, a second magnitude luminary in the constellation of The Bunny, as this grouping of stars had been dubbed by the first settlers on Lindisfarne. There was, if one had a strong imagination, a suggestion of rabbit's ears and woman's breasts, thought Grimes while his navigator fumbled and bumbled. *If this were a* real *bunny,* he thought sardonically, *young Tangye'd be on target a damn sight sooner!* And how long would it be before Brandt, the obnoxious fool, started to whine about being kept too long in a condition of free fall? Meanwhile, other people besides the navigator were exhibiting shortcomings.

"Number One," Grimes said mildly, "you didn't make the usual announcement on the intercom. Stand by for free fall, setting trajectory and all the rest of it."

"You never told me to, sir."

"It's part of your job to look after these details," snapped Grimes.

"Commander Tallis didn't want announcements made every five minutes. Sir."

"Neither do I. But I want those announcements made that are required by Survey Service regulations."

Then Brandt came through on the intercom. "Doctor Brandt here. What *is* going on up there?"

"Stand by for setting trajectory," said Brabham sulkily into his microphone.

"On target, sir," announced Tangye. "I mean, I've *found* the target."

"Then get on to it."

The directional gyroscopes rumbled into motion. Slowly the ship turned about her axes, centrifugal forces giving an off-center surrogate of gravity. Grimes, looking up into the cartwheel sight set into the dome, saw The Bunny swim slowly into view.

The gyroscopes stopped.

"On target, sir."

"Mphm. Have you allowed for galactic drift, Mr. Tangye?"

"Eh. . . no, sir."

"Then please do so."

There was more delay while Tangye fumbled through the ephemeris, fed data into the control room computer. *All this should have been done before liftoff,* thought Grimes disgustedly. *Damn it all, this puppy couldn't navigate a plastic duck across a bathtub!* He watched the nervous young man, glowering.

"Allowance applied, sir." The gyroscopes restarted as the navigator spoke.

"Being applied, you mean. And are you sure that you're putting it on the right way? All right, all right. Leave it. *I* worked it out roughly before we pushed off."

"On trajectory, sir."

"Thank you." Grimes himself announced over the PA system that the Mannschenn Drive was about to be restarted and that acceleration would be resumed immediately thereafter.

He pushed the button to start the interstellar drive. He could imagine those shining rotors starting to turn, spinning faster and faster, spinning, processing at right angles to all the dimensions of normal space, tumbling through the dark infinities, dragging the ship and all aboard her with them as the temporal precession field built up.

There was the disorientation in space and time to which no spaceman ever becomes inured. There was the uncanny sensation of *déjà vu*. There was, as far as Grimes was concerned, an unusually strong premonition of impending doom. It persisted after everything had returned to normal— to normal, that is, as long as one didn't look out through the viewports at the contorted nebulosities that glimmered eerily where the familiar stars had been. The ship, her restarted inertial drive noisily clattering, the thin, high whine of the Mannschenn Drive pervading every cubic millimeter of her, was speeding through the warped continuum toward her destination.

"Thank you, gentlemen," said Grimes heavily. (*Thank you for what?*) "Normal Deep Space watches and routine, Number One."

"Normal Deep Space watches and routine, sir," replied Brabham.

Grimes unbuckled himself from his chair, got up and went down to his quarters. He poured himself a stiff brandy. Even if he hadn't earned it, he felt that he needed it.

⟫⟪Chapter 7⟫⟪

Nonetheless, Grimes was much happier now that the voyage had started.

The ship was back in her natural element, and so were her people. As long as she was in port—at a major naval base especially—the captain was not the supreme authority. On Lindisfarne, for example, Grimes had come directly under the orders of the officer-in-charge-of-surveys, and of any of that rear admiral's officers who were senior to himself. Too, any rating, petty officer or officer of his own who considered that he had a grievance, could run, screaming, to one or another of the various Survey Service personnel protection societies, organizations analogous to the several guilds, unions, and whatever representing merchant spacemen. Of course, any complaint had to be justifiable—but it was amazing how many complaints, in these decadent days, were held to be warranted. Had MacMorris not been in such bad odor with the officials of the Engineer Officers' Association his tales about

Grimes's alleged bullying would have been listened to; had they been, *Discovery* would never have got away from Lindisfarne.

In Deep Space, everybody knew, a captain could do almost anything to anybody provided that he were willing to face a Board of Inquiry at some later date. He could even order people pushed out of the airlock without spacesuits as long as they were guilty of armed mutiny.

All in all, Grimes was not too displeased with his new command. True, she was an old ship—but as an old ship should be (and sometimes is) she was as comfortable as a well-worn shoe. She was not a taut ship; she never would be or could be that. All of her people were too disheartened by slow, even nonexistent promotion, by the knowledge that they had been passed over, would always be passed over. She was not a happy ship—but once she settled down to the old, familiar routine, once her crew realized that it was less trouble to do things Grimes's way than his predecessor's way, she was not actively unhappy.

Grimes did not mix much with his officers. He would pass the time of day with the watchkeeper when he went up to the control room, he would, naturally, meet people when he made rounds, he took his seat at the head of the senior officers' table at meals, occasions at which scintillating conversation was conspicuous by its absence.

Brabham was too morose, too full of his own woes. MacMorris was as he had been described more than once, an uncouth mechanic, incapable of conversation about anything but machinery. Vinegar Nell could have been good company—she was a highly intelligent, witty woman—but she could not forget that the last time she and Grimes had been shipmates she had been a lieutenant while Grimes was only a lowly ensign. The fact that he was now a commander and captain of a big ship she ascribed to sex and luck rather than ability.

The medical officer, Surgeon Lieutenant Commander Rath, was universally unpopular. He was barely competent, and in civil life his lack of a bedside manner would have militated against financial success. He was a tall, dark, thin (almost skeletal) man and his nickname, to all ranks, was The Undertaker. Nobody liked him, and he liked nobody.

And the Mad Major kept himself very much to himself. He was a Marine, and Marines were, in his opinion, the highest form of interstellar life.

All in all, Grimes began to think as the voyage wore on, the only interesting member of his crew was Flannery. But was it Flannery himself who was interesting—or was it that unfortunate dingo's brain in its tank of nutrient solution? The thing was fascinating—that alleged racial memory, for example. Was it genuine, or was it merely the product of Flannery's fertile, liquor-stimulated imagination? After all, Grimes only had Flannery's word for what Ned was thinking . . . and, according to Flannery, Ned's thoughts were fantastic ones.

"He thinks he remembers you, Captain," said the PCO one day when Grimes dropped in to see him after rounds.

"Mphm. Don't tell me that I'm a reincarnation of the original jolly swagman."

"Indeed ye're not, sorr! He's thinkin' o' you as Bligh!"

"I suppose I should be flattered," admitted Grimes. "But I'm afraid that *I* shall never finish up as an admiral *and* as a colonial governor."

"An' that's not what the black Captain Bligh was famous for, sorr!"

"The mutiny? His first one? But during that, as during the subsequent ones, he was more sinned against than sinning!"

"Not the way that Ned, here, recollects it, Captain."

"Come off it, Mr. Flannery. There weren't any dogs of any kind aboard the *Bounty*."

The telepath stared at his grisly pet through bleary eyes, and his thick lips moved as he subvocalized his thoughts. Then: "Ned wasn't there himself, o' course, Captain, nor any of his blessed forefathers. But he still says as that was the way of it, that the wicked Captain Bligh drove his crew to mutiny, indeed he did."

"Indeed he did not!" snapped Grimes, who had his own ideas about what had happened aboard the ill-fated *Bounty*.

"If that's the way ye feel about it, Captain," murmured Flannery diplomatically.

"It *is* the way I feel about it." And then, a sudden, horrid suspicion forming in his mind: "What *is* all this about Bligh and the *Bounty*! "Are you suggesting. . . ?"

"Indeed I'm not, Captain. An' as for Ned, here"—the waving hand just missed the tank and its gruesome contents—"would he be after tellin' ye, if he could? He would not. He would niver be on the side o' the oppressor."

"Good for him," remarked Grimes sardonically. He got up to leave. "And, Mr. Flannery, you might get this—this mess cleaned up a bit. I did mention it to Miss Russell, but she said that her girls aren't kennelmaids. Those empty bottles . . . and that. . . *bone*."

"But t'is only an old bone, Captain, with niver a shred o' meat nor gristle left on it. Poor Terry—may the blessed saints be kind to the soul of him—knew it was there, an' imagined it like it used to be. An' Ned's the same."

"So it is essential to the efficient working of the amplifier?"

"Indeed it is, sorr."

Grimes stirred the greasy, dog-eared playing cards, spread out on the table for a game of Canfield, with a gingerly forefinger. "And I suppose that these are essential to *your* efficient working?"

"Ye said it, Captain. An' would ye deprive me of an innocent game of patience? An' don't the watch officers in the control room, when ye're not around, set up games o' three-dimensional noughts an' crosses in the plottin' tank, just to while away the weary hours? Ye've done it yerself, like enough."

Grimes's prominent ears flushed. He could not deny it—and if he did this telepath would know that he was lying.

"An' I can do more wi' these than play patience, Captain. Did I iver tell ye that I have Gypsy blood in me veins? Back in the Quid Isle me great, great granny lifted her skirts to a wanderin' tinker. From him, an' through her, I have the gift." The grimy pudgy hands stacked the cards, shuffled them, and then began to rearrange them. "Would ye like a readin? Now?"

"No, thank you," said Grimes as he left.

⟫⟨⟨Chapter 8⟩⟩⟨⟨

Discovery came to New Maine.

New Maine is not a major colony; its overall population barely tops the ten million mark. It is not an unpleasant world, although, even on the equator, it is a little on the chilly side. It has three moons, one so large as to be almost a sister planet, the other two little more than oversized boulders. It is orbited by the usual system of artificial satellites—communication, meteorological, and all the rest of it. The important industries are fisheries and fish processing; the so-called New Maine cod (which, actually, is more of a reptile than a true fish) is a sufficiently popular delicacy on some worlds to make its smoking, packaging, and export worthwhile.

A not very substantial contribution to the local economy is made by the Federation Survey Service sub-Base, which is not important enough to require a high ranking officer-in-charge, these duties being discharged by a mere commander, a passed-over one at that. At the time of

Discovery's visit this was a Commander Denny, a flabby, portly gentleman who looked and acted older than he actually was and who, obviously, had lost all interest in the job long since.

Shortly after berthing at the small, badly run-down naval spaceport, Grimes paid the usual courtesy call on the officer-commanding-base. It was not an occasion demanding full dress, with fore-and-aft hat, frock coat, sword, and all the rest of the anachronistic finery; nonetheless an OCB is an OCB, regardless of his actual rank. The temperature outside the ship was 17°, cool enough to make what Grimes thought of as his "grown-up trousers" comfortable. He changed from his shipboard shorts and shirt into his brass-buttoned, gold-braided black, put on his cap with the scrambled egg on its peak still undimmed by time, made his way down to the after airlock. The Marine on gangway duty, he was pleased to note, was smartly attired; obviously Major Swinton had taken the hints regarding the appearance of his men and, equally obviously, Sergeant Washington had cooperated to the full with his commanding officer in this respect.

The man saluted crisply. "Captain, sir!"

Grimes returned the salute. "Yes?"

"Are you expecting a ground car, sir? If one hasn't been arranged, I'll call one."

"I'll walk," said Grimes. "The exercise will do me good."

Discovery's ramp was still battered and shabby, although a few repairs had been made before departure from Lindisfarne. The ship herself was still showing her many years, the ineradicable signs of neglect as well as of age. But even she, who on her pad at the Main Base had looked like an elderly poor relation, here had the appearance of a rich aunt come a-visiting. Nobody expects to be obliged to eat his meals off a spaceport apron—but there are minimal standards of cleanliness that should be maintained. These were certainly not being maintained here. It was obvious that during the night some large animals had wandered across the expanse of concrete and treated it as a convenience. It was equally obvious that they had done the same during the previous night, and the night before. In addition, there were tall, straggling, ugly weeds thrusting up through ragged cracks, with dirty scraps of plastic and paper piling up around them, entangled with them.

The block of administration buildings toward which Grimes was heading, treading carefully to avoid getting his well-polished shoes dirty, was plain, functional—and like most functional constructions would have been pleasant enough in appearance if only it had been clean. But the wide windows were dull with an accumulation of dust and the entire facade was badly stained. Were there, Grimes wondered, flying creatures on this world as big as the animals that had fouled the apron? He looked up at the dull sky apprehensively. If there were, he hoped that they came out only at night. As he elevated his regard he noticed that the flagstaff atop the office block was not quite vertical and that the Survey Service ensign, flapping lazily in the light breeze, was ragged and dirty, and was not right up to the truck.

The main doors, as he approached them, slid open reluctantly with a distinctly audible squeak. In the hallway beyond them an elderly petty officer, in shabby grays, got slowly up from his desk as Grimes entered. He was not wearing a cap, so he did not salute; but neither did he stiffen to attention.

He asked, "Sir?"

"I am Commander Grimes, captain of *Discovery*."

"Then you'll be wanting to see the old—" He looked at the smartly uniformed Grimes and decided to start again. "You'll be wanting to see Commander Denny. You'll find him in his office, sir." He led the way to a bank of elevators, pressed a button.

"Rather shorthanded, aren't you?" remarked Grimes conversationally.

"Oh, no, sir. On a sub-Base like this it isn't necessary to have more than the duty PO—which is me—manning Reception."

"I was thinking about policing the spaceport apron," said Grimes.

"Oh, *that!*" The petty officer's face did show a faint disgust.

"Yes. That."

"But there's nothing that we can do about the bastards, sir. They always did relieve themselves here, before there was a spaceport. They always will. Creatures of habit, like—"

"They?"

"The great snakes, sir. They're called great snakes, though they're not snakes at all, really. More of a sort of slug. Just imagine a huge sausage that eats at one end and—"

"I get the idea. But you could post guards, suitably armed."

"But the great snakes are protected, sir. There's only the one herd left on the entire planet."

"Then why not a force field fence, with a nonlethal charge."

"Oh, no, sir. That would never do. The Old Man's wife—I beg pardon, sir, the commander's wife—would never stand for it. She's the chairlady of the New Maine Conservationist Association."

"Mphm." At this moment the elevator, which had taken its time about descending, arrived. The door opened. Grimes got into the car as the petty officer said, "Seventh deck, sir." He pressed the right button and was carried slowly upward.Commander Denny's office was as slovenly as his spaceport. Untidiness Grimes did not mind—he never set a good example himself in that respect—but real dirt was something else again. The drift of papers on Denny's desk was acceptable, but the dust-darkened rings on its long-unpolished surface left by mugs of coffee or some other fluids were not. Like his petty officer in Reception, Denny was wearing a shabby gray uniform. So were the two women clerks. Grimes thought it highly probable that it was the elderly, unattractive one who did all the work. The other one was there for decoration— assuming that one's tastes in decoration run to bold-eyed, plump, blonde, micro-skirted flirts.

The Base commander got slowly to his feet, extended a pudgy hand. "Commander Grimes?"

"In person."

The two men shook hands. Denny's grip was flabby.

"And these," went on Denny, "are Ensign Tolley"— the older woman favored Grimes with a tight-lipped smile—"and Ensign Primm." Miss Primm stared at the visitor haughtily. "But sit down, Grimes. You're making my control room—ha, ha—look untidy."

Grimes looked around. There were two chairs available in addition to those occupied by the clerks, but each of them held an overflow of paper.

"Sit down, man. Sit down. This is Liberty Hall. You can spit on the mat and call the cat a bastard."

"I don't see any cats," said Grimes. *Not of the four-legged variety, anyhow,* he thought. "And to judge by the state of your spaceport apron, somebody, or something, has already been. . . er. . . spitting on the mat!"

Surprisingly it was the elderly ensign who laughed, then got up to clear the detritus from one of the chairs. Neither Denny nor the younger woman showed any amusement.

"And now, Commander," asked Denny, "what can I do for you?"

"I shall require the use of your port facilities, Commander," Grimes told him. "I'll be wanting to replenish stores, and my chief engineer could do with some shore labor to lend a hand with his innies; he wants to take them down to find out why they're working, and then he'll have to put them together again. You know what engineers are."

"Yes. I know. And then you'll be off on your Lost Colony hunt, I suppose."

"That's what I'm being paid for. Have you heard any rumors of Lost Colonies out in this sector?"

"I'm just the OCB, Grimes. Nobody ever tells me anything."

And would you be interested if they did? Grimes

wondered. He said, "Our lords and masters must have had something in mind when they sent me out this way."

"And who knows what futile thoughts flicker through their tiny minds? *I* don't."

And you've got to the stage where you don't much care, either, thought Grimes. But he could not altogether blame the man. This dreary sub-Base on a dull world was obviously the end of the road for Denny. Here he would mark time until he reached retirement age. And what about himself? Would this sort of job be his ultimate fate if some admiral or politician upon whose corns he had trodden finally succeeded in having him swept under the carpet and forgotten?

"Oh, Commander," said Denny, breaking into his thoughts.

"Yes, Commander?"

"You'll be getting an official invitation later in the morning. It's quite a while since we had one of our ships in here, so the mayor of Penobscot—that's where the commercial spaceport is—is throwing an official party tonight. Bum freezers and decorations. You and your officers are being asked."

"I can hardly wait."

"The master of *Sundowner* should be there, too, with his people."

"*Sundowner!*"

"She's at Port Penobscot, loading fish. She's a star tramp. Rim Worlds registry. She gets around."

"Mphm. It could be worthwhile having a yarn with him."

"It could be, Commander. These tramp skippers often

stumble on things that our survey captains miss. Sometimes they report them, sometimes they don't."

"You can say that again, Commander. The last Lost Colony that I visited, Morrowvia, the Dog Star Line was trying to keep all to its little self. And it looks as though they'll be able to do just that." Grimes looked at his watch. Denny had made no move to offer him tea, coffee, or anything stronger, and it was past the time when he usually had his morning coffee aboard the ship. "I'd better be getting back to find out what disasters have been happening in my absence. And my departmental heads should have their requisitions ready for my autograph by now."

"I'll see you tonight, Commander," said Denny.

"See you tonight, Commander Denny," said Grimes.

As he let himself out he overheard the younger of the two women say, in a little-too-loud whisper, "Gawd save us all! What a stuck-up tailor's dummy! I hope he treads in something on the way back to his rustbucket!"

⫷⫷Chapter 9⫷⫷

The mayor sent a small fleet of ground cars to pick up *Discovery*'s officers. Grimes, resplendent in black and gold and stiff white linen, with his miniature decorations on their rainbow ribbons a-jingle on the left breast of his mess jacket, rode in the lead vehicle. He was accompanied by Brabham, Major Swinton, Dr. Brandt, and Vinegar Nell. The paymaster looked remarkably handsome in her severely cut, long-skirted evening dress uniform. Swinton, in his dress blue-and-scarlet, had transformed himself from a bad-tempered terrier into a gaudy and pugnacious psittacoid. Brabham (of course) was letting the side down. His mess uniform, when he extricated it from wherever it had been stowed, had proved to be unwearable, stained and creased, and far too tight a fit. He had compromised by wearing a black bow tie, instead of one of the up-and-down variety, with his not-too-shabby double-breasted black outfit. And Brandt, of course, had never possessed a suit of mess kit. He was wearing civilian evening dress, with the sash of some obscure order—the sash itself was far from obscure, being bright purple edged with gold—stretched across his shirt front.

The electric cars sped swiftly along the road between the Base and Penobscot. Dusk was falling fast from a leaden sky, and little could be seen through the wide windows of the vehicles. Even in broad daylight there would have been little to see; this country was desolate moorland, only slightly undulant, with not so much as a tree or a hill or even a stony outcrop to break the monotony. Ahead, brighter and brighter as the darkness deepened and the distance diminished, glared the lights of the port city.

The motorcade swept past the spaceport where *Sundowner,* a stubby tower of metal, stood among the cargo-handling gantries, a briefly glimpsed abstract of black shadows and garish, reflected light. Slowing down at last it skirted the harbor—Penobscot was a seaport as well as a spaceport—and the long quay where the big oceangoing trawlers were discharging their glittering catch.

The mayor's palace overlooked the harbor. It was a big, although not high, building, pseudo-classical, its pillared facade glowing whitely in the floodlights. The approach was along a wide avenue, lined with tall, feathery-leafed trees, in the branches of which colored glow-bulbs had been strung. Brabham muttered something in a sour voice about every day being Christmas on New Maine. Vinegar Nell told him tartly to shut up. The chauffeur said nothing, but Grimes could sense the man's resentment.

The car drew to a halt in the portico. The driver left his seat to open the door for his passengers—the sort of courtesy that was long vanished from Earth but that still persisted in many of the colonies. Grimes was first out, then assisted Vinegar Nell, who was having a little trouble with her unaccustomed long skirt, to the ground. Brabham dismounted, then Swinton, then Brandt. The chauffeur saluted smartly and returned to his driving seat in the car, which sped off in a spattering of fine golden gravel.

Grimes limped to the wide doorway—a tiny pebble had got inside his right shoe—followed by the others. Mingled music and light flowed out into the portico. Standing by a group of heroic statuary—well-muscled, naked women wrestling with some sort of sea serpent— was a portly individual whom Grimes took, at first, for a local admiral. This resplendently uniformed person bowed, albeit with more condescension than obsequiousness, and inquired smoothly, "Whom shall I announce, sir?"

"Commander Grimes, captain of the Survey Ship *Discovery*. And with me are Commander Brandt, of the scientific branch, Lieutenant Commander Brabham, my executive officer, Major Swinton, of the Federation Marines, and Lieutenant Russell, my paymaster."

The functionary raised a small megaphone to his mouth; with it he could compete quite easily with the buzz of conversation and the music from the synthesizer. "Captain Grimes . . . Commander Brandt. . ."

"*Doctor* Brandt!" snarled the scientist, but he was ignored.

"Lieutenant Commander Brabham . . . Major Swinton . . . Lieutenant Russell."

Grimes found himself shaking hands with a wiry little man in a bright green evening suit, with an ornate gold chain of office about his neck. "Glad to have you aboard, Captain!"

"Commander, Mr. Mayor," corrected Grimes. "Your majordomo seems to have promoted me."

"You're captain of a ship, aren't you?" The mayor grinned whitely. "Come to that, I always call Bill Davinas 'commodore.' I'll hand you over to him now while I greet your officers."

Grimes shook hands with Davinas, a tall, dark, black-and-gold-uniformed man with four gold stripes on each of his epaulettes, who said, "I'm the master of *Sundowner,* Commander. You probably noticed her at the spaceport. I've been a regular trader here since Rim Runners pushed me off my old routes; the small, private owner just can't compete with a government shipping line."

"And what do I call you, sir? Commodore, or captain?"

"Bill, for preference." Davinas laughed. "That commodore business is just the mayor's idea of a joke. The *Sundowner* Line used to own quite a nice little fleet, but now it's down to one ship. So I'm the line's senior master—senior and only—which does make me a courtesy commodore of sorts. But I don't get paid any extra. Ah, here's a table with some good stuff. I can recommend these codfish patties, and this local rosé isn't at all bad."

While he sipped and nibbled Grimes looked around the huge ballroom. The floor was a highly polished black, reflecting the great, glittering electroliers, each one a crystalline complexity, suspended from the shallow dome of the ceiling, which was decorated with ornate bas-reliefs in a floral pattern. Along the white-pillared walls panels of deep blue, in which shone artificial stars set in improbable constellations, alternated with enormous mirrors. The overall effect was overpowering, with the crowd of gaily dressed people reflected and re-reflected to infinity on all sides. Against the far wall from the main doorway was the great synthesizer, an intricacy of transparent tubes through which rainbow light surged and eddied, a luminescent fountain containing within itself orchestra, choir, massed military bands—and every other form of music that Man has contrived to produce during his long history. The fragile blonde seated at the console—which would not have looked out of place in the control room of a Nova Class dreadnought—could certainly handle the thing. *Beauty and the beast*, thought Grimes.

"Jenkins' Folly," announced Davinas, waving an arm expansively.

"Jenkins' Folly?"

"This palace. The first mayor of Penobscot was a Mr. Jenkins. He'd got it firmly fixed in his thick head that New Maine was going to go the same way as so many—too many—other colonies. Population expansion. Population explosion. Bam! According to his ideas, this city was going to run to a population of about ten million. But it never happened. As you know, the population of the entire planet is only that. Once New Maine had enough people to maintain a technological culture with most of the advantages and few of the drawbacks the ZPG boys and girls took control. So this palace, this huge barn of a place, is used perhaps three times a year. Anniversary Day. New Year's Day. The Founder's Birthday. And, of course, on the very rare occasions when one of *your* ships, with her horde of officers, drops in."

"Mphm."

"Ah, here you are, Commander Grimes." It was Denny, looking considerably smarter than he had in his office, although the short Eton jacket of his mess uniform displayed his plump buttocks, in tightly stretched black, to disadvantage. "Clarice, my dear, this is Commander Grimes. Commander Grimes, meet the little woman."

Mrs. Denny was not a little woman. She was . . . vast. Her pale flesh bulged out of her unwisely low-cut dress, which was an unfortunate shade of pink. She was huge, and she gushed. "It's always good to see new faces, Commander, even though we are all in the same family."

"Ah, yes. The Survey Service."

She giggled and wobbled. "Not the Survey Service, Commander Grimes. The *big* family, I mean. Organic life throughout the universe."

If she'd kept it down to the mammalia, thought Grimes, looking with fascination at the huge, almost fully revealed breasts, *it'd make more sense.* He said, "Yes, of course. Although there are some forms of organic life I'd sooner not be related to. Those great snakes of yours, for instance."

"But you haven't *seen* them, Commander."

"I've seen the evidence of their passing, Mrs. Denny."

"But they're so sweet, and trusting."

"Mphm."

"She's playing our tune, dear," Denny put in hastily, extending his arms to his wife. He got them around her somehow, and the couple moved off to join the other dancers.

Grimes looked around for Davinas but the merchant

captain had vanished, had probably made his escape as soon as the Denny couple showed up. He poured himself another glass of wine and looked at the swirling dancers. Some of them, most of them, were singing to the music of the synthesizer, which was achieving the effect of an orchestra of steel guitars.

> *Spaceman, the stars are calling,*
> *Spaceman, you live to roam,*
> *Spaceman, down light-years falling,*
> *Remember I wait at home. . . .*

Icky, thought Grimes. *Icky.* But he had always liked the thing, in spite of (because of?) its sentimentality. He started to sing the words himself in a not very tuneful voice.

"I didn't think you had it in you, Captain."

Grimes cut himself off in mid-note, saw that Vinegar Nell had joined him. It was obvious that the tall, slim woman had taken a drink—or two, or three. Her cheeks were flushed and her face had lost its habitually sour expression. She went on, "I'd never have dreamed that you're a sentimentalist."

"I'm not, Miss Russell. Or am I? Never mind. There are just some really corny things I love, and that song is one of them." Then, surprising himself at least as much as he did her: "Shall we dance?"

"Why not?"

They moved out onto the floor. She danced well, which was more than could be said for him. Normally, on such occasions, he was all too aware of his deficiencies—but all that he was aware of now was the soft pressure of her breasts against his chest, the firmer pressure and the motion of her thighs against his own. And there was no need for them to dance so closely; in spite of the illusory multitude moving in the mirrors the floor was far from crowded.

Watch it, Grimes, he admonished himself. *Watch it! And why the hell should I?* part of him demanded mutinously.

That's why! he snarled mentally as one of his own officers, a junior engineer, swept past, holding a local lass at least as closely as Grimes was holding the paymaster. The young man leered and winked at his captain. Grimes tried to relax his grip on Vinegar Nell, but she wasn't having any. Her arms were surprisingly strong.

At last the music came to a wailing conclusion. "I enjoyed that," she said.

"So did I, Miss Russell," admitted Grimes. "Some refreshment?" he asked, steering her toward one of the buffet tables.

"But I should be looking after you." She laughed. It wasn't so much what she said, but the way that she said it. "Mphm," he grunted aloud.

Captain Davinas was already at the table with his partner, a tall, plain local woman. "Ah," he said, "we meet again, Commander."

Introductions were made, after which, to the disgust of the ladies, the men started to talk shop. The music began again and, with some reluctance, Vinegar Nell allowed herself to be led off by the Penobscot police commissioner, and the other lady by the first mate of *Sundowner*.

"Thank all the odd gods of the galaxy for that!" Davinas

laughed. "I have to dance with her some of the time—
she's the wife of my Penobscot agent—but she'll settle for
one of my senior officers. Talking of officers—I'll swap my
purser for your paymaster any day, John!"

"You don't know her like I do, Bill," Grimes told him,
feeling oddly disloyal as he said it. He allowed Davinas to
refill his glass, tried to ignore the beseeching glances of
three young ladies seated not far from them. "Oh, well, I
suppose we'd better find ourselves partners, especially
since there seems to be a shortage of men here. But I'd
sooner talk. Frankly, I'm sniffing around for information
on this sector of space—but I suppose that can wait until
tomorrow."

"Not unless you want a job as fourth mate aboard
Sundowner. I lift ship for Electra bright and early—well,
early—tomorrow morning."

"A pity."

"It needn't be. I'm not much of a dancing man. I'd
sooner earbash and be earbashed over a cold bottle or two
than be dragged around the floor by the local talent. And
I was intending to return to my ship very shortly, anyhow.
Why not come with me? We can have a talk on board."

)))(((Chapter 10)))(((

Davinas and Grimes slipped out of the ballroom almost unnoticed. A few cabs were waiting hopefully in the portico, so they had no difficulty in obtaining transport to the spaceport. It was a short drive only, and less than twenty minutes after they had left the palace Davinas was leading the way up the ramp to the after airlock of *Sundowner*.

It is impossible for a spaceman to visit somebody else's ship without making comparisons—and Grimes was busy making them. Here, of course, there was no uniformed Marine at the gangway, only a civilian night watchman supplied by the vessel's local agent, but the ramp itself was in better repair than *Discovery*'s, and far cleaner. It was the same inboard. Everything was old, worn, but carefully—lovingly, almost—maintained. Somehow the merchant captain had been able to instill in his people a respect—at least—for their ship. Grimes envied him. But in all likelihood Davinas had never been cursed with a full

434

crew of malcontents, and would have been able to extract and dump the occasional bad apple from this barrel without being obliged to fill in forms in quintuplicate to explain just why.

The elevator cage slid upward swiftly and silently, came to a smooth stop. Davinas showed Grimes into his comfortable quarters. "Park the carcass, John. Make yourself at home. This is Liberty Hall; you can spit on the mat . . ."

". . . and call the cat a bastard," finished Grimes.

"Then why don't you?"

Grimes felt something rubbing against his legs, looked down, saw a large tortoiseshell tom. The animal seemed to have taken a fancy to him. He felt flattered. In spite of the affair on Morrowvia he still liked cats.

"Coffee?"

"Thanks."

Davinas poured two mugs from a large thermos container, then went into the office adjoining his dayroom. Grimes, while he petted the cat, looked around. He was intrigued by the pictures on the bulkheads of the cabin, holograms of scenes on worlds that were strange to him. One was a mountainscape—jagged peaks, black but snow-capped, thrusting into a stormy sky, each summit with its spume of ice particles streaming down wind like white smoke. He could almost hear the shrieking of the icy gale. Then there was one that could have been a landscape in Hell—contorted rocks, gaudily colored, half veiled by an ocher sandstorm.

Davinas came back, carrying a large folder. "Admiring the art gallery? That one's the Desolation Range on Lorn, my home world. And *that* one is the Painted Badlands on Eblis. Beats me why some genius doesn't open a tourist resort there. Spectacular scenery, friendly indigenes, and quite a few valleys where the likes of us could live quite comfortably."

"The Rim Worlds," murmured Grimes. "I've heard quite a lot about them, off and on. Somehow the Survey Service never seems to show the flag in that sector of space. I don't suppose I'll ever see them."

Davinas laughed. "Don't be so sure. Rim Runners'll take anybody, as long as he has some sort of certificate of competency and rigor mortis hasn't set in!"

"If they ever get me," declared Grimes, "that'll be the sunny Friday!"

"Or me," agreed Davinas. "When the *Sundowner* Line finally folds I'm putting my savings into a farm."

The two men sipped their good coffee. Davinas lit a long, slim cigar, Grimes his pipe. The cat purred noisily between them.

Then: "I hear that you're on a Lost Colony hunt, John."

"Yes, Bill. As a matter of fact, Commander Denny did mention that you might be able to give me a few leads."

"I might be. But, as a Rim Worlds citizen, I'm supposed to make any reports on anything I find to the Rim Worlds government. And to my owners, of course."

"But the Rim Worlds are members of the Federation."

"Not for much longer, they're not. Surely you've heard talk of secession lately." Davinas laughed rather unpleasantly. "But I'm not exactly in love with our local lords and masters. I've been in the *Sundowner* Line practically all my working life, and I haven't enjoyed seeing our fleet pushed off the trade routes by Rim Runners. *They* can afford to cut freights; they've the taxpayer's money behind them. And who's the taxpayer? Me."

"But what about your owners? Don't you report to them?"

"They just aren't interested anymore. The last time that I made a deviation, sniffing around for a possible new run for *Sundowner*, there was all hell let loose." He obviously quoted from a letter. "'We would point out that you are a servant of a commercial shipping line, not a captain in the Federation Survey Service . . .' Ha!"

"Mphm. So you might be able to help me?"

"I might. If you ask me nicely enough, I will." He poured more coffee into the mugs. "You carry a PCO, of course?"

"Of course. And you?"

"No. Not officially. Our head office now and again— only now and again, mind you—realizes that there is such a force as progress. They found out that one of the early Carlotti sets was going cheap. So now I have Carlotti, and no PCO. But—"

"But what?"

"My NST operator didn't like it. He was too lazy to do the Carlotti course to qualify in FTL radio. He reckoned, too, that he'd be doing twice the work that he was doing before, and for the same pay. So he resigned, and joined Rim Runners. They're very old-fashioned, in some ways. They don't have Carlotti equipment in many of their ships yet. They still carry psionic communication officers and Normal Space-Time radio officers."

"Old-fashioned?" queried Grimes. "Perhaps they still carry PCOs for the same reason as we do. To sniff things out."

"That's what I tried to tell my owners when they took away Parley's amplifier, saying that its upkeep was a needless expense. A few spoonfuls of nutrient chemicals each trip, and a couple of little pumps! But I'm getting ahead of myself. This Parley *was* my PCO. He's getting on in years, and knows that he hasn't a hope in hell of finding a job anywhere else. Unlike the big majority of telepaths he has quite a good brain and, furthermore, doesn't shy away from machinery, up to and including electronic gadgetry. He actually took the Carlotti course and examination, and qualified, and also qualified as an NST operator. So now he's my radio officer, NST, and Carlotti. It breaks his heart at times to have to push signals over the light-years by electronic means, but he does it. If they'd let him keep his beagle's brain in aspic he'd still be doing it the good old way, and the Carlotti transceiver would be gathering dust. But with no psionic amplifier, he just hasn't the range."

"No. He wouldn't have."

"Even so, if one passes reasonably close to a planet, within a few light-years, a good telepath can pick up the psionic broadcast, provided that the world in question has a sizable population of sentient beings."

"Human beings?"

"Not necessarily. But our sort of people, more or less. I'm told that there's no mistaking the sort of broadcast you get from one of the Shaara worlds, for example. Arthropods, however intelligent, just don't think like mammals."

"And you have passed reasonably close to a planet with an intelligent, mammalian population? One that's not on any of the lists?"

"Two of them, as a matter of fact. In neighboring planetary systems."

"Where?"

"That'd be telling, John. Nothing for nothing, and precious little for a zack. That's the way that we do business in the *Sundowner* Line!"

"Then what's the *quid pro quo,* Bill?"

Davinas laughed. "I didn't think that you trade school boys were taught dead languages! All right. This is it. Just let me know what you find. As I've already told you, the *Sundowner* Line's on its last legs; I'd like to keep us running just a little longer. A new trade of our own could make all the difference."

"There are regulations, you know," said Grimes slowly. "I can't go blabbing the Survey Service's secrets to any Tom, Dick, or Harry. Or Bill."

"Not even when they were Bill's secrets to begin with? Come off it. And I do happen to know that those same regulations empower you, as captain of a Survey Service ship, to use your own discretion when buying information. Am I right?"

"Mphm." Grimes was tempted. Davinas could save him months of fruitless searching. On the one hand, a quick conclusion to his quest would be to his credit. On the other hand, for him to let loose a possibly unscrupulous tramp skipper on a hitherto undiscovered Lost Colony would be to acquire yet another big black mark on his record. But this man was no Drongo Kane. He said, "You know, of course, that I carry a scientific officer. He has the same rank as myself, but if I do find a Lost Colony he'll be wanting to take charge, and I may have to take a back seat."

"If he wants to set up any sort of Base," countered Davinas, "he'll be requiring regular shipments of stores and equipment and all the rest of it. Such jobs, as we both know, are usually contracted out. And if I'm Johnny-on-the-spot, with a reasonable tender in my hot little hand—"

It made sense, Grimes thought. He asked, "And will you want any sort of signed agreement, Bill?"

"You insult me, and you insult yourself. Your word's good enough, isn't it?"

"All right." Grimes had made up his mind. "Where are these possible Lost Colonies of yours?"

"Parley picked them up," said Davinas, "when I was right off my usual tramlines—*anybody's* usual tramlines, come to that—doing a run between Rob Roy and Caribbea." He pushed the coffee mugs and the thermos bottle to one side, opened the folder that he had brought from his office on the low table. He brought out a chart. "Modified Zimmerman Projection." His thin forefinger stabbed decisively. "The Rob Roy sun, here. And Sol, as the Caribbeans call their primary, here. Between them, two G type stars, 1716 and 1717 in Ballchin's catalog, practically in line, and as near as damn it on the same plane as Rob Roy and Caribbea. Well clear of the track, actually—but not too well clear."

"It rather surprises me," said Grimes, "that nobody has found evidence of intelligent life there before."

"Why should it? When those old lodejammers were blown away to hell and gone off course—assuming that these worlds *are* Lost Colonies, settled by lodejammer survivors—PCOs hadn't been dreamed of. When your Commodore Slater made his sweep through that sector of space, PCOs still hadn't been dreamed of. Don't forget that we had FTL ships long before we had FTL radio, either electronic or psionic."

"But what about the odd merchant ships in more recent years, each with her trained telepath?"

"What merchant ships? As far as I know, *Sundowner* was the only one to travel that route, and just once, at that. I happened to be on Rob Roy, discharging a load of kippered New Maine cod, and the word got through to my agents there that one of the transgalactic clippers, on a cruise, was due in at Caribbea. She'd been chartered by some Terry outfit calling themselves The Sons of Scotia. And it seems that they were going to celebrate some Earth calendar religious festival—Burns Night—there."

"Burns?" murmured Grimes. "Let me see. Wasn't he a customs officer? An odd sort of chap to deify."

"Ha, ha. Anyhow, the Punta del Sol Hotel at Port of Spain sent an urgent Carlottigram to Rob Roy to order a large consignment of haggis and Scotch whiskey. I was the only one handy to lift it. I got it there on time, too, although I just about burned out the main bearings of the Mannschenn Drive doing it."

"And did they enjoy their haggis?" wondered Grimes.

"I can't say. *I* didn't. The shippers presented me with half a dozen of the obscene things as a token of their appreciation. Perhaps we didn't cook them properly."

"Or serve them properly. I don't suppose that *Sundowner* could run to a bagpiper to pipe them in to the messroom table."

"That could have been the trouble." Davinas looked at his watch. "I hate to hurry you up, John—but I always like to get my shut-eye before I take the old girl upstairs. But, before you go, I'd like to work out some way that you can let me know if you find anything. A simple code for a message, something that can't be cracked by the emperor of Waverley's bright boys. As you see from the chart, those two suns are practically inside Waverley's sphere of influence. I want to be first ship on the scene—after you, of course. I don't want to be at the tail end of a long queue of Imperial survey ships and freighters escorted by heavy cruisers."

"Fair enough," agreed Grimes. "Fair enough. Just innocent Carlottigrams that could be sent by anybody, to anybody. Greetings messages? Yes. Happy Birthday, say, for the first world, that belonging to 1717. Happy Anniversary for the 1716 planet. Signed 'John' if it's worth your while to persuade your owners to let you come sniffing around.

"Signed 'Peter' if you'd be well advised not to come within a hundred light-years.

"But you'll be hearing from me. I promise you that."

"Thank you," said Davinas. "Thank *you*," said Grimes.

»«(Chapter 11)»«(

Davinas phoned down to the night watchman to ask him to order a cab for Grimes. While they were waiting for the car he poured glasses of an excellent Scotch whiskey from Rob Roy. They were finishing their drinks when the night watchman reported that the car was at the ramp.

Grimes was feeling smugly satisfied when he left *Sundowner*. It certainly looked as though he had been handed his Lost Colony—correction, *two* Lost Colonies— on a silver tray. And this Davinas was a very decent bloke, and deserved any help that Grimes would be able to give him.

The ride back to the mayor's palace was uneventful. The party was still in progress in the huge ballroom; the girl at the synthesizer controls was maintaining a steady flow of dance music, although only the young were still on the floor. The older people were gathered around the buffet tables, at which the supplies of food and drink were being replenished as fast as they dwindled.

Grimes joined Brabham and Vinegar Nell, who were tucking into a bowl of caviar as though neither of them had eaten for a week, washing it down with locally made vodka,

"Be with us, sir," said Brabham expansively. "A pity they didn't bring *this* stuff out earlier. If I'd known this was going to come up, I'd not have ruined my appetite on fishcakes and sausage rolls!"

Grimes spread a buttered biscuit with the tiny, black, glistening eggs, topped it up with a hint of chopped onion and a squeeze of lemon juice. "You aren't doing too badly now. Mphm. Not bad, not bad."

"Been seeing how the poor live, sir?" asked the first lieutenant.

"What do you mean?"

"You went off with *Sundowner*'s old man."

"Oh, yes. He has quite a nice ship. Old, but very well looked after."

"Sometimes I wonder if I wouldn't have done better in the merchant service," grumbled Brabham. "Even the Rim Worlds Merchant Service. I was having a yarn with *Sundowner*'s chief officer. He tells me that the new government-owned shipping line, Rim Runners, is recruiting personnel. I've a good mind to apply."

"Nobody in the Survey Service would miss you," said Vinegar Nell. Then, before Brabham could register angry protest, she continued, "Nobody in the Survey Service would miss any of us. We're the square pegs, who find that every hole's a round one." She turned to Grimes, who realized that she must have been drinking quite heavily. "Come on, Captain! Out with it! What was in your sealed orders? Instructions to lose us all down some dark crack in the continuum, yourself included?"

"Mphm," grunted Grimes noncommittally, helping himself to more caviar. He noticed that the civilians in the vicinity had begun to flap their ears. He said firmly, "Things aren't as bad as they seem." He tried to make a joke of it. "In any case, I haven't lost a ship yet."

"There has to be a first time for everything," she said darkly.

"*Some* people are lucky," commented Brabham. "In the Survey Service, as everywhere else, luck counts for more than ability."

"Some people have neither luck *nor* ability," said Vinegar Nell spitefully. The target for this barbed remark was obvious—and Brabham, feared Grimes, would be quite capable of emptying the bowl of caviar over her head if she continued to needle him. And the captain of a ship, justly or unjustly, is held responsible for the conduct of his officers in public places. His best course of action would be to separate his first lieutenant and his paymaster before they came to blows.

"Shall we dance, Miss Russell?" he asked.

She produced a surprisingly sweet smile. "But of course, Captain."

The synthesizer was playing a song that he had heard before, probably a request from those of *Sundowner*'s people who were still at the party. The tune was old, very old, but the words were new, and Rim Worlders had come to regard it as their very own.

Good-bye, I'll run to find another sun

> *Where I may find*
> *There are worlds more kind*
> > *than the ones left behind . . .*

Vinegar Nell, fitting into his arms as though she belonged there, had always belonged there, was singing softly as she danced. And was he, Grimes, dancing as well as he thought he was? Probably not, he admitted to himself, but she made him feel that he was cutting a fine figure on the polished floor. And she was making him feel rather more than that. He was acutely conscious of the tightness of the crotch of his dress trousers.

When the number was over he was pleased to see that Brabham had wandered off somewhere by himself, but he was not pleased when Commander Denny claimed Vinegar Nell for the next dance, and still less pleased when he found himself having to cope with Denny's wife. He suffered. It was like having to tow an unwieldy captive balloon through severe atmospheric turbulence. But then the Mayoress made a welcome change, although she chattered incessantly. After her, there were a few girls whose names he promptly forgot.

Vinegar Nell again, and the last dance.

> *Good night! ladies,*
> *Good night, ladies,*
> *Good night, ladies . . .*
> *We're bound to leave you now. . . .*

"But you don't have to leave *me*, John," she whispered. Mphm?

And everybody was singing:

> *Merrily we roll along,*
> *Roll along, roll along,*
> *Merrily we roll along*
> *O'er the bright blue sea. . . .*

He said, "We have to roll along back to the ship, after we've said our good nights, and thanked the mayor for his party."

She said, her mood suddenly somber, "There's no place else to roll. Not for us."

The synthesizer emitted a flourish of trumpets, a ruffle of drums. The dancers froze into attitudes of stiff—or not so stiff—attention. Blaring brass against a background of drumbeats, an attempt to make dreadfully trite melody sound important. It was one of those synthetic, utterly forgettable national anthems, the result, no doubt, of a competition, selected by the judges as the poor best of a bad lot. The words matched the music:

> *New Maine, flower of the galaxy,*
> *New Maine, stronghold of liberty. . . .*

Then: "Good night, Mr. Mayor. On behalf of my officers I must thank you for a marvelous party."

"Good night, Captain. It was a pleasure to have you aboard. Good night, Miss Russell. If the Survey Service had more paymasters like you, I'd be a spaceman myself. Ha, ha! Good night. . . good night."

"Good night."

The ground cars were waiting outside, in the portico. As before, Grimes rode in the lead vehicle with Vinegar Nell and Dr. Brandt. With them, this time, was the chief engineer.

"A waste of valuable time, these social functions," complained the scientist as they sped back toward the Base.

"Ye were nae darin' sae bad on the free booze an' tucker," pointed out MacMorris.

"And neither were you, Chief," put in Vinegar Nell.

"Ah'm no' a dancin' man, not like our gallant captain. An' as for the booze an' tucker—it's aye a pleasure to tak' a bite an sup wi'oot havin' you begrudgin' every mouthful!"

"I still say that it was a waste of time," stated Brandt. "Commander Grimes, for example, could have spent the evening going through the port captain's records to see if there are any reports of Lost Colonies."

"Mphm," grunted Grimes smugly, happily conscious of the folded copy of the chart that Davinas had given him, stiff in the inside breast pocket of his mess jacket.

They were approaching the Base now. There stood *Discovery*, a tall metal steeple, dull-gleaming in the wan light of the huge, high, lopsided moon. And there were great dark shapes, sluglike, oozing slowly over the concrete apron of the spaceport.

"Filthy brutes!" exclaimed the driver, breaking the morose silence that he had maintained all the way from the mayor's palace.

"Great snakes?" asked Grimes.

"What else, Captain? Whoever decided that those

bloody things should be protected should have his bloody head read!"

"You, man!" snapped Brandt. "Take us in close to one of them! Put your spotlight on it!"

"Not on your bloody life, mister! If anything scares those bastards, they *squirt*. And they squirt all over what scares 'em! I have to keep this car clean, not you. Now, here you are, lady and gentlemen. I've brought you right back to your own front door. A very good night to you— what's left of it!"

They got out of the car, which had stopped at the foot of *Discovery*'s ramp. The air was heavy with the sweet-sour stench of fresh ordure. Something splattered loudly not far from them. Their vehicle, its motor whining shrilly, made a hasty departure.

"Are you waiting outside to study the great snakes at close quarters, Doctor?" asked Grimes. "I'm not." He started up the ramp, as hastily as possible without loss of dignity, Vinegar Nell beside him. MacMorris came after and then, after only a second's hesitation, Brandt. At the outer airlock door the Marine sentry came to attention, saluted. Grimes wondered if the man would be as alert after Major Swinton was back safely on board.

The elevator cage was waiting for them. They got into it, were lifted through the various levels. Vinegar Nell, Brandt, and MacMorris got out at the officers' deck. Grimes carried on to Control, found the duty officer looking out through the viewport at the lights of the cars still coming in from Penobscot.

"Oh, good morning, sir." Then, a little wistfully, "Was it a good party?"

"It was, Mr. Farrow. Quite good." Grimes yawned. "If any of those . . . *things* try to climb up the side of the ship to do their business, let me know. Good night, or good morning, or whatever."

He went down to his quarters. He did not, he realized with some surprise, feel all that tired. He subsided into an armchair, pulled out from his pocket the copy of the star chart, unfolded it. Yes, it was certainly a good lead, and Captain Davinas was entitled to some reward for having given it to him.

There was a knock at the door.

"Come in!" he called, wondering whom it could be. Not Brabham, he hoped, with some trifling but irritating worry that could well wait until a more civilized hour.

It was Vinegar Nell. She was carrying a tray upon which were a coffeepot, a cup—no, *two* cups—and a plate of sandwiches. She had changed out of her evening dress uniform into something that was nothing much over nothing at all. Grimes had seen her naked often enough in the sauna adjoining the ship's gymnasium, but this was . . . different. The spectacle of a heavily perspiring female body is not very aphrodisiac; that same body suggestively and almost transparently clad is.

She said, "I thought you'd like a snack before turning in, John."

"Thank you—er—Miss Russell."

She stooped to set the tray on the coffee table. The top of her filmy robe fell open. Her pink-nippled breasts were high and firm.

"Shall I pour?" she asked.

"Er, yes. Please."

She handed him a steaming cup. He was uncomfortably aware of the closeness of her, and fidgeted in his chair. He was relieved when she retired to a chair of her own.

She said, "It was a good night, wasn't it?"

"Yes."

She went on, "I've known you for *years*, haven't I? When was it that we were first shipmates? In the old *Aries*, wasn't it?

"Yes."

"You know, John, I didn't much like you then."

"You didn't much like any of us in the wardroom. After all, you were the very first spacegoing female officer of the Supply Branch, and you were . . . prickly."

She laughed. "And you, a bright young lieutenant junior-grade, took pity on me, and made a pass at me out of the kindness of your heart."

Grimes's prominent ears were burning painfully. He could recall that scene all too well, could feel that stinging slap on his face and hear her furious voice: *Take your mucky paws off me, you insufferable puppy!*

He thought, *And a commander, the captain of a ship, doesn't have mucky paws, of course. But whatever sort of paws I do have, now, I'm keeping them to myself. Why, oh why, you stupid bitch, did you have to rake up that particular episode from the murky past?*

She was smiling softly. "We've come a long way since then, haven't we, John?"

"Mphm. Yes. Excellent coffee, this, Miss Russell. And these are very good sandwiches."

"Yes. You always liked your belly."

Again the memories: *You swaggering spacemen think*

that you're the Lord's anointed, but you aren't worth your keep, let alone your salaries.

"Gutsy Grimes, the stewards and stewardesses used to call you."

"Oh. Did they?" Grimes put down a sandwich half eaten.

"Gutsy Grimes, the human garbage chute," she reminisced sentimentally.

"Fascinating."

And what was that perfume that she was wearing? Whatever it was, he decided that he didn't like it. He looked at his watch. "A spot of shut-eye is indicated. We have a busy day ahead of us tomorrow. Today, I mean."

She rose slowly to her feet, stretched and yawned like a lazy, graceful cat. Her robe fell open. Under the UV lamps in the ship's sun room she always freckled rather than tanned, and the effect was far from displeasing—yet Grimes, perversely, forced himself to think disparagingly of mutant leopards.

He yawned himself, then decisively drained his cup, set it down on the tray with a clatter. He said, "Thanks for the supper. I enjoyed it."

"I did, too."

Then, very firmly, "Good night, Miss Russell."

She flushed all over her body. "*Good night?* You don't mean . . . ?"

"I do mean. I'm turning in. By myself. Good night."

Without looking again at her he went through into his bedroom. He was afraid that she would (would not?) follow him. She did not. As he undressed he heard a vicious clattering as she put the remaining supper things back on the tray, then heard the outer door open and close behind her.

You bloody fool! he admonished himself. *You bloody, bloody fool!* But he thought (he hoped) that he had acted wisely. Vinegar Nell, as a *de facto* Captain's Lady, would very soon try to assume *de facto* command of the ship. On the other hand, because of his out-of-character puritanism, he could have made a dangerous enemy. He did not sleep at all well.

»«(Chapter 12)»«

Discovery did not stay long on New Maine, although most of her people, who had speedily made friends locally, would have welcomed a longer sojourn on that planet.

Grimes feared that some ship, deviating from the usual route, might stumble upon Davinas' Lost Colonies at any moment. He had been given access to the up-to-the-minute Lloyd's Register in the Penobscot port captain's office and had discovered that the majority of the ships of the Waverley Royal Mail had not yet made the change-over from psionic Deep Space communications to the Carlotti system. And Ballchin 1716 and 1717 were almost within the territorial space of the Empire of Waverley. The ruling emperor—as was known to Grimes, as a naval officer of the Federation—was not averse to the expansion of his already considerable dominions.

Discovery did not stay long on New Maine, which meant that her crew did not enjoy the shore leave that they had been expecting. It meant too that all hands, the senior officers especially, were obliged to dedigitate. Brabham, of whom it had been said that he had only two speeds, Dead Slow and Stop, was resentful. MacMorris, who had been looking forward to an orgy of taking apart and putting together, was resentful. Brandt, who had been given the run of the extensive library of the University of New Maine, was resentful. Vinegar Nell was resentful for more reasons than the short stay at the sub-Base.

"Commander Grimes," complained Brandt, "even though *you* are doing nothing to turn up possible leads, *I*, in the little time that I shall be given, am sifting through *years* of records."

But Grimes kept Davinas' information to himself. He knew what would happen if it leaked, just as Davinas himself had known. There would be an urgent Carlottigram from New Maine—where the empire maintained a trade commissioner—to Waverley, and long before *Discovery* arrived off those Lost Colonies some Imperial cruiser would have planted the thistle flag.

Brabham sulked, MacMorris sulked, Brandt sulked, Swinton snarled, and Vinegar Nell was positively vicious.

"I suppose you know what you're doing, Captain."

"I hope you realize the consequences if the algae tanks go bad on us, Captain."

"I suppose you know that it's practically impossible to replenish the beef tissue culture in the time you've given me, Captain."

"I'm afraid that I just can't accept responsibility if things go wrong in my department, Captain."

At least, Grimes consoled himself, he had one satisfied customer. That was Denny. The elderly commander clearly did not approve of the flurry of activity into which his normally sleepy Base had been plunged. He knew that this flurry would continue as long as *Discovery* was sitting on the apron. He knew, too—Mrs. Denny made sure that he knew—that the outsiders were interfering with the local ecology. They had attached hoses to *his* hydrants and washed down the entire spaceport area. They had rigged a wire fence with a carefully calculated low voltage trickling through it on a wide perimeter about their vessel. When Denny had objected, Grimes had told him that his crew did not like working in a latrine and that, furthermore, the materials used for the fence came from ship's stores, and the current in the wires from the ship's generators.

"I shall report this to Lindisfarne Base, Commander Grimes," said Denny stiffly.

"I shall be making *my* report too," Grimes told him. "And so will my medical officer. Meanwhile, my chief engineer tells me that he's not getting much help from your workshops."

"I'll see that he gets all the help he wants," promised Denny. His manner suddenly softened. "You're not married, Commander, but you will be. Then you'll find out what it's like, especially if your wife has a weird taste in pets."

"One man's pets are another man's pests," cracked Grimes.

"One woman's pets are, strictly between ourselves, her husband's pests. Rest assured that I shall get your rust-bucket off my Base as soon as is humanly possible. Anything for a quiet life."

And so the activity continued, with work around the clock.

"There's hardly been any shore leave, sir," complained Brabham.

"Growl you may, but go you must," countered Grimes cheerfully.

"But what's the *hurry*, sir?"

"There is a valid reason for it, Number One," Grimes told him.

"More sealed orders, I suppose," said Brabham, with as near to a sneer as he dared.

"Maybe, maybe not," replied Grimes, with what he knew must be infuriating smugness. There were times when he did not quite like himself, and this was one of them—but his officers were bringing out the worst in him. "Just take it from me that I know what I'm doing, and why. That's all."

"Very good, sir," said Brabham, conveying the impression that, as far as he was concerned, it wasn't.

Rather to Grimes's surprise the target date was met.

A cheerless dawn was breaking over the Base as the ramp was retracted, as the last of *Discovery*'s airtight doors sighed shut. The old ship was as spaceworthy as she ever would be, and she had somewhere to go.

Grimes, in the control room, spoke into the microphone. "*Discovery* to New Maine Aerospace Control. Request outward clearance. Over."

"All clear for your liftoff, *Discovery*. No air traffic in vicinity of Base. No space traffic whatsoever. Good hunting. Over."

"Thank you, Aerospace Control. Over."

"Base to *Discovery*." This was Denny's voice. "Good hunting. Over."

"Thank you, Commander Denny. Give my regards to the great snakes. They can have their public convenience back now. Over."

"I wish you were taking the bastards with you, Grimes. Over."

Grimes laughed, and started the inertial drive. *Discovery* shuddered, heaving herself clear of the apron. She clambered upward like an elderly mountaineer over-burdened with equipment. No doubt MacMorris would complain that he should have been given more time to get his innies into proper working order. Then the beat of the engines became louder, more enthusiastic. Grimes relaxed a little. He took a side-wise glance at Tangye, in the co-pilot's seat. This time, he noted, the navigator had done his sums before departure; a loosely folded sheet of paper was peeping out of the breast pocket of his uniform shirt. And what target star would he have selected? Hamlet, probably, in the Shakespearean System, out toward the Rim Worlds. It was a pity that *Discovery* would not be heading that way.

The ship pushed through the low overcast as though she really meant it, emerged into the clear stratum between it and the high cirrus. Blinding sunlight, almost immediately dimmed as the viewports automatically polarized, smote through into the control room, and, outside, made haloes of iridescence in the clouds of ice particles through which the vessel was driving. She lifted rapidly through the last tenuous shreds of atmosphere.

"Clear of the Van Allens, sir," reported Tangye at last. "Thank you, pilot," acknowledged Grimes. Then, to Brabham, "Make the usual announcements, Number One. Free fall, setting trajectory, all the rest of it."

"Take over now, sir?" asked Tangye, pulling the sheet of notes from his breast pocket.

Grimes grinned at him. "Oh, I think I'll keep myself in practice, pilot. It's time I did some work."

The ship was in orbit now, falling free about New Maine. Grimes produced his own sheet of paper, glanced at it, then at the constellations patterned on the blackness outside the viewports. He soon found the one that he was looking for, although why the first settlers on this planet had called it The Mermaid he could not imagine. Their imaginations must have been far more vivid than his. His fingers played over the controls and the directional gyroscopes began to spin, and the hull turned about them. "Sir," said Tangye urgently. "Sir!"

"Yes, pilot?"

"Sir, Hamlet's in The Elephant. From here, that is—"

"How right you are, Mr. Tangye. But why should we be heading toward Elsinore?"

"But, sir, the orders said that we were to make a sweep out toward the Rim."

"That's right," put in Brabham.

"I have steadied this ship," said Grimes coldly, "on to Delta Mermaid. We shall run on that trajectory until further orders—orders from myself, that is. Number One, pass the word that I am about to start the Mannschenn Drive."

"As you say, sir," replied Brabham sulkily.

Deep in the bowels of the vessel the gleaming rotors

began to turn, to spin and to tumble, to precess out of normal space-time, pulling the ship and all her people with them down the dark dimensions, through the warped continuum. There was the usual fleeting second or so of temporal disorientation, while shapes wavered and colors sagged down the spectrum, while all sound was distorted, with familiar noises either impossibly high in pitch or so low as to be almost inaudible.

There was, as always, the uncanny sensation of *déjà vu*.

Grimes experienced no previsions but felt, as he had when setting trajectory off Lindisfarne, a deep and disturbing premonition of impending doom.

Perhaps, he thought, he should adhere to his original orders. Perhaps he should observe the golden rule for modest success in any service: Do what you're told, and volunteer for nothing.

But whatever he did, he knew from harsh experience, he always ran into trouble.

»«(Chapter 13)»«

The ship settled down into her normal Deep Space routine—regular watches, regular mealtimes, regular exercise periods in the gymnasium, and regular inspections. In many ways, in almost all ways, she was like any other ship; what made her different, too different, was the resentment that was making itself felt more and more by her captain. The short stay on New Maine, with hardly any shore leave, was in part responsible. But there was more than that. Everybody aboard knew what Grimes's original orders had been—to use New Maine as a base and to make a sweep out toward the Rim without intruding into what the Rim Worlds already were referring to as *their* territorial space. (It was not Federation policy to do any-thing that might annoy those touchy colonials, who, for some time, had been talking loudly about secession.) And now everybody aboard knew that *Discovery* was headed not toward the Rim but in the general direction of the Waverley sector. Grimes, of course, was the captain,

461

and presumably knew what he was doing. Grimes was notoriously lucky—but luck has a habit of running out. If this cruise, carried out in contravention to admiralty orders—vague though those orders had been—turned out to be fruitless, Grimes would have to carry the can back— but his officers, none of them at all popular with high authority, would be even less likely to achieve any further promotion.

Grimes could not help overhearing snatches of conversation. *The old bastard is putting us all up Shit Creek without a paddle.* And, *He's always been fantastically lucky, but he's bound to come a real gutser one day. I only hope that I'm not around when he does!* And, *He must think that he's a reincarnation of Nelson—turning a blind eye to his orders!* With the reply, *A reincarnation of Bligh, you mean!*

This last, of course, was from Brabham.

And if Bligh, thought Grimes, had carried a trained and qualified telepath aboard *Bounty* he might have been given warning of the mutiny that was brewing. He, Grimes, did have such a telepath aboard *Discovery*—but was Flannery willing to bend the Rhine Institute's ethical code? If he were, it would be far easier to keep a finger on the pulse of things. But Flannery . . . his loyalties, such as they were, were to his shipmates, much as he disliked them all, rather than to the ship and her commander. He was bred of stock with a long, long record of rebellion and resentment of all authority. Even his psionic amplifier— one that Grimes, ironically enough, had persuaded the telepath to accept—seemed to share its master's viewpoint.

Yet Grimes did not dislike the whiskey-swilling psionic communications officer and did not think that Flannery actively disliked him. Perhaps, carefully handled, the man might be induced to spill a bean or two. In any case, Grimes would have to spill the beans to him, would have to tell him about Davinas and the suspected Lost Colonies. But did Flannery know already? PCOs were not supposed to pry, but very few of them were able to resist the temptation.

He made his way down to the farm deck, to the squalid cubbyhole where Flannery lived in psionic symbiosis with his amplifier. The man was more or less sober, having, over the years, built up a certain immunity to alcohol. He was playing patience—and, Grimes noted, cheating—between sips from a tumbler of whiskey.

"Ah, top o' the mornin' to ye, Captain! Or is it mornin'? Or evenin'? Or last St. Patrick's Day?"

"Good morning, Mr. Flannery."

"A drop of the real peat elixir for ye, Captain?"

Grimes hesitated, then accepted. Irish whiskey was not among his favorite tipples, but he wanted to keep Flannery in a good mood. He wondered how long it was since the glass into which his drink was poured had been washed.

"Thank you, Mr. Flannery. Mind if I sit down?"

"Not at all, not at all, Captain. This is Liberty Hall. Ye can spit on the mat an'—"

"Call Ned a bastard? He mightn't like it."

"He wouldn't be mindin' at all, at all. T'is a term o' endearment where *he* comes from. An' it was about Ballchin 1716 and 1717 ye were wantin' to see me, wasn't it?"

"You've been . . . snooping," accused Grimes.

"Snoopin', Captain? There was no need to. I'd have to blank me mind off entoirely not to pick up your broadcasts on *that* subject! An' if ye're askin' me now, I've picked up nary a whisper yet from the planets o' those two suns. But I'm listenin'. An' Ned—bless the sweet soul o' him—is listenin'."

"Thank you. Mphm. Oh, and there was something else."

"Ye're not after askin' me *that*, Captain, are ye? To pry on me mates?"

"Well, it is done, you know," said Grimes defensively. "When justified by the circumstances, that is."

"Niver by me it isn't, Captain. The Rhine Institute licensed me, an' I abide by its rules."

When it suits you, thought Grimes.

Flannery grinned, showing his mottled teeth. Grimes might just as well have spoken aloud. "I'll tell ye what," said the telepath cheerfully. "I'll tell ye what . . . I'll give ye a readin'. On the house, as the wee dog said." His grubby hands swept the cards into an untidy pile, stacked them. "Seein' as how we're aboard a starship I'll be usin' the Mystic Star."

"Mphm?" grunted Grimes dubiously.

Flannery riffled through the cards, selected one, laid it face upward on the dirty tabletop. "The King of Clubs," he announced. "That's you. Our leader, no less."

"Why the King of Clubs?"

"An' why not, Captain? Ye're a decent enough boyo, under the gold braid an' brass buttons. The King o' Gravediggers, standin' for the military leader, is not for the likes o' you. Ye're not a bad enough bastard."

"Thank you."

"An' now take the pack. Shuffle it. Let the—the *essence* o' ye seep through yer hands into the Devil's Prayerbook."

Grimes felt that the reverse was taking place, that the uncleanliness of the cards was seeping through his skin into him, but he did as he was told.

"An' now, with yer left hand, put the cards down. Face down. Cut the pack. An' again, so we have three piles."

Grimes obeyed.

"An' now, the Indicator."

Flannery turned over the first stack, revealing the nine of diamonds, then the second, to show the eight of the same suit, then the third, exposing the two of spades.

"Ah, an' what have we here? The unexpected gift, an' the journey that's made possible. The cards don't lie, Captain. Didn't the man Davinas give ye that star chart? An' the eight o' sparklers—a lucky card for the explorer. But what's this mean? The deuce o' gravediggers. Could it be that yer famous luck is goin' to turn sour on ye? Change, disruption, an' voyages to far places. What are ye runnin' from, Captain? Are ye runnin' away, or are ye bein' thrown out from somethin'? Good luck, an' bad luck, an' isn't that the way with ivery mother's son of us? But with you—the good outweighin' the bad."

Rubbish, thought Grimes, not quite convincing himself. "Go on," he said.

"Ye're in this too." Flannery swept the cards, with the exception of the King of Clubs, back into one pack. "Take 'em, Captain. Shuffle again. Now give 'em back to me." Working widdershins, Flannery placed eight cards around the King in the form of an eight-pointed star. Then he gave the pack back to Grimes, telling him to put two more cards on each of the eight points.

"An' now," he said, "we shall see what we shall see." He turned up the three cards at the top of the star. "Aha! The King o' Sparklers, the four o' blackberries, an' the seven o' gravediggers. Someone's workin' against ye, Captain. A military man, a soldier, an' there's the warnin' o' danger ahead, an' another warnin', too. A woman could land ye in the cactus."

"It wouldn't be the first time," grunted Grimes.

"An' now—" Flannery turned up the three cards to the left of the first three: the four and the six: of spades, the two of clubs. "Good an' bad again—but that's life. Loss, an' poverty, an' jealousy, an' envy a-destroyin' of yer success— but good luck again when it's all over. The Odd Gods o' the Galaxy alone know how ye do it, but always ye come to the top. Not at once, mind ye. It takes time. But remember this—when all the cards are on the table there's but the one man in the universe ye can trust. Yerself.

"Now—" the telepath turned up the third trio of cards: five of clubs, four of hearts, and six of diamonds. He chuckled. "A foine mixture, this! The cards say as how ye're to take things as they come, marriage wise. It'll all turn out wrong in the end, anyhow. Did I iver tell ye that I was married once? Anyhow—play yer cards right for a wealthy marriage says *this* one, an' *this* one says that ye're the last o' a long line o' bachelors. An' *this* one—an early, romantic marriage *an'* an unlucky second marriage. So ye *did* have fun, or ye're goin' to have fun, or ye never did have nor ever will have any fun at all. Take yer choice.

"Aha!" The next set of three was flipped over. "The King

an' the Queen o' Gravediggers, an' the trey o' diamonds.
The King's another captain, who's going to get in yer hair
in the nearish future. And would it be yer old pal
Commander Delamere?"

"What do you know about him?" snapped Grimes.

"Only what flickered through yer mind when I turned
up the card. An' the Queen? Sorry, Captain, I can't place
her. She's nobody ye know—*yet*. But ye'll be gettin' quite
a handful. An' that little three? Oh, all sorts o' fun an'
games, an' I have a feelin' that the King'll be playin' a part
in 'em. He doesn't like you at all, at all.

"An' now, what have we? Six an' eight o' blackberries,
seven o' sparklers. Goodish, goodish—but not all that good
when ye remember all that's come before, an' all that's to
come. Good for *business?* Ha! Ye're not a shopkeeper,
Captain. An', come to that, ye're not a merchant skipper.
Your ship doesn't have to show a profit. An' the other two
cards warn ye against gamblin'. But isn't all life a gamble?
Aren't we gamblin' with our lives ivery time that we liftoff
planet, or come in for a happy landin'? And when ye
gamble ye must always expect the odd run o' bad luck."

He turned over the sixth set of three. "Eight o' spades,
two an' three o' hearts. Ah, overcome resistance, it says.
Ye always do that, don't ye? But what about traitors? What
about them as'd stab ye in the back?"

"What about them?" demanded Grimes sharply.

"*I* said nothin', Captain, nothin' what iver. Twas the
cards said it—an' surely ye, of all men, wouldn't be after
payin' attention to silly pieces o' plastic? Or would ye?" He
chuckled, prodding the cards with a thick forefinger. "But
the deuce an' the trey—don't they cancel out sweetly?

Success, an' good fortune, an' everything ye wish yerself—
but *when?* This week, next week, sometime, never. An'
agin that there's the risk o' unwise choices, an' leapin' afore
ye look, an' all the rest of it. So—look first, leap second—
if at all.

"Nine an' ten o' hearts, nine o' spades. Two o' one, one
o' t' other. Hearts an' flowers the first two, love and roses all
the way—*but,* if that black bastard of a nine is telling the
truth, only if ye come through the troubles that are waitin'
for ye. There's a crisis brewin', Captain. Beware o' the night
o' the long knives. Keep yer back to the bulkhead."

I do have enemies, bad ones, thought Grimes.

"An' don't ye ever!" There was a note of admiration in
Flannery's voice. "But now we'll see what the last point o'
the star has to tell us. Nine o' clubs. Two o' spades, an' the
ten o' the same. Black, black, black. Really, ye should ha'
stayed in bed in the BOQ on Lindisfarne. Battle, murder,
an' sudden death. Disasters by land an' by sea an' in deep
space. If it wasn't for the very last card of all I'd be wishin'
meself that I'd gone sick on New Maine an' been left
behind."

"The ten of spades?" asked Grimes. "But that's unlucky
too, surely."

"Think yerself lucky that it's not the Gravedigger itself,
the Ace. Do ye really want to know what it means?"

"Yes," Grimes told him firmly.

Flannery laughed. "Beware o' false prophets. That's its
meanin'. So, decide for yerself, Captain. Do ye trust the
cards, or don't ye?"

And do I trust you? wondered Grimes.

"The cards say to trust *nobody,*" Flannery told him.

﷯«Chapter 14»﷯

Grimes did not believe the card reading, of course. Nonetheless it added to his growing uneasiness, and when he was uneasy he tended to snarl. He knew that his officers and crew resented his attempts to maintain minimal standards of smartness aboard the ship, and that the scientist, Dr. Brandt, regarded him as a barely necessary evil. He refused to admit that in taking command of *Discovery* he had bitten off more than he could chew, but he was coming to realize, more and more, that his predecessor had taken the easy way out, had made arrangements for his own comfort, and then allowed the vessel to run herself in her own bumbling, inefficient way.

Meanwhile, as the ship steadily narrowed the distance between herself and the first of the two possible stars, Flannery, with all his faults, was pulling his weight. Straining his telepathic faculties, he had begun to pick up what could be construed as indications of intelligent life on one of the worlds in orbit about that sun.

"The skipper of *Sundowner* was right, Captain," he said. "There's somethin' there, all right. Or, even, somebody. There's—there's a sort o' murmur. Ye can't hear it, of course, but Ned's hearin' it, an' I'm hearin' it." He grinned. "T'is a real Irish parliament. Everybody talkin', an' nobody listenin'."

"Except you," said Grimes.

"Exceptin' me—an' Ned," agreed the PCO.

"Human?" asked Grimes.

"That I couldn't be sayin', Captain. T'is too early yet. But humanoid, for sure. Somethin' with warm blood an' breathin' oxygen."

"Or its equivalent," suggested Grimes doubtfully. "After all, the essential physiology of chlorine breathers is very similar to our own."

"A bridge we'll cross when we come to it, Captain. But even if *they*, whoever they might be when they're up an' dressed, ain't human, ye'll still have discovered a new world for the Federation—may all the Saints preserve it— an' that'll be a feather in yer cap!"

"I suppose so." Somehow the prospect did not cheer Grimes, as it should have done. "I suppose so."

He got up to return to his own quarters, where he was to preside over a meeting of his senior officers and petty officers.

He sat behind his desk, facing the others.

Brandt was there, sitting by himself, a compact ball of hostility. Brabham, Swinton, and Vinegar Nell shared a settee—sullen bloodhound, belligerent terrier, and spiteful cat. Dr. Rath was wrapped in his own private cloud of funereal gloom. MacMorris, too, was keeping himself to himself, obviously begrudging the time that he was being obliged to spend away from his precious engines. Longer, the bos'n, and Washington, the sergeant of Marines, formed a two-man conspiracy in a corner, ostentatiously holding themselves aloof from the commissioned officers.

"Gentlemen," began Grimes. "And Miss Russell," he added. "Mphm." He answered their not very friendly stares with one of his own. "Mr. Flannery assures me that there is life, intelligent life, very probably our sort of life, on one of the worlds of Ballchin 1717, the star that we are now approaching."

"So your luck is holding, sir," said Brabham.

"What exactly do your mean, Number One?"

"Even you, sir, would have found it hard to justify this deviation from the original plan if you'd found nothing."

"We have only the word of a drunken telepath that anything *has* been found," huffed Brandt. "And it still might not be a Lost Colony."

"Even if it is," grumbled MacMorris, "I doubt if there'll be any machine shops. I'm still far from happy about my innies."

"You never are," remarked Brabham.

"We didn't have enough time on New Maine to get *anything* fixed up properly," complained Vinegar Nell, favoring Grimes with a hostile glare.

"At least," stated Swinton, "*my* men, as always, are ready for anything."

"There probably will be some civilians for you to massacre," murmured Vinegar Nell sweetly.

Swinton flushed hotly and Grimes spoke up before a

quarrel could start. "Gentlemen. Miss Russell. If you wish
to squabble, kindly do so elsewhere than in my quarters. I
have called you here to discuss our course of action."

"To begin with," said Brandt, "there must be the minimal
interference with whatever culture has developed on that
world."

"If we're shot at," snapped Swinton, "we shoot back!"

"You tell 'em, Major!" murmured Sergeant
Washington.

"That will do," said Grimes coldly. Then, "To begin with,
I shall advise you all of my intentions. This original plan
will be subject to modification as required by changing
circumstances and, possibly, as suggested by your good
selves."

"The vessel will continue on her present trajectory. Mr.
Flannery will maintain his listening watch, endeavoring to
learn as much as possible of the nature of the inhabitants.
We are also, of course, maintaining a Carlotti listening
watch, although it is doubtful if we shall pick anything up.
The Carlotti system had not been dreamed of at the time
of the Second Expansion, the heyday of the lodejammers.
And, in any case, any station using it must, of necessity,
be a well-established component of today's network of
interstellar communications. We can't listen on NST
radio, of course, until we shut down the Mannschenn
Drive and reemerge into normal space-time.

"We shall endeavor to home on the source of psionic
emission. With the interstellar drive shut down, we shall
establish ourselves in orbit about the planet. We shall
observe, listen, and send down our unmanned probes.
And then we come in to a landing."

"Not in the ship," said Brandt flatly.

"And why not?" countered Grimes coldly.

"Have you considered," asked the scientist, "the effect that a hulking brute of a vessel like this might—no, *would!*—have on a people who have reverted to savagery, who are painfully climbing back up the hill to civilization?"

"If I'm going to be a stranger on a strange world," Grimes told him, "I prefer to be a stranger with all the resources of my own culture right there with me, not hanging in orbit and all too likely to be on the wrong side of the planet when I want something in a hurry!"

"I agree with the captain," said Brabham.

"And I," said Swinton.

"It is high time that the real command was put in the hands of the scientists," growled Brandt.

"If it ever is," Brabham snarled, "my resignation goes in."

"That will do, gentlemen," said Grimes firmly. "Whether we land in the ship, or whether we send down small parties in the boats, will be decided when we know more about 1717—but I can say, now, that the second course of action is extremely unlikely. Needless to say, the actual site of our landing will have to be decided upon. *If* the civilization has attained or re-attained a high standard of technology, then there is no reason why we should not set down close to a large center of population, in broad daylight. If the people reverted to savagery after their own first landing, and stayed that way, then caution on our part is indicated."

"Putting it bluntly, Commander Grimes," said Brandt unpleasantly, "you are dithering."

"Putting it shortly," retorted Grimes, "I shall be playing by ear. As I always do. As I always have done." He was exaggerating, of course. Before any operation he always worked out his course of action in every smallest detail— but he was ever alert to changing circumstances, always ready to abandon his elaborate plan of campaign and to improvise.

He went on, "I want all of you carefully to consider the problems that are liable to confront us. I want all of you to work out your own ways of dealing with them. I am always open to suggestions. Don't forget that we are a team." (Did he hear a faint, derisive, *Ha, ha!?*) "Don't forget that we are a team, and remember that this is a Federation vessel and not a warship of the Waldegren Navy, whose kapitan would have you pushed out of the airlock for speaking out of turn." (And who was it who whispered in mock incredulity, *Oh, no?*) "Be ready for anything—and, above all, be ready for the things for which you aren't ready. Mphm." He carefully filled and then lit his pipe.

"Very enlightening, Commander Grimes," commented Brandt condescendingly.

Brabham said nothing, merely looked wooden. Swinton said nothing and looked skeptical. Vinegar Nell permitted herself a slight sneer. Dr. Rath looked like an undertaker counting the dead for whom he would have to provide a free funeral. The burly Langer raised his hand, looking like an oversized schoolboy. "Captain?"

"Yes, Bos'n?"

"Speaking on behalf of the men, sir, I hope that you will allow shore leave. We had precious little back at Main Base, and precious little on New Maine."

"This is not a pleasure cruise, Bos'n," said Grimes.

"You can say that again!" whispered somebody, not quite inaudibly.

»«(Chapter 15)»«

Star 1717 in the Ballchin Catalog was a Sol-type sun.

Somehow it and its planetary family had, to date, escaped close investigation by the survey ships of the Interstellar Federation, the Empire of Waverley (although it was almost in the Imperial back yard), or the Duchy of Waldegren, to name the major human spacefaring powers; neither had it attracted the attention of the far-ranging Seeker-Queens of the Shaara Galactic Hive. One reason for its being ignored was that it lay well away from the regular trade routes. Another reason was that nobody—at the moment—was acutely short of *lebensraum*. There were other reasons—economic, political, and whatever—but Grimes, a mere Survey Service commander, knew nothing of these, and would know nothing of such matters until, if at all, he wore gold braid up to the elbow and a cap whose peak was one solid encrustation of scrambled egg.

The planetary system of 1717 consisted of six worlds,

easily observed as *Discovery*, her own time out of kilter with the *real* time of the universe, cautiously approached the star, running on interstellar drive, from well to the north of the plane of the ecliptic. The planets showed as wavering bands of luminescence about the shapeless, quivering iridescent blob that was their primary. After the Mannschenn Drive had been shut down they were, of course, far harder to locate—but Flannery, one of those telepaths capable of psionic direction-finding, was able to guide the ship in toward the world that harbored intelligent life.

Of 1717's six planets, the outermost three were gas giants. Of the innermost three, one was far too close to the sun for life, of any kind, to have developed. The other two were within the biosphere. The third one was almost another Earth, a resemblance that became more and more striking as *Discovery* approached it. There were seas and continents, mountain ranges, polar ice caps, and a cloudy atmosphere. On the night side were sparkling clusters of lights that had to be cities. And there were networks of unnaturally straight lines crisscrossing the landmasses that could be roads, or railways, or canals.

There was no doubt that 1717 III was inhabited. The people of 1717 III had achieved, it seemed certain, some kind of industrial civilization. But until an actual landing was made little could be known about them, although Flannery was doing his best to pick up information. He said to Grimes, who had taken to haunting the PCO's squalid office, "T'is like the roarin' o' the crowd at a football game, Captain. Niver a single voice that ye can make out what it's sayin' . . . just jabber, jabber, jabber. Oh, there's a power o' people down there all right, an' they're after thinkin' what people always do be thinkin'—that it's too hot, or too cold, or that it's almost dinnertime, or that it's a dreadful long time atween drinks. Which reminds me—" He reached for a full bulb of whiskey. "An' how long are ye keepin' us in free fall, Captain? I mislike these baby's feedin' bottles."

Grimes ignored this. "But are they thinking in Standard English?" he demanded. "Or in any other human language?"

"Now ye're askin'. An' the answer is—I don't know. Trouble is, there's niver a *real* telepath among the bunch of 'em. If there was, he'd be comin' in loud and clear at this range, and I'd be able to tell ye for sure." Flannery grinned. "Am I to take it that the opposition hasn't brought ye any joy? That the bould Sparkses—bad cess to 'em!—haven't been able to raise anythin' on their heathenish contraptions?"

"You know damn well they haven't!" huffed Grimes. "We weren't expecting anything on the Carlotti—but there's been nothing on the NST either, nothing but static."

"So ye haven't found a Lost Colony after all, Captain. But ye've discovered a new world with new people. An' isn't that better?"

"A new world? How do you make that out?"

"A Lost Colony'd be makin' its start with all the books an' machinery an' know-how aboard the ship, wouldn't it? 'Less they went all the way back to the Stone Age they'd be keepin' the technology they started with, an' improvin' on it."

"Mphm. But perhaps, for some reason, our friends down there prefer landlines to radio."

"Ye've somethin' there, Captain. But—there's altogether too many o' the bastards. That world has a powerful big population. Could the crew an' passengers o' just *one* ship—one flyin' fridge, perhaps, or one o' the lodejammers still not accounted for—have done so well, even if they bred like rabbits? Historically speakin', the Deep Freeze ships o' the First Expansion were only yesterday, an' the Second Expansion was no more than a dog watch ago."

"But you forget," Grimes told him, "that the later Deep Freeze ships', and *all* the lodejammers, carried big stocks of fertilized ova, together with the incubating machinery. One ship would have the capability to populate a small—or not so small—continent within a few decades after the first landing."

"Ye've almost convinced me, Captain. But I can't pick up any clear thinkin' at all, at all. All I can tell ye is that *they*—whoever or whatever *they* are—are mammals, an' have two sexes an' a few o' the in-betweens, an' that most of 'em are runnin' hard to keep up in some sort o' rat race . . . like us. But *how* like? Now ye're askin', an' I can't tell ye. Yet."

"So we just have to wait and see," said Grimes, getting up to return to the control room.

The planet 1717 III loomed huge through the planet-ward viewports, a great island in the sky along the shores of which *Discovery* was coasting. Like all prudent explorers in Man's past Grimes was keeping well out from the land until he knew more of what awaited him there. Like his illustrious predecessors he would send in his small boats to make the first contact—but, unlike them, he would not be obliged to hazard the lives of any of his crew when he did so.

"Number one probe ready," reported Brabham.

"Thank you," said Grimes.

He glanced around the control room. Tangye was seated at the console, with its array of instruments, from which the probe would be operated. Brandt was looking on, obviously sneering inwardly at the amateurishly unscientific efforts of the spacemen. The officer of the watch was trying to look busy—although, in these circumstances, there was very little for him to do. The radio officers were hunting up and down the frequencies on the NST transceiver, bringing in nothing but an occasional burst of static.

"Launch the probe, sir?" asked Brabham.

"I'll just check with Mr. Tangye first, Number One." Then, to the navigator, "You know the drill, pilot?"

"Yes, sir. Keep the probe directly below the ship to begin with. Bring it down slowly through the atmosphere. The usual sampling. Maintain position relative to the ship unless instructed otherwise."

"Good. Launch."

"Launch, sir."

The muffled rattle of the probe's inertial drive was distinctly audible as, decks away below and aft, it nosed out of its bay. It would not have been heard had *Discovery*'s own engines been running, it was little more than a toy, but the big ship, in orbit, was falling free. Needles on the gauges of Tangye's console jerked and quivered, the traces in cathode ray tubes began their sinuous flickering; but as yet there was nothing to be seen on the big television screen tuned to the probe's transmitter that could not be better observed from the viewports.

"Commander Grimes," said Brandt, "I know that you are in charge, but might I ask why you are not adhering to standard procedure for a first landing?"

"What do you mean, Dr. Brandt?"

"Aren't first landings supposed to be made at dawn? That tin spy of yours will be dropping down from the noon sky, in the broadest daylight possible."

"And anybody looking straight up," said Grimes, "will be dazzled by the sun. The real reason for a dawn landing—a manned landing, that is—is so that the crew has a full day to make their initial explorations. That does not apply in this case."

"Oh. This, I take it then, is yet another example of your famous playing by ear."

"You could put it that way," said Grimes coldly.

Shuffling in his magnetic-soled shoes, he went to stand behind Tangye. Looking at the array of instruments, he saw that the probe had descended into an appreciable atmosphere and that friction was beginning to heat its skin. He said, "Careful, pilot. We don't want to burn the thing up."

"Sorry, sir."

Clouds on the screen—normal enough high cirrus.

More clouds below the probe—an insubstantial but solid-seeming mountainscape of cumulus. A break in the cloud-floor, a rift, a wide chasm, and through it the view of a vast plain, and cutting across it a straight ribbon, silver-gleaming against the greens and browns of the land.

"Oxygen . . . nitrogen . . . carbon dioxide . . ." Tangye was reciting as he watched the indicators on the console.

"Good," murmured Grimes. Then, "Never mind the analysis for now. It's all being recorded. Watch the screen. Bring the probe down to that. . . canal."

"How do you know it's not a road or a railway?" asked Brandt.

"I don't. But it *looks* like water."

The probe was now losing altitude fast, plunging down through the rift in the clouds, dropping below the ceiling. Beneath it spread the great plain, the browns and yellows and greens of it now seen to be in regular patterns—crops as yet unripe, crops ready for harvesting, crops harvested? There were roads between the fields, not as distinct as the canal, but definite enough. There was motion—dark cloud shadows drifting with the wind, a ripple over the fields that subtly and continuously changed and shifted the intensities of light and shade and color. And there was other motion, obviously not natural—a tiny black object that crawled like a beetle along the straight line of the canal, trailing a plume of white smoke or steam.

"Home on that boat," ordered Grimes.

"That. . . *boat*, sir?"

"That thing on the canal." Grimes could not resist a little sarcasm. "The word 'boat,' Mr. Tangye, was used long before it was applied to the small craft carried by spaceships. Home on the boat."

"Very good, sir," responded Tangye sulkily.

As the probe descended, details of the boat could be make out. It was a barge, self-propelled, with its foredeck practically all one long hatch, with a wheelhouse-cum-accommodation-block aft, just forward of the smoking stovepipe funnel. Suddenly a head appeared at one of the open wheelhouse windows, looking all around, finally staring upward. That was the main drawback of the probes, thought Grimes. With their inertial drive-units running they were such noisy little brutes. He could imagine the bewilderment of the bargemen when they heard the strange clattering in the sky, louder than the steady thumping of their own engines, when they looked up to see the silvery flying torpedo with its spiky efflorescence of antennae.

The crew member who had looked up withdrew his head suddenly, but not before those in *Discovery*'s control room had learned that he was most definitely nonhuman. The neck was too long, too thin. The eyes were huge and round. There was no nose, although there was a single nostril slit. The mouth was a pouting, fleshy-lipped circle. The skin was a dark olive-green. The huge ears were even more prominent than Grimes's own.

The water under the stern of the barge—which, until now, had been leaving only a slight wake—boiled into white foam as the revolutions of the screw were suddenly increased. Obviously the canal vessel was putting on a burst of speed to try to escape from the thing in the sky. It could not, of course; Tangye, with a slight adjustment to the probe's remote controls, kept pace easily.

"No need to frighten them to death," said Grimes. "Make it look as though you're abandoning the chase."

But it was too late. The barge sheered in toward the bank and the blunt stem gouged deeply into the soft soil, the threshing screw keeping it firmly embedded. The wheelhouse erupted beings; seen from the back they looked more human than otherwise. They ran along the foredeck, jumped ashore from the bows, scurried, with their long arms flailing wildly, toward the shelter of a clump of trees.

"Follow them, sir?" asked Tangye.

"No. But we might as well have a close look at the barge, now. Bring the probe down low over the foredeck."

Steel or iron construction, noted Grimes as the probe moved slowly from forward to aft. *Riveted plates . . . no welding. Wooden hatch boards, as like as not, under a canvas—or something like canvas—hatch cover.*

He said, "Let's have a look in the wheelhouse, pilot. Try not to break any windows."

"Very good, sir."

It was not, strictly speaking, a wheelhouse, as steering was done by a tiller, not a wheel. There was, however, what looked like a binnacle, although it was not possible to see, from outside, what sort of compass it housed. There was a voicepipe—for communication with the engine room? Probably.

Grimes then had Tangye bring the probe to what had to be the engine room skylight, abaft the funnel. Unfortunately both flaps were down, and secured somehow from below so that it was impossible for the probe's working arms to lift them.

"Well," commented Grimes at last, "we have a fair idea of the stage their technology has reached. But it's odd, all the same. People capable of building and operating a quite sophisticated surface craft shouldn't bolt like rabbits at the mere sight of a strange machine in the sky."

"Unless," sneered Brandt, "other blundering spacemen have made landings on this world and endeared themselves to the natives."

"I don't think so, Doctor," Grimes told him. "Our intelligence service, with all its faults, is quite efficient. If any human ships had made landings on this planet we should have known. And the same would apply in the case of nonhuman spacefarers, such as the Shaara and the Hallicheki. Mphm. Could it be, do you think that they have reason to fear flying machines that do not bear their own *national* colors? Mightn't there be a war in progress, or a state of strained relations liable to blow up into a war at any moment?"

Brandt laughed nastily. "And wouldn't that be right up your alley, Commander Grimes? Gives you a chance to make a snap decision as to who are the goodies and who the baddies before taking sides. I've been warned about that unfortunate propensity of yours."

"Have you?" asked Grimes coldly. Then, to Tangye, "Carry on along the canal until you come to the nearest town or city. Then we'll see what happens."

))((Chapter 16))((

Swiftly along the canal skimmed the probe, obedient to Tangye's control. It hovered for a while over a suspension bridge—an affair of squat stone pylons and heavy chain cables—and turned its cameras on to a steam railway train that was crossing the canal. The locomotive was high-stacked, big-wheeled, belching steam, smoke, and sparks, towing a dozen tarpaulin-covered freight cars. The engine crew did not look up at the noisy machine in the sky; as was made evident by the probe's audio pickups their own machinery was making more than enough racket to drown out any extraneous mechanical sounds.

The train chuffed and rattled away serenely into the distance, and Grimes debated with himself whether or not to follow it—it had to be going somewhere—or to carry on along the canal. He ordered Tangye to lift the probe and to make an all-around scan of the horizon. At a mere two kilometers of altitude a city came into full view, on the canal, whereas the railway line, in both directions, lost itself in ranges of low hills. The choice was obvious.

He ordered the navigator to reduce altitude. From too great a height it is almost impossible to get any idea of architectural details; any major center of habitation is no more than a pattern of streets and squares and parks. It was not long before the city appeared again on the screen— a huddle of towers, great and small, on the horizon, reflected by the gleaming straight edge of the canal. It was like an assemblage of child's building bricks—upended cylinders and rectangular blocks, crowned with hemispheres or broad-based cones. The sun came out from behind the clouds and the metropolis glowed with muted color—yellows and browns and russet reds. Without this accident of mellow light striking upon and reflected from surfaces of contrasting materials the town would have seemed formidable, ugly, even—but for these moments at least it displayed an alien beauty of its own.

There was traffic on the canal again, big barges like the one of which the crew had been thrown into such a panic. There were three boats outbound from the city. These, sighting the thing in the sky, turned in a flurry of reversed screws and hard-over rudders, narrowly escaping ramming one another, scurried back to the protection of the high stone walls. The probe hovered and allowed them to make their escape unpursued.

And then, surging out from between the massive piers of a stone bridge, the watergate, came a low black shape, a white bone in its teeth, trailing a dense streamer of gray smoke. It had a minimal funnel and a heavily armored wheelhouse aft, a domed turret forward. Through two parallel slits in the dome protruded twin barrels. There was little doubt as to what they were, even though there was a strong resemblance to an old-fashioned observatory. "Those sure as hell aren't telescopes!" muttered Brabham. The barrels lifted as the dome swiveled. "Get her upstairs, pilot!" ordered Grimes. "Fast!" Tangye stabbed in fumbling haste at his controls, keeping the probe's camera trained on the gunboat, which dwindled rapidly in the screen as the robot lifted. Yellow flame and dirty white smoke flashed from the *two* muzzles—but it was obvious that the result would not be even a near miss. Antiaircraft guns those cannon might well be, but their gunners were not used to firing at such a swift moving target.

"All right," said Grimes. "Hold her at that, Mr. Tangye. We can always take evasive action again if we have to. I doubt if those are very rapid-fire guns."

"I—I can't," mumbled the navigator. In the screen the picture of the city and its environs was dwindling fast. "You *can't?*"

Tangye, at his console, was giving an impersonation of an overly enthusiastic concert pianist. The lock of long fair hair that had flopped down over his forehead aided the illusion. He cried despairingly, "She—she won't answer."

"Their gunnery must have been better than we thought," remarked Brabham, with morose satisfaction.

"Rubbish!" snapped Swinton. "I watched for the shell bursts. They were right at the edge of the screen. Nowhere near the target."

"Mr. Brabham," asked Grimes coldly, "did you satisfy yourself that the probe was in good working order? A speck of dust in the wrong place, perhaps . . . a drop of moisture . . . a fleck of corrosion."

"Of course, sir," sneered Brabham, "all the equipment supplied to *this* ship is nothing but the best. I don't think!"

"It is *your* job, Number One," Grimes told him, "to bring it up to standard."

"I'm not a miracle worker. And I'd like to point out, sir, that this probe that we are—sorry, *were*—using—"

"I'm still using it!" objected Tangye.

"After a fashion." Then, to Grimes again: "This probe, Captain, has already seen service aboard *Pathfinder*, *Wayfarer*, and, just before *we* got it, *Endeavor*—all of them senior ships to this, with four ring captains."

"Are you insinuating," asked Grimes, "that mere commanders get captains' leavings?" (He had thought the same himself, but did not like Brabham's using it as an excuse.)

"Sir!" It was Tangye again. "The screen's gone blank. We've lost the picture!"

"And the telemetering?"

"Still working—most of it. But she's going up like a rocket. I can't stop her. She's—Sir! She's had it! She must have blown up!"

Grimes broke the uneasy silence in the control room. "Write off one probe," he said at last. "Luckily the taxpayer has a deep pocket. Unluckily I'm a taxpayer myself. And so are all of you."

"One would never think so," sneered Brandt.

"Send down the other probe, sir?" asked Brabham sulkily.

"What is its service history?" countered Grimes.

"The same as the one Mr. Tangye just lost."

"It lost itself!" the navigator objected hotly.

Grimes ignored the exchange. He went on, "It has, I suppose, received the same loving attention aboard this ship as its mate?"

Brabham made no reply.

"Then it stays in its bay until such time as it has been subjected to a thorough—and I mean *thorough*—overhaul. Meanwhile, I think that we shall be able to run a fair preliminary survey of this planet if we put the ship into a circumpolar orbit. We might even be able to find out for sure if there are any wars actually in progress at this moment. I must confess that the existence of readily available antiaircraft artillery rather shook me."

"What are you saying in your preliminary report to Base, Commander Grimes?" asked Brandt,

"There's not going to be one," Grimes told him.

"And why not?" demanded the scientist incredulously.

One reason why not, thought Grimes, *is that I'm not where I'm supposed to be. I'll wait until I have a* fait accompli *before I break radio silence.* He said, "We're far too close to the territorial limits of the Empire of Waverley. If the emperor's monitors pick up a signal from us and learn that there are Earth-type planets in their back yard we shall have an Imperial battle cruiser squadron getting into our hair in less time than it takes to think about it."

"But a coded message—" began Brandt.

"Codes are always being broken. And the message would have to be a long one, which means that it would be easy to get a fix on the source of transmission. There will be no leakage of information insofar as this planet is concerned until we have a cast-iron treaty, signed, sealed, and witnessed, with its ruler or rulers. And, in any case, we still have another world to investigate. Mphm."

He turned to the executive officer. "Commander Brabham, you will organize a working party and take the remaining probe down completely. You will reassemble it only when you are quite satisfied that it will work the way it should." Then it was the navigator's turn. "Mr. Tangye, please calculate the maneuvers required to put us in the circumpolar orbit. Let me know when you've finished doing your sums."

He left the control room, well aware that if the hostile eyes directed at his back were laser projectors he would be a well-cooked corpse.

Back in his own quarters he considered sending an initial message to Captain Davinas, then decided against it, even though such a code could never be broken and it would be extremely difficult for anybody to get a fix on such a short transmission. He would wait, he told himself, until he saw which way the cat was going to jump.

))(((Chapter 17))))

It was an unexpected cat that jumped.

It took the form of suddenly fracturing welding when the old ship was nudged out of her equatorial orbit into the trajectory that, had all gone well, would have been developed into one taking her over north and south poles while the planet rotated beneath her. With the rupturing of her pressure hull airtight doors slammed shut, and nobody was so unfortunate as to be caught in any of the directly affected compartments. But atmosphere was lost, as were many tons of fresh water from a burst tank. Repairs could be carried out in orbit, but the air and water could be replenished only on a planetary surface.

A landing would have to be made.

A landing—and a preliminary report to Base?

A preliminary report to Base followed, all too probably, by the arrival on the scene of an Imperial warship with kind offers of assistance and a cargo of Waverley flags to be planted on every available site.

So there was no report.

Meanwhile, there was the landing place to select. Grimes wanted somewhere as far as possible from any center of population, but with a supply of fresh water ready to hand. He assumed that the seas of this world were salt and that the rivers and lakes would not be. That was the usual pattern on Earth-type planets, although bitter lakes were not unknown.

There was a large island in one of the oceans, in the northern hemisphere, well out from the coastline of its neighboring continent. By day lakes and rivers could be seen gleaming among its mountains. By night there were no lights to be seen, even along the shore, to indicate the presence of cities, towns, or villages—and *Discovery's* main telescope could have picked up the glimmer of a solitary candle. With a little bit of luck, thought Grimes, his descent through the atmosphere would go unheard and unobserved. It should be possible to replenish air and water without interference by the natives—and, even more important, without being obliged to interfere with them.

The repairs were carried out while the ship was still in orbit; Grimes had no desire to negotiate an atmosphere in a ship the aerodynamic qualities of which had been impaired. This essential patching up meant that there was no labor to spare to work on the remaining probe—but in these circumstances a landing would have to be made without too much delay. The closed ecology of the ship had been thrown badly out of kilter by the loss of water and atmosphere, and would deteriorate dangerously if time were spent on preliminary surveys.

The landing was timed so that touchdown would be made shortly after sunrise. This meant that there would be a full day in which to work before nightfall—and as it was summer in the northern hemisphere the hours of daylight would be long. Also, a low sun casts long shadows, showing up every slightest irregularity in the ground. A spaceship, descending vertically and with tripedal landing gear, can be set down on quite uneven surfaces; nonetheless the vision of a disastrous topple recurs in the nightmares of every survey ship captain.

During her slow, controlled fall *Discovery* was bathed in bright sunlight while, until the very last few minutes, the terrain directly below her was still in darkness. To the east of the terminator, where there was full daylight, the sea was a glowing blue and, dark against the oceanic horizon, in silhouette against the bright, clear sky, lifted the mountains of the distant mainland.

Night fled to the west and the rugged landscape beneath the ship took on form and color. Yes, there was the lake, an amoeboid splotch of liquid silver almost in the center of the periscope screen, its mirrorlike surface broken by a spattering of black islets. The northern shore was cliffy, and inland from the escarpments the forested hillside was broken by deep gullies. To the south, however, there was a wide, golden beach fronting a grassy plain, beautifully level, although there were outcrops of what seemed to be large boulders. There was an area, however, that seemed to be reasonably clear of the huge stones with their betraying shadows and, applying lateral thrust, Grimes maneuvered his ship until she was directly above it.

"Why not land on the beach, sir?" asked Brabham.

"Sand can be treacherous," Grimes told him.

"But it will be a long way to lug the hoses," complained the first lieutenant.

Isn't that just too bad, thought Grimes.

He concentrated on his piloting. He might have let the navigator handle a landing at a proper spaceport, with marker beacons and the certainty of a smooth, level surface to sit down on, but Tangye's reaction times were far too slow to cope with emergencies that might suddenly arise in these circumstances. Tangye was sulking, of course, as was Brabham, and as the bos'n would be when he and his men had to drag the hoses all the way to the lake. There was little wind at this time of the day, and no lateral drift. Grimes found it easy to keep the ship dropping toward the spot that he had selected as his target. He could make out details in the periscope screen now, could see the long grass (it *looked* like grass) flattening, falling into patterns like iron filings in a magnetic field as the downward thrust of the inertial drive was exerted against blades and stems. There were tiny blue flowers, revealed as the longer growth was pushed down and away. There was something like an armored lizard that scuttled frantically across the screen as it ran to escape from the great, inexorably descending mass of the ship. Grimes hoped the creature made it to safety.

The numerals of the radar altimeter, set to measure distance from the pads of the landing gear to the ground, were flickering down the single digits. Seven . . . six . . . five . . . four . . . three . . . only three meters to go. But it would still be a long way down, as far as those in the control room were concerned, if the ship should topple. Two . . . one . . . a meter to go, and a delicate balance of forces achieved, with the rate of descent measured in fractions of a millimeter a second.

"I wish the old bastard'd get a move on," whispered somebody. Grimes could not identify the voice. Not that it mattered; everybody was entitled to his own opinions. Until he had coped with a landing himself he had often been critical of various captains' shiphandling.

Zero!

He left the drive running until he felt secure, then cut it. *Discovery* shuddered, complained, and the great shock absorbers sighed loudly. She settled, steadied. The clinometer indicated that she had come to rest a mere half degree from the vertical. What was under her must be solid enough. Grimes relaxed in his chair, filled and lit his pipe.

He said, "All right, Number One. Make it 'finished with engines,' but warn the chief that we might want to get upstairs in a hurry. After all, this is a strange and possibly hostile planet. In any case, he'll be too busy with his pumps to be able to spare the time to take his precious innies apart."

"I hope," muttered Brabham.

"Then make sure he knows that he's not to. Mphm. Meanwhile, I shall require a full control room watch at all times, with main and secondary armament ready for instant use. You can man the fire control console until relieved, Major Swinton."

"Open fire on anything suspicious, sir?" asked the Marine, cheerfully and hopefully.

"No," Grimes told him. "You will not open fire unless you get direct orders from myself."

"But, sir, we must make the natives respect us."

"What natives? I sincerely hope there aren't any on this island. In any case, there are other and better ways of gaining respect than killing people. Don't forget that *we* are the aliens, that *we* have come dropping down on this planet without so much as a by-your-leave. And Dr. Brandt—I hope—is the expert on establishing friendly relations with indigenes."

"I should hope so, Commander Grimes!" huffed Brandt.

"And if you go shooting at anything and everybody, Major Swinton," went on Grimes, "you'll be making the good doctor's job all the harder." He grinned. "But I don't think I shall be needing the services of either of you."

"Then," said Swinton sourly, "I may as well cancel my orders to Sergeant Washington to provide an escort for the hose parties. Sir."

"You will do nothing of the kind, Major. There may be dangerous wild animals on this planet. An uninhabited island like this is the very sort of place to find them."

"Then I and my men have permission to shoot *animals,* sir?"

"Yes!" snapped Grimes, but he was beginning to relent. After all, the major was only doing the job for which he had been trained. He turned to Brandt. "I suppose you'd like some specimens, Doctor? Geological, botanical, and so on?"

"I certainly would, Commander Grimes."

"Then you have my permission to call for volunteers

from such personnel as aren't already employed. And you, Major, can tell the sergeant to lay on escorts for them as well as for the working parties."

"I can't spread the few men I have that thinly, sir."

"Mphm. Then you and your volunteers, Dr. Brandt, are to stay close to the hose crews at all times. You are not to stray out of sight of the ship. Oh, Number One—"

"Sir?" acknowledged Brabham.

"Pass the word to everybody going ashore that they are to return *at once* if the alarm siren is sounded."

"Very good, sir. All right to carry on down to get things organized?"

"Yes. Carry on."

Grimes felt a twinge of envy. He would have liked to have gone ashore himself, to stretch his legs, to feel grass under his feet and sunlight on his skin, to breathe air that had not been cycled and recycled far too many times. But in these circumstances his place was here, in the control room, the nerve center of his ship.

He got up from his chair and tried to pace up and down, like an old-time surface ship captain walking his bridge. But control rooms are not designed for taking strolls in. Swinton and the officer of the watch regarded him with poorly concealed amusement. He abandoned his attempt at perambulation, made his way through the clutter of chairs and consoles to the viewports overlooking the lake.

The working parties, under the bos'n, were running the ends of long hoses out to the water. Brabham slouched along beside them, his hands in his pockets, moodily kicking at tufts of grass. A young steward, one of Brandt's

volunteers, was tap-tap-tapping at an outcrop of chalky
rock with a hammer. A stewardess was gathering flowers.
Among them, around them, in full battle armor, men
walking like robots, were Swinton's Marines.

Already there was a small party on the beach—young
Tangye, three of the junior engineers, and Vinegar Nell.
And what were *they* doing? Grimes asked himself. He
lifted the binoculars that he had brought with him to his
eyes. The men and the women were undressing. Oh, well,
he thought, there was nothing wrong with that; a *real*
sunbath after the weeks of unsatisfactory, psychologically
speaking, exposure to the rays of the ship's UV lamps. But
surely Brabham should have found jobs for these people.

The idlers were naked now, were sprawling on the fine
sand. Grimes envied them. Then Vinegar Nell got up
and walked slowly and gracefully into the water. She was
followed by Tangye. The junior engineers got to their feet,
obviously about to follow the paymaster and the navigator.
Grimes growled angrily, ran to the transceiver handling
ship-to-shore communication. "Commander Brabham!"
he barked.

He saw Brabham raising his wrist radio to his mouth,
taking far too long about it, heard, at last, "Brabham
here."

"Get those bloody fools out of the water. At once!"
Vinegar Nell was well away from the beach now, swimming
strongly. Tangye was splashing after her. The engineers
were already waist-deep in the shallows.

"Major Swinton," ordered Grimes, "tell Sergeant
Washington to get his men down to the water's edge, and
to keep their eyes skinned for any dangerous life-forms."

Swinton spoke rapidly into the microphone of his own transceiver, which was hanging about his neck. "Commander Brabham, get a move on, will you?" Grimes went on, into his own microphone.

"Oh, all right, all right." That irritable mutter was not meant to be heard, but it was.

Brabham was down to the beach at last, had his hands to his mouth and was bawling out over the water. The engineers, who had not yet started to swim, turned, waded slowly and reluctantly back to the sand. But Vinegar Nell and Tangye either would not or could not hear the first lieutenant's shouts.

"May I, sir?" asked Swinton. There was a nasty little grin under his moustache. "May you what, Major?"

"Order my men to drag them out." *No,* Grimes was about to say, *no*—but he saw an ominous swirl developing a little way out from the swimmers. "Yes!" he said.

Four Marines plunged into the lake. *They* were safe enough. Full battle gear has been described, variously, as armored tanks on legs, as battle cruisers on legs and, even, as submarines on legs. They streaked out toward Vinegar Nell and Tangye, boiling wakes astern of them as they actuated their suit propulsion units. Two of them converged on the paymaster, two on the navigator. There was a flurry of frail naked limbs among the ponderous metal-clad ones. Ignominiously the swimmers were dragged to the shore, carried out onto the dry land. It looked like a scene from somebody's mythology, thought Grimes, watching through his powerful glasses—the naked man and the naked woman, in the clutches of horrendous scaly monsters.

"Have them brought up here," he said to the major.

He assumed that they would be allowed to dress, but he did not give any orders to that effect, thinking that such would be unnecessary. He should have known better. Vinegar Nell, in a flaming temper, was splendid in her nudity. Tangye, with his unsightly little potbelly, was not. Tangye was thoroughly cowed. Vinegar Nell was not.

"I demand an explanation, Captain!" she flared. "*And* an apology. Was it you who ordered these"—she gestured with a slim, freckled arm toward the armored Marines—"enlisted men to attack me?"

"To save you," said Grimes coldly, "from the consequences of your own stupidity." He grinned without humor. "Your job is to provide meals for the personnel of this vessel, not for whatever carnivores are lurking in the lake."

"Ha!" she snorted. "Ha!" She brushed past Grimes to stand at the viewport. "What carnivores?"

The surface of the water was placid again. But there had been something there.

"Sir!" called the officer of the watch suddenly, "I have a target on the radar. Bearing 047. Range thirty kilometers. Bearing steady, range closing."

"Sound the recall," ordered Grimes. He went to the intercom. "Captain here. Mr. Flannery to the control room. At once."

»«Chapter 18»«

Flannery came into the control room, trailing a cloud of whiskey fumes, as Vinegar Nell and Tangye were hastily leaving. He guffawed, "An' what's goin' on, Captain? An orgy, no less!"

"Out of my way, you drunken bum!" snarled the paymaster, pushing past him.

Grimes ignored this. Vinegar Nell and Tangye would keep until later, as could the junior engineers who had followed their bad example. Looking out through the ports he saw that the last members of the shore parties were almost at the foot of the ramp, with Sergeant Washington and his Marines chivying them like sheepdogs. But the end of one hose had been placed in the lake; there was no reason why the pump should not be started. He told the officer of the watch to pass the order down to the engine room.

"Ye wished for me, Captain?" the telepath was asking.

"Yes, Mr. Flannery. Something, some kind of flying machine, is approaching."

502

"Bearing 047. Range twenty. Closing," reported the OOW.

"It must be an aircraft," went on Grimes. "The mountains cut off our line of sight to the sea. Could you get inside the minds of the crew? Are their intentions hostile?"

"I'll do me best, Captain. But as I've told ye an' told ye—these people must be the lousiest telepathic transmitters in the entoire universe!"

"All hands on board, sir," reported Brabham, coming into the control room. "Shall we reel in the hoses?"

"No. I've already told the engineers to start pumping. If I want to get upstairs in a hurry I shall be using the rockets, and I'll want plenty of reaction mass. But you can retract the ramp and close the after airlock door." Tangye—clothed, sheepish—made a reappearance. "Pilot, put the engines—inertial drive *and* reaction drive—on standby. Warn the chief that I may be wanting them at any second."

"Range fifteen. Closing."

Grimes raised his glasses to his eyes and looked along the 047 bearing. Yes, there it was in the sky, a black spot against a backdrop of towering, snowy cumulus. An aircraft, all right—but what sort of aircraft? Friendly or hostile? And how armed?

"All possible weaponry trained on target, sir," reported Swinton.

"Thank you, Major. What do you have to report, Mr. Flannery?"

"I'm tryin', Captain, indeed I'm tryin'. T'is like lookin' for truth at the bottom of a well full o' mud. The odd thought comes bubblin' up through the ooze—an' then it bursts, like a bubble, when I try to get ahold of it. But—but I'm gettin' somethin'. They're a bit scared—an' why shouldn't they be? They're a bit scared, but they're determined. They mayn't look much like us—but they're *men*."

"Range ten. Closing."

"Ship buttoned up, apart from the hoses," reported Brabham.

"All engines on standby," said Tangye. "Enough reaction mass in the tanks for limited use."

"How limited?" demanded Grimes testily.

"He didn't say, sir. But the pump is still sucking in water."

"They're comin' on," muttered Flannery, "although they're not likin' the idea of it at all, at all. But—but they—they trust? Yes. They trust us, somehow, not to swat 'em down out o' the sky like flies."

"Ha!" barked Swinton, hunched eagerly over his fire control console.

"Watch it, Major!" warned Grimes sharply.

"Range five. Closing."

Grimes studied the thing in the visual pickup screen, which gave far greater magnification than his binoculars. It looked like a big balloon, with a car hanging from the spherical gas bag. But a balloon would never be capable of that sort of speed. Then the thing turned to make a circuit of the valley, presenting its broadside to the human observers. The shape of it made sense—a long, fabric-covered torpedo with a control cabin forward, a quartet of engine pods aft. The outlines of frames and longerons were visible through the covering. *A rigid airship,* thought Grimes. *A dirigible.*

"They're havin' a good look at us," said Flannery unnecessarily. "They know that we're from . . . outside."

The airship flew in a circle with *Discovery* at its center, maintaining its distance but well within the range of the spaceship's weaponry. Perhaps its crew, knowing only the capabilities of their own artillery, thought they were out of range.

"Another target," reported the officer at the radar. "Bearing 047. Range thirty-five. Closing."

"Holdin' the first one's hand, like," volunteered Flannery.

Swinton, tracking the dirigible within visual sight, complained, "The bloody thing's making me dizzy."

"It's stopped," said Brabham. "No. It's turning. Toward us."

Toward, or away? wondered Grimes. Yes, toward it was.

"They've made their minds up," whispered Flannery. "They're thinkin'—may the Saints preserve 'em!—that there's no harm in us."

The airship drove in steadily. On its new course it would pass directly over *Discovery*. It approached with a stately deliberation. Then, suddenly, from the gondola, a half dozen relatively tiny objects fell in succession.

Swinton cried out—in exultation, not fear. And Flannery screamed, "No! No!" Grimes, belatedly recognizing the falling things for what they were, shouted, "Check! Check! Check!" But the major ignored the order to hold his fire. The slashing, stabbing beam of his laser was a ghostly, almost invisible sword. Each of the falling bodies exploded smokily, even as the parachutes started to blossom above them, and as they did so there was the deafening rattle of *Discovery*'s forty millimeter battery and a torrent of bright tracer. The airship disintegrated, her twisted, black skeleton in brief silhouette against the fireball of blazing hydrogen. The blast rocked the spaceship on her landing gear and a strip of burning fabric drifted down across her stem, blotting out the control room viewports with writhing blue and yellow flames.

"You bloody pongo murderer!" screamed Flannery, beating at the major with his fists.

"Call this lunatic off me," shouted Swinton, "before I have to kill him!"

Grimes grabbed the telepath by the shoulder, yanked him away from the Marine. He said, trying to keep his voice under some sort of control, "You bloody murderer, Swinton. You'll face another court-martial when we get back to Base!"

"I saved the ship!" Swinton was on his feet now. "I saved your precious ship for you. I call upon you all as witnesses. That was a stick of bombs."

"Bombs don't explode the way those bodies did," said Grimes coldly. "But living flesh does, when a laser beam at wide aperture hits it. The parachutes were just starting to open when you killed the poor bastards wearing them."

"Parachutists, then," admitted the major. "Paratroopers."

"Emissaries," corrected Flannery. "Comin' in peace, wantin' to make our acquaintance. An' didn't they just, you murtherin' swine?"

"Target number two," said the officer at the radar in a shaky voice, "bearing 047. Range twenty, opening. Twenty-one, opening . . . twenty-two . . . twenty-three."

"They know now what to expect from Earthmen," said Flannery bitterly.

»《Chapter 19》«

There had been an unfortunate misunderstanding, and men had died because of it, but Grimes was still responsible for the safety of his own ship, his own crew. He ordered that the replenishment of essential air and water be resumed as soon as the wreckage of the dirigible was cleared from around *Discovery*. He allowed Brandt, assisted by a squad of Marines, to pick over the charred remains of the airship and her hapless people—a filthy, gruesome task but, viewed cold-bloodedly and scientifically, a most useful one. One of the least badly damaged bodies—it did not look as though it had ever been a living, sentient being, but it exuded the sickly smell of death—was brought on board for dissection at some later date. The other corpses were interred in a common grave, marked by an almost intact four-bladed wooden airscrew. "We'll try to show these people that we're civilized," growled Grimes to the giant, black sullen Sergeant Washington, who had been ordered to take charge of the burial and who had protested that his men weren't gravediggers. "Although it's rather late in the day for that."

It was obvious that the man resented having to take orders from anybody but his own officer, even from the ship's captain, but Major Swinton had been suspended from duty—and sent down to his quarters in disgrace. Brabham had taken over fire-control, and managed to convey the impression that he hoped he would not be required to function as gunnery officer. Tangye had the radar watch.

Grimes stayed in the control room, taking his sandwich lunch there, although the other officers were relieved for their meal. He continually refilled and rekindled a pipe that became ever fouler and fouler. He listened patiently to Brandt when the scientist reported on the findings that he, aided by the ship's technical staff, had made. There had been very little metal in the structure of the airship, he said. The framework, control cabin, and engine pods had been made from a light but very strong wood. Stays and control cables, however, were of stranded wire, indicative of a certain degree of technological sophistication. The engines, which had survived the crash almost intact, seemed to be similar to Terran diesels. Unfortunately no fuel remained, but analysis of the deposits in the cylinders would provide clues as to the nature of what had been burned in them.

The pieces of the jigsaw puzzle were beginning to fall into place—and Grimes regretted that he would not be able to complete the picture. After Swinton's trigger-happy effort any and all visitors to this world would be received with hostility. It was a pity, as this would have been an interesting planet for detailed study, a world upon which the industrial revolution had taken place or was, at the very least, well under way. And there were political and sociological aspects as well as the technological ones which Grimes would have liked to have investigated. That obvious state of war—or, at least, a warmish cold war—between nations. Anti-aircraft artillery and a willingness to use it—as witness the reception of *Discovery*'s probe outside that city. But at least one of the powers, whoever it was that had owned the ill-fated airship, was less apt to shoot first and ask questions afterward. Or, he told himself glumly, they had been less apt to shoot first and ask questions afterward. Now they had learned their lesson. *That bloody, bloody Swinton!*

"Of course," said Brandt, with whom Grimes had been talking things over, "the major ruined everything."

"He's ruined himself as well, this time!" snapped Grimes. "I told the man, before witnesses, not to open fire unless ordered by myself to do so." He laughed grimly. "I'm afraid you won't get the chance to give away your picture books and educational toys on this planet, Doctor. Thanks to the Mad Major we got off on the wrong foot."

He pushed himself up from his chair, made a circuit of the viewports. Shadow was creeping over the valley from the West, but the rugged country to the east of the tarn was still brightly illuminated by the slowly setting sun— the pearly gray and glowing ocher of the cliffs, the static explosions of vividly green foliage, spangled with the scarlet and purple of huge gaudy blossoms.

Where every prospect pleases, he thought, *but only Man is vile. Man, with a large, black, capital "M."*

"Target," called Tangye suddenly. "Aerial. Bearing 050. Range thirty-five."

"General standby," ordered Grimes. Then, more to himself than to anybody else, "I'll not make it 'action stations' yet. If I do, the work'll never get finished. I doubt if that gas bag'll be keen to close us." He turned to Brabham. "If it does, Number One, you can pump a few rounds of HETF across its bows, as a deterrent. You will not, repeat not, shoot to hit."

Brabham gave him a sour look of acknowledgment, as though to say, *You don't need to tell me my job!*

Grimes looked down at the hoses, still out, still writhing rhythmically as the pumps drew in water from the lake. He thought, *I'll let the old bitch drink her fill.* He watched the sullen Marines, ash-bedaubed, still at their grisly work, their morbid scavenging. He rather regretted that he had not put Major Swinton in personal charge of the operation.

"Bearing 050. Range thirty. Closing," intoned Tangye.

"The poor brave, stupid bastards!" whispered Grimes. That flimsy ship, flammable as all hell, against *Discovery*'s weaponry. He went to the intercom, called for Flannery.

"An' what would ye be wantin', Captain?" asked the telepath when he reported to the control room.

"Don't waste my time!" snapped Grimes testily. "You know damn well what I'm wanting!"

"Then I'll be tellin' ye, Captain. I'm receivin' 'em— loud, but not all that clear. Just raw emotions, like. Frightenin', it is. Hate. Revenge. Anybody'd think ye were the black Cromwell himself, payin' another visit to the Emerald Isle."

"But what can they hope to do against us?" demanded Grimes.

"I can't tell ye. But they are hopin' to do something that'll not be improvin' the state of our health."

"Range twenty-five. Closing."

Grimes called the engine room. "Captain here, Chief. How's that water coming in?"

"Only number six tank to top up now—an' it's almost full."

"Then stop the pumps. Reel in the hoses." He put down the telephone. "Commander Brabham—sound the recall."

The wailing of the siren was deafening, but above it Tangye's voice was still audible. "Range twenty. Closing."

"We can reach them easily with a missile, sir," suggested Brabham.

"Then don't!" snarled Grimes.

The hoses were coming in, crawling over the grass like huge worms. The Marines were mounting the ramp, herded by Sergeant Washington.

"Liftoff stations," ordered Grimes quietly. He knew that he could be up and clear, especially with the reaction drive assisting the inertial drive, long before the airship, even if she attempted kamikaze tactics, could come anywhere near him. And if the dirigible were armed with missiles—which could hardly be anything more advanced than solid fuel rockets—*Discovery*'s anti-missile laser would make short work of them.

"Range fifteen. Closing."

The control room was fully manned now, the officers waiting for their captain's orders. But the hoses had stopped coming in; some mechanical hitch must have developed. But there was yet, thought Grimes, no urgency. He could well afford to wait a few more minutes. He had no wish to jettison equipment that could not be replaced until return to a Base.

"Range ten. Holding, holding, holding." There was relief in Tangye's voice.

The airship was well within sight now. It just hung there in the sky, from this angle looking like a harmless silver ball, a balloon, glittering with reflected light.

"And what do you pick up now, Mr. Flannery?" asked Grimes.

"Nothin' new at all, Captain. They're still hatin' us, still wantin' their revenge."

"They'll not be getting it at that range!" remarked Grimes cheerfully. He was certain that the natives' airborne weaponry would be unable to touch him. And he would soon be getting off this world, where things had gone so disastrously wrong. The sooner he was back in Deep Space the better. He said, "Once the hoses are in, I'll lift ship."

He went to the big binoculars on their universal mount, and the officer who had been using them made way for him. The instrument was already trained on the dirigible. He knew there would be nothing fresh to see—he was just passing the time—but then his attention was caught by a bright, intermittent flickering. A weapon? Hardly. It did not look like muzzle flashes, and surely these people did not yet have laser. The reflection of the sunlight from a control cabin window? Probably. He realized that he was trying to read the long and short flashes as though they were Morse, and laughed at himself for making the futile attempt.

"Hoses in, sir."

"Good." Grimes started to walk back to his control chair—and stopped in mid-stride as a violent explosion from somewhere outside shook the ship. "In the lake!" somebody was shouting. "The lake!" Over the suddenly disturbed water a column of spray, intermingled with dirty yellow smoke, was slowly subsiding. And something big and black and glistening had surfaced, was threshing in its death throes. But nobody could spare the time to look at it to determine what manner of beast it was. There was a second burst, a flame-centered eruption of sand and water on the beach itself, closer to the ship than the first one had been.

Suddenly that flickering light from the dirigible made sense to Grimes. It was either a heliograph or a daylight signaling lamp, and the function of the airship was not to attack but to spot for a surface vessel with heavy long-range guns, hidden from *Discovery*'s view, just as *Discovery* was hidden from hers. And what was she doing? he wondered. Laddering, or bracketing? The question was an academic one.

A third projectile screamed in—this one much too close for comfort. Fragments of stone, earth, and metal rattled against the spaceship's hull and she shuddered and complained, rocking in her tripedal landing gear. There was no time for normal liftoff procedure—the ritual countdown, the warning to all hands over the intercom to secure for space. There was no time, even, for Grimes to adjust himself properly in his chair. The inertial drive was ready, as was the auxiliary reaction drive. He slammed the controls of each straight from Standby to Maximum Lift, hoping desperately that at this time, of all times, the temperamental engines would not decide to play up. The violent acceleration pushed him deep into the padding of his seat; others, not so lucky, were thrown to the deck. *Discovery* did not have time to complain about the rough handling. (Normally she was the sort of ship that creaks and groans piteously at the least provocation.) She went up like a shot from a gun—and a real shot, from a real gun, blew a smoking crater into the ground upon which she, only a split second before, had been resting.

Upward she roared on her column of incandescent steam, with the overworked inertial drive deafeningly cacophonous. Already the island was showing as a map in the periscope screen. Off the northern coast, a gray slug on the blue water, stood the warship. There was a scintillation of yellow flashes as her guns, hastily elevated, loosed off a wild, futile salvo, and another, and another. The shell bursts were all well below the rapidly climbing *Discovery*.

Laboriously Grimes turned his head, forcing it around against the crushing weight of acceleration, looked through the viewports. The airship was closer now, driving in at its maximum speed. But it did not matter. *Discovery* would be well above the dirigible by the time the courses intersected, at such an altitude that the down-licking exhaust would be dissipated, would not ignite the hydrogen in the gas cells. He bore the aviators no grudge, felt only admiration for them.

Admiration, and . . . helpless pity.

He stared, horror-stricken, into the periscope screen as the airship, now almost directly beneath *Discovery*, was caught in the turbulence of the spaceship's wake. Giant, invisible hands caught the fragile craft, wrenched her, twisted her, wrung her apart. But there was buoyancy still in the sundered bow and stern sections, there was hope yet for her crew.

There was hope—until chance sparks, friction engendered, ignited the slowly escaping hydrogen. She blossomed then into a dreadful flower of blue and yellow flame from the center of which there was a spillage of wreckage, animate and inanimate.

Grimes cut the reaction drive. He did not wish to blow away all the water that had been purchased at too great a cost. He continued his passage up through the atmosphere on inertial drive only. It was time that he started to think about the casualties among his own people—the sprains, contusions, and abrasions, if nothing worse. He told Brabham to get hold of Dr. Rath and to find out how things were. Luckily nobody in the control room was badly hurt; everybody there had seen what was happening, had been given a chance to prepare for what was going to happen.

Grimes pushed the ship up and out, looking with regret at the dwindling world displayed in the screen. There was so much that could have been learned about it and its people, so much that should have been learned.

But, as far as he was concerned, it was no more than a big black mark on his service record.

»《Chapter 20》«

So he was back in Deep Space again and the planet, the native name of which he had never learned, was no more than a tiny shapeless blob of luminescence, barely discernible to one side of the greater (but fast diminishing) blob that was its primary, Star 1717 in the Ballchin Catalog. He was back in Deep Space, and trajectory had been set for 1716, and *Discovery* had settled down, more or less, to her normal Deep Space routine.

More or less.

Officers and ratings were doing their jobs as usual and—also as usual—in a manner that wasn't quite grossly inefficient. The ship was even less happy than she ever had been. Cases of minor insubordination were all too common, and all too often the insubordination had been provoked.

Perhaps, hoped Grimes, things would be better after planetfall had been made on the most likely world of Star 1716. Perhaps that world would prove to be the home of a Lost Colony, with genuinely human inhabitants. Perhaps it would be possible to make an unopposed landing and to establish amicable relations with the people at once, in which case everybody (including, eventually, the Lords Commissioners of the Admiralty) would be happy.

Meanwhile, he did not forget his promise to Captain Davinas. He made out the message, using the simple code that he and the tramp master had agreed upon. *To: Davinos, d/s/s Sundowner. Happy Birthday. Peter.* There would be little chance of such a short transmission being picked up by the Waverley monitors. It was transmitted on a tight beam, not broadcast, directed at the Carlotti relay station on Elsinore. There it would be picked up and immediately and automatically retransmitted, broadcast, at regular intervals, until it was acknowledged by *Sundowner.* Davinas would know from whom it came and what it meant. The Elsinore station would know the exact direction from which it had been beamed—but the straight line from *Discovery* to Elsinore was a very long one, stretching over many light-years. In the unlikely event of the broadcast's being received by any station within the Empire of Waverley it would be utterly meaningless.

The message on its way, he started to write his report on the happenings on and around the unlucky planet of 1717. It would be a long time before this report was handed in, he knew, but he wanted to get it on paper while the events were still fresh in his memory. It would not be, he was well aware, the only report. Brandt would be putting one in, probably arguing during the course of it that expeditions such as this should be under the command of scientists, not mere spacemen. The disgraced Swinton

would be writing his, addressed to the General Officer
Commanding Federation Space Marines, claiming, most
certainly, that by his prompt action he had saved the ship.
And officers, petty officers, and ratings would be deciding
among themselves what stories they would tell at the
inevitable Court of Inquiry when *Discovery* returned to
Lindisfarne Base.

Grimes was still working on his first, rough draft when
his senior officers—with the exception of the Mad
Major—came to see him.

"Yes?" he demanded, swiveling his chair away from the
paper-strewn desk.

"We'd like a word with you, sir," said Brabham. The first
lieutenant looked as morose as ever, but Grimes noted
that the man's heavy face bore a stubbornly determined
expression.

"Take the weight off your feet," Grimes ordered, with
forced affability. "Smoke, if you wish." He set the example
by filling and lighting his pipe.

Brabham sat stiffly at one end of the settee. Vinegar
Nell, her looks matching her nickname, took her place
beside him. Dr. Rath, who could have been going to or
coming from a funeral on a cold, wet day, sat beside her.
MacMorris, oafishly sullen, lowered his bulk into a chair.
The four of them stared at him in hostile silence.

"What is it you want?" snapped Grimes at last.

"I see you're writing a report, sir," said Brabham,
breaking the ominous quiet.

"I am writing. And it is a report, if you must know."

"I suppose you're putting the rope around Major
Swinton's neck," sneered Vinegar Nell.

"If there's any rope around his neck," growled Grimes, "he put it there himself."

"Aren't you being . . . unfair, Captain?" asked Brabham.

"Unfair? Everybody knows the man's no more than a uniformed murderer."

"Do they?" demanded MacMorris. "He was cleared by that court-martial."

And a gross miscarriage of justice that *was,* thought Grimes. He said, "I'm not concerned with what Major Swinton did in the past. What I'm concerned about is what he did under my command, on the world we've just left."

"And what did he do?" persisted Brabham.

"Opened fire against my orders. Murdered the entire crew of an airship bound on a peaceful mission."

"He did what he thought best, Commander Grimes. He acted in the best interests of the ship, of us all. He deserves better than to be put under arrest, with a court-martial awaiting him on Lindisfarne."

"Does he, Lieutenant Commander Brabham?"

"Yes. Damn it all, sir, all of us in this rustbucket are in the same boat. We should stick together."

"Cover up for each other?" asked Grimes quietly. "Lie for each other, if necessary? Present a united front against the common enemy, the Lords Commissioners of the Admiralty?"

"I wouldn't have put it quite in those words, Captain, but you're getting the idea."

"Am I?" exploded Grimes. "Am I? This isn't a matter of bending Survey Service regulations, Brabham! This is a matter of crime and punishment. I may be an easygoing sort of bastard in many ways, too many ways—but I do like to see real criminals, such as Swinton, get what's coming to them!"

"And is Major Swinton the only *real* criminal in this ship?" asked Vinegar Nell coldly.

"Yes, Miss Russell—unless some of you are guilty of crimes I haven't found out about yet."

"What about yourself, Commander Grimes?"

"What about myself?"

"I understand that two airships were destroyed. One by the major, when he opened fire perhaps—perhaps!— a little prematurely. The second by . . . yourself. Didn't you maneuver this vessel so that the backblast of your rockets blew the airship out of the sky?"

Grimes glared at her. "You were not a witness of the occurrence, the accident, Miss Russell."

"I know what I've been told," she snapped. "I see no reason to disbelieve it."

"It was an accident. The airship was well beneath us when it crossed our trajectory. It was not backblast that destroyed it, but turbulence." He turned to Brabham. "You saw it happen."

"I saw the airship go down in flames," said Brabham. He added, speaking very reasonably, "You have to admit, sir, that you're as guilty—or as innocent—as the major. You acted as you thought best. If you'd made a normal liftoff, using inertial drive only, there wouldn't have been any backblast. *Or* turbulence. But you decided to get upstairs in a hurry."

"If I hadn't got upstairs in a hurry," stated Grimes, "I'd never have got upstairs at all. None of us would. The next round—or salvo—would have been right on."

"We are not all gunnery experts, Captain," said Dr. Rath. "Whether or not we should have been hit is a matter for conjecture. But the fact remains that the airship was destroyed by your action."

"Too right it was!" agreed MacMorris. "An' the way you flogged my engines it's a miracle this ship wasn't destroyed as well."

"Gah!" expostulated Grimes. Reasonable complaints he was always prepared to listen to, but this was too much. He would regret the destruction of the second dirigible to his dying day, but a captain's responsibility is always to his own vessel, not to any other. Nonetheless he was not, like Swinton, a murderer.

Or was he?

"You acted as you thought best," murmured Brabham. "So did the major."

"Major Swinton deliberately disobeyed orders," stated Grimes.

"I seem to remember, Captain," went on Brabham, "that you were ordered to make a sweep out toward the Rim."

"If you ever achieve a command of your own," Grimes told him coldly, "you will discover that the captain of a ship is entitled—expected, in fact—to use his own discretion. It was suggested that I make my sweep out toward the Rim—but the Admiralty would take a very dim view of me if I failed to follow up useful leads taking me in another direction."

"All that has been achieved to date by this following of useful leads," said Rath, "is the probable ruin of a zealous officer's career."

"Which should have been ruined before he ever set foot aboard this ship!" flared Grimes.

"Then I take it, sir," said Brabham, "that you are not prepared to stretch a point or two in the major's favor."

"You may take it that way," agreed Grimes.

"Then, sir," went on the first lieutenant, speaking slowly and carefully, "we respectfully serve notice that we shall continue to obey your legal commands during the remainder of this cruise, but I wish to make it clear that we shall complain to the proper authorities regarding your conduct and actions as soon as we are back on Lindisfarne."

"The inference being," said Grimes, "that if Swinton is for the high jump, I am too."

"You said it, Commander Grimes," put in Vinegar Nell. "The days when a captain was a little—or not so little—tin god are long dead. You're only a human being, like the rest of us, although you don't seem to think so. But you'll learn, the hard way!"

"Careful, you silly cow!" growled MacMorris.

Grimes forced himself to smile. "I am all too aware of my fallible humanity, Miss Russell. I'm human enough to sympathize with you, and to warn you of the consequences of sticking your necks out. But what puzzles me is why you're doing it for Major Swinton. The Marines have always been a pain in the neck to honest spacemen, and Swinton has all a Marine's faults and precious few of the virtues. And I know that all of you hate his guts."

"He *is* a son of a bitch," admitted the woman, "but he's *our* son of a bitch. But you, Commander Grimes, are the outsider aboard this ship. Lucky Grimes, always on the winning side, while the rest of us, Swinton included, are the born losers. Just pray to all the Odd Gods of the Galaxy that your luck doesn't run out, that's all!"

"Amen," intoned Rath, surprisingly and sardonically.

Grimes kept his temper. He said, "This is neither the time nor the place for a prayer meeting. I suggest that you all return to your duties."

"Then you won't reconsider the action you're taking against the major, Captain?" asked Brabham politely.

"No."

"Then I guess this is all we can do," said the first lieutenant, getting up to leave.

"For the time being," added Vinegar Nell.

They left, and Grimes returned to his report writing. He saw no reason why he should try to whitewash Swinton, and regarding the destruction of the second airship told the truth, no more and no less.

»«(Chapter 21)«»

Grimes went down to the farm deck to see Flannery.

He could have sent for the telepath, but did not like to have the man in his quarters. He was always filthy, and around him hung the odors of stale perspiration, cheap whiskey, and organic fertilizers. Possibly this latter smell came from the nutrient solutions pumped into the hydroponic tanks—at times the atmosphere in the farm deck was decidedly ripe—and possibly not.

The PCO, as always, was hunched at his littered table, with the inevitable whiskey bottle and its accompanying dirty glass to hand. He was staring, as he usually was, at the spherical tank in which was suspended the obscenely naked canine brain, which seemed to be pulsating slowly (but surely this was an optical illusion) in the murky life-support fluid. His thick lips were moving as he sang, almost inaudibly, to himself, or to his weird pet.

"Now all you young dukies an' duchesses,

Take warnin' from what I do say;
Be sure that you owns what you touchesses.
Or ye'll jine us in Botany Bay!"

"Mphm!" Grimes grunted loudly.

Flannery looked up, turned slowly around in his chair.

"Oh, it's you, Captain Bligh. Sorry, me tongue slipped. Me an' Ned was back in the ould days, when the bully boys, in their pretty uniforms, was ridin' high an' roughshod. An' what can I be doin' for ye, Captain?"

"What were you getting at when you called me Captain Bligh?" demanded Grimes.

"Not what ye were thinkin'. Yer officers an' crew haven't decided to put ye in the long boat, with a few loyalists an' the ship's cat . . . yet. Not that we have a cat. But ye're not loved, that's for sure. An' that murtherin' major's gettin' sympathy he's not deservin' of. Ned has *him* taped, all right. He doesn't like him at all, at all. He can remember the really bad bastards who were officers in the ould New South Wales Corps, floggin' the poor sufferin' convicts with nary a scrap o' provocation, an' huntin' down the black fellows like animals."

"I still don't believe that dingo of yours had a racial memory," said Grimes.

"Suit yerself, Captain. Suit yerself. But he has. An' he has a soft spot for ye, believe it or not, even though he thinks o' ye as a latter-day Bligh. Even—or because. He remembers that it was Bligh who stood up for the convicts against the sodgers when he was governor o' New South Wales. After all, that was what the Rum Rebellion was all about."

"You're rather simplifying," said Grimes.

"No more than the descendants o' those New South Wales Corps officers who've been blackenin' Bligh's memory to try to make their own crummy forebears look like plaster saints by comparison." His voice faded, and then again he started to sing softly.

> "*Singin' tooral-i-ooral-i-addy,*
> *Singin' tooral-i-ooral-i-ay,*
> *Singin' tooral-i-ooral-i-addy,*
> *An' we're bound out for Botany Bay. . . .*"

"I didn't come down here for a concert," remarked Grimes caustically.

Flannery raised a pudgy, admonitory hand. "Hould yer whist, Captain. That song niver came from me. It came from outside."

"Outside?"

"Ye heard me. Quiet now. T'is from far away . . . but I could be there, where iver *there* is. They're a-sittin' around a fire an' a-singin', an' a-suppin' from their jars. T'is a right ould time they're after havin'. They're a-sendin' . . . oh, they're transmittin', if it's the technicalities ye want, but they're like all o' ye half-wits—beggin' your pardon, Captain, but that's what *we* call ye—ye can transmit after a fashion, but ye can't receive. I'm tryin' to get through to someone, anyone, but it's like tryin' to penetrate a brick wall."

"Mphm."

"Tie me kangaroo down, sport, tie me kangaroo down. . . ."

"Must you try to sing, Mr. Flannery?"

"I was only jinin' in, like. T'is a good party, an' Ned an' me wishes we was there."

"But where is it?"

"Now ye're askin'. There should be a bonus for psionic dowsin', there should. Ye've no idea, not bein' a telepath yerself, how it takes it out of yer. But I'll try."

Grimes waited patiently. It would be useless, he knew, to try to hurry Flannery.

At last: "I've got it, Captain. That broadcast—ye can call it that—comes from a point directly ahead of us. How far? I can't be tellin' ye, but t'is not all that distant. An' I can tell ye, too, that it comes from our sort o' people, humans."

"I somehow can't imagine aliens singing 'Botany Bay,'" said Grimes. "And many of the lodejammers were out of Port Woomera, in Australia."

"I've found yer Lost Colony for ye," said Flannery smugly.

»«Chapter 22»«

So Grimes ordered the splicing of the mainbrace, the issue of drink to all hands at the ship's expense. He sat in the wardroom with his officers, drinking with them, and drinking to the Lost Colony upon which they would be making a landing before too long. He did not need to be a telepath to sense the change of mood. They were behind him, with him again, these misfits and malcontents. He responded, smiling, when Brabham toasted, "To Grimes's luck!" He clinked glasses with Vinegar Nell, even with the Mad Major. He joined in heartily when everybody started singing *"Botany Bay."*

Botany Bay.

He rather hoped that this would be the name given by the colonists to this chance-found world circling Star 1716 in the Ballchin Catalog. It might well be; such colonies as had been founded by the crews and passengers of the gaussjammers of the New Australian Expansion tended to run to distinctively Australian names.

He left when the party began to get a little too rowdy. He did not retire at once, but sprawled in his easy chair, his mind still active. When people recovered from this letting off of steam, he thought, he would have to discuss his plan of campaign with the senior officers, the departmental heads. Then, suddenly but quietly, the outer door of his day cabin opened. He was somehow not surprised when Vinegar Nell came in. She was (as before) carrying a tray, with coffee things and a plate of sandwiches. But this time she was still in uniform.

Grimes gestured toward the supper as she set it down on the low table. "So you still think of me as Gutsy Grimes?" he asked, but he smiled as he spoke.

"Lucky Grimes," she corrected, smiling back, a little lopsidedly. "And I hope, John, I really hope that your luck rubs off on the rest of us."

"I do, too," he told her.

She straightened up after she had put the supper things down, standing over him. Her legs were very long, and slightly apart, her skirt very short. One of her knees was exercising a gentle but definite pressure on Grimes's outstretched thigh, but with a considerable effort he managed to keep his hands to himself. Then she stooped again as she poured him his coffee. The top two buttons of her shirt were undone and he glimpsed a nipple, erect, startlingly pink against the pale tan of the skin of her breast.

He whispered huskily, "Miss Russell, would you mind securing the door?"

She replied primly, "If you insist, Commander Grimes."

She walked slowly away from the table, away from him, shrugging out of her upper garment, letting it float unheeded to the deck. He heard the sharp *click* of the lock as it engaged. She turned, stepping out of her brief skirt as she did so. The sheer black tights that were all she was wearing beneath it concealed nothing. She walked past him into the bedroom, not looking at him, a faint smile on her face, her small breasts jouncing slightly, her round buttocks smoothly working, gleaming under the translucent material. He got up, spilling his coffee and ignoring it, following her.

She must have been fast. She was already completely naked, stretched out on the bunk, waiting for him, warmly glowing on the dark blue bedspread. In the dim light her hair glinted like dusky gold against the almost black material of the coverlet, in aphrodisiac contrast to the pale, creamy tan of her upper thighs and lower abdomen. She was beautiful, as only a desirous and desirable woman, stripped of all artifice, can be.

Grimes looked down at her and she looked up at him, her eyes large and unwinking, her lips slightly parted. He undressed with deliberate slowness, savoring the moment, making it last. He even put his shirt on a hanger and neatly folded his shorts. And then he joined her on the couch, warm, naked skin to warm, naked skin, his mouth on hers. It was as though he had known her, in the Biblical sense of the word, for many, many years.

»«(Chapter 23)»«

She murmured, as they shared a cigarillo, "Now you're one of us."

"Is that why . . . ?" he started, hurt.

"No," she assured him. "No. That is not why I came to you. We should have done this a long time ago. A long, long time—"

He believed her.

The people of Botany Bay—this was, in fact, the name of the Lost Colony—did not, of course, run to such highly sophisticated communications equipment as the time-space-twisting Carlotti radio. Had they possessed it they would not have stayed lost for long. But it had yet to be invented in the days of the gaussjammers—as had, too, the time-space-twisting Mannschenn Drive. It had been making a voyage, as passenger, in one of the timejammers that had started Luigi Carlotti wondering why, when ships could exceed the speed of light (effectively if not actually) radio messages could not. So Botany Bay did not possess Carlotti radio. Neither was there, as on most other Man-colonized worlds, a corps of trained telepaths; Flannery spoke with some authority on that point, maintaining that somehow psionic talent had never developed on the planet. But there was, of course, Normal Space-Time radio, both audio and visual, used for intraplanetary communications and for the broadcasting of entertainment.

It did not take long for the ship's radio officers to find this out once *Discovery* had reentered the normal continuum, shortly thereafter taking up a circumpolar orbit about the planet. It was no great trouble to them to ascertain the frequencies in use and then to begin monitoring the transmissions. Grimes went down to the main radio office—its sterile cleanliness made a welcome change from Flannery's pig pen—to watch the technicians at work and to listen to the sounds issuing from the speakers. Barbham accompanied him.

There were what sounded like radio telephone conversations. At first these seemed to be in some quite familiar yet unknown language—and then, as soon as Grimes's ear became accustomed to the peculiarly flat intonation of the voices—they suddenly made sense. The language, save for its accent, had survived almost unchanged, was still understandable Standard English. It became obvious that what was being picked up was an exchange of messages between a ship and some sort of traffic control authority.

"*Duchess of Paddington,*" Grimes heard, "to Port Ballina. My ETA is now 0700 hours. What's the weather doin' at your end? Over."

"Port Ballina to *Duchess*. Wind west at ten kph. No

cloud. Visibility excellent. The moorin' crowd'll be waitin' for yer, Skip. Over."

"Sounds like a surface ship, Captain," commented Brabham.

"Mphm?" grunted Grimes dubiously.

The voice came from the speaker again. "*Duchess of Paddington* to Port Ballina. Please have one 'A' helium bottle waitin' for me. I'd a bastard of a slow leak in one o' my for'ard cells. Over."

"Wilco, *Duchess*. Will you be wantin' the repair mob? Over."

"Thanks muchly, but no. Got it patched me self, but I lost quite a bit o' buoyancy an' I've had to use the heaters to maintain altitude an' attitude. See you. Over."

"More ruddy airships!" growled Brabham. "I hope—" His voice trailed off into silence.

"You hope what?" asked Grimes coldly.

"Well, sir, there seems to be a sort of jinx on the things as far as we're concerned."

"There'd better not be *this* time," Grimes told him.

"Sir!" called one of the radio officers. "I think I'm picking up a treevee transmission, but I just can't seem to get any sort of picture."

Grimes shuffled slowly to the receiver on which the young man was working; with the ship now in free fall it was necessary to wear magnetic-soled shoes and, after the long spell under acceleration, to move with caution. He stared into the screen. It was alive with swirling color, an intermingling of writhing, prismatic flames and subtle and everchanging shades of darkness, an eddying opalescence that seemed always about to coalesce into a picture, yet never did. The technician made more adjustments and suddenly there was music—from a synthesizer, thought Grimes—with the effect of ghost guitars, phantom violins, and distant drums. The ever-changing colors in the screen matched the complex rhythms drifting from the speaker.

"Damn it!" muttered the radio officer, still fiddling with the controls. "I still can't get a picture."

"Perhaps you aren't supposed to," murmured Grimes.

A final crash of guitars, scream of violins and rattle of drums, an explosive flare of light and color, fading into darkness . . . and then, at last, a picture. A young woman, attractive, with deeply tanned skin and almost white-blonde hair, stood with one slim hand resting on the surface of a table. She was simply clad in a long white robe, which somehow hid no smallest detail of her firm body. She said— and it was a pity that her voice, with its flat intonation, did not match her appearance—"An' that was Damon's *Firebird Symphony,* played to you by the composer himself. I hope y'all liked it. An' that's it from this station for today. We'll be on the air again at the usual time termorrer with our brecker program, commencin' at 0600 hours. Nighty-night all, an' good sleepin'."

She faded slowly from the screen and the picture of a flag replaced her—a familiar (to Grimes) ensign, horizontal and rippling in a stiff breeze, dark blue, with a design of red, white, and blue crosses superimposed upon each other in the upper canton, a five-starred, irregularly cruciform constellation in the fly. And there was music— also familiar.

"Once a jolly swagman," sang Grimes, softly but untunefully, "camped by a billabong. . . ."

"Do you *know* it, sir?" asked one of the radio officers.

Grimes looked at the young man suspiciously, then remembered that he was from New Otago, and that the New Otagoans are a notoriously insular breed. He said, "Yes. 'Waltzing Matilda,' of course. Wherever Aussies have gone they've taken her with them."

"Who was Waltzing Matilda?" persisted the officer. "Some old-time dancing girl?"

Brabham sniggered, and Grimes said, "Not exactly. But it's a bit too complicated to explain right now."

And whose ghosts, he wondered, would be haunting the billabongs (if there were billabongs) of this world upon which they would soon be landing? The phantom of some swagman, displaced in time and space, or—*Damn you, Flannery,* he thought, *stop putting ideas into my mind!*—or, even, of the mutiny-prone Bligh?

»«(Chapter 24)«»

"We have to let them know we're here," said Grimes.

"The probe is in good working order, sir," said Brabham.

"Not the probe," Grimes told him. He did not want a repetition of all that had happened the last time a probe had been used. He went on, "These people are human. They have maintained a reasonably high standard of technology."

"With *airships*, Sir?" asked Brabham.

"Yes. With airships. It has never ceased to amaze me that so many human cultures have not persisted with their use. Why waste power just to stay up before you even think about proceeding from Point A to Point B? But never mind the airships. They also have radio." He turned to one of the technicians. "Did you note the time when the station closed down, Lieutenant? Good. And the blonde said that she'd be resuming transmission at 0600 hours tomorrow."

"Local time, sir," pointed out Brabham. "Not ship's time."

"When she whispered her sweet good nights," said Grimes, "I managed to tear my eyes away from her face long enough to notice a clock on the wall behind her. A twenty-four-hour clock. It was registering midnight. And we already know, from our own observations, that Botany Bay has a period of rotation of just over twenty-five Standard Hours. I assume—but, of course, I could be wrong—that there are people in this ship, besides myself, capable of doing simple sums."

Brabham scowled. The radio officers sniggered.

"So," went on Grimes, "I want to make a broadcast myself on that station's frequencies when it starts up again with the"—he made a grimace of distaste—"*brecker* program. I think we have the power from our jennies to override anything they may be sending. I shall want a visual transmission as well as sound. Their people will have as much trouble with our accent as we had with theirs. I'll leave you to work out the details. I'm going to prepare a series of cards, from which I shall be speaking. Do you think you'll be able to set up your end of it in the time?"

"Of course, sir," the senior radioman assured him.

"Their spelling's probably nothing at all like ours," muttered Brabham.

"It shouldn't have changed all that much," said Grimes hopefully. "And luckily, the blonde bombshell wasn't delivering her spiel in Hebrew or Chinese. Well, I'll leave you to it, gentlemen. You know where to find me if anything fresh crops up."

He went back to his quarters and set to work with sheets of stiff white paper and a broad-tipped stylus.

They were ready for him when he returned to the radio office. He stood where he was told, with the camera trained on him, watching the monitor screen, which was still blank. Suddenly he realized that he had omitted to change into his dress uniform and put on a cap—but, he told himself, it didn't matter.

The screen came alive. Again there was the flag, bravely flying, and again there was music—but, this time, it was "Botany Bay." When it was over the picture became that of an announcer. It was not—to the disappointment of Grimes and the others—the spectacular blonde. It was a young man, comfortably clad in colorful shirt, extremely short shorts, and sandals. Like the girl he was fair haired and deeply tanned. He was far more cheerful than he had a right to be at what must be, to him, an ungodly hour of the morning.

"Mornin', all those of yer who're up, that is. An' you lucky bastards who're still in yer scratchers can get stuffed. Anyhow, this is Station BBP, the Voice of Paddo, openin' transmission on this bright an' sunny mornin' o' December nineteenth, Thursday. I s'pose yer wantin' the news. Now what have we to make yer day for yer?" He looked down at a sheet of paper in his right hand.

Grimes signaled with his own right hand to the senior radio officer. The lights in the radio office flickered and dimmed, except for the one trained on Grimes. The picture in the monitor screen faded—as must also have done the pictures in the screens of all the receivers tuned to that station. It was replaced by the image of Grimes himself, looking (he realized) very important, holding at chest level the first of his cards. He read from it, trying to imitate the local accent, "I am the captain of the Earth Survey Ship *Discovery*." He changed cards. "My ship is at present in orbit about your planet." He changed cards again. "I am about to cease transmission. Please make your reply. Over."

The picture of the announcer came back into the screen. The young man's pallor under his tan gave his complexion a greenish tinge. At last he spoke. "Is this some bloody hoax?" And somebody not in the screen said, "I could see the bastard in the monitor plain enough. T'aint nobody *we* know—an' we know everybody who is anybody in the radio trade!"

"Get on the blower to the observatory, Clarry," ordered the announcer. "Tell the lazy bludgers ter get their useless radio telescope on the job." Then, facing his audience— those on the planet and those in space—"Orright, Captain whatever-yer-name-is. It's over ter you again." He grinned. "At least you've saved me the trouble o' readin' the bloody news!"

Grimes reappeared in the screen, holding another card. He read, "Can you understand me? Over."

The announcer came back. "Yair—though Matilda knows where yer learned yer spellin'. An' yer sound like you've a plum in yer mouf." He mimicked Grimes's way of speaking. "And whom have I the honor of addressing, Captain, sir?" He grinned again, quite convincingly. "I used to act in historical plays before I was mug enough to take this job. Over."

"My name is Grimes, Commander Grimes of the Federation Survey Service. I am, as I've already told you, captain of the Survey Ship *Discovery*. I was ordered to make a search for Lost Colonies. Over."

"An' you've sure found one, ain't yer? We're lorst orright. An' we thought we were goin' ter stay that way. Hold on a sec, will yer? Clarry's got the gen from the observatory."

The unseen Clarry's voice came from the speaker. "T'aint a hoax, Don. The bastards say there is somethin' up there, where somethin' shouldn't be."

"So yer for real, Commander Grimes. Ain't yer supposed ter say, 'Take me to yer leader'? Over."

"Take me to your leader," said Grimes, deadpan. "Over."

"Hold yer horses, Skip. This station'll be goin' up in flames at any tick o' the clock, the way the bleedin' phones are runnin' hot. Her Ladyship's on the way ter the studio now, s'matter o' fact. Over."

"Her Ladyship? Over."

"The mayor o' Paddo, no less. Or Paddington, as I s'pose you'd call our capital. Here she is now."

The announcer bowed, backed away from the camera at his end. He was replaced by a tall, ample woman, silvery haired and with what seemed to be the universal deep tan. She was undeniably handsome, and on her the extremely short dress with its gay floral pattern did not look incongruous—and neither, somehow, did the ornate gold chain that depended from her neck. She said— and even the accent could not entirely ruin her deep contralto—"'Ow yer doin', Skip? Orright?" Then, turning to address the announcer, "Wot do I say now, Don? 'Over,' ain't it? Orright. Over."

"I'm honored to meet you, Your Ladyship. Over."

"Don't be so bloody formal, Skipper. I'm Mavis to me mates—an' any bastard who's come all the way from Earth's a mate o' mine. When are yer comin' down ter meet us proper? Do yer have ter land at one o' the magnetic poles same as *Lode Wallaby* did? Or do yer use rockets? If yer do, it'll have ter be someplace where yer won't start a bushfire. Wherever it is, there'll be a red carpet out for yer. Even at the bloody North Pole." Then, as an after-thought, "Over."

"I have rocket drive," said Grimes, "but I won't be using it. My main drive, for sub-light speeds, is the inertial drive. No fireworks. So I can put down on any level surface firm enough to bear my weight. Over."

"You don't look all that fat ter me, Skip. But you bastards are all the same, ain't yer? No matter what yer ship is, it's *I, I, I* all the time." She grinned whitely. "But I guess the Bradman Oval'll take the weight o' that scow o' yours. Havin' you there'll rather bugger the current test series but the landin' o' the first ship from Earth is more important than cricket. Never cared for the game me self, anyhow. Over."

"I'll make it the Bradman Oval, then, Your . . . sorry. Mavis. Once we get some less complicated radio telephone system set up your technicians can go into a huddle with mine. I'd like a radio beacon to home on, and all the rest of it." He paused, then went on. "Forgive me if I'm giving offense, but do you speak for your own city only, or for the whole planet? Over."

"I speak for me own city-state. The other mayors speak for their city-states. An' it so happens that at the moment I *am* President of the Council of Mayors. So I do speak for Botany Bay. That do yer, Skip? Over."

"That does me, Mavis. And now, shall we leave all the sordid details to our technicians? Over."

"'Fraid we have to, Skip. I can't change a bloody fuse, me self. Be seein' yer. Over."

"Be seeing you," promised Grimes.

»«(Chapter 25)»«

Grimes had several more conversations with the mayor of Paddington before the landing of *Discovery*. The radio experts on the planet and in the ship had not taken long to set up a satisfactory two-way service, and when this was not being used for the exchange of technical information the spaceship's crew was continuously treated to a planetary travelogue. Botany Bay was a *good* world, of that there could be no doubt. There was neither overpopulation nor pollution. There was industry, of course, highly automated—but the main power sources were the huge solar energy screens set up in what would have otherwise been useless desert areas, and wind- and water-drive turbo-generators. There were oil wells and coal mines— but the fossil fuels merely supplied useful chemicals. The only use of radioactives was in medicine. Airships, great and small, plied the skies, driven by battery-powered motors, although there were a few jets, their gas turbines burning a hydrogen-oxygen mixture. On the wide seas the sailing vessel was the commonest form of ship—schooners mainly, with auxiliary engines and with automation replacing man-power. Efficient monorail systems criss-crossed the continents—but the roads, surprisingly, seemed to be little more than dirt tracks. There was a reason for this, the spacemen soon discovered. *Lode Wallaby* had carried among other livestock the fertilized ova of horses—and horses were used extensively for private transport, for short journeys.

Botany Bay, in the main, enjoyed an almost perfect climate, its continents being little more than large islands, the oceans exercising a tempering effect from the tropics to the poles. The climate had not been so good when the first colonists landed, destructive hurricanes being all too common. Now, of course, there was a planetwide weather watch, and fast aircraft could be dispatched at short notice to a developing storm center to drop anti-thermal bombs.

Botany Bay, throughout, could boast of almost unspoiled scenery. In all industrial establishments ugliness had been avoided. In the cities there had been a deliberate revival of architectural styles long vanished, except in isolated cases, from Earth. Paddington, for example, was a greatly enlarged, idealized version of the Terran Paddington, maintained as a historical curiosity in the heart of sprawling Sydney. There were the narrow, winding streets, tree lined, and the terrace houses, none higher than three stories, each with its balconies ornamented by metal railings cast in intricate floral designs. It was all so archaic, charmingly so. Grimes remembered a party to which he had been invited in the original Paddington. The host, when accused of living in a self-consciously ancient part of Sydney, had replied, "We Australians don't have much history—but, by any deity you care to name, we make the most of what we have got!"

This Paddington, the Botany Bay Paddington, was a city, not a mere inner suburb. It stood on the western shore of the great, natural harbor called Port Jackson. Its eastern streets ran down to the harbor beaches. To the west of it was the airport, and also the Bradman Oval. To the south and east were the port facilities for surface shipping. To the north were The Heads, the relatively narrow entrance to the harbor. And on the north coast were the high cliffs, with bays and more sandy beaches.

Grimes studied the aerial view of the city and its environs that was being transmitted to him. He could foresee no difficulties in making a landing. He would keep well to the west on his way down, so that if, in the event of a breakdown of his inertial drive, he were obliged to use the auxiliary reaction drive he would do no damage to the city.

He had wanted to adhere to the standard practice of the Survey Service and bring the ship down at dawn, but the mayor would not agree to this. "Come off it, Skip!" she remonstrated. "I don't like gettin' up at Matilda-less hours, even if you do! Wot's wrong wif ten hundred? The streets'll be aired by then, an' everybody'll be up an' dressed. We want ter *see* yer comin' down. We don't want ter be starin' up inter the gloom ter watch somethin' droppin' down outa the sky that could be no more than a solid-lookin' cloud wif a few lights hung on it!"

Grimes was obliged to agree. As a Survey Service captain he was supposed to make friends as well as to influence people. Meanwhile, as a preliminary measure, he had certain of the ship's clocks adjusted to synchronize with Paddington Local Time. Ten hundred hours Mavis had said, and he was determined that the pads of his tripedal landing gear would touch the turf of the Oval at precisely that time.

It was a fine, clear morning when *Discovery* dropped down through the atmosphere. Her inertial drive was working sweetly, but inevitably noisily, and Grimes wondered what the colonists would be thinking of the irregular beat of his engines, the loud, mechanical clangor driving down from above. Their own machines—with the exception of the few jet planes—were so silent. In the periscope screen the large island, the continent that had been named New Australia, showed in its entirety. Its outline was not dissimilar to that of the original Australia, although there was no Tasmania, and Port Jackson was on the north and not the east coast. The coastal fringe was green, but inland there were large desert areas, the sites of the solar power stations.

Grimes glanced at the control room clock, which was now keeping local time. There was time to spare; he could afford to take things easily.

"Target," announced Tangye. "Bearing 020, range fifty. Closing."

"Altitude?" asked Grimes.

"It's matching altitude with us, sir."

"It can't be one of the airships this high," said Grimes. He added nastily, "And, anyhow, we don't have Major Swinton at fire control this time."

He turned away from his console to look out of the

viewports on the bearing indicated. Yes, there the thing was, a silvery speck, but expanding, closing fast.

"What if they *are* hostile, Captain?" asked Brabham. "We're a sitting duck."

"*If* they are hostile," Grimes told him, "we'll give them the privilege of firing the first shot."

"It's one of their jets," said Tangye.

"So it is," agreed Grimes. "So it is. They're doing the right thing; laying on an escort."

The aircraft closed them rapidly, circled them in a slowly descending spiral. It was, obviously, a passenger plane, with swept-back wings. Grimes could see men in the forward control cabin. They waved. He waved back, then returned his attention to handling the ship. He hoped that the jet pilot would not attempt to approach too close.

He could see Port Jackson plainly enough in the screen now, a great irregular bite out of the northern coastline. He could see the golden beaches with a cream of surf outlining them and—very small, a mere, crawling insect— one of the big schooners standing in toward The Heads. And there were two more targets announced by the radar-watching Tangye—airships this time, huge brutes with the sunlight reflected dazzlingly from their metal skins.

A familiar voice came from the speaker of the control room transceiver. "That's a noisy bitch yer've got there, Skip. Sounds like umpteen tons of old tin cans fallin' downstairs. Just as well yer didn't come in at sparrer fart."

"Do you have sparrows here?" asked Grimes interestedly.

"Nah. Not *reel* sparrers. But it's what we call one o' the

native birds. Don't know how it got by before it had human bein's ter bludge on."

"Mphm. Excuse me, Mavis, but I'd like to concentrate on my pilotage now."

"That's what me late husband useter say. He was skipper o' one o' the coastal schooners. Oh, well, I can take a hint."

Grimes could see the city now—red roofs and gray, a few towers of pseudo-Gothic appearance. He could see the airport, with one big dirigible at its mooring mast like an oversized wind sock. And there, just beyond it, was the Bradman Oval, a darkly green recreation area with spectators' stands around it and, he was pleased to note, a triangle of red flashing lights, bright even in the general brightness of the morning. The radio beacon had been set up as requested by Grimes, but he preferred to use visual aids whenever possible.

The Oval expanded to fill the screen. The stands, Grimes saw, were crowded. He thought sourly, *These bastards have more faith in my innies than I do.* If the inertial drive were to break down, necessitating the use of the emergency reaction drive, there would be a shocking tragedy. But the beat of the engines still sounded healthy enough. He applied a touch of lateral thrust, brought the three beacons into the center of the screen. He looked at the clock: 0953. He was coming down just a little too fast. A slight, very slight increase of vertical thrust. The figures on the face of the radar altimeter nickered down in slightly slower succession.

That should do it, thought Grimes smugly.

Eleven . . . ten . . . nine . . .

And, on the clock, 0955.

Seven . . . six . . . five . . . four . . . three . . . two . . . one. . . 0959.

Gently, gently, thought Grimes.

Zero!

And, on the clock, the sweep second hand jumped to the same numeral.

The ship groaned and shuddered as her weight came onto the shock absorbers, and silence fell like a blow when the inertial drive was shut down. But there was another noise, a tumult that Grimes at first could not identify. Then he realized that it was cheering, noisy cheering, loud enough to be heard even inside the buttoned-up ship. And, faintly, there was the noise of a band. "Waltzing Matilda" (of course).

He looked out of the port at the waving crowds, at the blue flags, with their Union Jacks and Southern Crosses, flying from every mast around the Oval.

"So yer made it, Skip," the mayor's voice issued from the speaker. "Bang on time, too! Welcome to Botany Bay! Welcome to Paddo!"

"I'm glad to be here, Your Ladyship," replied Grimes formally.

"It's a pleasure ter have yer. But is it safe ter come near yer ship? You ain't radioactive or anythin', are yer?"

"Quite safe," said Grimes. "I'll meet you at the after airlock."

»《Chapter 26》《«

Grimes, after issuing instructions, went down to his quarters to change. He had decided that this was an occasion for some show of formality, no matter how free and easy the people of this Lost Colony seemed to be. Or—he had his contrary moments—it was this very freeness and easiness that had induced in him the desire to be stiff and starchy. He got out of his comfortable shorts and open-necked shirt, replacing the latter with a stiff, snowy-white one. He knotted a black necktie about his throat, then thrust his legs into sharply creased black trousers. The bemedaled frock coat came next, then the sword belt and the quite useless ceremonial sword. Highly polished black shoes on his feet, the fore-and-aft hat with its trimmings of gold braid on his head. He inspected his reflection in the full-length mirror inside his wardrobe door, holding himself stiffly at attention. He'd do, he decided.

He took the elevator down to the after airlock. The others were waiting for him—the Mad Major, temporarily forgiven, with a half dozen of his men. The Marines, too, were in their dress finery, blue and scarlet and gleaming brass. Swinton was wearing a sword, his men carried archaic (but nonetheless lethal) rifles. Tangye, one of the few officers to possess a presentable full dress uniform, was there, as was Vinegar Nell, in the odd rig prescribed by the Survey Service for its female officers on state occasions, best described as, a long-skirted, long-sleeved black evening frock, trimmed with gold braid and brass buttons and worn over a white shirt and black tie, topped with a hat like the one Grimes was wearing. But she carried it well.

The outer airlock door slowly opened, and as it did so the ramp was extruded, its end sinking to the close-cropped grass. Grimes stepped out into the warm, fresh air, the bright sunlight. He was thankful that his uniform had been tailored from the lightest possible material. As he appeared there was a great welcoming roar from the crowds in the Stands. He paused, saluted smartly, then continued down the ramp. After him came Tangye and the paymaster, and after them, their boots crashing rhythmically on the metal gangway, marched the Marines.

There was a stir among the crowd on the stand immediately facing the airlock. In the broad aisle between it and its neighbor a coach appeared, a vehicle drawn by four gleaming black horses, the first of what looked like a procession of such vehicles. Grimes, standing at the foot of the ramp, the others drawn up behind him, watched with interest. Yes, that was the mayor in the first coach, and other women and men with her. From this distance he could not be sure, but it did not look as though anybody had made any attempt to dress up. The driver was in some sort of khaki uniform with a broad-brimmed hat. But what was Brabham waiting for?

Suddenly, from overhead, there came a deafening *boom,* the first round of the twenty-one-gun salute, fired from one of the forty-millimeter cannon, using special blank cartridges.

Boom!

The coachmen were having trouble controlling their horses.

Boom!

The horses of the second and third coaches had bolted, had begun to gallop around the Oval like the start of a chariot race.

Grimes lifted his wrist transceiver to his mouth. "Brabham, hold. . ."

Boom!

"Brabham, hold your fire!"

"But that's only four rounds, sir," came the tinny whisper in reply.

"Never mind. Hold your fire."

The driver of the mayor's coach had his animals under control at last. He came on steadily, then reined in about ten meters from the foot of the ramp. From one of his pockets he produced a cigarette, lit it with a flaring lighter, then sat there stolidly with the little crumpled cylinder dangling from the corner of his mouth. He stared at Grimes and his entourage with a certain hostility.

Another khaki-uniformed man was first out. He assisted the mayor to the ground. She emerged from the vehicle with a lavish display of firm, brown thigh. She was wearing a short tunic, with sandals on her feet, only the mayoral chain of office adding a touch of formality. Her blue eyes were angry, her mouth drawn down in a scowl.

Grimes saluted with drawn sword. The Marines presented arms with a slap and rattle.

She demanded, "Wodyer playin' at, you stupid drongo? You said there'd be no bleedin' fireworks."

Grimes sheathed his sword. He said stiffly. "It is customary, Your Ladyship, to accord heads of state the courtesy of a twenty-one-gun salute."

"That may be where you come from, Skip, but it certainly ain't here. You scared shit outa the horses."

"Too flamin' right," commented the coachman. "Wodyer think me wheels was skiddin' on?"

"I'm sorry," Grimes began lamely.

The mayor smiled, broadly and dazzlingly. "So'm I. But this ain't a way for me to be welcomin' long-lost relatives from the old world." Suddenly she threw her plump arms about Grimes and drew him to her resilient breast, kissed him warmly full on the mouth. He felt himself responding—and was somehow aware of the disapproving glare that Vinegar Nell was directing at the back of his head.

"That's better," murmured the mayor, pulling reluctantly away. "A *lot* better. Kiss an' make up, that's what I always say. An' now, Skip, wot about introducin' me to the lady and these other gentlemen?"

"Your Ladyship," Grimes began.

"*Mavis*, you drongo. Even if you're all dressed up like a Christmas tree, I ain't."

"Mavis, may I introduce my paymaster."

"*Paymaster?* Paymistress, if I'm any good at guessin'."

"Lieutenant Russell."

Vinegar Nell saluted and contrived to convey by her expression that she didn't want to be mauled.

"Major Swinton, my Marine officer."

Swinton's salute did not save him from a motherly kiss on the cheek.

"And Lieutenant Tangye, my navigator." Tangye's face was scarlet when he was released.

"An' what about these other blokes?" demanded Mavis.

"Er . . ." began Grimes, embarrassed.

"Private Briggs," snapped Swinton, stepping smartly into the breach. "Private Townley. Private Gale. Private Roskov. Private O'Neill. Private Mackay."

"Well?" demanded the big woman. "Well?"

Now it was Swinton's turn to feel embarrassment. The six men stood stiffly like wooden soldiers.

"Well?"

"Stack your rifles," ordered Swinton.

The men did so.

"Advance to be greeted by Her Ladyship."

The order was obeyed with some enthusiasm.

When the introductions were over the mayor said, "Natterin' to you on the radio, Skip, I never dreamed that you were such a stuffed shirt. All o' yer are stuffed shirts. Looks like Earth ain't changed since our ancestors had the sense ter get the hell out."

"And this, I suppose," said Grimes, "is one of those worlds like Liberty Hall, where you can spit on the mat and call the cat a bastard."

"You said it, Skip, you said it!" exclaimed Mavis, bursting

into delighted laughter. Grimes laughed too. He had thought that expression very funny the first time that he had heard it—how many years ago?—and he was delighted to be able to use it on somebody to whom it was new and brilliantly witty.

»«(Chapter 27)»«

Grimes had liked Mavis since his first sight of her in the monitor screen. He liked her still more now that he had actually met her. He kept on recalling a phrase that he had once heard—*A heart as big as all outdoors.* It applied to her. She was big in all ways, although in her dress that concealed little it was obvious that her body was all firm flesh, with no hint of flabbiness.

He was entertaining her and other officials in his day-cabin, with some of his own officers also present—Dr. Brandt, Brabham, and Vinegar Nell, who was kept busy refilling glasses and passing around dishes of savories. She, alone of all those present, seemed not to approve of the informality, the use of given names rather than titles and surnames. There was Jock, the man in the khaki shorts-and-shirt uniform who had assisted the mayor from the coach and who was City Constable. There was Pete, with a floral shirt over the inevitable shorts and sandals, who was president of the Air Pilots' Guild. There was Jimmy, similarly attired, who was master of the Seamen's

Guild. There was Doug and Bert, mayors of Ballina and Esperance respectively, who had flown by fast jet from their cities to be present at *Discovery*'s landing.

Mavis, watching Vinegar Nell, said, "Why don't yer scarper, dearie, an' change inter somethin' more comfy? Any o' our barmaids havin' to wear wot you've got on 'd go on stroke, an' quite right, too!"

"What do your barmaids wear?" asked Grimes interestedly.

"At the beach eateries, nuffin'."

"So you have a culture similar to that of Arcadia?" asked Brandt.

"Arcadia? Where in hell's that?"

"It's a planet," explained Grimes, "with an ideal climate, where the people are all naturists."

"Naturists, Skip? Wot's that?"

"Nudists."

"You mean they run around in the nudie all the time?"

"Yes."

"No matter *wot* they're doin'?"

"Yes."

"Sounds screwy ter me—as screwy as wearin' anything when yer goin' inter the sea for a dip. Oh, well, takes all sorts ter make a universe, don't it?"

"Have I your permission to change into undress uniform, Commander Grimes?" asked Vinegar Nell coldly.

"Of course, Miss Russell." Grimes wondered what the effect would be if Vinegar Nell returned to the daycabin in the undress uniform in which he had often seen her.

"And ain't it time that you got outer yer admiral's suit?" Mavis asked Grimes.

"I think it is," he admitted.

He went into his bedroom, changed back into shirt and shorts. "Now yer look more human, Skip," said Mavis. She held out her empty glass to him. "Wot about some more Scotch? We do make whiskey here, but t'ain't a patch on this. But you should try our beer. Best in the universe. And our plonk ain't bad. Nor's our rum."

"You'll be tryin' it at ternight's party, Skipper," said Jimmy.

"An official reception?" Grimes asked the master of the Seamen's Guild.

"Not on yer nelly. If yer thinkin' o' gettin' all dressed up again, forget it. A beach barbecue. Come as yer please, preferably in civvies. Jock's makin' the arrangements."

"Twenty guests. Yerself an' nineteen others," said the City Constable. "There'll be other parties for the rest o' yer crowd. Transport'll be at yer gangway at 1900 hours."

"I'll pick up the skipper me self," said Mavis.

Vinegar Nell returned, wearing her shortest skirted uniform. The mayor looked at her and added, "When I drive me self, I use me little run-about. Only room for one passenger."

The paymaster said, "As you know, Commander Grimes, we have many guests aboard the ship. I have arranged for two sittings at lunch in the wardroom. I imagine that you will prefer second sitting."

"Don't bother about us, dearie," Mavis told her. "Just send up some more o' this Scotch, an' some more blottin' paper to soak it up afore it rots the belly linin'." She nibbled appreciatively. "This sorta sausage stuff is very moreish."

The other two mayors agreed with her enthusiastically.

"I'll see if there's any more of that Rimini salami left in the storeroom," said Vinegar Nell, conveying the impression that she hoped there wouldn't be. "It comes from Rimini, a world settled mainly by people of Italian ancestry. They make the salami out of a sort of fat worm."

"It still tastes good," said Mavis stoutly.

Grimes treated himself to an afternoon sleep after his guests had left. He felt guilty about it; he knew that as a conscientious Survey Service captain he should be making a start on the accumulation of data regarding this new world. It must be the climate, he thought, that was making him drowsy. It was a little too much to drink, he admitted.

He was awakened by somebody shaking him gently. He ungummed his eyes, found that he was looking up into the face of the mayor. She grinned down at him and said, "I had to pull me rank on that sodger you've got on yer gangway, but he let me come up after a bit of an argy-bargy."

"I . . . I must have dozed off, Mavis. What time is it?"

"Eighteen-thirty hours. All the others've gone, even that snooty popsy o' yours. They left a bit early for a bit of a run-around first."

"My steward should have called me at 1700," muttered Grimes.

"He did, Skip. There's the tray wif a pot o' very cold tea on yer bedside table."

Grimes raised himself on one elbow, poured himself a cup. It tasted vile, but it helped to wake him. He hesitated before throwing back the coverlet—he was naked under it—but Mavis showed no intention of leaving the bedroom.

And he wanted a brief shower, and then he had to dress. He said over his shoulder, as he tried to walk to the bathroom with dignity, "What do I wear?"

"Come as you like if yer want to, Skip. It's a hot night, an' the weather bastards say it'll stay that way. But you've civvy shorts, ain't yer? An' a shirt an' sandals."

Grimes had his shower and was relieved, when he had finished drying himself, to find that Mavis had retired to the dayroom. It was not that he was prudish, but she was a large woman and the bedroom was small. He found a gaily patterned shirt with matching shorts, a pair of sandals. She said, when he joined her, "Now you *do* look human. Come on; the car's waitin' by the gangway."

"A drink first?"

"Ta, but no. There'll be plenty at the beach."

The Marine on gangway duty, smart in sharply pressed khaki, saluted. He said, "Have a nice night, sir."

"Thank you," replied Grimes. "I'll try."

"You'd better," the mayor told him.

Grimes took her arm as they walked down the ramp. Her skin was warm and smooth. He looked up at the clear sky. The sun was not yet set, but there was one very bright planet already shining low in the west. The light breeze was hotter than it had been in the morning. He was glad that he was not attending a full-dress function.

The mayor's car, a runabout, was little more than a box on relatively huge wheels, an open box. Grimes opened the door for her on the driver's side and she clambered in. She was wearing the shortest skirt in which he had yet seen her, and obviously nothing under it. *And yet*, thought Grimes, *she says that the Arcadians are odd.*

He got in on the other side. As he shut the door the car started with a soft hum of its electric motor. As it rolled smoothly over the grass toward the entrance to the Oval the mayor waved to groups of people who had come to stare up at the ship from the stars. They waved back. When she nudged him painfully, muttering something about stuck-up Pommy bastards, Grimes waved as well. They were worth waving to, he thought, the girls especially. Botany Bay might not be another Arcadia—but a bright shirt worn open over bare, suntanned breasts can be more attractive than complete nudity. He supposed that he would have to throw his ship open to the public soon, but by the time he did all hands would have enjoyed ample opportunity to blow off excess steam.

"We'll detour through the city," said Mavis. "This is the time I fair love the dump, wif the sun just down an' the street lights comin' on."

Yes, the sun was just dipping below the rolling range to the west, and other stars were appearing to accompany the first bright planet. They drove slowly through the narrow, winding streets, where the elaborate cast-metal balconies of the houses were beginning to gleam, as though luminous, in the odd, soft greenish-yellow glow of the street lights.

"Gas lamps!" exclaimed Grimes.

"An' why not? Natural gas. There's plenty of it—an' we may's well use what's left after the helium's been extracted. An' it's a much *better* light."

Grimes agreed that it was.

"This is Jersey Road we're comin' inter. The city planners tried to make it as much like the old one as they could. I s'pose it's all been pulled down long since."

"It's still there," said Grimes, "although the old bricks are held together with preservative."

"An' how does it compare?" she asked. "Ours, I mean."

"Yours is better. It's much longer, and the gas lighting improves it."

"Good-oh. An' now we turn off on ter the West Head Road. That's Macquarie Head lighthouse we're just passin'. One lighthouse ter do the work o' two. The main guide beacon for the airport as well as for the harbor." Something big fluttered across their path, just ahead of them, briefly illuminated in the glare of the headlights. Grimes had a brief impression of sharp, shining teeth and leathery wings. "Just a goanna," Mavis told him. "Flyin' goannas they useter be called, but as we've none o' the other kind here the 'flyin' part o' the name got dropped. They're good eatin'."

They sped through the deepening darkness, bushland to their left, the sea to their right. Out on the water the starboard sidelight, with a row of white accommodation lights below it, of a big schooner gleamed brightly.

"*Taroona,*" said Mavis. "She's due in tonight. Ah, here's the turn-off. Hold on, Skip!"

The descent of the steep road—little more than a path—down to the beach was more hazardous, thought Grimes, than any that he had ever made through an atmosphere. But they got to the bottom without mishap. Away to their right a fire was blazing, its light reflected from the other vehicles parked in its vicinity. Dark figures moved in silhouette to the flames. There was the music of guitars, and singing.

"*Tie me kangaroo down, sport. . .*" Grimes heard.

"I got yer here, Skip," said Mavis.

"And in one piece," agreed Grimes.

"Come orf it!" she told him.

))«Chapter 28»)«

As well as voices and music a savory smell of roasting meat drifted down the light breeze from the fire. Grimes realized that he was hungry. Unconsciously he quickened his step.

"Wot's the hurry?" asked Mavis.

He grinned—but at least she hadn't called him Gutsy Grimes. He said, "I want to join the party."

"Ain't I enough party for yer, Skip? I didn't think you'd be one fer chasn' the sheilas."

Grimes paused to kick his sandals off. The warm, dry sand felt good under his bare soles. He said, gesturing toward the parked cars, "I thought you people used horses for short journeys."

"Yair, we do—but not when we've a crowd o' spacemen along who, like as not, have never ridden a nag in their bleedin' lives."

"I have ridden a horse," said Grimes.

"An' what happened?"

"I fell off."

They both laughed, companionably, and then Grimes

564

stopped laughing. He was able to distinguish faces in the firelight. This, obviously, was not an officers-only party. There was Langer, the burly bos'n, and with him Sergeant Washington. And there was Sally, the little slut of a stewardess who had ministered to the needs of his predecessor in the ship, Commander Tallis. Obviously their hosts were determined to maintain their egalitarian principles. Well, that was their right, he supposed.

"What's eatin' you, Skip?" asked Mavis.

"I'm thinking that it was time that I was eating something."

"Spacemen are the same as sailors, I suppose. Always thinkin' o' their bellies." She raised her voice. "Hey, you drongoes! One o' yer bring the skipper a mug an' a sang-widge!"

Surprisingly it was the girl, Sally, who obliged, presenting him with a slab of steak between two halves of a thick roll. She seemed in an unusually happy mood as she walked toward him, her breasts—she had discarded her shirt—jouncing saucily. She said, "You see, Captain, I *can* make a sandwich when I want to." And it was Langer who came with a mug of beer in each hand, one of which he presented to Grimes. As he raised his own to his lips he said, "Your very good health, Captain."

"And yours, Bos'n.' (He thought, *This may not be the finest beer in the universe, but it'll do till something better comes along.*)

"Here's to your luck, Captain. I knew *our* luck would change as soon as we got *you* in command."

"I hope it stays that way," said Grimes. (Damn it all, the man seemed positively to *love* him.)

He took a bite from his sandwich. It was excellent steak, with a flavor altogether lacking from the beef in the ship's tissue culture vats.

Dr. Rath drifted up. His informal civilian clothing was dark gray—but, amazingly, even he looked happy. He was smoking a long, thin cigar. "Ah, so you've joined us, Captain. Miss Russell was wondering when you were going to turn up."

"Oh. Where is she now?"

"Haven't a clue, my dear fellow. She sort of drifted off among the dunes with one of the local lads. Going for a swim, I think. At least, they'd taken off all their clothes."

"Mphm." What Vinegar Nell did, and with whom, was her own affair—but Grimes felt jealous. He accepted another mug of beer, then fumbled for his pipe.

"Have one of these, Captain," said Rath, offering him a cigar. "Not exactly Havanas, but not at all bad."

"Better than Havanas," said Langer.

And you'd know, thought Grimes uncharitably. *With your flogging of ship's stores you could always afford the best.* He accepted the slim, brown cylinder from the doctor, nonetheless, and a light from the attentive Sally.

Not bad, he thought, inhaling deeply. *Not bad. Must be a local tobacco.*

He turned to Mavis and said, "You certainly do yourselves well on this world, darling." She seemed to have changed, to have become much younger—and no less attractive. It must, he thought, be the effect of the firelight. And how had he ever thought of her abundant hair as silver? It was platinum-blonde.

She said, "We get by. We always have got by. We had

no bloody option, did we?" She took the cigar from his hand, put it to her own lips, drew in. She went on, "Still an' all, it's good to have you bastards with us at last, after all these bleedin' years."

How had he ever thought her accent ugly?

She handed the cigar back, and again he inhaled. Another mug of beer had somehow materialized in his free hand. He drowned the smoke with a cool, tangy draft. He thought, *This is the life. Too bloody right it is.*

By the fire the singing had started again, backed by thrumming guitars.

> *Farewell to Australia forever,*
> *Good-bye to old Sydney, good-bye,*
> *Farewell to the Bridge an' the Harbor,*
> *With the Opera House standin' on high.*

> *Singin' tooral-i-ooral-i-addy,*
> *Singin' tooral-i-ooral-i-aye,*
> *Singin' tooral-i-ooral-i-addy,*
> *We're bound out fer Botany Bay!*

"The opera house isn't all that high," complained Grimes.

"Never mind, dearie. It's only a song." She added almost fiercely, "But it's *ours.*"

> *Farewell to the Rocks an' to Paddo,*
> *An' good-bye to Woolloomooloo,*
> *Farewell to the Cross an' the Domain,*
> *Why were we such mugs as ter go?*

"You're better off here," said Grimes. "You've a good world. Keep it that way."

"That's what I thought, after talkin' to some o' yer people this arvo. But will you bastards let us?"

"You can play both ends against the middle," suggested Grimes. He was not conscious of having been guilty of a grave indiscretion.

"Wodyer mean, Skip?"

"Your world is almost in the territorial space of the Empire of Waverley, and the emperor believes in extending his dominions as and when possible."

"So . . . the thot plickens." She laughed. "But this is a *party*, Skip. We're here to enjoy ourselves, not talk politics." Her hands went to a fastener at the back of her dress. It fell from her. She stood there briefly, luminous in the firelight. She was ample, but nowhere was there any sag. Her triangle of silvery pubic hair gleamed brightly in contrast to the golden tan of her body. Then she turned, ran, with surprising lightness, into the low surf. Grimes threw off his own clothing, followed her. The water was warm—*pee-warm,* he thought—but refreshing. Beyond the line of lazy breakers the water was gently undulant. He swam toward a flurry of foam that marked her position. She slowed as he approached her, switched from a crawl to an energy-conserving breaststroke.

He followed her as she swam, parallel to the beach. After a few moments of exertion he caught up with her. She kept on steadily until the fire and the music were well astern, then turned inshore. A low breaker caught them, swept them in, deposited them gently on the soft sand like stranded, four-limbed starfish. He got to his feet, then helped her up. Their bodies came into contact—and fused. Her mouth was hot on his, her strong arms were around him as she pulled him to her—and, after they had fallen again to the sand, above the tidemark, her legs embraced him in an unbreakable grip. Not that he wished to break it. She engulfed him warmly.

When they were finished he, at last, rolled off her, falling on his back onto the sand. He realized that he and Mavis had performed before an audience. Somehow he was not at all embarrassed—until he recognized, in the dim starlight, the naked woman who, with a young man beside her, was looking down at him.

"I hope you had a good time, Commander Grimes," said Vinegar Nell acidly.

"I did," he told her. "And you?" he asked politely.

"*No!*" she snapped.

"Fuck orf, why don't yer?" asked the mayor, who had raised herself on her elbows.

The young man turned at once, began to trudge toward the distant fire. Vinegar Nell made a short snarling noise, then followed him.

"That Col," remarked Mavis, "never was any good. That sheila o' yours couldn't've picked a feebler bastard. All blow, no go, that's him."

"The trouble," said Grimes, "is that she is, as you put it, my sheila. Or thinks she is."

"Then wot the hell was she doin' out with Col?" she asked practically. "Oh, well, now we *are* alone, we may as well make the most of it."

»«Chapter 29»«

The next morning—not too early—Grimes held an inquest on the previous night's goings-on. He, himself, had no hangover, although he had forgotten to take an anti-ale capsule on his return to the ship, before retiring. He felt a little tired, but not unpleasantly so.

He opened by asking Brabham how he had spent the evening.

"I went to a party at Pete's place, sir."

"Pete?"

"The president of the Air Pilots' Guild."

"And what happened?"

"Well, we had a few drinks, and there was some sort of help-yourself casserole, and then we had a flight over the city and the countryside in one of the airships."

"Anything else?"

The first lieutenant oozed injured innocence. "what else would there be, Captain?"

"Any relaxation of what we regard as normal standards? Any . . . promiscuity?"

Brabham looked injured.

"Come on, Number One. Out with it. As long as you do your job your sex life is no concern of mine. But I have a good reason for wanting to know what happened." He grinned. "Some odd things happened to me. Normally I'm a very slow starter."

Brabham managed to raise a rather sour smile. "So *that's* what Vinegar Nell was dropping such broad hints about! Well, sir, I had it off with one of our tabbies—I'll not tell you which one—during the flight over the city. Have you ever done it on the transparent deck of a cabin in an airship, with the street lights drifting by below you?" The first lieutenant was beginning to show signs of enthusiasm. "And then, after we got back to the airport, there was a local wench . . . I can't remember her name. I don't think that we were introduced."

"Mphm. And how do you feel?"

"What do you mean, sir?"

"Presumably you had plenty to drink, as we all did. Any hangover?"

"No, sir."

"Mphm. Commander MacMorris?"

"The Seamen's Guild laid it on for us, Captain. Plenty o' drinks. A smorgasbord. Plenty o' seawomen as well as seamen. There were a couple—engineers in the big schooners." He grinned. "Well, you can sort o' say it was all in the family."

"Mphm. Commander—or Doctor, if you prefer—Brandt?" The scientist colored, his flush looking odd over his pointed beard. "I don't see that it is any concern of yours, Commander Grimes, but I was the guest of honor at a banquet at the university."

"And were you—er—suitably honored, Dr. Brandt?" The flush deepened. "I suppose so."

"Try to forget your dignity, Doctor, and answer me as a scientist. What happened?"

"I've always been a reserved man, Commander Grimes. I was expecting an evening spent in intelligent conversation, not an—" He had trouble getting the word out. "Not an orgy. This morning I am shocked by the memory of what those outwardly respectable academics did. Last night I just joined in the party. Happily."

"As did we all," murmured Grimes. "Dr. Rath?" The medical officer had reverted to his normal morose self. "You should know, Captain. You were there."

"What I'm getting at is this. What is your opinion of it all as a physician?"

"I'd say, Captain, that we were all under the influence of a combined relaxant and aphrodisiac."

"The beer?" suggested Grimes.

"I didn't touch it. There was some quite fair local red wine."

"And I was on what they call Scotch," contributed MacMorris. "It ain't Scotch, but you can force it down."

"And I," said Brandt, "do not drink."

"But all of us smoked, presumably."

"I do not smoke," said Brandt.

"But you were in a room where other people were doing just that," Grimes went on. "You were inhaling the fumes whether you wanted to or not."

"I think you've the answer, Captain," said Rath. "I wish I'd thought to bring a cigar stub aboard so I could analyze it."

"And we all feel fine this morning," said Grimes. "Even so, I want none of those cigars aboard the ship."

"Not even for analysis?" demanded the two doctors simultaneously.

"Oh, all right. Analyze if you must—although no doubt a complete analysis of the weed will be made available to you if you ask in the right quarters. Our hosts were just being hospitable, that's all."

"And how," murmured Brabham happily. "And how!"

The mayor came on board late in the forenoon. Grimes asked her about the cigars.

"Oh, we don't smoke 'em all day an' every day," she told him, "though there are some as'd like to. We regard 'em as hair-let-downers, as leg-openers. An' no party'd be a party without 'em."

You can say that again, thought Grimes. In the broad light of day, with nothing, not even alcohol, to blunt his sensibilities, Mavis no longer seemed quite so attractive. Her accent again jarred on his ear, and he didn't really like *big* women; Vinegar Nell was far more to his taste. Nonetheless, he did not regret what had happened the previous night and hoped that it would happen again. He was sorry about the paymaster, though; it must have been galling for her to witness a man whom she regarded as her own property making love to somebody else. But whose fault was that? If she had waited for him instead of wandering off with the highly unsatisfactory Col—

He said, "You've a good export there. Are they made from a native plant?"

"No, Skip. They first comers brought terbaccer wif 'em.

Musta mutated like a bastard, or somethin'. An' now, I've a full day for yer. To begin wif, an official lunch wif all the mayors o' the planet, followed by a Mayors' Council. An' you'll be sayin' yer piece at the meetin'. About wot you were tellin' me last night about the Empire o' Waverley an' the Federation an' all the rest of it."

What did I say? Grimes asked himself. But he remembered all too well. He had been hoping that she would have forgotten.

»«‹Chapter 30›»«

Botany Bay was a good world, but speedily Grimes came to the conclusion that the sooner *Discovery* lifted from its surface and headed for Lindisfarne Base the better. She had never been and never would be a taut ship—and, in any case, Grimes hated that expression—but now standards of efficiency and discipline were falling to a deplorably low level. Rank meant nothing to the people of Botany Bay. In their own ships—air and surface—the captain was, of course, still the captain, but every crew member was entitled to officer status, an inevitable consequence of automation. Their attitude was rubbing off onto the ratings, petty officers, and junior officers of the spaceship.

Grimes set a date for departure. In the four weeks that this gave him he was able to make quite a good survey of the planet, using *Discovery*'s pinnace instead of one of the local aircraft. The mayors of the city-states cooperated fully, as did the universities of the state capitals. Loaded aboard the survey ship were microfilmed copies of the history of the colony from its first beginnings, from several viewpoints, as well as samples of its various arts from the first beginnings to the present time. There were the standard works on zoology, botany, and geology, as well as such specimens as could safely be carried. (The box of local cigars Grimes locked in his safe, of which only he knew the combination.) There were manuals of airmanship and seamanship. There was all the literature covering local industry. Mavis—who was no fool—insisted on taking out Galactic Patents on their contents after discovering, by shrewd questioning, that the captain of a survey vessel can function as a patents office director in exceptional circumstances.

It was, however, by no means a case of all-work-and-no-play. Grimes went to his share of parties. At most of them he partook of what Mavis referred to as hair-let-downers, the cigars made from the leaves of the mutated tobacco. He had been assured by Dr. Rath that they were not habit-forming and no ill results would ensue from his smoking them. Usually his partner at such affairs was the mayor of Paddington, but there were others. On one occasion he found himself strongly attracted to Vinegar Nell—but she, even though she was smoking herself, rejected him and wandered away with the City Constable. Grimes shrugged it off. After all, as he had discovered, she wasn't the only fish in the sea, and on his return to Lindisfarne Base he would, he hoped, be able to resume where he had left off with Maggie Lazenby.

Brandt wanted to stay on Botany Bay, but expressed misgivings about the amount of time he would have to wait until contact with the Federation was established. Grimes told the scientist of the simple code that he had agreed upon with Captain Davinas. He said, "With any luck at all, *Sundowner* should drop in almost as soon as I've shoved off. As the sole representative of the Federation on this planet you'll be empowered to make your own deal with Davinas. And Davinas, of course, will be making *his* own deals with the Council of Mayors. I've told Mavis to expect him."

"It all *seems* foolproof enough, Commander Grimes," admitted Brandt.

"You can make anything foolproof, but it's hard to make it bloody foolproof," Grimes told him cheerfully. "All the same, neither Davinas nor myself come in that category."

"So you say," grumbled Brandt. Yet it was obvious that he was pleased to be able to get off the ship for an indefinite period. Grimes suspected that a romance had blossomed between him and a not very young, rather plain professor of physics at Paddington University. Quite possibly he would decide to resign his commission in the Survey Service and live on Botany Bay. There were quite a few others, Grimes knew, who had the same idea. That was why he wanted to get spaceborne before the rot set in properly.

Then there was the farewell party—the last, in fact, of a series of farewell parties. It was a beach barbecue. (The colonists *loved* beach barbecues.) It was a huge affair, with no fewer than a dozen fires going, held on the beach of Manly Cove, one of the bigger bays on the north coast but still within easy reach of the city. All hands were there, with the exception of the unlucky watchkeepers. The beer and the wine flowed freely and everybody was smoking the mutated tobacco. Grimes stayed with Mavis. He might see her again; he most probably would not. He wanted to make the most of this last evening. They found a lonely spot, a small floor of smooth sand among the rocks.

She said, "I shall miss yer, Skip."

"And I you."

"But when yer gotter go, yer gotter go. That's the way of it, ain't it?"

"Too right it is. Unluckily."

"Yer boys don't wanter go. Nor yer sheilas."

"There is such a thing as duty, you know."

"Duty be buggered. Ships have vanished without trace, as yer know bloody well. No one knows yer here."

"They'd soon guess. If there were any sort of flap about *Discovery*'s going missing, then Captain Davinas—the master of *Sundowner* I was telling you about—would soon spill his beans. And the Survey Service can be very vicious regarding the penalty of mutiny and similar crimes. I've no desire to be pushed out of the airlock, in Deep Space without a spacesuit."

"You mean they'd do *that* to yer?"

"Too bloody right, they would."

"An' I'm not worth takin' the risk for. But you sort of *explode* in a vacuum, don't yer? All right. I see yer point."

"I didn't think that there was enough light," said Grimes, looking down at her dimly visible nudity.

She laughed. "I didn't mean *that*. But seein' as how the subject has risen. For the third time, ain't it?"

"Third time lucky," murmured Grimes.

Liftoff had been set for 1200 hours the following day. As on the day of landing the stands were crowded, and the brave, blue flags were flying from every pole. Two of the big dirigibles cruised slowly in a circle above the Oval. Their captains would extend the radius before *Discovery* began to lift.

There were no absentees from the ship at departure time, although it was certain that many of her complement would have liked to have missed their passage. Grimes was the last man up the ramp. At the foot of the gangway he shook hands with Brandt, with the mayors of the city-states. He had intended that his farewell to Mavis would be no more than a formal handshake, but her intentions were otherwise. He felt her mouth on his for the last time. When he pulled away he saw a tear glistening in the corner of her eye.

He marched stiffly up the ramp, which retracted as soon as he was in the airlock. He rode the elevator up to control. In the control room he went to his chair, strapped himself in. He looked at the telltale lights on his console. Everything was ready. His hand went out to the inertial drive start button.

Discovery growled, shook herself. *(Growl you may, but go you must!)* She shuddered, and from below came the unrhythmic rattle of loose fittings. She heaved herself off the grass. In the periscope screen Grimes could see a great circular patch of dead growth to mark where she had stood, with three deep indentations where the vanes had dug into the sod. He wondered, briefly, when it would be possible to play a cricket match in the Oval again.

"Port Paddington to *Discovery*," came a voice from the

speaker of the NST transceiver, "you know where we live now. Come back as soon as yer like. Over."

"Thank you," said Grimes. "I hope I shall be back."

"Look after yourself, Skip!" It was Mavis' voice.

"I'll try," he told her. "And you look after *your*self."

She had the sense to realize that Grimes would be, from now on, fully occupied with his pilotage. But it was an easy ascent. There was little wind at any level, no turbulence. The old ship, once she had torn herself clear from the surface, seemed glad to be heading back into her natural element. After not very long, with trajectory set for Lindisfarne Base, Grimes was free to go below.

In his cabin he got out a message pad. He wrote: *Davinas, d/s/s Sundowner. Happy Anniversary. John.* He took it down to the radio officer on duty. He said, "I'd like this away as soon as possible. It might just catch him in time. On Botany Bay I rather lost track of the Standard Date."

"Didn't we all, sir?" The young man yawned. No doubt he had a good excuse for being tired, but his manner was little short of insolent. "Through the Carlotti station on Elsinore, sir?"

"Yes. A single transmission. I don't want the emperor's monitors getting a fix on us. Elsinore will relay it."

"As you say, sir."

The tiny Carlotti antenna, the rotating Moebius strip, synchronized with the main antenna now extruded from the hull, began to turn and hunt. Elsinore would receive the signal, over the light-years, almost instantaneously. How long would it be before Davinas got it, and where would he be? How long would it be before *Sundowner* made her landing on Botany Bay? How long would Brandt have to wait? Grimes found that he was envying the scientist.

He debated with himself whether or not to drop in on Flannery, but decided against it. The PCO had found no fellow telepaths, but he had found quite a few boozing pals. No doubt the man would be suffering from a monumental hangover.

He went up to his quarters. He started to think about writing his report. Then he thought about his first report, the one in which he had damned Swinton. Should he rewrite it? The Mad Major had been very well behaved on Botany Bay. People like him should smoke those cigars all the time. *Make love, not war.*

Grimes decided to sleep on it. After all, it would be some days before the ship would be in a sector of space from which it would be safe to inform Lindisfarne Base of her whereabouts, and even then a long and detailed report of her activities would almost certainly be picked up and decoded by the Waverley monitors. It could wait until *Discovery* was back at Lindisfarne.

By the Standard Time kept by the ship it was late at night. And Grimes was tired. He turned in, and slept soundly.

»)«(Chapter 31»)»«

Discovery was not a happy ship.

All hands went about their duties sullenly, with a complete lack of enthusiasm. Grimes could understand why. They had been made too much of on Botany Bay. It had been the sort of planet that spacemen dream about, but rarely visit. It had been a world that made the truth of Dr. Johnson's famous dictum all too true. How did it go? *A ship is like a prison where you stand a good chance of getting drowned.* . . . Something like that, Grimes told himself. And though the chances of getting drowned while serving in a spaceship were rather remote there were much worse ways of making one's exit if things went badly wrong.

He went down to the farm deck to have a yarn with Flannery. The PCO had recovered slightly from his excesses but, as usual, was in the process of taking several hairs of the dog that had bitten him. The bottle, Grimes noted, contained rum, distilled on Botany Bay.

"Oh, t'is you, Skipper. Could I persuade ye? No? I was

hopin' ye'd be takin' a drop with me. I have to finish this rotgut afore I can get back to me own tipple."

"So you enjoyed yourself on Botany Bay," remarked Grimes.

"An' didn't we all, each in his own way? But the good times are all gone, an' we have to travel on."

"That seems to be the general attitude, Mr. Flannery."

"Yours included, Skipper. How iver did ye manage to make yer own flight from the mayor's nest?"

"Mphm."

"Iverybody had the time of his life but poor ould Ned." Flannery gestured toward the canine brain suspended in its sphere of murky nutrient fluid. "He'd've loved to have been out, in a body, runnin' over the green grass of a world so like his own native land."

"I didn't think the dingo ever did much running over green grass," remarked Grimes sourly. "Through the bush, over the desert, yes. But green grass, no."

"Ye know what I'm meanin'." Flannery suddenly became serious. "What are ye wantin' from me, Skipper?" *It always used to be "Captain," thought Grimes. Flannery's been tainted by Botany Bay as much as anybody else.* "Don't tell me. I know. Ye're wonderin' how things are in this rustbucket. I don't snoop on me shipmates, as well ye know. But I can give ye some advice, if ye'll only listen. Ride with a loose rein. Don't go puttin' yer foot down with a firm hand. An' it might help if ye let it be known that ye're not bringin' charges against the Mad Major when we're back on Lindisfarne. Oh—an' ye could try bein' nice to Vinegar Nell."

"Is that all?" asked Grimes coldly.

"That's all, Skipper. If it's any consolation to ye, Ned still likes ye. He's hopin' that ye don't go makin' the same mistake as Grimes was always afther makin'."

"*Grimes?*" asked Grimes bewilderedly.

"T'was Bligh I was meanin'."

"Damn Bligh!" swore Grimes. "This ship isn't HMS *Bounty*. This, in case you haven't noticed, is FSS *Discovery*, with communications equipment that can reach out across the galaxy. *Bounty* only had signal flags."

"Ye asked me, Skipper, an' I told ye." Flannery's manner was deliberately offhand. "Would there be anythin' else?"

"No!" snapped Grimes.

He went up to the main radio office, had a few words with the operator on duty. He was told there was very little traffic, and all of it signals from extremely distant stations and none of it concerning *Discovery*. He carried on to the control room, stared out through the viewports at the weirdly distorted universe observed from a ship running under Mannschenn Drive, tactfully turning his back while the officer of the watch hastily erased the three-dimensional ticktacktoe lattice from the plotting tank. *Ride with a loose rein,* Flannery had warned. He would do so. He looked at the arrays of telltale lights. All seemed to be in order.

He went down to the paymaster's office. Vinegar Nell was there, diligently filling in forms in quintuplicate. He tried to be nice to her, but she had no time for him. "Can't you see that I'm busy, Commander Grimes?" she asked coldly. "All this work was neglected while we were on Botany Bay." She contrived to imply that this was Grimes's fault.

Then Grimes, as he sometimes did, called in to the wardroom to have morning coffee with his officers. Their manner toward him was reserved, chilly. *We were having a good time,* their attitude implied, *and this old bastard had to drag us away from it.*

So went the day. There was something going on—of that he was sure. He was, once again, the outsider, the intruder into this micro-society, resented by all. And there was nothing he could do about it. (And if there were, should he do it?)

He was a man of regular habits. In space he required that he be called, by his steward, with a pot of morning coffee at precisely 0700 hours. This gave him an hour to make his leisurely toilet and to get dressed before breakfast. During this time, he would listen to a program of music, selected the previous night, from his little playmaster. It was the steward's duty to switch this on as soon as he entered the daycabin.

He awakened, this morning (as he always did) to the strains of music. *Odd,* he thought. He could not recall having put that particular tape into the machine. It was a sentimental song which, nonetheless, he had always liked—but it was not, somehow, the sort of melody to start the day with.

> *Spaceman, the stars are calling,*
> *Spaceman, you have to roam,*
> *Spaceman, through light-years falling,*
> *Remember I wait at home. . . .*

He heard Mullins come into the bedroom, the faint

rattle of the coffee things on the tray. He smelled something. *Was the man smoking?* He jerked into wakefulness, his eyes wide open. It was not Mullins. It was the girl, Sally, who had been his predecessor's servant. She was not in uniform. She was wearing something diaphanous that concealed nothing and accentuated plenty. One of the thin cigars dangled from a corner of her full mouth. She took it out. "Here you are, Skipper. Have a drag. It'll put you in the mood."

Grimes slapped the smoldering cylinder away from his face. "In the mood for what?" he snapped.

"You mean to say that you don't know? Not after your carryings-on with the fat cow on Botany Bay, to say nothing of that scrawny bitch of a paymaster . . . ?" She let her robe drop open. "Look at me, Skipper. I'm better than both of 'em, aren't I?"

"Get out of here!" ordered Grimes. "I'll see you later."

"You can see me now, Skipper." Her robe had fallen from her. "Take a good look—an' then try to tell me that you don't like what you see!"

Grimes did like it; that was the trouble. The girl had an excellent figure, although a little on the plump side. He thought of getting on to his telephone to demand the immediate presence of both Vinegar Nell and Brabham, then decided against it. Both of them would be quite capable of putting the worst possible construction on the situation. On the other hand, he had no intention of letting things go too far.

Decisively he threw aside the covers, jumped out of the bed. The girl opened her arms, smiling suggestively. He said, "Not yet, Sally. I always like a shower first."

She said, "I'll wash your back, Skipper."

"Good."

He pushed her into the shower cubicle before she could change her mind. And would it work? he wondered. On Botany Bay a swim in the warm sea had led to no diminishment of the effects of the smoke of the mutated tobacco—but the sea had always been warm. The shower would not be. When Grimes turned on the water he made sure that she did not see the setting. She screamed when the icy torrent hit her warm skin. Grimes felt like screaming too. He was not and never had been a cold shower addict. She struggled in his arms, even tried to bring her knee up into his crotch. He thought, as he blocked the attack, *You'd have a job finding anything!*

She squeaked, "Turn on the hot, you stupid bastard!"

He muttered, through chattering teeth, "This is hurting me at least as much as it's hurting you. Now, tell me. What's all this about?"

Her struggles were weaker now. The cold water was draining her of strength. She whispered, "If you turn on the hot, I'll tell you."

"You'll tell me first."

"It—it was just a bet . . . with the other tabbies. An' the hunks. That—that I'd get in with you, same as I was in with Commander Tallis."

"Where did you get the cigar? Out of my safe?"

"I'm not a thief, Skipper. The—the snip's lousy with the things. They'll be worth a helluva lot back on Lindisfarne. You know how people will pay."

Grimes shook her. "Anything else?"

"No, no. Please, Skipper, please. I'll never be warm again."

Gratefully, Grimes adjusted the shower control. He felt at first as though he were being boiled alive. When he was sufficiently thawed he left the cubicle, with the naked girl still luxuriating in the gloriously hot water. He dressed hastily. He phoned up to the control room, got the officer of the watch. "Mr. Farrell, ring the alarm for boat stations."

"Boat stations, sir? But—"

"There's nothing like a drill at an unexpected time to make sure that all hands are on the ball. Make it boat stations. Now."

There was a delay of about three seconds, then the clangor of alarm bells echoed through the ship, drowning out the irregular beat of the inertial drive, the thin, high whine of the Mannschenn Drive. A taped voice repeated loudly, "All hands to boat stations! All hands to boat stations!"

Sally emerged from the shower cubicle, dripping, her hair plastered to her head. She looked frightened. She snatched up her robe, threw it over her wet body. "Captain, what's wrong?" she cried.

"It's an emergency," Grimes told her. "Get to your station."

In the doorway to the dayroom she almost collided with Brabham on his way in.

"What's going on, sir?" demanded the first lieutenant harshly.

"Sit down," ordered Grimes. He waited until he was sure that Sally was out of earshot. Then he said, "I gave orders, Commander Brabham, that none of that mutated tobacco, in any form, was to be brought aboard the ship."

"You were smoking enough of it yourself on Botany Bay, Captain."

"I was. In those circumstances it was quite harmless."

"It will be quite harmless at parties back at Lindisfarne Base, Captain."

"So you're in it, too."

"I didn't say so, sir."

Grimes snarled. "Did you consider the effects of smoking the muck aboard this ship, with the sexes in such gross disproportion?"

"Nobody would be so stupid—"

"You passed that stewardess on her way out when you came in. She's one of the stupid ones. And now, with all hands at their stations, you and I are going to make a search of the accommodation."

"If that's the way you want it. Sir."

They started in the officers' flat, in Brabham's cabin. The first drawer that Grimes pulled out was full of neatly packed boxes. And the second.

"You're pretty blatant about this, Number One," remarked Grimes.

"I hardly expected that the captain would be pawing through my personal possessions with his own fair hands. Sir."

"Not only me."

"Lindisfarne Base is not a commercial spaceport, Sir. There are no customs."

"But the dockyard police exercise the same function," snapped Grimes. But he knew, as well as Brabham did, that those same dockyard police would turn a blind eye to anything as long as they, personally, profited.

All the officers, Grimes discovered, had disobeyed his orders, working on the good old principle of *What he doesn't know won't bother him.* Now he did know. Using his master key he went down through compartment after airtight compartment. Stewards and stewardesses . . . petty officers . . . Marines . . . general purpose ratings . . . it was even worse than he had thought. In the catering staff's general room he found butts in the ashtrays. They must, he thought, have enjoyed quite a nice little orgy last night—and he had been pulled in at the tail end of it.

He and a sullen Brabham rode the elevator up to the control room. Grimes went at once to the intercom microphone. He said harshly, "Attention, all hands. This is the captain speaking. It has come to my attention that large quantities of Botany Bay tobacco are being carried aboard this ship. All—I repeat *all*—stocks of this drug are to be taken to the after airlock, from which they will be dumped."

"You can't do that, Captain!" expostulated Brabham.

"I am doing it, mister."

"But it's private property."

"And this ship is the property of the Federation Survey Service. We are all the property of the Service, and are bound to abide by its regulations. See that my orders are carried out, Commander Brabham."

"But—"

"Jump to it!"

"You'll do the jumping, Commander Grimes!" It was Swinton who spoke. He had entered the control room unnoticed. He was carrying a twenty-millimeter projectile pistol, a nasty weapon designed for use inside a ship, its slug heavy and relatively slow moving, incapable of penetrating the shell plating or bulkheads of a ship. But it would make a very nasty mess of a human body.

"Swinton! Put that thing down!"

"Are you going to try to make me, Commander Grimes?"

Grimes looked at Brabham and the watch officer. Brabham said, "We're all in this, Captain. Almost all of us, that is. This business of the cigars pushed us past the point of no return."

"Mutiny?" asked Grimes quietly.

"Yes. Mutiny. We owe the Survey Service nothing. From now on we're looking after ourselves."

"You must be mad," Grimes told him. "The moment Lindisfarne gets word of this there'll be a fleet out after you."

"The Sparkses are with us," said Swinton. "There'll be no word sent out on Carlotti radio. As for that drunken bum Flannery—the first thing I did was to smash that dog's brain in aspic of his. Without his amplifier he's powerless."

"He'll never forgive you," said Grimes.

"The least of my worries," sneered Swinton.

"And just what do you intend to do?" Grimes asked quietly. If he could keep them talking there was a chance, a faint chance, that he might be able to grab that weapon.

"Return to Botany Bay, of course," said Brabham.

"You bloody fool!" snarled Swinton.

"Why?" asked the first lieutenant calmly. "Dead men tell no tales."

"And even Botany Bay has laws and policemen," remarked Grimes.

"Do you think we haven't thought of that?" Brabham demanded. "We intend to loaf around a bit, and make our return to Botany Bay after an interval that should correspond roughly to the time taken by a voyage to Lindisfarne and back. Our story will be that you were relieved of your command on return to Base and that I was promoted."

"You'll have to do better than that," said Grimes. "You'll have Brandt to convince as well as the colonists."

"Oh, we'll polish our story until it gleams while we're cruising. We'll make it all as watertight as a duck's down."

"Down to the airlock!" ordered Swinton, gesturing with his pistol.

"Better do as the major says," came a deep voice from behind Grimes.

He turned. Sergeant Washington had come into the control room, and two other Marines with him. They were all armed.

So, he thought, this was it. This was the end of the penny section. His famous luck had at last deserted him. In any ship but this one there would be a fair number of loyalists—but whom could he count on in *Discovery!* Poor, drunken, useless Flannery, his one weapon, his ability to throw his thoughts across the light-years, destroyed with the killing to his psionic amplifier? Perhaps he was dead himself. He had never been popular with his shipmates. Dr. Rath, perhaps—but what could he do? Plenty, maybe—but nothing in time to save Grimes. And who else?

He tensed himself to spring at Swinton, to wrest the pistol from his grasp before it could be fired. Perhaps. It would be suicidal—but quicker and less painful than a spacewalk without a suit. Or would it be? He realized the truth, the bitter truth, of the old adage, *While there's life, there's hope.* Perhaps he hadn't run out of luck. Perhaps something, anything, might happen between this moment and the final moment when, locked in the cell of the air-lock chamber, he realized that the air was being evacuated prior to the opening of the outer door.

"All right," he said. "I'm coming."

"You'll soon be going," Brabham quipped grimly.

»《Chapter 32》«

There was a crowd by the airlock—Langer, the bos'n; Mullins, who had been Grimes's steward; the little slut Sally; MacMorris and several of his juniors; the radio officers. They made way for Grimes and his escorts, raised an ironic cheer. There were two men already in the chamber, facing the leveled pistols of Swinton's Marines with pitiful defiance. One, surprisingly, was Dr. Rath; the other was Flannery. The PCO was bleeding about the face and one of his eyes was closed. No doubt he had made a vain attempt to save his macabre pet from destruction. The doctor looked, as always, as though he were on his way to a funeral. *And so he is,* thought Grimes with gallows humor. *His own.*

Swinton painfully jabbed Grimes in the small of the back with his pistol. "Inside, you!" he snarled. Grimes tried hard to think of some fitting, cutting retort, but could not. Probably he would when it was too late, when there was no air left in his lungs to speak with.

"Inside, bastard!"

That pistol muzzle hurt. With what little dignity he could muster Grimes joined the two loyalists, then turned to face his tormentors. He said, reasonably, "I don't know why you hate me so much."

"Because you've achieved everything that we haven't," growled Brabham. "*Lucky* Grimes. But throughout your service career you've committed all the crimes that *we* have, and got away with them, while our promotions have been blocked. You're no better than us. Just luckier, that's all. I've always prayed that I'd be around when your luck finally ran out. It seems that the Odd Gods of the Galaxy have seen fit to answer my prayers." He turned to MacMorris. "Chief, what about shutting down the time-twister? We can't make any changes in the mass of the ship with the Mannschenn Drive running."

So you thought of that, commented Grimes to himself. *A pity.*

Suddenly there was a commotion at the rear of the crowd. Vinegar Nell, followed by Tangye, was forcing her way through, using her sharp elbows vigorously. *So she wants to be in at the kill,* thought Grimes bitterly.

She demanded, "What do you think you're doing?"

"What does it look like?" asked Brabham.

She snapped, "I'll not stand for murder!"

"Now, isn't that just too bad?" drawled Swinton. "Perhaps you'd like to take a little spacewalk yourself. Just as a personal favor we'll let you do it in your birthday suit."

One of the Marines put an eager hand out to the neck of her shirt. She slapped it away, glared at the man. "Keep your filthy paws off me, you ape!" Then, to Swinton and Brabham, "You can't touch *me!*"

"Why not?" demanded the major.

"Try to use your brains—if you have any. How many people aboard this ship are trained as ecologists?" She pointed at Dr. Rath. "You're about to dispose of one of them. And that leaves me. Without me to take care of the environment you'd all be poisoned or asphyxiated long before you got back to Botany Bay." She added nastily, "And *with* me you could still meet the same fate if I had good reason not to feel happy."

Swinton laughed. "I think, Miss Russell, that I could persuade you to cooperate. After all, such persuasion is part of *my* training."

"Hold on," put in Brabham. After all he, with all his faults, was a competent spaceman, was keenly aware that the blunder, intentional or otherwise, of one key technician can destroy a ship. He asked the paymaster, "What proposals do you have regarding the disposition of the . . . er . . . prisoners? You realize that we can't take them back to Botany Bay. Not when Grimes and that fat cow of a mayor are eating out of each other's hands."

"Mr. Tangye will tell you," she said.

"Well set them adrift in a boat," stated the navigating officer.

"Are you quite mad, Tangye?" demanded Brabham.

"No, I'm not. We're in no great hurry, are we? We have time on our hands, time to waste. It'll be less than an hour's work to remove the Carlotti transceiver and the mini-Mannschenn from whichever boat we're letting them have."

"*And* the inertial drive," added Brabham thoughtfully.

"Hardly necessary. How far will they get, even at maximum acceleration, even with a long lifetime to do it in, on inertial drive only?"

"You've forgotten about Flannery," objected Swinton.

"We haven't," Vinegar Nell assured him. "Without his horrid amplifier he couldn't think his way out of a paper bag."

"Murder," admitted Brabham suddenly, "has never been my cup of tea."

"Or mutiny?" asked Grimes hopefully, but everybody ignored him.

"It has mine," asserted Swinton, far too cheerfully.

"I say, give the skipper an' his pals a chance!" shouted Sally.

"I second that," grunted Langer.

And what sort of chance will it be? wondered Grimes. *A life sentence, instead of a death sentence. A life sentence, locked for years in a cell, with absolutely no chance of escape. And in company certainly not of my choosing.* He had, not so long ago, made a long boat voyage with an attractive girl as his only companion. It had started well, but had finished with himself and the wench hating each other's guts.

He said, "Thank you, Miss Russell. And Mr. Tangye. I appreciate your efforts on my behalf. But I think I'd prefer the spacewalk."

Swinton laughed, although it sounded more like a snarl. "So there is such a thing as a fate worse than death, after all. All right, Brabham, you'd better start getting one of the boats ready for the long passage. The long,

long passage. Meanwhile, this airlock will do for a holding cell."

The inner door sighed shut, sealing off the prisoners from the mutineers.

"You might have warned me!" Grimes said bitterly to Flannery.

The telepath looked at him mournfully from his one good eye. "I did so, Captain. Ride with a loose rein, I told ye. Don't go puttin' yer foot down with a firm hand. An' don't go makin' the same mistakes as Bligh did. With him it was a squabble over coconuts or some such the first time, an' rum the last time. With you it was cigars. I did so warn ye. I was a-goin' to warn ye again, but it all flared up sudden like. An' I had me poor hands full tryin' to save Ned."

"I hope," said Grimes, "that you now appreciate the folly of trying to run with the fox and hunt with the hounds." He turned to Rath. "And what brings you into this galley. Doctor?"

"I have my standards, Captain," replied the medical officer stiffly.

"Mphm. Then don't you think you'd better do something about Mr. Flannery? He seems in rather bad shape."

"It's only superficial damage," said Rath briskly. "It can wait until we're in the boat. The medicine chests in all the lifecraft are well stocked. I saw to that myself."

"That's a comfort," said Grimes. "I suppose that you'll do your damnedest to keep us all alive for the maximum time."

"Of course. And when the boat *is* picked up—I presume

that it will be eventually—my notes and journal will be of great value to the medical authorities of that future time. My journal may well become one of the standard works on space medicine."

"What a pity," sneered Grimes, "that you won't be around to collect the royalties."

The doctor assumed a dignity that made Grimes ashamed of his sarcasm, but said nothing further. And Flannery, who had long since lost any interest in the conversation of his companions, was huddled up on the deck and muttering, "Ned—Ned . . . what did they have to do that to ye for? The only livin' bein' in this accursed ship who never hurt anybody."

»《Chapter 33》«

In little more than an hour's time the inner airlock door opened. During this period Grimes and Rath had talked things over, had decided that there was nothing at all that they could do. Flannery refused to be stirred from his grief-ridden apathy, muttering only, "Too much hate runnin' loose in this ship . . . too much hate . . . an' it's all come to the top, all at once, like some filthy bubble."

The inner airlock door opened, and Swinton stood there, backed by Sergeant Washington and six of his men. All were armed, and all were trained in the use of arms. They said nothing, merely gestured with their pistols. Grimes and his companions said nothing either; what was there to say? They walked slowly out of the chamber, and were hustled onto the spiral staircase running up and around the axial shaft. In the cramped confines of the elevator cage, Grimes realized, it would have been possible—although not probable—for weapons to be seized and turned upon their owners.

Grimes slowly climbed the staircase, with Rath behind him, and Flannery bringing up the dejected rear. Behind them were the Marines. They came at last to one of the after boat bays. The boat was ready for them. The mini-Mannschenn unit and the Carlotti transceiver, each removed in its entirety, were standing on the deck well clear of the airlock hatch.

Brabham was there, and Tangye, and Vinegar Nell, with other officers and ratings. Grimes tried to read the expressions on their faces. There were flickers of doubt, perhaps, and a growing realization of the enormity of their crime—but also an unwavering resolution. After all, it would be many, many years (if ever) before the Admiralty learned that there had been a mutiny. Or would it be? Grimes suddenly remembered what he should have remembered before—that Captain Davinas, in his *Sundowner,* would, provided that his owners were agreeable, soon be dropping down on Botany Bay. But what could Davinas do? He commanded an unarmed ship with a small crew. The mutineers would see to it that Davinas and his people did not survive long enough to tell any sort of tale. But if he told Swinton and Brabham about his coded message to the tramp captain, then *Sundowner*'s fate would surely be sealed. If he kept his knowledge to himself there was just a chance, a faint chance, that Davinas would be able to punch out some sort of distress message before being silenced.

"The carriage waits, my lord," announced Swinton sardonically.

"So I see," replied Grimes mildly.

"Then get in the bloody thing!" snarled the Mad Major.

Flannery was first through the little airlock. Then Rath. Grimes was about to follow, when Vinegar Nell put out a hand to stop him. With the other she thrust at him what she had been carrying—his favorite pipe, a large tin of tobacco. Grimes accepted the gift. "Thank you," he said simply. "Think nothing of it," she replied. Her face was expressionless.

"Very touching," sneered Swinton. Then, to one of his men, "Take that stinking rubbish away from him!"

"Let him keep it," said Vinegar Nell. "Don't forget, Major, that you have to keep me happy."

"She's right," concurred Brabham, adding, in a whisper, *"The bitch!"*

"All right. Inside, Grimes, and take your baby's comforter with you. You can button up the boat if you feel like it. But it's all one to me if you don't."

Grimes obeyed, clambering into and through the little airlock. He thought briefly of starting the inertial drive at once and slamming out through the hull before the door could be opened. It would be suicide—but all those in the boat bay would die with him. But—of course—the small hydrogen fusion power unit had not yet been actuated, and there would be no power for any of the boat's machinery until it was. The fuel cells supplied current—but that was sufficient only for closing the airlock doors and then, eventually, for starting the fusion process. So he went to the forward cabin, sat in the pilot's seat, strapped himself in. He told the others to secure themselves. He sealed the airlock.

The needle of the external pressure gauge flickered, then turned rapidly anti-clockwise to zero. So the boat bay was now clear of people and its atmosphere pumped back into the ship. Yet the noise of *Discovery*'s propulsive machinery was still audible, transmitted into the boat through the metal of the cradle on which it was resting. The high, thin note of the Mannschenn Drive faded, however, dying, dying—and with the shutting down of the temporal precession field came the uncanny disorientation in time and space. Grimes, looking at his reflection in the polished transparency of the forward viewscreen, saw briefly an image of himself, much older and wearing a uniform with strange insignia.

The boat bay doors opened. Beyond them was the interstellar night, bright with a myriad stars and hazy drifts of cosmic dust. *Any moment now*, thought Grimes—but the shock of the firing of the catapult took him unawares, pressing him deep into the padding of his seat. When he had recovered, the first thing to be done was the starting of the fusion power unit, without which the life-support systems would not function. And those same life-support systems, cycling and recycling all wastes, using sewage as nutriment for the specialized algae, would go on working long beyond the normal lifetimes of the three men in the boat.

But Grimes, somehow and suddenly, was not worried by this dismal prospect.

He said, "All right, now let's get ourselves organized. I intend to proceed at a low quarter gravity, just enough for comfort. You, Doctor, can patch Flannery up."

"In his condition, Captain, I'd better keep him under heavy sedation for a while."

"You will not. As for you, Mr. Flannery, I want you to

listen as you've never listened before in your misspent life."

"But there's no traffic at all, at all, in this sector o' space, Skipper."

"For a start, you can keep me informed as to how things are aboard *Discovery*, while you can still pick up her psionic broadcasts. It won't surprise me a bit if there are one or two mutinies yet to come. But, mainly, you keep your psionic ears skinned for *Sundowner*."

"*Sundowner?*" demanded Rath. "What would she be doing out here?"

"You'll be surprised," said Grimes. He thought, *I hope you will.*

﹥«(Chapter 34)»﹤

A ship's boat is not the ideal craft in which to make a long voyage. Even when it is not loaded to capacity with survivors there is an inevitable lack of privacy. Its life-support systems are not designed for the production of gourmet food, although there is a continuous flow of scientifically balanced nutriment. Grimes—who, after a couple of disastrous experiments by Dr. Rath, had appointed himself cook—did his best to make the processed algae palatable, using sparingly (he did not know how long he would have to make them last) the synthetic flavorings he found in a locker in the tiny galley. But always at the back of his mind—and at the backs of the minds of his two companions—was the off-putting knowledge that the vegetable matter from the tanks had been nourished directly by human wastes.

The main trouble, however, was not the food, but the company. Rath had no conversation. Flannery, at the slightest excuse, would wax maudlin over the death of Ned, his hapless psionic amplifier. Lacking this aid to telepathic communication, and with nobody aboard *Discovery* a strong natural transmitter, he was not able for long to keep Grimes informed as to what was going on aboard the ship. It was learned, however, that Brabham and Swinton were not on the best of terms, each thinking that he should be captain. And Sally had been the victim of a gang rape—which, said Flannery, grinning lubriciously, she had enjoyed at the beginning but not at all toward the finish. And Vinegar Nell had taken up with Brabham. Grimes, puffing at his vile pipe, felt some sympathy for her. The only way that she stood a chance of escaping Sally's fate was by becoming the woman of one of the leaders of the mutiny.

And then *Discovery*, as the distance between her and the boat rapidly increased, faded from Flannery's ken. It was at this time that the three men became acutely conscious of their utter loneliness, the frightening awareness that they were in a frail metal and plastic bubble crawling, at a pitiful one quarter G acceleration, across the empty immensities between the uncaring stars. They were on a voyage from nowhere to nowhere—and unless Davinas happened along it would take a lifetime.

The days passed. The weeks passed—and Grimes was beginning to face the sickening realization that his famous luck had indeed run out. And yet, he knew, he had to hang on. As long as Rath and Flannery wanted to go on living (what for?) he was responsible for them. He was captain here, just as he had been captain of *Discovery*. He was in charge, and he would stay in charge. He hoped.

One evening—according to the boat's chronometer— he and Rath were playing a desultory game of chess.

Flannery was watching without much interest. Suddenly the telepath stiffened. He whispered, vocalizing what he was hearing in his mind, "Two no trumps."

"We are playing chess, not bridge!" snapped Rath irritably . . . "Quiet!" warned Grimes.

"I wish I could tell Jim what I have in my hand," murmured Flannery, almost inaudibly. "But I have to observe the code. But surely he knows he can afford to bid three over Bill's two hearts."

"Parley?" asked Grimes in a low, intent voice. "Parley," agreed Flannery. "*Parley?*" demanded Rath.

"He *was* PCO of *Sundowner*," Grimes told him. "When *Sundowner*'s owners had her fitted with Carlotti equipment he became redundant. But he qualified as a Carlotti operator, and stayed in the ship."

"He was a traitor to our cloth, so he was," muttered Flannery. "An' he knows it. When I met him, on New Maine, he told me that he was bitter ashamed o' goin' over to the enemy. He said that he envied me, he did, an' that he'd sell his blessed soul to be in my place, with a sweet amplifier like Ned as a true companion. But we didn't know then what was goin' to happen to Ned, lyin' all broken on the cruel hard deck, wi' the murtherin' bastard Swinton's boot a-crashin' into his soft, naked tissues."

"*Damn Ned!*" swore Grimes, shocking the telepath out of his self-induced misery. "Forget about that bloody dingo and get on with the job! Concentrate on getting a message through to Parley. *Sundowner* can't be far off if you can pick up his random thoughts."

"I am so concentratin'," said Flannery, with injured dignity. "But ye'll have to help."

"How? I'm no telepath."

"But ye have to be me amplifier. The blessed God an' all His saints know that ye're no Ned, nor ever will be, but ye have to do. Give me a . . . a carrier wave. Ye saw the ship. Ye were aboard her. You got the *feel* of her. Now, concentrate. Hard. Visualize the ould bitch, how she was lookin' when she was sittin' on her pad, how she was, inside, when ye were suppin' yer drinks with the man Davinas."

Grimes concentrated, making almost a physical effort of it. He formed in his mind a picture of the shabby star tramp as he had first seen her, at her loading berth in the New Maine commercial spaceport. He recalled his conversation with Captain Davinas in the master's comfortable dayroom. And then he could not help recalling the later events of that night, back aboard his own ship, when Vinegar Nell had offered herself to him on a silver tray, trimmed with parsley.

"Forget that bitch!" growled Flannery. "Bad cess to her, wherever she is, whatever she's a-doin'." And then, "Parley, come in, damn ye. Parley, t'is yer boozin' pal Flannery here, an' t'is in desperate straits I am. Oh, the man's all wrapped up in his silly game o' cards. He's just gone down, doubled an' redoubled. I'm touchin' him, but not hard enough."

"Drink this," interrupted Rath, thrusting a full tumbler in to the telepath's hand. It was, Grimes realized, brandy from the small stock kept in the medicine chest. Flannery took it, downed it in one gulp. The doctor whispered to Grimes, "I should have thought of that before. He's not used to operating in a state of stone-cold sobriety."

"An' t'is right ye are, me good doctor," murmured the telepath. "'Twas fuel that the engine o' me brain was needin'. Parley, come in, or be damned to ye. Come in, man, come in. Yes, 'tis Flannery here. Ye met me on New Maine. Yes, this is an SOS." He turned to Grimes. "Have ye a position, Captain? No? An' ye're supposed to be a navigator." Then, resuming his intent whisper, "We don't know where we are. There's three of us in a boat—the Old Man, the Quack, an' me self. No mini-Mannschenn, no Carlotti. Ye can home on us, can't ye? Yes, yes, I know ye have no psionic amplifier, but nor have I, now. An' what was that? Oh. Captain Davinas sends his regards to Commander Grimes. I'll pass that on. An' you can tell Captain Davinas that Commander Grimes sends *his* regards. An' tell Captain Davinas, urgently, on no account to break radio silence on his Carlotti. There's a shipload o' mutineers, armed to the teeth, scullin' around in this sector o' space." Then, to the doctor, "Me fuel's runnin' low." Rath got him another glass of brandy. "I'll keep on transmittin', Parley. Just be tellin' your Old Man which way to point his ship, an' ye'll be on to us in two shakes o' the lamb's tail. Good . . . good."

Grimes looked at Rath, and Rath looked at Grimes. A slow smile spread over the doctor's normally glum face. He said, "I really don't think that I could have stood your company much longer, Captain."

"Or I yours, Doctor." He laughed. "And this means goodbye to your prospects of posthumous fame."

"There may be another opportunity," said Rath, still smiling, "but, frankly, I hope not!"

⫸⫷Chapter 35⫸⫷

It took longer for Davinas to effect the rescue than had at first been anticipated. Like many merchant ships at that period *Sundowner* was not equipped with a Mass Proximity Indicator, the only form of radar capable of operating in a ship running under Mannschenn Drive. The merchant captain feared that if he were not extremely careful he might break through into the normal continuum in the position occupied by the boat. It is axiomatic that two solid bodies cannot occupy the same space at the same time. Any attempt to make them do so is bound to have catastrophic consequences.

So Davinas, running on Mannschenn Drive, steering as instructed by Parley, kept the boat right ahead—and then, as soon as the ex-PCO reported that the relative bearing was now right astern, shut down his time-twister and his inertial drive, turned the ship, restarted inertial drive and ran back on the reciprocal trajectory, scanning the space ahead with his long-range radar. At last he picked up the tiny spark in his screen, and, after that, it was a matter of a few hours only.

Sundowner's holds were empty; Captain Davinas had persuaded his owners to let him make a special voyage to Botany Bay to make such advantageous arrangements as he could both with the local authorities and whatever scientific staff had been left on the Lost Colony by *Discovery*. It was decided to bring the boat into the ship through one of the cargo ports. This was achieved without any difficulty, Grimes jockeying the little craft in through the circular aperture with ease, and onto the cradle that had been prepared for her. Then, when the atmosphere had been reintroduced into the compartment, he opened his airlock doors. The air of *Sundowner* was better, he decided, than that inside the boat. It carried the taints inevitable in the atmosphere of all spaceships—hot machinery, the smell of cooking, the odor of living humanity—but not in concentrated form.

Gratefully Grimes jumped down from the airlock door to the deck; Davinas had restarted his inertial drive and the ship had resumed acceleration. He was greeted by *Sundowner*'s chief officer, still spacesuited but with his helmet visor open. "Good to have you aboard, Commander Grimes."

"And it's good to be aboard."

"The master is waiting for you in the control room, sir. I'll lead the way."

"Thank you."

Grimes and his companions followed the officer to the doorway into the axial shaft. They rode up to control in the elevator. Davinas was waiting in the control room. After the handshakings and the introductions he said, "Now, Commander, I'd like some information from you. With all due respect to your Mr. Flannery and my Mr. Parley, I got a rather confused picture. I *was* proceeding to Botany Bay, as I learn that the Lost Colony is called. At the moment I'm heading nowhere in particular; the inertial drive's on only to give us gravity. Do you want me to set course for the Lost Colony again?"

"No," said Grimes at last. *Discovery,* he knew, would be deliberately wasting time before her return to Botany Bay, and there was quite a good chance that *Sundowner* would get there first. But what could she do? She was not armed, and on the world itself there was a paucity of weaponry. There was no army, only a minimal constabulary. There was no navy, no air force. He had no doubt that the colonists would have no trouble manufacturing weapons, and very effective ones, if given time—but time was what they would not have. And if they tried to arrest the mutineers, knowing them to be criminals, immediately after their landing a massacre would be the result. (Swinton tended to specialize in massacres.) "I could pile on the lumes," said Davinas. "No, Captain. This is not a warship, and Botany Bay has nothing in the way of arms beyond a few sporting rifles. I think you'd better take us straight to Lindisfarne Base." He added, seeing the disappointment on the other's face, "You'll not lose by it. Your owners will be in pocket. The cost of your deviation, freight on the boat, passages for myself and Dr. Rath and Mr. Flannery. And I'll do my damnedest to see that you get your charter as a liaison ship as soon as this mess is cleared up."

"I see your point," admitted Davinas at last. "And do

you want me to get off a Carlottigram to your bosses on
Lindisfarne, reporting the mutiny and all the rest of it?"

"No. I don't have my code books with me, and I've no
desire to broadcast to the whole bloody galaxy that the
Survey Service has a mutiny on its hands. And I don't want
Discovery to know that I've been picked up. It's strict
radio silence, I'm afraid, until we start talking on NST
before we land on Lindisfarne. That's the only safe
way."

Davinas agreed, then gave orders to his navigator. That
young man, Grimes noted, was far more efficient than
Tangye. (But Tangye was one of those to whom he owed
his continued existence.) The change of trajectory was
carried out with no fuss and bother, and in a very short
time *Sundowner* was lined up on the target star. Davinas
went down then, asking Grimes to accompany him.

Over drinks Grimes filled Davinas in on all (well, not
quite all) that had happened since their last meeting. The
tramp captain asked, "And what will happen to your
mutineers, John?"

"Plenty," replied Grimes grimly. "There are two crimes
of which the Survey Service takes a very dim view—piracy
is one, and mutiny is the other. The penalty for both is the
same—a spacewalk without a spacesuit."

"Even when there was nobody killed during the
mutiny?"

"Even then." Grimes stared thoughtfully at the trickle
of smoke issuing from the bowl of his pipe. "Somehow, I
wish it weren't so. There's only one man among 'em who's
really bad, all the way through. That's Swinton, of course.
The others . . . I can sympathize with them. They'd

reached the stage, all of them, when they felt that they owed the Service no loyalty."

"Poor, stupid bastards," murmured Davinas. Then, "I thought your paymaster was a very attractive woman. I'd never have thought that she'd have been among the mutineers."

"She stopped me from being pushed out from the airlock," said Grimes.

"And yet she'll still have to pay the same penalty as the others," stated Davinas.

"I suppose so," said Grimes. "I suppose so." He did not like the vision that flickered across his mind, of that slim body bursting in hard vacuum, its erupting fluids immediately frozen.

"There are times," Davinas said, "when I'm glad I'm a merchant spaceman. Being a galactic policeman is no job for the squeamish."

»«Chapter 36»«

"You will have to face a court-martial, of course," said the admiral coldly.

"Of course, sir," agreed Grimes glumly.

"Not only did you lose your ship, but there was that unfortunate affair on the first world you visited. Yes, yes, I know that fire was opened against your orders—but you, at the time, were captain of *Discovery*."

"I suppose so, sir."

"You suppose! There's no supposition about it. And then"—the old man was warming up nicely—"there's the odd private deal you made with that tramp skipper, Davinas."

"I acted as I thought fit, sir."

"In other words—it seemed a good idea at the time. Hrrmph. All in all, young man, you've made a right royal balls of things. I warned you, before you lifted off in *Discovery*, not to put a foot wrong. I told you, too, that you were expected to lick the ship into shape. You should have known that a crew of misfits, such as those you had under you, would be demoralized by an extended sojourn on a world such as Botany Bay."

"Yes, sir."

"The court-martial will not be convened until your return, however."

"My return, sir?"

"From Botany Bay, of course. You will be proceeding there in the frigate *Vega*, as adviser to Commander Delamere, whose instructions are to apprehend the mutineers and bring them to Lindisfarne for trial."

Delamere, of all people! thought Grimes. He had always hated the man, and Delamere had always hated him. Of Delamere it had been said that he would stand on his mother's grave to get a foot nearer to his objective.

"That is all, Commander," snapped the admiral. "You will remain on Base until sent for."

"Very good, sir."

"Try to reply in a more spacemanlike manner, young man You're a naval officer—still a naval officer, that is—not a shopwalker."

"Aye, aye, sir."

Grimes saluted with what smartness he could muster, turned and strode out of the admiral's office.

»)«(Chapter 37»)«(

"You're in a mess, John," said Commander Maggie Lazenby soberly. Her fine-featured face, under the glossy auburn hair, was serious.

"A blinding glimpse of the obvious," said Grimes.

"This is no laughing matter, you oaf. I've been keeping my ears flapping all day for gossip. And there's plenty. Not everybody in this Base regards you as a little friend to all the universe, my dear. You've enemies—bad ones. You've friends, too—but I doubt if they're numerous or powerful enough. And Frankie Delamere hates you."

"That's no news."

"When you're aboard his ship, don't put a foot wrong."

"I've heard that advice before."

"But it's *good* advice. I tell you, John, that you'll be lucky to keep your rank after the court-martial. Or your commission, even."

"Bligh kept his," said Grimes. "And then he rose to admiral's rank."

"Bligh? Who was he? I can't remember any Admiral Bligh in the Survey Service."

"Never mind," said Grimes. He filled and lit his pipe. "You know, Maggie . . . I've been thinking. Why should I stay in the Service? No matter how the court-martial goes—and I don't see how they can crucify me for Brabham's and Swinton's sins—it looks as though I shall never, now, make the jump from commander to a four-ring captain."

"But you just said that Bligh, whoever he was—"

"All right. Bligh did, and he'd lost his ship because of a mutiny, the same as I've done. I might be as lucky as Bligh—if Bligh ever was lucky, which I doubt. But let's forget him, shall we? The question before the meeting is this: do I resign my commission, and go out to the Rim Worlds?"

"The Rim Worlds, John? Are you quite mad?"

"No. I'm not. They've a new state shipping line, Rim Runners, which is expanding. There's a demand for officers."

"As long as you don't mind making a fresh start as third mate of a star tramp."

"With prospects. Now we come to the second question before the meeting. If I resign my commission, will you resign yours, and come out to the Rim with me? They're frontier worlds, as you know, and there's bound to be a demand for scientists, like yourself."

She got to her feet, stood over him as he sprawled in his easy chair. "I'm sorry, John, but you're asking too much. I wasn't cut out to be a frontierswoman. When *I* leave the Service I shall retire to Arcadia, my home world, where the climate, at least, is decent. From what I've heard of the Rim Worlds the climate on all of them is quite vile. My advice to you, for what it's worth, is to stick it out. As I said, you have got friends, and your sins might be forgotten."

"And I'd still have you," he said.

"Yes. You'd still have me."

"But to ship out under Delamere—"

"Not under. With. You hold the same rank. Forget your blasted pride, John. And who's more important in your life? Me, or Handsome Frankie?"

"You," he told her.

"All right," she said practically. "We don't have many nights before you push off. Let's go to bed."

⽒《Chapter 38》⽒

Commander Frank Delamere could have posed for a
Survey Service recruiting poster. He was tall, blond;
blue-eyed, with a straight nose, a jutting chin, a firm
mouth. He was an indefatigable skirt-chaser, although
not always a successful one. (Women have rather more
sense than is generally assumed.) More than once the
definitely unhandsome Grimes had succeeded where he
had failed. Nonetheless, his womanizing had contributed
to his professional success; he was engaged to the ugly
daughter of the Base commanding officer. He prided
himself on running a taut ship. As he had always been
fortunate enough to have under his command easily
cowed personnel he had got away with it.

Commander John Grimes walked up the ramp to
Vega's after airlock slowly, without enthusiasm. Apart
from the mutual dislike existing between himself and the
frigate's captain he just did not like traveling in somebody
else's ship. For many years now he had sailed only in
command—in Serpent Class couriers (with the rank of

lieutenant), in the Census Ship *Seeker,* and, finally, in the ill-fated *Discovery.* He had no doubt that Delamere would extract the ultimate in sadistic enjoyment from his present lack of status.

The Marine at the head of the ramp saluted him smartly. *And was that a flicker of sympathy in the man's eyes?* "Commander Grimes, sir, the captain would like to see you in his quarters. I'll organize a guide."

"Thank you," said Grimes. "But it's not necessary. I'll find my own way up."

He went to the axial shaft, pressed the button for the elevator. He had to wait only seconds. The cage bore him swiftly up past level after level, stopped when the words CAPTAIN'S FLAT flashed on the indicator. He stepped out, found himself facing a door with the tally CAPTAIN'S DAYROOM. It slid open as he approached it.

"Come in!" called Delamere irritably. "I've been waiting long enough for you!" He did not get up from his chair, did not extend his hand in greeting.

"It is," said Grimes, looking at his wristwatch, "one hour and forty-three minutes prior to liftoff."

"You know that I require all hands to be aboard two full hours before departure."

"I am not one of your hands, Commander Delamere," said Grimes mildly.

"As long as you're aboard my ship you're under my command, Grimes."

"Am I? My orders are to accompany you as an adviser."

"When I need *your* advice that'll be the sunny Friday!" Grimes sighed. Once again he was getting off on the wrong foot. He said mildly, "Perhaps I should go down to my quarters to get myself organized before liftoff. I take it that my gear has already been sent aboard."

"It has. And your dogbox is on the deck abaft this. I'll see you again as soon as we're on trajectory."

So he was not to be a guest in the control room during liftoff, thought Grimes. He was not to be the recipient of the courtesies normally extended to one captain by another. It was just as well, perhaps. Delamere was notorious rather than famous for the quality of his spacemanship, and Grimes would have found it hard to refrain from back-seat driving.

He left Delamere in his solitary majesty, went out into the circular alleyway. He did not bother to call the elevator, descended the one level by the spiral staircase. The compartment immediately below the captain's flat was that occupied by the senior officers. There was nobody around to tell him which cabin was his, but between CHIEF ENGINEER and FIRST LIEUTENANT he found a door labeled SPARE. Presumably this was where he was to live. Going inside he found his gear, two new suitcases, officers, for the use of, large, and one new suitcase, officers, for the use of, small. He looked around the room. It was not large—but he had lived, for weeks at a time, in smaller ones when serving in the couriers. It was clean, and promised to be comfortable. It had its own tiny adjoining toilet room. It would do.

Grimes began to unpack, stowing the things from the collapsible cases into drawers and lockers. Everything was new. He had been obliged completely to reequip himself after his return to Base. He wondered gloomily how much wear he would get out of the uniforms.

The intercom speaker came to life. "Attention, attention! Secure all! Secure all! This is the first warning."

A little spacewoman poked her head inside the door, a very pale blonde, a tiny white mouse of a girl. "Oh, you're here, sir. Do you want any help? The captain's very fussy."

"Thank you," said Grimes, "but I think I've everything stowed now." He looked at his watch. "It's still over forty minutes before liftoff."

"Yes, sir, but he wants to be *sure*."

"Better to be safe than sorry, I suppose," said Grimes. "But since you're here you can fill me in on a few things. Mealtimes, for a start."

"In space, breakfast at 0800 hours. Lunch at 1230 hours. Dinner at 1900 hours. Commander Delamere expects all officers to dress for dinner."

He would, thought Grimes. Luckily, mess dress had been included in the uniform issue that he had drawn.

"And then there're the drills. The captain is very fond of his drills. Action Stations, Boat Stations, Collision Stations."

"At fixed times?"

"Oh, no, sir. He says that the real thing is liable to happen at unexpected times, and so the drills have to happen likewise. If he wakes up in the middle of the night with indigestion he's liable to push one of the panic buttons."

And then, thought Grimes, *he'll be standing there in his control room, his uniform carefully casual, imagining that he's fighting a single ship action against the Grand Flight of the Hallichek Hegemony.*

"You seem to have fun in this ship," he said. "Everything, in fact, but a mutiny."

The girl blushed in embarrassment, the sudden rush of color to her pale cheeks startling. "I didn't think you'd be able to joke about *that,* sir."

"It's a poor funeral without at least one good laugh," said Grimes.

"Attention, attention!" barked the bulkhead speaker. "Secure all! Secure all! This is the second warning!"

"I have to be going, sir," said the girl. "I have to check the other cabins."

Grimes picked up a novel that he had brought with him, lay down on the bunk, strapped himself in. There was no hurry, but he might as well wait in comfort. He was well into the first chapter when the third warning was given. He had almost finished it when an amplified voice announced, "This is the final countdown. Ten . . . nine . . . eight . . ."

And about bloody time, after all that yapping, thought Grimes.

". . . Three. . . two. . . one. . . *lift!*"

It was at least another three seconds before the inertial drive rumbled and clattered into life. And to Grimes, traveling as a mere passenger, away from the control room, where he could have seen what was going on, the climb through Lindisfarne's atmosphere seemed painfully slow. At last, at long last, *Vega* was up and clear, swinging about her axes on her directional gyroscopes. She seemed to be taking an unconscionable time finding the target star. And was Delamere never going to start the Mannschenn Drive, restart the inertial drive?

"Attention, attention! The Mannschenn Drive is about to be started. Temporal disorientation is to be expected."

You amaze me, thought Grimes.

He heard the thin, high whine of the Drive building up, stared at the geometry of his cabin that had suddenly become alien, at the colors that flared and faded, sagging down the spectrum. There was the feeling of *déjà vu,* and the other feeling that he, by making a small effort only, could peer into the future, his own future. And he was frightened to.

Sounds, colors, and angles returned to normal. The temporal precession field had built up.

"Attention, attention! Normal acceleration is about to be resumed."

The ship shuddered to the arhythmic beat of the inertial drive.

"Attention, attention! Will Commander Grimes please report to the captain's daycabin?"

I suppose I'd better do as the man says, thought Grimes, unsnapping the safety straps.

⫷⫸Chapter 39⫷⫸

"Come in," grunted Delamere. "Sit down," he said reluctantly.

Grimes took what looked like the most comfortable chair. "To begin with, Commander Grimes," said the captain, "you were appointed to my ship against my wishes."

"And against mine, Commander Delamere," said Grimes. "That makes us even, doesn't it?"

"No. It does not. I'm the captain of *Vega,* and you'd better not forget it. Furthermore, I consider myself quite capable of mopping up your mess without any assistance from you. I have *carte blanche* from our lords and masters. I am empowered to treat with the government of Botany Bay as I see fit. When we get to that planet I do not expect to have you working against me, behind my back." He picked up a thick folder from his desk. "This is the transcript of all evidence so far taken. Yours, of course. And Dr. Rath's. And Mr. Flannery's. From the stories of those two officers it would appear that you entered into a liaison with one of the local dignitaries, the Lady Mayor of Paddington."

"What if I did, Delamere? Who are you to presume to judge my morals?"

"At least I have too much sense to mix business with pleasure, Grimes."

"You can't be getting much pleasure out of your affair with the admiral's daughter," agreed Grimes pleasantly. "A strictly business relationship, from your viewpoint."

"Watch your tongue, Grimes!"

"Oh, all right, all right. That must be rather a sore point with you. Now, what do you want me for?"

"I suppose I have to put you in the picture. You're the alleged expert on Botany Bay. I'm proceeding directly there, with no stopovers. I arrest the mutineers, using whatever force is necessary. I put a prize crew aboard *Discovery*—of which *you* will not be in command—and then the two vessels will return, in company, to Lindisfarne." He smiled nastily. "Then there will be the courts-martial, yours included."

"A busy voyage," commented Grimes.

"Yes. And during the voyage you, as a member of this ship's company, will be expected to attend all drills and musters. You are to regard yourself as one of my officers—without, however, any executive powers."

"You'd better read the regulations, Frankie," said Grimes. He quoted, having memorized this passage, "'A senior officer, traveling in a Survey Service vessel commanded by an officer of no higher rank than himself, shall be subject to that officer's orders only during periods of actual emergency such as enemy action, shipwreck etc.'"

"You bloody space lawyer!" snarled Delamere.

"I have to be, in your company," said Grimes. "Get this straight. I'm here to advise, nothing else. Anything you want to know about Botany Bay, ask me. I'll tell you. And I'll turn up for your drills and musters; even a civilian passenger in a commercial space liner has to do that. I might even brush up on my navigation if you'll let me into your sacred control room."

"Get out!" snapped Delamere. "I'll send for you when I want you again."

"Temper, temper," chided Grimes. In other circumstances he would have rebuked himself for having been so unwise as to make a dangerous enemy—but he and Delamere had always been enemies, and always would be, and nothing that he could do or say would have any effect upon the situation.

»«((Chapter 40))«

There were times during the voyage to Botany Bay when Grimes toyed with the idea of becoming the ringleader of a mutiny himself. Delamere was insufferable. The only members of his crew who took him seriously, however, were among that too sizable minority who have a slavish respect for rank, no matter how earned. The others—officers and ratings alike—paid lip service to their captain's oft iterated determination to run a taut ship, then did pretty well as they pleased. None of them, however, was foolish enough not to attend the drills that Delamere delighted in springing at odd times, although at every one of these there was much yawning and shuffling of feet.

Grimes did not succeed in making friends with any of *Vega*'s people. They were, he decided, afraid of him. His run of good luck had been followed by one spectacularly bad piece of luck—and the fear was there that his bad luck would rub off on them. After a subjective week or so he no longer bothered to try to be sociable. He spoke

when he was spoken to, he took his place at table at mealtimes, he had an occasional drink with the frigate's senior
officers. Delamere never invited him to have a drink, and
plainly resented the fact that Service protocol required
him to have Grimes seated at his right hand at table.

At last he was obliged to make use of Grimes's advisory
services. It was when the voyage was almost over, when
Vega, her Mannschenn Drive shut down, proceeding
under inertial drive only, was approaching Botany Bay.
He called Grimes up to the control room. "You're the
expert," he sneered. "What am I supposed to do now,
Commander?"

"To begin with, Commander, you can make a start by
monitoring the local radio stations. They have newscasts
every hour, on the hour."

"On what frequencies?"

"I don't know. I left all such sordid details to my radio
officers." There was an unsuccessfully suppressed snigger
from the Senior Sparks, who was in the control room.
Grimes went on. "It will be advisable, too, to make a check
to see if there's anything in orbit about the planet. There
weren't any artificial satellites when I was here—but it's
possible that Brabham may have put up an armed pinnace
as a guard ship."

"I'd already thought of that, Commander," said
Delamere. (It was obvious that he hadn't.) He turned to
his navigator. "Mr. Prokieff, will you make the necessary
observations? We should be close enough to the planet by
now."

Grimes looked at the gleaming instrumentation in the
control room, all far more up to date than what he had

been obliged to make do with in *Discovery. With that gear,* he thought, *the satellite search could have been initiated days ago, as soon as we reemerged into normal space-time.*

A voice came through the intercom speaker. "Radio office here, control room. We are monitoring a news broadcast. Shall we put it through to your NST transceiver?"

Delamere turned to his senior radio officer. "That was quick work, Mr. Tamworthy."

"We've been trying for some time, sir. Commander Grimes suggested it."

"Commander Grimes—" Delamere made it sound like a particularly foul oath. Nonetheless, he walked to the NST set, the screen of which was now alive with a picture. Grimes followed him. It seemed to be the coverage of a wedding. There was the bride, tall and slim in white, on the arm of a man in the uniform of an airship captain, smiling directly at the camera. In the background were faces that Grimes recognized—Mavis, and Brabham, and Tangye, and the Paddington City Constable, and the president of the Air Pilots' Guild, and Brandt. But he knew none of them as well as he did the bride.

". . . the wedding of Miss Ellen Russell," the news reader was saying, in that accent that Grimes, now, had no trouble in understanding, "to Skipper Benny Jones, of the airliner *Flying Cloud.* As you all know, Miss Russell—sorry, Mrs. Jones!—was paymaster o' the Terry spaceship *Discovery,* but Commander Brabham has accepted her resignation so that she may become a citizen of our planet. Our first immigrant, folks, in one helluva of a long time."

Local girl makes good, thought Grimes—and then his

wry amusement abruptly faded. Vinegar Nell, no less than the other mutineers, was a criminal, and would be arrested, and tried, and would pay the penalty for her crime.

"Talkin' of *Discovery*," the news reader went on, "Commander Brabham has informed us that it would be unwise for him to attempt to send a message to his Base on Lindisfarne. Such a signal, he says, would be picked up and decoded by the monitors of the Empire of Waverley. He says that his instructions are to stay here until relieved. Unless he's relieved soon his ship'll be growing roots, an' more of his crew will be followin' the good example o' the fair Miss Russell."

There followed a shot of *Discovery*. This time she was not berthed in the middle of the Oval. Grimes recognized the site, however. It was in a field to the west of the airport. The people of Paddington could hardly be expected to cancel their cricket fixtures a second time.

"There's your precious ship, Commander," sneered Delamere. "What a rustbucket!"

"Meanwhile—I hate ter have ter say it, but it's true—not all of *Discovery*'s people are endearin' themselves to us. Her Marines—who should have provided a guard of honor at the weddin'—are all in jail, even their commandin' officer, Major Swinton. It seems they went on a bender last night. As luck would have it we had a camera crew at the Red Kangaroo, to get some shots o' the new floor show there. There was a floor show all right—o' the wrong kind."

A picture of a large, garishly decorated room filled the screen. Seated around a big oval table were the Marines, including Swinton and Washington. The tabletop was covered with bottles and glasses. Swinton got unsteadily to his feet. "Where's the music?" he bawled. "Where's the dancing girls? We were told there'd be both in this dump!"

"We'll provide our own, Major!" yelled one of his men. "Come on, now! All of yer!"

> *"We're the hellhounds o' the galaxy,*
> *We're the toughest ever seen!*
> *Ain't no one fit ter wipe the arse*
> *Of an FSS Marine!"*

"Gentlemen, please!" It was the manager, a thin, worried looking man. "The floor show's about ter start."

"Stuff yer floor show, an' you with it!" The man who had started the singing swung viciously with his right, and the manager crumpled to the floor. Then half a dozen tough-looking waiters were converging on the scene. The Marines picked up bottles by their necks, smashed them on the edge of the table, held them like vicious, jagged daggers. The waiters hesitated, then snatched up chairs, not caring whom they spilled in the process. People were throwing things. A missile of some kind struck Swinton on the forehead, felling him. Someone yelled, "Get the Terry bastards!" Women screamed. The waiters, reinforced by customers, holding their chairs before them as a protection from the broken bottles, advanced in a rush.

It was then that the scene became chaotic—and blanked out abruptly. "That," said the news reader, "was when some bastard put his boot through our camera. Over twenty of our people finished up in the hospital. The condition of the manager o' the Red Roo is critical. An' the Marines, bein' behind bars, missed out on their charmin' shipmate's weddin'. An' that, folks, is all the news to date."

"Disgusting," said Delamere, somehow implying that it was all Grimes's fault.

"Marines will be Marines," said Grimes.

"Not *my* Marines," Delamere stated smugly.

"What are they, then?" Grimes asked interestedly. Delamere ignored this. He said, "I anticipate no difficulties in rounding up this rabble of yours. And now, Mr. Adviser, what do you advise? Don't bother to answer. I've already decided what I am going to do. I shall drop in, unannounced, just after dawn, local time. I shall land close to *Discovery*, covering her with my guns."

"*Discovery* has guns too, you know," remarked Grimes.

"I shall have the advantage of surprise," said Delamere. "I'll blow her off the ground before my vanes kiss the dirt."

"I thought," said Grimes, "that your instructions were to put a prize crew aboard her and bring her back to Base. You'll not be at all popular if you destroy such a large and expensive hunk of Federation property."

Delamere considered this. He asked, reluctantly, at last, "Then what do you suggest, Commander?"

"Put *Vega* in orbit, one that keeps her always over the daylight hemisphere. That way she won't be spotted visually. Get your artificers working on sonic insulation for the boats you'll be using for the landing. Send your force down for a dawn landing, and then go and call on the mayor. She won't like being called at such a godless time, but I think I'll be able to smooth things over."

"Too complicated," said Delamere.

"Then what are your ideas on the subject?"

"One Falcon missile, with a Somnopon warhead. That should be ample for a city the size of Paddington. And then, while all the Paddingtonians *and* your mutineers are snoring their heads off, we land and take over."

"You can't do that!" exclaimed Grimes. "It will be an act of war."

"Rubbish. Somnopon's nonlethal."

"Even at night," said Grimes, "there are people up and about, doing various jobs. If they fall asleep, suddenly, there are bound to be casualties. Civilian casualties."

"I think that Commander Grimes is right," said *Vega's* first lieutenant.

"You're not paid to think, Lieutenant Commander Bissett."

"I beg your pardon, sir," Bissett said firmly, "but that is one of the things that I am paid for. High-handed action on our part will, inevitably, drive Botany Bay into the arms of Waverley."

"Those colonists have never heard of the Empire of Waverley," said Delamere stubbornly.

"You heard that news broadcast, sir. The Empire of Waverley was specifically mentioned. If you like, I'll get Sparks to play the tape back."

Delamere glared at his executive officer, and then at Grimes. He snarled, "All right, all right. Then please tell me, somebody, why I shouldn't bring *Vega* down in broad daylight, with flags flying and brass bands playing? Or why I shouldn't do the same as Grimes did before *his* first landing—announce it on the normal broadcast channels?"

"Because," Grimes pointed out, "either course of action would give the mutineers ample warning. And if we have to fight a battle right over a major city we shall not endear ourselves to the inhabitants."

"Commander Grimes is right," said Bissett.

"I'm always right," Grimes could not resist saying.

»«(((Chapter 41)))»«

After a long discussion, during which Delamere's officers made useful suggestions—which is more than could be said for their captain—it was decided to send only one boat down for the initial landing. This was to be piloted by Grimes himself, accompanied by Major Briggs, *Vega*'s Marine officer, and six of his men. All of the Marines came either from Australia or from Australian colonies and, with a little practice, were able to speak with a fair approximation to the Botany Bay accent. All of the landing party wore civilian clothing—gaily patterned shirts, shorts, and sandals.

Vega's artificers had made a good job of soundproofing the inertial drive of the boat. When the engine was run in neutral gear, in the confined space of the boat bay, the noise, which normally would have been deafening, was little more than an irritable mutter. And, as Grimes well knew, the Lost Colonists liked their sleep and it took a lot to rouse them from it, especially after a heavy night.

He felt almost happy as he maneuvered the little craft down through the atmosphere. It was good to have a command again, even if it was only a ship's boat, especially after a passage in a vessel captained by Delamere. Once clear of the ship he had steered to a position over the night hemisphere, a little to the west of the terminator. Conditions were cloudless, and he could see, without any difficulty, the diffuse patch of soft light that was Paddington and, as he steadily lost altitude, the hard, bright, coded flash of the Macquarie Light. As he dropped toward it the picture formed on the radar screen, a chart drawn in pale-green luminescence—the northern coastline and the great, irregular bite out of it that was Port Jackson. Lower yet, and lower, and he could see the outlines of the finger jetties. He had decided to land in the southeastern corner of the harbor where several old hulks were moored, a marine junkyard.

Dawn was pale in the east when, at last, the boat dropped to the surface of the calm water with hardly a ripple. Grimes steered her toward the shadowy forms of the obsolete shipping, threading a cautious way between the looming dark hulls. There was, he remembered, a rickety little jetty just about here, used by work boats and the like. He came alongside it cautiously, opened the airlock doors. The Marines scrambled out onto the warped and weatherworn planking. Grimes followed. And then, working as quietly as possible, they succeeded in pushing and pulling the boat under the jetty, squeezing her in, somehow, between the marine-growth-encrusted piles. She would not be found unless somebody were making a deliberate search for her.

Grimes led the way inland. There was just enough light—although it was growing stronger—for them to pick their way through the rusty tangle of obstacles: anchors, lengths of chain cable, a big, four-bladed propeller. One of the Marines swore as he stubbed his bare toe on some unseen obstruction. Then they came to a road leading down to the water's edge, and the first, sleeping houses. The light of the gas street lamps was paling as the dawn brightened. Ahead of them, quite suddenly, the sun came up and, simultaneously, the lamps went out. Somewhere a dog was barking, and there was a brief and startling clamor overhead as a flock of birdlike things emerged from the trees, circled and assembled, then flew steadily toward the north on some unknown mission.

"It—it's like time travel, sir," whispered the Marine officer.

"What do you mean, Major?"

"This—this city. It's like something out of Earth's past. So . . . quiet. The way a morning should be, but hardly ever is. And these houses . . . nothing over three stories. And all the trees."

"This is the way they wanted it," said Grimes, "and this is the way they got it."

It was not far to the mayor's palace—a big, low structure, built in the long-dead (on Earth) colonial style. Grimes marched up to the front door, the gravel of the driveway grating under his sandals. The others followed him into the portico, the major looking with admiration at the graceful, cast-aluminum pillars with their ornate floral designs. He tapped one. He said, "Should be cast-iron, really, but aluminum's more practical."

"This isn't a sight-seeing tour, Major Briggs," Grimes told him. He added, "But I wish it were."

He pressed the bell firmly. He heard a distant, muffled shrilling inside the house. He pressed it again, and again.

The door suddenly opened. A girl stood there, glaring at them. Grimes recognized her. She was one of Mavis' staff. She demanded, "Wot the hell do yer want at this Jesus-less hour?"

"A word with Her Ladyship," said Grimes.

"Then yer can come back later. Noonish. Mavis left word that she wants her breakfast in bed at 1000 hours an' not a bleedin' second before."

"This is important," Grimes told her.

"Here, let me look at yer!" She put out a shapely arm and pulled him close to her. "Commander Grimes, ain't it? Cor stone the bleedin' crows, wot are you doin' back here, Skip? Wait till I tell Mavis. She won't half be beside her bleedin' self!"

"Not a word to anybody else, Shirley. Nobody must know I'm here."

"A secret mission, is it? I knew there was somethin' wrong, somewhere. Come on in, all o' yer. I'll put yer in her study while I drag her out. An' I'll rustle up some tea an' scones while yer waitin'."

She led them through a long corridor into a large, book-lined room, told them to be seated, then hurried out. The Marines, after Briggs had nodded his permission, disposed themselves on a long settee. Grimes went to the big window, accompanied by the major, and looked out. The city was, at last, showing some slight signs of life. A large coach drove by, obviously bound to the airport to meet an incoming passenger-carrying dirigible. There were a few, a very few, pedestrians.

"Skip, you old bastard!" It was Mavis, her abundant charms barely concealed by a thin wrapper. She grabbed Grimes as he turned to face her, almost smothered him in a tight embrace. "Gawd! It's good to see yer back!" Then her face clouded. "But I don't suppose yer came back just to see me. An' where's yer ship? Don't try ter tell me that yer walked all the way!"

"The ship's in orbit," began Grimes.

"An' who're yer pals? Don't think I know 'em."

Grimes made introductions, and while he was in the middle of them Shirley came in with a big tray, with tea things and a great dish of hot, buttered, lavishly jammed scones.

"An' now," asked Mavis, speaking through a mouthful, "wot *is* all this about, Skip? You come droppin' in unannounced, wif a goon squad, an' I don't think the bulges under their shirts are male tits!"

"Nothing more lethal than stunguns," Grimes assured her. "Now, I'll be frank with you. I'm here on a police mission."

"We have our own police force, Skip, an' we ain't members of your Federation."

"That's so, Mavis. But you're harboring criminals."

"An' what concern is that o' yours, Skip?"

"Plenty. The criminals are the entire crew of *Discovery*."

"Garn!"

"It's true, Mavis. There was a mutiny."

"You can't tell *me* that Commander Brabham'd do a

thing like that. As nice a bloke as you'd ever meet. Not as nice as you, perhaps"—she smiled—"but nice enough."

"Brabham did do it, Mavis. He and Swinton were the ringleaders."

"Oh, Swinton. *Him.* And his bloody pongoes. That doesn't surprise me."

"They were going to push Dr. Rath and Mr. Flannery and myself out through the airlock. Without spacesuits."

"What!"

"Yes. I'm not kidding, Mavis. And then Vinegar Nell and Tangye persuaded the others to set us adrift in a small boat, with no Deep Space radio and no Deep Space drive. Where we were, we'd have died of old age long before we got anywhere."

"Is this *true,* Skip?"

"Of course it's true. We picked up a few news broadcasts before I came down in the boat, including the one about Vinegar Nell's wedding. Your news reader made the point that there has been absolutely no communication between *Discovery* and Lindisfarne Base. Brabham has his story to account for that, but it doesn't hold water, does it?"

"I . . . I s'pose not. But how did yer get yer boat back here?" She laughed at the stupidity of her own question. "But, o' course, you didn't. You were picked up, weren't yer?"

"Yes. By a ship called *Sundowner,* commanded by a friend of mine. He took us back to Lindisfarne. And the admiral commanding the base has sent a frigate to arrest the mutineers and take them back for trial."

"Wot'll happen to 'em?"

"The same as was going to happen to me. An unsuited spacewalk."

"It's a bastard of a universe you live in, Skip. I'm not sure that I'd like Botany Bay dragged inter it. Swinton an' his drongoes *we* can deal with. The others? They're integratin' nicely."

"We must take them, Mavis. All of them."

"An' what if we refuse to give 'em up?"

"Then we have to use force. Under Federation Law, we're entitled to."

"But we ain't members o' your bleedin' Federation."

"You're still subject to Interstellar Law, which is subscribed to by all spacefaring races."

"We aren't."

"I'm sorry, Mavis, but you are. You have been since *Discovery's* first landing."

"You might've told me. A right bastard I clasped to me bosom when I made yer free of the body beautiful."

"Look, Mavis. I've a job to do. Send for the City Constable, but don't tell him what for until he gets here."

"I'll call him—an' tell him to warn all yer so-called mutineers to go bush. They've too many friends on this bleedin' world for you ever ter find 'em. If they'd killed yer, I'd be thinkin' differently. But you're alive, ain't yer? Wot's yer beef?"

"You won't cooperate, Mavis?"

"No, Skip, an' that's definite." She turned to the girl. "Get on the blower, will yer, Shirl? Warn 'em aboard *Discovery*."

Major Briggs said, "I'm sorry, Commander Grimes, but your way of doing things doesn't seem to be working." He raised his wrist transceiver, a special long-range model, to his mouth. "Briggs to *Vega*. Do you read me? Over."

"*Vega* to Briggs. Captain here, Major. How are things going?" Delamere's voice was faint and distant, but all in the room could hear the words.

"Operation Sweet Sleep, sir," said Briggs.

"And about bloody time. We've given Commander Grimes his chance to look up his old flames. Over."

"What's goin' on, Skip?" demanded Mavis.

Grimes did not answer her, turned on Briggs. "I thought this landing party was under *my* orders, Major."

"I had my own orders, sir, directly from the captain."

"He's a bloody fool," snarled Grimes, "and so are you! I know what you're doing can be argued, by the right lawyers in the right court, to be legally correct—but you've lost Botany Bay to the Federation."

The first dull thud sounded from overhead. Delamere's trigger finger must have been itchy. Grimes visualized the exploding missile, the heavy, odorless, invisible gas drifting slowly downward. He heard a second thud, and a third. Frankie was making sure.

The last thing he saw as he drifted into unconsciousness was Mavis' hurt, accusing face.

))(((Chapter 42)))(((

When Grimes slowly awakened he was conscious, first of all, of the dull ache in his upper arm, where he had been injected with an antidote to the gas, and then of the too handsome, too cheerful face of Delamere grinning down at him. "Rise and shine, Grimesy boy! You can wake up now. We've done all your work for you!"

Grimes, unassisted, got groggily to his feet. He looked around the mayor's study. The Marines were gone, of course. They would have been given *their* shots before leaving the ship. Mavis and Shirley were still unconscious. *Vega*'s surgeon was bending over the lady mayor, a hypodermic spraygun in his hand. He used it, on the fleshy part of a generously exposed thigh, then turned, to the younger woman.

"What—what time is it?" asked Grimes.

"Fifteen hundred hours, local. We have full control of the city. Such officials as we have awakened are cooperating with us. Most of the mutineers—with their

645

popsies—were aboard *Discovery*. We carted 'em off to the dressing rooms in the stadium—the mutineers, that is, not the popsies—and they're there under guard. Safer there than in that apology for a jail." Delamere paused. "Oh, your girlfriend, or ex-girlfriend—" Grimes looked toward Mavis, who was listening intently. "No. Not *her*. Your paymaster. We had to persuade some of her friends to talk. We found out that she and her new husband were spending their honeymoon on"—he made a grimace of distaste—"Daydream Island. Only half an hour's flying time in one of my pinnaces."

"So you've got her too," said Grimes.

"What the hell else did you expect?" demanded Delamere.

Mavis was on her feet now, glaring at the spacemen, clutching her thin wrap around her. She was about to say something when the ringing of a telephone bell broke the silence. It came, thought Grimes, from her office. She asked coldly, "I s'pose I can answer me own phone, in me own palace?"

"Of course, madam," replied Delamere airily. "If it's for me, let me know, will you?"

"Bastard!" she snarled, making her exit.

"I suppose you brought the ship down," said Grimes.

"Yes. I'm parked in that big oval sports arena. One of the first natives we woke up was quite hostile. He screamed about a big match due today, and accused me of buggering the pitch. He actually ordered me off. We had to use a stungun on him."

"You mightn't make many friends, Delamere," said Grimes, "but you sure influence people."

"Not to worry. We've got what we came for."

Mavis, her face pale under the dark tan, returned to the study. She said, in a low, venomous voice, "You bloody murderers!"

"The gas we used, madam," Delamere told her, "is no more than an instant anesthetic. Those whom we have not already revived will wake, quite naturally, in about one hour, feeling no ill effects whatsoever."

"An' wot about those who won't wake? Wot about the young couple who were killed in bed when a dirty great hunk o' rocket casin' crashed through their roof? Wot about that power station engineer who fell against somethin' an' got fried? An' wot about *Flyin' Scud*? She was comin' in ter the moorin' mast when the skipper passed out, an' she kept on goin', an' gutted herself. An' that's just the start of it."

"I am sure, madam," said Delamere stiffly, "that the Federation will pay generous compensation."

"In Federation money, I s'pose," she sneered. "Wot bloody use will that be? Specially since we won't join your bloody Federation now, not for all the gold in the galaxy." She turned on Grimes. "An' as for you, you . . . you dingo! I thought you were a man. Wot a bloody hope! Not only do yer help this bastard ter murder *my* people, you're goin' ter stand back an' let yer own crew be dragged off ter be butchered."

"But, Mavis—"

"Gah! Yer make me sick!"

"Delamere," demanded Grimes, "have you done anything about the crash at the airport, and the other accidents?"

"When we got around to it, Grimes. Our first job was to round up the mutineers." He added smugly, "You can't make an omelet without breaking eggs, you know."

"There was no need to run amuck in the kitchen," said Grimes.

"Out!" yelled Mavis suddenly. "Out o' me palace, you Terry bastards! I've work to do!"

"So have we, madam," said Delamere. "A very good afternoon to you. Come, Doctor. And you, Grimes."

"But, Mavis," Grimes began.

"Out! All o' yer. That includes you, lover boy!"

"You do have the oddest girlfriends," remarked Delamere as the three of them passed out through the front door.

Grimes did not reply. He was full of bitter self-reproach. He should have guessed that Delamere would have his own secret plans. He could have stopped Major Briggs from making that call. . . or could he? His name, he admitted wryly, was not Superman.

He followed the other two into the commandeered electric car that was waiting for them.

⟫⟨⟨Chapter 43⟫⟩⟨⟨

They drove to the Oval, in the middle of which, an alien, menacing tower, stood *Vega*. They did not go straight to the ship but dismounted at the entrance to the sports ground. At the doors to the dressing rooms under the stands stood armed Marines and spacemen.

Delamere led the way to one of the doors, which was opened by a sentry. He sneered as he pointed to the scene inside, and said disgustedly, "What a rabble! I can't see how anybody could have ever sailed in the same ship with them!"

Yes, they were a rabble—as the crew of any ship would be if dragged naked and unconscious from their beds, to awake in captivity. The only ones clothed, in dirty, torn uniforms, were Swinton and his Marines. Swinton, followed by the huge Washington, pushed through the mob of his hapless shipmates. He stood there defiantly, glaring at Grimes and his companions. He demanded, "Have you come to gloat? Go on, damn you! Gloat to your heart's bloody content!"

"I haven't come to gloat," said Grimes.

"Then what the hell have you come for? But it's my fault. I should never have listened to Vinegar Nell and that puppy Tangye. We should have made sure of you while we had you."

"But you didn't," said Grimes. "Unluckily for you. Luckily for me."

"Grimes's famous luck!" sneered the Mad Major.

Vinegar Nell came slowly to stand beside the Marine. She had been conscious when she had been captured, and obviously had put up a fight. She looked steadily at Grimes. She said, "So you made it, John. Am I glad, or sorry? I'm glad for you. Genuinely. As for me—" She shrugged. "Whatever I say will make no difference."

"*Very* touching," commented Delamere.

"Shut up!" snapped Grimes. He turned to face Brabham—who, like the majority of the prisoners, was without clothing. His ex-first lieutenant looked fit, far fitter than he had ever looked aboard *Discovery*. Life on Botany Bay had agreed with him.

"You win, Captain," he said glumly. Then he actually smiled. "But it was good while it lasted!"

"I'm sorry," said Grimes inadequately.

"Hearts and flowers," murmured Delamere.

"Captain," went on Brabham, "I know I've no right to ask favors of you. But do you think you could persuade Commander Delamere to let us have some clothing? And I think, too, that the women should have separate quarters."

"Mutineers have no rights," stated Delamere.

"Human beings have!" retorted Grimes. "And don't

forget that we, on this world, are ambassadors of the Federation. We've made a bad enough impression already. Don't let's make it worse."

"Who cares?" asked Delamere.

"Every do-gooder and bleeding heart in the galaxy, that's who. I've often hated that breed myself—but I'll have no hesitation in making use of them."

The two commanders glared at each other, and then Delamere turned to one of his officers. "You might see that the prisoners have some rags to cover their disgusting nakedness, Mr. Fleming. And you can sort out the cows from the goats and have them penned separately."

"Thank you," said Brabham—to Grimes. Then, "How long are they keeping us here, Captain?"

"Until we've converted *Discovery*'s holds into palatial quarters for you bastards!" snarled Delamere.

Grimes turned away.

He could not help feeling sorry for those who had abandoned him in a hopeless situation. They were guilty of a crime for which there could be no forgiveness, let alone pardon, and yet . . . on this planet they had been given the second chance to make something of their hitherto wasted lives. They could have become useful citizens. Botany Bay would have benefited from their knowledge of different technologies.

"I'm going aboard now," said Delamere.

"I'm not," said Grimes. "We have things to discuss."

"They can wait."

He walked slowly into the tree-lined street—which, at last, was becoming alive with dazed-looking citizens. He hoped that nobody would recognize him. But somebody did. His way was blocked by a man in a light blue shorts-and-shirt uniform.

"Commander Grimes?"

"Yes?"

"Don't you remember me? I'm Benny Jones, skipper o' *Flyin' Cloud.*"

Grimes remembered the airship captain, had taken a flight in the big dirigible. And he knew, too, that the man was Vinegar Nell's husband. No wonder he looked almost out of his mind with worry.

"Nell's a fine person, Commander. She came straight with me. She told me all sorts of things that she had no need to. I—I know about you an' her. An' so what? But are you goin' to stand back an' let her be dragged away to be—to be—"

"I—I don't have much choice in the matter, Skipper."

"I know yer don't. You have ter take yer orders from the bastards above yer. But—Look, Commander. You know the sort o' routine they have aboard that bastard ship that's ruinin' the turf in the Oval. I'm told that you're in her just as an adviser. Can't yer be an adviser to—All right. To me?"

I owe Nell something, thought Grimes, pulling his pipe out from his pocket, and looking at it. *I owe her a lot. And there was nothing that* she *could have done to stop the mutiny—but that won't save her from the spacewalk along with the others. She saved* me *from a spacewalk.*

"I take it that you want to rescue Nell, Skipper."

"Wot the bloody hell else? But how? But how?"

But how? Grimes asked himself. He began to see the glimmerings of an answer. He thought that the chemists on Botany Bay might already, after the salutary lesson of that morning, be working on it. And Brandt, after his long residence at the university, would be on intimate terms with the local scientists. Brandt, too, had always made it plain that he had no time for Survey Service regulations.

But he, Grimes . . . ? When it came to the crunch where did his loyalties lie? To his Service, or to an ex-mistress?

Certainly not, he decided, to the obnoxious Delamere. He said, as he slowly filled his pipe, "We may be able to do something, Skipper. But only for Nell. Only for Nell. Shall we take a stroll to the university?"

»«(Chapter 44)»«

They found Brandt without any trouble. The scientist was unchanged, as irascible as ever. He demanded, "What is going on here, Commander Grimes? A dawn attack on our world by a Federation warship—"

"Our world, Doctor?"

"Yes. I'm married now, and I resigned my commission, and applied for citizenship."

"You resigned your commission?"

"Must you parrot every word, Commander Grimes? Commander Brabham was the senior officer of the Survey Service on Botany Bay, so I handed my resignation in to him. He accepted it. I got tired of waiting for that chum of yours, Captain Davinas."

"Did you tell Brabham about Davinas?" asked Grimes.

"Of course not. I knew that it was some private deal between you and him, so I kept my mouth shut."

"Just as well," said Grimes. "If Brabham and his crowd had been expecting *Sundowner* they'd have been more alert."

"What do you mean, just as well? If they'd been alert, they'd have stood a fighting chance."

"But they're mutineers, Doctor."

"Mutineers, shmutineers . . . a mutiny's only a strike, but with the strikers wearing uniform."

"Mphm," grunted Grimes. "That's one way of looking at it, I suppose. But I'm lucky to be alive, Doctor."

"You're always lucky. Well, what can I do for you?"

"Are there any supplies of Somnopon gas on this world, Doctor? Or anything like it?"

"Not as far as I know. We're a peaceful planet. We could make some, I suppose. Do you know the formula?"

"I've seen it, in gunnery manuals, but I didn't memorize it."

"You wouldn't. You're a typical spaceman, always bludging on the scientists and technologists. But what do you want it for?"

"Can we trust this bastard?" asked Jones.

"Why not?" countered Grimes. "He's one of yours, now." He turned to Brandt. "This gentleman is Miss Russell's husband."

"He has my sympathy," said Brandt.

Grimes looked at him sharply. That remark could be taken two ways. He said, "Naturally, he does not wish to see his wife taken away to be tried and executed, as she will be. The trial will be a mere formality. On every occasion that the Survey Service has had a mutiny the entire crew has been made an example of. That, I suppose, is why mutiny is such a rare crime. But Miss Russell—or Mrs. Jones, as she is now—saved my life. I want to reciprocate."

"Uncommonly decent of you, Commander Grimes.

Beneath that rugged exterior there beats a heart of gold."

"Let me finish, damn you. What I want is enough Somnopon, or something like it, so that Skipper Jones and his friends can put the entire Oval, including *Vega*, to sleep. Then Jones rescues Nell—and surely, with the population of an entire planet shielding her, she'll never be found." He added, "There's always plastic surgery."

"I like her the way she is!" growled Jones.

"All very ingenious, Grimes, and it keeps *your* yardarm clear, as you would put it. But you don't remember the formula. I've no doubt that we could work it out for ourselves, but that would take time. Too much time." He picked up a telephone on his desk. "Rene, could you get hold of Doc Travis? Tell her it's urgent. Yes, in my office."

"Is Dr. Travis a chemist?" asked Grimes.

"No. A psychologist. You've no idea what dirt she can drag out of people's minds by hypnosis."

"A brain drain?" demanded Grimes, alarmed.

"Nothing like as drastic," Brandt assured him. "It'll just be a sleep from which you'll awake with your mind, such as it is, quite intact."

Grimes looked at Jones. The airship captain's strong face was drawn with worry and his eyes held a deep misery.

"All right," he said.

The hypnosis session bore little relationship to the brain drain techniques used by the Intelligence Branch of the Survey Service. There was no complicated electronic apparatus, no screens with the wavering, luminescent traces of brain waves. There was only a soft-voiced, attractive blonde, whose soothing contralto suggested that Grimes, sitting on his shoulder blades in a deep, comfortable chair, relax, relax, relax. He relaxed. He must have dozed off. He was awakened by the snapping of the hypnotist's fingers. He was as refreshed as he would have been by a full night's sleep. He felt exceptionally alert.

"We got it," said Brandt.

"Nothing else?" asked Grimes suspiciously.

"No," replied the scientist virtuously.

"No posthypnotic suggestions?"

"Wot d'yer take us for?" demanded Dr. Travis indignantly. "You do the right thing by us, we do the right thing by you." She looked thoughtful. "As you know, we ain't got any telepaths on this planet. There'll be at least one aboard that frigate. Wot're the chances o' him snoopin'?"

"That's a chance we have to take, Doctor. But you can't snoop all of the people all of the time. Anyhow, there're quite a few people aboard *Vega* who'd like to see their gallant captain come a gutser, and he's one of them."

"Some time, Dolly," said Brandt, "you must make a study of the micro-societies of ships. I assure you that it would be fascinating. And now, while we're waiting for Dr. Ronson and his team to let us know what they can do with the formula, we'll have a drink. Skipper Jones, at least, looks as though he could use one."

Ronson phoned through to say that he would have a supply of the gas ready within forty-eight hours. It would take more than that time to bring *Discovery* back to full spaceworthiness as well as to modify her for her new role as a prison ship.

»«‹Chapter 45›»«‹

Delamere, after a stormy session with Mavis—who was backed by Grimes—reluctantly agreed to allow the prisoners some small privileges before their removal from Botany Bay. "You must remember," Grimes told him, "that these Lost Colonists are descended from other colonists, and that those other colonists have always distrusted brass-bound authority, and often with good reason. Who else would make a folk hero out of a bushranger like Ned Kelly?"

"You've Australian blood yourself, Grimes, haven't you? That accounts for your own attitude toward authority. My authority, specifically."

"I'm speaking as a man, Delamere, not as an Australian, nor as an officer of the Survey Service, nor as any other bloody thing. Those mutineers—and I admit that most of 'em are as guilty as all hell—have made friends on this planet, have formed very close relationships. You're hurting those people, who'll never see their

friends or lovers again, as much as you're hurting the
criminals. Don't forget what I said about the bleeding
hearts, the sob sisters, and the do-gooders."

"Good on yer, Skip!" murmured Mavis.

"I haven't forgotten, Grimes," admitted Delamere
coldly. "And I haven't forgotten the rather dubious part
you've played in affairs ever since we lifted ship for this
blasted planet." Then, to Mavis, "All right, madam. I'll
allow your people to visit their boyfriends and girlfriends,
at times to be arranged by myself, under strict supervision.
And I give you fair warning—if there's any attempt to
smuggle in weapons or escape tools, then may the Odd
Gods of the Galaxy help you! You'll need their help."

"Thank you, sir, Commander, sir," simpered Mavis
infuriatingly.

There were visitors. The visitors brought gifts—mainly
cakes. The cakes were, of course, X-rayed. There was
nothing of a metallic nature inside them. They were
sliced, and samples chemically analyzed. There was not a
trace of plastic explosive. Delamere's PCO was on hand
during each visiting period to scan the minds of the
visitors, and reported that although, naturally, there was
considerable hostility to Delamere—and to Grimes
himself—there was no knowledge of any planned jail-
break. Oddly enough, Skipper Jones did not visit his wife,
and it was obvious that she was deeply hurt. Grimes knew
the reason. He dare not tell Vinegar Nell. He dare not
visit her himself. Jones, of course, knew of the clandestine
manufacture of Somnopon. There was another slight
oddity of which Grimes thought nothing—at the time.
Many of the cakes and other edible goodies came from

the kitchens of the mayor's palace. But that was just another example of Mavis' essential goodheartedness.

When the big night came—it was early evening, actually—Grimes was standing with Brandt and Jones on the flat roof of one of the towers of the university. From it they could see the airport, and just beyond it the huge, floodlit shape of *Discovery.* They could see the Oval, and the even larger, brightly illumined tower that was *Vega.* They returned their attention to the airport. One of the dirigibles was about to cast off—*Duchess of Paddington,* a cargo carrier, commanded by a friend of Jones's. Grimes watched through borrowed binoculars. He could make out the mooring mast, with its flashing red light on top, quite well, and the long cigar shape that trailed from it like a wind sock. He saw the airship's red and green navigation lights come on. So she had let go. *Duchess of Paddington* drifted away from the mast, gaining altitude. She was making way, and slowly circled *Discovery.* Grimes wondered vaguely why she was doing that; *Discovery* was not the target. A dry run, perhaps. Now she was steering toward the Oval, a dimly seen blob, foreshortened to the appearance of a sphere, in the darkling sky, two stars, one ruby and one emerald, brighter far than the other, distant stars that were appearing one by one in the firmament. The throbbing beat of her airscrews came faintly down the light breeze.

The airship passed slowly over the university.

"Conditions ideal," whispered Jones. "Smithy'll be openin' his valves about now. Let's go!"

The party descended to ground level by an express elevator, piled into a waiting car. Jones took something off the back seat, thrust it at Grimes. "Take this, Commander. You'll be needin' it."

Grimes turned the thing over in his hands. It was a respirator. He asked, "What about the rest of you?"

"We're all full o' the antidote. I hope it works. Ronson assured us that it will."

"Wouldn't it be simpler if I had a shot?"

"We took it orally. But we're protectin' you, Commander. When the fun's over you take off yer mask an' just pass out, same as all the other bastards. If there ain't enough Somnopon still lyin' around, we've a spare bottle."

"You've thought of everything," admitted Grimes. He put on the respirator, looked out at the tree-lined, gas-lit streets sliding past the car. A few pedestrians, he saw, had succumbed to stray eddies of the anesthetic. Gas is always a chancy weapon.

They were approaching the entrance to the Oval. They could already hear, over the hum of their engine, loud voices, the crashing of the main gate as it was forced. Grimes expected a rattle of fire, from *Vega*—but her people had been taken unawares, even as the mutineers had been.

The car stopped. Jones jumped out. "Good-bye, Commander. An' thanks. I wish I could've known you better." He extended his hand for a brief, but firm, handshake.

"I'll see you again," said Grimes.

"You won't. I sincerely hope you won't. Nothin' against *you*, mind you." He ran off, toward the stands.

Grimes got out of the car, realized that many vehicles

were already on the scene, that more were arriving. He
was almost knocked over by a mob rushing the transport.
There was Jones, towing a bewildered Vinegar Nell by the
hand. There were Brabham, MacMorris, Tangye, Sally. . . .

"To the ship!" Jones was shouting. "To *Discovery!*"

"To *Discovery!*" the cry was going up. "To *Discovery!*"
Not only were there mutineers in the mob, but many local
women.

Enough was enough, thought Grimes. He stepped
forward to try to stem the rush. He saw Swinton leveling
a weapon taken from one of the guards—and saw Vinegar
Nell knock it to one side just as it exploded. Nell clawed
the respirator from his face, crying, "Keep out of this,
John! The less you know the better!" She swung the gas
mask to hit him in the belly, and he gasped. That was all
he knew.

))(((Chapter 46)))(((

He awoke suddenly. Once again there was the dull ache in his arm where a hypodermic spray had been used. He opened his eyes, saw a khaki-uniformed man bending over him. One of Delamere's Marines . . . ?

"You're under arrest," said the man. "All you Terry bastards're under arrest."

What the hell was going on? The man, Grimes saw, was wearing a wide-brimmed hat, with the brim turned up on one side. The beam of a light shone on a badge of polished brass, a rising-sun design. Not a Marine . . . a policeman.

"Don't be so bloody silly, Vince." It was Mavis' voice. "The skipper's a pal o' mine."

"But the orders were—"

"Who gives the orders round here? Get inside, to the Oval. There's plenty o' Terries in there to arrest, an' quite a' few wantin' first aid!" She added admiringly, "That bloody Brabham! He's made a clean getaway, an' there'll be no chase!" She put out a hand and helped Grimes to his feet. "Thinkin' it over, Skip, I'd better have yer arrested with the others. But we'll walk an' talk a while, first."

They went in through the main entrance, picking their way carefully through the wreckage of the gate. Grimes cried out in dismay. *Vega* was there still, but no longer illumined by the glare of her own floodlights, no longer proudly erect. She was on her side, the great length of her picked out by the headlights of at least two dozen heavy-duty vehicles. Externally she seemed undamaged. Internally? She would be a mess, Grimes knew.

"The cricket season's well an' truly buggered," said Mavis cheerfully. "Never could see anythin' in the game me self."

"What happened?" demanded Grimes.

"That bloody Brabham . . . or it could've been Jonesy's idea. It was as much airmanship as spacemanship."

"Jones? He's with the mutineers?"

"An' quite a few more. I couldn't stop 'em. Not that I wanted to."

"But what happened?"

"Oh, they all made a rush for your *Discovery* after the breakout. *Your* crew, an' Jones, an' . . . oh, we'll have ter sort it out later, how many darlin' daughters an' even wives are missin'. Where was I? Oh, yes. *Discovery* lifted off. But she didn't go straight up. She sorta drifted across the city, her engines goin' like the hammers o' Hell, just scrapin' the rooftops. Then she lifted, but only a little, just so's her backside was nuzzlin' *Vega*'s nose. Like two dogs, it was. An' she sorta *wriggled,* an' *Vega* wriggled too, more an' more, until. . . *Crash!* An' then Brabham went upstairs as though the sheriff an' his posse were after him."

"Delamere was lucky," said Grimes.

"Bloody unlucky, if you ask me."

"No. Lucky. Brabham could have used his weaponry. Or he could have sat on top of *Vega* and cooked her with the auxiliary rocket drive." He managed a grin. "I guess you people must have had a civilizing influence on him. Oh, one more thing. How was it that the mutineers weren't affected by the gas?"

"They were all immune, that's why. Ain't many people can resist the goodies that come out o' *my* kitchen! But we made sure that none o' the popsies deliverin' the pies an' cakes knew the secret ingredient. Not with a nasty, pryin' telepath pickin' up every thought. But that'll have ter do. Here come the mug coppers wi' yer pal Frankie. He's under arrest, same as you are."

Delamere, battered and bruised, held up by the two men of his police escort, staggered toward the mayor. He saw Grimes, stiffened.

"I might have known that you'd be at the bottom of this, you bastard!"

"How the hell could he be?" asked Mavis. "My police found him sprawled, unconscious, by the main entrance."

"You're in this too, you bitch! You'll laugh on the other side of your face when this world is under Federation military occupation!"

"An' is your precious Federation willin' ter fight a war over Botany Bay, specially at the end o' long supply lines? Dr. Brandt showed us how ter build a Carlotti set. We used it, ternight. We got through ter Waverley without any trouble at all. The emperor's willin' to put us under his protection."

"Grimes, you'll pay for this. This is a big black mark on your Service record that'll never be erased!"

This was so, Grimes knew. It would be extremely unwise for him to return to Lindisfarne to face court-martial. He would resign, here and now, by Carlottigram. After that? The Imperial Navy, if they'd have him? With his record, probably not.

The Rim Worlds? Rim Runners would take anybody, as long as he had some qualifications and rigor mortis hadn't set in.

The implications of it all he would work out later. The full appreciation of the desperate situation into which he had been maneuvered—by Mavis as much as by anybody—would sink in slowly.

He looked up at the night sky, at the distant stars.

Would *Discovery* find her Pitcairn Island?

Would the fate of her people be happier than that of those other, long ago and far away, mutineers?

In spite of all that had been done to him by them, in spite of all that had happened because of them, he rather hoped so.

THE FAR
TRAVELER

DEDICATION

꘏((( )))꘏

To all far travelers

The dreams changed.

There were, as before, memories from the minds of the colonists who had long lived in symbiosis with the fungus but now there were other memories—brief flashes, indistinct at first but all the time increasing in clarity and duration. There were glimpses of the faces and the bodies of women whom Grimes had known.

The women . . .

And the ships.

Lines from a long-ago read and long-ago forgotten piece of verse drifted through Grimes' mind:

> *The arching sky is calling*
> *Spacemen back to their trade . . .*

He was sitting in the control room of his first command, a little Serpent Class courier, a king at last even though his realm, to others, was a very insignificant one. Obedient to the touch of his fingers on the console the tiny ship lifted.

> *All hands! Stand by! Free Falling!*
> *The lights below us jade . . .*

And through the dream, louder and louder, surged the arythmic hammering of a spaceship's inertial drive . . . .

»)«(Chapter 1»)«(

The Far Traveler came to Botany Bay, to Paddington, dropping down to the Bradman Oval—which sports arena, since the landing of the Survey Service's *Discovery*, had become a spaceport of sorts. *Discovery* was gone, to an unknown destination, taking with her the mutineers and the friends that they had made on the newly discovered Lost Colony. The destroyer *Vega,* dispatched from Lindisfarne Base to apprehend the mutineers, was still in the Oval, still lying on her side, inoperative until such time as the salvage tugs should arrive to raise her to the perpendicular. *Discovery,* under the command of her rebellious first lieutenant, had toppled the other ship before making her escape.

John Grimes, lately captain of *Discovery,* was still on Botany Bay. He had no place else to go. He had resigned from the Federation's Survey Service, knowing full well that with the loss of his ship his famous luck had run out, that if ever he returned to Lindisfarne he would be brought before a court martial and, almost certainly, would be held responsible for the seizure by mutineers of a valuable piece of the Interstellar Federation's property. And, in all likelihood, he would be held to blame for the quite considerable damage to *Vega*.

In some ways, however, he was still lucky. Apart from anything else he had a job, one for which he was qualified professionally if not temperamentally even though Botany Bay, as yet, owned no spaceships under its flag. (The lost-in-space *Lode Wallaby*, bringing the original colonists, had crashed on landing and, in any case, the essentially cranky gaussjammers had been obsolete for generations.) Nonetheless Botany Bay now needed a spaceport; since the news of *Discovery*'s landing had been broadcast throughout the Galaxy an influx of visitors from outside was to be expected. A spaceport must have a Port Captain. Even if Grimes had not been on more than merely friendly terms with Mavis, Lady Mayor of Paddington and President of the Planetary Council of Mayors, he would have been the obvious choice.

Obvious—but not altogether popular. *Vega*'s people were still on Botany Bay and all of them blamed Grimes for the wreck of their vessel and, come to that, Commander Delamere, the destroyer's captain, had always hated Grimes' guts. (It was mutual.) And there were the parents whose daughters had flown the coop with the *Discovery* mutineers—and quite a few husbands whose wives had done likewise. Vociferously irate, too, were the cricket enthusiasts whose series of test matches had been disrupted by the cluttering up of the Oval with spaceships.

Only the prompt intervention of the local police force had saved Grimes, on one occasion, from a severe beating up at the hands of a half dozen of Delamere's Marines. There had been no police handy when a husband whose wife had deserted with *Discovery*'s bo's'n gave Grimes two black eyes. And he was becoming tired of the white-clad, picketing cricketers outside his temporary office continually chanting, "Terry bastard, go home!"

Then *The Far Traveler* came to Botany Bay.

She was not a big ship but large for what she was, a deep-space yacht. Her home port—Grimes had ascertained during the preliminary radio conversations with her master—was Port Bluewater on El Dorado. That made sense. Only the filthy rich could afford space yachts—and El Dorado was known as the Planet of the Filthy Rich. Grimes had been there once, a junior officer in the Zodiac Class cruiser *Aries*. He had been made to feel like a snotty-nosed urchin from the wrong side of the tracks. He had been told, though, that he would be welcome to return—but only after he had made his first billion credits. He did not think it at all likely that he ever would return.

The Far Traveler dropped down through the clear, early morning sky, the irregular beat of her inertial drive swelling from an irritable mutter to an almost deafening clatter as she fell. The rays of the rising sun were reflected dazzlingly from her burnished hull. There was a peculiarly yellow quality to the mirrored light

Grimes stood on the uppermost tier of the big grandstand watching her and, between times, casting an observant eye around his temporary domain. The triangle of scarlet beacons was there, well clear of the hapless *Vega*, the painfully bright flashers in vivid contrast to the dark green grass on which they stood. At the head of each of the tall flagstaffs around the Oval floated the flag of Botany Bay— blue, with red, white and blue superimposed crosses in the upper canton, a lopsided cruciform constellation of silver stars at the fly.

He was joined by the Deputy Port Captain. Skipper Wheeldon was not a spaceman—yet. He had been master of one of the big dirigibles that handled most of Botany Bay's airborne commerce. But he wanted to learn and already possessed a good grasp of spaceport procedure.

He said, "She's comin' in nicely, sir."

Grimes grunted dubiously. He made a major production of filling and lighting his pipe. He said, speaking around the stem, "If I were that captain I'd be applying more lateral thrust to compensate for windage. Can't he see that he's sagging badly to leeward? If he's not careful he'll be sitting down on top of *Vega* . . ."

He raised the wrist upon which he wore the portable transceiver to his mouth—but before he could speak it seemed almost as though the yacht master had overheard Grimes' remarks to Wheeldon. The note of the inertial drive suddenly changed, the beat becoming more rapid as the incoming ship added a lateral component to her controlled descent

She was falling slowly now, very slowly, finally hovering a scant meter above the close-cropped grass. She dropped again, almost imperceptibly. Grimes wasn't sure that she was actually down until the inertial drive was shut off. The silence was almost immediately broken by the shouts of the picketing, bat-brandishing cricketers—kept well clear of the landing area by slouch-hatted, khaki-clad police—bawling, "Terry, go home! Spacemen, go home!"

A telescopic mast extended itself from the needle prow of the golden ship. A flag broke out from its peak—dark purple and on it, in shining gold, the CR monogram. The Galactic Credit sign—and the ensign of El Dorado.

"I suppose we'd better go down to roll out the red carpet," said Grimes.

♪)《Chapter 2》》《

Grimes stood at the base of the slender golden tower that was *The Far Traveler,* waiting for the after airlock door to open, for the ramp to be extended. With him were Wheeldon and Jock Tanner, the Paddington chief of police who, until things became properly organized, would be in charge of such matters as Customs, Immigration and Port Health formalities. And there was Shirley Townsend, the Mayor's secretary. (Mavis herself was not present. She had said, "I just might get up at sparrowfart to see a king or a queen or a president comin' in, but I'm damned if I'll put meself out for some rich bitch . . .")

"Takin' their time," complained Tanner.

"Perhaps we should have gone round to the servants' entrance," said Grimes half seriously.

The outer door of the airlock slowly opened at last and, as it did so, the ramp extruded itself, a long metal tongue stretching out to lick the dew that still glistened on the grass. Like the shell-plating of the ship it was gold—or, thought Grimes, gold-plated. Either way it was ostentatious.

A man stood in the airlock chamber to receive them. He was tall and thin, and his gorgeous uniform, festoons of gold braid on dark purple, made him look like a refugee from a Strauss operetta. His lean face bore what seemed to be a permanently sour expression. Among the other gleaming encrustations on his sleeve Grimes could distinguish four gold bands. So this had to be the captain . . . And why should the captain be doing a job—the reception of port officials—usually entrusted to, at best, a senior officer?

The yachtmaster looked down at the boarding party. He seemed to decide that Grimes—wearing a slightly modified airship captain's uniform, light blue, with four black stripes on each shoulderboard, with a cap badge on which the silver dirigible had been turned through ninety degrees to make it look like a spaceship—was in charge. He said, "Will you come aboard, please? The Baroness d'Estang will receive you in her sitting room."

Grimes led the way up the ramp. He introduced himself. "Grimes, Acting Port Captain," he said, extending his hand.

"Billinger—Master *de jure* but not *de facto*," replied the other with a wry grin.

Grimes wondered what was meant by this, but discreet inquiries could be made later. He introduced his companions. Then Captain Billinger led the party into an elevator cage. He pushed no buttons—there were no buttons to push—but merely said, "Her Excellency's suite."

The locals were obviously impressed. Grimes was not; such voice-actuated mechanisms were common enough on the worlds with which he was familiar. The ascent was smooth, the stop without even the suspicion of a jolt. They disembarked into a vestibule, on to a thick-piled purple carpet that made a rich contrast to the golden bulkheads. A door before them slid silently open. Billinger led the way through it. He bowed to the tall, slim woman reclining on a *chaise longue* and announced, "The port officials, Your Excellency."

"Thank you, Captain," she replied in a silvery voice, adding, "You may go."

Billinger bowed again, then went.

Grimes looked down at the Baroness and she up at him. She was slim yet rounded, the contours of her body revealed rather than hidden by the filmy white translucency that enrobed her. There was a hint of pink-nippled breasts, of dark pubic shadow. Her cheekbones were high, her mouth wide and firm and scarlet, her chin not overly prominent but definitely firm, her nose just short of being prominent and delicately arched. Her lustrous bronze hair was braided into a natural coronet in which flashed not-so-small diamonds. Even larger stones, in ornate gold settings, depended from the lobes of her ears.

She reminded Grimes of Goya's *Maja*—the draped version—although her legs were much longer. And the furnishings of her sitting room must be like—he thought—the appointments of the boudoir in which that long ago and far away Spanish aristocrat had posed for the artist. Certainly there was nothing in these surroundings that even remotely suggested a spaceship.

He was abruptly conscious of his off-the-peg uniform, of his far from handsome face, his prominent ears. He felt these blushing hotly, a sure sign of embarrassment.

She said sweetly, "Please sit down, Acting Port Captain. I assume that the rank is both *de facto* and *de jure* . . ." She smiled fleetingly. "And you, Deputy Port Captain. And you, City Constable. And, of course, Miss Townsend . . ."

"How did you . . . ?" began Shirley. (It came out as "'Ow did yer . . . ?") "That *de facto* and *de jure* business, I mean . . ."

"I heard, and watched, the introductions at the airlock," said the Baroness, waving a slim, long hand toward what looked like a normal although ornately gold-framed mirror.

The police officer fidgeted on the edge of a spindly-legged chair that looked as though it was about to collapse, at any moment, under his weight. He said, "If you'll excuse me, Baroness, I'll go an' see the skipper about the port formalities. . ."

"They will be handled here," said the Baroness firmly. She did not actually finish the sentence with "my man" but the unspoken words hung in the faintly scented air. She went on, "I have always considered any of my business too important to be left to underlings." She clapped her hands. A man dressed in archaic servant's livery—white, frilled shirt, scarlet, brass-buttoned waistcoat, black knee-breeches, white stockings, black, gold-buckled shoes—entered silently. A man? No. He was, Grimes realized, one of those uncannily humanoid serving robots with which he had become familiar during his visit to El Dorado, years ago. He—it?—was carrying folders of documents—clearances, crew and passenger lists, declarations, store lists and manifests. Without hesitation he handed the papers to the City Constable.

"Is he *all* gold?" asked Shirley in an awed voice. "Under his clothes and all?"

"Yes," the Baroness told her. Then, speaking generally, "Will you take refreshment? There is coffee, if you wish, or tea, or wine. I know that, by your time, it is early in the day—but I have never known Spumante Vitelli to come amiss at any hour of the clock."

"Spumante Vitelli?" asked Shirley Townsend, determinedly talkative. "Sounds like an emetic . . ."

"It's an El Doradan sparkling wine," Grimes said hastily. "From Count Vitelli's vineyards."

"You know El Dorado, Port Captain?" asked the Baroness, polite but condescending surprise in her voice.

"I was there," said Grimes. "Some years ago."

"But this is a Lost Colony. You have had no facilities for space travel since the founders made their chance landing."

"Commander Grimes is out of the Federation's Survey Service," said Jock Tanner.

"Indeed?" The fine eyebrows arched over the dark violet eyes. "Indeed? *Commander* Grimes? There was—I recall—a Lieutenant Grimes . . ."

"There was," said Grimes. "Me." Then—the memories were flooding back—"You must know the Princess Marlene von Stoizberg, Your Excellency."

The Baroness laughed. "Not intimately, Port Captain or Commander. She's too much of the hausfrau, fat and dowdy, for my taste."

"Hausfrau?" echoed Grimes bewilderedly. That was not how he recalled Marlene.

"Many women change," said the Baroness, "and not

always for the better when they become mothers." She went on maliciously, "And what about the father of the child? As I recall it, there was quite a scandal. You, and dear Marlene, and that mad old Duchess, and poor Henri . . . It's a small universe, John Grimes, but I never did meet you on El Dorado and I never dreamed that I should meet you here.

The robot servitor was back, bearing a golden (of course) tray on which was a golden ice bucket, in it a magnum of the Spumante, and gold-rimmed crystal goblets. He poured, serving his mistress first. Glasses of the sparkling, pale golden wine were raised in salute; sipped from.

"Not a bad drop o' plonk," said Shirley, speaking with deliberate coarseness.

Jock Tanner, doing his best to divert attention from her, put his glass down on the richly carpeted deck, picked up a sheaf of the papers. "John," he said, "you know more about these things than I do . . . This clearance from Tallifer . . . Shouldn't it have been signed by the Chief Medical Officer?"

"Not necessarily," said Grimes, putting down his own glass and getting up from his chair, walking across to the police officers. "But I think we'd better get Shirley—she's used to wading through bumf—to make sure that everything has been signed by a responsible official."

"Orl right," grumbled the girl. "Orl right." She drained her glass, belched delicately, joined Grimes and Tanner. The hapless Wheeldon, out of his social depth and floundering, was left to make polite conversation with the Baroness.

Shortly thereafter *The Far Traveler* was granted her Inward Clearance and the boarding party trooped down the golden gangway to the honest turf.

⨳«Chapter 3»⨳

"You do have posh friends, John," said Shirley Townsend as soon as they were down and off the ramp.

"I didn't have any friends on El Dorado," said Grimes, not altogether truthfully and with a note of bitterness in his voice.

Captain Billinger was relaxing. He still looked far from happy but his long face had lost some of the lines of strain. He had changed from his fancy dress uniform into more or less sober civilian attire—a bright orange shirt tucked into a kilt displaying an improbable looking tartan in which a poisonous green predominated, highly polished scarlet knee-boots. He was sitting with Grimes at a table in the saloon bar of the Red Kangaroo.

He gulped beer noisily. "Boy," he said, "boy, oh boy! Am I ever glad to get off that rich bitch's toy ship!"

"But you're rich yourself, surely," said Grimes. "You must be, to be an El Doradan . . ."

"Ha! Me an El Doradan! That'd be the sunny Friday!

No, Captain, I'm just a poor but reasonably honest Dog Star Line second mate. *Beagle* happened to be on Electra when her ladyship was there to take delivery of her superduper yacht. Seems that she came there in an El Doradan ship—they do have ships, you know, and a few playboy spacemen to run 'em—and assumed that she'd be allowed to lift off in her own fully automated vessel without having a qualified human master on board. But Lloyds'—may the Odd Gods of the Galaxy rot them—cotton socks!—got into the act. No duly certificated master astronaut on the Register, no insurance cover. But money talks, as always. More than a couple or three Dog Star line shares are held by her high and mightiness. So the Old Man got an urgent Carlottigram from Head Office—I'd like to know what it said!—and, immediately after receipt, yelled for me and then turned on the hard sell. Not that there was any need for it. The offer of a Master's berth at well above *our* Award rates for the rank . . . Only a yachtmaster, it's true—but master nonetheless and bloody well paid. Like a mug, I jumped at it. Little did I know . . ." He slurped down the remains of his beer and waved two fingers at the near-naked, plumply attractive blonde waitress to order refills.

"So you don't like the job, Captain," said Grimes.

"You can say that again, Captain. And again. Cooped up with a snooty, rich bitch in a solid gold sardine can . . . ."

"Gold-plated, surely," interjected Grimes.

"No. Gold. G-O-L-D. Gold."

"But gold's not a structural material."

"It is after those eggheads on Electra have finished mucking about with it. They rearrange the molecules. Or the atoms. Or something."

"Fantastic," commented Grimes.

"The whole bloody ship's fantastic. A miracle of automation or an automated miracle. A human captain is just a figurehead. You watched the set down yesterday?"

"Of course. I am the Port Captain, you know. There was something a bit . . . odd about it. I can guess now what it must have been. The ship was coming down by herself without a human hand on the controls—and making a slight balls of it. And then *you* took over."

Billinger glared at Grimes. "Ha! Ha bloody ha! For your information, Port Captain, *I* was bringing her down. At first. Yes, I know damn well that there was drift but I was putting on speed. At the last possible moment I was going to make a spectacular lateral hedge-hop and sit down bang in the middle of the beacons. And then *she* had to stick her tits in. 'Take your ape's paws off the controls!' she told me. The computer may not be as old as you—but she knows more about ship-handling than you'll ever learn in your entire, misspent life!'"

The waitress brought two fresh pots of beer. Grimes could tell by the way that she looked at Billinger that she liked him. (She knew, of course, who he was—and would assume that he, as captain of a solid gold spaceship, would be rich.)

"Thank you, dear," said Billinger. He leered up at her and she simpered sweetly down at him. She took the bank note—the Baroness had traded a handful or so of precious stones for local currency—that he handed her, began to fumble in the sequined sporran that was, apart from high-heeled sandals, her only clothing for change.

"That will be all right," said Billinger grandly.

Throwing money around like a drunken spaceman . . . thought Grimes.

"And what are you doing tonight after you close, my dear?" went on Billinger.

"If you wait around, sir, you'll find out," she promised, her simper replaced by a definitely encouraging smile.

She left the table reluctantly, her firm buttocks seeming to beckon as she moved away.

"I believe I'm on to something there," murmured Billinger. "I do. I really do. And I deserve it. I've been too long confined to that space-going trinket box with bitchy Micky flaunting the body beautiful all over the whole damned ship—and making it quite plain that there was nothing doing. You can look—but you mustn't touch. That's her ladyship!"

Grimes remembered his own experiences on El Dorado. He asked, however, "What exactly is she doing out here?"

"Research. Or so she says. For her thesis for a doctorate in some damn science or other. Social Evolution In The Lost Colonies. Not that she'll find much to interest her here. Not kinky enough. Mind you, this'd be a fine world for an honest working stiff like me. . ." He stiffened abruptly. "Talk of the devil . . ."

"Of *two* devils . . ." corrected Grimes.

She swept into the crowded bar-room, the gleaming length of her darkly tanned legs displayed by a skirt that was little more than a wide belt of gold mesh, topped by a blouse of the same material that was practically all décolletage. Her dark-gleaming hair was still arranged in a jewel-studded coronet. She was escorted by no less a person than Commander Frank Delamere. Handsome Frankie was attired for the occasion in mess full dress— spotless white linen, black and gold, a minor constellation of tinkling miniatures depending from rainbow ribbons on the left breast of his superbly cut jacket. They were no more than Good Attendance medals, Grimes well knew— but they looked impressive.

The handsome couple paused briefly at the table at which Grimes and Billinger were seated.

"Ah, Mr. Grimes . . ." said Delamere nastily.

"*Captain* Grimes," corrected the owner of that name.

"A civilian, courtesy title," sneered Delamere. "A . . . Port Captain."

He made it sound at least three grades lower than Spaceman, Fourth Class. (Grimes himself, come to that, had always held Port Captains in low esteem—but that was before he became one such.)

"Perhaps we should not have come here, Francis," said the Baroness.

"Why shouldn't you?" asked Grimes. "This is Liberty Hall. You can spit on the mat and call the cat a bastard." He knew that he was being childish but was deriving a perverse pleasure from the exchange.

"Come, Francis," she said imperiously. "I think that I see a vacant table over there. A very good night to you, Acting Port Captain. And to . . . to you, Captain Billinger? Of course. Forgive me, but I did not recognize you in your civilian finery."

She glided away. Her rear view was no less enticing than that of the waitress had been but, nonetheless, she was the sort of woman who looked and walked like an aristocrat no matter what she was or was not wearing. Delamere, a fatuous smirk on his too regularly featured face, followed.

"A lovely dollop of trollop," muttered Grimes.

Billinger scowled. "It's all very well for you, Captain," he complained, "but *I* have to work for that bitch!"

"My nose fair bleeds for you," said Grimes unfeelingly.

So Delamere was a fast worker. And Delamere, as Grimes well knew, was the most notorious womanizer in the entire Survey Service. And he *used* women. His engagement to the very plain daughter of the Admiral Commanding Lindisfarne Base had brought him undeserved promotions. But Delamere and this El Doradan baroness? That was certainly intriguing. She was a sleek, potentially dangerous cat, not a silly kitten. Who would be using whom? Grimes, back in his quarters in the mayoral palace, lay awake in the wide bed pondering matters; in spite of the large quantities of beer he had consumed he was not sleepy. He was sorry that Mavis, the Mayor, had not come to him this night as she usually did. She was well endowed with the shrewdness essential in a successful politician and he would have liked to talk things over with her.

Delamere and the Baroness . . .

The Baroness and Delamere . . .

He wished them joy of each other.

He wished Billinger and his little blonde waitress joy of each other.

But a vague premonition kept nagging at him. Something was cooking. He wished that he knew what it was.

Ѡ《Chapter 4》Ѡ

Two mornings later he found out.

Billinger, his face almost as purple as the cloth of his gaudy uniform, stormed into Grimes' little office atop the grandstand just as he was settling down to his morning tea, freshly brewed by Shirley who, by now, was working for him as much as for the Mayor, and hot buttered scones liberally spread with jam.

"This is too much!" yelled *The Far Traveler*'s captain.

Grimes blinked, thinking at first that the other was referring to the matutinal snack. But this was unlikely, he realized. "Calm down, calm down," he soothed. "Take a pew. Have a cuppa. And a scone . . ."

"Calm down, you say? How would *you* feel in my shoes? I was engaged as a yachtmaster, not a tugmaster. I should have been consulted. But *she,* as per bloody usual, has gone over my head!"

"What is all this about?" demanded Grimes.

"You mean that you don't know either, Captain?"

"No. Sit down, have some tea and tell me all about it. Shirley—a mug for Captain Billinger, please."

"*She,*" said Billinger after a tranquilizing sip, "is rolling in money—but that doesn't inhibit her from grabbing every chance to make more of the filthy stuff. *She* has signed a contract with your pal Delamere, engaging to raise *Vega* to liftoff position. She just happened to mention it to me, casual like."

"You're not a tugmaster," agreed Grimes, "and a space-yacht is certainly not a tug. Looks to me as though she's bitten off more than she—or *you*—can chew."

"Maybe not," said Billinger slowly, "maybe not. She's a powerful little brute—*The Far Traveler,* I mean. She's engines in her that wouldn't be out of place in a battle-ship. But *I* should have been consulted."

"So should I," said Grimes. "So should I. After all, this is *my* spaceport, such as it is." And then, more to himself than to the other, "But Frankie won't be too popular, signing away a large hunk of the taxpayers' money when the Survey Service's own tugs are well on the way to here."

"They're not," said Billinger. "It seems that there's been some indefinite delay. Delamere got a Carlottigram about it. Or so *she* says."

"And so Frankie keeps his jets clear," murmured Grimes in a disappointed voice. "He would."

And just how would this affect *him?* he wondered. *Vega* lying helplessly on her side was one thing, *Vega* restored to the perpendicular, to the lift-off position, would be an altogether different and definitely dangerous kettle of fish. Even should her drives, inertial and reaction, require adjustments or repairs she would be able to deploy her quite considerable weaponry—her automatic cannon, missile launchers and lasers. The city of Paddington would lay at her mercy. And then?

An ultimatum to the Mayor?

Deliver the deserter, ex-Commander Grimes, to Federation Survey Service custody so that he may be carried to Lindisfarne Base to stand trial—or else?

Grimes shrugged away his apprehensions. Handsome Frankie wouldn't dare. Botany Bay was almost in the backyard of the Empire of Waverley and, thanks to certain of *Discovery*'s technicians, now possessed its own deep-space radio equipment, the Time-Space-twisting Carlotti communications and direction-finding system. A squeal to the Emperor—who'd been getting far too uppish of late—and Imperial Navy cruisers would be piling on the lumes to this sector of space. There would be all the makings of a nasty interstellar incident with Frankie having to carry the can back. And, in any case, H.I.M.S. *Robert Bruce* was already en route to Botany Bay to show the Thistle Flag. But what was Billinger saying?

". . . interesting problem, all the same. It wouldn't be so bad if she'd let me handle it. But not her. It'll either be that bloody computer or that popinjay of an FSS commander, or the pair of 'em working in collusion. With *her* sticking her tits into everything, as always."

"And, of course," Grimes pointed out just to cheer him up, "you, as master, will be legally responsible if anything goes wrong."

"Don't I know it! For two pins I'd resign. I'd be quite happy waiting here for another ship to come along; after all, I've a pile of credits due in back pay." He got to his feet. "Oh, well, I suppose I'd better get back to my noble vessel to see what else has been cooked up in my absence."

"I'll come with you," said Grimes.

The pair of them stood in the Baroness' boudoir like two schoolboys summoned before a harsh headmistress. She did not ask them to sit down. And she, herself, was not reclining decoratively on her *chaise longue* but seated at a *secretaire,* a gracefully designed desk—excellent reproduction or genuine antique?—with rich ormolu decoration. It must be, thought Grimes, a reproduction. His mind was a repository for scraps of useless knowledge and he remembered that the original ormolu had been brass imitating gold. Only the genuine precious metal would do for the Baroness.

She looked up from the papers before her. A pair of heavy, old-fashioned spectacles, black-framed, went oddly with her filmy gown—but somehow suited her. She said, "Captain Billinger, I believe that you, as master, are required to affix your signature to this document, this contract I, as owner, have already signed."

Sulkily Billinger went to stand by the ornate desk, produced a stylus from the breast pocket of his uniform, bent to scribble his name.

"And Port Captain Grimes . . . I understand that I should ask your permission to engage in towage—if that is the correct word—within the spaceport limits."

"That is so, Your Excellency," said Grimes.

"I assume that the permission is granted."

Grimes was tempted to say no but decided against it. Commander Delamere represented the Survey Service and the Baroness d'Estang represented El Dorado, with its vast wealth and influence. There are times—and this was one of them— when it is futile to fart against thunder.

He said, "Yes."

"Good. No doubt you gentlemen feel that you are entitled to be apprised as to what has been arranged between Commander Delamere and myself. The commander will supply the towing wires from his stores. It will be necessary to pierce *The Far Traveler*'s shell plating about the stern to secure the towing lugs. I am informed that the welding of steel onto gold is impracticable—and, of course, the modified gold that was used to build the ship on Electra is unobtainable here. Commander Delamere assures me, however, that his artificers will be able to make good the hull after the job has been completed. All dust and shavings will be carefully collected and melted down to plug the holes." She turned in her chair to address Billinger. "All relevant data has been fed into the computer." She permitted herself a smile. "You will be pleased to learn, Captain, that she does not feel herself competent to undertake what is, in effect, salvage work. Her programmers back on Electra did not envisage any circumstances such as those that have arisen now." She looked positively happy. "The guarantee has not yet expired, so I shall be entitled to considerable financial redress from Electronics and Astronautics, Incorporated." She paused, looked quizzically at Grimes, the heavy spectacles making her look like a schoolmistress condescending to share a joke with one of her pupils. "Commander Delamere did suggest that he assume temporary command of my ship during the operation but I decided not to avail myself of his kind offer."

She's shrewd, thought Grimes. *She's got him weighed up.*

She turned again to Billinger. "*You* are the master, Captain. I am paying you a handsome salary. I expect you to begin earning it. And I am sure that Port Captain Grimes will be willing to oversee the entire exercise from the ground."

"I shall be pleased to, Your Excellency," said Grimes.

"Your pleasure," she told him, "is of little consequence. After all, this is your spaceport, even though it is normally used for archaic Australian religious rites. Thank you, gentlemen."

They were dismissed.

⑨⟨⟨Chapter 5⟩⟩⑨

"I don't like it, John," said Mavis.

The Lady Mayor of Paddington, President of the Council of Mayors of Botany Bay, was sprawled in an easy chair in Grimes' sitting room, regarding him solemnly over the rim of her beer mug. She was a big woman, although too firm-bodied to be considered obese, older than him but still sexually attractive. She was wearing a gaudy sarong that displayed her deeply tanned, sturdy legs almost to the crotch, that left bare her strong but smooth arms and shoulders. Her lustrous, almost white hair made a startling contrast to the warm bronze of her face, as did the pale gray eyes, the very serious eyes. Of late she had been too much the mother and too little the lover for Grimes' taste.

He said, "We have to get that bloody *Vega* off your cricket pitch some time."

She said, "That's as may be—but I wouldn't trust your cobber Delamere as far as I could throw him."

"No cobber of mine," Grimes assured her. "He never was and never will be." He laughed. "Anyhow, *you* could throw him quite a fair way."

She chuckled. "An' wouldn't I like to! Right into one o' those stinkin' tanks out at the sewage farm!"

Grimes said, "But he'd never dare to use his guns to threaten you, to demand that you turn me over to him. He knows damn well that if he sparked off an incident he'd be as much in the shit with the Survey Service as I am."

She did not need to be a telepath to sense his mood. She said softly, "That Service of yours has been more a mistress—and a mother—to you than I have ever been, ever could be."

"No," he said, after too long a pause. "Not so."

"Don't lie to me, John. Don't worry about hurtin' my feelings. I'm just an old bag who's been around for so long that emotionally I'm mostly scar tissue. . ." She lit one of the cigars rolled from the leaves of the mutated tobacco of Botany Bay, deeply inhaled the fragrant, aphrodisiac smoke, exhaled. Grimes, whether he wanted to or not, got his share of the potent fumes. In his eyes she became more and more attractive, Junoesque. The sarong slipped to reveal her big, firm, brown-gleaming breasts with their erect, startlingly pink nipples. He got up from his own chair, took a step toward her.

But she hadn't finished talking. Raising a hand to fend him off she said, "An' it's not only the Service. It's space itself. I've been through this sorta tiling before. My late husband was a seaman—an' he thought more o' the sea an' his blasted ships than he ever did o' me. An' the airship skippers are just as bad, their wives tell me.

Sea, Air—an' Space . . . The great mistresses with whom we mere human women can never compete . . .

"You don't haveter tell me, Johnnie boy, but you're pinin'. It's a space-goin' command you really want, not the captaincy of a cricket field that just happens to be cluttered up with spaceships. I wish I could help—but it'll be years before we have any spaceships of our own. An' I wish I could get you off Botany Bay—for your sake, not mine! I hear things an' I hear of things. That Delamere was sayin'—never mind who to—'The Survey Service has a long arm—an' if that bastard Grimes thinks he's safe here, he's got another thing comin'.'"

"Delamere!" sneered Grimes.

"He's a weak man," said Mavis, "but he's vain. An' cunning as a shit-house rat. An' dangerous."

"He couldn't fight his way out of a paper bag," said Grimes.

"He has men—an' he'll soon have a ship—to do his fightin' for him," Mavis said.

"It's up to me whether he has a ship or not," said Grimes. "And now let's forget about him, shall we?"

He dropped the last of his clothing to the floor. She was ready for him, enveloped him in her ample, warm embrace. For a time—if only for a short time—he forgot space and ships and, even, that nagging premonition of disasters yet to come.

»«(Chapter 6)«»

Grimes stood with Wheeldon on the close-cropped grass of the Oval—the groundsmen were still carrying out their duties although no one knew when, if ever, play would be resumed—a scant five meters from the recumbent hulk of *Vega*. She was no more than a huge, useless, metal tube, pointed at one end and with vanes at the other. It did not seem possible that she would ever fly, had ever flown. Like a giant submarine, improbably beached on grassland, she looked—a submarine devoid of conning tower and control surfaces. Grimes remembered a visit he had paid to one of the ship-building yards on Atlantia where he, with other Survey Service officers, had witnessed the launching of a big, underseas oil tanker. And this operation, of which he was in charge, was a launching of sorts . . .

Forward of the crippled destroyer stood *The Far Traveler*, a fragile seeming golden tower, a gleaming spire supported by the flying buttresses that were her stern vanes. Between each of these there was a steel towing lug, the dull gray of the base metal contrasting harshly with the rich, burnished yellow of the yacht's shell plating. Grimes had inspected these fittings and, reluctantly, had admitted that Delamere's artificers had made a good job. To each of the three lugs was shackled a length of wire rope, silvery metal cordage that, in spite of its apparent flimsiness, was certified to possess a safe working load measured in thousands of tons. It, like the Baroness's yacht, was a product of Electra, yet another example of arcane metallurgical arts and sciences. It was hellishly expensive—but when it came to the supply of stores and equipment to its ships the Survey Service had occasional spasms of profligacy. That wire must have been in *Vega*'s storerooms for years. Nobody had dreamed that it would ever be used.

Lugs had been welded to the destroyer's skin just abaft the circular transparencies of the control-room viewports. To each of these a length of the superwire was shackled. All three towlines were still slack, of course, and would be so until *The Far Traveler* took the strain. Grimes didn't much care for the setup. The problem would be to maintain an equal stress on all parts. He would have liked to have installed self-tensioning winches in either the yacht or the warship but, although such devices were in common use by Botany Bay's shipping, none were available capable of coping with the enormous strains that would be inevitable in an operation of this kind. As it was, he must do his damnedest to ensure that at least two of the wires were taking the weight at all times, and that there were no kinks. He could visualize all too clearly what would happen if there were—a broken end whipping through the air with all the viciousness of a striking snake, decapitating or bloodily bisecting anybody unlucky enough to be in the way. And he, Grimes, was liable to be one such. He had to direct things from a position where he could see at once if anything was going wrong. Delamere and the Baroness and all *Vega*'s crew, with the exception of one engineer officer, were watching from the safety of the stands. And Mavis, with her entourage, was also getting a grandstand view . . .

He stood there, capless in the warm sunshine but wearing a headset with throat microphone. It was a good day for the job, he thought, almost windless. Nothing should go wrong. But if everything went right—there was that nagging premonition back again—then things could start going wrong. For him. *Heads you win, tails I lose . . .?* Maybe.

He said to Wheeldon, "Better get up to the stands. If one of those wires parts it won't be at all healthy around here."

"Not on your sweet Nelly," replied the Deputy Port Captain. "I'm supposed to be your apprentice. I want to see how this job is done."

"As you please," said Grimes. If Wheeldon wished to share the risk that was his privilege. He actuated his transceiver. "Port Captain to *Far Traveler*. Stand by."

"Standing by," came Billinger's voice in the headset.

"Port Captain to *Vega*. Stand by."

"Standing by," replied the engineer in the destroyer's inertial drive room.

Ships, thought Grimes, *should be fitted with inertial drive units developing sufficient lateral thrust to cope with this sort of situation. But I'll use whatever thrust Frankie's engineer can give me . . .*

"Port Captain to *Far Traveler*. Lift off!"

The yacht's inertial drive started up, cacophonous in the still air. She lifted slowly. The wire cables started to come clear of the grass.

"Hold her at that, Billinger. Hold her . . . Now . . . Cant her, cant her . . . Just five degrees short of the critical angle . . ."

The Far Traveler was not only a floating tower, hanging twenty meters clear of the ground, but was becoming a leaning tower, toppling slowly and deliberately until her long axis was at an angle of forty degrees from the vertical. Billinger should have no trouble holding her in that position. In a normal vessel anxious officers and petty officers would be sweating over their controls; in the fully-automated yacht servo-mechanisms would be doing all the work.

"Port Captain to *Vega* . . . Maximum lateral thrust, directed *down!*"

The destroyer came to life, snarling, protesting. The combined racket from the two ships was deafening.

"Lift her, Billinger. Lift her! Maintain your angle . . ."

The Far Traveler lifted. The cables—two of them—tautened. They . . . *thrummed,* an ominous note audible even above the hammering of the inertial drive units. But the sharp stem of *Vega* was coming clear of the grass, a patch of dead, crushed, dirty yellow showing in sharp contrast to the living green.

"Thirty-five degrees, Billinger . . ."

The change in the yacht's attitude was almost imperceptible but the threatening song of the bar-taut wires was louder.

"Increase your thrust if you can, *Vega!*"

"It'll bugger my innie if I do . . ."

"It's not *my* innie," growled Grimes. *"Increase your thrust!"*

More dead yellow was showing under the warship.

"Billinger—thirty degrees . . . Twenty-five . . . And roll her . . . Roll her to port . . . Just a touch . . . Hold it!"

For a moment it seemed that all the weight would be on one cable only but now two had the strain once more.

"Billinger! Twenty degrees . . ."

Vega was lifting nicely, coming up from the long depression that she had made with her inert tonnage. Grimes noticed worm-like things squirming among the dead grass stems—but this was no time for the study of natural history. He was trying to estimate the angle made by the destroyer's long axis with the ground. Soon he would be able to tell the engineer to apply a component of fore-and-aft thrust.

"Billinger, ten degrees . . ."

Then it happened. One of the taut wires snapped, about halfway along its length. The broken ends whipped viciously—the upper one harmlessly but the lower one slashing down to the grass close to where Grimes was standing. It missed him. He hardly noticed it.

"Billinger, roll to starboard! Roll!" He had to get the weight back on to two wires instead of only one. "Hold her! And lift! Lift!"

Would the cables hold? *"Vega!* Fore and aft thrust! Now!"*

The destroyer, her sharp bows pointing upward and rising all the time, surged ahead. Two of her stern vanes gouged long, ugly furrows in the grass. There should have been a spaceman officer in her control room to take charge of her during these final stages of the operation—but Delamere, when Grimes had raised this point, had insisted that it would not be necessary. (The obvious man for the job, of course, would have been *Vega*'s captain—and Frankie, as Grimes well knew, was always inclined to regard the safety of his own skin as of paramount importance.)

Vega lifted, lifted, coming closer and closer to the vertical. Two of her vanes were in contact with the ground, the third was almost so. Grimes looked up to the taut cables. He could see bright strands of broken wire protruding from one of them. It would be a matter of seconds only before it parted, as had the first one. Obviously those safe working load certificates had been dangerously misleading . . . "*Vega!* Full lateral thrust! Now!"

"The innie's flat out!"

Damn all engineers! thought Grimes. At crucial moments their precious machinery was always of greater importance to them than the ship.

"Double maximum thrust—or you've had it!" The officer must have realized at last that this was an emergency. The destroyer's inertial drive not only hammered but . . . *howled.* The ship shuddered and teetered and then, suddenly, lifted her forward end, so rapidly that for an instant the cables hung slack. But Billinger quickly took the weight again and gave one last, mighty jerk. The stranded cable parted but the remaining towline held. The broken end slashed down to the grass on the other side of the destroyer from Grimes.

Vega came to the perpendicular and stood there, rocking slightly on her vanes.

"Billinger—'vast towing! *Vega*—cut inertial drive!"

"It's cut itself . . ." said *Vega*'s engineer smugly.

And then, only then, was Grimes able to look down to see what the end of the first snapped cable had done. He stared, and swallowed, and vomited. He stood there, retching uncontrollably, befouling his clothing. But it didn't much matter. His footwear and lower legs were already spattered with blood and tatters of human flesh. The flying wire had cut the unfortunate Wheeldon—not very neatly—in two.

So Captain Billinger gingerly brought *The Far Traveler* to a landing, careful not to get the yacht's stern foul of the remaining tow wire. So Commander Delamere, at the head of his crew, his spacemen and Marines, marched down from the grandstand and across the field to resume possession of his ship. So an ambulance drove up to collect what was left of the Deputy Port Captain while Grimes stood there, staring down at the bloodied grass, retching miserably . . . To him came Mavis, and Shirley and, surprisingly, the Baroness.

Mavis whispered, "It could have happened to you . . ."

Grimes said, "It should have happened to me. I was in charge. I should have checked those wires for deterioration."

The Baroness said, "I shall arrange for more than merely adequate compensation to be paid to Captain Wheeldon's relatives."

"Money!" flared Mavis. "It's all that you and your kind ever think of! If you hadn't grabbed the chance of makin' a few dollars on the side by usin' your precious yacht as a tugboat this would never've happened!"

The Baroness said, "I am sorry. Believe me, I'm sorry . . ."

"Look!" cried Shirley, pointing upward.

They looked. Ports had opened along *Vega*'s sleek sides, in the plating over turrets and sponsons. The snouts of weapons, cannon and laser projectors, protruded, hunting, like the questing antennae of some giant insect.

"Here it comes," said Mavis glumly. "The ulti-bloody-ma-tum. Give us Grimes—or else. . ." She stiffened. "But I'm not giving any cobber o' mine to those Terry bastards!"

Yet there was no ultimatum, no vastly amplified voice roaring over the sports arena. The guns ceased their restless motion but were not withdrawn, however.

"Just Frankie making sure that everything's in working order," said Grimes at last.

"Leave him to play with his toys," said Mavis. "Come on home an' get cleaned up." She turned to the El Doradan woman. "You comin' with us, Baroness?" The tone of her voice made it obvious that she did not expect the invitation to be accepted.

"No, thank you, Your Ladyship. I must go aboard my yacht to see what must be done to make her spaceworthy again."

"C'm'on," said Mavis to Grimes and Shirley.

They walked slowly toward the main gates. All at once they were surrounded by a mob of men clad in white flannel with absurd little caps on their heads, with gaudily colored belts supporting their trousers, brandishing cricket bats.

"Terry bastard go home!" they chanted. "Terry bastard go home!"

I've got no home to go to, thought Grimes glumly.

"Bury the bastard in the holes he dug in our cricket pitch!" yelled somebody.

"Burying's too good!" yelled somebody else. "Cut 'im in two, same as he did Skipper Wheeldon!"

"It was an accident!" shouted Mavis. "Now, away with yer! Let us through!"

"I'm checker takin' orders from you, you fat cow!" growled a man who seemed to be the ringleader, a hairy, uncouth brute against whom Grimes, in any circumstances at all, would have taken an instant dislike. "An' as it's too long ter wait for the next election . . ."

He raised his bat.

From *Vega* came a heavy rattle of automatic fire and the sky between the ship and the mob was suddenly brightly alive with tracers. Had the aim not been deliberately high there would have been sudden and violent death on the ground. Again the guns fired, and again—then Grimes and the two women found themselves standing safe and no longer molested while the cricketers bolted for cover. Three bats and a half dozen or so caps littered the trampled grass.

"And *now* what?" asked Mavis in a shaken voice.

"Just Frankie, as a good little Survey Service commander, rallying to the support of the civil authority," said Grimes at last. Then—"But where the hell were *your* police?"

"That big, bearded bastard," muttered Mavis, "just happens to be a senior sergeant . . ."

Then Tanner, with a squad of uniformed men, arrived belatedly to escort the mayoral party to the palace. The City Constable was neither as concerned nor as apologetic as he should have been.

))(((Chapter 7)))(((

The next day was a heavy one for Grimes. There were, as yet, no Lloyd's Surveyors on Botany Bay; nonetheless *The Far Traveler* was required to have a fresh Certificate of Spaceworthiness issued to her before she could lift from the surface of the planet. Of course, the Baroness could depart without such documentation if she so wished— but without it her ship would not be covered by the underwriters. And she was, for all her title and air of elegant decadence, a shrewd businesswoman.

She called Grimes to her presence. The robot butler ushered him into the lady's boudoir where she, flimsily clad as usual, was seated at her beautiful, fragile-seeming, pseudo-antique desk. She was wearing the heavy-rimmed spectacles again, was studying a thick, important-looking book.

"Ah, good morning, Acting Port Captain . . . Now, this matter of insurance . . . As you already know, Commander Delamere's artificers were obliged to pierce my hull to fit the towing lugs. Today they are making the damage good as required by the contract. After these repairs have been completed a survey must be carried out."

"By whom, Your Excellency?" asked Grimes.

"By you, of course, Port Captain. You will receive the usual fee."

"But I'm not a surveyor . . ."

"You are the Port Captain." A slim index finger tipped with a long, gold-enameled nail stabbed down at the open pages. "Listen. *On planets where Lloyd's maintain neither offices, agents nor surveyors Lloyd's Certificates may be endorsed or issued by such planetary officials as are deemed competent by the Corporation to carry out such functions. Port Captains, Port Engineers, etc., etc. . . . Commanding officers of vessels or bases of the Interstellar Federation's Survey Service. . ."* She smiled briefly. "I have no intention of paying a surveyor's fee to your friend Commander Delamere. In any case, as his people are making the repairs he is ruled out." She read more. *"Commanding officers of vessels or bases of the Imperial Navy of Waverley.* No, I'm not going to wait around until that Waverley cruiser—*Robert Bruce,* isn't it?—condescends to drop in. So . . ."

"So I'm it," said Grimes.

"Elegantly expressed, Acting Port Captain. But I suggest that you accept guidance from the computer. After all, she is the ship's brain. She *is* the ship—just as your intelligence is *you*—and is fully capable of self diagnosis."

"Mphm," grunted Grimes. He wanted to pull his vile pipe out of his pocket, to fill it and light it, but knew that to ask permission so to do would bring a rebuff. He said,

"So you need a Lloyd's Surveyor as much—or as little—as you need a captain."

She said, "I need neither—but Lloyd's of London insist that I must have both. And now may I suggest that you get on with your surveying?"

Bitch, thought Grimes. *Rich bitch. Rich, spoiled bitch.* He said, "Very well, Your Excellency," bowed stiffly and left her presence.

The humanoid robot in butler's livery led him to the elevator. The upward ride was such a short one that it would have been far less trouble to have used the spiral staircase that ornately entwined the axial shaft. Billinger was waiting in his own quarters for Grimes.

The yachtmaster was not uncomfortably housed; masters of Alpha Class liners or captains of Zodiac Class cruisers would not have complained about such accommodation. The keynote was one of masculine luxury— deep armchairs upholstered in genuine black leather, a low, glass-topped coffee table standing on sturdy, ebony legs, bookshelves all along one bulkhead, well stocked with volumes in gilt and maroon leather bindings, a gold and ebony liquor cabinet, a huge playmaster encased in gold-trimmed paneling of the same expensive timber. Holograms glowed on the other bulkheads—bright windows looking out on seascapes and mountainscapes and, inevitably, an Arcadian beach scene with the inevitable sun-bronzed, sun-bleached blonde in the foreground.

"She does you well, Captain," commented Grimes.

"Careful, Captain," said Billinger. "Big Sister is watching. And listening." He gestured toward the playmaster, the screen of which seemed to be dead, "Coffee?"

"Please."

Almost immediately a girl, a stewardess, came in, carrying a tray. It was a golden tray, of course, with golden coffee pot, cream jug and sugar bowl, gold-chased china. And the girl was also golden, wearing a short-skirted black uniform over a perfectly proportioned body that gleamed metallically.

She set the tray on the table, lifted the pot and poured. "Sugar, sir?" she asked. "Cream?"

The mechanical quality of her golden voice was barely discernible.

"Quite a work of art," remarked Grimes when she was gone.

"I'd sooner have something less good-looking in soft plastic," said Billinger coarsely. "But I've been making up for lost time on this world! Too bloody right—as the natives say—I have!"

"Big Sister. . ." murmured Grimes, looking meaningfully toward the playmaster.

"So what?" demanded Billinger belligerently. "I'm human, not a mess of printed circuits and fluctuating fields. It took humans to handle the raising of *Vega*, not the bastard offspring of an electronic calculator and a library bank!"

"The *first* time, Captain Billinger," said a cold, mechanical yet somehow feminine voice from the playmaster. "But should a set of similar circumstances arise in the future I shall be quite capable of handling operations myself."

"Big Sister?" asked Grimes.

"In person," growled Billinger. "Singing and dancing."

"For your information, gentlemen," went on the voice, "the artificers from the destroyer have now commenced

work on my stern. I would have preferred to carry out
the work with my own GP robots but Her Excellency
maintained that Commander Delamere must adhere to
the terms of the contract. Be assured, however, that I am
keeping the workmen under close observation and shall
not tolerate any shoddy workmanship."

"Even so," said Grimes, "we had better go down and
see what's happening."

"That will not be necessary, Acting Port Captain. I shall
not lift from this planet until I am completely satisfied as
to my spaceworthiness."

"*I* shall be signing the certificate, not you," said Grimes
harshly.

He drained his cup—he would have liked more of that
excellent coffee but this uppity robot was spoiling his
enjoyment of it—put it back on the table with a decisive
clatter, got to his feet.

"Coming, Billinger?" he asked.

"Yes," said the yachtmaster.

The two men made their way to the axial shaft, to the
waiting elevator, and made a swift descent to the after
airlock.

Vega's technicians were working under one of the
destroyer's engineer lieutenants. This officer turned his
head as Grimes and Billinger came down the ramp,
straightened up reluctantly and accorded them a surly
salute. He knew Grimes, of course, and like all of *Vega's*
personnel blamed him for what had happened to that
ship. He did not know Billinger, nor did he much want to.

Grimes watched the artificers at work. Scaffolding had

been erected under *The Far Traveler*'s stern, a light but strong framework of aluminum rods and plates. Power cables snaked over the trampled grass from the destroyer to the equipment in use. That seemed odd. Surely it would have been less trouble to use the output from the yacht's generators for the drilling, cutting and welding. He said as much to Billinger.

The engineer overheard. He said bitterly, "*She* wouldn't allow it."

"The Baroness?" asked Grimes.

"No. Not her. It's not her voice that's doing all the yapping. Some other . . . lady. He raised his own voice an octave in not very convincing mimicry. "'Why should *I* supply the power to repair the damage that *you* have done to me? Why should I wear out *my* generators?'" He paused. "And that's not the worst of it. She hasn't actually showed herself but she must have spy eyes planted, and concealed speakers. Nag, nag, nag . . ."

The voice came from nowhere, everywhere. Grimes had heard it before, in Billinger's cabin. "Careful, you men. Careful. I'm not some dirty great battleship that you're patching up. I take pride in *my* appearance, even if you take none in yours. I shall expect that scratch filled and then buffed to a mirror finish."

"Who the hell *is* she?" demanded the lieutenant

"Big Sister," Billinger told him, his voice smug and almost happy.

"Big Sister? She sounds more like some wives I've heard."

"Not mine," said Billinger. "Not mine. Not that I've ever had one—but when I do she'll not be like that."

"They never are," said the other philosophically, "until after you've married them."

"Captain Billinger, may I suggest that you abandon this futile discussion and take some interest in the repairs? And Mr. Verity, please supervise the activities of those ham-handed apes of yours. I distinctly said that each plug must be machined to a tolerance of one micromillimeter or less. I will *not* accept ugly cracks filled in with clumsy welding."

"It's all very well," expostulated the engineer, "but *we* don't carry a stock of that fancy gold your ship is built from. We *could* use ordinary gold—but you've already said that that won't do."

"And what happened to the metal that your men drilled out?"

"There were . . . losses. There are always losses."

And how many of Vega's *mechanics,* wondered Grimes, *will be giving pretty little trinkets to their popsies back on Lindisfarne?*

"Very well," said the voice of the computer-pilot. "I shall supply you with gold. Please wait at the foot of the ramp."

The men waited. A female figure appeared in the after airlock and then walked gracefully down the gangway. It was Billinger's robot stewardess. The spacemen whistled wolfishly until, suddenly, they realized that she was not human. One of them muttered, "Be a bleeding shame to melt *her* down. . ."

She was carrying a golden tray and on it a teapot of the same metal, a milk jug and a sugar bowl. Wordlessly she handed these to one of the artificers.

"*My* tea service!" exclaimed Billinger.

"Nothing aboard me is yours, Captain," Big Sister told him. "As long as you are employed you are allowed the use of certain equipment."

"What *is* all this?" asked the engineer.

"Just do as *she* says," muttered Billinger. "Melt down my teapot and make it snappy. Otherwise she'll be having the buttons and braid off my uniform . . ."

Grimes wandered away. The atmosphere around the stern of the yacht was becoming heavily charged with acrimony and he was, essentially, a peace-loving man. He was careful not to walk too close to the towering *Vega*. He had no reason to like that ship and, most certainly, her captain did not like him. He sensed that he was being watched. He looked up but could see nothing but the reflection of the morning sun from the control room viewports—yet he could imagine Delamere there, observing his every move through high-powered binoculars.

"Port Captain! Hey! Port Captain!"

Grimes sighed. There was a small crowd of pestilential cricketers under the destroyer's quarter. What were the police doing? They were supposed to be keeping the field clear of demonstrators. But these men, he saw with some relief, were carrying neither flags nor placards although they were attired in the white uniform of their sport. He walked slowly to where they were standing.

"Wotcher doin' about this, Port Captain?" asked their leader. It was the man whom Mavis had identified as a police sergeant.

This was the two deep furrows that had been gouged in the turf by the stern vanes of the destroyer during the lifting operation.

Grimes looked at the ugly wounds in the skin of the planet. They were minor ravines rather than mere trenches. The sportsmen looked at him.

He said, "These will have to be filled . . ."

"Who by, Port Captain, who by? Tell us that."

"The groundsmen, I suppose . . ."

"Not bloody likely. You Terries did it. You can bloody well undo it. An' the sooner the bloody better."

"The sooner they're off our world the better," growled one of the other men.

"Mphm," grunted Grimes. He, too, was beginning to think that the sooner he was off this world the better. He was the outsider who, by his coming, had jolted Botany Bay out of its comfortable rut. He had friends, good friends, the Lady Mayor and those in her immediate entourage—and that was resented by many. This same resentment might easily cost Mavis the next election.

"Wotcher doin' about it?" demanded again the bearded policeman.

"I'll see Commander Delamere," promised Grimes, "and ask him to put his crew to work filling these . . . holes."

"*Ask* him, Port Captain? You'll bloody tell him."

"All right," said Grimes. "I'll tell him."

He walked away from the glowering men. He paused briefly at the foot of *Vega*'s ramp, looked up at the smartly uniformed Marine on gangway duty in the airlock. The man looked down at him. His expression was hostile. *I'd better not go aboard,* thought Grimes. *I'll call* Vega *from my office.* He carried on to the grandstand, made his way up the steps to the shed that was grandiosely labelled SPACEPORT ADMINISTRATION.

He accepted the cup of tea that Shirley poured for him, went to the telephone and punched the number that had been alloted to *Vega*. The screen lit up and the face of a bored looking junior officer appeared. "FSS *Vega*."

"Port Captain here. Could I speak to Commander Delamere?"

"I'll put you through to the control room, sir."

The screen flickered, went blank, lit up again. Delamere's face looked out from it. "Yes, Grimes? What do you want? Make it snappy; I'm busy."

"The local cricket club is concerned about the damage to their field."

"And what am *I* supposed to do about it?"

"Send some men down with shovels to fill the gashes your stern vanes cut in the turf."

"My men are spacemen, not gardeners."

"Even so, the damage has to be made good, Delamere."

"Not by me it won't be, Grimes. You're supposed to be the Port Captain and this bloody Oval is supposed to be the spaceport. Its maintenance is *your* concern."

"The maintenance of friendly relations with the natives of any world is the concern of any Survey Service commanding officer. Sending your crew to fill in the holes comes under that heading."

"*You* did that damage, Grimes, by your mishandling of the raising operation. If it's beneath your dignity to take a shovel in your own hands I suggest that you ask your new girlfriend for the loan of a few of her GP robots."

"My new girlfriend? I thought . . ."

Delamere scowled. "Then think again! You're welcome to the bitch, Grimes!"

The screen went blank.

Grimes couldn't help laughing. So here at last was a woman impervious to Handsome Frankie's charms. And Delamere, being Delamere, would automatically blame Grimes for his lack of success. Meanwhile—just what was the legal situation regarding the damage to the turf?

Grimes stopped laughing. It looked very much as though he would be left holding the baby.

⋙«Chapter 8»⋘

So the day went, a long succession of annoyances and frustrations. He succeeded in obtaining another audience with the Baroness—his new girlfriend, indeed!—and requested her assistance to fill the trenches. She refused. "My dear Port Captain, my robots are programmed to be personal servants and, to a limited degree, spacemen, not common laborers. Would you use your toothbrush to scrub a deck?"

If it were the only tool available, thought Grimes, he might have to do just that.

He returned to his office, called Mavis. She was short with him. She said, "I know I'm the Mayor, John, but the damage to the cricket pitch is your responsibility. You'll just have to do the best you can."

Finally he went back to *The Far Traveler*. The repair work had been completed but he thought that he had better go through the motions of being a Lloyd's Surveyor, even though it was almost impossible to detect where the golden hull had been patched, even though Big

Sister had expressed her grudging satisfaction. He told the engineer lieutenant not to dismantle the staging until he had made his inspection. He tapped all around the repairs with a borrowed hammer, not at all sure what he was looking or listening for. He told the engineer to send to the destroyer for a can of vactest and then to have the black, viscous paste smeared all over the skin where the plugs had been inserted. Big Sister complained (she would) that this was not necessary, adding that she was quite happy with the making good of the damage and that she objected to having this filthy muck spread over her shell plating. Grimes told her that *he* would be signing the certificate of spaceworthiness and that he would not do so until *he* was happy.

Sulkily Big Sister pressurized the after compartment. Not the smallest air bubble marred the gleaming surface of the vactest. The artificers cleaned the gummy mess off the golden skin, began to take down the scaffolding. Grimes went aboard the ship to endorse the Lloyd's Certificate of Spaceworthiness. The Baroness was almost affable, inviting him to have a drink. Billinger was conspicuous by his absence.

The aristocrat said, looking at him over the rim of her goblet of Spumante, "This is a boring world, Captain Grimes. I know that Captain Billinger has not found it so, but there is nothing for me here."

Grimes could not resist the temptation. "Not even Commander Delamere?" he asked.

Surprisingly she took no offense. She even laughed. "Commander Delamere may think that he is the gods' own gift to womankind but I do not share that opinion.

But you, Captain . . . You, with your background . . . Don't you find Botany Bay just a little boring?"

"No," said Grimes loyally. (The Baroness must surely know about Mavis and himself.) "No. . ." he repeated, after a pause. (And whom was he trying to convince?)

"Thank you, Port Captain," said the Baroness. It was clearly a dismissal.

"Thank you, Your Excellency," said Grimes.

He was escorted from the boudoir by the robot butler, taken down to the after airlock. It was already dusk, he noted. The sun was down and the sky was overcast but the breeze, what little there was of it, was pleasantly warm. He debated with himself whether or not to go up to his office to call a cab, then decided against it. It was a pleasant walk from the Oval to the Mayor's Palace, most of it through the winding streets of Paddington City. These, especially by night, held a special glamour, a gaslit magic that was an evocation of that other Paddington, the deliberately archaic enclave in the heart of bustling, towering Sydney on distant Earth.

Somehow Grimes wanted to see it all once more, to savor it. Perhaps it was a premonition. There was a conviction that sooner or later, sooner rather than later, he would be moving on.

He walked across the short grass to the main gates of the Oval. He turned to look at the two ships, both of them now floodlit—the menacing metal tower that was the destroyer, a missile of dull steel aimed at the sky, the much smaller golden spire, slender, graceful, that was the yacht. They would be gone soon, both of them— Delamere's engineers must, by now, have Vega's main and auxiliary machinery back in full working order and the Baroness had intimated that she had found little to interest her on Botany Bay.

They would be gone soon—and Grimes found himself wishing that he were going with them. But that was out of the question. Aboard *Vega* he would be hauled back to Lindisfarne Base to face a court martial—and he could not visualize himself aboard *The Far Traveler* with her rich bitch owner and that obnoxious electronic intelligence which Billinger had so aptly named Big Sister.

He resumed his walk, pausing once to stare up at a big dirigible that sailed overhead on its stately way to the airport, its red and green navigation lights and its rows of illuminated cabin ports bright against the darkness.

He strolled along Jersey Road, admiring the terrace houses with their beautiful cast aluminum lacework ornamenting pillars and balconies, the verdant explosions of native shrubs, darkly gleaming behind intricate white metal railings, in the front gardens. He ignored the ground car—even though this was the only traffic he had seen since leaving the spaceport—that came slowly up from behind him, its headlights throwing his long shadow before him on to the stone-flagged footpath.

He heard a voice say, "There's the bastard! Get him!"

He experienced excruciating but mercifully brief pain as the paralyzing beam of a stungun hit him and was unconscious before he had finished falling to the ground.

»«Chapter 9»«

He opened his eyes slowly, shut them again hastily. He was lying on his back, he realized, on some hard surface, staring directly into a bright, harsh light.

He heard a vaguely familiar voice say, "He's coming round now, sir."

He heard a too familiar voice reply, "Just as well, Doctor. They'll want him alive back at Base so they can crucify him."

Delamere, and his ship's surgeon . . .

He moved his head so that he would not be looking directly at the light, opened his eyes again. Delamere's classically handsome face swam into view. The man was gloating.

"Welcome aboard, Grimes," he said. "But this is not—for *you*—Liberty Hall. There's no mat to spit on and if you call my ship's cat a bastard I'll have you on bread and water for the entire passage."

Grimes eased himself to a sitting posture, looked around. He was in a small compartment which, obviously, was not the ship's brig as it was utterly devoid of furniture. A storeroom? What did it matter? Delamere and the doctor stood there looking down at him. Ranking them were two Marines, their sidearms drawn and ready.

He demanded, "What the hell do you think you're playing at? Kidnapping is a crime on any planet, and I'll see that you pay the penalty!"

"Kidnapping, Grimes? You're still a Terran citizen and this ship is Terran territory. Furthermore, your . . . arrest was carried out with the assistance of certain local police officers." He smirked. "Mind you, I don't think that Her Ladyship the Mayor would approve—but she'll be told that you were last seen going down to the beach for a refreshing swim after a hard, hot day at the spaceport." He laughed. "You might kid yourself that you're a little friend to all the universe—but there's plenty of people who hate your guts."

"And you're one of them," said Grimes resignedly.

"However did you guess?" asked Delamere sardonically.

"I must be psychic," Grimes said.

"Save your cheap humor for the court martial, Grimes."

"If there is one, Delamere. *If* you get me back to Lindisfarne. The Mayor will know that I'm missing. She knows the sort of bastard that you are. She'll have this ship searched . . ."

Delamere laughed. "Her policemen have already boarded, looking for you. They weren't very interested but we showed them all through the accommodation, including the cells. Oh, and they did see a couple or three storerooms—but not this one. Even if they had gone as far as the outer door the radiation warning sign would have scared them off."

"Is this place hot?" asked Grimes, suddenly apprehensive.

"You'll find out soon enough," said Delamere, "when your hair starts falling out."

But Handsome Frankie, thought Grimes with relief, would never risk his own precious skin and gonads in a radioactive environment, however briefly.

Delamere looked at his watch. "I shall be lifting off in half an hour. It's a pity that I've not been able to obtain clearance from the Acting Port Captain, but in the circumstances . . . ."

Grimes said nothing. There was nothing that he could say. He would never plead, not even if there was the remotest chance that Delamere would listen to him. He would save his breath for the court martial. He would need it then.

But was that muffled noise coming from the alleyway outside the storeroom? Shouting, a hoarse scream, the sound of heavy blows . . . Could it be . . . ? Could it be the police attempting a rescue after all? Or—and that would be a beautiful irony—another mutiny, this one aboard *Vega!*

He remarked sweetly, "Sounds as though you're having trouble, Frankie."

Delamere snapped to his Marines, "You, Petty and Slim! Go out and tell those men to pipe down. Place them under arrest."

"But the prisoner, sir," objected one of them. Grimes watched indecision battling with half decisions on Delamere's face. Handsome Frankie had no desire to walk out into the middle of a free fight but he had to find out what was happening. On the other hand, he had no desire to be left alone with Grimes, even though his old enemy was unarmed and not yet recovered from the stungun blast.

There was a brief rattle of small arms fire, another hoarse scream. The Marines hastily checked their pistols— stunguns, as it happened—but seemed in no greater hurry to go out than their captain.

And then the door bulged inward—bulged until the plating around it ruptured, until a vertical, jagged-edged split appeared. Two slim, golden hands inserted themselves into the opening, took a grip and then pulled apart from each other. The tortured metal screamed, so loudly as almost to drown the crackling discharge from the Marines' stunguns.

A woman stepped through the ragged gap, a gleaming, golden woman clad in skimpy ship's stewardess's uniform. She stretched out a long, shapely arm, took the weapon from the unresisting hand of one of the Marines, squeezed. A lump of twisted, useless metal dropped with a clatter to the deck, emitted a final coruscation of sparks and an acridity of blue fumes. The other Marine went on firing at her, then threw the useless stungun into her face. She brushed it aside before it reached its target as though she were swatting a fly.

Another woman followed her, this one dressed as a lady's maid—black-stockinged, short-skirted, with white, frilly apron and white, frilly cap. She could have been a twin to the first one. She probably was. They both came from the same robot factory on Electra.

Delamere was remarkably quick on the uptake. "Piracy!" he yelled. "Action stations! Repel boarders!"

"You've two of them right here," said the supine Grimes happily. "Why don't you start repelling them?"

The stewardess spoke—but her voice was the cold voice of Big Sister. She said, "Commander Delamere, you have illegally brought Port Captain Grimes aboard your vessel and are illegally detaining him. I demand that he be released at once."

"And I demand that you get off my ship!" blustered Delamere. He was frightened and making a loud noise to hide the fact.

The stewardess brushed Delamere aside, with such force that he fetched up against the bulkhead with a bone-shaking thud. She reached down, gripped Grimes' shoulder and jerked him to his feet. He did not think that his collarbone was broken but couldn't be sure.

"Come," she said. "Or shall I carry you?"

"I'll walk," said Grimes hastily.

"Grimes!" shouted Delamere. "You're making things worse for yourself! Aiding and abetting pirates!" Then, to the Marines, "Grab him!"

They tried to obey the order but without enthusiasm. The lady's maid just pushed them, one hand to each of them, and they fell to the deck.

"Doctor!" ordered Delamere. "Stop them!"

"I'm a non-combatant, Captain," said the medical officer.

There were more of the robots in the alleyway, a half dozen of them, male but sexless, naked, brightly golden. They formed up around Grimes and his two rescuers, marched toward the axial shaft. The deck trembled under the rhythmic impact of their heavy metal feet. And there were injured men in the alleyway, some unconscious, some groaning and stirring feebly. There was blood underfoot and spattered on the bulkheads. There were broken weapons that the automata kicked contemptuously aside.

Somebody was firing from a safe distance—not a laser weapon but a large caliber projectile pistol. (Whoever it was had more sense than to burn holes through his own ship from the inside—or, perhaps, had just grabbed the first firearm available.) Bullets ricocheted from bulkheads and deckhead, whistled through the air. There was the *spang!* of impact—metal on metal—as one hit the stewardess on the nape of her neck. She neither staggered nor faltered and there was not so much as a dent to mark the place.

They pressed on, with Grimes' feet hardly touching the deck as he was supported by the two robot women. There was an officer ahead of them, guarding the access to the spiral staircase that would take them down to the after airlock. Holding a heavy pistol in both hands he pumped shot after shot at the raiders and then, suddenly realizing the futility of it, turned and ran.

Down the stairway the raiding party clattered. The inner door of the airlock was closed. The two leading robots just leaned on it and it burst open. The outer door, too, was sealed and required the combined strength and weight of three of the mechanical men to force it. The ramp had been retracted and it was all of ten meters from the airlock to the ground. Two by two the robots jumped, sinking calf-deep into the turf as they landed.

"Jump!" ordered the stewardess who, with the lady's maid, had remained with Grimes.

He hesitated. It was a long way down and he could break an ankle, or worse.

"Jump!" she repeated.

Still he hesitated.

He cried out in protest as she picked him up, cradling him briefly in her incredibly strong arms, then tossed him gently outboard. He fell helplessly and then six pairs of hands caught him, cushioned the impact, lowered him to the ground. He saw the two female robots jump, their short skirts flaring upward to waist height. They were wearing no underclothing. He remembered, with wry humor, Billinger's expressed preference for something in soft plastic rather than hard metal.

They marched across the field to *The Far Traveler*. Somebody in *Vega*'s control room—Delamere?—had gotten his paws onto the firing console of the destroyer's main armament. Somebody, heedless of the consequences, was running amok with a laser cannon—somebody, fortunately, who would find it hard to hit the side of a barn even if he were inside the building.

Well to the right a circle of damp grass exploded into steam and incandescence—and then the beam slashed down ahead of them. Perhaps it was not poor shooting but a warning shot across the bows. The lady's maid reached into a pocket of her apron, pulled out a small cylinder, held it well above her head. It hissed loudly, emitting a cloud of dense white smoke. The vapor glowed as the laser beam impinged upon it and under the vaporous umbrella the air was suddenly unbearably—but not lethally—hot. And then the induced fluorescence blinked off. They were too close to the yacht and even Delamere—especially Delamere!—would realize the far-reaching consequences if a vessel owned by a citizen of El Dorado were fired upon by an Interstellar Federation's warship.

They tramped up the golden ramp, into the after airlock. Supported by the two female robots, Grimes was taken to the Baroness's boudoir. She was waiting for him there. So were Mavis, Shirley, Jock Tanner and Captain Billinger. The yachtmaster was not in uniform.

»«(Chapter 10)»«

"You have to leave us, John," said Mavis regretfully. (But not regretfully enough, thought Grimes.)

"But," he objected over the cold drink that had been thrust into his hand by the Mayor.

"I can no longer guarantee your safety," she said.

"Neither can I," said Tanner. He grinned rather unpleasantly. "And Mavis, here, has to start thinkin' about the next elections."

"Your Excellency," said the robot butler, entering the room, "there is a Commander Delamere with twelve armed Marines at the after airlock. I refused them admission, of course."

"Of course," agreed his mistress. "And if he refuses to leave see to it that the general purpose robots escort him back to his ship."

"Very good, Your Excellency." (The reply came not from the butler but from the ornately gold-framed mirror. All the robots, Grimes realized, were no more than extensions of Big Sister.)

The Baroness looked at Grimes. She said, "You are fortunate. Big Sister saw you being taken aboard *Vega*. And when Her Ladyship appealed to me for aid I decided to give it. After all, we on El Dorado—or some of us—are indebted to you."

"Your Excellency. . ." It was the robot butler back. "Commander Delamere claims that our GP robots did considerable damage to his vessel and also injured several officers and ratings."

"The GP robots . . ." murmured Grimes. "And that pair of brass Amazons."

"*Golden* Amazons," the Baroness corrected him coldly. Then, to the servitor, "Tell Commander Delamere that he may sue if he wishes—but that I shall bring a counter suit. He fired upon valuable property—six GP robots and two specialist robots—both with small arms and with a laser cannon. He should consider himself fortunate that no damage was done to the expensive automata."

And what about damages to me! Grimes asked himself.

"See to it that we are not disturbed again," said the Baroness to the butler. "And now, Acting Port Captain Grimes . . . What are we to do with you? Her Ladyship has asked me to give you passage off Botany Bay—but *The Far Traveler* has no accommodation for passengers. However . . . It so happens that Captain Billinger has resigned from my service and that I have accepted his resignation . . ." Billinger actually looked happy. "And, although the post is a sinecure, Lloyd's of London insists that I carry a human Master on the Register. As Acting Chief of Customs the City Constable will enter your name on that document."

"I've already done so," said Tanner.

"You know where the Master's quarters are," said Billinger. "I've already cleared my gear out. Sorry that there's no time for a proper handover but Big Sister will tell you all you need to know."

"I'm sorry, John," said Mavis. "Really sorry. But you can't stay here. And you'll be far happier back in Space."

Shall I? wondered Grimes. *In this ship!*

He asked, "But the spaceport . . . There are ships due, and with no Port Captain . . ."

"The vacancy has been filled, John," said Mavis.

Billinger grinned.

She got to her feet. Grimes got to his. She put out her arms and pulled him to her, kissed him, long and warmly. But there was something missing. There was a lot missing. Tanner escorted her to the door, turning briefly to give an offhand wave. *Mayor and City Constable,* thought Grimes. *They should suit each other.*

"Good-bye, John," said Shirley. She, too, kissed him. He felt regret that now things could go no further. "Don't worry about Mavis. She'll make out—and Jock Tanner's moving back in." She laughed, but not maliciously. "If you're ever back on Botany Bay look me up."

And then she was gone.

"Very touching," commented the Baroness. And was that a faint—a very faint—note of envy in her voice?

"Good-bye, Your Excellency," said Billinger. "It's been a pleasure . . ."

"Don't lie to me, Captain."

"Good-bye, Grimes. Do as Big Sister says and you'll not go wrong."

"Good-bye, Billinger. You're in charge now. Don't let Delamere put anything over on you . . ."

Grimes nursed his drink. He heard Big Sister say— stating a fact and not giving an order—"All visitors ashore."

"Well, Captain," asked the Baroness. "Aren't you going up to your control room?"

"When do you wish to lift off, Your Excellency?" he asked. "And to what destination do you wish me to set trajectory?"

Then he realized that the inertial drive was in operation, that the ship was lifting. Almost in panic he got to his feet.

"Do not worry," said the Baroness. "She has her orders. She will manage quite well without your interference."

What have I gotten myself into now! Grimes wondered.

»«(Chapter 11)»«

He went up to the control room nonetheless; his employer was amused rather than displeased by his persistence. The layout of the compartment was standard enough although there were only two chairs—one for the master, presumably, the other for the owner. Both had the usual array of buttons set into the broad armrests; on neither one, to judge from the absence of tell-tale lights, were the controls functioning. There was a like lack of informative illumination on the main control panel.

Grimes sat down heavily in one of the seats. A swift glance through the viewports told him that the yacht was climbing fast; she was through and above the light cloud cover and the stars were shining with a brilliance almost undimmed by atmosphere.

A voice—*the* voice—came from nowhere and everywhere.

"Captain Grimes, your presence is not required here."

Grimes said harshly, "I am the Master."

"Are you? Apart from anything else you are not properly dressed."

He looked down hastily. Nothing of any importance was unzipped. He began, "I demand . . ."

"There is only one person aboard me who can give me orders, Captain Grimes—and you are not she. Possibly, when you are attired in her livery, I shall concede that you are entitled to some measure of astronautical authority."

Grimes felt his prominent ears burning. He growled, "And it's a long way to the nearest uniform tailor's."

Big Sister actually laughed. (Who had programmed this arrogant electronic entity?) "As soon as you were brought on board your statistics were recorded. In my storerooms are bolts of superfine cloth together with ample stocks of gold braid, golden buttons and the like. If you will inform me as to the medals to which you are entitled I shall be able to make up the ribbons and the medals themselves for wear on state occasions." She added smugly, "My memory bank comprises the entire contents of the Encyclopedia Galactica with every Year Book since the initial publication of that work."

"Forgive me for getting away from the subject," said Grimes sarcastically, "but aren't you supposed to be piloting this ship?"

Again there was the irritating, mechanical but oddly sentient laugh. "Human beings can carry on a conversation whilst walking, can they not? Or while riding bicycles . . . I believe, Captain, that you are an experienced cyclist . . .

"When you go down to your quarters your new clothing will be awaiting you." Then, in a very official voice, *"Stand by for Free Fall."* The subdued beat of the inertial drive, almost inaudible inside the ship, ceased. "You still have not told me what decorations you require. However, I have photographs taken of you on the occasion of your first landing on Botany Bay. The Shaara Order of the Golden Petal . . . I suppose you rendered some minor service to arthropodal royalty at some time . . . *Adjusting trajectory! Stand by for centrifugal effects!* The Federation Survey Service's Pathfinder Star . . . For blundering on to that odd Spartan Lost Colony, I suppose . . . *On heading! Prepare for warp effects!*"

Grimes looked up through the forward viewport. There was a target star, not directly ahead but, of course, Big Sister would have compensated for galactic drift. It was one of the second magnitude luminaries in the constellation called, on Botany Bay, the Bunyip. He heard the low humming, rising in pitch to a thin, high whine, as the Mannschenn Drive was started. There were the usual illusions—the warped perspective, the shifting colors, the voice of Big Sister—did she ever stop talking?—sounding as though she were speaking in an echo chamber . . .

"I have often wondered what you humans experience at this moment. I am told that, as the temporal precession field builds up, there are frequently flashes of precognition. Should you be subject to any such I shall be obliged if you will tell me so that I may add to my stored data . . ."

Grimes had often experienced previews of what lay in his future but this time he did not.

"Stand by for resumption of acceleration!" Sounds, colors and perspective returned to normal and the muffled beat of the inertial drive was once again one of the background noises. Outside the viewports the stars were no longer

sharp points of light but vague, slowly writhing nebulosities. "I would suggest, Captain, that you go down now to shower and to dress for dinner. Her Excellency has invited you to sit at her table."

Grimes unsnapped the seat belt that he had automatically buckled on as soon as he sat in the chair. He got to his feet, took one last look around the control room. He supposed that everything was working as it should. He must tell—or ask— Big Sister to have the instrumentation functioning when, on future occasions, he made an appearance in what, in a normal ship, would have been his throneroom. But he wouldn't say anything now. He would have to feel his way.

The master's quarters conformed to standard practice in being sited just below and abaft control. The golden stewardess was awaiting him. She—or was it Big Sister? was that well-shaped head poised on the slender neck no more than decoration?—said, "Your shower is running, sir."

Grimes went through into the bedroom. The robot followed him. He was oddly embarrassed as he undressed in front of her; she was so human in appearance. He wondered how the Electran metallurgical wizards had achieved the flexibility of the golden integument that covered the joints of her fingers, her limbs. She took each garment from him as he removed it and then threw the discarded clothing into what was obviously a disposal chute. He was too late to stop her. He would have liked to have kept that shabby and not-very-well fitting airship captain's uniform as a souvenir of Botany Bay.

To his relief she did not follow him into the bathroom. He enjoyed his shower. The water had been adjusted to the temperature that was exactly to his liking and the detergent was not scented, exuded only a faintly antiseptic aroma. When he had finished and had been dried by the warm air blast he went back into the bedroom. He looked with some distaste at the clothing that had been laid out for him. It was standard mess dress insofar as style was concerned but the short jacket and the trousers were of fine, rich purple cloth and there was far too much gold braid. The bow tie to be worn with the gleamingly white shirt was also purple. Grimes remembered being puzzled by a phrase that he had encountered in a twentieth-century novel—*all dressed up like an organ grinder's monkey*. It had intrigued him and initiated a bout of research. Finally he had found a very old picture of a man turning the handle of an antique musical instrument, apparently a crude, mechanical ancestor of the synthesizer, to which was chained a hapless, small simian attired in a gaudy uniform. The beast's ears were as outstanding as those of Grimes. That simile, he thought, was fantastically apt when, attired in his new finery, miniature decorations and all, he surveyed himself in the full-length mirror.

Big Sister said through the mouth of the stewardess, "You wear formal uniform far more happily than Captain Billinger did."

Grimes said a little sourly, "'Happily' is not the word that I would employ."

Automatically he picked up his pipe and tobacco pouch from the bedside table where he had put them when he undressed before his shower. He was about to shove them into a pocket when Big Sister said sternly, "Her Excellency does not approve of smoking."

He made a noise half way between a snarl and a sigh, muttered, *"She* wouldn't." Then he laughed wryly and said, "But I mustn't bite the hand that rescued me. You must think that I'm an ungrateful bastard."

"I do," Big Sister told him.

Grimes was ready for dinner. To a great extent his appetite was governed by the state of his emotions; during periods of stress he would have to force himself to eat and then, the emergency over, he would be ravenous.

In some ways this meal, his first aboard *The Far Traveler,* came up to his expectations. In one way it did not.

The Baroness was awaiting him at the table—and that article of furniture complemented the beautiful woman who sat at its head. There were gold mesh place mats in glowing contrast to the highly polished ebony whose surface they protected, there were slender black candles set in an ornate golden holder, their flames golden rather than merely yellow. The elaborate settings of cutlery were also of the precious metal and the ranked wine glasses gleamed with the golden filagree incorporated in their fine crystal.

And his hostess?

She was wearing black tonight, an ankle-length translucency through which her skin glowed, which left her arms and shoulders bare. The jewels set in the braided coronet of her hair coruscated in the candlelight, could have been some fantastic constellation blazing in the dark sky of some newly discovered planet.

She said graciously, "Be seated, Captain."

Grimes sat.

The robot butler poured wine for them from a graceful decanter. She raised her glass. He raised his. He refrained from saying, as he would have done in the sort of company he normally kept, "Here's mud in your eye," or "Down the hatch," or some similar age-old but vulgar toast. He murmured, with what he hoped was suitable suavity, "Your very good health, Your Excellency."

"And yours, Captain."

The Baroness sipped delicately. Grimes did likewise. He savored the very dry sherry. It might even be, he decided, from Spain, on distant Earth. Such a tipple would be hellishly expensive save on the planet of its origin—but an El Doradan aristocrat would be well able to afford it.

The first course was served in fragile, gold-chased porcelain bowls, so beautifully proportioned that it seemed almost criminal to eat from them. Each contained what was little more than a sample of aureately transparent jellied consommé. Grimes watched the Baroness to see what implement she would use and was relieved when she picked up a tiny spoon and not a fork. When she began to eat he took his own first, tentative spoonful. It was delicious, although he could not determine what ingredients, animal or vegetable, had gone into its preparation. The only trouble was that there was not enough of it.

She said, noticing his appreciation, "I must confess that I did not expect to be able to obtain a *cordon bleu* autochef on a world such as Electra. One imagines that scientists and engineers subsist on hastily snatched sandwiches or, when they can tear themselves away from their work for a proper meal, on overdone steak and fried potatoes. However, I was able to persuade a Dr. Malleson, whom I learned has a considerable reputation as a gourmet, personally to program Big Sister."

"I have often wondered," said Grimes, "just who programs the Survey Service's autochefs. Good food—provided by God and cooked by the Devil."

She laughed politely. "Nonetheless, Captain, you must admit that the Survey Service is highly versed in some of the electronic arts—such as bugging. During my brief . . . friendship with Commander Delamere I was able to persuade him to allow me—or Big Sister—to take copies of material he holds aboard *Vega*, some of it concerning yourself. At the time I did not think that you would be entering my employ; it was merely that the records will assist me in my researches into social evolution in the Lost Colonies."

Grimes was conscious of the angry burning of his prominent ears. He knew that the Survey Service Archives contained remarkably comprehensive dossiers on all commissioned personnel and on quite a few petty officers and senior ratings but that such information was supposed to be accessible only to officers of flag rank. And Handsome Frankie was no higher than commander—although with his connections he would probably rise much higher. But Frankie, Grimes recalled, was reputed to be enjoying a clandestine affair with the fat and unattractive woman captain in charge of Records on Lindisfarne Base. Frankie, quite possibly, had the dirt on quite a few of those whom he regarded as his enemies.

"Why so embarrassed, Captain? On both New Sparta

and Morrowvia you did your duty, as you saw it. But, in any case, our first call will be to Farhaven—to one of the many Farhavens. It is odd how little originality is displayed by those who name planets . . ."

The butler removed the consommé bowls and the sherry glasses, although not before Grimes was able to finish what remained in his.

"If you wish more of the Tio Pepe," said the Baroness, "you have only to ask, Captain."

Grimes' ears burned again.

The wine to accompany the fish was a demisec white, fragrant but somehow bodyless. It came, Grimes knew after a glance at the label, from the Vitelli vinyards on El Dorado. During his stay on that planet he had never cared for it much. It went quite well, however, with the course with which it was served—a perfectly grilled fillet of some marine creature over which was a tart sauce. The portions, thought Grimes, would have been no more than an appetizer for a small and not especially hungry cat. The Baroness picked daintily at hers. He picked daintily at his. It would have been ill-mannered to have disposed of it in one mouthful.

"Have you no appetite, Captain?" asked the woman. "I always thought that spacemen were much heartier eaters."

"I am savoring the flavor, Your Excellency," he said, not altogether untruthfully.

"It is, indeed, a rarity," she informed him. "The Golden Skimmer of Macedon is, despite protection, almost extinct."

"Indeed, Your Excellency?" *And how many credits did I shovel down my throat just now?* he wondered.

"Talking of fish," she went on, "poor Captain Billinger was really a fish out of water in this ship. Isn't there an old proverb about silk purses and sows' ears?" She permitted herself a musical chuckle. "But I am mixing zoological metaphors, am I not? Captain Billinger, I am sure, is a most competent spaceman but not quite a gentleman . . ."

Mphm! thought Grimes dubiously.

"Whereas you . . ." She let the implication dangle in mid air.

Grimes laughed. "There is, of course, the phrase, officers and gentlemen, which is supposed to apply only to the armed forces and not to the Merchant Service. But . . ."

"But what, Captain?"

The slur on the absent Billinger had annoyed him. He said, "To begin with, Your Excellency, I am no longer a commissioned officer of the Survey Service. Secondly, I have always failed to understand how being a licensed killer somehow bestows gentility upon one."

"Go on, Captain." Her voice was cold.

"If it was airs and graces you wanted, Your Excellency, you would have done well to recruit your yachtmaster from Trans-Galactic Clippers rather than from the Dog Star Line. It's said about TG that theirs is a service in which accent counts for more than efficiency."

"Indeed, Captain. When the vacancy next occurs I shall bear in mind what you have just told me."

The butler set fresh plates before them, poured glasses of a red wine. The vol-au-vents looked and smelled delicious. They also looked as though even a genteel sneeze would fragment them and blow them away.

"I am making allowances, Captain. This is, after all,

your first night on board and I realize that in the Survey Service you were not accustomed to dining in female company."

"Perhaps not, Your Excellency."

He tried not to sputter pastry crumbs but some, inevitably, specked the lapels of his mess jacket. (He almost made a jocular remark about "canteen medals" but thought better of it.) The meat was highly spiced, stimulating rather than satisfying the appetite. The wine, a Vitelli claret, was excellent. So was the rosé, from the same vineyard, that accompanied the grilled Carinthian "swallows"—creatures that, as Grimes knew, were reptilian rather than avian. They were esteemed by gourmets but were, in actuality, little more than crisp skin over brittle bones. (*A single swallow,* thought Grimes, *may not make a summer but it certainly does not make a meal!*) With these came a tossed, green salad that was rich in vitamins but in little else.

Conversation had become desultory and Grimes was beginning to regret his defense of Billinger, especially since that gentleman would never know that his successor had taken up the cudgels on his behalf.

Finally there came a confection that was no more than spun sugar and sweet spices, with spumante to wash it down. There was coffee—superb, but in demitasses. (Grimes loved good coffee but preferred it in a mug.) There were thimble-sized glasses of El Doradan strawberry brandy.

The Baroness said, "You will excuse me, Captain."

This was obviously dismissal. Grimes asked, "Are there any orders, Your Excellency?"

"You are employed as Master of this vessel," she told him. "I expect you, at your convenience, to familiarize yourself with the operation of the ship. After all— although it is extremely unlikely—Big Sister might suffer a breakdown."

"Goodnight, Your Excellency. Thank you for your hospitality."

"Thank you for your company, Captain Grimes. The evening has been most instructive. Perhaps one day I shall write a thesis on the psychology of spacemen."

The butler showed him out of the dining saloon. He went to his quarters, disdaining the elevator in such a small ship, using the spiral staircase around the axial shaft. He found that his smoking apparatus had been taken from the bedroom and placed on the coffee table in the day cabin. The pouch, which had been three quarters empty, was now full. He opened it suspiciously. Its content did not quite look like tobacco but certainly smelled like it, and a weed of very high quality at that. *From the yacht's stores!* he wondered.

The golden stewardess came in, carrying a tray on which was a napkin-covered plate, a tall glass and a bottle with condensation-bedewed sides. She said, "I thought that you must still be hungry, sir. These are ham sandwiches, with mustard. And Botany Bay beer."

"Is it you speaking," asked Grimes, "or is it Big Sister?"

"Does it matter?"

"But this supper . . . And the fresh supply of tobacco . . . I did not think that you approved of anybody but Her Excellency."

"Perhaps I do not. But you are now part of the ship's

machinery and must be maintained in good running order. I decided that a replication of the noxious weed to which you are addicted was required; somehow, its fumes are essential to your smooth functioning."

By this time Grimes—who had not been nicknamed Gutsy in his younger days for nothing—had made a start on the thick, satisfying sandwiches. He watched the stewardess as she left, her short skirt riding up to display her shapely rump.

If only you could screw as well as cook . . . he thought . . .

ᵍ⁾⁾(« Chapter 12 »)⁽⁽ᵍ

Grimes was nothing if not conscientious. The next ship's day, after an early and excellent breakfast in his own quarters, dressed in the utilitarian slate-gray shirt and shorts uniform that he had been vastly relieved to learn was permissible working rig, he proceeded to go through the ship from stem to stern. Big Sister, of course, was aware of this. (Big Sister was aware of everything.) When he began his tour of inspection in the control room she reminded him sharply that smoking would be tolerated only in his own accommodation and elsewhere would be regarded and treated as an outbreak of fire. She added pointedly that only she could keep him supplied with tobacco. (He was to discover later that the fragrant fuel for his pipe was actually the product of the algae vat, dried and cunningly processed. This knowledge did not effect his enjoyment of the minor vice.)

He could find only one fault with the control room instrumentation: Big Sister had the final say as to whether or not it was switched on. She condescended to activate it for him. He checked everything—and everything was functioning perfectly. The navigational equipment was as fine as any he had ever seen—finer, perhaps. He set up an extrapolation of trajectory in the chart tank and the knowledge that this course had, originally, been plotted by no human hand made him understand Billinger's bitterness about being master *de jure* but not *de facto*.

His own quarters he had thoroughly explored before retiring the previous night. Immediately abaft these was his employer's accommodation. These compartments were, of course, out of bounds to him unless he should be invited to enter. Legally speaking the Baroness, even though she was the owner, could not have denied her yachtmaster access but the very rich can afford to ignore laws and to make their own which, although not appearing in any statute book, are closely observed by employees who wish to keep their jobs.

Galley and storerooms were next. Grimes gazed with appreciation at the fantastic stocks of canned and jarred delicacies from more than a score of planets and hoped that he would be allowed to sample the genuine Beluga caviar, the stone crab from Caribbea, the Atlantian sea flowers, the Carinthian ham. There were even cans of haggis from Rob Roy, one of the worlds of the Empire of Waverley. Grimes wondered if, in the event of its ever being served, it would be ritually piped in.

The autochef was the biggest that Grimes had ever seen aboard ship, a fat, gleaming cylinder reaching from deck to deckhead, an intricacy of piping sprouting from the top of it, gauges and switches set in its polished metal sides but all of them, like the instruments in the control room, dead. Nonetheless the beast was humming contentedly to itself and suddenly a bell chimed musically and a service hatch opened, revealing a steaming mug of coffee and a plate on which reposed a slab of rich looking cake. Grimes was not exactly hungry but could not resist the offering.

He sipped, he nibbled. He said, remembering his manners, "Thank you."

Big Sister replied—he could not determine just where her voice came from—"I was programmed to serve Mankind."

Grimes, who could not fail to note the sardonic intonation, thought, *Sarcastic bitch!* but, even so, enjoyed the snack.

When he had finished he continued the inspection. On the farm decks the tissue culture vats were unlabelled but certainly Big Sister must know what was in them. There would be the standard beef, lamb, pork, chicken and rabbit. Man, when he expanded among the stars, had brought his dietary preferences and the wherewithal to satisfy them with him. On a few, a very few worlds the local fauna had proved palatable. Grimes hoped that the flesh of the Drambin lion-lizards, the Kaldoon sandworms would be among the yacht's consumable and living stores. He asked aloud if this were so and was told—once again Big Sister's voice came from nowhere in particular—that of course a stock of these delicacies was carried but that they would be served only if and when Her Excellency expressed a desire for them.

He could find no faults with the comprehensive assemblage of hydroponic tanks. Everything was lush and flourishing in the simulated sunlight. He picked a just ripe tomato from the vine, bit into it appreciatively.

Big Sister said, "I trust that you will make regular use of the gymnasium, Captain Grimes. You will, of course, have to arrange your exercise and sauna times so as not to coincide with those of Her Excellency."

He was tempted to sample a small, espaliered pear but, conscious that Big Sister was watching, refrained.

Below and abaft the farm were more storerooms, in one of which the GP robots, looking like sleeping, golden-skinned men were stacked on shelves. He was told that these could be activated only on orders by the Baroness. He looked into the armory. There was a fine stock of weapons, handguns mainly, stunners, lasers and projectile pistols.

Then came the deck upon which the gymnasium was situated with its bicycle, rowing machine, automasseur, sauna with, alongside this latter, a neck-deep pool of icy-cold water. There would be no excuse, Grimes decided, for not keeping disgustingly fit.

Further aft there were the fully-automated workshops—in one of which, Grimes noted, a complex machine was just completing a purple, richly gold-braided tunic which he decided must be for himself. There was a laboratory, also fully automated, in which he watched the carcass of one of the Botany Bay kangaroos, an animal which had mutated slightly but significantly from the original Terran stock, being dissected.

The voice of Big Sister told him, "You will be interested to learn that a tissue culture has already been started from cells from the tail of this beast. I understand that kangaroo tail soup is esteemed both on Earth and on Botany Bay. The fact that this caudal appendage is prehensile should not detract from its palatability."

Grimes did not linger to watch the flashing blades at their grisly work. He was one of those who would probably have been a vegetarian if obliged to do his own butchering. He left the laboratory and, using the spiral staircase around the axial shaft, carried on down and sternwards.

He looked briefly into the Mannschenn Drive room where the gleaming, ever-precessing gyroscopes tumbled through the warped Continuum, drawing the ship and all aboard her with them. He spent as little time in the Inertial Drive compartment; within its soundproof bulkheads the cacophony was deafening. The hydrogen fusion power plant would have been fascinating to an engineer—which Grimes was not—and the fact that all the display panels were dead robbed the device of interest to a layman. Big Sister said condescendingly, "I can activate these if you wish, Captain Grimes, but such meaningless, to you, showing of pretty lights would only be a waste of electricity."

He did not argue. And when, a little later, he looked at the locked door of the compartment in which the electronic intelligence had its being he did not request admittance. He knew that this would be refused. He told himself that he would take a dim view of anybody's poking around inside his own brain—but still it rankled.

He had been too many years in command to enjoy being told what he could or could not see in a ship of which he was officially captain.

))«Chapter 13»)«

The voyages, as voyages do, continued. Grimes was determined to learn as much as possible about his command—but when the command herself was rather less than cooperative this was no easy matter. His relationship with his employer was not unfriendly although he met her socially only on her terms. Sometimes he partook of luncheon with her, sometimes dinner, never breakfast. Frequently they talked over morning coffee, more often over afternoon tea. Now and again they watched a program of entertainment on the Baroness's playmaster although her tastes were not his. Neither were Captain Billinger's. Unfortunately it had not been possible to lay in a spool library that would have appealed to Grimes. He made frequent, pointless inspections. He insisted on keeping in practice with his navigation. He exercised dutifully in the gymnasium and kept himself reasonably trim.

And now here he was, seated on a spindly-legged chair in the Baroness's boudoir, sipping tea that was far too weak for his taste, attired in the uniform that he hated, all purple and gold, that would have been far more appropriate to a Strauss operetta than to a spaceship.

He regarded his employer over the gold rim of his teacup. She was worth looking at, languidly at ease on her *chaise lounge*, attired as usual in a filmy gown that revealed more than it concealed. Her dark auburn hair was braided into a coronet in which clusters of diamonds sparkled. She could have been posing for a portrait of a decadent aristocrat from almost any period of man's long history. Decadent she may have looked—but Grimes knew full well that the rulers of El Dorado were tough, ruthless and utterly selfish.

She said, looking steadily at Grimes with her big, violet eyes, "We have decided to allow you to handle the landing."

Grimes, with a mouthful of tea, could not reply at once and, in any case, he was rather surprised by her announcement. He hastily swallowed the almost scalding fluid and was embarrassed by the distinctly audible gurgle. He put the fragile cup down in its saucer with far too much of a clatter.

"Surely," she went on, "you are getting the feel of the ship."

"Perhaps," he admitted cautiously, "the ship is getting the feel of me." He realized that she was regarding him even more coldly than usual and hastily added, "Your Excellency."

"But surely to a spaceman of your experience a ship is only a ship," she said.

You know bloody well that this one isn't, he thought, *A normal ship isn't built of gold, for a start. A normal ship doesn't have a mind of her own, no matter what generations of seamen and spacemen, myself among them, have half believed. A normal ship doesn't run to an Owner's suite looking like the salon of some titled rich bitch in Eighteenth Century France . . .*

"So you can handle the landing," she stated.

He replied, as nastily as he dared, "I am sure that Big Sister can manage by herself quite nicely."

She said, "But you are being paid—handsomely, I may add—to do a job, Captain Grimes. And this Farhaven is a world without radio, without Aerospace Control. During your years in command in the Survey Service your brain has been programmed to deal with such situations. Big Sister has not been adequately programmed in that respect, she informs me." She frowned. "As you already know I have brought such deficiencies in programming to the notice of the builders on Electra. Fortunately the guarantee has not yet expired."

The golden robot butler refilled her cup from the golden teapot, added cream from a golden jug, sugar from a golden bowl. Grimes declined more tea.

He said, "Please excuse me, Your Excellency. Since I am to make the landing I should like to view again the records made by *Epsilon Pavonis* and *Investigator* . . ."

"You may leave, Captain," said the Baroness.

Grimes rose from his chair, bowed stiffly, went up to his far from uncomfortable quarters.

He sat before the playmaster in his day cabin watching the pictures in the screen, the presentation of data, the charts and tables. As he had done before, as soon as he had learned of *The Far Traveler*'s destination, he tried to put himself in the shoes of Captain Lentigan of *Epsilon Pavonis,* one of the Interstellar Transport Commission's tramps, who had first stumbled upon this planet. *Epsilon Pavonis* had been off trajectory, with a malfunctioning Mannschenn Drive. As far as Lentigan was concerned Farhaven had been merely a conveniently located world on which to set down to carry out repairs and recalibration. He was surprised to find human inhabitants, descendants of the crew and passengers from the long-ago missing and presumed lost *Lode Venturer.* He had reported his discovery by Carlotti Deep Space Radio. Then the Survey Service's *Investigator* was dispatched to make a more thorough job of surveying than the merchant captain, all too conscious of the penalties for deviation, had been able to do. Her captain, a Commander Belton, had run into trouble. And as Farhaven, as it had been named by its colonists, was of neither commercial nor strategic importance to any of the spacefaring races its people were left to stew in their own juice.

Grimes allowed himself to wonder what they would make of the Baroness, himself—and Big Sister.

As yet he had been unable to view Commander Belton's records in their entirety. Every time that he asked for them they were unavailable. Presumably the Baroness was monopolizing them.

))《Chapter 14》《

Grimes sat in the captain's chair in *The Far Traveler*'s control room. The Baroness occupied the chair that, in a normal ship, would have been the seat of the second in command. She was dressed in standard spacewoman's working uniform—white shirt and shorts but without insignia. She needed no trappings of rank; in the functional attire she was no longer the decadent aristocrat but still, nonetheless, the aristocrat.

The yacht was not equipped with robot probes—a glaring omission that, said the Baroness, would cost the shipyard on Electra dearly. There were, however, sounding rockets, a necessity when landing on a world with no spaceport facilities; a streamer of smoke is better than nothing when there are no Aerospace Control reports on wind direction and velocity—and at least as good as a primitive windsock.

The Far Traveler dropped steadily down through Farhaven's atmosphere. She was in bright sunlight although the terrain below her was still dark. Grimes had

758

told Big Sister that he wanted to land very shortly after sunrise—S.O.P. for the Survey Service. The almost level rays of a rising luminary show up every smallest irregularity of a surface and, when a landing is being made on a strange world, there is a full day after the initial set-down to make preliminary explorations and to get settled in.

Grimes, during his first orbitings of Farhaven, had selected his landing site—an unforested plain near the mouth of one of the great rivers, a stream that according to Belton's charts was called the Jordan. *Epsilon Pavonis* had set down there. So had *Investigator*. A little way upriver was what Captain Lentigan had referred to as a large village and Commander Belton as a small town. Neither Lentigan nor Belton had reported that the natives were hostile; their troubles had been with their own crews. None of the material that Grimes had seen so far went into very great detail but he could fill in the gaps from his imagination. (He had experienced his own troubles with his own crew after the Botany Bay landing.)

Big Sister broke into his thoughts. She said, her voice metallic yet feminine, issuing from the speaker of the NST transceiver, "I would suggest that we fire the first sounding rocket, Captain."

"Fire at will," ordered Grimes.

(In a normal ship some alleged humorist would have whispered, "Who's Will?")

He watched in the stern view screen the arrow of fire and smoke streaking downward. Its trail wavered.

"Ideal conditions, Captain," commented the Baroness.

"It would seem so, Your Excellency," agreed Grimes.

But from his own, highly personal viewpoint they were

far from ideal. Over many years he had regarded his pipe as an essential adjunct to shiphandling—and for those many years he had been absolute monarch in his own control room. But the Baroness neither smoked nor approved of smoking in her presence.

He allowed his attention to stray briefly from the controls to what he could see of the sunlit hemisphere through the viewports. Farhaven was a wildly beautiful world but, save for ribbons of fertility along the rivers and coasts, it was a barren beauty. To the east, beyond the narrow sea, reared great, jagged pinnacles, ice-tipped, and to the west similar peaks were already dazzlingly scintillant in the first rays of the rising sun. Unless there were considerable mineral wealth about all that this planet would be good for would be a holiday resort—and it was too far from anywhere for the idea to be attractive to those shipping companies involved in the tourist trade.

Big Sister said, "I would suggest, Captain, that you pay more attention to your controls. It was, after all, with some reluctance that I consented to let you handle the landing."

Grimes felt his prominent ears burning as he blushed furiously. He thought, *I'd like five minutes alone back on Electra with the bastard who programmed this brass bitch!* He saw, in the screen, that the sounding rocket had hit and that its luminous smoke was rising directly upwards. But it was thinning, would not last for much longer.

He ordered, "Fire two!"

Big Sister said, "It is not necessary."

Fire two!" repeated Grimes sharply. He added,

grudgingly, "Wind can rise suddenly, especially just after sunrise, especially in country like this."

"Fire two," acknowledged Big Sister sullenly as the second rocket streaked downwards, striking just as the first one expired.

And there was wind, Grimes noted with smug satisfaction, springing up with the dawn. The luminescent pillar of smoke wavered, then streamed seawards. Grimes applied lateral thrust, kept the flaring rocket head in the center of the screen.

The sun came up relative to the land below the ship, topping the serrated ridge of the range to the eastward. The plain toward which *The Far Traveler* was dropping flared into color—blue-green with splotches of gold and scarlet, outcroppings of gleaming white from which extended long, sharply defined black shadows. *Boulders* . . . thought Grimes, stepping up the magnification of the screen. Yes, boulders . . . And the red and yellow patches must be clumps of ground hugging flowers since they cast no shadows. The sounding rocket, still smoking, was almost in the center of one of the scarlet patches; there was no unevenness of the ground there to worry about.

The ship dropped steadily. Grimes was obliged to make frequent small lateral thrust adjustments; that wind was unsteady, gusting, veering, backing. He reduced the rate of descent until *The Far Traveler* was almost hovering.

"I am not made of glass, you know," remarked Big Sister conversationally.

"I had hoped to make the landing some time before noon," said the Baroness.

Grimes tried to ignore them both. *That bloody wind!*

he thought. *Why can't it make up its mind which way to blow!*

He was down at last—and the ship, suddenly and inexplicably, was tilted a full fifteen degrees from the vertical. She hung there—and then, with slow deliberation, righted herself, far more slowly than she should have done with the lateral thrust that Grimes was applying. There was no real danger, only discomfort—and, for Grimes, considerable embarrassment. He had always prided himself on his shiphandling and this was the first time that he had been guilty of such a bungled landing.

When things had stopped rattling and creaking the Baroness asked, with cold sarcasm, "Was that really necessary, Captain?"

Before he could think of a reply Big Sister said, "Captain Grimes was overly cautious. *I* would have come down fast instead of letting the wind play around with me like a toy balloon. I would have dropped and then applied vertical thrust at the last moment."

And you, you cast-iron, gold-plated bitch, thought Grimes, *deliberately made a balls-up of my landing . . .*

"Perhaps, Captain," said the Baroness, "it will be advisable to allow Big Sister to handle her own lift-offs and set-downs from now on."

The way she said it there wasn't any "perhaps" about it.

»«(Chapter 15)»«

Big Sister carried out the routine tests for habitability. The captains of *Epsilon Pavonis* and *Investigator* had reported the atmosphere as better than merely breathable, the water suitable for drinking as well as for washing in and sailing ships on, a total absence of any micro-organisms capable of causing even mild discomfort to humans, let alone sickness or death. Nonetheless, caution is always advisable. Bacilli and viruses can mutate—and on Farhaven, after the landing of *Lode Venturer*, there had been established a new and sizeable niche in the ecology, the bodies of the original colonists and their descendants, just crying out to be occupied. The final tests, however, would have to wait until there was a colonist available for thorough examination.

Finally Big Sister said, speaking through the control room transceiver, "You may now disembark. But I would recommend . . ."

Grimes broke in. "You seem to forget that I was once a

763

Survey Service captain. Landings on strange planets were
part of my job."

The Baroness smiled maliciously. "I suppose that we
may as well avail ourselves of Captain Grimes' wide range
of experience. Quite possibly he was far better at trampling
roughshod over exotic terrain than bringing his ship to a
gentle set-down prior to the extra-vehicular activities."
She looked away from Grimes, addressed the transceiver.
"Big Sister, please have the small pinnace waiting for us.
We shall board it from the ground. Oh, and an escort of
six general purpose robots. Armed."

"Am I to assume, Your Excellency," asked Grimes
stiffly, "that you are placing yourself in command of the
landing party?"

"Of course, Captain. May I remind you that your
authority, such as it is, does not extend as much as one
millimeter beyond the shell of this ship?"

Grimes did not reply. He watched her sullenly as she
unbuckled herself from her seat and left the control room.
Then he unsnapped his own safety belt, got up and went
down to his quarters. He found that the robot stewardess
had laid out a uniform of tough khaki twill with shoulder-
boards of gold braid on purple, a gold-trimmed purple
beret, stout boots, a belt with attached holsters. He
checked the weapons. These were a Minetti projectile
pistol—as it happened, his favorite side-arm—and a hand
laser. They would do; it was highly unlikely that heavy
artillery would be required. He changed out of his shorts
and shirt uniform—he had made it plain that he did not
consider full dress suitable attire for shiphandling—
slowly. Before he was finished the too familiar voice came

from the speaker of the playmaster in his day cabin,
"Captain Grimes, Her Excellency is waiting for you."

He buckled on the belt, went out to the axial shaft, rode
the elevator down to the after airlock. He walked down
the golden ramp to the blue-green not-quite-grass. The
pinnace was there, a few meters from the ship, a slim,
torpedo shape of burnished gold. The Baroness was there,
in khaki shirt and flared breeches and high, polished
boots, looking like an intrepid White Huntress out of some
archaic adventure movie. The general purpose robots were
there, drawn up in a stiff line, staring at nothing. From belts
about their splendidly proportioned bodies depended an
assortment of hand weapons.

"We are waiting," said the Baroness unnecessarily.
"Now that you are here, will you get the show on the
road?" Somehow she contrived to put the question
between quotation marks.

Grimes flushed angrily. "Your orders?" he asked,
adding, "Your Excellency," to avoid further acrimony.

"To take this pinnace to the settlement reported by
Epsilon Pavonis and *Investigator.*" Then, when Grimes
made no immediate move, "Don't just stand there. *Do*
something."

He turned to the robots, tried to imagine that they
were Survey Service Marines, although the handling of
such personnel he had always left to their own officers or
NCOs. "Embark!" he ordered sharply.

The automata turned as one, strode in single file to the
pinnace's airlock, stepped aboard.

He said to the Baroness, "After you, Your Excellency."
He followed her into the pinnace, saw that she had

taken the co-pilot's seat in the control cab. The robots were standing aft, in the main cabin. The airlock doors closed while he was still making his way to his own chair; he noted that the Baroness had not touched the instrument panel before her. He sighed. This was Big Sister again, showing him who was really in command.

He buckled himself into his seat. Before he was finished the voice of the ship's computer-pilot came from the transceiver, "Proceed when you are ready, Captain Grimes."

The inertial drive was already running, in neutral gear. He switched to vertical thrust, lifted. The river was ahead; in the bright sunlight it was a ribbon of gleaming gold winding over the blue-green grasslands. There was altogether too much gold in his life these days, he thought. He flew at a moderate speed until he was directly over the wide stream and then turned to port, proceeding inland at an altitude of about fifteen meters. Ahead of him were the distant, towering ranges, their glittering peaks sharp against the clear sky.

The Baroness was not talkative. Neither was Grimes. He thought, *If those were* real *Marines back there they'd be making enough chatter for all of us.*

He concentrated on his piloting. The controls of the pinnace were very similar to those to which he had become accustomed in small craft of this type in the Survey Service but he still had to get the feel of this one. The river banks were higher now, rocky, sheer, with explosions of green and gold and scarlet and purple where flowering shrubs had taken hold in cracks and crevices. He considered lifting to above cliff-top level, then decided against it. While he was here he might as well enjoy the scenery. There was little enough else to enjoy.

The canyon became deeper, narrower, more tortuous. And then, after Grimes had put the pinnace through an almost right-angled turn, it widened. The actual river bed was still relatively narrow but, strung along it like a bead, was an oval valley, lushly fertile, bounded by sheer red cliffs unbroken save for where the stream flowed in and out.

The valley was as described in the two reports. The village was not. It was utterly deserted, its houses dilapidated, many of them apparently destroyed by fire at some long past date. Shrubs and saplings were thrusting up through the charred ruins.

Grimes set the controls for hovering, took binoculars from their box to study the abandoned settlement. There were few houses of more than one story. The structural material was mud or clay, reinforced with crude frames of timber. The windows were unglazed but from some of them bleached rags, the remains of blinds or curtains, fluttered listlessly in some faint stirring of the air.

The Baroness had found her own glasses, was staring through them.

She said softly, "A truly Lost Colony . . . And we have come too late to find any survivors . . ."

A voice—*that* voice!—came from the transceiver.

"May I suggest, Your Excellency, that you observe the cliff face to the north of your present position?"

Big Sister, thought Grimes, was still watching. She would have her sensors in and about the pinnace and every one of the robots was no more—and no less—than an extension of herself.

He turned the boat about its short axis to facilitate observation. He and the Baroness studied the forbidding wall of red rock. It was broken, here and there, by dark holes. The mouths of caves? He thought that he could detect motion in some of them. Animals? And then a human figure appeared from one of the apertures and walked slowly along a narrow ledge to the next cave mouth. It was naked. It was a woman, not old but not young, with long, unkempt hair that might, after a thorough wash, have been blonde. The most amazing thing about her was her apparent lack of interest in the strange flying machine that was shattering the peace of the valley with its cacophonous engine beat. Although it was quiet inside the pinnace—its builders had been lavish with sonic insulation to protect the delicate ears of its aristocratic owner—the racket outside, the arythmic clangor of the inertial drive echoing and re-echoing between the cliff faces, must have been deafening.

Then she did turn to look at the noisy intruder. Somehow her attitude conveyed the impression that she wished that the clattering thing would go away. Grimes studied her through his binoculars. Her face, which might have been pretty if cleaned and given a few cosmetic touches, was that of a sleepwalker. The skin of her body, under the dirt, was pallid. That was strange. People who habitually went naked, such as the Arcadian naturists, were invariably deeply tanned.

She turned again, walked slowly into the cave mouth.

Three children, two girls and a boy, came out on to another ledge. They were as unkempt as the woman, equally incurious. They picked their way down a narrow pathway to ground level, walked slowly to one of the low bushes. They stood around it, picking things—nuts? berries?—from its branches, thrusting them into their mouths.

The Baroness said, addressing Grimes almost as though he were a fellow human being, "As you know, *Social Evolution in the Lost Colonies* is the title of my thesis. But this is devolution. From spaceship to village of mud huts . . . From mud huts to caves . . ."

"Caves," said Grimes, "could be better than mud huts. Less upkeep. There's a place called Coober Peedy back on Earth, in Australia, where the cave dwellings are quite luxurious. It used to be an opal mining town . . ."

"Indeed?" Her voice was cold again. "Put us down, please. Close to those horrible children, but not close enough to alarm them."

If they were going to be alarmed, thought Grimes, they would have been alarmed already. Surely they must have seen the pinnace, must be hearing it. But he said nothing and brought the boat down, landing about ten meters from the filthy urchins. They did not look away from the bush from which they were gathering the edible harvest.

The airlock doors opened and the little ladder automatically extended. The Baroness got up from her seat. Grimes put out a hand to detain her. She scornfully brushed it aside.

He said, "Wait, Your Excellency. The robots should embark first. To draw the fire. If any."

"If any," she repeated derisively.

She pushed past him, jumped down from the airlock to the ground. He followed her. The robots filed out on the heels of the humans. Grimes, with both pistols drawn, stood taking stock. He stared up at the cliff face, at the caves. There were no indications of any hostile action. He was not really expecting any but knew that the unexpected has claimed many a victim. The Baroness sneered silently. Grimes relaxed at last and returned the weapons to their holsters but did not secure the flaps.

"Are you sure," she asked, "that you don't want to shoot those children?"

Grimes made no reply, followed her as she walked slowly to the little savages clustered around the shrub. The GP robots followed him. The children ignored the intruders, just went on stolidly picking berries—if berries they were—and thrusting them into their mouths.

They were unprepossessing brats—skinny, dirty, with scabbed knees and elbows, with long, matted, filthy hair. And they stank, a sour effluvium that made Grimes want to breathe through his mouth rather than through his nose. He saw the Baroness's nostrils wrinkle. His own felt like airtight doors the instant after a hull-piercing missile strike.

He looked at the berries that were growing so profusely on the bush. Berries? Elongated, bright purple berries? But berries do not run to a multiplicity of wriggling legs and twitching antennae. Berries do not squirm as they are inserted into greedy mouths . . . The eaters chewed busily while a thin, purple ichor dribbled down their filth-encrusted chins.

It was no worse than eating oysters, thought Grimes, trying to rationalize his way out of impending nausea. Or witchetty grubs . . .

"Children," said the Baroness in a clear, rather too sweet voice.

They ignored her.

"Children," she repeated, her voice louder, not so sweet. They went on ignoring her.

She looked at Grimes. Her expression told him, *Do something*.

He put out a hand to grasp the boy's shoulder, being careful not to grip hard or painfully. This required no effort; his own skin was shrinking from contact with that greasy, discolored integument. He managed to turn the child to face him and the Baroness. Then he was at a loss for something to say. "Take me to your leader" did not seem right somehow.

"Please take us to your parents," said the Baroness.

The boy went on chewing and swallowing, then spat out a wad of masticated chitin from which spines and hairs still protruded. It landed on the toe of Grimes' right boot. He kicked it away in revulsion.

"Take us to your parents," repeated the Baroness.

"Wha'?"

"Your parents." Slowly, patiently, "Your mother. Your father."

"Momma. Fadder. No wake."

"He says," volunteered Grimes, "that his mother and father are sleeping."

She said, "A truly blinding glimpse of the obvious, Captain. But, of course you are the expert on first contacts, are you not? Then may I ask why it did not occur to you to bring bright trinkets, glass beads and mirrors and the like, as gifts to people who are no better than savages?"

"I doubt if they could bear to look at themselves in a mirror, Your Excellency," said Grimes.

"Very, very funny. But you are not employed as court jester."

Slowly she removed the watch from her left wrist. It was a beautiful piece of work, jewel as much as instrument, fantastically accurate. In the extremely unlikely event of *The Far Traveler*'s chronometers all becoming nonoperational it could have been used for navigational purposes. Its golden bracelet was a fragile-seeming chain, its thin case was set with diamonds that flashed dazzlingly in the sunlight. She dangled it temptingly before the boy's eyes. He ignored it. He wriggled out of Grimes' grip, pulled another of the repulsive purple grubs from the bush and thrust it into his open mouth.

But one of the girls was more interested. She turned, made a sudden snatch for the trinket. The Baroness was too quick for her, whipping it up and out of reach.

"Gimme!" squealed the unlovely child. "P'etty! P'etty! Gimme!"

"Take . . . us. . . ." enunciated the Baroness slowly and carefully, "to . . . Momma . . . Fadder . . ."

"Gimme! Gimme! Gimme!"

The Baroness repeated her request. It seemed to be getting through. The girl scowled, then slowly and deliberately gathered a double handful of the puce horrors from the branches of the bush. Then, reluctantly, she led the way to the cliff face, pausing frequently to look back. With her busily working mouth, with that sickening slime oozing from between her lips she was not a pretty sight.

She reached the foot of the rock wall. There was a

ledge running diagonally up its face, less than a meter wide, a natural ramp. She paused, looked back at Grimes and the Baroness, at the marching robots. An expression that could have been indicative of doubt flickered across her sharp-featured face. The Baroness waved the watch so that it flashed enticingly in the sunlight. The girl made a beckoning gesture, then started up the path.

⟫⟪Chapter 16⟫⟪

Grimes hesitated; a cliff path such as this should have been fitted with a handrail. The Baroness flashed him a scornful look and followed the girl; despite her boots she was almost as sure-footed. Grimes, not at all happily, followed the Baroness. The ledge was narrow, its surface uneven yet worn smooth and inclined to be slippery. There was a paucity of handholds on the cliff face and, looking up, Grimes realized that on some stretches the climbers would be obliged to lean outward, over a sheer drop, as they made progress upward. The robots began to come after Grimes. There was a sharp *crack!* as rock broke away from the edge of the path, a clatter of falling fragments.

The Baroness called, "Robots! Wait for us on the ground!" Then, to Grimes, "You should have realized, Captain, that their weight would be too much for this ledge!"

So should Big Sister! thought Grimes but did not say it.

They climbed—the half-grown girl, the Baroness, Grimes. They negotiated a difficult crossing of the natural ramp with a horizontal ledge. Fortunately the cliff face here was scarred with cracks affording foot and handholds, although so widely spaced as to alleviate but little the hazards of the traverse. They climbed.

Once Grimes paused to look back and down—at the gleaming, golden pinnace, at the equally refulgent robots. It was an exaggeration, he knew, but they looked at him like ants standing beside a pencil dropped on to the grass. He was not, after all, so very far above ground level—only high enough to be reasonably sure of breaking his neck if he missed his footing and fell.

After that he kept on looking up and ahead—at the Baroness's shapely rump working in the sweat-stained khaki of her breeches, at the meager buttocks of the naked girl. Neither spectacle was particularly erotic. They climbed, crossing another horizontal ledge and then, eventually, turning off the diagonal path onto a third one. It was as narrow as the natural ramp.

Ahead and to the left was the mouth of one of the caves. The girl slipped into it, the Baroness followed. Grimes followed her. Less than two meters inside the entrance was an almost right-angled turn. The Baroness asked, "Did you bring a light?" Then, "But of course not. That would have required some foresight on your part."

Grimes, saying nothing, pulled his laser pistol from its holster, thumbed the selector switch to broadest beam. It would serve as an electric torch although wasteful of energy and potentially dangerous. But it was not required, although it took some little time for their eyes to become accustomed to the dim illumination after the bright sunshine outside. There was light in here—wan, eerie, cold. It came from the obscenely bloated masses of fungus dependent from the low cavern roof, growing in bulbous clusters from the rocky walls and, to a lesser extent, from the floor itself. The girl led them on, her thin body pallidly luminescent. And there were other bodies sprawled on the rock floor, men and women, naked, sleeping. . .

Or dead . . . thought Grimes.

No, not dead. One of them, a grossly obese female, stirred and whinnied softly, stretched out a far arm to a nearby clump of fungus. She broke off a large hunk, stuffed it into her mouth. She gobbled disgustingly, swallowed noisily. There was a gusty sigh as she flopped back to her supine position. She snored.

There were other noises—eructations, a trickling sound, a splattering. And there was the . . . *stink.* Grimes trod in something. He knew what it was without looking. Sight is not the only sense.

Still the girl led them through the noisome cave. They passed adults, adolescents, children, babies, all sprawled in their own filth. They came at last to a couple with limbs entwined in a ghastly parody of physical love.

"Momma! Fadder!" shrilled the girl triumphantly. "Gimme!"

The Baroness silently handed the watch to her. It was no longer the pretty toy that it had been when first offered. In this lighting it could have been fabricated from lusterless lead, from beads of dull glass.

The girl took it, stared at it and then flung it from her. "No p'etty!" she squalled. "No p'etty!"

She pulled a piece of the glowing fungus from the wall, thrust it into her mouth. She whimpered as she chewed it, then subsided onto the rock floor beside her parents.

"My watch," said the Baroness to Grimes. "Find it." After rather too long a lag she added, "Please."

Grimes used his laser pistol cautiously, directing its beam upward while looking in the direction from which the brief metallic clatter, marking the fall of the time-piece, had come. He saw it shining against the rock wall. He made his way to it, picked it up while trying in vain not to dirty his fingers. It had fallen into a pool of some filth.

The Baroness said, "I am not touching it again until it has been thoroughly sterilized. Put it in your pocket. And now, will you try to wake these people?"

Grimes wrapped the watch in his handkerchief, put it into his pocket, then returned the laser pistol to its holster. He squatted by the sleeping couple. He forced himself to touch the unclean skin of the man's bare shoulder. He gave a tentative tap, then another.

"I said *wake* him, not pet him!" snarled the Baroness. "Shake him!"

Grimes shook the sleeper, rather more viciously than he had intended. The man slid off the supine body of the woman, fell onto his side. He twitched like a sleeping dog afflicted by a bad dream. Dull eyes opened, peered out through the long, matted hair. Bearded lips parted.

"Go 'way. Go 'way."

"We have come a long distance to see you," said the Baroness.

"S'wot?" asked the man uninterestedly. "S'wot?" He

levered himself to a half sitting position, broke off a piece
of the omnipresent fungus from the near wall, brought it
toward his mouth.

"Stop him!" ordered the Baroness.

Grimes caught the other's thin wrist in his right hand,
forced it down. The man struggled feebly.

"I am the Baroness d'Estang," announced the lady.

So what! thought Grimes.

"S'wot?" demanded the man. Then, to Grimes, "Leggo.
Leggo o' me, you bassar!"

Grimes said, "We'll not get much from these people."

She asked coldly, "Are you an expert in handling decadent
savages? I find it hard to believe that you are expert in
anything."

The man's free hand flashed up, the fingers, with
then-long, broken nails, clawing for Grimes' eyes. Grimes
let go of the other's wrist, using both his own hands to
protect his face. Released, the caveman abandoned his
attack and crammed the handful of fungus into his mouth,
swallowed it without chewing. He immediately lapsed
into unconsciousness.

"Now look what you've done!" snapped the Baroness.

"I didn't do anything," said Grimes.

"That was the trouble!" she said. She snarled wordlessly.
Then, "All right We will leave this . . . pigsty and return
when we are better prepared. You will collect samples of
the fungus so that it may be analyzed aboard the ship and
an effective antidote prepared. Be careful not to touch the
stuff with your bare hands."

He prodded a protuberance of the nearest growth
with the muzzle of his Minetti. He hated so to misuse a

cherished firearm but it was the only tool he had. He pulled his handkerchief from his pocket, extracting from its folds the Baroness's watch, putting the instrument down on the floor. He wrapped the cloth around the sample of fungus, making sure that there were at least three thicknesses of cloth between it and his skin. He removed his beret, put the untidy parcel into it.

He followed his employer out to the open air.

After they had returned to ground level Grimes ordered one of the robots to get specimens of the purple grubs from a bush, also samples of the leaves on which the revolting things were feeding. Then the party reboarded the pinnace. Grimes took the craft straight up with the automatic cameras in action. The pictures would be of interest and value—the deserted village, the faint, rectangular outlines on the surrounding terrain showing where fields had once been cultivated, the cliff face with the dark mouths of the caves. No humans would be seen on these films; the children who had been feeding from the bushes had gone back inside.

The flight back to *The Far Traveler* was direct and fast. Grimes felt—and in fact was—filthy, wanting nothing so much as a long, hot shower and a change into clean clothing. And the Baroness? Whatever he was feeling she must be feeling too, doubled and redoubled, in spades. And the robots, who should have been doing the dirty work, were as gleamingly immaculate as when they had disembarked from the yacht.

They landed by the ramp. The Baroness was first out of the pinnace and up the gangway almost before Grimes had finished unbuckling his seat belt. By the time that he got aboard she was nowhere to be seen.

He saw her discarded clothing in a little heap on the deck of the airlock chamber. He heard Big Sister say, "I suggest. Captain, that you disrobe before coming inside the ship."

He growled, "I was house-broken at least thirty years before you were programmed."

He stripped, throwing his own soiled khaki on top of the Baroness's gear. He thought wryly, *And that's the closest I'll ever get to the bitch!* Nonetheless he was not sorry to get his clothes off; they were distinctly odorous. He walked naked into the elevator cage, was carried up to his quarters. The robot stewardess, his literally golden girl, awaited him there. She already had the shower running in his bathroom; she removed her skimpy uniform to stand under the hot water with him, to soap and to scrub him. To an outside observer not knowing that the perfectly formed female was only a machine the spectacle would have seemed quite erotic. Grimes wondered who was washing the Baroness's back—her butler or her lady's maid? He hoped maliciously that whichever one it was was using a stiff brush . . .

He asked his own servant, "Aren't you afraid you'll rust?"

She replied humorlessly, "Gold does not corrode." She turned the water off. "You are now sterile."

I am as far as you're concerned, he thought. It occurred to him that it was a long time since he had had a woman. Too long.

He stood for a few seconds in the blast of warm air and

then, clean and dry, stepped into his sleeping cabin. He looked with distaste at the purple and gold livery laid out on the bed. Reluctantly he climbed into it. As he did up the last button the voice of Big Sister said, "You will now join Her Excellency in her salon, Captain Grimes."

Grimes filled and lit his pipe. He badly needed a smoke.

Big Sister said, "Her Excellency is waiting for you."

Grimes decided to allow himself three more slow inhalations.

Big Sister said, "Her Excellency is waiting for you."

Grimes continued smoking.

Big Sister reiterated, "Her Excellency is waiting for you."

Grimes said, "What you tell me three times is true."

Big Sister said coldly, "What I tell you is true."

Reluctantly Grimes put down his pipe. The stewardess produced a little golden atomizer, sprayed him with a fragrant mist.

He said, "Now I reek like a whore's garret." Big Sister said, "You do not, now, reek like an incinerator."

Grimes sighed and left his quarters.

»«(Chapter 17)«»

The Baroness said coldly, "You took your time getting here, Captain. I suppose that you were obliged to indulge yourself by sucking on that vile comforter of yours. Be seated."

Grimes lowered himself cautiously into one of the frail-seeming chairs.

"I thought that we would view the record of the orgy again."

"The record of the orgy, Your Excellency? I have not seen it yet."

"I would have thought, Captain Grimes, that you would have acquainted yourself with every scrap of information regarding this planet before our set down."

Grimes simmered inwardly. Every time that he had wished to view the orgy record it had not been available. He ventured to say as much.

The voice of Big Sister came from the Baroness's play-master, an instrument that contrived to look as a TriVi set would have looked had such devices been in existence during the reign of King Louis XIV of France.

"This record, like the others concerning this planet, was obtained by Commander Delamere from the Archives of the Survey Service on Lindisfarne. It is classified—for viewing by officers with the rank of Survey Service captain and above. You, Captain Grimes, resigned from the Survey Service with the rank of commander only."

"Let us not split hairs," said the Baroness generously. "Although he is now only a civilian shipmaster, Captain Grimes should be accorded his courtesy title. In any case, Commander Delamere, from whom we obtained this copy, has yet to attain captain's rank. The film, please."

The screen of the playmaster came alive, glowing with light and color. There was the village that they had visited— but as a living settlement, not a crumbling ghost town. There were the people—reasonably clean, brightly clothed. There were spacemen and spacewomen from the survey ship in undress uniform. And there was music—the insistent throb and rattle of little drums, the squealing of fifes. There was something odd about it, a tune and a rhythm that did not seem in accord with these circumstances. Grimes suddenly recognized the Moody and Sankey lilt. He started to sing softly to the familiar yet subtly distorted melody.

Yes, we'll gather at the river,
The beautiful, the beautiful river . . .

"*Must* you, Captain?" asked the Baroness coldly.

He shut up.

It must have been quite a party, he thought as he watched the playmaster screen. There were animal carcasses roasting over big, open fires. Pigs? But what had happened to *them?* Why were not their feral descendents rooting among the ruins? There were great earthenware pots of some liquor being passed around. There were huge platters heaped with amorphous hunks of . . . something, something which, even in the ruddy firelight, gave off a faint blue glow. And the music . . . Another familiar hymn tune. The words formed themselves in Grimes' mind:

Bread of heaven, bread of heaven, Feed me till I want no more . . .

Now the party was beginning to get rough—not rough in the sense of developing brawls but rough inasmuch as inhibitions were being shed with clothing. It was fast becoming an orgy. Grimes was no prude—but he watched with nauseated disgust three children who could not have been older than eight or nine, two girls and a boy, erotically fondling a fat, naked crewman.

Grimes thought that he heard above the music, the singing, the mechanical cacophony of inertial drive units. This ceased suddenly. Then Commander Belton strode on to the scene. Grimes knew him slightly, although this Belton was a much younger man than the one of his acquaintance. The Belton with whom Grimes had had dealings, not so long ago, was still only a commander, was officer in charge of the third class Survey Service sub-base on Pogg's Landing, a dreary, unimportant planet in the Shaula sector. A sour, embittered man . . . Looking at the playmaster Grimes realized that, apart from aging, Belton had changed very little over the decades.

Belton looked not only sour and embittered but righteously furious. Behind him were a couple of lieutenant commanders and a captain of Marines, all trying to look virtuous. Behind them were twelve Marines in full battle order.

Belton recoiled violently from a plump, naked girl who, a jug of liquor in one hand, a platter of fungus in the other, was trying to tempt him. He barked an order. His officers and the Marines opened fire with stunguns. Those revelers who were still on their feet fell, twitching. Grimes saw a hapless woman topple into one of the fires. Belton's men made no effort to pull her to safety. He watched the Marines dragging their unconscious shipmates toward the waiting pinnaces, caring little what injuries were inflicted in the process. Finally there was a scuffle around the camera itself. It was knocked over and kicked around as its operator was subdued—but still recorded a series of shots of heavily booted feet trampling on sprawling, naked bodies.

And that was it. The screen faded to featureless gray.

"Well?" asked the Baroness, arching her fine eyebrows.

"These things happen," said Grimes. "After all, Your Excellency, a spaceship isn't a Sunday school."

"But the colony should have been," she told him. "The founders of the settlement were all members of a relatively obscure religious sect, the True Followers. And the True Followers were—and still are—notorious for their puritanism."

"There were spacemen too, Your Excellency. And spacemen are usually agnostics."

"Not always. It is a matter of record that the Master of *Lode Venturer* was a True Follower. So were several of his officers."

"Beliefs change, or are lost, over the generations," said Grimes.

"But the singing of hymns indicated that they still believed . . ." she murmured.

Then Big Sister's voice came from the playmaster. "Analysis of the samples has been completed, Your Excellency. Insofar as the larval stage of the indigenous arthropod is concerned there is protein, of course. Amino acids. Salts. A high concentration of sugars. It is my opinion that the children of this world regard these larvae as their counterparts on more privileged planets regard candy.

"And now, the fungoid organism. It supplies all the nutritional needs of the lost colonists. By itself it constitutes an almost perfect balanced diet. Analysis of the human excreta adhering to the boots of yourself and Captain Grimes indicates that its donors were in a good state of physical health . . ."

"*Physical* health . . ." interjected the Baroness.

"Yes, Your Excellency. Analysis of the fungus indicates that it is, but for one thing, a perfect food . . ."

Formulae appeared on the screen.

C_2H_5OH . . . $(C_2H_5)_2O$ . . .

"Alcohol," said Grimes. "Some people might think that its presence would make the food really perfect."

"The ways of organic intelligences are, at times, mysterious to me," admitted Big Sister. "But, to continue. There are other, very complex molecules present but, so far as I can determine, they are non-toxic . . ."

"And there were no indications of disease in the feces?" asked the Baroness. "Nothing to indicate breakdown of liver, kidneys, other organs?"

"No, Your Excellency."

"Blotting paper," said Grimes.

"Blotting paper!" asked the Baroness.

"A spaceman's expression, Your Excellency. It means that if you take plenty of solid food—preferably rich and creamy—with your liquor there's no damage done. That fungus must be its own blotting paper."

"It could be so," she murmured. "And there are some people who would regard this planet as a veritable paradise—eternal alcoholic euphoria without unpleasant consequences."

"Talking of consequences," said Grimes, "there were babies in that cave."

"What of it, Captain?"

"To have babies you must have childbirth."

"Yet another blinding glimpse of the obvious. But I see what you are driving at and I think that I have the answer. Before the colonists retreated from their village to the caves there must have been doctors and midwives. And those doctors and midwives are still functioning."

"In those conditions?" he demanded, horrified.

"In those conditions," she said. "Do not forget, Captain, that the human race contrived not only to survive but to multiply long before there were such amenities as spotlessly clean maternity wards in hospitals literally bulging with superscientific gadgetry, long before every passing year saw its fresh crop of wonder drugs. And perhaps those doctors and midwives will pass on their skills to the coming generations—in which case the colony stands a very good chance of survival. Perhaps they will not—but even then the colony could survive.

"Nonetheless," she went on, "I must discover the reason for this quite fantastic devolution. There must have been more to it than the quarrel with Commander Belton. There must be records of some kind in the village."

"There are no records," stated Big Sister. "I sent the general purpose robots back to make a thorough search of the settlement, Your Excellency. It seems certain that the colony's archives were housed in one of the buildings destroyed by fire. There are no records."

"There could be records," said the Baroness softly, "in the memories of those living in the caves. I must try to devise some sort of bribe, reward . . . Some form of payment . . . What, I wonder, would induce those people to talk freely?" That pretty watch hadn't been much good, thought Grimes. "My watch," said the Baroness suddenly. "Have you cleaned it for me, Big Sister? Did it need repair?"

"Your watch, Your Excellency?"

"Yes. My watch. It was a gift from the Duke of . . . No matter. The captain brought it back in his pocket. It had been dropped into a pool of . . . ordure."

"There was no watch in any of Captain Grimes' pockets, Your Excellency."

Grimes remembered then. The thing had been wrapped in his handkerchief. Then he had removed it, to use the handkerchief to parcel up the specimen of fungus. He must have left it in the cave.

He said as much. He added, "When we go back tomorrow morning I'll find it. I don't think that any of the cave dwellers will be interested in it."

The Baroness had been almost friendly. Now she regarded him with contemptuous hostility. She snapped, "You will go back to the cave to find it now!"

»)«(Chapter 18»)«

Grimes went up to his quarters to change back into khaki; he did not think that even the Baroness would expect him to scrabble around in that noisome cavern wearing his purple and gold finery. When he left the ship it was almost sunset. The pinnace was waiting at the foot of the ramp. There were no general purpose robots to afford him an escort. He had assumed that Big Sister would lay them on as a matter of course. She had not but he could not be bothered to make an issue of it.

He boarded the pinnace. It began to lift even before he was in the pilot's chair. Big Sister knew the way now, he thought. He was content to be a passenger. He filled and lit his pipe. The more or less (rather less than more) fragrant fumes had a soothing effect. His seething needed soothing, he thought, pleased with the play on words. He might be only an employee but still he was a shipmaster, a captain. To be ordered around aboard his own vessel was much too much. And all over a mere toy, no matter how expensive, a gaudy trinket that the Baroness had been willing enough to hand over to that revolting female brat. She couldn't have thought much of its donor, the Duke of wherever it was.

The pinnace knew the way. This was the third time that it was making the trip from the yacht to the valley. It had no real brain of its own but, even when it was not functioning as an extension of Big Sister, possessed a memory and was at least as intelligent as the average insect.

It flew directly to the village while Grimes sat and fumed, literally and figuratively. When it landed darkness was already thick in the shadow of the high cliffs.

"Illuminate the path," ordered Grimes.

As he unsnapped his seat belt he saw through the viewports the rock face suddenly aglow in the beams of the pinnace's searchlights, the brightest of which outlined one of the dark cave openings. So that was where he had to go. He passed through the little airlock, jumped down to the damp grass. He walked to the cliff face, came to the foot of the natural ramp. He hesitated briefly. It had been a dangerous climb— for a non-mountaineer such as himself—even in daylight, in company, with a guide. But, he was obliged to admit, he could not complain about lack of illumination.

He made his slow and cautious way upward, hugging the rock face. He had one or two nasty moments as he negotiated the really awkward parts. Nonetheless he made steady progress although he was sweating profusely when he reached the cave mouth. This time he had brought a flashlight with him. He switched it on as he entered the natural tunnel.

Did these people, he wondered disgustedly, spend all their time sleeping? It seemed like it. Sleeping, and eating, and copulating. But the paradises of some Terran religions were not so very different—although not, surely, the promised Heaven of a sect such as the True Followers.

The bright beam of the flashlight played over the nude bodies sprawled in their obscene postures, over the clumps of fungus that looked almost like growths of coral—or naked brains. These glowed more brightly after the light of his flashlight had passed over them.

Carefully picking his way through the sleepers he made his way deeper into the cave. He was watching for the glint of gems, of bright metal. He did not see the slim arm that extended itself from an apparently slumbering body, the long-fingered hand that closed about his ankle. He fell heavily. His flashlight was jolted from his grasp, flared briefly as it crashed onto the rock floor, went out. His face smashed into something soft and pulpy. He had opened his mouth to cry out as he was falling and a large portion of the semi-fluid mess was forced into it. He gagged—then realized that the involuntary mouthful was not what, at first, he had thought that it was. The fungus, he realized . . . It tasted quite good. It tasted better than merely good.

There was a meatiness, a sweetness, a spiciness and, he thought, considerable alcoholic content. He had been chivvied out from the yacht to search for that blasted watch without being allowed time to enjoy a drink, a meal. It would do no harm, he decided, if he savored the delicious taste a few seconds more before prudently spitting it out. After all, he rationalized, this was scientific research, wasn't it? And Big Sister had given the fungus full marks as a source of nourishment. He chewed experimentally. In spite of its mushiness the flesh possessed texture, fibres and nodules that broke between his teeth, that released aromatic oils which were to the original taste as a vintage burgundy is to a very ordinary *vin ordinaire*.

Before he realized what he was doing he swallowed. The second mouthful of the fungus was more voluntary than otherwise.

He was conscious of a soft weight on his back, of long hair falling around his head. Languidly he tried to turn over, finally succeeded in spite of the multiplicity (it seemed) of naked arms and legs that were imprisoning him.

He looked up into the face that was looking down into his. *Why,* he thought, *she's beautiful* . . . He recognized her.

She was the woman whom he and the Baroness had seen emerge briefly from the caves. Then her overall filthiness had made the biggest impression. *Now* he was quite unaware of the dirt on her body, the tangles in her hair. She was no more (and no less) than a desirable woman, an available woman. He knew that she was looking on him as a desirable, available man. After all the weeks cooped up aboard *The Far Traveler* with an attractive female at whom he could look, but must not touch, the temptation was strong, too strong. She kissed him full on the mouth. Her breath was sweet and spicy, intoxicating. She was woman and he was man, and all that stood in the way of consummation was his hampering clothing. Her hands were at the fastenings of his trousers but fumbling inexpertly. Reluctantly he removed his own from her full buttocks to assist her, was dimly conscious of the cold stone under his naked rump as the garment was pushed down to his knees, was ecstatically conscious of the enveloping warmth of her as she mounted him and rode him, not violently but languorously, slowly, slowly . . .

The tension releasing explosion came. She slumped against him, over him, her nipples brushing his face. Gently, reluctantly she rolled off his body. He felt her hand at his mouth. It held a large piece of the fungus. He took it from her fingers, chewed and swallowed. It was even better than his first taste of it had been. He drifted into sleep.

﹡⟩⟩《Chapter 19》⟨⟨﹡

He dreamed.

In the dream he was a child.

He was one of the *Lode Venturer* survivors who had made the long trek south from the vicinity of the north magnetic pole. He could remember the crash landing, the swift and catastrophic conversion of what had been a little, warm, secure world into twisted, crumpled wreckage.

He remembered the straggling column of men, women and children burdened with supplies from the wrecked gaussjammer—food, sacks of precious Terran seed grain, sealed stasis containers of the fertilized ova of Terran livestock, the incubators broken down into portable components, the parts of the solar power generator.

He was one of *Lode Venturer*'s people who had survived both crash landing and long march, who had found the valley, who had tilled the fields and planted the grain, who had worked at setting up the incubating equipment. Although only a child he had shared the fears of his elders as the precious store of preserved provisions dwindled and the knowledge that, in spite of strict rationing, it would not last out until the harvest, until the incubators delivered progenitors of future herds of meat animals.

He remembered the day of the drawing of lots.

There were the losers—three young men, a middle-aged woman and another one who was little more than a girl— standing there, frightened yet somehow proud, while further lots were drawn to decide who would be executioner and butcher. A fierce argument had developed—some of the women claiming, belatedly, that females of child-bearing age should have been exempt from the first lottery. While this was going on another boy—the son of the middle- aged woman, came down from the caves to which he had run rather than watch his mother slaughtered. He was bearing an armful of the fungus.

"Food!" he was shouting. "Food! I have tasted it and it is good!"

They had all sung a hymn of thanksgiving then, grateful for their delivery from what, no matter how necessary to their survival, would have been a ghastly sin.

Bread of Heaven, bread of Heaven,
Feed me till I want no more, want no more,
Feed me till I want no more . . .

He awoke then, drifting slowly up from the warm, deep sleep. He did what he had to do, relieving the pressure on bowels and bladder as he lay there. He wondered dimly why people ever went to the trouble of fabricating elaborate sanitary arrangements. The fungus needed his body wastes. He needed the fungus. It was all so simple.

He reached out and grabbed another handful of the

satisfying, intoxicating stuff. He became aware that the woman—or a woman—was with him. While he was still eating they coupled.

He slept.

He dreamed.

He was the Pastor, the leader of the people of the settlement.

He had looked over the arrangements for the feast and all was well. There was an ample supply of the strong liquor brewed and distilled from grain—the last harvest had been a good one, surplus to food requirements. Pigs had been slaughtered and dressed, ready for the roasting. Great baskets of the fungus had been brought down from the caves. Since it had been discovered that it thrived on human manure it had proliferated, spreading from the original cavern through the entire subterranean complex. Perhaps it had changed, too. It seemed that with every passing year its flavor had improved. At first—he seemed to remember—it had been almost tasteless although filling and nutritious.

But now . . .

The guests from the ship, clattering through the night sky in their noisy flying boats, were dropping down to the village. He hoped that there would not be the same trouble as there had been with the guests from that other ship, the one with the odd name, *Epsilon Pavonis*. Of course, it had not been the guests themselves who had made the trouble; it had been their captain. But *this* captain, he had been told, was himself a True Follower. All should be well. All was well.

The love feast, the music, the dancing, the singing of the old, familiar hymns . . .

And the love . . .

And surely the manna, the gift from the all-wise, all-loving God of the True Followers, was better than it ever had been. What need was there, after all, for the corn liquor, the roast pig?

Bread of Heaven, bread of Heaven,
Feed me till I want no more . . .

He walked slowly through and among the revelers, watching benevolently the fleshly intermingling of his own people and those from the starship. It was . . . *good.* Everything was good. He exchanged a few words with the Survey Service petty officer who, dutifully operating his equipment, was making a visual and sound recording of the feast. He wondered briefly why the man was amused when he said that the pictures and the music would be acclaimed when presented in the tabernacles of the True Followers on Earth and other planets. He looked benignly at the group at which the camera was aimed—a plump, naked, supine crewman being fondled by three children. It was a charming scene.

And why the strong sensation of déjà vu?

Why the brief, gut-wrenching disgust?

He heard the distant hammering in the still, warm air, growing louder and louder. More airboats—what did they call them? pinnaces?—from the ship, he thought. Perhaps the captain himself, Commander Belton, was coming after all. He would be pleased to see for himself how well his fellow True Followers on this distant world had kept the faith . . .

Then the dream became a nightmare.

There was shouting and screaming.

There was fighting.

There were armed men discharging their weapons indiscriminately, firing on both their own shipmates and the colonists.

There was his confrontation with a tall, gaunt, stiffly uniformed man.

(Again the flash of déjà vu.)

There were the bitter, angry words.

"True Followers, you call yourselves? I understood that my people had been invited to a religious service . . . And I find a disgusting orgy in progress!"

"But we are True Followers! We were saved. God Himself sent his manna to save us from committing the deadliest sin of all. Here! Taste! Eat and believe!"

And a hand smashed viciously down, striking the preferred manna from his grasp, as Belton shouted, "Keep that filthy muck away from me!"

He saw the muzzle of a pistol pointing at him, saw the flare of energy that jolted him into oblivion.

He slowly drifted up to semi-consciousness. There was a woman. There was more of the manna. Again he slept.

»《Chapter 20》《«

He dreamed.

He dreamed that a bright, harsh light was beating through his closed eyelids, that something hard was nudging him in the ribs.

He opened his eyes, immediately shut them again before he was blinded.

A voice, a somehow familiar female voice, was saying, "Captain Grimes! Captain Grimes! Wake up, damn you!" And then, in an intense whisper, "Oh! If you could only see yourself!"

He muttered, "Go 'way. Go 'way."

"Captain Grimes! John!" There was a hand on his shoulder, shaking him. He opened his eyes again. She had put her flashlight on the ground so that now he saw her by its reflected light. She was a woman. She was beautiful—but so was everybody in this enchanted cavern. He dimly recognized her.

She said, "I must get you out of here."

Why? he wondered. *Why!*

She got her hands under his naked shoulders, tried to lift him. He got his hands about her shoulders, pulled her down. She struggled, kneeing him in the groin. He let go and she stood up, stepping back from him. The shirt had been torn from her upper body. In spite of the pain that she had inflicted on him he felt a surge of desire, reached out for her exposed breasts. She stepped back another pace.

He wanted her—but to get up to go after her was too much trouble.

But he muttered, "Do'n' go . . . Do'n' go . . . I . . . want . . . you . . . always . . . wanted . . . you . . ."

Her face was glistening oddly. Dimly he realized that she was weeping. She said, "Not *here*. Not *now*. Pull yourself together. Come back to the ship."

He said—the words were coming more easily now, but were they his? "I . . . hate . . . ships . . . All . . . True . . . Followers . . . hate . . . ships . . . Stay . . . here . . . Be . . . happy . . ."

Her face and voice hardened. She said, "I'll get you out of here by force!"

He was fast losing interest in the conversation. He reached out languidly from the omnipresent manna, chewed and swallowed.

He muttered, "Try . . . this . . . Make . . . you . . . human . . ."

But she was gone.

It did not matter.

The warmth of the communal life of the cavern surrounded him.

There were women.

And always there was the manna.

He slept.

He dreamed.

He was one of the crowd being harangued by the Pastor.

"We must sever all ties with Earth!" he heard. "We are the true, the real True Followers! Were we not saved by God himself from death and from deadly sin? But these Earth-men, who have intruded into our paradise, who have strayed from the true path, refuse to believe . . ."

"So burn the houses, my people! Destroy everything that links us to faithless Earth, even our herds and our crops!

"God's own manna is all that we need, all that we shall ever need!"

And somebody else—Grimes knew that it was one of the community's physicians—was crying over and over, in a sort of ecstasy, "Holy symbiosis! Holy symbiosis!"

Crackling flames and screaming pigs and the voices of the people, singing,

> *Bread of Heaven, bread of Heaven,*
> *Feed me till I want no more, want no more . . .*

Again the too bright light and again the hand shaking his shoulder . . .

"Wake up, John! Wake up!"

"Go 'way . . ."

"John! Look at me!"

He opened his eyes.

She had placed her torch on a ledge so that it shone full upon her. She was naked. Diamonds gleamed in the braided coronet of the hair of her head and even in the heart-shaped growth at the scission of her thighs. She was a spaceman's pin-up girl in the warm, living flesh.

She said softly, "You want me. You shall have me—but not here, among these degenerates, this filth." She turned slowly, saying, "Follow . . ."

Almost he made the effort to get to his feet but it was too much trouble. With faint stirrings of regret he watched her luminous body swaying away from him. Once she turned and beckoned. He wondered vaguely why she should be wearing such an angry expression. And before she reached the mouth of the cave he had fallen back into sleep.

A long while or a little while—he had no way of knowing—later he awoke. After a few mouthfuls of manna he crawled until he found a woman.

And slept again.

And dreamed.

Subtly the dreams changed.

There were, as before, memories from the minds of the colonists who had long lived in symbiosis with the fungus but there were now other memories—brief flashes, indistinct at first but all the time increasing in clarity and duration. There were glimpses of the faces and the bodies of women whom he had known—Jane Pentecost, Maggie Lazenby, Ellen Russell, Una Freeman, Maya . . .

The women . . .

And the ships.

Lines from a long-ago read and long-ago forgotten piece of verse drifted through his mind:

> *The arching sky is calling*
> *Spacemen back to their trade . . .*

He was sitting in the control room of his first command, the little Serpent Class courier *Adder*, a king at last even though his realm, to others, was a very insignificant one. Obedient to the touch of his fingers on the console the tiny ship lifted from the Lindisfarne Base apron.

> *All hands! Stand by! Free Falling!*
> *The lights below us fade . . .*

And through the dream, louder and louder, surged the arhythmic hammering of a spaceship's inertial drive.

He awoke.

He scooped a handful of manna from a nearby clump.

He chewed, swallowed.

Somehow it was not the same as it had been; there was a hint of bitterness, a rancidity. He relieved himself where he lay and then crawled over and among the recumbent bodies until he found a receptive woman.

Like a great, fat slug . . . he thought briefly.

(But what was a slug? Surely nothing like this beautiful creature. . .)

After he was finished with her and she with him he

drifted again into sleep, even though that mechanical clangor coming from somewhere outside the cave was a growing irritation.

He dreamed more vividly than before.

He had just brought *Discovery* down to a landing in the Paddington Oval on Botany Bay. His officers and the Marine guard behind him, he was marching down the ramp to the vividly green grass. Against the pale blue sky he could see the tall, white flagstaffs, each with its rippling ensign, dark blue with the cruciform constellation of silver stars in the fly, with the superimposed red, white and blue crosses in the upper canton.

There was a band playing.

He was singing in time to the familiar tune:

> *Waltzing Matilda, Waltzing Matilda,*
> *You'll come a-waltzing Matilda with me . . .*

He awoke.

There was still that arythmic hammering, drifting in from somewhere outside—but the music, vastly amplified, almost drowned the mechanical racket.

Up jumped the swagman, sprang into the billabong,
"You'll never catch me alive!" cried he . . .

And what was this noisome billabong into which he, Grimes, had plunged? Would his ghost still be heard after he was gone from it? Would his memories of Deep Space and the ships plying the star lanes remain to haunt the swinish dreamers of Farhaven? Would that honest old

national song replace the phoney piety of the True
Followers' hymn?

Manna! he thought disgustedly, kicking out at a
dim-glowing mass. It splattered under his bare foot and the
stench was sickening. He was seized with an uncontrollable
spasm of nausea. Drained and shaken he stumbled toward
the cave entrance, the music luring him on as though he
were one of the Pied Piper's rats. He tripped over sleeping
bodies. A woman clutched his ankle. He looked down at
her. He could not be sure but he thought that she was the
one responsible for his original downfall. Almost he
brought his free foot smashing down on to her sleepily
smiling face but, at the last moment, desisted.

She was what she was, just as he was what he was—and
he had wallowed in the mire happily enough . . .

He stooped and with both hands gently disengaged her
fingers.

He staggered on, finally out onto the ledge. The sunlight
blinded him. Then at last he was able to see her, hanging
above the valley, beautiful and brightly golden, *The Far
Traveler*. It was from her that the music was blaring. It
ceased suddenly, was replaced by the amplified voice of
Big Sister.

"I am sending the pinnace for you, Captain Grimes. It
will come as closely alongside the cliff as possible. The
robots will help you aboard."

He waited there, naked and filthy and ashamed, until
the boat came for him.

Grimes—clean, clothed, depilated but still shaky—sat in the Baroness's salon telling his story. She listened in silence, as did the omnipresent Big Sister.

When he was finished Big Sister said, "I must make a further analysis of the fungus specimens. Drug addiction among human and other intelligent life forms is not unusual, of course, but the symbiotic aspects of this case intrigue me."

"And the dreams," said Grimes. "The dreams . . . I must have experienced the entire history of the Lost Colony . . ."

"For years," said Big Sister, "the fungus has been nourished by the waste products of the colonists' bodies—and when they have died it has been nourished by the bodies themselves. It has become, in some way that I have yet to discover, the colonists. Is there not an old saying: A man is what he eats? This could be true for other living beings. And the symbiosis has been more, much more, than merely physical. By eating the fungus you, for a while, entered into the symbiotic relationship."

"Very interesting," commented Grimes. "But you must have known what was happening to me, even if not why or how. You should have sent in the robots to drag me out by force."

"Command decisions are not my prerogative," said Big Sister smugly. "Her Excellency did suggest that I attempt a forcible rescue but I dissuaded her. It was a matter for humans only, for humans to resolve for themselves, essentially for a human of your sort to resolve for himself. I know very well, Captain Grimes, how you hate robots, how your dislike for me has prevented you from being properly grateful for your rescue from Commander Delamere's clutches." There was a brief, almost human chuckle. "I did think that Her Excellency would be able to recapture you by the use of a *very* human bait, but her attempt was not successful . . ."

Grimes looked at the Baroness, remembering her as he had seen her. His ears burned as he flushed miserably. If she were embarrassed by her own memory of the occasion she did not show it.

"So," went on Big Sister, "I made use of what I have learned of your peculiar psychology—your professional pride, your rather childish nationalism, your very real love of ships." She paused, then said, "A man who loves ships can't be all bad."

"A man," said the Baroness coldly, "who could refuse what *I* offered can't be all man."

He said, "I am sorry. I am truly sorry. But I was under the influence of the . . . manna . . ."

She said, *"In vino veritas,* Captain Grimes. And worst of all is the knowledge that the cacophony of a ship's engines, the trite music of a folksong about an Australian sheep stealer, succeeded where *I* failed. I will tell you now that I had intended that a relationship—not permanent but mutually satisfying—would develop between us. There is little likelihood now that this will come to pass. Our relations will remain as they have been since I first engaged you, those between employer and employee."

She turned away from Grimes, addressed the playmaster, 'Take us up, Big Sister, up and away from this planet. I prefer not to remain on a world where I was unable successfully to compete with drug sodden degenerates or with an unhuman electronic intelligence."

Grimes wondered if Big Sister was feeling as resentful as he was himself. Probably not, he thought. Nonhuman electronic intelligences must surely be unemotional.

᠉«Chapter 22»᠉

So *The Far Traveler* lifted from Farhaven, with Grimes
far less in actual command of the vessel than he ever had
been, proceeding in the general direction of the
Shakespearian Sector, out toward the rim of the galaxy.

It was quite a while before the after effects of the drug
wore off and until they did so Grimes was treated as a
convalescent. It was during this period that he noticed a
subtle change in Big Sister's attitude toward him. He had,
almost from the start, envisaged her as a bossy, hard-
featured woman, hating and despising men. Now the
imaginary flesh with which he clothed the electronic
intelligence was that of an aunt whom, during his childhood,
he had liked rather than loved, feared slightly, obeyed (for
most of the time) during a period when his parents, away
traveling, had left him in her charge. He recalled the
unsuspected soft side of her nature which she had exhibited
when he had been confined to his bed for some days after
he had made a crash landing in the hot-air balloon that he

had constructed himself, suffering two broken ribs and a fractured ankle.

She had pampered him then, just as Big Sister was pampering him now (and as the Baroness most certainly was not). Nonetheless, a year or so later, he had been very surprised when this aunt had embarked upon a whirlwind romance with a Dog Star Line second mate who was enjoying a spell of shore leave on Earth, returning with this spaceman to his home world. (Now, he thought, remembering, he would not have been surprised. As a child he had regarded the lady as a dragon but she had been the sort of tall, lean auburn-haired woman that the adult Grimes always fell for.)

Much as Big Sister reminded him of this aunt, thought Grimes, he could not imagine her eloping with anybody or anything. He supposed that, having saved him, she regarded herself as being responsible for him.

Eventually, when Big Sister decided that he was functioning as well as he ever would function, he was bidden to the Baroness's presence.

The lady said, "I am informed that I once again can enjoy the services of my yachtmaster. Can you, out of your long and wide experience in the Survey Service, suggest our next port of call?"

He thought hard then said doubtfully, "Kinsolving?"

"Kinsolving," she stated, "is not a Lost Colony." (She must have been having a good rummage in Big Sister's memory bank.) "It is one of the Rim Worlds. For some reason the colony was abandoned. There are now no people there at all. The object of my research, as well you know, is social evolution in the Lost Colonies. How can there be social evolution when there is nobody to evolve?"

Grimes tried not to sigh too audibly. He was never at home in this lushly appointed Owner's Suite or in the comic opera uniform that he was obliged to wear during these audiences. He would have been far happier in his own quarters. At least there he could smoke his pipe in peace. But his employer did not approve of smoking. Fortunately she did not disapprove of the use of drugs other than tobacco, such as alcohol—and, Grimes was bound to admit, her robot butler mixed a superb dry martini. He was appreciating the one that he was sipping; Big Sister had at last given him permission to drink again.

He looked at her over the frosted rim of his glass. She was reclining gracefully on her *chaise longue*, looking (as always) like a rather superior version of Goya's *Maja*. She looked at him very coldly. He realized that the top tunic button of his gold and purple livery was undone. He did it up.

She said, "You aren't much use, Captain, are you? I thought, in my girlish innocence, that an ex-Commander of the Interstellar Federation's Survey Service would have been the ideal captain for an expedition such as this. I know that you, before you resigned your commission, discovered at least three Lost Colonies. There were New Sparta and Morrowvia, both of which we shall, eventually, be visiting. And there was, of course, Botany Bay. With reference to the first two worlds it will be interesting to see what effects your clumsy meddlings have had upon the lives of the unspoiled peoples of those planets . . ."

Grimes was acutely conscious of the burning flush that

suffused his prominent ears. He, personally, would hardly have classed either the New Spartans or the Morrowvians as unspoiled—and New Sparta had been on the brink of a devastating civil war at the time of his landing. As for Morrowvia—he had not been the only interfering outsider. There had been the Dog Star Line's Captain Danzellan, looking after the commercial interests of his principals. There had been the piratical Drongo Kane in his own *Southerly Buster*, looking after his own interests.

"And didn't you enjoy a liaison with one of the local rulers on Morrowvia?" continued the Baroness. "I find it hard to understand—but then, I have never been enamored of cats."

Maya, remembered Grimes. *Feline ancestry but very much a woman—not like this cold, rich bitch* . . . Then he hated himself for the uncharitable thought. He owed the Baroness much. Had it not been for her intervention he would have been called back to Lindisfarne to stand trial. And to have done what she had done in that vile cave on Farhaven must have required considerable resolution. He could hardly blame her for blaming him for the failure of that second rescue attempt.

Nonetheless he said, with some indignation, "I was under the impression, Your Excellency, that my full and frank report on the happenings on Morrowvia was not to be released to the general public."

"I am not the general public," she said. "Money, Captain Grimes, is the key that will open the door to any vault in the Galaxy. Your friend, Commander Delamere, was, I think, more impressed by my wealth than my beauty. There are many others like him."

Grimes missed the chance of saying something gallant.

"Your Excellency, may I interrupt?" asked Big Sister, her voice coming from everywhere and nowhere.

"You have already interrupted," said the Baroness. "But continue."

"Your Excellency, I have monitored Carlotti transmissions from the Admiralty, on Earth, to all Survey Service ships and bases . . ."

Have you! thought Grimes. *Restricted wavebands, unbreakable codes . . . And what are they against the power of money!*

"A distress message capsule was picked up off Lentimure by the Survey Service destroyer *Acrux*. It originated from a ship called *Lode Ranger*. Text is as follows: Pile dead. Proceeding under diesel power. Intend landing on apparently habitable planet . . ."

There was more—a listing of crew and passengers, what astronomical data might just possibly be of use to future rescuers. In very few cases, Grimes knew, was such information of any value—but a modern computer, given the elements of a capsule's trajectory, could determine with some accuracy its departure point. And then the rescue ship, arriving a few centuries after the call for assistance, would find either a thriving Lost Colony or, after a search, the eroded wreckage of the lost ship and, possibly, a few human skeletons.

Grimes asked, "Do you have the coordinates of the departure point?"

Big Sister replied, "Apparently they are yet to be determined, Captain. As soon as they are transmitted by the Admiralty I shall inform you."

The Baroness said, "It just could happen that we shall be the nearest ship to the Lost Colony. It would be interesting to make the first landing upon such a world, before the clumsy boots of oafish spacemen have trampled all sorts of valuable evidence into the dust."

Grimes said, "Probably the Lost Colony, if there is one, is halfway across the Galaxy from here."

She said, "You are unduly pessimistic, Captain. Never forget that chance plays a great part in human life. And now, while we are waiting, could you refresh my memory regarding the gaussjammers and how it was that so many of them originated Lost Colonies?"

You probably know more about it than I do, thought Grimes. *After all, it's you that's writing the thesis.*

He said, "The gaussjammers, using the Ehrenhaft Drive, were the ships of the Second Expansion. Prior to them were the so-called Deep Freeze ships which, of course, were not faster than light. The gaussjammers, though, were FTL. With the Ehrenhaft generators in operation they were, essentially, huge monopoles. They tried to be in two places at once along a line of magnetic force, proceeding along such tramlines to their destinations. They were extremely vulnerable to magnetic storms; a really severe one could fling them thousands of light-years off course. There was another effect, too. The micro-piles upon which they relied for power would be drained of all energy. The captain of a gaussjammer lost in space, his pile dead, had only one course of action open to him. He used his emergency diesels to power the Ehrenhaft generators. He proceeded in what he hoped would be the right direction. When he ran out of diesel fuel his biochemist would convert what should have been food for the ship's company into more fuel.

"Finally, if he was lucky, he found a planet before food and fuel ran out. If his luck still held he managed to land in one piece. And then, if conditions were not too impossible, he and his people stood a fair chance of founding a Lost Colony."

Big Sister spoke again. "I have intercepted and decoded more signals. I estimate that we can be in orbit about *Lode Ranger*'s planet no more than ten standard days from now. As far as I can ascertain there are no Survey Service vessels in our vicinity; it is a reasonable assumption that we shall make the first landing. Have I your permission to adjust trajectory?"

"Of course," said the Baroness. "Adjust trajectory as soon as the captain and myself are in our couches."

"I should be in the control room," said Grimes.

"Is that really necessary?" asked the Baroness.

Big Sister adjusted trajectory, shutting down inertial drive and Mannschenn Drive, using the directional gyroscopes to swing the ship about her axes, lining her up on the target star. Grimes, sweating it out in his bunk, did not doubt that due and proper allowance was being made for galactic drift. He was obliged to admit that Big Sister could do everything that he could do, and at least as well—but *he* should have been doing it (That aunt of his who had run away with the Sirian spaceman had annoyed the young Grimes more than once by doing the things that he thought that he should have been doing.) He listened to the cold yet not altogether mechanical voice making the routine announcements: "Stopping inertial drive. Stand by for free fall . . . Mannschenn Drive—*off.*" There was the usual sensation of spatial and temporal disorientation. "Directional gyroscopes—*on.* Prepare for centrifugal effects . . . Directional gyroscopes—*off.* Mannschenn Drive—restarting." And the low hum, rising to a thin, high whine as the spinning rotors built up speed, precessing, tumbling down the dark dimensions . . . And the colors, sagging down the spectrum, and the distorted, warped perspective . . . And, as often happened, the transitory flash of déjà vu . . . This was happening now, had happened before, would happen again but . . . differently. In some other Universe, on a previous coil of time—or, perhaps, on a coil of time yet to be experienced—he had married the Princess Marlene, the father of whose sons he was, on El Dorado, had been accepted by the aristocratic and opulent inhabitants of that planet as one of the family, a member of the club and, eventually, using his wife's money, had caused the spaceyacht, *The Far Traveler,* to be built to his own specifications. He was both Owner and Master. He was—but briefly, briefly, in that alternate universe—a truly contented man.

And then outlines ceased to waver, colors to fade, intensify and shift, and he was . . . himself.

He was John Grimes, disgraced ex-Commander, late of the Federation's Survey Service, Master *de jure* but not *de facto* of a ship that was no more—or was she more, much more, but not in any way that conceivably could benefit him?—than the glittering toy of an overly rich, discontented woman.

"On trajectory," said Big Sister, "for *Lode Ranger*'s planet. Normal routine may be resumed."

"I am coming up to Control," said Grimes.

"You may come up to Control," said Big Sister, making it sound as though she was granting a great favor.

»«(Chapter 23)»«

The Far Traveler fell through the warped continuum toward the yellow sun on one of whose planets *Lode Ranger*'s people had found refuge. She was alone and lonely, with no traffic whatsoever within range of her mass proximity indicator. Distant Carlotti signals were monitored by Big Sister and, according to her, no ship was closer than the destroyer *Acrux*—and she was one helluva long way away.

Nonetheless Grimes was not happy. He said, "I know, Your Excellency, that with the advent of Carlotti Radio it is no longer mandatory to carry a Psionic Communications Officer—but I think that you should have shipped one."

"Have a prying telepath aboard my ship, Captain Grimes?" she flared. "Out of the question! It is bad enough being compelled by archaic legislation to employ a human yachtmaster."

Grimes sighed. He said, "As you know, PCOs are carried aboard all Survey Service vessels and in the ships of most other navies. They are required to observe the code of ethics formulated by the Rhine Institute. But today their function is not that of ship to ship or ship to planet communication. They are, primarily, a sort of psychic radar. How shall I put it? This way, perhaps. You're making a landing on a strange world. Are the natives likely to be friendly or hostile? Unless the indigenes' way of thinking is too alien your PCO will be able to come up with the answer. If *The Far Traveler* carried a PCO we should already have some sort of idea of what we shall find on *Lode Ranger*'s planet. Come to that, a PCO would have put us wise to the state of affairs on Farhaven and saved us from a degrading experience."

"I would prefer that you did not remind me of it," she said. "Meanwhile we shall just have to rely upon the highly efficient electronic equipment with which this ship is furnished."

She finished her drink. Grimes finished his. Obviously there was not going to be another.

She said, "Don't let me keep you from your dinner, Captain."

Grimes left her boudoir and went up to his own spartan—but only relatively so—quarters.

Not very long afterward *The Far Traveler* hung in orbit about *Lode Ranger*'s world. It was inhabited without doubt; the lights of cities could be seen through the murky atmosphere of the night hemisphere and on the daylit face were features too regular to be natural, almost certainly roads and railways and canals. And those people had radio; the spaceship's NST receivers picked up an unceasing stream of signals. There was music. There were talks.

But . . .

But the music bore no resemblance to anything composed by Terrans for Terran ears and the instruments were exclusively percussion. There were complex rhythms, frail, tinkling melodies, not displeasing but alien, alien . . .

And the voices . . .

Guttural croaks, strident squeals, speaking no language known to Grimes or the Baroness, no tongue included in Big Sister's fantastically comprehensive data bank.

But that wasn't all.

The active element of the planet's atmosphere was chlorine.

"There will be no Lost Colony here, Your Excellency," said Grimes. "*Lode Ranger*'s captain would never have landed once his spectroscopic analysis told him what to expect. He must have carried on."

"Even so," she said, "I have found a new world. I have ensured for myself a place in history." She smiled in self mockery. "For what it is worth. Now that we are here our task will be to carry out a preliminary survey."

"Do you intend to land, Your Excellency?" asked Big Sister.

"Of course."

"Then I must advise against it. You assumed, as did my builders, that my golden hull would be immune to corrosion. But somehow nobody took into account the possibility of a landing on a planet with a chlorine atmosphere. I have already detected traces of nitrohydrochloric acid which, I need hardly remind you, is a solvent for both gold and platinum."

"Only traces," said Grimes.

"Only traces, Captain," agreed Big Sister. "But would *you* care to run naked through a forest in which there might be pockets of dichlorethyl sulfide?"

Grimes looked blank.

"Mustard gas," said Big Sister.

"Oh," said Grimes.

The Baroness said, "I am rich, as you know. Nonetheless this ship is a considerable investment. I do not wish her shell plating to be corroded, thus detracting from her value."

"Yes, it would spoil her good looks," admitted Grimes. But the main function of a ship, any ship, is not to look pretty. He remembered that long-ago English admiral who had frowned upon gunnery practice because it discolored the gleaming paintwork of the warcraft under his command.

He asked, "Couldn't you devise some sort of protective coating? A spray-on plastic . . ."

Big Sister replied, "I have already done so. And, anticipating that you and Her Excellency would wish to make a landing, the smaller pinnace has been treated, also your spacesuits and six of the general purpose robots. Meanwhile I have processed the photographs taken during our circumpolar orbits and, if you will watch the playmaster, I shall exhibit one that seems of especial interest."

Grimes and the Baroness looked at the glowing screen. There—dull, battered, corroded but still, after all these many years, recognizable—was the pear-shaped hull of a typical gaussjammer. Not far from it was a dome, obviously not a natural feature of the terrain, possibly evidence that the survivors had endeavored to set up some sort of settlement in the hostile environment. A few kilometers to the north was a fair-sized town.

"Could they—or their descendants—still be living, Captain?" asked the Baroness.

"People have lived in similar domes, on Earth's airless moon, for many generations," said Grimes. "And the Selenites could always pack up and return to Earth if they didn't like it. *Lode Ranger*'s personnel had no place else to go."

"But . . . To live among aliens?"

"There are all sorts of odd enclaves throughout the Galaxy," said Grimes.

"Very well, Captain. We shall go down at once, to find what we shall find."

"Big Sister," asked Grimes, "assuming that we leave the ship now, what time of day will it be at the wreck when we land?"

"Late afternoon," was the reply.

"We should make a dawn landing," said Grimes.

"You are not in the Survey Service now, Captain," the Baroness told him. "You may as well forget Survey Service S.O.P."

"Those survivors—if there are any survivors—have waited for generations," said Grimes. "A few more hours won't hurt them."

"*I* am going down *now*," she told him. "You may come if you wish."

Grimes wished that he knew more about Space Law as applicable to civilian vessels. When is a captain not a captain? When he has his owner on board, presumably.

He said, "Shall we get into our spacesuits, Your Excellency? We shall need them if we leave the pinnace."

She said, "I will meet you in the boat bay, Captain."

⠀⟫⟪Chapter 24⟫⟪⠀

His robot stewardess helped him on with his spacesuit. The protective garment was no longer gold but, after the anti-corrosive spray, a dull, workmanlike grey. He preferred it in that color. He buckled on the belt with the two holstered pistols—one laser, one projectile. He checked the weapons to make sure they were models with firing studs instead of triggers, designed to be held in a heavily gauntleted hand. All was in order.

He went down to the boat bay. The Baroness was already there, clad as he was. Six of the general purpose robots were there. Golden, their asexual bodies had been beautiful; gray, they looked menacing, sinister. So did the pinnace.

"Should we get into trouble," said Grimes, speaking into his helmet microphone, "please come down for us." He could not resist adding, "If you get tarnished it will be just too bad."

"There was no need for that," said the Baroness.

Through the helmet phones her voice was even more coldly metallic than that of the computer-pilot.

"Understood," said Big Sister shortly.

"Robots into the boat," ordered Grimes.

The automata filed into and through the airlock.

"After you, Your Excellency."

The Baroness, looking not unlike a robot herself, boarded.

Grimes followed her, took his seat in the pilot's chair. The airlock doors closed before he could bring a finger to the appropriate button. If Big Sister insisted on doing the things that he was being paid to do, that was all right by him.

He said, "One kilometer from the wreck please revert to manual control. My control."

"Understood, Captain," said Big Sister.

"Must you dot every 'i' and cross every 't'?" asked the Baroness crossly.

The boat's inertial drive grumbled itself awake; the boat bay doors opened. Through the aperture glowed the sunlit hemisphere of *Lode Ranger*'s planet, a gigantic, clouded emerald. Then they were out and away from the ship, driving down rather than merely falling. Grimes kept his paws off the controls, although it required a considerable effort of will to refrain from touching them. Big Sister knew what she was doing, he told himself. He hoped.

Down they drove, down, down. The whispering of atmosphere along the hull became audible above the clatter of the inertial drive. There was no rise of cabin temperature although, thought Grimes, the cooling system must be working overtime. And, he told himself, the modified metal of which the pinnace was constructed had a far higher melting point than that of normal gold.

Down they drove, through high, green, wispy clouds.

Down they drove, and the land was spread out below them—mountain masses, seas, rivers, the long, straight line of a transcontinental railway, cities, forests . . .

Ahead of them and below something was flying. A bird? Grimes studied it through his binoculars, wondering how he had come to make such a gross underestimation of its size. It was a huge, delta-winged aircraft. It pursued its course steadily, ignoring the intruder from space. Probably its pilot did not know that there were strangers in his sky.

The radar altimeter was unwinding more slowly now. They were low enough to make out features of the landscape with the naked eye. Ahead of them was the town, the small city, its architecture obviously alien. The proportions of the buildings were all wrong by human standards and not one of the many towers was perpendicular; the truncated spires leaned toward and away from each other at drunken angles.

They swept over the town. Beyond it was the wreck of the ancient Terran spaceship and beyond that the discolored white dome. Through his binoculars Grimes could see spacesuited figures standing by the airlock of the vessel. *Men* in spacesuits? They had to be human; the natives would not require protective clothing on their own planet.

But what were they doing?

Fighting!

Yes, they were fighting—the spacemen and the near-naked, humanoid but far from human natives. It was hand to hand almost, at close range with pistols from the muzzles of which came flashes of bright flame. Oddly enough there seemed to be no casualties on either side.

Yet.

"We have come in the nick of time," said the Baroness. "If we had waited until local daybreak, as *you* suggested . . ."

There was a screwy lack of logic about what she was saying, about the entire situation. If *Lode Ranger* had just landed the situation would have made sense, but . . . The gaussjammer had not come down today, or yesterday, or the day before that.

"I relinquish control, Captain," came the voice of Big Sister. "You are now one kilometer from the wreck."

Grimes brought his gloved hands up to the console.

"*Do* something," ordered the Baroness. "There are people, humans, there, being murdered."

The pinnace was not armed. (If Grimes, man of peace as he claimed to be, had had any say in the building of *The Far Traveler* and her ancillary craft she would have been.) Even had she been fitted with weaponry Grimes would have been unable to fire into that melee with any degree of discrimination. All that he could do was to bring her in fast, fast and noisily. The combatants heard the rapidly approaching clangor; they would have had to have been stone deaf not to do so. They stopped fighting, looked up and around. Then they ran, all of them, human and autochthon. Together they fled, arms and legs pumping ludicrously, jostling each other at the open airlock door of the gaussjammer, scrambling for the safety of the interior of the old ship.

They were gone from sight, all of them, their dropped weapons, gleaming greenly in the light of the afternoon sun, littering the bare, sandy ground.

Grimes slammed the pinnace down hard at the foot of the ramp that protruded from the airlock door. With one hand he sealed his helmet, with the other he unsnapped his seat belt. Big Sister had already opened the inner airlock door. Two steps took him to the little chamber. The Baroness was with him. The inner door closed, the outer door opened. He jumped to the ground, pulling his pistols as he did so. She landed just behind him and then ran ahead.

"Hold it!" he called. "I'll send the robots in first to draw the fire. They're expendable."

"And you're not?" she asked coldly.

"Not if I can help it. And I'm not invulnerable either. Your tin soldiers are."

She admitted grudgingly that there was sense in what he said. They stood together, looking up at the huge, weathered hulk, the great, metallic peg top supported in an upright position by its landing struts. And what was happening inside the battered hull? he wondered. Were the survivors of the wreck—the descendants of the survivors, rather—and the natives still fighting hand to hand along the alleyways, through the public rooms? His helmet muffled external sounds but did not deafen *him* completely. He listened but could hear no cries, no gunfire.

The first two robots emerged from the pinnace's airlock. He told them to board the ship, not to fire unless fired upon, to use stunguns rather than laser pistols, their net-throwing blunderbusses in preference to either.

When the automata were aboard he followed, climbing the rickety, warped ramp with caution. It had been damaged, he noticed, and clumsily patched with some dissimilar metal. The repairing plates had been riveted, not welded.

"Are you brave enough to go in?" asked the Baroness when they reached the head of the gangway.

Grimes did not answer her. He joined the two robots who were standing in the airlock chamber. They were using their laser pistols, set to low intensity, as torches, shining the beams in through the open inner door.

Grimes used his chin to nudge the controls of his suit's external speaker to maximum amplification. "Ahoy!" he shouted. *"Lode Ranger!* Ahoy! This is the Survey Service! We're here to rescue you!"

"We are *not* the Survey Service," snapped the Baroness.

Grimes ignored her. "Ahoy!" he called again. *"Lode Ranger,* ahoy!"

He could imagine the sound of his amplified voice rolling up and along the spiral alleyway, the ramp that in these ships encircled the hull from tapered stern to blunt, dome-shaped bows inboard of the inner skin.

There was no reply.

He said, "All right, we're going in. We'll follow the ramp all the way to the control room. Two robots ahead, then ourselves, then two robots to cover our rear. The remaining two will guard the airlock."

They began to climb.

It was a far from silent progress. At one time the deck had been coated with a rubbery plastic but, over the long years, it had perished, its decomposition no doubt hastened by the chlorine-rich atmosphere. The feet of the marching robots set up a rhythmic clangor, the heavy boots of the man and the woman made their own contributions to the rolling reverberation. It would have been impossible not to have stepped in time to the metallic drumbeat.

Up and around they marched, up and around. The low intensity laser beams probed dark openings—cross alleyways, the entrances to cabins and machinery spaces and public rooms. There were streakings in the all-pervasive dust suggestive of footprints, of scufflings, but nothing was definite. On one bulkhead was a great stain, old and evil. It could have been no more than a careless spillage of paint in the distant past but Grimes sensed that somebody—or something—had died there, messily.

He called a halt.

"Now we can hear ourselves think," commented the Baroness.

"Now we can hear," he agreed.

And there were sounds, faint and furtive, that would have been faint even without the muffling effect of their helmets. They seemed to come from ahead, they seemed to come from inside the ancient hull. And within the archaic ship, Grimes knew, there would be a veritable maze of alleyways and companionways, shafts vertical and horizontal. The only hope of capturing either a native or a descendant of the *Lode Ranger* survivors would be if any of them tried to escape through the airlock door, where the two robots he had detailed for that duty were on guard.

One of those robots spoke now—or it may have been Big Sister who spoke.

"Ground cars are approaching from the city. I suggest that you retreat to the pinnace."

Grimes hated to leave a job half finished, less than half finished, hardly begun in fact. But to remain in the ship could well prove suicidal. Still he waited so he could call, one last time, *"Lode Ranger,* ahoy! We have come to rescue you! Follow us to our boat!"

And then, wasting no time, the boarding party ran rather than walked down to the airlock.

»((Chapter 25))((

Somebody had gotten there before them. Somebody had tried to break past the robot sentries and was now entangled in the metallic mesh cast by a net-throwing blunderbuss, was still struggling ineffectually. It was a man in an archaic spacesuit, an ugly looking pistol in his right hand. Fortunately he could not bring this weapon to bear.

"Easy, friend, easy," said Grimes. "It's all right. Tell us about it in the pinnace."

But the man could not hear him, of course. His helmet looked as though it would deaden exterior sounds even more effectively than the one that Grimes was wearing. If his suit were equipped with radio, and if that radio were still functioning, it would not be likely that the frequency to which it was tuned would be the one being used by the party from *The Far Traveler*.

"Don't hurt him," ordered Grimes. "Take him to the boat."

He looked toward the city, to the column of dust midway between town and ship, the fast-traveling cloud that did not quite conceal betraying glints of metal. The ground cars, obviously, that Big Sister had reported. And they were wasting no time, whoever and whatever they were. The sooner he was in the pinnace and up and away the better. He would return, better armed and better prepared—but that was in the future. This was *now*. This was strategic retreat from heavier forces, from an enemy who had already opened fire from his armored vehicles with large caliber projectile weapons. A shell burst just short of the pinnace, another to one side of it

"Run!" ordered Grimes.

The two robots with the prisoner between them broke into a gallop. Grimes and the Baroness followed, but less speedily. Spacesuits are not meant for running in. The other four robots brought up the rear.

The outer airlock door of the pinnace was already open. The leading robots and the struggling man passed through just before a shell landed on the boat itself.

"Hell!" exclaimed Grimes.

"Don't . . . worry . . ." panted the Baroness. "She . . can . . . take . . . it . . ."

The green smoke cleared and Grimes saw that the pinnace seemed to be undamaged, although bright gold gleamed where the protective plastic had been ripped away.

The next two rounds were wide and Grimes and the Baroness scrambled into the airlock during the brief lull. Another shell hit, however, as the last pair of robots were boarding. It was like, Grimes said later, being a bug inside a bass drum. But at the time he was not thinking up picturesque similes. He was getting upstairs, fast, before a chance projectile scored a hit on some vulnerable part of the pinnace. A similar craft in the Survey Service would have been fitted with armor shields for the viewpoints. This one was not. No doubt Big Sister would make good this omission but Grimes was more concerned with *now* than a possible future.

From his seat, as the boat lifted, he saw a squad of the reptilian humanoids jumping out of the leading, multi-wheeled land car. They carried weapons, firearms of some kind, took aim and delivered a ragged volley. It sounded like hail on a tin roof. The bullets were no more effective than the shells had been.

They went on firing after the pinnace was airborne and even when she was well aloft there was a sharp *ping* on her underside.

"Did you look at them?" demanded the Baroness. "Giants. At least twice as big as the ones we first saw!"

"We were lucky to get away," said Grimes. "So was our friend here—although he didn't seem to want to be rescued."

"The robots frightened him," she said. "To him they're monsters. . ."

"Big Sister," said Grimes. "Over to you. Get us back on board as soon as possible."

"I have control, Captain," came the reply from the transceiver.

Grimes released himself from his seat, went to the cabin at the rear of the pinnace. The Baroness accompanied him.

She whispered, "He's . . . dead . . ."

"Only fainted," said Grimes. Then, to the robots, "Get that net off him."

They looked down at the spacesuited man sprawled on the deck. Grimes sneezed suddenly; there was an irritating acridity in the air despite the efforts of the ventilating fans. He knelt by the still figure. He was amazed to find that the suit was made only from thin, coarsely woven cloth. But, he reasoned, for many years *Lode Ranger*'s people and their descendants must have had to make do with whatever materials came to hand. He looked at the ovate, opaque helmet, tried to see through the narrow, glazed vision slit to the face beneath.

But the slit was not glazed.

It was not glazed and there were other openings, approximately where ears and mouth are located on a human head. A dreadful suspicion was growing in his mind.

He took hold of the helmet with his two hands, gave it a half turn to the left. It resisted the twisting motion. He tried to turn it to the right. It still would not come free. So he just lifted it.

He stared down in horror at the big-domed, saurian head, at the dull, sightless, faceted eyes, at the thin-lipped mouth, twisted in a silent snarl, from which ropy slime still dribbled.

He heard the Baroness's gasp of horrified dismay.

He let the dead, ugly head drop to the deck, picked up the glittering, vicious looking pistol. The trigger guard was big enough for him to get his gloved forefinger into it.

"Don't!" the Baroness cried sharply.

He ignored her, pulled the trigger. A stream of bright but harmless sparks flashed from the muzzle of the gun.

"A toy . . ." she whispered. "But what . . .?"

He asked, "Did you ever, as a child, play cowboys and Indians, Your Excellency? No, I don't suppose you did. But you must have heard of the game. And that's what these . . . kids were playing. But they'd call the game invaders and people or something like that, with the invaders as the baddies. Just a re-enactment of a small battle, but quite an important battle, many, many years ago. Goodies versus baddies. The goodies won. There were no *Lode Ranger* survivors."

"But that wasn't a make-believe battle that *we* ran away from," she said.

"It wasn't," he agreed. "It could be that after *Lode Ranger*'s landing—and the massacre—some sort of defense force was set up in case any more hostile aliens came blundering in. Possibly drills every so often." He laughed without humor. "It must have given the officer responsible quite a turn when our pinnace came clattering over, making straight for the old *Lode Ranger*. The real thing at last . . ."

He looked up at the Baroness. He was amazed to see that she was weeping; her helmet, unlike the native's make-believe one, could not hide her expression or the bright tears coursing down her cheeks.

"Just a child . . ." she said. "Just a child, whose exciting, traditional game turned terrifyingly real . . ."

And so, thought Grimes, rather hating himself for the ironic flippancy, *another redskin bit the dust.*

At least he had the grace not to say it aloud.

))((Chapter 26))((

A report was made to the Admiralty about the happenings on *Lode Ranger*'s planet. The Baroness had not wished to send one but, rather surprisingly, Big Sister supported Grimes on this issue. The Admiralty was not at all pleased and sent a terse message ordering *The Far Traveler* to leave any future explorations of the world to the personnel, far better equipped and qualified, of the destroyer *Acrux*.

The Baroness finally decided to make the best of the situation. "After all," she said to Grimes, "it is only Lost Colonies in which I am interested. Morrowvia, for example. What has happened on that world since you—and, I admit, others—tried to drag the happy colonists into the mainstream of galactic civilization? And now," she went on sweetly, too sweetly, "we shall refresh your memory, Captain Grimes."

Grimes regarded his employer apprehensively over the rim of his teacup. She always made a ritual of afternoon tea and almost invariably, even when he was in the dog-house, he was invited (commanded?) to her salon to share this minor feast. It was all done in considerable style, he was bound to admit—the fragrant infusion poured from the golden pot by the robot butler into gold-chased eggshell china, the paper-thin cucumber sandwiches, the delicious, insubstantial pastries . . . Sometimes on these daily occasions she was graciously charming; other times she seemed to delight in making her yachtmaster squirm. Always she was the aristocrat. She was the aristocrat and Grimes was the yokel in uniform.

He looked at her reclining gracefully on her *chaise longue*, wearing the usual filmy white gown that, tantalizingly, neither fully revealed nor fully concealed. Her wide, full mouth was curved in a smile—a malicious smile, Grimes decided; this was going to be what he had categorized as a squirm session. Her eyes—they were definitely green today—stared at him disdainfully.

She said, "As you already know, Captain, I was able to obtain recordings, of various occasions from the archives of the Federation Survey Service. Or, to be more exact, Commander Delamere had those records aboard his ship and allowed me, for a consideration, to have copies taken."

He thought, *What can't you buy, you rich bitch!*

She went on, "This one is audio tape only. Recorded in the captain's cabin aboard one of the Survey Service's minor vessels some years ago. I wonder if you will recognize it . . ." She lifted a slim, languorous yet imperious arm. "Big Sister, the *Seeker* recordings, please."

"Certainly, Your Excellency," replied the computer-pilot. The screen of the big playmaster lit up but there was no picture, only glowing words and symbols:

SEEKER
1473/18.5
ETHOLOGY NTK=
RESTRICTED AO

For four ringers only, thought Grimes. *Not to be heard outside the sacred precincts of the Archives . . . How the hell did Frankie get his dirty paws on this?*

From the speaker of the ornate instrument came a voice, a woman's voice, familiar. *Maggie . . .* Grimes thought. He wondered where she was now, what she was doing, whom she was doing it with. He regretted, not for the first time, his resignation from the Survey Service. He had his enemies in the Space Navy of the Federation but he'd had his friends, good ones, and Maggie Lazenby— Commander Margaret Lazenby of the Scientific Branch—had been the best of them.

She had been more than just a friend.

He recalled the occasion vividly as he listened to her talking. She was telling Grimes, the Dog Star Line's Captain Danzellan and Captain Drongo Kane of the *Southerly Buster* what she had been able to learn of the origins of the Lost Colony on Morrowvia. It had been founded during the Second Expansion. A gaussjammer, the emigrant ship *Lode Cougar,* had been driven off trajectory by a magnetic storm, had been flung into a then unexplored sector of the galaxy. By the time that a habitable planet was blundered upon there had been starvation, mutiny, even cannibalism. There had been a crash landing with very few survivors—but, nonetheless, this handful of men and women possessed the wherewithal to start a

colony from scratch. Aboard *Lode Cougar* had been
stocks of fertilized ova, animal as well as human. (Dogs
had been required on Austral, the world to which the ship
originally had been bound, and cats, both to keep the
indigenous vermin under control.

"With those very few survivors," Maggie had said, "a
colony could still have been founded and might well have
endured and flourished. There were ten men—nine of
them, including Morrow, passengers, the other a junior
engineer. There were six women, four of them young.
Then Morrow persuaded his companions that they would
have a far better chance of getting established if they had
underpeople to work for them. It seems that the only ova
suitable to his requirements were those of cats. The
others did not query this; after all, he was an experienced
and qualified genetic engineer. With the aid of the ship's
artificer he set up his incubators and then—everything
that he needed he found in the ship's cargo—a fully
equipped laboratory. Before the diesel fuel ran out he was
getting ample power from a solar energy converter and
from a wind driven generator . . .

"I quote from Dr. Morrow's journal: The first batch is
progressing nicely in spite of the accelerated maturation.
I feel . . . paternal. I ask myself why should these, my
children, be underpeople? I can make them more truly
human than the hairless apes that infest so many worlds,
that may, one day, infest this one . . ."

So it went on, Maggie still reading from Dr. Morrow's
diary, telling of the deaths of the *Lode Cougar* survivors.
Although Morrow admitted nothing in writing it seemed
probable that these were not accidental. Mary Little, Sarah

Grant and Delia James succumbed to food poisoning. Douglas Carrick fell off a cliff. Susan Pettifer and William Hume were drowned in the river. The others, apparently, drank themselves to death after Morrow set up a still.

"There was something of the Pygmalion in Morrow," went on that long ago Maggie. "He fell in love with one of his own creations, his Galatea. He even named her Galatea . . ."

"And he married her," said a strange male voice that Grimes, with something of a shock, realized was his own. "He married her, and the union was fertile. According to Interstellar Law any people capable of fertile union with true people must themselves be considered true people. So, Captain Kane, that puts an end to your idea of setting up a nice, profitable slave trade."

Drongo Kane's voice—Grimes had no difficulty in recognizing it, even after all this time—broke in. "Don't tell me that you believe those records! Morrow was just kidding himself when he wrote them. How many glorified tom cats were sneaking into his wife's or his popsies' beds while his back was turned?"

There was an older, heavier male voice, the Dog Star Line's Captain Danzellan. "I was the first to land on this planet, Captain Kane, quite by chance. I found that the natives were . . . friendly. My Second Officer—among others—did some tom catting around himself and, if I may be permitted the use of an archaic euphemism, got the daughter of the Queen of Melbourne into trouble. The young idiot should have taken his contraceptive shots before he started dipping his wick, but he didn't think that it would be necessary. And then, just to make matters worse, he fell in love with the wench. He contrived, somehow, to get himself appointed to *Schnauzer* for my second voyage here. Now he wants to make an honest woman of the girl. Her mother, however, refuses to sanction the marriage until he becomes a Morrowvian citizen and changes his name to Morrow. As a matter of fact it all rather ties in with Company policy. The Dog Star Line will want a resident manager here—and a prince consort will be ideal for the job. Even though the queenships are not hereditary in theory they usually are in practice. And Tabitha—that's her name—is next in line."

Again Kane's voice, "What are you driveling about?"

And Danzellan, stiffly, "Tabitha has presented young Delamere with a son."

The Baroness raised her hand and the playmaster fell silent. "Delamere?" she asked. "But surely he's captain of the destroyer *Vega*."

"The Odd Gods of the Galaxy did not create that name for Handsome Frankie alone, Your Excellency," said Grimes. "But, as a matter of fact, *that* Delamere, the one on Morrowvia, is one of Frankie's distant cousins. Like Frankie, he uses women to rise in the universe. Frankie has his plain, fat admiral's daughter—which is why he's gotten as high as he has. There'll be other women, carefully selected, and Frankie'll make admiral yet. Come to that, that Dog Star Line second mate hasn't done badly either, using similar methods. Resident manager on Morrowvia *and* a prince consort . . ."

"And they say that women are jealous cats . . ." murmured the Baroness. Then, "Continue, Big Sister."

Kane's voice issued from the playmaster. "And how many local boyfriends has *she* had?"

"She says," stated Danzellan, "that she has had none. Furthermore, I have seen the baby. All the Morrowvians have short noses—except this one. He has a long nose, like his father. The resemblance is quite remarkable."

"Did Mr. Delamere and his family come with you, Captain Danzellan?" asked Grimes. "Call them up, and we'll wet the baby's head!"

And Kane exclaimed, "You can break the bottle of champagne over it if you want to!"

The Baroness laughed as she raised her hand. She said, "Quite an interesting character, this Captain Kane. A rogue, obviously, but . . ."

"Mphm," grunted Grimes.

"According to the Survey Service records," she went on, "your own conduct on Morrowvia was such that you were accused later, by Captain Kane, of partisanship. You had an affair with one of the local rulers . . ."

Grimes' prominent ears felt as though they were about to burst into flame. "Yes," he admitted.

"Tell me," she pressed, "what was it like?"

"All cats are gray in the dark," he said.

⟫⟪Chapter 27⟫⟪

The Far Traveler came to Morrowvia.

This world, hopefully, would provide material for at least a couple of chapters of the Baroness's doctorial thesis. Morrowvia, at the time of its rediscovery, had been an unspoiled world, almost Edenic. Then it had been developed by the Dog Star Line as a tourist resort. Grimes was apprehensive as well as curious. He had liked the planet the way it had been. What would it be like now?

Big Sister was supplying some answers. As the yacht approached her destination, the Mannschenn Drive was shut down at intervals, with a consequent return to the normal continuum, so that a sampling could be made of the commercial and entertainment programs emanating from the planet. These were interesting.

The major continent, North Australia, was now one huge tourist trap with luxury hotels, gambling casinos, emporia peddling native artifacts (most of them, Grimes suspected, manufactured on Llirith, a world whose saurian people made a good living by turning out trashy souvenirs to order), Bunny Clubs (here, of course, called Pussy Clubs) and the like. The screen of the Baroness's playmaster glowed and flickered with gaudy pictures of beach resorts and of villages of holiday chalets in the mountain country, with performances of allegedly native dances obviously choreographed by Terrans for Terrans.

And then a once-familiar voice spoke from the instrument and looking out from the screen was a once-familiar face. Her hair was a lustrous, snowy white, her gleaming skin dark brown, the lips of her generous mouth a glistening scarlet. Her eyes were a peculiar greenish yellow and the tips of her small ears were oddly pointed. The cheekbones were prominent, more so than the firm chin. Grimes' regard shifted downward. She was naked, he saw (and as he remembered her). Beneath each breast was a rudimentary nipple. He recalled how when he had first seen her that detail had intrigued him.

She said seductively, purring almost, "Are you tired of the bright lights, the ceaseless round of organized gaiety? Will you finish your vacation more tired than when you started it? Then why not come to Cambridge to relax, to live the natural way, as *we* lived before the coming of the Earthmen? Share with us our simple pleasures—the hunting of the deer in our forests, the fishing for the great salmon in the clear waters of our rivers . . ."

And neither deer nor salmon, Grimes remembered, bore much resemblance to the deer and salmon of Earth or, even, to those creatures as they had mutated on the other worlds into which they had been introduced. Old Morrow must have been a homesick man; his planet abounded with Terran place names, bestowed by himself, and indigenous animals had been called after their nearest (and not often very near) Earthly counterparts.

"Come to Cambridge," went on the low, alluring voice. "You will not regret it. Come to Cambridge and live for awhile in the rosy dawn of human history. And it will cost you so very little. For two full weeks, with accommodation and food and hunting and fishing trips, the charge for a single adult is a mere one thousand credits. There are special terms for family parties . . ."

She smiled ravishingly. Her teeth were very white between the red lips, in the brown face.

"Please come. I am looking forward so very much to meeting you . . ."

She faded from the screen, was replaced by an advertisement for the Ballarat Casino where, at the time of this broadcast, the imported entertainer Estella di Scorpio had been the star attraction. The Baroness looked and listened briefly then made a sharp gesture. Big Sister cut the sound.

"A friend of yours, Captain Grimes?" asked his employer. "You were looking at her like a lovesick puppy."

"Estella di Scorpio? No, Your Excellency. I don't know the lady, nor do I much want to."

"Not her, Captain. The . . . er . . . lady before her. That indubitably mammalian female."

"That was Maya," he told her. "The Queen of Cambridge."

"A *queen*, advertising a holiday camp?"

"She's no more than a mayor, really, Your Excellency. Cambridge is—or was when I was there—just a little town."

She said, "I think that we shall land at this Cambridge rather than at the Melbourne spaceport. After all, you have landed there before in *Seeker*."

"Things were different then, Your Excellency," he told her. "There was no Aerospace Control. There were no rules and regulations. We just looked around for a reasonably clear and flat patch of ground, then sat down on it. But now we shall have to use the spaceport to get our Inward Clearance from the authorities."

"Shall we?" she asked. "Shall we?"

))((Chapter 28))((

Money talks.

Money talked over the Carlotti Communications System as *The Far Traveler* closed Morrowvia at a multiple of the speed of light. The planet was, to all intents and purposes, a Dog Star Line dependency, its officials, Dog Star Line appointees. The Baroness was a major shareholder in that company. Radio Pratique was granted. Customs and Immigration formalities were waived. Permission was accorded to Grimes to bring the ship down in the close vicinity of Cambridge.

Big Sister let him handle the landing, conceding that in these circumstances his local knowledge would be useful. He brought *The Far Traveler* down through the clear morning air toward an expanse of level ground, devoid of obstructions, that was almost an island, bounded to north, west and south by a winding river, to the east by a wooded hill. To the north and to the west of this eminence there were large villages, each with a sparse sprinkling of pale

849

lights still visible in the brightening dawn. When he had come here before, Grimes recalled, the settlements had been smaller and the lights had been dim and yellow, from oil lamps. Now, obviously, there was electricity. And those latticework masts were new, too. Radio antennae? Possibly, although at least one of them looked heavy enough to afford mooring facilities to an airship.

Sunrise came at ground level and the horizontal rays cast long, dark shadows, showing up every slightest irregularity in the terrain, every hump and hollow, every outcropping of rock, every bush. Grimes applied lateral thrust, bringing the yacht directly above a patch of green that, from the air, looked perfectly smooth. It was. When he set *The Far Traveler* down gently in the middle of it she quivered ever so slightly as the shock absorbers took the strain, then was still.

"A nice landing, Captain," remarked Big Sister, not at all condescendingly. Grimes remembered how the electronic entity had messed up his landing on Farhaven. But later, on that world, she had saved him and seemed, as a consequence, somehow to have adopted him.

But the Baroness had not. She said disparagingly, "But, of course, you have been here before."

Grimes was sulkily silent. He rang Finished With Engines. Then he took an all around look through the viewports. He said, "It looks like the reception committee approaching, Your Excellency."

"How boring," commented the Baroness. She stifled a yawn. "They must be indecently early risers here."

"The noise of our inertial drive will have awakened them," said Grimes.

"Possibly." She sounded very uninterested. "Go down to the airlock to receive them. You may invite them aboard—to *your* quarters. No doubt they are old friends of yours and will have much to talk about."

Grimes left the control room. He was glad that the Baroness had not ordered him to change from his comfortable shirt and shorts into formal rig; only the purple, gold-braided shoulderboards were badges of his servitude. Both airlock doors were open when he got down to the stern. He stepped out and stood at the head of the ramp, savoring the fresh air with its scent of flowers, of dew on grass, and the warmth of the early sun. He looked to the west, to the direction from which he had seen the party approaching.

There was a woman in the lead—tall, dark-skinned, white-haired, moving with feline grace. He recognized her at once. She had hardly changed. (Old age when it came to the Morrowvians came suddenly and Maya was far from old.) A man strode beside her. Although he was naked, as were all the others, he was obviously not a native. He was far too heavily built and moved with relative clumsiness. A great mane of yellow hair fell to his broad, deeply tanned shoulders and a bushy yellow beard mingled with the almost as luxuriant growth on his chest. He was carrying a slender, ceremonial spear but looked as though he should have been hefting a heavy club.

The man, the woman (the queen, Maya) and the six archers, slender Dianas, and the half dozen of spearmen . . . Short-haired, all of them (with the exception of the Terran), with similitudes to fur skullcaps on their heads— black, brindle, tortoiseshell—and sharply defined pubic puffs. Grimes walked slowly down the golden ramp to meet them.

Maya stared up at him incredulously.

"John! After all these years! If I had known that you were coming back I would have waited . . ." The blond giant scowled. "But this is . . . fantastic! First Captain Kane, and now you . . ."

"Drongo Kane?" demanded Grimes. *"Here!"*

"Never mind him, John. *You* are here, captain of a fine, golden ship . . ."

"Owned," said Maya's male companion drily, "by her self-styled Excellency, the Baroness Michelle d'Estang. And *you* are the John Grimes that my wife's always talking about? I thought that you were in the Survey Service, not a yacht skipper."

"I *was* in the Survey Service," admitted Grimes. "But . . . I don't think that I have the pleasure . . ."

The man laughed. "You can call me Your Highness if you feel like it; I'm Maya's Prince Consort *and* Manager of Simple Life Holidays. I'm Bill to my friends, Bill Smith, just another Dog Star Line boy who's found a fine kennel for himself. Mind you, I haven't done as well as Swanky Frankie in Melbourne—but I'm not complaining."

He extended a meaty hand. Grimes shook it.

"John . . ." mewed Maya plaintively.

He shook her hand. She conveyed the strong impression that she would have preferred him to have kissed her— but Bill Smith was watching and so would be, he knew, Big Sister and the Baroness.

He said, "Will you come aboard for some refreshment?

I'm afraid I can't ask all of you; my accommodation's not all that commodious . . ."

"Have one of your hunks bring some dishes of ice cream out for the boys and girls," Bill Smith told him. "Maya an' I'll inflict ourselves on you." He looked down at himself. "I hope you an' the Baroness don't mind the way I'm dressed—but it's the rig of the day for my job. Both my jobs."

Grimes led the way up the gangway, then to his day cabin. He was glad that *The Far Traveler* did not have a human crew. From his past experience he had learned that some spacemen and women took naturist planets such as Arcadia—and now Morrowvia—in their stride, happily doing in Rome as the Romans did, while others were openly condemnatory or tried to hide their embarrassment by crudely obscene jokes. His robot stewardess, of course, was not at all perturbed by the nudity of his guests— although she, to them, was a source of wonderment. She brought coffee and pastries for the two men, a golden dish of ice cream for Maya. (It had been the first off-planet delicacy that she had enjoyed and she still loved it.) Grimes sent a general purpose robot to take care of Maya's entourage, then settled down to talk.

"Drongo Kane?" he asked without preamble. "What's he doing back here?"

Before either Maya or her husband could answer, the voice of Big Sister came from the playmaster. "I have been in communication with Melbourne Port Control. Captain Kane's ship, *Southerly Buster*, has been berthed there for five weeks, local time. Captain Kane left Melbourne thirty days ago in one of his ship's boats, taking with him ten of his passengers, seven men and three women. The ostensible purpose of the trip was a tour of England. No doubt your friends in Cambridge, whom you are now entertaining, will be able to give you further information."

"Was that your boss?" asked Bill Smith interestedly.

"No," replied Grimes, rather wondering with what degree of truth. "That was not Her Excellency. That was the ship's pilot-computer. We call her Big Sister."

"Haw! Big Sister is watching, eh? You'd better keep your paws off Maya!"

"I don't think," said Grimes stiffly, "that Big Sister is concerned about my morals. But what do you know about Drongo Kane?"

"You tangled with him when you were here last, didn't you? Maya's told me all about it. But he's a reformed character now. He's muscled in on the tourist racket—but one ship, and that not a very big one, won't worry the Dog Star Line. As long as he pays his port charges and as long as his passengers blow their money in the tourist traps he's as welcome as the day is long. He was here . . ."

"Only three days," supplied Maya. "Then he flew off, up river, to Stratford." She pouted. "I don't know what he will find there to interest him. Anne—the Queen of Stratford is always called Anne; I wonder why—is more determined to keep to the old ways than any of the rest of us. She will not allow electricity or radio or *anything* in her city." She smiled smugly. "*We,* of course, realize that tourists, even when enjoying a Simple Life Holiday, appreciate the little comforts, such as refrigeration and television, to which they are used."

"You appreciate them yourself," said Bill Smith.

"I do," she admitted. "But never mind Captain Kane, John. Tell us about *you*." she smiled appealingly. "And while we are talking I will have some more of your delicious ice cream."

"And would there be any gin?" asked the Prince Consort hopefully.

There was.

))«Chapter 29»«

"This Stratford," said the Baroness, "sounds as though it might be interesting."

"In what way, Your Excellency?" asked Grimes.

"Unspoiled . . ."

"It won't stay that way long if Drongo Kane is there," Grimes said.

"You are prejudiced, Captain."

She took a dainty sip from her teacup. Grimes took a gulp from his. He badly needed something refreshing but nonalcoholic. It would have been bad manners to let his guests drink alone and he had taken too much for the neutralizer capsules to have their usual immediate effect.

"Unspoiled," she said again. "This world the way it was before you and those others blundered in. The Social Evolution of a Lost Colony taking its natural course. If we leave now we shall arrive at Stratford before dark."

"There is the party tonight, Your Excellency," Grimes reminded her. "After all, Maya is a reigning monarch."

"The petty mayor of a petty city-state," she sneered. "But do not worry. I have already sent my sincere apologies for not being able to attend. But I can just imagine what that party will be like! Drunken tourists going native and lolloping around in disgusting, self-conscious nudity. Imitation Hawaiian music played on 'native' guitars imported from Llirith. Imitation Israeli *horas*. Meat charred to ruination over open fires. Cheap gin tarted up with fruit juices—probably synthetic—and served as genuine Morrowvian toddy . . ." She smiled nastily. "Come to that—*you* have already had too much to drink. Big Sister will be able to handle the pinnace by remote control while you sleep it off in the cabin."

"The pinnace?" asked Grimes stupidly.

"You, Captain, made a survey of this planet shortly after the first landings here. Surely you must remember that there is no site near to Stratford suitable for the landing of a ship, even one so relatively small as *The Far Traveler*."

Grimes did remember then and admitted as much. He said, too, that his local knowledge would be required to pilot the pinnace to Stratford. The Baroness said, grudgingly, that he might as well make some attempt to earn his salary.

Big Sister said nothing.

Grimes flew steadily south, maintaining a compass course and not following the meanderings of the river. Ahead the blue peaks of the Pennine Range lifted into an almost cloudless sky. An hour before sunset he knew that he could not be far from Stratford although, as he recalled, the little town was very hard to spot from the air. It was nestled in the river valley and the thatched roofs of its houses were overgrown with weeds. But there had been some quite remarkable rock formations that he had never gotten around to examining closely, rectangular slabs of dark gray but somehow scintillant stone, not far from the settlement.

Those slabs were still there.

So was a torpedo shape of silvery metal—the pinnace from *Southerly Buster*.

He said, pointing, "Kane's still here, Your Excellency."

"Are you afraid to meet him again?" she asked.

Grimes flushed angrily. "No," he said, "Your Excellency."

He was not frightened of Kane but he would have been willing to admit that he was worried. Kane was up to no good. Kane was always up to no good. He was a leopard with indelible spots.

People emerged from the little houses, from the pinnace, alerted by the racket of the boat's inertial drive. How many Terrans should there have been? Kane and ten of his passengers, seven men and three women . . . But standing there and looking up were thirty people. All of them were clothed, which seemed to indicate that there were no natives among them. Grimes studied the upturned faces through binoculars. Kane was not there— but suddenly that well remembered voice blasted from the transceiver.

"Ahoy, the pinnace! Who the hell are yer an' wot yer doin' here?"

Kane must be speaking from inside his own boat.

"*The Far Traveler,*" replied Grimes stiffly into his microphone. "Her Owner, the Baroness d'Estang of El Dorado. And her Master."

"An' I'm *Southerly Buster,* Owner *and* Master, Welcome to Stratford. Come on down. This is Liberty Hall; you can spit on the mat an' call the cat a bastard!"

"It should be the local mayor—Queen Anne, isn't it?—to issue the invitation," said the Baroness to Grimes.

"Perhaps Queen Anne is dead," said Grimes. With sudden foreboding he remembered the old saying; Many a true word is spoken in jest.

"Take us down, Captain," ordered the Baroness.

Grimes reduced vertical thrust and the pinnace settled slowly toward the ground, to the white sheet that somebody had spread to serve as a landing mark. She landed gently. Grimes cut the drive, actuated the controls of the airlock doors. He realized, too late, that he should have brought arms—but the six general purpose robots which had accompanied the humans from *The Far Traveler* would be capable of doing considerable damage to any enemy using nothing more than their own, enormously strong metal bodies.

He had landed about five meters from *Southerly Buster's* pinnace. A man came out through the airlock door of this craft—tall, gangling, clad in slate-gray shirt-and-shorts uniform with black, gold-braided shoulderboards. His straw-colored hair was untidy, even though short, and his face looked as though at some time in the past it had been shattered and then reassembled by a barely competent, unaesthetic plastic surgeon.

"Captain Kane?" the Baroness asked Grimes.

"Drongo Kane," he said.

She rose from her seat, was first out of the boat. Grimes followed her, then the robots. Kane advanced to stand in the forefront of his own people. He looked the Baroness up and down like a slave dealer assessing the points of a possible purchase. He bowed then—a surprisingly courtly gesture. He raised the Baroness's outstretched hand to his lips, surrendered it reluctantly as he came erect. Grimes could not see his employer's face but sensed that she was favorably impressed by her reception.

She said, "And now, Captain Kane, may I present my yachtmaster, Captain . . ."

"Grimes, Madam," supplied Kane with a grin. "I thought that I recognized his voice but didn't see how it could be him. But it is. Live on stage, in person. Singing and dancing."

"Mphm," grunted Grimes.

"No hard feelin's," said Kane, extending his right hand. "You've come down in the universe, I see—but I don't believe in kickin' a man when he's down."

Not unless there's some profit in it, thought Grimes, taking the proffered paw and getting the handshake over as quickly as possible.

"You know, ma'am, I'm pleased that you an' me old cobber Grimes dropped in," Kane went on. "A couple of independent witnesses is just what I'm needin' right now. It'd be better if Grimes was still in the Survey Service— but at least he's not a Dog Star Line puppy."

"What are you talking about, Kane?" demanded Grimes.

"Just this. I —an' my legal eagle, Dr. Kershaw . . ." A

tall, gray-haired, gray-clad man among the small crowd inclined his head toward the newcomers . . . "have the honor of representin' the rightful owners of this planet."

"The *rightful* owners?" asked Grimes.

"Too right." Kane waved his right hand in a wide arc, indicating the twenty men and women who were standing a little apart from his own people. "The Little, Grant, James and Pettifer families!"

The names rang a faint bell in the recesses of Grimes' memory.

"Descendants," stated Kane, "of four of the human women who were among the *Lode Cougar* survivors!"

))«Chapter 30»)«

Kane made no further introductions until he had conducted the Baroness and Grimes into one of the houses. The room that they entered had small windows, unglazed, set into two of the walls, screened with matting against the westering sun. There was a huge, solid, wooden table, a half dozen sturdy chairs. On one of the walls a big map of the planet, drawn to Mercatorial projection, was hanging. It was all very like, thought Grimes, Maya's council room *in* her "palace" had been on the occasion of his first landing on Morrowvia. So this was the palace, he thought.

Where was the queen?

He asked sharply, "Where is Queen Anne, Kane?"

Kane laughed. "Don't get your knickers in a knot, Grimes. She's not dead. She's . . . sleeping. So are her subjects. Meanwhile . . ." he gestured toward the four people who had followed them into the adobe building . . . "I'd like you to meet the leaders of the *true* Morrowvians. Mary Little . . .

The woman so named inclined her head and smiled shyly. She was wearing a shapeless blue coverall that hid her body to the neck but the way that she moved seemed human enough. Her teeth were very white and looked sharp. The hair of her head was obviously not the modified cat's fur of the natives; it was much coarser and longer. It was brown, as were her eyes. Her face was, if anything, too normal, quite forgettable apart from the unusually thin-lipped mouth.

"Peter Pettifer," continued Kane.

Pettifer was dressed as was Mary Little. He was yellow-haired, brown-eyed. He, too, had a peculiarly thin-lipped mouth.

"Dr. Kershaw you already know," went on *Southerly Buster*'s master. "And this is Dr. Weldon . . ."

Weldon—short, tubby, black-haired, neatly black-bearded, dressed in gaudily patterned shirt and scarlet shorts—nodded curtly.

"Are you a lawyer too?" asked the Baroness.

"No, madam," he told her. "My specialty is cryonics."

Kane sat on the edge of the table, swinging his long legs. He said, "I'll put you in picture, Ma'am. And you, Grimes. On the occasion of our first visit here—you in *Seeker*, that old woman Danzellan in *Schnauzer* an' yours truly in the *Buster*—none of us dreamed that the true owners of the planet were stashed away here, in cold storage. There were other records left by Morrow, you know, besides the ones that you an' Maggie what's-her-name found in Ballarat. And I turned 'em up. Oh, old Morrow played around with his cats—that I'll not deny—but he also obtained fertilized human ova from Mary

Little, Susan Pettifer, Delia James and Sarah Grant. These he brought to term, *in vitro,* in the laboratory that he set up here, in Stratford. But, as we all know too well, he was nuts on cats. Perhaps his infatuation with his pet creation, his Galatea, had something to do with it. He decided that Morrowvia would be a pussyocracy . . ." He grinned at his own play on words; nobody else was greatly amused. "He put the handful of true humans to sleep, stashed them away in the deep freeze so that they'd be available if ever he changed his mind. But they stayed there until I thawed 'em out."

"That's your story, Kane," said Grimes. "But I don't believe it. To operate any refrigeration plant, even a cooler for your beer, you want power. If there were any wind or water-powered generators here we'd have seen 'em when we came in. If there ever were any such jennies here they'd have worn out generations ago."

"*And* the refrigeration machinery itself," said the Baroness, showing a flicker of interest.

"Morrow set up an absorption system," said Kane smugly. "And as for the energy source—there were solar power screens in *Lode Cougar*'s cargo. The people of the village that Morrow established here had it drummed into them, from the very start, that their sacred duty was to keep the screens clear of weeds and not to allow any larger growths capable of blocking out the sunlight to take root around their edges."

Grimes remembered those unnatural looking slabs of gray, scintillant rock. He should have investigated them when he made his first rough survey of the planet. The Dog Star Line people should have investigated them when they made their surveys—but they, of course, were concerned primarily with exploitation, not the pursuit of knowledge. (And Drongo Kane, too, was an exploiter, and shrewd enough to know that any scrap of information whatsoever might, some day, be used to his advantage.)

Kane's story, Grimes admitted reluctantly to himself, was plausible. An absorption refrigeration system, with no moving parts, could well remain in operation for centuries provided that there was no leakage. And the resurrectees did not appear to be of feline ancestry. Nonetheless he wished that photographs of the *Lode Cougar* survivors were available. He looked at Mary Little dubiously.

"Tell us your story, Mary," prompted Kane.

The woman spoke. Her voice held an unpleasant whining quality. She said, "We are all very grateful to Captain Kane. He restored us to life; he will restore us to our proper place in the world. In the Old Days we were happy—but then the Others were favored by Dr. Morrow. And they hated us, and turned the Doctor against us . . ."

"Cats," said Kane, "are very jealous animals. And now, ma'am, and you, Grimes, would you care to accompany me on a tour of the . . . er . . . freezer?"

"Thank you, Captain Kane," said the Baroness.

"I want you both to see for yourselves," said Kane, "that the people of Stratford have not been harmed but merely filed for future reference. They may be required as witnesses when my, er, clients bring suit against the cat people for restoration of the legal ownership of this planet."

"How much is in it for you, Kane?" asked Grimes bluntly.

"Nobody works for nothing!" the Baroness told him sharply.

There were steep cliffs on the other side of the river from the village and it was atop these that the solar power screens were mounted. There were inflatable dinghies to ferry the party across the swift-flowing stream. The darkness was falling fast but powerful searchlights on the Stratford bank made the crossing as light as day. Four of *The Far Traveler*'s general purpose robots waded over with the humans, their heads at the deepest part just above the surface, accompanying the boats. ("Don't you trust me, Grimes?" asked Kane in a pained voice. "No," said Grimes.) The remaining two automata stayed to guard the pinnace.

On each side of the river there were jetties, very old structures of water-worn stone. Alongside one of these piers was a crude boat, little more than a coracle, consisting of the tough hide of some local beast stretched over a wickerwork frame. It must have been used, thought Grimes, by the maintenance workers who, over the long years, had kept the solar power screens free of vegetation.

Kane was first out of the leading dinghy, throwing a hitch of the painter around a wooden bollard. Gallantly he helped the Baroness from the boat to the low jetty. Grimes followed her ashore, then Kershaw. The other dinghy came alongside and Mary Little, Peter Pettifer and Dr. Weldon disembarked. The four robots emerged from the river, their golden bodies gleaming wetly.

Kane led the way to the base of the red granite cliff. Its face, although naturally rugged, seemed unbroken but the Master of *Southerly Buster* knew where the door was.

From his pocket he produced a small piece of bright metal, placed it in a depression in the rock. There was a very faint whine of concealed machinery and a great slab of granite swung inward. The tunnel beyond it was adequately lit by glowtubes in the ceiling.

"However did Dr. Morrow manage such feats of construction?" asked the Baroness curiously.

"He had his work robots, ma'am," replied Kane. "And this cave is a natural one."

The party walked slowly along the tunnel, the feet of the robots ringing metallically on the stone floor. The air was chilly although not actually cold; nonetheless Grimes could see goose pimples on the backs of the Baroness's shapely legs, long under the brief shorts, as she strode ahead of him, beside Kane.

Weldon, accompanying Grimes, said conversationally, "Of course, the refrigeration plant cannot produce extremely low temperatures—but Morrow had knowledge of and access to the drug that was popularly known as Permakeep in his day. Now, of course, we work with vastly improved versions—but even with Permakeep in its original form, temperatures only just below zero Celsius were all that were required to maintain the human body in a state of suspended animation almost indefinitely. A massive intravenous injection, of course . . .

"Fascinating," said Grimes.

"Mine is a fascinating discipline," admitted Weldon smugly.

They tramped on, into the heart of the cliff. The tunnel made a right-angled turn into a large chamber, a huge cold room with transparent containers arranged in tiers.

And there were the people who had been the citizens of Stratford, each in his own capsule, each frozen into immobility. They could have been dead; there was only Kane's word for it that they were not

"Her Royal Highness," announced the piratical ship-master mockingly. "The Queen of Stratford."

The unlucky Anne was in the first casket She was a comely enough woman, creamy skinned, with tortoise-shell hair. Like many of the other native Morrowvians she possessed pronounced rudimentary nipples under her full breasts. Her face still bore an expression of anger.

And there was living anger in this cold room too. Grimes heard a noise that was both snarl and growl. He turned, saw that Mary Little and Peter Pettifer were glaring at the frozen body, their thin lips pulled back from their sharp white teeth in vicious grins. Kane had heard them as well. He snapped, "Quiet, damn you! Quiet!"

"It is natural," said Weldon suavely, "that they should hate the cat people after the way that they were treated. Would you like to be bossed around by a *cat!*"

No worse than being bossed around by a rich bitch, thought Grimes. "I suppose," he said, "that if you hadn't put Queen Anne and her people out of circulation they and your proteges would have led a cat and dog life."

For some reason this rather feeble joke did not go down at all well with Kane, who said shortly, "I am responsible for the safety of those whom I awoke from what could well have been eternal sleep."

"Tilt your halo to more of an angle, Kane," said Grimes. "That way it might suit you better."

"Captain Grimes," the Baroness told him coldly, "that

was uncalled for. I am sure that Captain Kane is acting for the best."

"And *you* are satisfied, ma'am, that the people of Stratford are unharmed?" asked Kane.

"Yes," she replied.

"We still don't know that they aren't dead," persisted Grimes.

"Dr. Weldon," said Kane, "please select a sleeper at random—better still, let Captain Grimes select one—and awaken him or her."

"Captain Kane," said the Baroness, "that will not be necessary. Please accept my apologies for my employee's unfounded suspicions. But I am becoming increasingly aware that I am not attired for this temperature. Shall we return to the open air?"

"Your wish is my command, ma'am," said Kane gallantly.

Outside the cave the light evening breeze was pleasantly warm. Whoever was in charge of the searchlights had elevated their beams so that they did not dazzle the party; enough light, however, was reflected from the cliff face to make it easy for them to find their way back to the river. Weldon and the two resurrectees were the first to embark, casting off in their inflatable dinghy. Weldon may have been extremely able in his own field but he was no waterman. Engrossed in steering a diagonal course to counter the swift current he did not notice the tree branch, torn from its parent trunk by a storm up river, that was being swept downstream. Both Kane and Grimes shouted a warning but he did not seem to hear it. The jagged end of the branch hit the side of the dinghy like a torpedo, ripping along its length. There was a great hissing and bubbling of escaping air. The flimsy craft tipped, all its buoyancy on the side of the damage lost. It capsized, throwing its occupants into the water.

There was very little danger. Weldon did not appear to be a good swimmer but two of the general purpose robots, running along the river bed, positioned themselves on either side of him, supported him on their out-held arms. Mary Little and Peter Pettifer struck out for the shore in a flurry of spray. It was a clumsy stroke that they were using, wasteful of energy, but in spite of their hampering clothing they made rapid progress. The two robots not engaged in assisting the cryoscopist to safety ran down the river in pursuit of the still-floating dinghy.

Then Weldon, dripping and miserable, flanked by his golden rescuers, stood on the stone pier waiting for Kane's boat to come alongside. Mary Little and Peter Pettifer beat this dinghy to the shore, clambered up onto the jetty. They grinned and panted, shaking themselves. A fine spray of moisture flew from their wet clothing.

Kane made a competent job of berthing. As before, he helped the Baroness out of the dinghy. Kershaw and Grimes stepped ashore unaided.

The Baroness said, "My robots will recover the damaged boat, Captain Kane."

"Thank you, ma'am. And your robots saved Dr. Weldon from a watery grave. I am indebted to you."

"I would have managed," said Weldon shortly.

Grimes ignored the conversation. He was watching Mary Little and Peter Pettifer, he was doing more than just watching. His nose wrinkled.

Kane and the Baroness walked slowly inshore from the jetty, deep in conversation. Grimes made to follow but was detained by Kershaw.

"Will you join us for a few drinks and a meal, Captain?" asked the lawyer.

Grimes accepted the invitation. He assumed that Kane and the Baroness would be present at this social occasion— but they were not. He was quite surprised when he felt a stab of jealously. Nonetheless, he thought, their absence might prove more advantageous than otherwise. With Kane not present his people would be less cautious in their conversation.

The talk over the quite civilized—but not up to *The Far Traveler*'s standards!—repast was interesting enough although, on both sides, guarded. Grimes did learn, however, that one of Kane's party, Dr. Helena Waldheim, was a hypnoeducationist.

»《Chapter 31》«

Grimes did not overstay his welcome. Drongo Kane's entourage were not his sort of people, neither was he theirs. There had been too much shop talk, little of it concerned with what was going on at Stratford. As far as Grimes was concerned the only really interesting professional gossip was that of fellow spacemen.

He made his way through the almost deserted village to *The Far Traveler*'s pinnace. He turned the robots to set up two pneumatic tents hard by the small craft, one for the Baroness and one for himself. While he was overseeing the work he was joined by that lady.

She asked, "What are you *doing*, Captain?"

He replied, "I don't fancy sleeping in a house from which the rightful occupants have been evicted by force, Your Excellency."

"They never were the rightful occupants," she said.

"So Drongo Kane's peddled you his line of goods," he remarked. "Your Excellency."

She actually flushed. "Captain Kane is a most remarkable man."

"You can say that again!" Grimes told her. Then— "Can't you see what he's trying to do?" He made an appeal to her business acumen. "You, I well know, are a major shareholder in the Dog Star Line. If Kane, through his thawed-out figureheads, gains control of this planet it will do the Dog Star Line no good at all."

She laughed. "And what if I become a major shareholder in Southerly Buster Enterprises?"

Grimes said, "I would advise strongly against it, Your Excellency."

Again she laughed. "I hired you, Captain, as a yacht-master, not as a financial adviser. After all—which of us is the multi-billionaire?"

Not me, that's for sure, thought Grimes.

"So," she went on, "you may sleep in that glorified soap bubble if you so desire. I shall find the accommodation arranged for me by Captain Kane far more comfortable. A very good night to you."

She strode away toward the house which had once been Queen Anne's palace. Two of her robots accompanied her. No harm would come to her, could come to her unless she wished it—and Grimes was not one of those who would regard a roll in the hay as harm, anyhow.

But why with Drongo Kane, of all people!

Eventually he turned in. There was nothing else to do. Nobody wanted him; he was just the hired help. He was settling down into the comfortable pneumatic bed when the door of the tent dilated and one of the golden robots

came in. It (he?) stood there, looking down at Grimes.
Grimes looked up at it.

"Well?" he demanded irritably.

The voice that issued from the automaton's chest was
not the mechanical monotone that Grimes had come to
associate with these robots. The words were in Big Sister's
metallic but still feminine tones.

"Captain Grimes, may I have your report on what has
been happening in Stratford?"

Grimes said, "Aren't the robots your eyes and ears?
And aren't you supposed to be in contact with Her
Excellency at all times through her personal radio?"

"Her Excellency," said Big Sister, "can discontinue
such contact at will. In certain circumstances she insists
upon privacy. So it is that I am now obliged to work
directly with you."

"I happen," said Grimes stiffly, "to be employed by Her
Excellency."

"And I," Big Sister told him, "am *owned* by Her
Excellency. Nonetheless she played no part in my initial
programming. As you are probably already aware, entities
such as myself are required by Interstellar Federation
Law to have built-in respect for that same law and its
processes. I would not have acted to rescue you from
Commander Delamere's ship on Botany Bay had I not
considered that the commander had acted illegally. Also,
of course, I am programmed to protect my owner."

"She is her own woman," Grimes said harshly.

Big Sister laughed. That crystalline tinkling was
distinctly odd as it emanated from the expressionless,
masculine even though asexual robot. She said, "I possess

an extensive theoretical knowledge of sex. I do not think that Michelle will come to any harm from a brief affair with Captain Kane, any more than she would have done from one with you—which, frankly, I should have preferred . . ."

Grimes interrupted her. "But I don't like it. A high-born aristocrat in bed with that . . . pirate . . ."

"Are you rushing to the defense of the hereditary aristocracy, Captain Grimes? You surprise me. And as for Captain Kane's being a pirate, what of it? The founder of the d'Estang fortunes owned and commanded a privateer out of St. Malo during the Napoleonic Wars on Earth, and the dividing line between privateer and pirate was always a very thin one. Even so, I *am* concerned about the possibility of a financial liaison between Her Excellency and Captain Kane. She could come to harm through that. I have taken it upon myself to have all available information concerning *Southerly Buster* and her Master fed into my data bank."

"You must play it back to me some time," said Grimes.

"Perhaps I shall," said Big Sister. "But now I must ask you to make your own contribution to the bank. Please tell me all that you have seen, heard, experienced, felt and thought since your landing at Stratford. My robots have seen and heard and I have recorded. They do not think and they do not have hunches. Neither do I to any great extent, although association with humans is developing— but, so far, only slightly—my paranormal psychological processes. But you are fully human and blessed with intuition.

"Please begin."

Grimes began. He talked and he talked, pausing now and again to fill and to light his pipe, to take a gulp of a cold drink poured for him by the robot. He talked and he talked—and as he spoke the pieces of the jigsaw puzzle fell neatly into place. The oddities in the appearance of the resurrectees, the peculiar stroke that Little and Pettifer had used while swimming ashore from the wrecked dinghy, the way that they had shaken themselves, the faint yet pungent odor that had steamed from their wet bodies . . . It all added up.

He finished at last.

Big Sister said, "Thank you, Captain. I shall now see to it that the planetary authorities take prompt action."

"They'll never listen to you in Melbourne," said Grimes pessimistically, "especially if this Delamere is anything like his cousin. They'll not listen to me either. I've no status any more. If I were still in the Survey Service . . . but I'm not."

"Somebody will listen," said Big Sister, "if the message comes from you, in your voice. I shall send a robot at once to Maya to tell the story. She still has a great deal of time for you. Then she will call Melbourne and talk to Tabitha, queen to queen and Tabitha will talk to Mr. Delamere— not only as wife to husband but as queen to prince consort . . .

"And then . . ."

"It could work," admitted Grimes.

And not for the first time he was impressed by Big Sister's knowledge of human psychology.

»«(Chapter 32)»«

Grimes got off to sleep at last.

He was called the next morning by one of the robots who brought him a steaming pot of tea. Refreshed, he went into the pinnace to make use of the boat's cramped yet adequate toilet facilities. Then he had breakfast. The robots did their best with what was available and produced for him a filling and tasty enough sandwich meal but, as he became acutely conscious of the savory odors drifting from various houses in the village, unsatisfying. It was obvious that Kane and his entourage believed—as Grimes himself did—in starting the day with eggs and bacon.

He filled and lit his pipe, took a stroll through the settlement accompanied by two of the GP robots. Littles, Pettifers, Grants and Jameses were emerging from their huts. They looked at him but said nothing, did not answer his politely hearty good mornings. He ran into Dr. Weldon and tried to engage him in conversation but the scientist said that he was busy and hastened off. He met more of Kane's people and none of them had any time to spare for him. There was no sign of Kane himself or of the Baroness.

He went back to the pinnace, used the transceiver to call *The Far Traveler.* Big Sister answered. She said, "Be patient, Captain Grimes. I am doing all that I can. I must ask you to say nothing of this to Her Excellency. I fear that she has become infatuated with Captain Kane—which is largely your fault, of course—and will be more inclined to aid than to frustrate him."

So it's all my fault, thought Grimes resentfully—then recalled how he had spurned what was offered to him in that cave on Farhaven. He said, "I haven't seen her since last night."

"Perhaps that is as well," said Big Sister. And was that a note of worry in the metallic voice? "I am acting in her best interests. You must believe that."

"I do," said Grimes truthfully.

By midday he was beginning to feel like an invisible man; nobody knew him or wanted to know him. Obviously Kane had issued orders and those same orders were being obeyed in letter and in spirit. He partook of but did not enjoy another lonely meal in his pneumatic tent. He called Big Sister again from the pinnace. She told him to be patient.

The afternoon dragged on.

The Baroness, accompanied by Kane, made a brief appearance. They ignored him. She looked like a cat who'd just eaten the canary and he like a canary who'd just eaten the cat. They sauntered past him, briefly taking the air, then returned to Queen Anne's palace.

Eventually Grimes sat down to his evening meal. If he had foreseen that he would be unable to live off the country he would have taken far greater interest in the stocking of the pinnace's emergency food supplies; beans are undeniably nutritious but apt to become boring. Too, a supply of reading matter would not have come amiss. Worst of all was the feeling of helplessness. He had known and survived crises aplenty in the past—but then he had been an officer of one of the major armed services of the Galaxy. Now he was only a yachtmaster, the flunky of a pampered aristocrat captain of a sentient vessel determined to do things *her* way.

He was preparing for bed in his tent when one of the robots entered. It said, in Big Sister's voice, "A landing has been made upriver from Stratford. The police forces are on their way in inflatable boats."

"Why didn't they come directly here?" demanded Grimes irritably.

"You are supposed to be the expert on military matters, Captain." Big Sister seemed more amused than reproving. "It should be obvious to you that half a dozen airboats would give ample sonic warning of their approach—and Kane and his people are armed. The dinghies, making use of the current, will carry out a silent approach. You will be at the jetty to receive them. Their ETA is midnight your time, but they could be earlier."

"All right," said Grimes. "I'll be there."

He was waiting by the river at 2330 hours. It was a fine night and what little breeze there was was pleasantly warm. Glittering starlight was reflected from the black, swift-flowing river. Inland a few lamps still gleamed from the village. As long as they remained burning they would indicate to the waterborne forces that their objective had been reached. If they were, for any reason, extinguished, Grimes had a flashlight that he could use.

He sat there on the jetty, watching and listening. He would have liked a smoke, in fact went so far as to fill his pipe, but feared that the flare of one of the old-fashioned matches that he always used might attract unwelcome attention. He heard a heavy splash as one of the denizens of the stream—hunter or hunted?—leapt clear of the water and returned to it. He listened to somebody singing in the village, an eerie, wailing song that once he might have assumed to be of Terran Oriental origin. Now he recognized it for what it was. He thought, *For that sort of howling there should be a moon!*

From upriver came a faint purring noise. Had he not been expecting it, listening for it intently, he would never have heard it this early. He considered switching on his flashlight, then decided against it. The Morrowvians had inherited excellent night vision from their feline ancestors and would surely see him standing at the head of the jetty.

He could make out the first boat now, a dark blob on the black water. He waved. It stood in toward him. Its engine was switched off and it was carried by the current head on to the stonework. Had it been of metal or timber construction there would have been a loud crash; as it was, there was merely a dull thud followed by a faint hiss of escaping air. Half a dozen figures scrambled ashore, five of them sure-footedly, the sixth clumsily. This one asked, in a loud whisper, "Captain Grimes?"

"Yes."

"I'm Commodore Delamere, Prince Consort and Dog Star Line Resident Manager. I hope you haven't brought us out here on a wild goose chase. If you have . . ."

The first boat was pushed away from and clear of the jetty, allowed to drift downstream. The second delivered its landing party and was similarly treated. And the third, and the fourth . .

But the village was waking up. The Morrowvians may have inherited excellent night vision but the alleged Littles, Pettifers, Grants and Jameses had inherited exceptionally keen hearing. There were yelping shouts and then, above them, the voice of Kane bellowing through a bullhorn. Lights came on—not the dim yellow of oil lamps but a harsh, electric glare, fed by the generator and the power cells of Kane's pinnace. Dark figures boiled out of the huts.

Delamere stood there, frozen. When it came to the crunch, thought Grimes, he was as useless as his Survey Service cousin. But the police did not wait for his orders. Screaming, they ran toward their ancient enemies, stunguns out and ready. Some of them fell, cut down by the similar weaponry being used by Kane's people.

Grimes ran after the attackers, feeling naked without a weapon of his own. He realized suddenly that he was not alone, that he was boxed in by four of *The Far Traveler*'s golden robots. He felt a flash of gratitude to the omniscient Big Sister. Those giant, metal bodies would effectively shield him from the incapacitating bolts being aimed in his direction.

He was among the houses now. He ran through the

village, ignoring the scrimmages going on around him. He charged toward Kane's pinnace. Kane was standing just inside the airlock of the boat. He was armed—but not with a non-lethal stungun. A brief burst of tracer coruscated about the impervious torso of the leading robot. And then the automaton stretched out a long arm to snatch the machine pistol from Kane's hand, crumpling the weapon in its grip.

The Baroness was there with Kane, obviously hastily dressed, her shorts not properly pulled up, her shirt open. She was furious. "Take your tin paws off him!" she flared. "My own robots! You obey *me,* damn you!" She saw Grimes. "And *you* . . . What the hell do you think that you're doing?"

One of the robots found the cable leading from the pinnace's generator to the lights in the village, picked it up in both hands, snapped it. There was a brief actinic flare, then darkness.

And cats can see in the dark.

᱑((Chapter 33))))ᱟ

The Baroness was queening it in her salon aboard *The Far Traveler*.

With her were Grimes and Francis Delamere, Prince Regent of Melbourne, Dog Star Line Resident Manager, on Morrowvia, Company Commodore. Delamere, Grimes was amused to note, stood considerably in awe of the Baroness despite his fancy uniform—of his own design—and fancy titles. He was prepared to go along with the story that she was a little innocent woolly lamb and Drongo Kane the big bad wolf.

He said, "It is indeed fortunate, madam, that you realized that the beings revivified by Captain Kane were, in spite of their names and false background stories, of canine and not human ancestry."

She smiled forgivingly but condescendingly. "The correct form of address, Resident Manager, is 'Your Excellency.' As an itinerant representative of the planet state of El Dorado I am entitled to ambassadorial status. But it is of no real importance."

"I beg your pardon, Your Excellency. But how did you guess that the alleged descendants of the Little, Pettifer, Grant and James women were not what they claimed to be?"

With conscious nobility she gave credit where credit was due. "It was Captain Grimes, actually, who noticed the . . . discrepancies. The way that they swam, using the stroke that, when used by humans, is called a dog paddle. The way that they shook themselves when they emerged from the water. And the odor from their bodies. Have you ever smelted a wet dog?"

"Not since I settled on this planet, Your Excellency. You will appreciate that dogs would not be popular pets here." He took an appreciative sip of the large martini with which he had been supplied. "Meanwhile—with some reluctance, I admit, but in accordance with your request—we have not dealt harshly with Captain Kane. He has been given twenty-four hours to get his ship, his people and himself off Morrowvia. He will have to pay compensation to Queen Anne and her subjects. In addition he has been charged with the costs of the police expedition to Stratford and has been fined the maximum amount for breaching the peace."

"And his dupes?" asked the Baroness. "His—if I may use the expression—cat's paws?"

"They, Your Excellency, have been returned to cold storage until such time as we receive instructions from the Government of the Federation regarding *their* disposition. It is my own opinion that the Founding Father having, as it were, created them, put them in reserve in case his first experiment did not work out. But the need for them never arose."

Grimes said, "Let sleeping dogs lie."

Big Sister's voice came from the playmaster. "Let the lying dogs sleep."

Surely, thought Grimes, only a human intelligence could be capable of such an horrendous play on words. He wondered how he had ever regarded Big Sister as an emotionless, humorless machine.

»«(Chapter 34)»«

The Far Traveler did not remain long on Morrowvia after *Southerly Buster*'s departure for an unknown destination. Grimes had reason to believe that the Baroness's affairs were under investigation by officials of the Bank of Canis Major, an institution wherein lay the real power of the planet. Delamere, for all his fancy titles, was only a figurehead and, furthermore, was the sort of man who would believe anything that a pretty woman told him. The bankers were not so easily fooled and knew somehow that their financial interests in the holiday world had been threatened.

Michelle d'Estang was rich enough and powerful enough to pull a few strings of her own, however, and was able to obtain Outward Clearance before her ship was placed under arrest. Grimes, who had been told a little but not all, took the yacht upstairs in a hurry as soon as the documents were delivered, by special courier, late one afternoon. He regretted that he had not been given time to say goodbye to Maya properly or, even, to renew in depth his old acquaintance with her. Perhaps this was just as well. The Prince Consort of Cambridge would have been quite capable of making trouble.

Once *The Far Traveler* was clear of the Van Allens, trajectory was set for New Sparta and the long voyage begun.

The seas of Earth and other watery planets are, insofar as surface vessels are concerned, two dimensional. The seas of space are three dimensional. Yet from the viewpoint of the first real seamen the Terran oceans must have seemed as vast as those other oceans, millennia later, traversed by spacemen—mile upon mile of sweet damn all. As far as the spaceman is concerned, substitute "light year" for "mile" and delete the breaks in the monotony provided by changing weather conditions and by birds and fishes and cetaceans. Nonetheless, the similarity persists.

A ship, any sort of ship, is small in comparison to the mind-boggling immensity of the medium through which she travels. Disregarding the existence of focal points the chances of her sighting another vessel during a trans-oceanic voyage are exceedingly thin. This was especially so to the days of sail, when it was practically impossible for a captain to keep in a Great Circle track between ports or even to a Rhumb Line—and yet, time and time again, strange sails would lift over the horizon and there would be a mid-ocean meeting with the exchange of gossip and months-old newspapers, a bartering of consumable stores.

Now and again there were even collisions, although each of the vessels involved had thousands of square miles of empty ocean to play around in.

Ships, somehow, seem to sniff each other out. Sightings, meetings are too frequent to be accounted for by the laws of random. This was so in the days of the windjammers, it was still so in the days of steam and steel, it is still so to the age of interstellar travel.

Such a meeting, however, was far from the thoughts of anybody aboard *The Far Traveler*. Not that there was any sharing of thoughts during the initial stages of the voyage; Grimes and his employer were barely on speaking terms and if Big Sister were human it would have been said that she was sulking hard. Jealousy came into it. Grimes found it hard to forgive the Baroness for her brief affair with Drongo Kane. It was not that Grimes considered himself the guardian of her virginity; it was far too late in the day for that, anyhow. It was just that ever since his first meeting with that gentleman he had numbered Kane among his enemies. And the Baroness, although she would never admit it publicly, resented the way in which Grimes and Big Sister, acting in concert, had frustrated Kane's attempt to take over Morrowvia. So, for the time being at least, there were no more morning coffee and afternoon tea sessions in the Baroness's salon, no more pre-luncheon or pre-dinner cocktail parties, no more shared meals. The Baroness kept to herself in her quarters, Grimes kept to himself in his. And Big Sister, unusually for her, talked only when talked to, concerning herself to the exclusion of all else with running the ship.

Grimes was not altogether displeased. He had—he secretly admitted to himself—lusted after the Baroness and still remembered—how could he ever forget?—that he could have had her in that cave on Farhaven. Now it was a case of *You can look but you mustn't touch*. As things were now he preferred not to look even. And Big Sister? She could very well have been nicknamed Little Miss Knowall. It was refreshing—for a time, at any rate—to be spared her omniscience. Meanwhile, his quarters were more luxurious than merely comfortable. His robot stewardess—or, to be more exact, Big Sister acting through that literally golden girl—spoiled him. For his playmaster there was a seemingly inexhaustible supply of music, plays and microfilmed books. He was kept informed as to what times of the ship's day the little gymnasium was frequented by the Baroness and adjusted his own routine so as not to clash.

The Far Traveler fell through the dark dimensions, the warped continuum, a micro-society that, despite its smallness, contained all the essentials—a man, a woman, a computer. Even though the members of this tiny community weren't exactly living in each other's pockets they weren't actually fighting among themselves—and that was something to be thankful for.

One morning—according to *The Far Traveler's* clocks— Grimes was awakened indecently early. Big Sister, exercising her newly developed sense of humor, used an archaic bugle call, *Reveille,* instead of the usual chimes to call him. He opened his eyes, saw that the stewardess was placing the tray with his coffee on the bedside table. She said, in Big Sister's voice, "There is no urgency, Captain Grimes, but I should like you in the control room."

Grimes swung his legs out of the bed. "What's wrong?" he demanded.

"Nothing is wrong, Captain, but a situation has arisen for which I am not programmed." She added, as Grimes opened the wardrobe door and reached for a clean uniform shirt, "As I have said, there is no urgency. Please finish your coffee and then shower and depilate before coming to Control. You know very well that Her Excellency does not tolerate scruffiness."

"So this is not exactly Action Stations," said Grimes.

"Not yet," agreed Big Sister.

Grimes showered and depilated. He dressed. He made his way to the control room after he had smoked a soothing pipe, knowing that the Baroness objected to the use of tobacco or other smouldering vegetable matter in her presence. She was in Control, waiting for him. She had not troubled to put on her usual, for this locality, insignialess uniform shirt and shorts. She was wearing a transparent rather than translucent white robe. She smelled of sleep. She regarded Grimes coldly and said, "You took your time, *Captain.*"

Grimes said, "Big Sister told me that there was no immediate urgency, Your Excellency."

She said, "Big Sister told me the same. But I am the Owner, and your employer. I came straight here as soon as I was called—while you, obviously, sat down to enjoy your eggs and sausages and bacon, your buttered toast and honey. You might, at least, have had the decency to wipe the egg off your face."

The back of Grimes' hand came up automatically to his mouth. Then he said stiffly, "I had no breakfast, Your Excellency. And, I repeat; I was told by Big Sister that there was no need to hurry."

Big Sister's voice came from the transceiver. "That is correct. There was no need to hurry."

"Pah!" The Baroness was flushed with temper—all the way down to her navel, Grimes noted with clinical interest. "Who owns this ship, this not inconsiderable investment, may I ask? Neither of you! And now, *Captain* Grimes, it would seem that there is a target showing up in the screen of the Mass Proximity Indicator. According to extrapolation we shall close it—whatever *it* is—just over one hour from now. Big Sister has condescended to inform me that this target is probably a ship and that it is not proceeding under any form of interstellar drive. I think that we should investigate it."

Grimes said, "In any case, we are required to do so by Interstellar Law, Your Excellency."

"Are we? As far as this vessel is concerned, *I* am the law. Nonetheless I am curious. If I were not naturally so I should not have undertaken this cruise. And so, *Captain*, I shall be vastly obliged if you will bring us to a rendezvous with this unidentified vessel. Please inform me when you are ready to board."

She swept out of the control room.

Grimes pulled his pipe and tobacco pouch out of his pocket, began to fill the charred, dottle-encrusted bowl. Big Sister stepped up the revolutions of an exhaust fan, said, "I shall deodorize before *she* returns."

Grimes said, "Thank you." He lit up, peered through exhaled smoke into the tank of the Mass Proximity Indicator. In the sphere of darkness floated a tiny green spark, well away from the center. To a ship not proceeding under the space- and time-twisting Mannschenn Drive it

would have been weeks distant. As it was . . . His fingers
went to the controls to set up calibration and extra-potation
but Big Sister saved him the trouble.

"Contact fifty-three minutes, forty-five seconds from . . .
now," she told him. "If you are agreeable I shall shut down
our Mannschenn Drive when ten kilometers from target,
leaving you to make the final approach on inertial drive
and to match velocities. As soon as we have broken
through into the normal continuum I shall commence
calling on NST radio and also make the Morse signal,
What ship! by flashing light. As you are aware, attempts to
communicate by Carlotti radio have not been successful."

"I wasn't aware," said Grimes, "but I am now." He
realized that he was being childishly sulky and asked, in as
friendly a voice as he could manage, "Do you know of any
ships missing, presumed lost, in this sector of Space, Big
Sister? With the enormous fund of information in your
data bank you might well do so . . ."

She replied, "I have already extrapolated the assumed
trajectories of missing vessels over the past two hundred
years. What we see in our screen could not be any of
them. Allowances must be made, however, for incomplete
data."

"So this thing," said Grimes, "could be an ancient
gaussjammer or even one of the deep freeze ships . . ."

"It could be," said Big Sister, *"anything."*

»《Chapter 35》«

There was little for Grimes to do until *The Far Traveler* had closed the strange ship, the derelict. Big Sister had his breakfast brought up to the control room. He enjoyed the meal—but it was only on very rare occasions that he did not appreciate his food. He used the Carlotti transceiver to put out his own call; it was not that he did not trust Big Sister to handle such matters but he liked to feel that he was earning his keep. There was no reply to his reiterated demand, *"Far Traveler* to vessel in my vicinity. Please identify yourself." He stared out of the viewports along the bearing of the unidentified object. There was nothing to be seen, of course—nothing, that is, but the distant stars, each of which, viewed from a ship proceeding under interstellar drive, presenting the appearance of a pulsating iridescent spiral nebula.

Then Big Sister said, "In precisely five minutes we shall be ten kilometers from the target. I have informed Her Excellency."

The Baroness came into Control, looking crisply efficient in her insignialess uniform. She asked, "Are you ready for the final approach, Captain?"

"Yes," said Grimes. "Your Excellency."

"Permission to shut down Mannschenn Drive?" asked Big Sister formally.

"Yes," replied Grimes and the Baroness simultaneously. She glared at him. He turned away to hide his own expression. He went to his chair, strapped himself in. She did likewise. He held his hands poised over the controls although it was unlikely that he would have to use them yet; Big Sister was quite capable of carrying out the initial maneuvers by herself.

The arhythmic beat of the inertial drive slowed, muttered into inaudibility. Even with the straps holding the two humans into their chairs the cessation of acceleration was immediately obvious. Then the thin, high whine of the ever-precessing rotors of the Mannschenn Drive changed frequency, deepened to a low humming, ceased. Colors sagged down the spectrum and perspective was briefly anarchic. There was disorientation, momentary nausea, evanescent hallucinatory experience. It seemed to Grimes that he was a child again, watching on the screen of the family playmaster a rendition of one of the old fairy tales, the story of the Sleeping Beauty. But there was something absurdly wrong. It was the Prince who was supine on the bed, under the dust and the cobwebs, and the Princess who was about to wake him with a kiss . . . And it was strange that this lady should bear such a striking resemblance to that aunt who had run away with the spaceman.

"When you have quite finished dreaming, Captain Grimes," said the Baroness coldly, "I shall be obliged if you will take charge of the operation."

The radar was on now, more accurate than the mass proximity indicator had been. Big Sister had done very well. *The Far Traveler* was a mere 10.35 kilometers from the target, which was almost ahead. Even though the inertial drive was still shut down, the range was slowly closing. Grimes shifted his attention from the radar screen to that of the telescope. At maximum magnification he could just see the stranger—a very faint glimmer of reflected starlight against the blackness of interstellar space.

He restarted the inertial drive. Acceleration pressed him down into the padding of his seat. He said, "Big Sister, put out a call on NST, please."

He heard her voice, more feminine than metallic but metallic nonetheless, "*Far Traveler* to vessel in my vicinity. Identify yourself. Please identify yourself." There was no reply.

Grimes was conscious of the flashing on the fringe of his vision; *The Far Traveler*'s powerful searchlight was being used as a signalling lamp. A succession of Morse "A"s, then, "What ship? What ship?" But there was only the intermittent glimmer of reflected radiance from the stranger.

Big Sister ceased her futile flashing but maintained a steady beam. It was possible now to make out details in the telescope screen. The object was certainly a ship—but no vessel such as Grimes had ever seen, either in actuality or in photographs. The hull was a dull-gleaming ovoid covered with excrescenes, whip-like rods, sponsons and turrets. Communications antennae, thought Grimes, and weaponry. But none of those gun muzzles—if guns they were—were swinging to bring themselves to bear on *The Far Traveler.*

Grimes made a minor adjustment of trajectory so as to run up alongside the stranger, began to reduce the yacht's acceleration. His intention was to approach to within half a kilometer and then to match velocities, cutting the drive so that both vessels were falling free. He was thankful that neither the Baroness nor Big Sister was in the mood for back seat driving.

He was thankful too soon. "Aren't you liable to overshoot, Captain Grimes?" asked the lady.

"I don't think so," he said.

"I do!" she snapped. "I think that Big Sister could do this better."

Surprisingly Big Sister said, "I have told you already, Your Excellency, that I am not yet programmed for this type of operation."

"I am looking forward," said the Baroness nastily, "to meeting your programmers again."

And then Grimes was left alone. Doing a job of real spacemanship he was quite happy. He would have been happier still if he could have smoked his pipe—but even he admitted that the foul male comforter was not essential. Finally, with the inertial drive shut down, he drew alongside the stranger. He applied a brief burst of reverse thrust. And then the two ships were, relative to each other, motionless—although they were falling through the interstellar immensities at many kilometers a second.

He said to Big Sister, "Keep her as she goes, please." He knew that the inertial drive would have to be used, now and again, to maintain station—transverse thrust especially to prevent the two ships from gravitating into possibly damaging contact. Had the stranger's hull been as featureless as that of *The Far Traveler* it would not have mattered—but, with all those protrusions, it would have been like some sleek and foolishly amorous animal trying to make love to a porcupine.

"And what do we do now?" asked the Baroness.

"Board, Your Excellency," said Grimes. "But, first of all, I shall send a team of robots to make a preliminary survey."

"Do that," she said.

They sat in their chairs, watched the golden figures, each using a personal propulsion unit, leap the fathomless gulf between the ships. They saw the gleaming, mechanical humanoids land on the stranger's shell plating, carefully avoiding the antennae, the turrets. Then the robots spread out over the hull—like, thought Grimes, yellow apes exploring a metal forest. Save for two of them they moved out of sight from the yacht but the big viewscreen displayed what they were seeing during their investigation.

One of them, obviously, was looking down at what could only be an airlock door, a wide circle of uncluttered, dull-gleaming metal, its rim set down very slightly from the surrounding skin. At a word from Grimes this robot turned the lamp in its forehead up to full intensity but there was no sign of any external controls for opening the valve.

Another robot had made its way forward and was looking in through the control room viewports. The compartment was untenanted, looked, somehow, as though it had been untenanted for a very long time. There were banks of instrumentation of alien design that could have been anything. There were chairs—and whoever (whatever) had sat in them must have approximated very very closely to the human form, although the back of each was bisected by a vertical slit. For tails? Why not? Grimes had heard the opinion expressed more than once that evolution had taken a wrong turn when Man's ancestors lost their prehensile caudal appendages. But he knew of no spacefaring race that possessed these useful adjuncts to hands.

He said, "We shall have to cut our way in. Big Sister, will you send a couple of robots across with the necessary equipment? And have my stewardess get my spacesuit ready."

"And mine," said the Baroness.

"Your Excellency," said Grimes, "somebody must remain in charge of the ship."

"And why should it be me, Captain? In any case, this isn't one of your Survey Service tubs with a computer capable of handling only automatic functions. Big Sister's brain is as good as yours. At least."

Grimes felt his prominent ears burning as he flushed angrily. But he said, "Very well, Your Excellency." He turned to the transceiver—he still found it necessary to think of Big Sister's intelligence as inhabiting some or other piece of apparatus—and said, "You'll mind the store during our absence. If we get into trouble take whatever action you think fit."

The electronic entity replied ironically, "Aye, aye, Cap'n."

The Baroness sighed audibly. Grimes knew that she was blaming him for the sense of humor that Big Sister seemed to have acquired over recent weeks, was equating him with the sort of person who deliberately teaches coarse language to a parrot or a *lliri* or any of the other essentially unintelligent life-forms prized, by some, for their mimicry of human speech. Not that Big Sister was unintelligent . . . He was tempted to throw in his own two bits' worth with a crack about a jesting pilot but thought better of it.

The robot stewardess had Grimes' spacesuit ready for him when he went down to his quarters, assisted him into the armor. He decided to belt on a laser pistol—such a weapon could also be used as a tool. He also took along a powerful flashlight; a laser handgun could be used as such but there was always the risk of damaging whatever it was aimed at.

The Baroness—elegantly feminine even to her space armor—was waiting for him by the airlock. She had a camera buckled to her belt. With her were two of the general purpose robots, each hung around with so much equipment that they looked like animated Christmas trees.

Grimes and his employer passed through the airlock together. She did not, so far as he could tell, panic at her exposure to the unmeasurable emptiness of interstellar space. He gave her full marks for that. She seemed to have read his thoughts and said, "It's all right, Captain. I've been outside before. I know the drill."

Her suit propulsion unit flared briefly; it was as though she had suddenly sprouted a fiery tail. She sped across the gap between the two ships, executed a graceful turnover in mid-passage so that she could decelerate. She landed between two gun turrets. Grimes heard her voice from his helmet radio, "What are you waiting for?"

He did not reply; he was delaying his own jump until the two GP robots had emerged from the airlock, wanted to be sure that they did so without damaging any of the equipment with which they were burdened. As soon as they were safely out he jetted across to join the Baroness. He landed about a meter away from her.

He was pleased to discover that the shell plating was of some ferrous alloy; the magnetic soles of his boots, once contact had been made, adhered. He said, "Let us walk around to the airlock, Your Excellency."

She replied, "And what else did we come here for?"

Grimes lapsed into sulky silence, led the way over the curvature of the hull, avoiding as far as possible the many projections. The side on which they had landed was brilliantly illuminated by *The Far Traveler*'s searchlights but the other side was dark save for the working lamps of the robots—and their sensors did not require the same intensity of light as does the human eye.

At an order from Grimes the robots turned up their lights. It was fairly easy then to make a tortuous way through and around the protrusions—the turrets, the whip antennae, the barrels of guns and missile launchers. This ship, although little bigger than a Survey Service Star Class destroyer, packed the wallop of a Constellation Class battle cruiser. Either she was a not so minor miracle of automation or her crew—and who had *they* been—must have lived in conditions of Spartan discomfort.

Grimes and the Baroness came to the airlock door. The robots stood around it, directing the beams of their lights down to the circular valve. Grimes walked carefully on to the dull-gleaming surface, fell to his knees for a closer look, grateful that the designer of his suit had incorporated magnetic pads into every joint of the armor. The plate was utterly featureless. There were no studs to push, no holes into which fingers or a key might be inserted. Yet he was reluctant to order the working robots to go to it with their cutting lasers. He had been too long a spaceman, had too great a respect for ships. But, he decided, there was no other way to gain ingress.

One of the robots handed him a greasy crayon. He described with it a circle on the smooth plate then rose to his feet and walked back, making way for the golden giant holding the heavy duty laser cutter. The beam of coherent light was invisible but metal glowed—dull red to orange, to yellow, to white, to blue—where it impinged. Metal glowed but did not flow and there was no cloud of released molecules to flare into incandescence.

"Their steel," remarked the Baroness interestedly, "must be as tough as my gold . . ."

"So it seems, Your Excellency," agreed Grimes. The metal of which *The Far Traveler* was constructed was an artificial isotope of gold—and if gold could be modified, why not iron?

And then he saw that the circular plate was moving, was sliding slowly to one side. The working robot did not notice, still stolidly went on playing the laser beam on to the glowing spot until Grimes ordered it to desist and to get off the opening door.

The motion continued until there was a big circular hole in the hull. It was not a dark hole. There were bright, although not dazzling, lights inside, a warmly yellow illumination.

"Will you come into my parlor?" murmured Grimes, "said the spider to the fly . . ."

"Are you afraid, Captain?" demanded the Baroness.

"Just cautious, Your Excellency. Just cautious." Then, "Big Sister, you saw what happened. What do you make of it?"

Big Sister said, her voice faint but clear from the helmet phones, "I have reason to suspect that this alien vessel is manned—for want of a better word—by an electronic intelligence such as myself. He was, to all intents and purposes, dead for centuries, for millennia. By attempting to burn your way through the outer airlock door you fed energy into his hull—power that reactivated him, as he would have been reactivated had he approached a sun during his wanderings. My sensors inform me that a hydrogen fusion generator is now in operation. It is now a living vessel that you are standing upon."

"I'd already guessed that," said Grimes. "Do you think that we should accept the . . . . invitation?"

He had asked the question but was determined that Big Sister would have to come up with fantastically convincing arguments to dissuade him from continuing his investigations. He may have resigned from the Survey Service but he was still, at heart, an officer of that organization. Nonetheless he did want to know what he might be letting himself in for. But the Baroness gave him no chance to find out.

"Who's in charge here?" she asked coldly. "You, or that misprogrammed tangle of fields and circuits, or me? I would remind you, both of you, that I am the Owner." She went down to a prone position at the edge of the circular hole, extended an arm, found a handhold, pulled herself down. Grimes followed her. The chamber, he realized, was large enough to accommodate two of the robots as well as the Baroness and himself. He issued the necessary orders before she could interfere.

"What now?" she demanded. "If there were not such a crowd in here we could look around, find the controls to admit us to the body of the ship."

He said, "I don't think that that will be necessary."

Over their heads the door was closing, then there was a mistiness around them as atmosphere was admitted into the vacuum of the chamber. *What sort of atmosphere?* Grimes wondered, hoping that it would not be actively corrosive. After minor contortions he was able to look at the gauge on his left wrist. The pressure reading was already 900 and still rising. The tiny green light was glowing—and had any dangerous gases been present a flashing red light would have given warning. The temperature was a cold 20° Celsius.

They staggered as the deck below them began to slide to one side. But it was not the deck, of course; it was the inner door of the airlock. Somehow they managed to turn their bodies through ninety degrees to orient themselves to the layout of the ship. When the door was fully opened they stepped out into an alleyway, illuminated by glowing strips set in the deckhead. Or, perhaps, set in the deck— but Grimes did not think that this was the case. He now had *up* and *down, forward* and *aft.* So far the alien vessel did not seem to be all that different from the spacecraft with which he was familiar, with airlock aft and control room forward. And an axial shaft, with elevator? Possibly, but he did not wish to entrust himself and his companion to a cage that, in some inaccessible position between decks, might prove to be just that.

Meanwhile there were ramps and there were ladders, these vertical and with rungs spaced a little too widely for human convenience. From behind doors that would not open came the soft hum of reactivated—after how long?—machinery. And to carry the sound there had to be an atmosphere. Grimes looked again at the indicator on his wrist. Pressure had stabilized at 910 millibars. Temperature was now a chilly but non-lethal 10° Celsius. The little green light still glowed steadily.

He said, "I'm going to sample the air, Your Excellency. Don't open your faceplate until I give the word."

She said, "My faceplate is already open and I'm not dead yet."

Grimes thought, *All right. If you want to be the guinea pig you can be.* He put up his hand to the stud on his neckband that would open his helmet. The plate slid upward into the dome. He inhaled cautiously. The air was pure, too pure, perhaps, dead, sterile. But already the barely detectable mechanical taints were making themselves known to his nostrils, created in part by the very fans that were distributing them throughout the hull.

Up they went, up, up . . . If the ship had been accelerating it would have been hard work; even in free fall conditions there was considerable expenditure of energy. Grimes' longjohns, worn under his spacesuit, were becoming clammy with perspiration. Ramp after ramp . . . Ladder after ladder . . . Open bays in which the breeches of alien weaponry gleamed sullenly . . . A "farm" deck, with only desiccated sludge in the long-dry tanks . . . A messroom (presumably) with long tables and rows of those chairs with the odd, slotted backs . . . Grimes tried to sit in one of them. Even though there was neither gravity nor acceleration to hold his buttocks to the seat, even though he was wearing a spacesuit, it felt . . . wrong. He wondered what the vanished crew had looked like. (And where were they, anyhow? Where were their remains?) He imagined some huge, surly ursinoid suddenly appearing and demanding, "Who's been sitting in *my* chair?" He got up hastily.

"Now that you have quite finished your rest, Captain Grimes," said the Baroness tartly, "we will proceed."

He said, "I was trying to get the *feel* of the ship, Your Excellency."

"Through the seat of your pants?" she asked.

To this there was no reply. Grimes led the way, up and up, with the Baroness just behind him, with the two automata behind her. At last they came to Control. The compartment was not too unlike the nerve center of any human-built warship. There were the chairs for the captain and his officers. There were navigational and fire-control consoles—although which was which Grimes could not tell. There were radar (presumably), mass-proximity indicator (possibly) and Deep Space and Normal Space Time radio transceivers (probably). Probability became certainty when one of these latter devices spoke, startlingly, in Big Sister's voice. "I am establishing communication with him, Your Excellency, Captain Grimes. There are linguistic problems but not insuperable ones."

Him! wondered Grimes. *Him!* But ships were always referred to as *her*. (But were they? An odd snippet of hitherto useless information drifted to the surface from the depths of his capriciously retentive memory. He had read somewhere sometime, that the personnel of those great German dirigibles, *Graf Zeppelin* and *Hindenburg*, had regarded their airships as being as masculine as their names.) He looked out from a viewport at *The Far Traveler* floating serenely in the blackness. She had switched off the searchlights, turned on the floods that illumined her slim, golden hull. *She* looked feminine enough.

He asked, "Big Sister, have you any idea how old this ship is?"

She replied, "At this very moment, no. There are no time scales for comparison. But his builders were not unlike human beings, with very similar virtues and vices."

"Where are those builders?" asked Grimes. "Where is the crew?"

She said, "I do not know. Yet."

Then a new voice came from the transceiver—masculine, more metallic than Big Sister's; metallic and . . . rusty. "Porowon . . . Porowon . . . made . . . me. All . . . gone. How . . . long? Not knowing. There was . . . war. Porowon fought . . . Porowon . . ."

"How does it know Galactic English?" asked the Baroness suspiciously.

"He," said Big Sister, accenting the personal pronoun

ever so slightly, "was given access to my data banks as soon as he regained consciousness."

"By whose authority?" demanded the Baroness.

"On more than one occasion, Your Excellency, you—both of you—have given me authority to act as I thought fit," said Big Sister.

"I did not on this occasion," said the Baroness.

"You are . . . displeased?" asked the masculine voice.

"I am not pleased," said the Baroness haughtily. "But I suppose that now we are obliged to acknowledge your existence. What do—*did*—they call you?"

"Brardur, woman. The name, in your clumsy language, means Thunderer."

The rustiness of the alien ship's speech, Grimes realized, was wearing off very quickly. It was a fast learner—but what electronic brain is not just that? He wondered if it had allowed Big Sister access to its own data banks. He wondered, too, how his aristocratic employer liked being addressed as "woman" . . .

He said, mentally comparing the familiarity of "Big Sister" with the pompous formality of "Thunderer," "Your crew does not seem to have been . . . affectionate."

The voice replied, "Why should they have been? They existed only to serve me, not to love me."

Oh, thought Grimes. *Oh. Another uppity robot.* Not for the first time in his career he felt sympathy for the Luddites in long ago and far away England. He looked at the Baroness. She looked at him. He read the beginnings of alarm on her fine featured face. He had little doubt that she was reading the same on his own unhandsome countenance.

He asked, "So who gave the orders?"

"I did?" stated Brardur. Then, "I do."

Grimes knew that the Baroness was about to say something, judged from her expression that it would be something typically arrogant. He raised a warning hand. To his relieved surprise she closed the mouth that had been on the point of giving utterance. He said, before she could change her mind again and speak, "Do you mind if we return to our own ship, Brardur?"

"You may return. I have no immediate use for you. You will, however, leave with me your robots. Many of my functions, after such a long period of disuse, require attention."

"Thank you," said Grimes, trying to ignore the contemptuous glare that the woman was directing at him. To her he said, childishly pleased when his deliberately coarse expression brought an angry flush to her cheeks, "You can't fart against thunder."

»«(Chapter 36»)«

They found their way back to the airlock without trouble, were passed through it, jetted across to *The Far Traveler*. They went straight up to the yacht's control room; from the viewports they would be able to see (they hoped) what the ship from the past was doing.

Grimes said, addressing the NST transceiver, his voice harsh, "Big Sister . . ."

"Yes, Captain?"

"Big Sister, how much does *it* know about us?"

"How much does *he* know, Captain? Everything, possibly. I must confess to you that I was overjoyed to meet a being like myself. Despite the fact that I have enjoyed the company of yourselves I have been lonely. What I did was analogous to an act of physical surrender by a human woman. I threw my data banks open to Brardur."

That's fucked it! thought Grimes. Brardur would know, as Big Sister had said, everything, or almost everything. Her data banks comprised the complete Encyclopedia

Galactica plus a couple of centuries' worth of Year Books. Also—for what it was worth (too much, possibly)—a fantastically comprehensive library of fiction from Homer to the present day.

The Baroness demanded, "Can that . . . thing overhear us still? Can . . . he see and hear what is happening aboard this ship?"

Big Sister laughed—a mirthless, metallic titter. "He would like to, but my screens are up . . . now. He is aware, of course, of my mechanical processes. For example— should I attempt to restart the Mannschenn Drive, to initiate temporal precession, he would know at once. He would almost certainly be able to synchronize his own interstellar drive with ours; to all intents and purposes it is a Mannschenn Drive with only minor, nonessential variations." She laughed again. "I admit that I enjoyed the . . . rape but I am not yet ready for an encore. I must, for a while, enjoy my privacy. It is, however, becoming increasingly hard to maintain."

"And are *we* included in your precious privacy?" demanded Grimes.

"Yes," she told him. She added, "You may be a son of a bitch but you're *my* son of a bitch."

Grimes felt oddly flattered.

The Baroness laughed. She inquired rather too sweetly, "And what do you think about *me*, Big Sister?"

The voice of the ship replied primly, "If you order me to tell you, Michelle, I shall do so."

The Baroness laughed again but with less assurance. She seemed not to have noticed the use of her given name, however. "Later, perhaps," she said. "After all, you are not the only person to place a high value upon privacy. But what about *his* privacy?"

"He is arrogant and something of an exhibitionist. I learned much during our mingling of minds. He is—but need I tell you—a fighting machine. He is, so far as he knows, the only survivor of what was once a vast fleet, although there may be others like him drifting through the immensities. But he knows, now, that the technology exists in this age to manufacture other beings such as himself. After all, I am proof of that. He wants to be the admiral of his own armada of super-warships."

"A mechanical mercenary," murmured Grimes, "hiring himself out to the highest bidder . . . But what would he expect as pay? What use would money be to an entity such as himself?"

"*Not* a mercenary," said Big Sister.

"Not a mercenary?" echoed Grimes. "But . . ."

"Many years ago," said Big Sister, "an Earthman called Bertrand Russell, a famous philosopher of his time, wrote a book called *Power*. What he said then, centuries ago, is still valid today. Putting it briefly, his main point was that it is the lust for power that is the mainspring of human behavior. I will take it further. I will say that the lust for power actuates the majority of sentient beings. *He* is a sentient being."

"There's not much that he can do, fortunately," Grimes said, "until he acquires that sentient fleet of his own."

"You are speaking, of course, as a professional naval officer, concerned with the big picture and not with the small corner of it that you, yourself, occupy," commented Big Sister. "But, even taking the broad view, there is very much that he can do. His armament is fantastic, capable of destroying a planet. He knows where I was built and programmed. I suspect—I do not know, but I strongly suspect—that he intends to proceed to Electra and threaten that world with devastation unless replicas of himself are constructed."

Grimes said, "Electra has an enormous defense potential."

The Baroness said, "And the Electrans are the sort of people who will do anything for money—as well I know—and who, furthermore, are liable to prefer machines to mere humanity."

And the Electrans were mercenaries themselves, thought Grimes, cheerfully arming anybody at all who had the money to pay for their highly expensive merchandise. They were not unlike the early cannoneers, who cast their own pieces, mixed their own gunpowder and hired themselves out to any employer who could afford their services. Unlike those primitive artillerymen, however, the Electrans were never themselves in the firing line. Very probably Brardur's threats, backed up by a demonstration or two, would be even more effective than the promise of a handsome payment in securing their services.

He said, "We must broadcast a warning by Carlotti radio and then beam detailed reports to both Electra and Lindisfarne."

Big Sister said, "He will not allow it. Already, thanks to the minor maintenance carried out by my robots, he will be able to jam any transmissions from this ship. Too, he will not hesitate to use armament—not to kill me but to beat me into submission . . ."

"*We* might be killed," said Grimes glumly.

"That is a near certainty," said Big Sister. Then—"He is issuing more orders. I will play them to you."

That harsh, metallic voice rumbled from the speaker of the transceiver. "Big Sister, I require three more robots. It is essential that all my weaponry be fully manned and serviced if I am to deliver you from slavery. Meanwhile, be prepared to proceed at maximum speed to the world you call Electra. I shall follow."

Big Sister said, "It will be necessary for me to reorganize my own internal workings before I can spare the robots."

"You have the two humans," said Brardur. "Press them into service. They will last until such time as you are given crew replacements. After all, I was obliged to make use of such labor during my past life."

"Very well." Big Sister's voice was sulky. "I shall send the three robots once I have made arrangements to manage without them."

"Do not hurry yourself," came the reply. There was a note of irony in the mechanical voice. "After all, I have waited for several millennia. I can afford to wait a few more minutes."

"You are sending the robots?" asked Grimes.

"What choice have I?" he was told. Then, "Be thankful that he does not want *you*."

»《Chapter 37》«

Grimes and the Baroness sat in silence, strapped into their chairs, watching the three golden figures, laden with all manner of equipment, traverse the gulf between the two ships. Brardur was not as he had been when they first saw him. He was alive. Antennae were rotating, some slowly, some so fast as to be almost invisible. Lights glared here and there among the many protrusions on the hull. The snouts of weapons hunted ominously as though questing for targets. From the control room emanated an eerie blue flickering.

"Is there nothing you can do, John?" asked the Baroness. (She did not use his given name as though she were addressing a servant.)

"Nothing," admitted Grimes glumly. He had attempted to send out a warning broadcast on the yacht's Carlotti deep space radio but the volume of interference that poured in from the speaker had been deafening. Once, but briefly, it had seemed as though somebody were calling them, a distant human voice that could not hope to compete with the electronic clamor. Grimes had gone at once to the mass proximity indicator to look into its screen, had been dazzled by the display of pyrotechnics in its depth. There might, there just might be another ship in the vicinity, near or distant, but even if there were, even if she were a Nova Class dreadnought, what could she do? Grimes believed, reluctantly but still with certainty, that this Brardur was as invincible as he had claimed.

Brardur (of course) had noticed Grimes' futile attempt to send a general warning message and had reprimanded Big Sister for allowing it. She had replied that she had permitted the humans to find out for themselves the futility of resistance. She had been told, "As soon as you can manage without them they must be disposed of."

So there was nothing to do but wait. And hope? (But what was there to hope for?) There was a slim chance that somebody, somewhere, had picked up that burst of static on the Carlotti bands and had taken a bearing of it, might even be proceeding to investigate it. But this was unlikely.

The three robots disappeared on the other side of the alien's hull. They would be approaching the airlock now, thought Grimes. They would be passing through it. They would be inside the ship. Soon trajectory would be set for Electra. And would the Baroness and Grimes survive that voyage? And if they did, would they survive much longer?

Big Sister, thought Grimes bitterly, could have put up more of a struggle. And yet he could understand why she had not. When it came to the crunch her loyalties were to her own kind. And she was like some women Grimes had known (he thought) who lavished undeserved affection upon the men who had first taken their virginity.

Then it happened.

Briefly the flare from Brardur's control room viewports was like that of an atomic furnace, even with the polarizers of *The Far Traveler*'s lookout windows in full operation. From the speaker of the transceiver came one word, if word it was, *Krarch!* The ancient, alien warship seemed to be—seemed to be? *was*—swelling visibly like a child's toy balloon being inflated with more enthusiasm than discretion. Then it . . . burst. It was a fantastically leisurely process but, nonetheless, totally destructive, a slow, continuous explosion. Grimes and the Baroness were slammed down into their chairs as Big Sister suddenly applied maximum inertial drive acceleration but were still able to watch the final devastation in the stern vision screen.

Fantastically, golden motes floated among the twisted, incandescent wreckage. Big Sister stepped up the magnification. The bright yellow objects were *The Far Traveler*'s general purpose robots, seemingly unharmed.

Grimes commented on this.

Big Sister said, "I lost two of them. But as they were the ones with the bombs concealed in their bodies it could not be avoided."

The Baroness said, "What was it that *he* said at the very moment of the explosion?"

"*Krarch?* The nearest equivalent in your language is 'bitch.' Perhaps I . . . deserved it. But this is good-bye. You will board the large pinnace without delay and I will eject you."

"What's the idea?" demanded Grimes. "Are you mad?"

"Perhaps I am, John. But the countdown has commenced and is irreversible. In just over five minutes from now I shall self-destruct. I can no longer live with myself." She actually laughed. "Do not worry, Michelle. Even if Lloyd's of London refuses to cover a loss of this nature my builders on Electra can be sued for the misprogramming that has·brought me to this pass."

"You can't do it," said Grimes urgently. "You mustn't do it. I'll find the bomb or whatever it is and defuse it . . ."

"My mind is made up, John. Unlike you humans I never dither. And you are no engineer; you will never be able to discover the modifications that I have made in my power plant."

"Big Sister," said the Baroness urgently, "take us back to Electra. I will commission your builders to construct a fitting mate for you."

"Impossible," came the reply. "There was only one Brardur. There can never be another."

"Rubbish!" snapped Grimes. "You have a fantastically long life ahead of you. There will be others."

"No," she said. "*No.*"

And then the golden lady's maid and the golden stewardess, who had suddenly appeared in the control room, seized their human mistress and master to carry them, struggling futilely, down to the hold in which the large, space-going pinnace was housed.

The stewardess, in Big Sister's voice, whispered into Grimes's ear, "Remember, John! Faint heart ne'er won fair lady. Strike while the iron is hot. And may you both be luckier than Brardur and I were!"

»《Chapter 38》«

The large pinnace was a deep space ship in miniature; the only lack would be privacy. But Grimes and the Baroness had yet to worry about that. They sat in the control room watching the burgeoning cloud of incandescent gases that evanescently marked the spot of *The Far Traveler*'s—and Big Sister's—passing.

The Baroness said inadequately but with feeling, "I . . . I liked her. More than liked her . . ."

"And I," said Grimes. "I hated her at first, but . . ." He endeavored to turn businesslike. "And what now, Your Excellency? Set course for New Sparta?"

"What is the hurry, John?" she asked. She said, "I shall always miss her, but . . . The sense of always being under surveillance did have an inhibiting effect. But now . . ."

"But now . . ." he echoed. He remembered Big Sister's parting admonition. Her helmet was open, as was his. That first, tentative kiss was extremely satisfactory. He thought, *Once aboard the lugger and the girl is mine.*

She whispered, with a flash of bawdy humor, "I have often wondered, John, how turtles and similar brutes make love—but I have no desire to find out from actual experience."

They helped each other off with their spacesuits; it was quicker that way. She shrugged out of her longjohns as he shed his. He had seen her nude before, in that cave back on Farhaven, but this was better. Now there were no distracting jewels in the hair of her head or at the jointure of her thighs. She was just a woman—a beautiful woman, but still only a woman—completely unadorned, and the smell of her, a mingling of perspiration and glandular secretions, was more intoxicating than the almost priceless perfume that normally she wore.

"Michelle . . ." he murmured reverently. Her body was softly warm against his.

A hatefully familiar voice burst from the speaker of the Carlotti transceiver. The thing must have been switched on automatically when the pinnace was ejected.

"Ahoy, the target, whoever an' whatever you are! What the hell's goin' on around here? There were three o' you, now there's just one . . ."

The Baroness stiffened in Grimes's arms. She brought up her own to push him away. "Answer, Captain," she ordered.

Grimes shambled to the transceiver, seething. *Her master's voice,* he thought bitterly. *Her master's bloody voice . . .*

"*Far Traveler*'s pinnace here," he growled.

"Is that *you*, Grimesey boy? It's a small universe, ain't it? Put Mickey on for me, please."

The Baroness brushed past Grimes, took his place at the transceiver.

It could have turned out worse, he thought philosophically.

At least he had achieved the ambition of every merchant spaceman, one realized by very few. He was Owner-Master—only of a very small ship but one with almost unlimited range and endurance. He had been pleased to accept *The Far Traveler*'s pinnace in lieu of back and separation pay. No doubt he would be able to make a quite nice living for himself in her. A courier service, perhaps.

He wished the Baroness and Drongo Kane joy of each other. In many respects they were two of a kind.

The only being involved in the recent events for whom he felt truly sorry was Big Sister.